READER'S DIGEST CONDENSED BOOKS

THE PAINTING OPPOSITE: *HELD UP* BY NEWBOLD TROTTER

READER'S DIGEST
CONDENSED BOOKS

Volume 3 • 1975

THE READER'S DIGEST ASSOCIATION

Pleasantville, New York

Reader's Digest Condensed Books are published five times a year at Pleasantville, N.Y.

CONTENTS

MRS. 'ARRIS GOES

TO MOSCOW

A CONDENSATION OF THE BOOK BY

Paul Gallico

ILLUSTRATED BY Alan Manham

The inimitable Mrs. 'Arris is on the go again, this time to Moscow with her friend Violet Butterfield. In this hilarious and lighthearted adventure, Mrs. 'Arris gets into things right up to her neck. It all begins with a photograph of a pretty girl named Lisabeta and a sad tale of Kremlin-thwarted love.

When tickets to Moscow appear as if by magic, the ladies are off, despite Mrs. Butterfield's real reservations about the whole project. But the Kremlin is no match for Ada 'Arris. True love, Mrs. 'Arris and the reader all triumph in this rollicking Russian romp.

Chapter One

THE photograph definitely had never been there before.

Of this Mrs. Harris was certain, being sharp-eyed, observant and most particular about the little objects, pictures and mementos which cluttered the London flats of the clients for whom she did daily work, since the majority of clients were fussy about their knickknacks and irritable when things were moved.

Some eight by ten inches, framed to stand up, the photograph now reposed on Mr. Lockwood's desk. Against a curious background of snow and a great wall topped by a strange tower, it revealed, fur-clad, the head and shoulders of a lovely-looking girl.

Mrs. Harris, whose purpose had been to dust Mr. Lockwood's desk, his typewriter, reference books and the various toys that all writers seem to keep about their working area, picked up the mystery photo and examined it more closely. It was obviously a blowup from a snapshot, but even the graininess of the enlargement did not conceal the luminous melancholy of the eyes. Those eyes looking straight into the camera were trying to convey a message, and to Mrs. Harris, who was both imaginative and incurably romantic, the communication was one of sadness and longing. Winter, snow, an unhappy girl and behind her some kind of grim fortress.

This sadness transferred itself to Mrs. Harris or, rather, crystallized the emotion she realized was always present around Mr. Lockwood's small apartment. For, from the beginning six months ago when she had answered his ad and taken on to "do" for him for a couple of hours a day, she had felt him to be a distracted man with some secret sorrow.

She stood there, a thin wiry figure, armed head to toe for the battle against dust and dirt, in apron, felt slippers and headcloth; the long handle of the floor-polishing mop held upright in the crook of her arm; the picture in one hand, a dustrag in the other. She had little darting mischievous eyes which were now aglow with the excitement of her discovery, rounded cheeks like frosted crab apples, and her chirpy sparrow's face was a campaign map of lines and furrows of a lifetime of struggle.

Thus engrossed, she did not hear Mr. Geoffrey Lockwood let himself into the flat and march into his study to catch her at what she would have called "snooping" at the picture. Ada Harris was not basically a snooper and, nipped *in flagrante*, she began to rub the glass in the frame vigorously with her duster.

Mr. Lockwood, with a curiously stern look upon his otherwise pleasant and rather handsome countenance, came over and without a word took the photograph from her hand and replaced it.

The awful silence absolutely shrieked to be broken. Mrs. Harris said, "Ain't she beautiful."

Mr. Lockwood did not reply, and because his back was partially turned to her she could not see the expression on his face, which was dark and lowering and did not suit him at all. He was about thirty-five, sandy-haired, blue-eyed, with a rugged maleness of features, but his face in repose always had an air of bewilderment and absentmindedness that from the very first had awakened Mrs. Harris' motherly instincts. These were never too far from the surface, since she herself had a married daughter and grandchildren.

Mrs. Harris, her remark left unanswered, felt that yet another was called for and asked, "Where is it? That plyce looks like a jail."

Mr. Lockwood replied, "The Kremlin," then suddenly shouted, "Damn them!" with such ferocity that Mrs. Harris jumped.

"I'm sorry, sir, I wasn't meanin'—"

"I didn't mean *you*, Mrs. Harris. It's *them*. And the bloody don't-give-a-damn Foreign Office as well."

"Nor did I mean to snoop neither," said Mrs. Harris. "It's just that I hadn't never seen it before and when I come in today there it was and 'er lookin' so loverly I couldn't 'elp—"

"I know," Mr. Lockwood admitted. "I couldn't bear to have it out before, but when I thought the Foreign Office was finally going to do something for me . . ." He didn't finish that sentence but added another equally baffling. "She's a Russian girl."

Baffling was hardly the word to describe Mrs. Harris' emotions, or her flaming curiosity which required every bit of her self-control to be contained. Who was that "Russian girl"? Wife? Sweetheart? Where was she? And why? Unquestionably she was the key to that melancholy that was always wrapped around Mr. Lockwood. But it was a key which Mrs. Harris' innate sense of propriety refused to let her turn.

Ada Harris belonged to that vanishing breed of London char-ladies who for fifty pence an hour visited small London flats or offices and cleaned them. She herself specialized in dwellings, because she was fascinated by other people's lives and that was where one encountered them. Her clients eventually found her to be not merely a conscientious drudge but a woman primed with a fabulous fund of wisdom garnered through a lifelong attendance at the school of hard knocks. She could give advice to the lovelorn, had a list of all the best hairdressers, shops and bargain counters at her fingertips, understood the two-legged male animal, could counsel on marital problems and was herself a member of the chars' underground which passed back and forth succulent tidbits of gossip of marriage, divorce and scandal, acquired at first hand.

She was, however, as she had said, not a snooper, nor did she ever pry into the personal affairs of her clients. Though once such a one asked for a bit of advice, Ada was ready to hold forth. Propped up by her mop handle, she could let them have anything from a half hour to forty-five minutes without drawing a deep breath. She loved nothing better than a good heart-to-heart chat, oft to the considerable distress of employers who had rendezvous at beauty parlors, milliners, dressmakers or had a taxi ticking over outside. But a client would have to volunteer.

11

To his own eternal surprise Mr. Lockwood found himself volunteering. He had sat himself down at his desk and was regarding his typewriter morosely. "She's an Intourist guide in Moscow," he said. "We met while I was last there for my book, *Russia Revealed.*"

Ada Harris could hardly credit her ears. Lockwood, a man she always felt to be impervious to her ministrations, appeared to be about to come clean. Mrs. Harris' reaction and the whole miserable unhappy affair came crowding in on him. He was ready to unload. And to what better dead-end safety valve than this semianonymous woman who appeared daily and then vanished into limbo?

"She's an Intourist guide," he repeated. "Intourist, Mrs. Harris, is the Russian tourist agency. This girl's name is Lisabeta Nadeshda Borovaskaya, but I called her Liz. I suppose we just sort of went up in flames." And as he looked at the tiny figure of his listener, mouth open, eyes popping, hanging on his every word, he fell prey to sudden embarrassment. He averted his eyes. "I mean, we wanted to get married—I've never known anyone like her before—well, you've seen her picture— Forgive me, I'm talking like a schoolboy."

But Mrs. Harris was not going to have the tap turned off. She said, "What 'appened? Why didn't you?"

Lockwood's eyes looked away from what seemed to him to be no future and into the past. He replied in one word, "Russia," as though that were the answer to all questions. And then, seeing his audience still agog for information, he said, "They're dead set against foreigners and forbid any of their people marrying one. We were lucky to be able to keep it completely secret, and then I had to leave. If they'd ever found out . . ." He realized that his cryptic sentences were getting neither him nor his audience anywhere and thereupon launched into a more consecutive narrative.

They had met, fallen in love and pledged themselves to one another at the very outset of Lockwood's tour of Russia. Moscow had been his first stop on a planned Intourist itinerary which, however, Lockwood intended to evade at several points to acquire material for the book his publishers had commissioned, *Russia Revealed.* They had been extraordinarily fortunate in that their love affair had not been uncovered during his three weeks in Moscow.

Discreet inquiries, as though for a book, into the problems connected with a Russian marrying a foreigner exposed the enormity of the problem. Such a marriage might take place after unraveling reels of red tape, but even then there was no guarantee that the wife or the husband, whichever was the Russian citizen, would be allowed to leave the country.

The prospects were bleak, but the two had the courage and tenacity of people in love, and Lockwood had friends in the Foreign Office in London as well as some contacts in the embassy in Moscow. They agreed that first Lockwood must complete his trip, which would last about three months and take him as far east as the Chinese border and as far south as Russia's Black Sea resorts. They would not communicate during his absence. Upon his return a mutual friend would introduce them as though they were meeting for the first time. They would risk letting the friendship develop openly. Only then would they tackle both problems, getting married and arranging for her to be allowed to return to England with him.

While Lockwood told his tale, Mrs. Harris tried to follow with her alert mind and "see" some of what he was telling, but she had no point of reference beyond the photograph with its grim background. Only in general was she aware that life behind the iron curtain was not all it might be. But the important thing was to keep him going, for at that point he had ceased to speak and was sitting miserably regarding the photograph.

"Oh blimey," she said. "Wouldn't they let you get married?"

Lockwood came out of his reverie. "Worse than that. I never saw her again." This was what was killing him, he confessed, as he again picked up the story, which was one of overconfidence and betrayal. During the trip he had managed to interview a dissident writer, exiled from Moscow having served a term in a Russian labor camp, and who in addition had been given the treatment in a lunatic asylum until protest from the West had secured his release. The meeting with this man had been discreet but not sufficiently so, and when Lockwood had stepped off the train in Moscow, he had been immediately picked up. Someone, maybe even the Soviet writer himself, had tipped off the KGB, the Russian secret police.

Had not another part of Lockwood's plans worked out, it would have gone hard with him. He had kept two sets of notes on the journey. The ones that mattered, the dangerous ones, he had smuggled out through Turkey during his visit to Sochi on the Black Sea, and at the last minute something had made him include the photo of Lisabeta in the packet. So when the KGB pulled him in for twenty-four hours of grilling, he was clean. He had only his travel notes. However, his visit to the dissident writer had made him *persona non grata*. The KGB confiscated his notes, escorted him from the interrogation cell to the airport, and five hours later he found himself back in London.

The full implications of Lockwood's dilemma had not yet struck Mrs. Harris, but as usual when faced with a client's problem, her mind was already searching for a way out and she was beginning to experience the thrill of participating vicariously in someone else's trouble. She said, "But can't you get back some'ow? A lot of people now is takin' trips to Russia. A friend of a lidy I work for has just come back and she said it was loverly."

"Vodka, caviar, coddling—the smiling mask." Lockwood spoke bitterly. "They'd never give me a visa, especially after my book comes out. And if I were to contact Liz, they'd have her in one of those cells so fast she wouldn't know what hit her."

Mrs. Harris was beginning to see a little. That cell would be somewhere behind that wall. "Ow," she said. "You're prop'ly in the cart, ain't you?" which was the strongest expression she knew for a crushing defeat. "But she'll understand."

The full import of Lockwood's tragedy was then revealed. "How can she?" he groaned. "Don't you see? There was no report about my expulsion. I'd promised to be in touch with her when I got back to Moscow. That was six months ago. What I can't bear besides everything else is her thinking I've run out on her."

Mrs. Harris drew on her fund of experience. "If she loves you, she'd never think that."

Lockwood cried, "What else should she believe?"

"Come on now, luv, use yer nut. Write 'er a letter."

"It won't do," said Lockwood. "All foreign mail is intercepted. At the slightest indication that she had any connection with me she'd be arrested. They'd see a plot at once."

Some of Mr. Lockwood's despair entered Mrs. Harris' sympathetic soul. "You poor man," she said. "You are for the 'igh jump, ain't you? What about yer pals in the Foreign Office? Didn't you say—"

She only succeeded in rekindling Lockwood's rage. "Bloody hypocrites! Up to yesterday they said they might do something. That's why I dared look at her photo again. This morning it's 'Sorry, old boy, can't rock the boat, you know.' Change in the political situation."

The impasse was quite clear now. If he tried to get through to the girl, she would be implicated. If he didn't, she would go on believing the man she loved had cruelly deserted her, and in the meantime two lovers were suffering broken hearts.

Mrs. Harris, moved to the depth of her being and close to tears, said, "Lord, Mr. Lockwood, I wish I could 'elp you."

"Nobody can," Lockwood said gloomily, and he picked up the photograph and put it into his desk drawer.

Mrs. Harris said, "Don't put 'er away. You never know what might 'appen. She'll 'elp you keep yer tucker up."

He replaced the photo and then they both fell silent, and during that silence Mrs. Harris indulged in a fantasy, the kind that often came to her when people were in trouble, or she herself fell prey to an ambition. It was in two parts, neither of them sensible or practical. In one she was facing a group of men behind that fortress wall and giving them a piece of her mind about separating two unhappy lovers. In the second she was ringing Mr. Lockwood's doorbell and at her side was Liz. When he opened the door Mrs. Harris would cry, " 'Ere she is, Mr. Lockwood, I've been to Russia and brought 'er back for you!"

Lockwood now cleared his throat and said, "Well," and made motions of one about to go to work.

Mrs. Harris could take a hint and said, "I'll be gettin' on," and proceeded to her next rendezvous with dust and dirt.

Chapter Two

Mrs. Harris brooded all the way home that Saturday, and Mr. Lockwood's dilemma was still coloring her mood when her bosom friend and neighbor, Mrs. Violet Butterfield, arrived for their nightly path-crossing cup of tea and gossip.

Bosom was an apt word to apply to Mrs. Butterfield, as she was as round as Ada Harris was spare. Only the features in the full-moon face were small—a mouth that formed into a tiny "o" above a triple row of chins, a button nose and small startled eyes. The shape of the mouth was just right for the instant emission of shrieks of fright.

For whereas Ada Harris was the complete optimist and the soul of courage often to the point of recklessness, Mrs. Butterfield was timid, wholly pessimistic and given to pronouncements of doom and disaster, particularly when her best friend was taking one of her notions.

At one time Violet had been a member of that gallant band of women who arose daily at four a.m. and sallied forth to clean London's offices, but lately she had succeeded in acquiring the job of attendant in the ladies' room of the Paradise Club.

It was this that solidified the nightly ritual, for just as Mrs. Harris was closing down her day's work, so to speak, Violet Butterfield was starting off on hers, enabling them to spend an hour or so together over the teapot and the evening papers.

Mrs. Butterfield would supply tidbits of scandal gleaned from ladies who visited her domain, while Mrs. Harris narrated tales of the vagaries of her smarter or more eccentric clients. Oddly that night, however, Ada did not feel inclined to pass on Mr. Lockwood's story. The plight of the young lovers seemed somehow too sacred for tittle-tattle. Besides which there shortly began a turn of events which temporarily drove it out of her head—the fur coat and the color-television set.

"You and yer fur coat!"

"You and yer bloomin' telly!"

It was Violet Butterfield who for years had had her eye on a fur coat of musquash, a species of water rat, which each autumn would appear in the window of Arding & Hobbs, the department store where they did their shopping. It was a losing game. For while Violet scrimped and saved the price of last year's coat, by the time the new season rolled around, the galloping inflation had added another twenty pounds to the price and whipped it out of reach again.

As for Mrs. Harris, her television set was black and white, cantankerous, ancient and out of date and given to collapse during crucial moments of favorite programs. She yearned for the new giant-screen color set that would turn her basement flat at number 5 Willis Gardens, Battersea, into a veritable theater. The price of such a one was over four hundred pounds, as out of reach as her chum's musquash wrapping. But that did not stop her from wishing. And often on her way home she would pause before a shop displaying such and look with longing upon the machines in the window, all projecting the same scene in gorgeous colors.

The teapot was empty, the "sangwidges" had been disposed of and Mrs. Butterfield was aware that her friend was unusually silent. She found an item in the *Evening News* that she thought would awaken her interest.

"'Ullo, 'ullo," she said, "'ere's somefink about a friend of yers." And she read aloud a dispatch from Paris which revealed that the Marquis Hypolite de Chassagne was ending his tour of duty as ambassador of France to the United States, and upon his return to Paris would take up an appointment as senior adviser on foreign affairs at the Quai d'Orsay. "A real pal, wasn't 'e?" She added, "Maybe 'e'd be comin' over to London like 'e used ter. . . ."

But Mrs. Harris only nodded morosely.

"Blimey, luv," exclaimed Violet, "yer tucker's down, ain't it? One of them as you do for turn narsty on you?"

Mrs. Harris shook her head but remained mute.

"Well then," Mrs. Butterfield said, "why don't we see what's on the telly?" She went over, switched it on and twiddled the knob for ITV, where she got a violent blizzard on the screen and a vicious growl from the speaker. The BBC 1 hissed and crackled, and the picture was scrambled like an egg. The third channel offered a total blank.

Ada Harris suddenly became articulate. "Bloody 'ell!" she cried. "I only 'ad it fixed last week. And me wantin' to see 'Stars on Sunday' tomorrow. Turn it off, Vi, before I put me foot through it. Maybe I will take on more jobs until I can get me a color set."

Ada's outbursts of temper were rare and usually frightened Vi into saying the wrong thing. "Oh, you could never do it. It's like me fur coat. They always keep twenty quid ahead of you."

"You and yer fur coat," said Mrs. Harris.

"You and yer telly," Mrs. Butterfield was compelled to answer, but was immediately contrite, besides which she'd had an idea to reclaim her chum's ruined Sunday.

She said, "Look 'ere, Ada, the TUC which our Office Cleaners' Union is connected wif is givin' a big charity do in Bermondsey tomorrow night. We all 'ad to buy two tickets. 'Ow about us goin'?"

Mrs. Harris said contemptuously, "Unions," for she was an independent soul and steered clear of them. But she recognized the peace offering and her heart flooded with warmth. "Okay, Vi, we might as well 'ave a look."

The affair the next night turned out to be a happy and relaxed occasion for the two. There were friends and music, food and a floor show; but best of all, there was a grand lottery for which the rewards were dazzling. Tickets were priced at a pound each, and the array of loot was headed by a maroon Mini Minor car, mounted on a rotating pedestal, with further valuables displayed and listed in a roped-off enclosure. Refrigerators, washing machines, tours for two to foreign climes, stereos, cameras.

But Mrs. Harris did not so much as glance at any of those prizes, for there among them it was: her television set.

Oh, the beauty of it. In a polished mahogany cabinet, its doors thrown wide, the set was in operation, and on its giant screen a pair of ballet dancers in multicolored costumes were leaping and pirouetting through the air. Even the music was flawless.

While Mrs. Butterfield wandered around the display, Mrs. Harris remained riveted. A pound was a great deal of money to her and translated into two hours of hard labor on her knees. But against that treasure trove displayed before her eyes? And yet for another moment she hesitated and waited, for she knew that she was on the verge of playing one of the hunches which occasionally would suffuse her and were received as messages dispatched to her by her Personal Deity, sitting in His office somewhere behind the firmament and part of whose job it was to concern Himself with her affairs. By and large, Ada could look back upon the fact that up to that point He had not done too badly by His client.

Mrs. Harris waited, and the message came through loud and clear: Buy the ticket, Ada. She opened her purse, handed a pound note to the pretty girl selling the chances and received a piece of white pasteboard bearing the number 49876TH. She was filling in a stub with her name and address as Mrs. Butterfield reappeared. "Look, Vi!" She waved her lottery ticket. "I've got me telly."

Violet looked confused and the pretty girl smiled.

"Well, I mean I will 'ave it," explained Ada.

All Mrs. Butterfield's pessimism rose to hand. "Ada! A quid! You ain't got that kind of money to spend. They're sellin' thousands of those tickets all over London. You ain't got a chance."

Mrs. Harris' dark eyes twinkled. "I 'ad a 'unch. You know me and me 'unches. It's as good as in me front room. 'Ere, look at me number. You know what the TH stands for? Television Harris. Come on, I'll buy you a drink to celebrate."

Hence Mrs. Harris was not unduly surprised three and a half weeks later when she returned from work to find a letter, on the envelope of which was the imprint TUC Charity Committee Grand Annual Lottery. The telly, of course. Nevertheless, she had the fortitude to wait for the evening tea so that Violet could share in the excitement.

It therefore came as a considerable shock when the envelope produced a letter advising Mrs. Ada Harris that as holder of number 49876TH she was the winner of a five-day tour to Moscow for two, all expenses paid, and enclosing vouchers to be presented at the Intourist bureau in Regent Street. Congratulations!

THE result of this astonishing sideswipe by Lady Luck was to draw almost immediate battle lines between Vi and Ada and furnish the subject of the first serious rift in the long-standing friendship of the two women.

For when the vouchers upon the London office of Intourist to supply them with two round-trip tickets for Package Tour 6A, three days and four nights in Moscow, were produced and lay on the table, Mrs. Butterfield, with as much horror as though they had been a pair of black mambas, shrieked, "Roosha! I wouldn't go there if you gave me a million pounds. Torturers, murderers, savidges is what they are. I've read all about 'em in the newspapers and so 'ave you, Ada 'Arris. And don't get any idea of takin' any trips to where we can get our 'eads cut off or get put in some dungeon for the rest of our lives."

But Mrs. Harris did not reply to this tirade. She sat there staring at those bits of paper without a qualm of disappointment, for although she was saying farewell to her color telly, she was bidding hello to something much more exciting and beautiful. The fantasy she had entertained arising out of Mr. Lockwood's dilemma now came sweeping back with double impetus. To her suddenly inflamed imagination there came a vision of what surely must have been almost a direct communication from on high: Forget about that telly, Ada Harris. You go off to Russia and get Mr. Lockwood's girl out for him. And here are the tickets I have provided. There was no doubt in Ada's mind but that this was the message.

Her first impulse was to hurry off to Mr. Lockwood's flat and announce the news of a possible line of communication between himself and his lost love when she remembered that he was out of town for a week. A week's grace, and perhaps this was for the best.

It would give her time to work on Violet, for Mrs. Harris was far from being a fool, and while she did not subscribe to Mrs. Butterfield's portrait of unrestrained violence, she was not completely happy at the thought of penetrating that sinister barrier known as the iron curtain by herself. Two was a safety measure.

The speed with which an entire filmstrip of thought can unreel through a person's head is well known, and so hardly a second had elapsed from Mrs. Butterfield's anguished outburst before Mrs. Harris replied calmly, "Oh, I don't know, Vi, you carn't believe everything you read in the papers. It might be nice for us to take a little 'oliday what's been dropped in our laps."

"'Oliday amongst them monsters?" squealed Violet. "Ada, you carn't be serious. You wouldn't get me to go," and she added, "not for a million pounds." And here the small "o" of her mouth fell silent as she gazed at her friend in complete terror. In the world of Mrs. Butterfield one million pounds was the absolute *summum* of impossibility of attainment and yet, looking at Ada's calm countenance and knowing her and what she was like if ever she made up her mind to something, it was almost as if she expected Ada to open her handbag and lay the money on the table or borrow it from The Bank of England.

Mrs. Harris was aware that she was going to have her work cut out. She forced a laugh. "Oh, come on, Violet Butterfield, use yer nut. Maybe it's true about some of them bigwigs killin' each other off, but 'oo'd ever want to make trouble for the likes of us?"

"The likes of them and the likes of us ain't no different to them Rooshans, Ada 'Arris. The way I've seen you carry on, they'd 'ave you in one of them cells pullin' out yer fingernails quicker than you could say Dick Robertson."

"Garn," scoffed Mrs. Harris, "you've got rats in yer loaf. 'Oo 'ave I ever given any trouble to? 'Oo do you fink in Moscow would ever 'ave 'eard of Mrs. 'Arris, char?"

Six o'clock in London was eight o'clock Moscow time. It might not have been at the exact moment when Mrs. Harris asked her rhetorical question that her name did come up in that far-off city, but appear it did in a file lying upon the desk of that conscientious servant of the KGB, Comrade Inspector Vaslav Vornov.

Comrade Vornov served his organization with unending zeal, as evidenced by the fact that he was at this hour still at his desk, working his way through a pile of clippings from the capitalist press. His job in the vast system of Russian espionage and internal security was to ferret out the movements of the enemies of the Soviet Union, ticket them and label them and, should they cross the boundaries of Holy Mother Russia, see to it that steps were taken to render them harmless.

The clipping near the bottom of the pile which now commended itself to his study was the same one from the British newspaper which Mrs. Butterfield had recently called to the attention of Mrs. Harris, the one that dealt with the change of post of the Marquis Hypolite de Chassagne. Comrade Vornov read through the item, then pushed a button and commanded a junior officer to produce from the enemies file the dossier on the marquis. If the marquis was again to become a power in French foreign policy, it was certain that his voice would be raised once more in resistance to the Soviet master plan of a phony détente, designed to lull the West into false security.

The dossier was as thorough a compendium of a hostile subject as could only be amassed by the far-flung tentacles of the KGB and contained a list of names of practically everyone with whom the marquis had ever come into contact. Many of them were familiar to the comrade inspector; others far down the list he had never heard of and their position indicated that they were not considered important, but in casting his eyes over the names, he came upon that of one Ada Harris of 5 Willis Gardens, Battersea, London, S.W. 11. There were no details as to the who, what, why or wherefore of her connection with the marquis and so the inspector read on, making a note of the more familiar associates who from that time on were to be closely watched.

Whoever has heard of Ada Harris in Moscow? Mrs. Harris had asked. Comrade Inspector Vaslav Vornov of the KGB had. And one reason that Vornov had attained his position in the organization was that he possessed a memory such as might be encompassed by a herd of elephants, but of this Ada was blissfully ignorant. Not that it would have worried her at this stage. She was too busy planning her counterattack to weaken the defenses of Mrs. Butterfield.

Mrs. Harris' opening skirmish in her campaign was to stop in at the Intourist office in Regent Street. Here she picked up a dozen highly colored brochures extolling and reproducing the grandeurs of Russia. When Violet produced smudgy paragraphs of newsprint detailing the horrors suffered by the citizens of the U.S.S.R. as well as anyone caught messing into their business, Ada had her antidote to spread out onto the tea table.

Here were pictures of neat white boats upon the blue Moskva River and palaces of glorious proportions. The red brick of the fascinating Kremlin dominated almost every scene—ancient monuments, colorful churches and fabulous modern buildings. There were multicolor portraits of ballerinas, opera singers, folk dancers and circus performers, all in action. Hotel brochures showed rooms as luxurious as any that Ada had cleaned at the Savoy when she had done temporary stints there as chambermaid.

But the most significant thing was the joy upon the faces of the citizens depicted, diverting themselves by the sea or dancing, singing, playing, smiling, happy, happy, happy. It would have been quite obvious to anyone looking in of an evening into number 5 Willis Gardens during the duels between the two friends with both their exhibits spread out that somewhere, someone wasn't telling the exact truth. But the two sides of the coin produced no more than a standoff.

Chapter Three

Mrs. Butterfield had been right to worry that her assessment of a million pounds as the price for which she might be persuaded to make the trip was, in Ada's determination, not enough; for Ada's forces of will and coercion were so redoubtable and well known that the million pounds tended to dwindle in efficacy.

Thus, one evening Ada counterattacked from, of all bases, Violet Butterfield's main citadel, the press. She looked up from her paper to remark casually, "I guess if 'er mum can let 'er daughter go ridin' around over there, it carn't be so turrible and there ain't nuffink goin' to 'appen to a couple of old biddies like us."

Mrs. Butterfield bit. "What mum? 'Oos daughter?"

"The queen," replied Mrs. Harris. "'Ere, read it. Princess Anne's goin' to Roosha to ride on her 'orse wif her boy friend, and her dad's goin' too. Now, what 'ave you got to say to that?"

It was true. The World Horse Trials Championships were to take place at Kiev, and Mrs. Butterfield was compelled to assimilate the news that Princess Anne, her father and her fiancé were planning to journey thither to take part.

It was a blow. "Them's royalty," Violet countered feebly. "'Oo'd dare do anything to them? It's us would be treated shymeful. I've been readin' what it's like. No 'ot water in the barf, and when you pull the chain, nuffink 'appens. 'Oo wants five days of that?"

At this point something clicked in Mrs. Butterfield's brain and she opened up a surprise sally which almost destroyed Mrs. Harris' forces. "Look 'ere, Ada, it's all very well for them royals to go gallyvantin'. They ain't got nuffink else to do. But what about me job? You! You can just tell yer people you won't be back for a week and they got to lump it. The Paradise ain't like that. If I took one day off they'd give me the push quick as a wink. The job's cushy and the tips are good and there's a dozen that would be waitin' to take me place. I'll bet you ain't thought of that, Ada 'Arris. And so let's 'ave an end to all this palaver. And good luck to the princess on 'er bloomin' 'orse."

For once Mrs. Harris was silenced. In these tough times a job was a job. For three days the visit to Moscow was not mentioned while Mrs. Harris wondered how to get over that hurdle. Help arrived from a most unexpected quarter. For it seemed that the Great Manipulator who dwelt behind the stars had His own ideas on the subject and for some reason in His infinite wisdom and omnipotence wanted Mrs. Harris in Moscow.

He went about the matter in His usual roundabout but effective way by sending an inspector from the fire department to look over the layout of the Paradise Club.

For two days Mrs. Butterfield had Mrs. Harris fooled by arising from their teatime conference at her usual hour, saying, "Well, luv, I'd better be gettin' on," and taking her departure as usual. But the third day the jig was up.

Mrs. Harris was still in the pages of her *Evening News* when Violet went through her formula, and without looking up, Ada said quietly, "Must be off, must you? Where to? The flicks?"

Stopped at the door, Mrs. Butterfield swung her huge bulk about and looked at her friend with some alarm. "What flicks?" she said. "I don't know what yer talkin' about."

Ada said, "Come sit down. 'Ere, listen to this," and she read:

"FIRE PREVENTION OFFICER CLOSES DOWN FAMOUS NIGHT SPOT
Paradise Club Infringes Safety Regulations

"Fire Prevention Officer John Reach announced the closure of the Paradise Club in Upper Mount Street for failing to comply with certain fire prevention and safety regulations. Club manager Silk Mathieson said that the changes ordered would take over a month to complete, during which period the club would remain closed. Mr. Mathieson added that the staff was being given a month's holiday with pay during the reconstruction."

Mrs. Butterfield sat quivering in a position usually described as rooted to the spot, staring guiltily at her friend, who now lowered her newspaper and said, "Violet Butterfield, 'ow could you do this to me? A month's 'oliday wif pay and you pretending to be orf to work. 'Ow about a little 'oliday trip wif me to Moscow, old girl?"

Caught, Mrs. Butterfield reacted with a burst of anger which was unusual for her. "I ain't goin' to be told where to go and where not to go, Ada 'Arris, and when it comes to one of the plyces I ain't goin', Roosha's it. And that's final!" And having said this she fell to trembling again as she waited for her friend's counter-explosion. To her surprise it didn't come.

Instead, Mrs. Harris said quietly, "I understand, Violet." For she was hurt not because Mrs. Butterfield was frightened of going behind the iron curtain but because she had tried to conceal the fact that she was not required in her job for a month or more. She went over to the sideboard and removed the two vouchers from the china soup tureen where she kept important papers. She pushed one voucher across the table in Violet's direction, saying, "There you are. You invited me to the party and paid for me ticket to get in so that's yers. You do wif it what you like. As for me, I'm goin'."

Mrs. Butterfield immediately fell apart, all anger drained from her. "Ada, yer not finkin' of goin' *alone?*" she cried.

Very much on her dignity, Mrs. Harris replied, "If me best friend carn't accept me invitation, I suppose I'll 'ave to."

When Mrs. Butterfield wept she did not dissolve into tears, she flooded the premises with them. "Oh, Ada," she wailed, "don't talk like that. You *are* me best friend, the only one I've got in the world. I don't care what 'appens to me, I'll come wif you. Someone's got to look arfter you."

Her surrender would have melted the proverbial heart of stone. Mrs. Harris rose with arms outstretched, and with tears furrowing her cheeks cried, "Oh, Vi, I knew you would," while Vi said, "Ada, I wasn't meanin' to tell a lie. We can use me 'oliday pay for spendin' money." And they melted into a damp embrace, the tiny Mrs. Harris practically vanishing into Mrs. Butterfield's bosom.

After they had dried off and brewed a fresh pot of tea, Ada said brightly, "And you know what, Vi? You could get yer fur coat."

"I *could?* Really?"

"Russia's where they come from. Cheap. Look 'ere, in these pitchers. Everybody's wearin' fur 'ats. You'll 'ave yer coat yet. We'll go tomorrow and get our tickets."

HAVING been to the Intourist office before to collect brochures and found there nothing more menacing than the normal confusion of any thriving travel bureau, and having noted that apparently all transactions were conducted in understandable English, Mrs.

Harris took Mrs. Butterfield along with her the next morning, hoping that the normality of it would help to allay her fears.

The gambit worked, since the bureau was situated among such comforting British establishments as a tobacconist, a sweetshop, the Regent Street Typewriter Company, Raine's Bag Emporium and the National Westminster Bank. This location did much to calm Mrs. Butterfield.

Violet was further soothed by the atmosphere within the office, with its huge blown-up color photographs of Moscow in spring as well as under its winter mantle of snow. And when they stepped up to a counter and the girl behind it said, "Can I 'elp you? 'Ave you seen our list of tours already?" Mrs. Butterfield whispered to Ada, "Blimey, why them Rooshans speak just like the rest of us," and was shooshed by Mrs. Harris. "Don't be stupid, Vi, she's as English as you and me."

Mrs. Harris thought how clever it was of the Russians to staff their office mainly with British assistants, and the fact that she did think this and was listening and looking with a calculating ear and a sharp eye was a measure of what was always present now in her head. If she was going to succeed in getting Lockwood's girl out of the country, she would want to know everything there was to know about these people.

Yet now that she was actually on the threshold of putting her self-imposed mission into action, Ada found herself entertaining a qualm in that her timorous friend, having consented to accompany her to Russia, had no idea of what she, Ada Harris, proposed to do when she got there. She did not wish to tell her since she was certain it would cause Mrs. Butterfield to go up in flames. Nevertheless, she was prepared to gamble and give her the chance for an out. Therefore, with generous heart she turned to her friend and said, "What do you fink, Vi? Shall we? I wouldn't like to see you un'appy. I suppose we could go somewhere else for a bit of a 'oliday. We could call it orf if you say so."

But Mrs. Butterfield was really captivated by the beauty of the posters. No bewhiskered characters bearing bombs from which burning fuses extended were standing about, nor was there anything in the slightest way sinister to be observed, and furthermore the cockney girl behind the counter was a touch of home. Looking up at the huge colored panels she said, "Ain't it pretty. If it's all like that, I wouldn't mind 'avin' a look."

Ada gave Vi's soft fleshy arm a squeeze and said, "Ducks, yer a friend after me own 'eart." Then she presented the vouchers to the girl, who turned them over to a handsome young man who might have been Russian but who spoke perfect English. He examined the vouchers, found them valid and produced application forms.

"Passports, ladies?" he queried, turning glowing dark eyes on them. "And we'll be needing three photographs."

"Got 'em!" exclaimed Mrs. Harris triumphantly. "And our birf certificates."

The young man gave them a charming smile. "I can see you ladies are experienced travelers. No, no, only the photographs." These latter were left over from a trip Mrs. Harris and Mrs. Butterfield had taken to the United States.

"Now, if you will just fill out these papers for me," he went on. "You will find pen and ink at the table."

One sheet was a booking form on which the young man had already entered the number of their package tour. The other sheets, the visa applications, looked somewhat more formidable, the questions printed in Cyrillic letters as well as the English transliteration. Mrs. Harris ran rapidly down the list of questions to see to what extent the Russians might be prying into her private life. Name, citizenship, date of birth, profession and so on—she found them astonishingly innocuous.

Calligraphy was not exactly the strong point of either Mrs. Butterfield or Mrs. Harris, and often one of the latter's clients would exclaim in despair to her husband, "Oh dear, somebody phoned while we were out; Mrs. Harris has left a note and I can't make head or tail of the name." The two women embarked upon the job of filling out the forms, writing painfully and slowly, with considerable blotting and crossing out, so that at the end of a half hour, much of which was consumed by argument, they had finished and the documents were almost legible. Their longest debate had taken place over the question of their professions, which they had to put down beneath their names. Neither of them was ashamed of what she did for a living; it just seemed difficult to find a satisfactory wording.

"Char" would be unintelligible to foreigners. What then? Cleaning Woman? Daily? Household Help? Mrs. Harris decided that a char she was and they'd have to make the best of it, but to have it look a little more imposing she wrote "Char Lady."

Mrs. Butterfield was equally at a loss. A description of her functions at the Paradise seemed too complicated. What was one to call it? Washroom? Powder Room? Ladies' Room? The queries addressed by those in search of her place of work usually curtailed it to "Where's the Ladies'?" The compromise reached with Ada's assistance was that she called herself "Ladies' Attendant."

The completion of this task filled them both with a sense of accomplishment. Ada took the batch back to the counter, where the young man checked them. "Very good," he said. "When the visas are ready, in about two weeks, we will notify you at the address you have given. Package Tour Six A departs from Heathrow on a Sunday at ten thirty a.m., arriving in Moscow at three, where you will remain Monday to Thursday. You will be met at the airport by an Intourist guide who will advise you as to the hotel into which you have been booked. Of course, we cannot give you the exact date of departure until your visas have been granted, or your hotel bookings, but have no worries, everything will be arranged."

Both women left, excited and in good spirits. Mrs. Harris had expected a good deal more red tape, and in her elation at the concurrence of her friend she forgot to be suspicious. Suspicious, that is to say, of the fact that everything had gone so well. Life had taught her that nothing was easy, particularly when one wanted something, and if the realizations of one's desires and ambitions moved too smoothly, that was the time to watch out. However, she was not clairvoyant and hence could not follow what was happening to the documents she and Mrs. Butterfield had left behind them in the Intourist bureau.

Chapter Four

A CHAPTER in Mr. Geoffrey Lockwood's forthcoming book, and one which the Russians were not going to like, stated that the U.S.S.R. was a nation partially paralyzed by a bureaucracy still using methods hung over from the imperial past. The government was a vast conglomeration of ignorant stubborn men, hamstrung as well by terror, a maze from which there were no exits. Each department, wrote Mr. Lockwood, regarded itself as a little independent kingdom answerable to no one, with the chiefs up to ministry level acting entirely upon whim. The result was that any sensible suggestion emanating from the olympus of the Presidium got diluted, reversed, or totally lost in a morass of bureaucracy before it had so much as a chance for the breath of life.

One of the Soviet Union's most important windows to the West was its big travel bureau, Intourist, the visible part of which was reasonably efficient. The same could not be said of some of the Russian bureau staff connected with it.

The two women had hardly left the building in Regent Street when the staff in the back office went to work upon the documents deposited by them. Civil servants began picking their way through the hen-track replies to the questionnaires, which were then promptly photocopied, analyzed and digested for dispatch to the departments that would have to deal with them. Copies would go to the consulate and embassy in London, to Intourist's own headquarters in Moscow and to the all-important KGB's intelligence service, which received immediately a photocopy of the original by electronic transmission.

The clerk called upon to make a précis of the Harris-Butterfield forms, and faced with the problem of deciphering the aforementioned hen tracks, dispatched to his superiors a remarkable document. It revealed that one Lady Ada Harris Char, accompanied by her personal maid, Violet Butterfield, had made application for the five-day tourist trip to Moscow.

Mrs. Harris' elevation to the British aristocracy had been a matter of a simple stroke of the pen. Since the words "Char Lady" meant nothing to the clerk, he had judged it to be an error of reversal and so had corrected it to "Lady Char." The case of who and what was Mrs. Butterfield gave him more trouble, but he solved it by a piece of brilliant deduction. Having decoded her profession as Ladies' Attendant, he reasoned that no British milady would think of traveling without her personal servant, and thus Mrs. Butterfield became attached to "Lady Char" as "and maid."

At Intourist headquarters in Moscow the machinery started at once to put Mrs. Harris and Mrs. Butterfield, along with their fellow passengers, on Package Tour 6A. This called for an unbudgeable routine of visits to historic places, institutes, monuments, and an evening at the Bolshoi Ballet. But there was also a branch of Intourist appointed to sift through the visitors' list in case anyone of importance appeared thereon. Anyone of title fell into that category. British aristocrats in particular were to be handled with kid gloves. This special branch had a neatly concealed budget to supply visiting VIPs with caviar, champagne, chauffeur-driven limousines, country dachas, shoots and other privileges. In due course the précis concerning the impending arrival of Lady Char and maid reached this branch, and the subjects thereof were scheduled for the program called for by Lady Char's eminence.

This exquisite muddle augured most auspiciously for the holiday planned by the two friends. By chance the photocopy of the original applications sent to the KGB wound up on the desk of Comrade Inspector Vaslav Vornov, he of the elephantine memory.

These documents were merely part of the batch of some twenty-five or so comprising just one more scheduled departure of Package Tour 6A. And Comrade Vornov's practiced eye found no suspect who might be doing a bit of spying on the side. There appeared to be simply a group of normal tourists who would, of course, as a precaution, be photographed anyway as they descended from the plane and naturally kept under constant surveillance by the Intourist guide, hotel staff and in particular the "Dragon Lady" who sits by the elevator of every floor of every hotel, handing out the room keys.

Vornov was about to stamp the batch when he was aware that something was niggling at his mind. A name? A profession? Wait. He had it! A name: Mrs. Ada Harris. Hadn't it in some way been connected with that archenemy of the Russian people, the Marquis Hypolite de Chassagne? Yes, there it was on the application: Ada Harris, plus a traveling companion, Violet Butterfield. He picked up the telephone, called the computer section, gave them both names and said, "Run those through and give me the results immediately."

The computer section complied at once. Within a few moments their monster disgorged a fund of most satisfying information. By a brilliant inspiration of total recall Vornov felt himself on the verge of serving Mother Russia and his own career by exposing yet another capitalistic spy plot. He reached for pen and paper and composed the following memo:

Comrade Colonel Gregor Mihailovich Dugliev
Chief of Foreign Division Internal Security
Dear Comrade Colonel Dugliev:

I have been so fortunate as to have uncovered a capitalistic plot on the part of the British to infiltrate spies into the Soviet Union in the guise of tourists on Package Tour 6A, scheduled to leave London for Moscow on Sunday, August 26. It would appear from information supplied by our computer system that over a period of years, a woman by the name of Ada Harris has acted as a courier for a number of known enemies of the Soviet Union, whose dossiers I will be sending you under separate cover. These include the Marquis Hypolite de Chassagne, of whose activities you have been aware for some time.

In 1958 Mrs. Harris made a trip to Paris to contact de Chassagne. The cover she has employed over the years has been that of a char, the British word for a daily cleaning woman, which as you will note appears upon the enclosed copy of her visa application.

Of her companion, Mrs. Violet Butterfield, nothing is known and I consider that our operatives in London have been highly remiss in failing to penetrate the activities of this unquestionably likewise dangerous woman.

It is my recommendation that these two spies be allowed to enter the Soviet Union in order that we may ascertain the nature of their mission. Naturally they will be kept under constant surveillance, but I would presume to counsel that particular attention be paid to the one known as Mrs. Butterfield, who must obviously be the more dangerous of the two since she has been able to operate so long and successfully without her objectives being known. Our branch will supply you with all photographs and information as soon as available.

I sign myself, dear Comrade Gregor Mihailovich, as your faithful and obedient servant.

Vaslav Vornov
Inspector Foreign Division
Internal Security

TEN days later Mrs. Harris and Mrs. Butterfield received a notification from Intourist that their visas had been granted, that they were leaving for Moscow on Aeroflot Flight 101 at ten thirty Sunday morning, August 26, and would they kindly come to Regent Street to collect their tickets, documents, instructions, etc.

MRS. Harris hovered over Geoffrey Lockwood.

She was clad in her going-into-action clothes—felt slippers, overalls, headcloth—and armed with her long-handled dry mop. She was also loaded to the eyebrows with her news, but was unable to find the break to impart it. Mr. Lockwood was reading page proofs of *Russia Revealed.*

He had once instructed her: "When I'm home or working when you come, Mrs. Harris, take no notice of me." He often had been. And never had she dared to initiate a chat. However, at this point she might have to do so.

She tried doing a little banging about with her mop, hoping he might look up and say, Must we have all this noise, Mrs. Harris? but he didn't. She then stood stock-still not far from his desk and simply stared at him hypnotically. Somewhere she had read that if you did that long enough, the other party was bound to look up. Mr. Lockwood didn't.

And so, as was inevitable, Mrs. Harris burst. "Mr. Lockwood, I'm goin' to Russia. Me and me friend, Mrs. Butterfield!"

Mr. Lockwood was vaguely aware that a sentence from the outside world had assailed his ears, and so he said, "That will be nice for you," at which point the one word of the sentence that could have import for him registered, and he looked up. "What? What? Where?"

The breach had been made. Mrs. Harris spilled, "To Russia, to Moscow for five days. Next Sunday. We won the tickets in a lottery. . . ." And here she suddenly dried up, but fixed her glance upon the girl in the photograph on the desk.

Mr. Lockwood laid down his pen and looked up at Mrs. Harris with eyes staring out of a face that had gone quite pale. He said, "Moscow? You? I don't understand."

But he had understood very well, which was the reason for the draining of all color from his face, caused by the sudden whirlwind of impossibilities, fears, yearnings and the barest, hardly even to be considered, thought of salvation. Here was the familiar figure of this spry old lady, leaning on her mop handle, telling him, in effect, that the following Sunday evening she would be in Moscow. Moscow! Liz! Communication! Of course it was out of the question. Impossible!

The astute cockney mind of Ada Harris read him like a book. She knew exactly what he was thinking, which, of course, was the same as she herself had in her mind. "Package Tour Six A," she said. "A proper lark. I . . ." She stopped because Mr. Lockwood had suddenly turned bright red and put his head in his hands. She decided to come right out with it, and said, "Why couldn't I try to get in touch wif yer young lady for you? Maybe give 'er a letter or a message?"

Mr. Lockwood removed his hands from his fevered brow. "Oh, Mrs. Harris, could you? Would you? Oh, my God, a letter. Something for us both to hold on to. A thread." But immediately the reaction set in. "You're very kind to offer, Mrs. Harris, but it's utterly impossible. It's too dangerous."

"Why? What's dangerous?" scoffed Mrs. Harris. "Everything's

fixed up for the 'ole of the trip and tickety-boo. I arranges to meet the young lady and slips 'er the letter. 'Oo's to know?"

"Mrs. Harris, the Russians are the most suspicious people on earth. They're constantly looking for spies, not only under the bed, but in, on top and over and everywhere else. Nothing sets them off like a foreigner trying to contact a Russian national. . . ." His eyes lingered on the photograph of the beautiful Liz. Then he said, "If they were to find the letter on you, you would be in great trouble, and she too."

The more he talked, the happier and more determined Mrs. Harris became. It was not the actual delivery of the missive but the great design of exporting Liz which was so exciting her. She laid her mop aside. "Come on now, Mr. Lockwood, 'oo's goin' to be lookin' for anything on an old biddy like me, admirin' the sights wif a bunch of tourists? I ain't no fool, Mr. Lockwood, what do you fink, I'd be carryin' the bloomin' letter in me 'and and 'avin' the young lady paged? 'Ere's a chance if you've ever 'ad one."

Mr. Lockwood succumbed as he had known he would. The image of the letter he would write to Lisabeta Nadeshda Borovaskaya had formed in his mind, flaming words already curling up from the pages. "Mrs. Harris, if you were to do that for me, I would be grateful to you to the end of my days. I'd forgotten that you'd be with a crowd all the time."

"Then it's settled," said Mrs. Harris happily.

"I'll write the letter immediately. And I'll read it to you as well."

"Read it to me!" exclaimed Mrs. Harris. "I wouldn't dream of it, pryin' into a person's personal affairs."

"But in this instance you must," insisted Mr. Lockwood. "I shall be writing it in Russian, and it would be wrong to ask you to take a letter into Russia without your knowing its contents."

Mrs. Harris' mischievous eyes were all aglow. She felt crowned with romance like a halo. "By the way," she said, "'ow will I find Miss Liz?"

Mr. Lockwood looked up from the typewriter into which he had slipped a sheet of letter paper. He said, "You won't have any difficulty. Perhaps you noticed my agitation when you mentioned

35

the number of your tour. Liz is the regular Intourist guide for Package Tour Six A."

Like so many first-class professional writers, Mr. Lockwood wrote rotten love letters—his cool literacy deserting him for such treacle as "There never has been, there isn't now, there never will be anyone but you, my darling," plus explanations of how it all happened, and that he was trying to "move heaven and earth" to bring their separation to an end.

But Mrs. Harris as he read it to her felt uplifted. She sniffed audibly, tears gathered in her eyes, and if her thought about extracting Liz from behind the iron curtain had begun as a sweet daydream, it had now become a steely determination.

If Mr. Lockwood had had so much as a hint of this, he would, of course, have put an end to the entire operation immediately, but how could he suspect such a thing of the little char? As it was, he had the good sense to take normal precautions for the protection of Mrs. Harris as well as Liz. He folded the sheets, put them into a plain envelope and sealed it without signature or address. He then repeated half a dozen times how deeply grateful he was, adding, "You need only tell her whom it is from. As to money, can I perhaps . . ." and he gestured toward his wallet.

"No, sir, oh no," protested Mrs. Harris. "The trip is all pyde for and we 'ave all we want." She wasn't going to have the exquisite beauty of this romance sullied by the squalor of cash.

Chapter Five

Sunday was one of those azure days provided occasionally by the Celestial Management to reassure the inhabitants of planet Earth that things aren't really as bad as they might think, and Mrs. Harris and Mrs. Butterfield were packed and ready to go.

Ada was elegantly clad in a dark blue Norman Hartnell (By Appointment to Her Majesty the Queen) suit, with white print blouse, patent leather shoes, white gloves, and handbag from Aspreys in Bond Street, an outfit whose parts had once graced two well-liked long-standing clients, Lady Dant and Lady Corrison, who in sudden fits of generosity had bestowed them upon Ada.

Mrs. Butterfield had somehow confined the bulges of her rotund person into a modest traveling outfit which was also a gift. She looked neat but not dowdy, the perfect satellite to Ada. They carried suitcases bearing blue and white stickers and, in addition to tickets and passports, clutched several Intourist folders plus a small booklet instructing visitors to the Soviet Union on how to behave upon arrival there.

In the very last moment, while the taxi that was to take them to the West London Air Terminal was ticking over, Mrs. Harris went to the china soup tureen on her sideboard and removed therefrom an envelope and, with every appearance of not being really very interested in what she was doing, put it into the Aspreys handbag and snapped it shut.

But Mrs. Butterfield, whose nerves had been brought to the very edge by this moment of departure to a land from which she never really expected to return, saw her and queried, "What's that?"

Mrs. Harris replied noncommittally, "Nuffink. Just a letter."

If Mrs. Butterfield had been equipped with bells, she would have jangled like a dozen fire alarms. "A letter?" she cried. "To 'oo? What's it about? What was it doin' 'idin' away in yer soup dish? Ada 'Arris, what are you keepin' from me?"

Ordinarily this inquisition would have irritated Mrs. Harris to the point of a snappish retort. But her conscience was not entirely clear on the subject of dragging her friend off to a place to which she didn't want to go. And there was a further question of ethics. She had been at no pains to conceal her hurt when Vi had tried to hide from her that the Paradise Club had closed down. And now she herself, Ada Harris, was proposing to keep from Mrs. Butterfield that she was acting as a courier for Mr. Lockwood.

"Oh, very well, Vi," she said. "Keep yer hair on. It's a letter to Mr. Lockwood's sweetheart in Moscow 'oo he can't get in touch wif and the both of them dyin' of worry and love," and she quickly recounted the saga of Geoffrey Lockwood and his Liz.

Mrs. Butterfield did not keep her hair on. In fact her coiffure was practically standing up straight as she shouted, "Ada 'Arris,

'ave you gone barmy? Don't you know what 'appens to people
what carries secret papers to Roosha? I just read a harticle where
you carn't even bring a Bible into Roosha. You put that letter right
back where you got it from or I ain't goin'!"

The clickety-clack of the taxi engine outside added to Ada's exasperation and she cried, "Violet Butterfield, yer a silly goose.
There's nuffink in this letter that nobody couldn't read. And what's
more it ain't got any nyme or address on it of anybody, it's just a
poor bloke apourin' out 'is 'eart to 'is sweetie 'oo 'e's lost. All I
know is that 'er name is Liz, I've seen 'er photer, she's the guide on
our tour and when I get 'er alone for a moment I slips 'er the letter
and what's the 'arm in that?" She picked up her suitcase and made
for the door, leaving Mrs. Butterfield stranded in mid-room.

Thus, the latter, compelled to a somewhat ignominious surrender, picked up her own luggage and followed Mrs. Harris out
of the flat, muttering, "Suicide, that's what it is. Daft in the 'ead.
I carn't see any good comin' of this."

This grumbling went on in the taxicab until Ada finally said,
"Oh, Vi, do shut up. We're goin' off on a free 'oliday to enjoy ourselves." The two then sat silent all the way to the air terminal,
which was not exactly the most auspicious beginning to a carefree
vacation. Mrs. Butterfield regarded Mrs. Harris' handbag as
though it contained a bomb.

Nor was Heathrow Airport exactly soothing to the nerves, for
this happened to be the period of the great IRA attack upon
London. Bombs were arriving in the letter post, incendiaries were
being stuffed among the dry goods in department stores, and one
never knew when a car parked at a curb was going to blow sky-
high. Guerrilla action and sabotage were in the air, and Heathrow
was seething with police in uniforms and in plain clothes, intelligence and security officers, not to mention inspection devices for
turning up illicit hardware.

Mrs. Harris caught the atmosphere at once but didn't say anything, not wishing further to alarm Violet. Violet, however, had
her own built-in seismograph. "Ada, what's up? The plyce is
crawlin' wif rozzers." Her mind was simply unable to adjust to the

letter that her friend was carrying, equating it now with the bombs for which the police were so industriously searching, and once more she tackled the subject. "Ada, supposin' one of them cops arsks to look into yer 'andbag and finds that there letter? They'd 'ave the darbies on you quicker than a wink."

Mrs. Harris wanted to say, Don't be a fool, Vi, this ain't Russia, but thought better of it. Besides which, Vi was still at her.

"Come on, Ada, tear it up. You can chuck it over there in that litter bin. When you see the girl you can *tell* 'er all about 'er boy friend."

For a moment Mrs. Harris was of half a mind to do just that, except that there is something connected with a love letter which makes it impossible to dispose of in such a manner. Just then the loudspeaker came to her rescue, announcing Aeroflot Flight 101 to Moscow. Ada said, "That's us, Vi. We're off."

The inspection of passports was cursory, but then they found themselves guided to an enclosure before the departure lounge. There was a long counter in the room, a number of uniformed policemen and two policewomen. It took only the first glimpse of the blue to set Mrs. Butterfield off again. "I told you, Ada," she quavered. "We're for it."

"Shut up, Vi. It's the syme for everybody. Carn't you see?"

Although Mrs. Harris had never before been through one of these airport frisks, she was knowledgeable from complaints of some of her employers as to what a bore it was to travel by air these days with all this inspecting. Indeed the routine has now become familiar to every airline traveler who, unless he is packing a .38 or a hand grenade, goes through it with relief that precautions are taken to make sure that the party sitting next to him isn't loaded for bear.

Handbags, briefcases and packages were given a swift but thorough inspection and then returned to their owners, who were then moved on to a pair of technicians holding electronic metal detectors which they passed over the contours of the passengers. These gadgets would signal the presence of any untoward hardware concealed about their persons.

The effect upon Mrs. Butterfield when the inspector opened Mrs. Harris' handbag and the fatal letter showed between the brochures was shattering. Her round florid face quivered, and gobbets of perspiration gathered on her forehead. If the police were looking for anyone acting in a suspicious manner, they had a beauty. However, the searchers merely dug their fingers into the corners, feeling for small-caliber artillery and, not finding any in the bags of the two ladies, handed them back.

In her agitation Mrs. Butterfield at first did not notice that she had been given Mrs. Harris' handbag while Ada had hers. It was not until she reached the men with the metal detectors that she realized that it was now she who carried the letter. Thus she arrived before them in a state of abject terror which was wholly justified apparently by the results, for as the technicians performed their little contour pantomime both the gadgets gave forth high-pitched screams of triumph.

From Mrs. Butterfield emerged one anguished moan. "Oh my Gawd, the bloody letter." She then melted to the floor in a dead faint. The metal detectors continued to cheer.

Mrs. Harris stared horrified at her friend. Would she have been so foolish because of what she had been told of Mr. Lockwood as to have concealed a weapon upon her person? But no, she had only known about the letter at the last moment.

The police were quietly efficient. They surrounded Mrs. Butterfield. Smelling salts were produced, and when she returned to life, the two policewomen escorted her into a side room. Ada, fuming, swept aside official protest and followed.

Mrs. Butterfield was propped up in a chair, and one of the policewomen was expertly running her hands over her torso when suddenly she started to smile. "Madge," she whispered to her partner, "you won't believe this." Then she turned to Mrs. Butterfield. "Madam, will you please stand up for a moment?"

Mrs. Harris said, "Look 'ere, what's all this? Leave me friend alone. She ain't got nuffink."

Madge had begun to smile too. "I think it's her stays. If madam would be so good as to let us look."

"Stays?" cried Mrs. Harris. "What's that got to do with that thing makin' noises like somebody was cuttin' its throat? Stays is made of plastic. Vi? What the 'ell is it you've got on you?"

Sanity began to return to Mrs. Butterfield and with it, understanding. She raised her skirts. The three women stared. Mrs. Harris said, "Cor blimey, Violet, where did you get that?"

"That" turned out to be one of those long old-fashioned laced-up corsets stiffened with steel ribs.

"What's wrong wif it?" Violet said. "I only wears it when I dresses up because it 'olds me up comfortablelike."

The policewoman explained. "We apologize, madam. Of course, it's the steel. Here, we'll let you out this other door and then you won't be embarrassed."

As the two women at last proceeded to the loading bay, Violet whispered, "I thought their bleedin' machines had found the letter. 'Ere, take yer handbag back. I want nuffink to do wif it."

Chapter Six

IF THE departure from Heathrow was less than soothing to the two travelers, their arrival before the glittering glass façade of Sheremetyevo International Airport in Moscow was chaotic, terrifying, and for Mrs. Harris and all her plans a disaster of the first magnitude. For here not only was there all of the turmoil of the great airport, but it was conducted some fifty decibels louder, in a foreign language among foreign uniforms, with every sign in an unintelligible alphabet, the Cyrillic lettering. Different sounds, different smells, different tempo. Although she had not set foot on the ground, she had entered a foreign country which in no way that she could define had about it a slight feeling of menace.

There had been nothing during the three-and-a-half-hour flight from London to instill this sensation of unease. The plane was clean, its appurtenances neat and the stewardesses crisp in beige linen uniforms, and extraordinarily pretty. The girls had served up an excellent meal with even a dollop of caviar. Both women had announced that at least in the culinary department the

Rooshans were a little bit of all right. And when a stewardess pushing a trolley offered them vodka, wine, beer or Russian champagne, Mrs. Butterfield had exclaimed, "Cor blimey! 'Eavens above. Caviar and champagne and all that lot for free."

Even Mrs. Harris, who was difficult to impress, was affected by this largesse. "I'll 'ave a bit of that white stuff," she had said to the stewardess, pointing to the vodka. "And maybe a glass of beer to 'elp it go down."

Thereafter, somnolence had descended upon the two voyagers and all early misgivings were forgotten.

Touchdown at an airport after having been whizzed through the air seemingly against all the laws of nature is likely to crowd all emotions except relief from the minds of most passengers, and Mrs. Harris and Mrs. Butterfield were at first no different. At last, when the wheels had stopped turning and the jets sighed and whispered to a stop, the chief stewardess had taken a microphone in hand and said, "Please, all keep your seats. Your Intourist guides are here and will call for you by your tour number and you may then leave the plane."

Mrs. Harris felt a small cold chill trickle down her spine. The moment was at hand upon which she had reflected and dreamed many a night since the arrival of the tickets. In another instant she would lay her eyes upon the lost love of Geoffrey Lockwood, Liz the beautiful, Liz in the flesh.

The door in the side of the plane slid open and a dozen or so men and women piled aboard.

"There," said Mrs. Harris. "Them must be the guides!" In her excitement at trying to spot Liz she did not focus too clearly, but there seemed to be three girls who were undeniably pretty. She remembered that in the picture Liz had been wearing a fur hat, so that one could not see her hairstyle.

Three groups of passengers were called and marched down the aisle and into Russia, two of them under the aegis of a pair of the pretty ones. Mrs. Harris had calmed down now, so she saw and heard quite clearly what happened next.

Visually it was that a woman who must have been in her late

fifties and looked as though she had been carved out of weathered wood stepped to the fore and with a strong no-nonsense gesture possessed herself of the microphone from the last user. Two small suspicious eyes glared out of the square face unrelieved by a bitter turned-down mouth and flaring nostrils. Her stiff gray clothes might have been carved out of wood too, and a nondescript hat was perched on a bun of gray hair. She spoke with slightly more of an accent than had the other guides, and the words that fell upon Mrs. Harris' horrified and unbelieving ears were the following: "I am Praxevna Lelechka Bronislava. I am your Intourist guide for Package Tour Six A. All peoples from Package Tour Six A raising their hands."

Twenty-nine went up. Mrs. Harris found herself unable to lift hers so much as a centimeter out of her lap.

"I will show to you Moscow. We will be friends. If you do as I tell you, there will be no trouble. Come, I take you to customs and immigration. If you have obeyed the rules in the little booklet about what you may or may not bring to Russia, you need not be afraid. We will go."

Icy panic had Ada Harris in its grip. Stunned, she gazed after the square retreating back of the Intourist guide. What name? Praxevna Lil-somethin'-or-other. Liz! Liz! What's 'appened to you? What am I to do? For from the moment Mr. Lockwood had revealed that his sweetheart was the guide for Package Tour 6A, Mrs. Harris had never for a single instant doubted that all would go well. Had she known that the Soviet's second government, the KGB, had for this particular tour substituted Praxevna Lelechka Bronislava for Lisabeta Nadeshda Borovaskaya, and placated the latter by temporarily moving her "upstairs," Mrs. Harris might well have lapsed into one of those strange comas that immobilized her in moments of extreme crisis, particularly when brought on through her own actions.

It was Violet who was the first to give vent to an opinion. "Looks like Mr. Lockwood's girl friend is a bit long in the tooth."

The remark started Mrs. Harris' adrenaline flowing again, and she hissed viciously, "Oh Gawd, Vi, that ain't 'er."

44

"No?" said Mrs. Butterfield. "Where is she then?"

The full nature of the calamity now was plain to Ada as she replied, "I don't know," for she was realizing for the first time that she had no means of finding or indentifying the girl beyond her memory of the photograph.

Mrs. Butterfield's system of alarm bells became activated again. "You don't know! That's a fine one. What about that bleedin' letter? You 'eard what that old bag said. If we weren't bringing nuffink in, there wouldn't be nuffink to worry about. Couldn't you go to the loo and stuff it down?"

"For the good Lord's sake, stop worryin', Vi. I've *been* to the loo. It ain't in me 'andbag anymore."

By this time almost all the passengers had passed up the aisle, and there was nothing for the pair to do but follow on, practically the last ones to emerge from the giant airliner and into the focus of the telescopic lenses of the KGB.

IN A concealed room in the upper story of the airport building, one of the KGB agents observing the plane through field glasses gave an exclamation, glanced at two photographs on the table before him and then, using the glasses again, said, "There they are. The small one in blue is the courier, Mrs. Harris. The other is the Butterfield person, whose cover we have not been able to penetrate." He motioned to the camera crew. "The fat one, comrades; concentrate on her. We want every angle, and the pictures had better be good." The cameras, with their long zooming lenses, began to whirr and click. Turning to his companion at the table, the field-glass man asked, "Who is handling this tour?"

The other KGB man replied, "Didn't you see her? It's Praxevna Lelechka Bronislava."

Field Glasses grunted. "She's one of our best. If anyone can break the fat woman's cover, she will."

THE startling development of the nonappearance of Liz had assumed a completely disproportionate importance in the mind of Mrs. Harris, as though she had incurred some great personal loss.

In a state of semishock, she endured the interminable waits in customs and immigration, the rudeness of the inspectors and the thorough search of her belongings. She was not even stirred by Mrs. Butterfield's constant agitation that the now useless letter would be found, which it wasn't because Mrs. Harris had artfully concealed it upon her person.

Nor did she remember much of the bus ride at dusk, first through forests of birch and pine and later past blocks of flats, identical rectangles of glass and concrete or stone. She was only subliminally aware of the pandemonium reigning in the Hotel Tolstoy with the arrival of their busload of thirty tourists to augment another hundred or so already milling about the reception desk.

The Tolstoy was one of the older hotels in Moscow, situated near a corner of Krasnaya Square with an excellent view of some of the city's more sensational architecture. However, because of its state of dilapidation, the hotel was allocated to package tours, a classification which did not improve the temperaments of management and service, who were jealous of the glittering new Rossiya Hotel and of the other hostelries that received the cream of the visitors. And so any time the staff did not spend snarling at the clients was passed shouting and waving their arms at one another. Tourists whose reservations turned out to be unconfirmed or nonexistent were now jostling and angry, women were weeping with fatigue and frustration, luggage was piled up helter-skelter. It was into this inferno that Praxevna Lelechka brought her little flock.

Observation and intuition were two of Mrs. Harris' strong points. Had her mind not been so fogged by disappointment, she certainly would have been suspicious at the ease with which their guide elbowed her way to the reception desk and in a moment returned and, ignoring the rest of the tour, said to Ada and Violet, "Come, I have your room." Even the sluggish elevator appeared to obey her will, and when its doors opened, she rudely but efficiently shouldered a path through the waiting throng with the two in tow, giving an order to the operator, who immediately closed out the rest of the horde and took them up to the seventh floor.

In the corridor, when they got off the elevator, they were confronted by a woman seated at a desk, an obese creature who like their guide was a decorated veteran of the KGB. But whereas Praxevna Lelechka resembled a wood carving, the other was like a large gray bloated spider ready to pounce. Her eyes were as malevolent as a spider's and her mouth seemed to be especially molded for stinging. She had no neck; the gross head simply sat upon her corpulency. She was named and engraved in Ada's mind as "Mrs. 'Orrible."

The two women exchanged a few words in Russian, Mrs. 'Orrible handed over the key and the guide said, "Come, I show you your room." She led the Englishwomen down the corridor, unlocked a door and ushered them into room 734. Immediately, a middle-aged maid in a neat apron and cap appeared and was addressed, again in Russian, by their escort. She looked frightened and Mrs. Harris automatically registered this.

"So," said the guide, "see the view. Wonderful. Remain here. I will come and take you to your dinner. Thank you." She left, but before she closed the door Mrs. Harris did see that the maid, who had left the room, had stationed herself in a corner of the corridor outside.

During her career as a daily, Ada Harris had encountered every kind of dwelling and type of decoration, and here she found herself immersed not unpleasantly in neo-Victorian red plush tassels, brass bedsteads, fringed bedcovers and on second glance a considerable amount of dirt and dilapidation. The chambermaid obviously wasn't much of one.

It was this assessment of the room's frowsiness that brought Mrs. Harris back to the simple facts of who and where she was, and that in indulging her fancies about Mr. Lockwood and his Liz she was being a bit of a fool. He had said that Liz was the Intourist guide for Package Tour 6A and would be greeting them in the airport. Well, she wasn't, and she hadn't. And in the meantime here Ada was on a paid-up holiday on which she had dragooned her best friend against her will, and what any sensible person would do would be to forget Lockwood and Company and begin to enjoy herself. This settled, she glanced out of the window and her enjoyment began at once, for she was gazing upon a scene that was breathtaking.

She had no idea of their location and thus did not know that this window gave onto an extended part of the formidable Kremlin wall, St. Basil's Cathedral, the tomb of Lenin and Red Square. Night had supplanted dusk, lighting was in full blaze, and Mrs. Harris found herself looking upon a wondrous illumination of colored walls, belfries, church steeples—some shaped like onions, others wearing what appeared to be oriental turbans. Giant red stars gleamed from tower pinnacles, and the bulbous tops of the churches were picked out in blues and yellows. She could only think of it as a bejeweled fairy city. She was genuinely moved and felt suddenly glad she had come.

Then Mrs. Butterfield emerged from the bathroom, to which she had repaired immediately they were alone. She said, "There's no loo paper."

This bald statement threw Mrs. Harris off the track of her windowside reverie. "What?" she said. "No what?"

"Loo paper," repeated Mrs. Butterfield. "And what's more, when you pulls the flush, nuffink 'appens. You call this a 'otel?"

"What's all this?" said Mrs. Harris. "Let's 'ave a look." She went into the bathroom and came out carrying the cardboard centerpiece usually found in the heart of rolls of toilet tissue. "No loo paper and not no other kind of paper either," she said. "And no stopper for the barftub. Flyspecks on the mirror and the light don't work. Let's get on the blower and 'ave a little word wif somebody."

The telephone, however, wasn't having any. It gave forth clicks, buzzes and a roar of grating static, but no human voice.

"Is this rotten old dump the best they got?" asked Mrs. Harris. In spite of the elegant view and the excitement of travel, the room not properly cleaned or in working order put her out of sorts.

She was suddenly aware that Mrs. Butterfield, eyes bulging with terror, had gone into a most extraordinary pantomimic dance, lifting first one foot, then the other from the floor; then pointing to the chandelier; next sealing her lips with her fingers.

"Crikey, luv," said Mrs. Harris, "what's got into you?"

Violet went "Shhhhhh," and putting her mouth practically into Ada's ear, whispered, "Bugs. Ain't you read all the 'otels in Roosha got microphones? They can 'ear every word yer sayin'."

"Oh, they can, can they?" cried Mrs. Harris, aloud to Violet's horror. "Bugs, eh?" and looking up into the tarnished brass chandelier, she bawled, "You up there, anybody what's listenin', we need loo paper!"

This challenge having gone unregarded, Mrs. Harris said, "Come on, we'll go and 'ave a word wif Mrs. 'Orrible."

When she went to the door and yanked it open, the chambermaid practically fell into the room. Mrs. Harris said, "What's all this? Listenin' at key'oles?"

The maid let out a frightened squeak of "*Nyet,*" and immediately began to polish the doorknob.

"Look 'ere, we want some loo paper," said Mrs. Harris.

"She don't understand English," Violet said, which was right on the nose.

"*Loo paper!*" cried Ada, exhibiting the cardboard tube and pitching her voice up to the decibels used by foreigners who think that if they shout in their own language, they will be understood.

The chambermaid shook her head and said, "*Nyet.*"

"Come on, Vi," Ada said. "Maybe old 'Orrible speaks English." But this decision, implemented by action as they came out of the room, sent the chambermaid into a perfect flurry of *nyets* and finger wavings. She tried to push both women back inside. Mrs. Harris' ire reached a fast boiling point. "'Ere, 'ere, what's this, a bloody jail? Get yer 'ands off me. Go on, scarper, before I loses me temper."

Aided by Violet's bulk, the woman was brushed out of the way. She burst into tears and fled.

"Now, what got into 'er?" Mrs. Harris said. "Funny people, them Rooshans." At that moment she had not yet the faintest suspicion that they were under the strictest kind of surveillance, and that behind the service door through which the maid had disappeared was a KGB operative, who reported to headquarters that the occupants of room 734 had left the premises.

The said occupants marched down the corridor to where the spider woman sat silently and stolidly, with only the glitter of her eyes to show she was alive.

Mrs. Harris, her dander still up, said, "We want loo paper," and exhibited her cardboard tube. "Understand? What you find in any harfway decent run 'otel."

From Mrs. 'Orrible's mouth emerged the chilly words, "No more."

Mrs. Harris was not going to be put off. "What do you mean, no more paper? Then why don't you bleedin' well send out and buy some? Plenty is bein' paid for our room."

The stinger of a mouth twitched. "No more. Go away."

Mrs. Harris now went into full spate. "Go away, me foot. Where's yer manners? We're visitors 'ere. No more where? In the 'otel? In the 'ole bloody country? Get me the manager, or I'll 'ave yer 'otel down around yer ears."

At this point there occurred an unexpected diversion. The door opposite Mrs. 'Orrible's desk, numbered 701, opened partly to let the most extraordinary head, which at first glance resembled an interested beaver's, pop forth. "It won't do you any good. There ain't any in the whole country. Hullo," said the head. "Someone from home." Keen amused eyes stared through outsize spectacles. "How would you two ladies like to join me in a little drink?" The head then introduced itself. "Sol Rubin, Rubin's Consolidated Paper Company Limited."

Chapter Seven

WHILE a few more seconds ticked away into eternity, the tableau in the corridor remained static, like a stopped film, except that an inviting smile had spread over the features of Mr. Rubin. His face was a conglomeration of contradictions, much too small for the enormous swatch of dark bushy hair. His mouth with the protruding front teeth gave it its beaver aspect, plus the inevitable businessman's mustache that spread above it. His nose was sufficiently prominent to hold up his large thick-lensed glasses. The thing about Mr. Rubin was his infectious gaiety. His overall effect

upon Ada was a calming one; she always regretted it when she lost her temper. And he seemed to know something about this paper situation. She said, "I'm sure that's very kind of you, sir. Ada 'Arris is the name, and this is me friend, Violet Butterfield. If we wouldn't be puttin' you out . . . ."

"Not at all, ladies, not at all. An unexpected pleasure." His speech was that of the reeducated ex-cockney. He opened the door to show that attached to the unusual head was a spry little body, snappily clad in the latest style, and invited them to enter with a grandiose wave of his arm.

The grating voice of Mrs. 'Orrible spoke from the pulpit. "Is not allowed for ladies to visit gentlemen's rooms."

"Oh, come orf it," Ada said. "At our age, what do you fink's goin' to 'appen? The gentleman's invited us for a drink."

"That's it," said Mr. Rubin, enlarging his gesture of welcome so that he now struck the attitude of a dancing master. "Don't pay no attention. She's new anyway. I don't know what happened to Annie, the one that's been on this floor. Annie was a little bit of all right. Knew how to close an eye. Come in!"

The two sailed in beneath the malevolent glare of Mrs. 'Orrible, and as soon as the door had closed behind them, she reached for the telephone and dialed the number of her superior.

"Pavel? Tashka. They have made contact."

"With whom?"

"With the Jew, Rubin, in 701. They went into his room."

"Ah!" Pavel's voice grew heavy with sarcasm. "Right under your nose? And you did not try to prevent it?"

"I have no orders to resort to violence, Comrade."

"That is true. Besides, the orders are to be very careful with Rubin. There are two ministries involved."

The obese woman sighed in relief. "Perhaps it is for the best, for you will be able to monitor all that is said in the room. They will surely disclose the nature of the contact."

There was rather too long a pause from the other end of the telephone, followed by: "There have been some temporary complications. The necessary repairs have not yet been made. That department has never really been cooperative. Install, yes. Repair, no."

"Boris and Anoutchka are on the floor. Boris has a listening device. Do you want him to attach it to the door?" Boris was the KGB man concealed with the chambermaid and quarreling with her behind the service door.

Pavel's voice spoke sharply. "Don't be a fool, Tashka. I told you the Rubin area is highly sensitive. If it ever comes out why he is here, we will be taking residence in Siberia. Find the guide Praxevna Lelechka and get those two out of there." This was followed by an expressive Russian oath and a clunk as the phone was hung up.

WITHIN the confines of room 701, which was in the same state of crumbling Victorian glory as that of Violet's and Ada's, Mr. Rubin was holding a bottle of London gin, saying, "How do you like yours?"

"With just a drop of water," replied Mrs. Harris, "and me friend 'ere likes it straight. Ain't that right, Vi?"

Mrs. Butterfield said, "If the gentleman doesn't mind." She was not wholly at ease, for any unusual situation in which she found herself was always fraught with possible doom.

While Mr. Rubin was pouring, Ada's bright mischievous eyes were exploring the room to see if she could guess who and what this attractive little man might be. "Salesman" was the answer she rang up from a pile of sample books she saw upon a table.

Mr. Rubin raised his own glass of clear liquid and said, "To you ladies," and then half under his breath added, "and to Ivan."

The two women raised theirs, and Mrs. Harris replied to the toast. "Yer very good 'ealth, sir, and we're very much obliged to you for yer kindness," and then her curiosity getting the better of her she asked, " 'Oo's Ivan?"

"Ah, Ivan," repeated Mr. Rubin. "Ivan, the master of the hot ruble. He's the hotel porter. You want it, he'll get it for you if you've got the lolly. That is, the hard stuff—you know—foreign currency." He held up the gin bottle. "Where do you think this came from? I can't stand that vodka. And like I said, Annie—I call her Annie but her name is Anoutchka—knew when not to look. I don't know how this new bag is going to work if she stays on permanent."

Mr. Rubin needn't have worried. The new bag had been briefed to let anything except shooting irons or people go into room 701; for not only was Ivan a pillar of the thriving black market, but he was also a trusted connection of the KGB, which had ordered him to see that Mr. Rubin was supplied with anything he wanted to keep him in good temper and quiet. Ivan, furthermore, was compelled to split half of his hard-currency take with his KGB contact, but of none of this was Mr. Rubin aware.

"Cheers," he said, and raised his glass once again. "And what are you two ladies doing in this godforsaken town?"

This last phrase agitated Mrs. Butterfield to the point where she took a big gulp of straight gin and went into a splutter.

"We won it in a raffle," replied Mrs. Harris. "I mean the trip. We couldn't afford it otherwise. I work as a daily and me friend 'ere looks after the ladies in the Paradise Club."

"To Britain's bulwark," Mr. Rubin toasted. "I love you both."

Mrs. Harris didn't quite know how to take this affection, but put it down to gin. "Nice of you to say so, Mr. Rubin." Then she inquired, "Just what is it you travel in, Mr. Rubin?"

"Aha!" he said. "So you've guessed. By the way, you can call me Sol," and he took another solid slug. As the gin took effect it tended to elimate his "h's." Then he said, "Paper, I'm the biggest bloody paper concern in the 'ole United Kingdom. Rubin's Grade A Soft-as-Silk toilet tissue—say 'soft-as-silk' and you know it's Rubin's."

"Oh," said Ada Harris, making a lightning calculation. "And what they ain't got any of here is—"

"Exactly," concluded Rubin. "And if they knew that I was admitting to you or anybody else that such was the case, they might even put me away. They got a lot of stinkers running this country."

Here Mrs. Butterfield exploded into her pantomimic dance of the bug, and Rubin laughed uproariously.

"Oh, them," he said. "I've got 'em all. Nothing else to do to keep busy. Do you know how long I've been 'ere? Eight weeks! While they're trying to make up their mind. I could give you a guided tour of Moscow, only when I go out there's this KGB bloke on my tail all the time. So mostly I stick to me room and try to amuse myself. This last lot they don't even seem to have tried to repair. 'Ere, I'll show you."

Mr. Rubin then took the two women on an electronic tour of the premises and pointed out the minute microphones, each one with the wires carefully snipped.

Mrs. Harris was fascinated. "'Oo'd have believed it? But are you sure you got them all?"

"Oh, yes," replied Rubin. "You get to know their minds."

"But what's the big secret?" Mrs. Harris asked, puzzled.

"Ha!" exclaimed Rubin. "*Nekulturni.* That's a word I picked up here. Not cultured. The Russ is trying to impress everyone with 'is culture. It's not cultured to be caught with your pants down without—" He interrupted himself, as Mrs. Butterfield was showing signs of embarrassment. "It's not like it was only 'ere," he continued. "They're queuing up for it in Japan, and the Chinese have a mission in London right now trying to buy the stuff. Shortages all over, and me sitting on three 'undred and eighty million rolls. That's what the Ministry of Supply sent for me for. I'm the only firm that's got it."

"Then why don't you sell it to 'em?" Ada asked.

"Because the minister of Purchase doesn't like Jews and won't okay the tab. The big boys in the government don't want to know about it and are letting the two departments fight it out, and I'm stuck 'ere."

The ever practical-minded Ada asked, "Why don't you scarper and sell it to somebody else?"

"Can't," snapped Rubin. "They've picked up me passport."

Mrs. Butterfield gave a little shriek. "See, Ada, I told you what they were like!"

Ada, torn between calming her friend's ever-present fears and not denying Mr. Rubin, said, "But they've got to give it back—"

Rubin snorted. "Not them. We're in Russia, ladies, where anything can 'appen. I'll give you an example. They 'ad their own

55

factory where they made their own rolls—enough to supply everybody. Well, the bloke that managed it had been allocated a big shipment of paper. 'E never got it. The chappie that runs the greeting-card syndicate got to somebody in Supply first, and diverted the load to his own factory. So now they've got a couple of billion greeting cards and no rolls of tissue. But greeting cards ain't what you need when—"

"I think we'd better be goin'," put in Mrs. Butterfield.

"Just one more little drinkie first," urged Mr. Rubin. And, having replenished, he raised his glass and shouted, "To paper! Everybody wants paper! Wallpaper, blotting paper, paper 'andkerchiefs, paper plates— You can't buy it, and soon there won't be enough trees left to make it."

There was a stiff rap on the door and it opened to reveal the dead-tree figure of their guide. Behind her, at her desk, loomed Mrs. 'Orrible. It was a depressing sight.

The guide said, "Did I not say to you to stay in your room?"

"Did you now, dearie?" Mrs. Harris replied. "I suppose we must 'ave forgot."

Mr. Rubin waved the gin bottle. "Come in, girls, and have a drink. Plenty more where this came from."

The two Russians exchanged glances of anger and bafflement. Whatever was being cooked up by the KGB with regard to the two Englishwomen, this scene was not included.

The guide finally said, "Is not time for drinking. Is time for eating. Come, I take you. Good Russian dinner."

Violet said, "Maybe we'd better, Ada," and then to Rubin, "Thanks ever so."

Ada added, "It's been a treat and we're much obliged. I 'opes as you makes out wif the you-know-what."

Mr. Rubin waved them out of the door. "It's been a pleasure."

The exit was managed with fair dignity.

When they returned upstairs after their meal, their guide, who to Ada and Violet had become "Auntie Praxie," still hung about. She had sat with them during dinner, and now something that Mrs. Harris had felt as a kind of growing irritation snapped and she

56

asked, "You sleepin' with us, dearie? That'll be a fair treat but no extra charge I 'ope."

The guide said impassively, "I just like to see things right for you. I come in the morning and show you breakfast. Sleep nice."

They entered their quarters and Mrs. Harris' eyes did a hundred and eighty degrees about the room. She said, "Well, at least the maid's been 'ere, turned the beds down and done a bit of tidyin' up. It's been a day, 'asn't it?"

This chatter she continued for a moment or two in order to distract Mrs. Butterfield from what she hoped her friend would not notice. The room and their belongings had been searched.

It was only then that she realized what had been biting her ever since their arrival. They had been under constant watch, except for their temporary escape into the dispensary of Mr. Rubin.

She pressed her hand to her side and felt the crackle of Mr. Lockwood's letter, but it was reassuring no longer. Was Violet right, and was there really some danger connected with it? Was that why Liz had not been there—was she already in trouble? Remembering the photo and Mr. Lockwood's expression, a feeling of sadness rather than fear pervaded her.

However, the discovery that they were being watched was disturbing, sufficiently so that while Mrs. Butterfield was wrestling with the bathroom amenities, Ada took certain precautions with regard to the letter and then returned it to her handbag.

Chapter Eight

THE next day Mrs. Harris and Mrs. Butterfield with the rest of the visitors were swept away on the inflexible routine of Package Tour 6A. When the tourist party was assembled at the hotel entrance to board the bus, Ada's sharp powers of observation, plus the warning of the search the night before, led her to an examination of their fellow travelers. Two of them were men she had not seen before, and there was a subtle something in the cut of their clothes which just wasn't right for foreigners. Were these then watchers? And if so, what on earth for?

For a moment she was almost tempted to excuse herself, go back to their room and do what Violet had bidden her—tear up the letter if that was what this was all about and flush it down the loo—until she remembered that the loo didn't flush. But something else also prevented this: the thought that somehow she might yet encounter Liz, by accident even see that lovely melancholy face somewhere in a crowd.

Marveling, they paraded across the cobbled stones of Red Square. Wherever they went, Mrs. Harris was aware that the odd pair out were always managing to be close behind her and Mrs. Butterfield. They traipsed past the fabulous-colored turban-topped St. Basil's Cathedral, the GUM state department store, which didn't look like a store but like a palace, and the thirty-two-hundred-room Rossiya Hotel, which didn't look like a hotel but like a store. Ultimately they approached the *pièce de résistance* of the morning's tour, Lenin's tomb. It was strangely squat and square after all the curves and peaks of churches and towers, a solid edifice of red granite with a single band of black labradorite across the front bearing the name Lenin in Cyrillic lettering. A long dark line of figures, patient men and women in rough ill-cut clothes, had been standing for hours waiting to get in.

The guide said, "We will now visit the tomb of Lenin, our most glorious hero. Because you are tourists you will be permitted to go in before the others. You will go quietly and move along quickly, for many people are waiting."

Violet said, "'Oo did she say it was?"

"Lenin. 'E's the one made the Revolution. They got 'im buried 'ere, but you can 'ave a look at 'im."

They filed through the entrance porch between two immaculate soldiers standing guard with bayonets fixed, and then down a flight of stairs by barely enough light to see. They found themselves in an underground chamber that appeared to be lit only by the glow emerging from the glass case around Lenin's coffin. At the open sarcophagus they paused and looked down upon the extraordinary figure of the man with the high brow and small pointed beard, clad in a black suit, his eyelids closed as if in sleep.

"Lor' luv ya," Mrs. Butterfield hissed. "Don't 'e look natural?"

Somewhere in the darkness a guard whispered, "Ssssshhh!"

"No, 'e don't," replied Mrs. Harris and felt a sudden sadness and pity gripping her heart. "He looks like 'e's from Madame Tussaud's Waxworks." And suddenly she found she could almost not bear it, and her whisper was too audible as she said, "It's a rotten shyme. Why couldn't they give the little man a decent burial if they thought so much of 'im? Tarting 'im up and every Tom, Dick and 'Arry starin' down at 'im through the glass cover and 'im not bein' able to say so much as bugger off."

She felt herself pushed from behind. "Go please, move along."

"Narsty for the poor little feller," was Ada's final comment as she did so.

Moscow, Mrs. Harris was finding, was a constant and often delightful series of prize packages. You never knew what anything was going to be like. Driving through the streets in the tour bus, she was depressed by the drab shapeless clothing of the inhabitants and even more dispirited by the sight of the old women in black, and young ones too, sweeping the streets with brooms made of twigs. She did not fail to notice the big black chauffeur-driven cars with men lounging comfortably in the back, and she whispered to Mrs. Butterfield, "Looks like some are more communist than others around 'ere. They ain't no different from us. Women gets the dirty work." In spite of the grandiose architecture, she sniffed the sour aroma of universal poverty.

And then, the next minute, they were shuffling through the fabulous Kremlin museum known as the Armory. Here they were blinded by the display of swords, thrones, icons, Bibles, robes, headgear of solid gold encrusted with diamonds, emeralds and rubies, copes embroidered with pearls, crowns blazing with diamonds and emeralds, and a scepter and orb set with ancient rubies. Here was wealth that defied the imagination, from the delicate Fabergé jeweled Easter eggs to the imperial coaches glittering with gold paint.

"Cor blimey," Violet said. " 'Oo owns all this stuff?"

Ada said, "I wouldn't know, but makes our crown jewels look like

Woolworth's, don't it? Maybe if they divvied it up so everybody 'ad a share like they talk about, there'd be enough for everyone to 'ave a decent suit of clothes and maybe get things workin' in the barfroom as well."

The guide appeared at their elbow. "We show you examples of wonderful Russian workmanship. They belong to the people."

From the Kremlin, Ada and Violet found themselves transported to a drab hotel dining room where they were served an almost inedible meal by surly waiters who practically threw the dishes at them. From thence they were wafted to the splendors of the Bolshoi Opera and Ballet Theater, where *The Sleeping Beauty* was being performed. But even here Ada was aware of the weird contrast between the audience—drab, square-bodied men and women who looked as though they had all been chiseled out of granite—and the slender dancers onstage, all grace and beauty, floating through the air. She could hardly believe that those beautiful airy creatures in their glowing costumes and the thickset masses watching them were the same people, Russians all.

So exciting and novel was their prize-package tour turning out to be that the time flew by and the affair of Mr. Lockwood and his lost ladylove began to dim, and even the fact that someone seemed obviously keeping a watch over them faded rather into the picture of what this marvelous city and astonishing people were really like. Mrs. Harris had even forgotten about the letter now hidden in a compartment of her handbag.

If there had been one disappointment, neither Mrs. Harris nor Violet had seen fit to mention it. This was the matter of Mrs. Butterfield's fur coat. Ada kept quiet because they had not seen such an article on the horizon or anywhere else, and Mrs. Butterfield refrained from calling attention to it since as a lifelong pessimist she never expected anything good to happen to her. The only furs they encountered were the tattered garments to be seen on the backs of peasants from the northern regions. Of the modest musquash there was no sign, even in the great GUM department store. Fur hats peeled from some nondescript quadruped were worn by most Russian men, and that was that.

There was gossip among the tour members that there was a shop called the Berioska that was stocked with treasures which could be bought with foreign currency. However, none of the members of this particular package tour having shown any signs of the necessary affluence, no visit to this super emporium was scheduled. And now their time was running out.

Ada Harris, who wished to make certain that there was actually nothing in the pelt line within her friend's reach, had asked whether they might be let off for an afternoon's shopping at this mart. "*Nyet.* Impossible," the guide had replied. "It is not scheduled in this tour. Besides which, you would find the articles are far too expensive."

Praxevna Lelechka had her orders. Never for a moment were the two women to be allowed out of sight. And so, with regret at the disappointment she had caused her friend, Ada was compelled to admit defeat. But this was before a telephone conversation took place between Comrade Colonel Gregor Mihailovich Dugliev, chief of Foreign Division Internal Security, and Vaslav Vornov, inspector, Foreign Division Internal Security, in which the chief, having demanded a report on the activities of the two Englishwomen and having received it, gave his subordinate seven different kinds of Russian hell. It went something like this:

GREGOR MIHAILOVICH DUGLIEV: Comrade Inspector Vaslav Vornov, have you a report upon the two Englishwomen spies, Harris and Butterfield?

VASLAV VORNOV: Right here before me, Comrade Chief.

DUGLIEV: Well?

VORNOV: Nothing. Outside of the regrettable incident in the room of the paper merchant, from which time surveillance was increased, there has not been a second when they have not been with a group or under even heavier observation.

DUGLIEV: What are you saying? [Dugliev's voice was ominous.] Do you mean to tell me that this pair has never been permitted to be off by themselves, naturally thoroughly shadowed but so that we would have had the opportunity to arrest and interrogate them?

VORNOV: But, Comrade, my orders were plain that they were to be handled under Regulation Twelve. Their effects have been searched. No codes or suspicious articles have been found. All the electronic devices in their room are in working order. The medicament which induces talking in one's sleep has been administered during their evening meal. The usual approaches to tempt them to commit misdemeanors—offers of special currency-exchange rates and illegal spirits, bids to purchase their belongings at tempting prices—all have been rejected. In view of the ah . . . ah . . . advanced ages of the suspects, the sexual approach has been omitted. But every moment of their presence is accounted for.

DUGLIEV: Idiot! Imbecile! Clown! Dolt! [And he followed with a number of Russian epithets too difficult for translation.] Do you not know that a Section A has been added to Regulation Twelve? Suspects on a package tour are to be given a half day by themselves in order that they may have the opportunity of carrying out whatever their assignment might be, so an *agent provocateur* may plan some . . . Half-wit! Numbskull!

VORNOV: But, Comrade, no such Section A has reached my desk. . . .

DUGLIEV: Bungler! Oaf! You should have thought of it yourself.

VORNOV: But, Comrade Gregor Mihailovich, my report shows that these women are either too clever for us or innocent. As I told you, they have resisted every effort we have made to tempt them. What good would a shopping tour do, surrounded by the entire secret police?

DUGLIEV: Featherbrain! Donkey! Dunce! Don't you know that it is impossible for any foreigner, or even Soviet citizen, to walk from Gorky Street to Red Square without committing at least three misdemeanors, not to mention felonies, for which they may be arrested and interrogated for up to three days? If this pair has asked for any free time, see that it is granted immediately. Then alert Section Five of the *agents provocateurs* and see that there are special operatives along their route.

AND thus it was that at a quarter to four on that sunny afternoon, Ada Harris and Violet Butterfield were informed by Praxevna Lelechka that they could go on their shopping tour. "Do not get lost. If so, simply say the name of your hotel. Someone will help you find it."

A moment later they were standing alone in the heart of Moscow. "Which way shall we go?" asked Ada.

"I don't know," quavered Mrs. Butterfield, for, suddenly separated from the security of the group, apprehension had closed in again. "Maybe we shouldn't 'ave left them. Somefink awful might 'appen."

"Nonsense," replied Ada, delighted to be on the loose. "We'll 'ave a go at that Berioska Shop. It's just around the corner."

Chapter Nine

BUT the Berioska Shop was exactly what their guide had indicated, a mart for millionaires and a waste of time for anyone whose pockets were not loaded with traveler's checks. When the Soviets went out after foreign currency, they weren't kidding. The brochures handed to the tourist promised the best that Russia had to offer in precious stones, antique gold and silver, exquisite carvings, carpets, handwoven silks and laces, not to mention valuable fur overcoats once worn by a variety of small animals.

Ada and Violet wandered through this tastefully set out treasure-house goggle-eyed. The prices were marked in dollars, pounds, francs and marks. "Lor' luv us," said Mrs. Harris, "what are we doin' in 'ere? Five quid would be just about the price of the wrappin'."

Nevertheless, an article marked anywhere from three thousand to ten thousand dollars when you haven't got it can, in an odd way, give pleasure, particularly if one is able to say, as Mrs. Butterfield did of several items, "Blimey, I wouldn't 'ave that in me own 'ouse if you give it to me." And so, after having thoroughly enjoyed their first half hour of liberty, Mrs. Ada Harris and Mrs. Violet Butterfield emerged from the shop into the street and to that which was waiting for them, namely the *crème de la crème* of the KGB and *agents provocateurs* in varying disguises. The irony of the affair was that this horde of special agents was not needed to induce Mrs. Harris and Mrs. Butterfield to violate any of the hundreds of regulations designed to ensnare the Soviet citizen or visitor and put him or her temporarily into pokey. It all happened neatly and cleanly by itself.

As the two women walked onto the sunlit pavement, wondering in what direction they should go, a dusty, battered, vintage Bentley drew up. It was packed with people, six young men and four girls. All were clad in jeans and sweat shirts, bearing the names and insignia of various American universities such as Yale, Princeton and the University of Oklahoma. The sweat shirts were fashionable abroad at that time and could be bought all over Europe.

The weird vehicle and the very un-Russian-looking occupants emerging from it caused passersby to stop out of curiosity, and in a moment a small crowd had gathered. At this point the leader of the group, a tall boy with a gaunt face and fiery eyes, began intoning, "The Lord is always with us. Let us all sing together in praise of the Lord who is our Saviour and support." Another young man produced a cornet and blew the first notes of that fine old hymn "Rock of Ages." Nine youthful voices took up the refrain.

Mrs. Harris was enchanted, for they were singing in English. "Now, 'oo would 'ave thought there'd be something like this 'ere in Moscow?" she said. "C'mon, Vi, let's let 'em 'ear us," and she joined in lustily. The Russian bystanders remained mute but were fascinated.

They had finished "Rock of Ages" and were in the middle of "Jesus Wants Me for a Sunbeam" when two large black Zim cars loaded with men in uniform were seen approaching.

The youthful group then performed a miracle which could only have been the result of long experience. They whipped out handbills, pressed one upon each of the spectators, piled into their jalopy and were off around the corner and out of sight. The spectators were not far behind with the vanishing act, and by the time the two black Zims drew up, only Mrs. Harris and Mrs. Butterfield were left standing there reading their handbills.

The documents were smudgy but the message was clear. FORSAKE NOT JESUS AND HE WILL NOT FORSAKE THEE. CARRY THE MESSAGE OF JOY TO THY RUSSIAN BROTHERS FOR THE LORD IS AT

HAND AND HE WILL BE THY SUCCOR. PRAY FOR HIS LIGHT TO SHINE THROUGH THE DARKNESS OF THIS BENIGHTED COUNTRY, and more of the same. At the bottom was imprinted in smaller type: Victoria Evangelical Missionary Bible Society, 31 Stratton Street, Victoria, London, W.1.

Ada was just saying, "What do you know, Stratton Street . . ." when the Zims disgorged their contents of a mixed bag of Russian lawmen, who promptly placed Mrs. Harris and Mrs. Butterfield under arrest for possession of religious tracts containing statements inimical to the security of the Union of Soviet Socialist Republics. The women were well and truly nobbled, since they were the only people in sight and were clutching the incriminating documents.

Among the force deployed against Ada and Violet were not only Colonel Gregor Mihailovich Dugliev and Inspector Vaslav Vornov, but an even higher KGB official who had read the dossier of the two alleged spies. But to his delight—because when a foreigner was framed in this manner there were always likely to be repercussions in the Western press—it so happened that the arrest of this dangerous pair could be carried out by an ordinary policeman on the relatively minor charge of being in possession of illicit foreign religious literature. The point was the KGB had them.

At first the two women did not know what was happening, for all the talk was conducted in Russian until the policeman, pointing to the incriminating evidence, said in English, "Forbidden! You are under arrest. Come with us," and at that juncture, and just before they were bundled into one of the Zims, they knew.

At this moment there occurred an incident which happened completely outside the ken of the KGB crowd, as well as Ada's and Violet's. A car drove by which attracted no attention whatsoever; nor should it have, for it was one of the Intourist vehicles usually reserved for VIPs. There was a lone rider in the back who saw the knot of police and their quarry, but being used to such scenes gave it no heed. Then, looking once more, just as Ada was being helped into a car, the person reacted violently. The Intourist car was already well past the scene before the passenger's knocking upon the window behind the driver brought the car to a halt. Upon instruction, the driver remained awaiting further orders.

The KGB officials were for immediate incarceration of the two women in the dread Lubyanka prison, but even for the KGB there were regulations to be observed. Since the arrest had been for a minor breach of law, not to mention the fact that the persons in custody were foreigners, to have dragged them off to a cell would have been diplomatically inadvisable. The proper procedure was to book them in an ordinary police station. From there on the KGB could move in.

The Zims accordingly headed for the nearest police station. The lurking Intourist car made for the same destination.

The curious thing about the reaction of the two women to what had hit them out of the blue, so to speak, was a kind of inversion. Mrs. Butterfield had been expecting something of the sort ever since the Russian plane had taken off from the safety of the Heathrow runway. Mrs. Harris had not. Therefore, it was actually Ada who was the more frightened of the two and was now fervently wishing she had never heard of Mr. Lockwood's love. If listening to a band of itinerant hymn shouters and being caught holding specimens of their creed was a crime sufficient in this country to bring out apparently the bulk of the coppers, what penalties might not be incurred when it was discovered that she was illicitly transporting communication to a Soviet citizen? And discovered it would be, for Mr. Lockwood's love letter—or what he had claimed was his love letter—was still in her handbag, which would unquestionably be thoroughly searched. Her own moral courage was such that she did not really care what might happen to her, but she was in despair over where she might have led her friend.

Police stations in all countries practically look, smell and behave alike. The odor is a combination of disinfectant, unwashed bodies and human fear. The decor is depressing and the human operatives act like robots.

Ordinarily the booking would have taken place at the Soviet equivalent of the sergeant's desk, but with so much KGB brass around, they were all crowded into a side room where there was a table and some chairs. Ada and Violet were addressed by the interpreter as follows: "We must inform you that you are both under arrest for the contravention of the Soviet code against introducing into the Soviet Union forbidden religious material such as books, pictures, tracts or handbills of the nature of those which we have found upon your persons. The brochures issued by the Intourist bureau and the instructions delivered verbally by your Intourist guide have clearly indicated that such articles are in contravention of Soviet law. You are, therefore, charged with breach of these laws and are subject to all penalties to which lawbreakers in this country are liable, no matter what nationality. If you reply honestly to all our inquiries, we may be able to deal with you leniently. Now, your names?"

"Me nyme, eh?" The reply emerged from the usually gentle lips of Mrs. Butterfield with such grating venom that, in probably what was the most surprising moment of her life, Ada Harris turned and watched her friend blow her stack.

"What's me nyme, is it? Well, you can bloody well go and look it up in all them flippin' papers I've signed to get meself into yer rotten country. If you don't know me nyme by now, you never will so you can go and bloody well look it up."

There was a moment's shocked pause which gave Mrs. Butterfield time for an intake of breath, and she being, as noted, rotund, had the lung capacity for a good and lasting supply on one draw. "And what's more, if you carn't run a bleedin' country, you ain't got the right to take good money from furriners to come and look at it. Call yerselves a country? That's a laugh. Try and get a decent mouthful of food 'ere wifout an hour and a 'alf's wait, stone-cold when it gets there and a dirty look from the waiters thrown in. Manners? You got words in yer rotten language for please and thank you, but I ain't never 'eard 'em yet. 'Be 'ere, go there. Get in the bus, don't talk.' You call that a 'oliday?"

It was time for another breath. Mrs. Butterfield gulped at it and waved a fat forefinger under the nose of Colonel Dugliev. "And it's a crime, is it, to raise me voice in praise of the Lord from whom all blessings flow, includin' yer own? 'Oo do you fink gave you all them sparklers and jewels you got tucked away? You ought to be down on yer knees 'arf of the day givin' thanks to Him that looks after the ugly lot of you."

Mrs. Butterfield took aboard another generous helping of the stale air and, to Ada's horror, continued. Mrs. Harris had no doubt that if they had not been doomed before, they would be now. "And what's all this me friend 'ere tells me about searchin' through our private belongin's? What's that kind of a way to treat visitors comin' over 'ere to see all them plyces like in them loverly photygraphs? And then bein' treated like spies. That's a good one. What would anybody want to be spyin' on a country for that gets its plumbin' mixed up with its electricity. And 'as us follered about by cops. It's me nyme you want to know, do you? Well, it's Violet Mabel Ernestine Butterfield and you can all kiss me royal—"

Mrs. Harris was just in time to choke off the conclusion of the sentence by laying her hand on her friend's arm and saying, "Violet," for she had been observing the mounting choler in Dugliev, which now burst. With a thunderous thump of his fist on the table he shouted,"Quiet! *We* are asking the questions. You will be lucky if you do not spend the rest of your life in a labor camp. We know you are spies and couriers." He now rounded upon Ada. "Your name?"

Recognizing his mood, she replied, "Ada Millicent Harris."

"Give me your handbag. You will both be searched."

Violet Butterfield turned a sickly green. All the fight went out of her; she knew what was inside the bag and so did Ada Harris, who thought to herself, We're done for. What a fool I've been. For goodness knows whether Mr. Lockwood's tender missive was not a call for comrades to arise in revolution. She had not even the forlorn hope that her little silly ruse would succeed, for what she had done was to cover the envelope with little notes such as "Send postcards to Frank and Aunt Mary," "Buy doll for Annie," "Fur coat," "Souvenirs" and other such memory joggers to make it look like a bit of scrap and a shopping list. But all the things that had been happening since their arrival—the search, the shadowing and now the arrest—served to make her realize that this was far more serious than she had thought. What she had marked upon the envelope wouldn't fool these grim men in this grim place for a second. The envelope would certainly be opened. They were lost.

The colonel had his arm outstretched to seize the handbag when there came an interruption in the form of footsteps and voices at a distance, torrents of voluble Russian in which the voice of a young woman could be heard mingling with those of the police. It culminated with the door of the interrogation room flying open and momentarily framing the figure of a lovely girl, wearing the Intourist badge and on her youthful face a look of indescribable perturbation. Within a moment she had flung herself into the room and fallen upon her knees before Mrs. Harris.

"Lady Char!" the girl cried. "I am so glad to have found you at last. But why are you here?" White with fury, she arose and faced the KGB group and demanded in Russian, "What is the meaning of this? Are you aware of who this is?"

Colonel Dugliev said, "These are dangerous spies and who are you and what is the meaning of this interference?"

Not in the least intimidated, the girl turned upon them with still greater anger. "Spies? You must all be out of your minds. You have laid your hands upon one of Britain's most important aristocrats, Lady Char. The Special Branch for International Culture has been searching for her since she arrived, and I have been delegated to look after her," and then switching to English, "My dear Lady Char, however can you forgive us? Someone has muddled your papers, but now that I have found you, all will be well. We must hurry, as you are on the list of guests for the Foreign Office reception which begins in an hour. You will just have time to change."

Things had suddenly taken such a bizarre turn that Dugliev, instead of having the girl thrown out or arrested, said, "What nonsense are you talking about an aristocrat? And how dare you interfere in KGB affairs? This pair here is dangerous. . . ."

The girl must either have been highly courageous or have known the firmness of the ground upon which she stood, or both, for she now said cuttingly, "I assumed that having reached your lofty rank in the KGB you must have learned to read at some time. So please read these," and she slapped down some documents onto the table. Colonel Dugliev and Inspector Vornov leaned over and examined them. The first was the set of applications of Ada Harris, Lady Char, and her attendant, Violet Butterfield, for visas, covered with official stamps and various Russian versions of Examined and Passed and Special Treatment. The second was a document of instructions from the Special Branch for International Culture advising whomever that Ada Harris, Lady Char, and her attendant were important guests of the Soviet Union and were to be shown every courtesy at all times. The documents bore the likenesses of Ada Harris and Violet Butterfield.

The silence as these two formidable pieces of paper were examined was broken only by Mrs. Butterfield's murmuring, "'Oo's Lady Char?" and a hissing rejoinder from Mrs. Harris, "Shut up."

The colonel was worried; the documents were undeniably genuine. He said, "There must be a mistake. But one does not speak, my girl, in this fashion to the KGB if one is in command of one's senses. This matter will have to be looked into."

The girl went up in flames again, Russian flames which Ada gathered were all on their side. She had stolen a look at the papers, and it was no problem to see if one moved a single word of her original application one would get Ada Harris, Lady Char.

"It is you who have made the mistake!" shouted the girl. "I have no further time to argue. My job is to present these ladies at the reception. If you wish to ignore these documents, you will do so at your own risk when the Presidium hears about it," and then in English to Ada and Violet, "My car is waiting outside." She gestured to them to arise. "We will move you and your belongings immediately to the quarters reserved for you at the Rossiya Hotel, where you will receive the personal apologies of the assistant vice-commissar of the Special Branch for International Culture." She picked the papers up off the table. "Come," she said.

The colonel hesitated and was lost. He represented one of the most powerful agencies of terror and coercion in the world, an

entire administration responsible only to the Presidium. But he knew that while the Presidium wielded the KGB as a deadly instrument, it also had its pet and that was the Special Branch for International Culture, one of whose purposes was to flatter British milords and ladies, Italian dukes and American millionaires into giving Communist Russia what it wanted. The colonel knew that the cultural organization's name was only a cover, that its real purpose was to achieve a détente which would be to Russia's commercial benefit. If the girl was right, and certainly the documents looked genuine, he could be in trouble. So he stood mutely by as the young Intourist guide, followed by Mrs. Ada Millicent Harris and Mrs. Violet Mabel Ernestine Butterfield, marched through the door and out the front entrance to freedom.

The guide said, "We will go first in the car to this inferior hotel and move you to your proper quarters." Mrs. Harris said nothing, and Mrs. Butterfield, having been told to shut up, remained shut.

At the Tolstoy they went up in the jerky elevator, received a key from Mrs. 'Orrible and entered the room. When the door was closed, Ada turned quietly to the girl and said, "'Ullo, Liz."

Chapter Ten

When the letter had been read and the crying, the laughing, the jubilation, the hugging and kissing were over, Lisabeta Nadeshda Borovaskaya dried her eyes and, in deference to concealed microphones, whispered, "Oh, Lady Char, you have made me the happiest girl in the world. I have never stopped loving Geoffrey, but life has been agony not knowing whether he was alive or dead or in prison or perhaps had stopped loving me. I shall be grateful to you and the good God for the rest of my life and never, never doubt again. Oh, I must not even think of it, but perhaps you, milady, might be able to help me to go to Geoffrey."

The thought that arrowed through the mind of Mrs. Ada Harris in view of what they had just been through was, Not bloody likely, but in consideration of the girl's ecstatic happiness, she could not bear to discourage her and she said, "We'll see." However, there was another danger to be dealt with. Violet Butterfield was a large woman who entertained a larger than normal supply of female curiosity. She had seen her old friend suddenly addressed as Lady Char, rescued from the secret police and hugged and kissed, while she herself, in this ridiculous muddle, had been relegated to the position of personal servant to Lady Char. A casual side-look at Mrs. Butterfield told Ada that Violet was nearing the point where her safety valve would go, and this peculiar game which had popped up in the very nick of time might be blown.

Whatever happened, this girl and her superiors, whoever they were, must continue to believe that the blood coursing through Ada Harris' veins was as blue as the River Danube.

Rescue came again from the charming girl, and Ada Harris now fully understood the agony of Mr. Lockwood at losing her, and for an instant fell prey to all the old fantasies. Liz looked at her watch and said, "Oh dear, we must be at the reception as quickly as possible, but first I will make sure that your suite in the Rossiya is ready." She picked up the telephone, which reacted no differently than ever it had before, and after a wait she banged down the receiver. "I'll call from the desk by the elevator. Wait here, I'll be right back," and she was flying down the hall.

No sooner had the door closed than Mrs. Butterfield's mouth opened and Ada rushed to put her hand across the orifice, pointing up to the ceiling as she did so. She dragged Mrs. Butterfield over to the window, where they both leaned out. There the roar of early evening traffic and the tolling of the great church bells provided cover for Violet's outburst.

"What's all this about, Ada? 'Oo's this Lady Char and all this kowtowin' to 'er? You ain't no lady. Not that you ain't a lady, luv, but what's all this got to do wif me waitin' on you and the letter bein' for this girl and changin' hotels? One minute we're about to get hung, like I told you we would, and the next we're goin' to a reception and I don't know where I am."

There not being much time, Ada made it short. "Listen to me, luv," she said, "you've got to keep yer 'ead on yer shoulders now or they will tyke it off for you. There's been a muddle. You know

75

them forms we filled out. Well, I wrote down me profession, Char Lady, and somebody turned around and made it Lady Char and has got us in with the nobs. As long as they think that, nothin' can 'appen to us. I'm the one they're in a mix-up about, so just let me do the talkin' and if I arsk you to 'and me a 'andkerchief, try to do it grycefully and don't forget to call me milady, even if it kills you."

Footsteps were heard down the hall, and they quickly drew away from the window as Liz burst in on them. "It's ready," she cried, "and the assistant vice-commissar of the Special Branch for International Culture is there waiting to make his apologies."

"Loverly," said Mrs. Harris, and then to Mrs. Butterfield, "Pack me bag, Violet, and don't be long about it."

"Yes, milady," Mrs. Butterfield just managed to say.

THE effect upon Mrs. Harris and Mrs. Butterfield of the fabulous mountain of glass and marble known as the Rossiya Hotel, after the tatty hotel to which they had been assigned, was staggering. The building was twelve stories high, boasted four separate lobbies, nine restaurants, the biggest ballroom in the world and ninety-three elevators. Their two-room suite was elegantly furnished, and the amenities even worked, although Mrs. Butterfield's immediate report after they had entered was, "There's no loo paper."

Before they had been there a few minutes, a young man in a smart uniform appeared and made a graceful speech of apology for the fact that they had been missed at the airport. Every effort would be undertaken to make up for whatever discomfort they might have suffered, and as for the arrest, they would receive a written apology. Then he glanced at his watch and said, "If I might beg you to hurry, the reception begins in half an hour. Lisabeta Nadeshda and I will wait downstairs while you change. Fortunately, the Palace of Congress is close by."

BLIMEY, Ada thought, for a country that ain't supposed to care about knickknacks and everybody 'avin' no money, these Rooshans don't do too badly for themselves Cor, just look at this plyce.

They had been ushered into the great hall of the Palace of Congress, illuminated by gigantic chandeliers. There were golden chairs, silken curtains, a vast buffet table covered with troughs of caviar, whole sturgeons, meats and roast game birds of every variety, with drinks to match. Somewhere unseen an orchestra was playing soft music, and the room was aglitter with splendid be-medaled Soviet and foreign uniforms. The entire diplomatic corps must have been present. There was a roar of conversation, much laughter and a clinking of glasses. They couldn't do a better job at Buckingham Palace, Ada thought, and guided by Liz, who had produced the credentials for their entrance, they moved toward a receiving line in the center of the great hall.

As they started off, Mrs. Harris felt a touch at her elbow and she recognized a voice. " 'Ullo, luv, what are you doin' 'ere?"

It was their erstwhile friend Mr. Rubin, obviously half-seas over, and Ada trembled for fear he might give the game away. "We've come because we were arsked, but what are you doin' 'ere?"

Mr. Rubin's face took on a most wily expression. Leaning close to Mrs. Harris, he said, "I'm 'ere because I'm so bloody important they 'ad to 'ave me. I got a secret. It's such a blowser I got three cops on me tail, but I've give 'em the slip."

"Why?" asked Mrs. Harris. " 'Ave you done somefink?"

" 'Ave I done somefink?" repeated Mr. Rubin, who by then had imbibed enough gin to go cockney all the way. "Nuffink like this has ever 'appened before. A real blockbuster. We've got a deal. 'Ere's to it." He raised the glass in his hand, swallowed half its contents and then, leaning even closer to Mrs. Harris, whispered, "The biggest bulk sale of Rubin's Grade A Soft-as-Silk toilet tissue in the history of the bloomin' world. Three hundred and eighty million rolls. Cleaned us out and put in an order for more. Top, top secret."

Mrs. Harris was pleased for the little man, but the practical side of her was irritated and she said, "Oh, come off it wif all that secret stuff. 'Ow you gonna keep a sale that big quiet?"

Mr. Rubin's eyes took on an incandescent glitter. He grabbed Ada's arm and whispered, "Birdseed. Me and my company's agreed not never to let anybody know. It'll be shipped into Russia in containers labeled Fenway's Birdseed. 'Ow about that now?"

Ada had a good look at Mr. Rubin and saw that although he was not half, but three-quarters seas over, he was telling the truth. Curiosity made her ask, "What became of the government feller that didn't want to buy?"

"Diggin' ditches somewhere up around the Arctic Circle. You carn't afford to guess wrong in this country. When this shindig is over come up to room 701 and we'll 'ave a drink on it."

As he released her arm and strayed off, three large uniformed Russians appeared at his side, smiling, but Ada saw that they were crocodile smiles. They were obviously guarding him. It was true then that he had indeed become a highly important personage. The meaning of it all and the need for such stringent secrecy was not entirely clear to Mrs. Harris, but the story of the exile imposed upon the poor man who had guessed wrong added to the revulsion that had been building up in her against those who held this country in their grip.

At which point she felt her elbow taken again, but this time it was Mrs. Butterfield who was behind her in what now turned out to be the reception line that they had joined. Mrs. Butterfield said, "I fink I'm goin' to faint," and then thought to add, "milady."

Irritably, Ada said, "Oh for Gawd's sakes, Vi, carn't you—"

Violet broke in. "Tyke a look at 'oo we're goin' to meet."

Mrs. Harris did. About ten people ahead in the reception line, flanked on one side by a tall graying man in striped trousers and black tailcoat and on the other by a Russian general, stood a distinguished, rather youngish-looking man in a lounge suit.

"Oh my Gawd, Vi," Ada whispered, "I might faint meself. It's 'Is 'Ighness, Prince Philip, the Duke of Edinburgh. I'd forgot 'e was 'ere. 'Eaven 'elp us, Vi, what are we goin' to do and say?"

Mrs. Butterfield replied, "I just 'opes I don't fall over when I does me bobs, and I ain't sayin' nuffink. You said you was goin' to do all the talkin', milady."

The line moved up another ten feet.

And then Mrs. Harris found herself standing face-to-face with the husband of the queen of all the British, gazing into a pair of quizzical blue eyes and hearing herself announced. "Your Royal Highness, may I present Lady Ada Char from London."

She was now staring straight into those eyes, and something happened inside the Mrs. Harris which was her, the only thing ever that she had been able to be, and that was herself. She made her little bob and then blurted out, "Beggin' Yer 'Ighness' pardon, but it ain't really so. I ain't no lydy. I'm just ordinary Ada 'Arris from Battersea, 'ere on a 'oliday. Me work's charrin' and they got it muddled on me papers and I 'opes you'll forgive me."

The duke broke into a broad grin. "Ada Harris," he said. "I'm delighted to meet you," and he held out his hand.

Ada warmed to him like an old friend. Suddenly the vast distance that separated them no longer seemed to exist. The duke asked, "Are you enjoying your stay in Russia? Are you being properly looked after?"

And then it was that something else happened within Mrs. Harris, triggered perhaps by the fact that across the room she caught sight of Colonel Dugliev, but more from the fact that such a homely rapport had been established between the duke and herself. If there was anyone to whom she could explain the indignities that had been heaped upon her, who but the husband of the queen of England? And, to the horror of the director of protocol and one or two other English-speaking dignitaries, it suddenly poured forth.

"Properly looked arfter Yer 'Ighness? Properly treated like I was a criminal. Searched and follered and listened to, arrested because some poor revivalist stuck a 'andbill in me fingers, carted off to a jail with me friend 'ere, Mrs. Butterfield" (Violet went into a series of bobs at this mention) "shouted at and called a spy. Me, a 'ardworkin' woman 'oo never so much as opened up a bureau drawer of any of me clients to see what was inside."

The smile vanished from the face of the duke. He said, "I suggest you tell your story to Sir Harold Barry over there, adviser on Russian affairs to His Excellency our ambassador here, and in the meantime let me repeat that it has been a pleasure to meet you."

Mrs. Harris moved off in the direction of the dignitary the duke had indicated. Some five yards away from His Royal Highness, Mrs. Butterfield was still bobbing.

Sir Harold was clad in striped-trouser diplomatic regalia, and with his thinning white hair, military mustache and spectacles above a beak nose he had the appearance of a formidable owl, and rather intimidated Mrs. Harris. Without realizing she was doing so, she had blown her top to the consort of the queen. In addition to which, and in the hearing of Liz, she had exposed her phony aristocracy. But to have to come up with the details of her story to this grand-looking gentleman was something else again. However, the fierceness of his expression was replaced by a bland smile as she stood before him and he said, "How do you do. I saw His Royal Highness tell you to have a word with me. Come, come, you mustn't be afraid. Somebody try to nobble your passport or put buckshot in your caviar? We'll go over there with your friend and sit down and have a little chat."

This chat turned out to be rather a long one. Ada soon saw from the questions he asked that the diplomat was no fool. Finally he brushed his mustache with a finger and said, "Rum lot some of these chaps. They're worse than we are at seeing Reds under the bed. More frightened of themselves than they are of anybody else. And one thing they can't stand is making fools of themselves. They won't like it when they find out they've done that. I suggest you go back to your hotel and wait there until you hear from me. Not to worry. Cheers," and he raised his glass in what was simultaneously a toast and a dismissal.

BACK in the sitting room of their luxury suite, Liz, Mrs. Butterfield and Mrs. Harris clustered together by the open window with the radio full on and held a whispered council of war, or rather a council of love, which dealt mainly with what seemed to be the insuperable problem of uniting Lisabeta Nadeshda Borovaskaya with Geoffrey Lockwood. Mrs. Harris would be able to take back verbal messages of undying affection, but anything beyond that seemed to be blocked at every turn.

To begin with, while Liz had a solid job with Intourist for VIPs, she was not that far trusted as to be allowed to make trips to any of their Western offices. Somewhere, somebody had suspected that she had been more than a guide to a certain British writer. Therefore, even though her life and work in Moscow were not interfered with, she was aware that she was under surveillance. One false move and she would be lost.

The Soviet Union is probably the most gigantic jail in the world, with several thousand doors to entry and exit, locked instantaneously by the turn of one handle. Escape over a border is impossible, and to leave by any ordinary means of transportation calls for enough documents to paper a room. The more questions Mrs. Harris asked, the more Liz was able to prove that she would be unable to leave the country, much less reach England. And the tighter the doors appeared to be locked, the more Mrs. Harris refused to accept the impossibility of bringing together the lovers. She said, "Now, dearie, don't you despair. I've always found that if you want somethin' bad enough and keep on at it, you can get it. I'll fink of somethin'."

Ordinarily such apparently blockheaded optimism might have irritated Liz, but there was something in Mrs. Harris' faith which could not be denied. Mrs. Harris did not know herself whence it came except that she remembered how powerful her fantasy had been, when first Mr. Lockwood had broached the subject, that one day she would be ringing his doorbell and saying, "Mr. Lockwood, 'ere's a friend of yers come to see you." It appeared unthinkable for this not to happen. And then there was something else rattling around at the back of her head. There was something Sir Harold had said about the Russians which, if she could only remember it, might help her open all the locked doors.

Tears were falling from the eyes of Lisabeta. "Don't you see," she sobbed, "you aren't even a real lady. Oh dear, I don't mean that. You *are* a darling to want to help me, but you see if you had really been Lady Char they might have listened to you."

Ada said, "Now don't you worry about that one bit." Sir Harold had said, "Not to worry." And he had said something else.

There came a knock on the door, and when they said, "Come in," it produced a most handsome young man in striped trousers who said, "I'm Byron Dale, from the British embassy, and Sir Harold Barry sent me. He feels that you and your friend might be better off if you came and stayed at the embassy until your departure. I see you haven't unpacked your bags yet. That's good."

Ada understood. Whatever dangers had threatened them since their entry into the Soviet Union were not yet over, and now that Liz had so violently defied the KGB on their behalf, she too was involved. "I won't go unless Liz 'ere can come too," Ada said.

The young man looked doubtful for a moment and then, having regarded Liz, lost his doubts. "All right. No one said she was not to come, but I think we ought to hurry. I have a car downstairs." He picked up the bags and the three women followed him out of the room. Halfway down the corridor, Mrs. Harris suddenly shrieked, "Eureka!" and while Liz and Mrs. Butterfield looked at her as though she had gone mad she said, "I've suddenly remembered what it was Sir 'Arold said. We'll 'ave you in London yet, my girl."

At that moment their good fortune was that the delegation from the KGB chose elevator number 7 to rise to Lady Char's suite. Elevator number 7 had been cranky for days. Now, loaded with the KGB operatives, it gave up between the third and fourth floors. By the time a cure had been effected and they reached their objective there were no more birds in the nest of the pseudo Lady Char, who was about to be arrested for impersonation and half a dozen other crimes they would manage to fasten upon her.

Chapter Eleven

ANATOLE Pavlovich Agronsky, vice-foreign minister who for eight years had been Russian ambassador to England, and Sir Harold Barry, adviser to the British ambassador, were old friends, tennis opponents and bridge partners, and so they were on first-name terms, relaxed and understanding with one another except when it came to business, when each retired to his side of the diplomatic chessboard. Then, still quietly, with only thoughts of the problem at hand and the benefit of their countries, moves were made and the impasse discussed. Such a session took place this morning.

This meeting, being one which might be trivial but also could suddenly turn serious, was held on neutral ground and probably the only spot the Russians had not yet managed to bug successfully, a bench in the heart of the Park of Culture and Rest, where the sounds of traffic and of children playing provided cover.

"You see, my dear Harold," Agronsky was saying, "that the situation has been removed from our purview. Rest assured, I will use my own good offices. But as you must see, the women are undoubtedly spies, at least the one who calls herself Mrs. Harris, she having also conspired to pass herself off as a British aristocrat. Impersonation, as you know, is looked upon with extreme disfavor, as I gather it is in your country. By now the KGB will have taken both the women into custody, as well as Lisabeta Nadeshda Borovaskaya, the Intourist guide who was obviously a participant in the plot."

Sir Harold, who for the last ten minutes of the discourse had remained at his most introspective owlishness, said nothing.

"The women," continued Agronsky, "will be subjected to no physical harm, but as you know the KGB has its own methods of extracting information. My judgment of the affair is that there will be a trial, a confession, a sentence and, after the case is forgotten, in all likelihood a parole and expulsion from the country."

Sir Harold turned toward his friend so as to benefit from the sound cover of a screaming baby. He said, "Except for one thing, Anatole Pavlovich, everything you say might be taken as gospel but for the fact that the lift carrying your KGB goons chose to succumb to the shoddy material used by your crooked contractors in constructing it, and quit. By the time it resumed its functions the ladies had been removed to our embassy, along with the girl, who Mrs. Harris insisted accompany her."

Agronsky gave vent to a long sigh and remarked, "There is an old Russian saying: 'It is more difficult to find an honest contractor than a diamond in a suet pudding,'" and Sir Harold smiled.

"You have, my friend," Sir Harold said, "succeeded in making thorough asses of yourselves. Mrs. Harris is no more a spy than you are the prima ballerina at the Bolshoi. Your dossier on Mrs. Harris is nothing but an invention of your operatives in search of promotion. But let us return to the situation as it now stands."

Agronsky was irritated. "The case of the two women will be considered in accordance with our laws. Until then they may remain in your embassy. The girl, of course, must be turned over immediately to our authorities. As a sensible chap, Harold, you must see that we cannot do otherwise."

"As your personal friend, I say no to that," was Sir Harold's rejoinder. "Mrs. Harris is no spy, courier or anything else subversive. You have my word for it and you know that I have never lied to you. I gather then that your representatives of the utopia for the proletariat of the world are about to prosecute one of Britain's favorite characters, their daily, the char, a hardworking woman who arises at four in the morning and does not end her day until long after sundown. She receives the equivalent of half a ruble an hour, is usually a widow, feeds and educates her children and is one of the mainstays of our way of life. Put this workingwoman in the dock and our newspapers will raise such a hue and cry that you will wish you had never heard of her. You have lived in England. You should know that."

"But the impersonation of Lady Char," expostulated Agronsky.

"Oh come," replied Sir Harold. "Your clerks are as blockheaded as your contractors are crooked. We have obtained a copy of her original visa application, and one of your brighter civil servants got Char Lady and Lady Char back to front. Besides which everyone heard her denying it to Prince Philip himself. If you will listen to the counsel of an old friend who is genuinely fond of you, Mrs. Harris and Mrs. Butterfield will be allowed to complete their bizarre Moscow package tour tomorrow as scheduled on the noon jet for London."

Agronsky suddenly burst into laughter. "You are, of course, quite right. The whole thing is utterly absurd. The pair may depart. And if the KGB takes it out on me, you'll have lost your tennis partner. But the girl must be returned."

Sir Harold brushed his mustache with a forefinger and said, "I am afraid Mrs. Harris has attached a condition to her departure. She wishes Lisabeta Nadeshda Borovaskaya to be given an exit visa and allowed to accompany her to London."

Agronsky's explosive "What?" drowned out the squalling baby.

"A matter of the heart," replied Sir Harold quietly, and then launched into the narrative of the unhappy affair involving Lisabeta Borovaskaya and Geoffrey Lockwood.

For the first time Agronsky became truly incensed and said angrily, "That is impossible. You know it is. Who is this scrubbing woman to make conditions to the Russian government? And what's more, you are a fool for having told me, for now I cannot remain silent as to this past liaison and as a result the girl will be severely punished. Within an hour there will be KGB representatives at the embassy and I demand that the girl be turned over to them at once. You, I know, will not be anxious to kick up an international rumpus during our mutual attempts at détente. Do you agree?"

Curiously the British diplomat did not reply to this question, but looked rather sad as he said, "What is it about you Russians that you take such delight in keeping young lovers apart, in denying people who cherish one another the right to be together? Your cruelty in this respect is well known. And yet you are a warm sentimental folk. Can you explain this, Anatole Pavlovich?"

"Come now, Harold," replied Agronsky. "If you have not yet learned to distinguish between Russian sentimentality and political hardheadedness . . ."

"Of course," said Sir Harold. "I was only thinking of the newspapers. Mention unrequited love on Fleet Street and the presses begin to turn almost automatically."

Agronsky sighed. "We are used to abuse in the press."

"I was mainly thinking of the charwomen's underground."

"Underground!" exclaimed Agronsky. "So there *is* something—"

"Really, Anatole," said Sir Harold. "You were in London for a decade. Surely you encountered the dailies' gossip grapevine?"

The Russian broke into a charming smile. "Dear Mrs. Minby."

"Exactly," agreed Sir Harold. "How was it that you knew three days before we did that the Ngonbian African Middle States government was breaking off relations with us?"

Here the Russian diplomat clapped his hand to his forehead. "Oh my God, but of course, Mrs. Minby! She had it from Mrs. Cranshaw, whose friend cleaned in the Ngonbian embassy."

"Precisely," said Sir Harold. "Communication with the press is not the practice of a person like Mrs. Harris. Of course, eventually the journalists get wind of the story, but then as you say, with all the fuss being raised over your dissidents, you're used to such abuse. Very well, the two women go tomorrow. I shall rely upon you that there will be no last-minute interference by the KGB."

"You needn't worry," Agronsky said. "When that division sorts out its blunders on this case, it will be having problems of its own."

"Thank you," said Sir Harold, then he looked suddenly uneasy. "Look here, Anatole, I have a slightly embarrassing request to make of you—purely on the basis of friendship. Could you accompany me to the embassy for a moment to listen to a personal plea that Mrs. Harris would like to make on behalf of this girl?"

Agronsky stiffened. "A personal plea? But it would be useless."

"Of course," concluded Sir Harold. "But it would be a kindness. She is a good woman, utterly sincere, and really believes that if she could only speak to someone in authority, it might soften your hearts. At least then she will know that she has tried and will not be plagued by that awful thought that it might have worked if only she had had the chance."

The Russian regarded his friend for a moment. "You are a good fellow, Harold. In memory of our Mrs. Minby I'll come."

The two men left the park bench and entered Sir Harold's car. On the way to the embassy, Agronsky was thinking that this was probably the silliest thing he had ever done in his life. On the way back, he was thinking the opposite and thanking his lucky stars.

The plea of Ada Harris was sentimental, genuine and touching. Liz was waiting in another room. There were only Ada, the two men and Mrs. Butterfield, who occasionally wiped a tear from her eyes as her friend spoke of the lovers' constancy.

"'E's a gent, is Mr. Lockwood," explained Ada. "'E could 'ave put it down to a passin' fancy and forgot about 'er. But not 'im. Moonin' like a schoolboy over 'er photer, tryin' to move 'eaven and earth to 'ave 'er join 'im. And Liz is a hangel from above. She give 'er word and never broke it. It ain't often, sir, that two people separated by circumstances like what's 'appened stand by their word. When it does, then you know yer talkin' about real love, not like what's on the telly. You know what would 'appen if you let 'er go? Two people would love yer country like it ain't never been loved before. Sir, what 'ave you got to lose? Let 'er come. You yerself would be feelin' all the better for it."

Vice-Foreign Minister Agronsky was indeed moved by Mrs. Harris, but not budged; from every aspect, including the security of his own skin, the situation was unbudgeable. It was the first time that the vice-foreign minister had seen Mrs. Harris, since he had been minding the store while his superiors attended the reception. He now looked upon the tiny figure and the lines in the face that marked, in a way, each stopping place on the long road of years of manual work. His thoughts turned to the millions upon millions of Russians, equally battered by life and hard work, begging some minor civil servant for some permission or necessary document and being rudely turned down just for the sheer joy of showing power. Well, this was Russian bureaucracy and he was a part of it. But he took no satisfaction out of the necessity for his reply. "I'm afraid, madam, that nothing can be done. Lisabeta Nadeshda Borovaskaya has broken Russian law and must suffer the consequences."

"What law 'as she broke?" Ada inquired. "To fall in love?"

The vice-foreign minister, preoccupied, failed to see the stiffening of Mrs. Harris' frail body or the fire come into the little eyes that a moment before had been soft and beguiling. He said, "That is neither here nor there."

Mrs. Harris turned to Sir Harold. "What will they do to 'er?"

For the life of him, later, Sir Harold could not remember why he told the truth. "Probably give her ten years in a labor camp."

Mrs. Harris turned upon Agronsky. "You monster! You barstid! Except for that poor girl, I ain't come across a livin' soul in this

87

country that ain't got the devil in 'im. You Rooshans 'ate everybody, includin' yer own selves. You 'ate Christians carryin' on the inno- cent work of the Lord, and you 'ate the Jews until you need 'em. Like poor little Mr. Rubin. 'Im and 'is toilet rolls and keepin' 'im tipsy for eight weeks. *Birdseed* indeed! There ain't one of you does anything straight—" And here Mrs. Harris broke off as she saw the change come over the vice-foreign minister. He had turned sheet white, swayed as though he were about to faint.

"W-w-what," he stammered, "did you say about birdseed?"

Mrs. Harris was not sure yet that she had struck gold, but it was clear that she had unstrung this rigid man. She rubbed it in.

"You 'eard me. Millions of rolls of you-know-what paper to be sent into the country labeled as birdseed. I suppose when you buys a load of tractors you mark it complexion cream."

Sir Harold was regarding Mrs. Harris with wonder and great awe, for he had got it. Mrs. Harris somehow had come into posses- sion of information that the Russians wanted hidden.

For a moment Agronsky tried to bluff it out. "Birdseed? Paper? You must be out of your mind, my good woman."

Nobody could challenge Mrs. Harris' veracity. "Come orf it," she snapped. "Out of me mind, am I? There ain't a roll of loo paper in the 'ole bloomin' country, and you ain't the only ones. They queue up for it in Japan, China's all out, the Africans ain't got nuffink but palm leaves. So, you buy up the 'ole load we got in our warehouses, only you ain't got the guts to say what yer buyin' so you ship it in as birdseed."

Sir Harold had to turn his back or explode with laughter.

"Who told you this monstrous lie?" croaked Agronsky.

"Monstrous lie, me foot," said Ada. "Mr. Rubin. And if you want me to, I'll give you the nyme of the birdseed company it's comin' in under. I know all about the 'ole bloomin' story."

The vice-foreign minister wiped a deluge of moisture from his anguished countenance, took a deep breath to regain command of himself and said, "Sir Harold, could we perhaps speak privately?"

"But of course," agreed the British adviser. "Come up to my office." He turned to the two ladies and said, "If you will excuse us for just a moment?" And since his back was turned to Agronsky, he was able to throw Mrs. Harris a large wink.

In Sir Harold's office, with the doors carefully closed, the two men sat down and gathered their resources for the duel that each knew was about to take place.

Agronsky came to the point immediately. "You realize, of course, the two women cannot now be allowed to leave. Somehow they have come into possession of information which if disseminated might do enormous damage to the prestige of the Soviet Union. It is heartless indeed, but as a diplomat whose country has done equally heartless things at times, you will understand. You know the KGB. Two women, traveling alone, they disappear . . ."

Sir Harold nodded gravely and replied, "Yes, I can see that. But how do you plan to make *me* disappear?"

"What?" queried the Russian sharply.

"Well, you see," replied Sir Harold mildly, "now I know it too. That makes—let me see—Mr. Rubin, Mrs. Harris, Mrs. Butterfield and myself. And unless, my dear Anatole, you're prepared to shoot me dead on the spot, His Excellency the ambassador will be informed. The coding secretary will know. So will the decoder in London, and after that, the foreign secretary. That makes quite a gathering in which the Mesdames Harris and Butterfield become insignificant—except perhaps for the charwomen's underground. You see, dear boy, that any talk of these two innocents vanishing is quite ridiculous."

The Russian official, second-in-command to the Soviet foreign minister, was reeling under the apprehension of the complications and possible loss of face for his government all because of a few words spoken by a London cleaning woman.

Sir Harold slowly filled a pipe, then continued. "Of course Whitehall could put a stop to the sale, which would not be a catastrophe for you. A leak to the press, however, would be. Birdseed. Whatever made you people hit upon something quite so absurd?"

Agronsky said nothing. His mind was working frantically.

Sir Harold lit his pipe and said, "I do not think that your top boys would enjoy becoming the laughingstock of the world, as they would if the birdseed story was printed in the foreign press. And can you visualize the cartoonists' field day all over Europe? Oh my dear fellow!"

The vice-foreign minister groaned. "Oh my God, what shall I do? I shall be blamed. The KGB will see to that."

Sir Harold puffed on his pipe, then said quietly, "Make a deal. Send the girl back with Mrs. Harris. In exchange, she and her friend will keep their mouths shut. It's that simple."

The Russian stared. Suddenly an avenue seemed open. He said, "But how could you trust—the charwomen's underground?"

Sir Harold replied, "Hadn't you noticed? Mrs. Harris is a woman of honor. If she gives her word, she will keep it."

Color began to come back into the face of Agronsky. "But what about you? The ambassador, the Foreign Office, your duties?"

"If Mrs. Harris' plea failed to touch you, Anatole Pavlovich, it reached me. Send the girl with them and I will give you my promise, along with Mrs. Harris' and Mrs. Butterfield's, that what transpired here will go no further. The secret will be safe. You have the power and the courage. Within twelve hours you could arrange for an exit visa for Lisabeta Nadeshda."

Agronsky's mind revved up another hundred RPMs. A shortcut here, a word there, a fiddle there, and the visa could be produced. Then he had a black moment. "The KGB . . ."

"The KGB is rattled. As our American friends would put it, they goofed and haven't yet found out just where. If you work fast, the girl will be out of the country before they know what's happened."

The dark cloud passed from Agronsky.

Sir Harold arose. "Shall we go and talk to the girls?"

Sir Harold picked up the telephone and said to a secretary, "Send Lisabeta Nadeshda Borovaskaya to the reception room to join Mrs. Harris and her friend." And a few moments later Liz was there, shy, worried, confused, and when she saw Agronsky, frightened. Mrs. Butterfield was blubbing and Mrs. Harris hardly dared look at her.

Agronsky was casting quick looks about the room. "Is it safe?"

"I doubt it," said Sir Harold. "However, we will have our little conference in the one room in the embassy we never much worry about—it's been specially built. It gets a little stuffy in there and so we've named it the Turkish Bath. I think it floats on something or other, but the point is you can rely on it."

They went down several corridors and then entered a room through double doors that had a curious kind of corrugated threshold in between. The room was compact, comfortably furnished, with a small conference table and chairs. Sir Harold locked the inner door and pressed a button beside it, and a red light appeared. He remarked cryptically, "We're shooting," then switched on an air-conditioning apparatus and said, "and soundproof. Sit."

They did as bidden and Sir Harold, after a moment's embarrassed silence, said, "Well, someone's got to start this." He turned to the girl. "If you had permission, would you of your own free will like to go to London into political asylum—that is, to be accepted as a resident and allowed to live unmolested in freedom?"

The girl stared at him in disbelief. "Can you mean it? Are you serious? Or is this just another form of torture?"

"No," replied Sir Harold. "I mean it."

"Oh yes, yes, yes! Yes, please. Oh, I'd give anything."

"Another question. Have you any relatives living in Russia?"

Liz glanced at Vice-Foreign Minister Agronsky before she replied. "My father disappeared in 1952 when—when I was three years old. My mother died two years ago. I have an uncle in Kiev, but I doubt whether he even knows if I'm alive."

"Well," said Sir Harold, "you heard the girl, Minister. No coercion, no problems. I suggest you make your proposal."

Agronsky now addressed Mrs. Harris. "Sir Harold and I have discussed your plea for this girl. It was indeed touching. Under the circumstances we are prepared to let her go."

With a cry of joy Liz threw herself upon Mrs. Harris. "You, you, it is you who have done it. Oh, how can I thank—"

Mrs. Harris, alert as a terrier, disengaged from the girl. "'Ang on a minute, luv, until we 'ear what the catch is."

Agronsky now said, "There is one condition."

Ada nodded and said, "There's always one. Let's 'ear it."

There now took place something which the average person would have said was impossible, a meeting of the minds of a highly trained, highly sophisticated diplomat and an uneducated working-class widow. Of the five persons in the room, there was one who knew nothing about the secret Soviet purchase and its ramifications. This was Liz. For a moment Agronsky looked through and into Mrs. Harris and she looked back. Then he said carefully, "What exactly do you know about the—what was it—mentioned a little while ago? Yes, I remember—birdseed."

Oh yes, they were in harmony, the two minds. "Nuffink," Mrs. Harris replied. "I carn't remember the subject bein' referred to."

"And your friend here?"

Mrs. Harris looked fondly at Vi. "You needn't worry about 'er."

"And you?" asked Agronsky, and in his breast he was feeling the most delightful connection between his own inner self and this little woman who understood exactly his meaning.

Mrs. Harris said, "I give me word."

Agronsky said, "I can trust you," and Ada, looking squarely into his broad face, said quietly, "Are you arskin' or tellin' me?"

"Telling you. The girl will be allowed to go with you."

There occurred another damp interlude, in which the girl clutched at Ada. "I can't believe it. I've never been so happy."

"It's all right, luv," said Mrs. Harris, and stroked the girl's hair, adding grimly, "I've got the password."

Agronsky sighed. Could he trust that common ordinary woman not to betray him once she was safely in England? And regarding her again, he knew that she was neither common nor ordinary but a warm and gallant human being, a valiant fighter in the battle for survival. He said, "We will have Lisabeta Nadeshda Borovaskaya at the airport at eleven o'clock tomorrow morning."

Sir Harold said, with just the slightest emphasis, "*We* will have Miss Borovaskaya at the airport at eleven, along with Mrs. Harris and Mrs. Butterfield. *You* bring the visa and passport."

Agronsky smiled at his friend and said, "Very well. If I were in your situation, I should do the same." He suddenly felt a sweet relief. The deal might be a black mark against him, but when the details reached the top via the foreign minister, he knew that the hardheads in the government would realize that he had had no choice and had done the right thing.

Freed now momentarily from the cast-iron suit of bureaucratic armor, Anatole Pavlovich Agronsky said, "You are really a most remarkable woman, Mrs. Harris. By a set of extraordinary circumstances you were in control of a situation which would have affected the reputation of the Soviet Union, and yet you made no attempt to use this information for your own advantage. And when the opportunity presented itself, you asked for nothing for yourself but only for the happiness of two young people. Is there nothing that you would like for your own, some little memento? I realize that you have been very much put upon here, and I feel ashamed."

"Nuffink, thank you, sir," replied Ada Harris. "What you've done for Liz is the greatest thing that ever 'appened to me and I'll never forget it or you neither, and I'm sayin' thank you."

And then suddenly a curious expression came over the face which a moment before had been so full of the grandeur of dignity. The old mischievous apple-cheeked twinkle-eyed Mrs. Harris reappeared. "Beggin' yer pardon, sir, come to think of it there is somefink I'd like. A fur coat."

Agronsky was conscious of a sudden chill of disappointment in Mrs. Harris. The demand for a fur coat had a certain greediness and vulgarity about it. He suppressed a sigh. Oh well, what did you expect? he thought. He said, "I see. A fur coat."

Mrs. Harris said, "Not for me, sir, but for me friend 'ere. She's been wantin' a fur coat for years, she 'as, and savin' up for one, but the stores keep gettin' ahead of 'er. Inflytion, they calls it. Every time she thought she 'ad the money, the price was twenty quid up. Well, sir, it was me persuaded 'er she could buy a fur coat cheap in Russia like it said in them little booklets you get out. She didn't want to come on this trip because she was frightened, but I said, 'Look 'ere, Vi, 'ere's yer chance of a lifetime to get yer fur coat cheap. But, cor blimey, when we got into that store you can buy things in with foreign money—the prices! Two and three thousand quid!" She hesitated. "It ain't nothin' like them in that shop I'd be arskin' for 'er, just the kind maybe a girl like Liz would buy for 'erself 'ere when it got cold in winter."

Relief coursed through the heart of Anatole Pavlovich Agronsky. The feet which for a moment had begun to take on a certain clay texture had now shown themselves again pure gold. Mrs. Harris was asking for something once more not for herself. "Your friend," Agronsky said, "shall have her fur coat." He looked at his watch. "Well, if I'm to produce a passport and visa by tomorrow morning, I'd best be about the business." To Liz he said, "Will you give me your identification card and all of your papers?"

Liz looked up in alarm. A Russian without his cards and papers upon him became an unperson. But Ada said, "I trust 'im, Liz," and the girl did as he asked.

Anatole Pavlovich Agronsky felt as though he had been knighted. He shook hands with Liz and said, "Good luck," and with Mrs. Butterfield; but with Mrs. Harris he leaned over and kissed her wrinkled cheek before he departed.

Sir Harold felt he'd better break it up. He said, "There are two rooms upstairs where you ladies can make yourselves comfortable, but under no circumstances are you to leave this building."

Mrs. Harris said, "Sir, excuse me, but would it be possible for me to send a cable to London? I'll pay for it."

"Yes, yes, of course, Mrs. Harris. Just write it out."

Mrs. Harris wrote on a pad he handed her. The diplomat glanced at it and saw nothing in it which did not appear to be quite justified. He had, of course, no idea of the final sacrifice to the ending of a dream that it entailed. What he was wondering was how the last act of this drama was going to turn out.

Chapter Twelve

THE departure of British Airways Flight 801 Moscow-London the next midday was, from the standpoint of Mrs. Harris and Mrs. Butterfield, everything that could be desired in the way of smoothness and comfort. Sir Harold Barry was there to see them off. So was

Anatole Pavlovich Agronsky. They carried bouquets of flowers for the women. Mrs. Harris was aware of a curious undercurrent of excitement, but put this down to the joy she was experiencing at having brought off the impossible.

The formalities of departure all seemed to go with a wave and a nod. Nor did Mrs. Harris feel any astonishment that after they had passed the last barrier both Sir Harold and Agronsky accompanied them across the tarmac to the aircraft. There did seem to be a larger contingent than usually boarded an aircraft, and among them some very hard-looking men. The three women mounted the stairs and turned at the entrance to the plane to wave to the two diplomats. There were then a great many of these tough-looking characters left over on the ground, who as the door of the jet slid shut turned and trooped back to the airport building.

Sir Harold took out a handkerchief and mopped the perspiration from his face. His heart was filled with affection for his friend and enemy, Anatole Pavlovich Agronsky, who had kept his word.

There is a simplicity to the politics of power. If one side has more muscle than you have, you don't start anything. The KGB had the airport loaded with agents to prevent Lisabeta Nadeshda Borovaskaya from departing the Soviet Union, but the Foreign Office, which the Presidium knew dealt with matters often of the greatest delicacy, had a pipeline to the head of the special police known as the militia. There were twice as many militiamen at the airport as there were KGB. There was peace. Moscow-London Flight 801 had vanished into the western sky.

ANYONE who failed to share in the reunion of Geoffrey Lockwood and Lisabeta Nadeshda Borovaskaya at Heathrow Airport, via television, radio, newspaper or magazine features, got it *viva voce* from those who had. Someone had got wind of the impending drama, probably from the telegraph operator, and when Liz came down the steps of the aircraft and into the waiting arms of Mr. Lockwood, there was such a popping of flashbulbs, flaring of floodlights and shoving of microphones as Heathrow had not seen in years. One of the finest pictures to result was Mr. Lockwood crushing not his ladylove but a wizened little old charwoman to his breast and looking down upon her with a rare expression of love and gratitude. All this took place on the tarmac.

When the happy lovers moved into the VIP lounge, someone produced champagne and the celebration went into high gear.

Fortunately no one inquired into the reason for the sudden release of Lisabeta to join her lover, in British asylum, but then the Russians were notoriously unpredictable. Vice-Foreign Minister Anatole Pavlovich Agronsky had a chuckle over several fulsome editorials in British journals praising the Russians for their generosity in this case, which would undoubtedly have favorable results upon the détente.

By the time Mr. Lockwood had expressed his gratitude and wonderment to Mrs. Harris for the thousandth time, Ada and Violet finally managed to break away. An hour later they were sitting in number 5 Willis Gardens in old comfortable clothes, having enjoyed their evening cup of tea, Ada filled with the richness of the happiness she had created, both of them slightly tiddly from the airport champagne.

"I say," said Mrs. Butterfield, "'ow did that there Mr. Lockwood know Liz was on the plane? I thought 'e was goin' to 'ave a surprise, 'im openin' 'is door, and there you'd be."

"I cabled 'im," replied Ada. "Knockin' on 'is door was the dream of a silly old woman, and enough to give a man who wouldn't be expectin' it a 'eart attack. That would 'ave been nice, wouldn't it? ''Ere's yer sweetie,' and 'e drops down dead."

"Ada," said Vi, "you always do the right fing. It was beautiful. I cried me eyes out. Let's see what's on the telly."

Even though Mrs. Harris had had it repaired before their departure, no picture appeared. The screen was streaked with what looked like the heaviest snowfall in the Hebrides. Suddenly Violet exclaimed, "The bloody Rooshans, they forgot me fur coat! All that there stuff that looks like snow reminded me of it."

"Oh, Vi," said Ada. "I never . . . It's all my fault."

Violet was immediately defending her friend. She said, "No, it isn't, and when it comes to it, I wasn't really expectin' one. Look

'ere, we got out wif Liz and what's more wif our lives, and sittin' in that there perlice station, I wasn't so sure we would."

"You were marvelous," Ada praised. "You let 'em 'ave it."

"They got me dander up," said Vi, and so as they reminisced over the adventure through which they had just passed, the evening drew to a close. Next day they were back at their labors.

Four weeks later, on a Saturday, Mrs. Harris' doorbell went mad at eight a.m. She found Mrs. Butterfield trembling on the doorstep, holding a highly official-looking envelope with the crest of the Soviet embassy upon it. "Ada, I'm frightened. Look what's come, delivered by 'and. Do you suppose they're arfter me?"

"Why don't you open it?" said Mrs. Harris, all curiosity.

They did. There was a card inside which read, "His Excellency Valery Zornyn, Ambassador from the Union of Soviet Socialist Republics to Great Britain, begs the attendance of Mrs. Violet Butterfield at the Embassy at four o'clock this afternoon." At the bottom, handwritten, was a little note: "She may, if she likes, bring her friend, Mrs. Harris." For the rest there was only the address of the embassy at Kensington Palace Gardens, W.8.

Violet was all atremble. "They'll send me back there."

But Mrs. Harris, who had been studying the card with steadier nerves, said, "Silly, if they were goin' to do anything like that they wouldn't 'ave said I could accompany you. We go."

It was His Excellency the Russian ambassador himself, standing by an exquisite marquetry table on which reposed a large cardboard box, who made the following speech that afternoon: "Madam Butterfield, during your visit to our country a promise was made to you. The Soviet government and its people always fulfill their promises and it is therefore with the greatest pleasure that I present you with . . ." and here one assistant raised the cover of the box, another scrabbled tissue paper out of the way and a third raised from it, fluffed up and spread out, a most magnificent rich brown sable coat. "Allow me to present you with it. There will be no duty. It has entered the country legally."

Pale, shaking with excitement as well as astonishment, Mrs. Butterfield was enveloped in the coat, and there stood Yogi Bear, only twice as huge as though expanded with a bicycle pump. She looked about as impossible as it was for anyone to look wrapped in such an exquisite garment. It was gorgeous, it was the best ever, but it wasn't Mrs. Butterfield. Ada Harris was too touched at the Russians having fulfilled their promise, and with such grandeur, to laugh, but she wanted to.

The ambassador smiled benignly. The secretary replaced the coat in the box. And Mrs. Butterfield and Mrs. Harris emerged unscathed from the Soviet embassy.

UNSCATHED? Hardly. For now it weighed upon them both.

"What am I to do with it?" Violet asked. "I carn't wear the bleedin' fing. It makes me look like a helifant."

"Well, not exactly a helifant," Ada said, "though it does round you out a bit."

"What's it worth?"

"About ten thousand quid," Ada replied.

"Oh Lordy, we'll be robbed and murdered in our beds for it. And 'ow am I goin' to show up at the Paradise Club for cleanin' out lavatories, wearin' a sable coat? I'd better give it back."

"You carn't. They'd be insulted. We've got to fink." Ada went into her thinking pose, chin in hand. Suddenly she leaped up and cried, "Oh my Gawd, what's 'appened to me brynes. We flog it."

"Flog it to 'oo?" said Violet, wide-eyed. "You know we don't want no questions arsked. 'Oo's goin' to pay ten thousand quid?"

"I wouldn't say exactly ten," replied Ada. "We sell it privately for a bit less, but you'll 'ave a fortune for yer old age. It just came to me mind. Once when I was doin' the cleanin' for Lady Corrison, I 'eard 'er badgerin' 'er 'usband to buy 'er a sable coat, and 'im sayin' 'e'd be 'anged if 'e'd put out ten thousand quid for a bit of hide. Them kind is always lookin' for a bargain, and this would fit 'er perfect. We could let 'er 'ave it for seven. She could work 'er 'usband for that. Then, you buys your musquash coat at Arding and Hobbs and you puts the rest in stocks and bonds and never 'ave another worry for the rest of yer life."

"Oh Lordy," said Mrs. Butterfield, "do you fink she would?"

"It's as good as done."

"Ada," said Vi, "I don't know what in the world I would do wifout you, or what I could do to thank you."

But she did know one way how to thank her friend who managed to squeeze six thousand five hundred pounds out of the Corrisons, and before another day had passed, Mrs. Butterfield was proud and happy in her musquash coat and the rest of the money, or almost the rest, safely stowed away. One evening a week or so later, returning home from her labors, Mrs. Harris found to her surprise and delight that the old television was gone and in its place reposed a magnificent giant-screen color set. Then Mrs. Butterfield appeared and was hugged and kissed and given the rounds of "You shouldn't 'ave done it. Oh, Vi, I ain't never been so thrilled in me life. How on earth did you get it in 'ere?"

"I nipped yer spare key last night," Vi replied. Then with moist kisses and hugs added, "We'll both enjoy it, dearie, and you 'ad it comin' to you. If it 'adn't been for you I'd never of got me musquash and all that money in the bank. Let's try it."

"Loverly," agreed Mrs. Harris. "I'm dyin' to see it work." She pushed the ON button and the voice came before the picture and was saying, "British Airways Special Tour Contest just for you."

Then the picture, in glorious color, bloomed onto the screen, and as the two women stared, they were back in Red Square. "British Airways package holiday tours offer *you* a chance to win two tickets for five days in glorious Moscow. Send for our brochure and fill out the coupon. You may be the lucky one."

Red Square zoomed in again, the queue still waiting outside Lenin's tomb. Mrs. Harris and Mrs. Butterfield fell into one another's arms, screaming with laughter, and remained there shouting helplessly until the commercial faded from the screen.

Paul Gallico has been introduced to readers of Condensed Books through two earlier adventures of the unique London char (*Mrs. 'Arris Goes to Paris* and *Mrs. 'Arris Goes to New York*), as well as two other stories, *The Hand of Mary Constable* and most recently *The Boy Who Invented the Bubble Gun.*

Paul Gallico

Born in New York City in 1897, Gallico spent much of his childhood traveling with his parents throughout Europe. He remembers his father, a concert pianist, as a great raconteur of adventure tales which provided constant entertainment and inspiration. Young Gallico wrote his first piece of fiction when he was only ten, thus beginning a lifelong passion for storytelling.

He graduated from Columbia University in 1921 and in 1922 went to work for the New York *Daily News,* where he quickly built a reputation as an outstanding sportswriter. In 1936 he left the paper to devote his time to free-lance writing. The huge success of an early book, *The Snow Goose,* soon thereafter established him as a novelist of unique quality.

Wherever he has lived since, from Mexico to Liechtenstein, and whatever his job, from war correspondent to screenwriter, he has cast the same humorous, affectionate and concerned eye on the human beings around him, and from them has created the characters who delight his millions of readers.

Paul Gallico now divides his time between London and the south of France, where he works daily on one writing project or another. His purpose is to entertain, and in the process he finds himself thoroughly entertained as well. At seventy-eight he seems to share with his own Mrs. 'Arris an enthusiastic pleasure in life's possibilities.

THE MONEY-CHANGERS

A CONDENSATION OF THE BOOK BY

ARTHUR HAILEY

ILLUSTRATED BY
DON STIVERS

The Moneychangers unlocks the door of the
First Mercantile American Bank as the
founder's imminent death sets off a power
struggle for the bank's presidency. But while
the giants of the institution lock horns, a
series of dramas is taking place: a vulnerable
girl teller's cash shortage points the way to
the terrifying depths of the underworld and a
credit card counterfeiting ring; fearful
depositors start a run on a suburban
branch. . . . Money. People. Banking. This
fast-paced, exciting novel is the inside story
of all three.

As he did in *Hotel* and *Airport,* Arthur
Hailey takes us behind the façade of an
institution that touches us all. The engaging
and dramatic stories of the individual
moneychangers make *The Moneychangers*
the most human story about banking ever
written.

Chapter 1

Long afterward, many would remember those two days in the first week of October with vividness and anguish.

It was on Tuesday of that week that old Ben Rosselli, president of First Mercantile American Bank and grandson of the bank's founder, made an announcement—startling and somber—which reverberated through the bank and far beyond. And the next day, Wednesday, the bank's "flagship" downtown branch discovered the presence of a thief—beginning a series of events which few could have foreseen, and ending in financial wreckage and human tragedy.

The bank president's announcement occurred without warning; remarkably, there were no advance leaks. Ben Rosselli had telephoned a number of senior employees of FMA early in the morning at their homes. To each the message was the same: "Please be in the Headquarters Tower boardroom at eleven a.m."

Now all except Ben were assembled in the boardroom, twenty or so, talking quietly in groups, waiting. All were standing; no one chose to be first to pull a chair back from the gleaming directors' table, longer than a squash court, which seated forty.

A voice cut sharply across the talk. "Who authorized that?"

Heads turned. Roscoe Heyward, executive vice-president and comptroller, had addressed a white-coated waiter who was pouring sherry into glasses.

Heyward was a zealous teetotaler. He glanced pointedly at his watch in a gesture which said clearly, Not only drinking, but this *early*. Several who had been reaching for the sherry withdrew their hands.

"Mr. Rosselli's instructions, sir," the waiter stated. "And he especially ordered the best sherry."

A stocky figure, fashionably dressed in light gray, said easily, "Whatever time it is, no sense passing up the best."

Alex Vandervoort, blue-eyed and fair-haired with a touch of gray at the temples, was also an executive vice-president. Genial and informal, his easygoing ways belied the tough decisiveness beneath. The two men—Heyward and Vandervoort—represented the second management echelon, immediately below the presidency, and while both were seasoned and capable of cooperation, they were, in many ways, rivals. Their differing viewpoints permeated the bank, giving each a retinue of supporters at lower levels.

Now Alex took two glasses of sherry, passing one to Edwina D'Orsey, brunette and statuesque, FMA's ranking woman executive.

Edwina saw Heyward glance toward her, disapproving. Well, it made little difference. Roscoe knew she was a loyalist in the Vandervoort camp. "Thank you, Alex," she said, and took the glass.

There was a moment's tension, then others followed the example. Roscoe Heyward's face tightened angrily.

At the boardroom doorway the vice-president for security, Nolan Wainwright, a towering, Othello-like figure and one of two black executives present, raised his voice. "Mrs. D'Orsey and gentlemen— Mr. Rosselli."

The hum of conversation stopped.

Ben Rosselli stood there, smiling slightly. As always, his appearance struck a median point between a benevolent father figure and the solid pillar of strength to whom thousands entrusted their money for safekeeping. He looked both parts and dressed them: in statesman-banker black, with the inevitable vest, across its front a thin gold chain and fob. It was striking how closely he resembled the first Rosselli—Giovanni—who had founded the bank in the basement of a store a century ago. It was Giovanni's patrician head, with flowing silver hair and full mustache, which the bank reproduced on passbooks and traveler's checks as a symbol of probity.

The here-and-now Rosselli had the silver hair and mustache, almost as luxuriant. But what no reproduction showed was the family drive, the ingenuity and boundless energy which had raised First Mercantile American to its present eminence. Today, though, in Ben Rosselli the usual liveliness seemed missing. He was walking with a cane; no one present had seen him do so before.

Now he reached out, as if to pull one of the heavy boardroom chairs toward him. But Nolan Wainwright moved more quickly. The security chief placed the chair for him. With a murmur of thanks the president settled into it and waved a hand to the others. "This is informal. If you like, pull chairs around. Ah, thank you." He accepted a glass of sherry from the waiter, who went out, closing the door.

A few others seated themselves, but most remained standing. It was Alex Vandervoort who said, "We're obviously here to celebrate." He motioned with his sherry glass. "The question is—what?"

Ben Rosselli smiled fleetingly. "I wish this were a celebration, Alex. It's simply an occasion when I thought a drink might help." He paused, and suddenly tension permeated the room.

"I'm dying," Ben Rosselli said. "My doctors tell me I don't have long. I thought all of you should know." He raised his own glass, contemplated it, and took a sip of sherry.

Where the boardroom had been quiet before, now the silence was intense. No one moved or spoke. Ben leaned forward on his cane. "Come now, let's not be embarrassed. We're all old friends; it's why I called you here. And, oh yes, to save anyone asking, what I've told you is definite; if I thought there was a chance it wasn't, I'd have waited longer. The trouble is lung cancer, well advanced, I'm told. It's probable I won't see Christmas." He paused, and all the frailty and fatigue showed. Softly he added, "So now, as and when you choose, you can pass the word to others."

Edwina D'Orsey thought, There would be no choosing the time. The moment the boardroom emptied, what they had just heard would spread through the bank, and beyond, like prairie fire.

She was dazed, and sensed that the reaction of others was the same.

"Mr. Ben," said old Pop Monroe, a senior clerk in the trust department, "I guess you floored us good." His voice wavered. "I reckon nobody knows what the hell to say." There was a murmur, almost a groan, of assent and sympathy.

Above it Roscoe Heyward injected smoothly, "What we can say, and must"—there was a hint of reproof in the comptroller's voice, as if others should have waited for him to speak first—"is that while this terrible news has shocked and saddened us, we pray there may be hope. Doctors' opinions are seldom exact. Medical science can achieve a great deal in halting, even curing—"

"Roscoe, I said I'd been over all that," Ben Rosselli said, betraying his first trace of testiness. "As to doctors, I've had the best. Wouldn't you expect me to?"

"I would," Heyward said. "But we should remember there is a higher power, and it must be the duty of us all"—he glanced around the room—"to pray to God for at least more time."

The older man said wryly, "I get the impression God has already made up His mind."

Alex Vandervoort observed, "Ben, we're all upset. I'm especially sorry for something I said earlier."

"About celebrating? Forget it! You didn't know." The old man chuckled. "Besides, why not? I've had a good life; surely that's a cause to celebrate." He patted his pockets, then looked around him. "Anybody have a cigarette? Those doctors cut me off."

Several packs appeared. Roscoe Heyward queried, "Are you sure you should?" Ben Rosselli looked at him sardonically. It was no secret that these two had never achieved personal closeness.

Alex Vandervoort lighted the cigarette which the bank president took. Alex's eyes, like others in the room, were moist.

"At a time like this there are some things to be glad of," Ben said. "Being given a little warning is one, the chance to tie loose ends." Smoke from his cigarette curled around him. "Of course, on the other side there are regrets for the way a few things went. You sit and think about those, too."

No one had to be told of one regret—Ben Rosselli had no heir.

An only son had been killed in action in World War II; more recently a promising grandson had died in Vietnam.

A fit of coughing seized the old man. Nolan Wainwright accepted the cigarette from shaking fingers and stubbed it out. Now it became evident how weakened Ben Rosselli really was, how much the effort of today had tired him. Though no one knew it, it was the last time he would be present at the bank.

They went to him individually, shaking his hand gently, groping for words to say. When Edwina D'Orsey's turn came, she kissed him lightly on the cheek and he winked.

Roscoe Heyward was one of the first to leave the boardroom. The executive vice-president–comptroller had two urgent objectives: to ensure a smooth transition of authority after Ben Rosselli's death and to make certain of his own appointment as president.

Wise in the ways of bank politics, Heyward had begun planning his campaign even while this morning's session was in progress. Now he headed for his office suite, paneled rooms with a breathtaking view of the city far below. Seated at his desk, he summoned the senior of his two secretaries, Mrs. Dora Callaghan, and instructed her to telephone all outside directors. He had been quick to observe that only two members of First Mercantile American's board, other than senior management officers, had been present—both old friends of Ben's. That meant that fifteen board members were uninformed of the impending death. Heyward would make sure that all fifteen received the news from him. The facts were so shattering that there would be an instinctive alliance between anyone receiving the news and whoever conveyed it. Also, some directors might resent not having been informed in advance. Roscoe Heyward intended to capitalize on this resentment.

Half an hour after he began phoning, he was informing the Honorable Harold Austin earnestly, "We're overwhelmingly distressed, of course. What Ben told us simply does not seem real."

"Not possible!" The other voice on the telephone still reflected the dismay expressed moments earlier. "And to have to let people know personally!" Harold Austin was from one of the city's oldest families, and long ago had served a term in Congress—hence the title Honorable, a usage he encouraged. Now he owned the state's largest advertising agency and was a veteran director of the bank with strong influence on the board.

The comment about a personal announcement gave Heyward his opening. "I understand exactly what you mean about the method of letting this be known. It did seem unusual. What concerned me most is that the directors were not informed first. I felt it my duty to advise you and the others immediately." Heyward's aquiline, austere face showed concentration; behind rimless glasses his gray eyes were cool.

"I appreciate that, Roscoe. We should have been told."

"Thank you, Harold. At a time like this, one is never sure exactly what is best. Only that someone must exercise leadership."

The use of first names came easily to Heyward. He was old family himself. His personal connections extended far beyond state boundaries, to Washington and elsewhere. Heyward was proud of his social status and friendships in high places. He also liked to remind people of his direct descent from a signer of the Declaration of Independence. Now he suggested, "Another reason for informing board members is that this sad news about Ben is going to have tremendous impact. And it will travel quickly."

Austin concurred. "No doubt of it. Chances are, by tomorrow the press will be asking questions."

"Exactly. And the wrong kind of publicity could make depositors uneasy, as well as depress the price of our stock." Roscoe Heyward could sense wheels turning in his fellow director's mind. The Austin Family Trust, which the Honorable Harold represented, held a big block of FMA shares.

Heyward prompted, "Of course, if the board takes energetic action to reassure shareholders, depositors, and the public generally, the effect could be negligible."

"What do you have in mind, Roscoe?"

"Continuity of authority. There should be no vacancy in the office of chief executive, even for a day. With the greatest respect to Ben, this bank has been regarded for too long as a one-man institution.

But no bank among the nation's top twenty is or could be individually run. Sad as this time is, the directors have an opportunity to dissipate that legend."

Heyward could visualize Austin—a handsome, aging playboy, a flamboyant dresser, with flowing iron-gray hair, probably, as usual, smoking a large cigar. Yet the Honorable Harold was nobody's fool. At length he declared, "Your point is valid. Ben Rosselli's successor needs to be decided on, and probably his name announced before Ben's death. I happen to think you are that man, Roscoe. You've the qualities, experience, the toughness, too. So I'm willing to pledge you my support, and there are others on the board whom I can persuade to go the same route."

"I'm certainly grateful. . . ."

"Of course, in return I may ask an occasional quid pro quo."

"That's reasonable."

"Good! Then we understand each other."

The conversation, Heyward decided as he hung up, had been eminently satisfactory. Austin was a man who kept his word.

The next call, to Philip Johannsen, president of MidContinent Rubber, gave Heyward another opportunity. Johannsen volunteered that frankly he didn't get along with Alex Vandervoort, whose ideas he found unorthodox.

"Alex *is* unorthodox," Heyward said. "Of course, he has some personal problems. I'm not sure how much the two go together."

"What kind of problems?"

"Women, actually. One doesn't like to . . ."

"This is important, Roscoe. Also confidential. So go ahead."

"Well, Alex has marital difficulties. And he's involved with another woman. She's a left-wing activist, frequently in the news, not in a context which would be helpful to the bank. I sometimes wonder how much influence she has on Alex."

"You were right to tell me, Roscoe," Johannsen said. "It's something the directors ought to know. Left-wing, eh?"

"Yes. Her name is Margot Bracken."

"I think I've heard of her. And what I've heard I haven't liked."

Heyward smiled. He was less pleased, however, two telephone

calls later, when he reached an out-of-town director, Leonard L. Kingswood, chairman of the board of Northam Steel.

Kingswood had begun his working life as a furnace melder in a steel plant. He said, "Don't hand me that line, Roscoe," when Heyward suggested that the bank's directors should have had advance warning. "I would have handled it the same way myself. Tell the people you're closest to first, directors and other stuffed shirts later."

As to the possibility of a price decline in FMA stock, Len Kingswood's reaction was, "So what? FMA will dip a point or two on the big board when this news gets out, because most stock transactions are on behalf of nervous Nellies who can't distinguish between hysteria and fact. But the stock will go back up within a week because the bank is sound and all of us on the inside know it."

And later in the conversation: "Roscoe, this lobbying of yours is as transparent as a fresh-washed window, so I'll make my position just as plain. You're a topflight comptroller, the best moneyman I know anywhere. Any day you get an urge to move over here to Northam, with a fatter paycheck and a stock option, I'll put you at the top of our financial pile. That's an offer. But good as you are, Roscoe, you're not an overall leader. That's the way I'll call it when the board convenes to decide on who's to follow Ben. My choice is Vandervoort. I think you ought to know that."

Heyward said evenly, "I'm grateful for your frankness, Leonard."

"And if ever you want to talk about that offer, just call me."

Roscoe Heyward had no intention of working for Northam Steel. His pride would not permit it after Leonard Kingswood's biting verdict of a moment earlier. Besides, he was still fully confident of obtaining the top role at FMA.

Again the telephone buzzed. Dora Callaghan announced one more director on the line. "It's Mr. Floyd LeBerre."

"Floyd," Heyward began, his voice pitched low and serious, "I'm sorry to be the one to convey some sad and tragic news."

NOT all who had been at the momentous boardroom session left as speedily as Roscoe Heyward. A few lingered outside, still with a sense of shock, conversing quietly. Pop Monroe said softly to

Edwina D'Orsey, "This is a sad, sad day." Edwina nodded. Ben Rosselli had been important to her as a friend and had taken pride in her rise to authority in the bank.

Alex stopped beside Edwina, then motioned to his office several doors away. "Do you want to take a few minutes out?"

She said gratefully, "Yes, please."

The offices of the bank's top-echelon executives were on the same floor as the boardroom—the thirty-sixth, high in FMA Headquarters Tower. Alex Vandervoort's suite, like others here, had an informal conference area, and there Edwina poured herself some coffee. Vandervoort produced a pipe and lit it.

The camaraderie between the two was of long standing. Although Edwina, who managed First Mercantile American's main downtown branch, was several levels lower than Alex in the bank's hierarchy, he had always treated her as an equal, and often, in matters affecting her branch, dealt with her directly, bypassing the layers of organization between them. By unspoken consent they avoided, for the moment, the subject closest to their minds.

He asked, "How's business at the branch this month?"

"Excellent. And I'm optimistic about next year."

"Speaking of next year, how does Lewis view it?" Lewis D'Orsey, Edwina's husband, was owner-publisher of a widely read investors newsletter.

"Gloomily. He foresees another big drop in the value of the dollar."

"I agree with him." Alex mused, "You know, one of the failures of American banking is that we've never encouraged our clients to hold accounts in foreign currencies—Swiss francs, deutsche marks, others—as European bankers do. Oh, we accommodate the big corporations because they know enough to insist. But if we'd promoted European currency accounts even five years ago, some of our smaller customers would have gained from dollar devaluations, instead of lost."

"Wouldn't the U.S. Treasury object?"

"Probably. But they'd back down under public pressure."

"Have you ever broached the idea?"

"I tried once. I was shot down. To bankers, the dollar—no matter how weak—is sacred. It's a head-in-sand concept we've forced upon the public and it's cost them money." Alex stopped. They sat for several moments without speaking.

Through the wall of windows which made up the east side of Alex's office suite, they could see the robust midwest city spread before them. Closest were the business canyons of downtown, the larger buildings only a little lower than First Mercantile American's tower. Beyond the downtown district, coiled in a double S, was the wide, traffic-crowded river. A latticework of bridges, rail lines, and freeways ran outward to industrial complexes and suburbs, hazy in the distance. Nearer than the suburbs, though just beyond the river, was the inner residential city labeled by some the city's shame.

In the center of this last area a large new building and the steelwork of a second stood out against the skyline.

Edwina pointed to the buildings. "If I were Ben, and wanted to be remembered for something, I'd like it to be Forum East."

"I suppose so." Alex's gaze followed Edwina's. "Without him it would have stayed just an idea."

Forum East was an ambitious attempt to rehabilitate the city's core. Ben Rosselli had committed First Mercantile American to the project, and Alex Vandervoort was in charge of the bank's involvement. The main downtown branch, run by Edwina, handled the project's construction loans and mortgages.

"I was thinking," Edwina said, "about changes which will happen here. I hope none will affect Forum East." She sighed. "It isn't an hour since Ben told us. . . ."

"And we're discussing future bank business before his grave is dug. Well, we have to, Edwina. Ben would expect it. Some important decisions must be made soon."

"Including who's to succeed as president. A good many of us have been hoping it would be you."

"Frankly, so was I."

What both left unsaid was that Alex Vandervoort had been viewed, until today, as Ben Rosselli's chosen heir. But not this soon. Alex had been at First Mercantile American only two years. Ben Rosselli had persuaded him to move over from the Federal Reserve, holding out the prospect of eventual advancement to the top.

"Five years or so from now," Ben had told Alex, "I want to hand over to someone who can cope with big numbers and show a profitable bottom line. But I want a man who won't ever forget that small depositors—individuals—have always been our strong foundation. The trouble with bankers nowadays is that they get too remote." He was making no firm promise, Ben Rosselli made clear, but added, "My impression, Alex, is that you are the kind of man we need. Let's work together for a while and see."

So Alex moved in, bringing his experience and a flair for new technology, and with both had quickly made his mark. As to philosophy, he found he shared many of Ben's views.

Long before, Alex had also gained insights into banking from his father—a Dutch immigrant who became a Minnesota farmer. Pieter Vandervoort had burdened himself with a bank loan and, to pay the interest on it, labored from predawn to darkness, seven days a week. He died of overwork, impoverished, and the bank sold his land, recovering not only arrears of interest but its original investment. His father's experience showed Alex that the other side of a bank counter was the place to be. His route to banking was a Harvard scholarship and an honors degree in economics.

"It may still work out," Edwina D'Orsey said. "Length of service isn't everything."

"It counts."

Mentally, Alex weighed the probabilities. He knew he had the talent and experience to head the bank, but chances were that the directors would favor someone who had been around longer—Heyward, for example, who had worked for FMA for twenty years.

Yesterday the odds favored Alex. Today they had been switched. He knocked out his pipe. "I must get back to work."

"Me, too."

But Alex, when he was alone, sat silent, thoughtful.

Edwina took an express elevator from the directors' floor to the main-floor foyer of FMA Headquarters Tower—an architectural mix of Lincoln Center and the Sistine Chapel. The foyer surged with people—hurrying staff, visitors, sightseers. Through the curving glass front she could see Rosselli Plaza, with its trees, benches, sculpture, and gushing fountain. In summer, office workers ate their lunches there, but now it was bleak, inhospitable. A raw fall wind swirled leaves and sent pedestrians scurrying for indoor warmth. It was the time of year Edwina liked least. It spoke of melancholy, winter soon to come, and death.

Involuntarily she shuddered, then headed for the tunnel, carpeted and softly lighted, which connected the bank's headquarters with the main downtown branch. This was her domain.

CHAPTER 2

WEDNESDAY, at the main downtown branch, began routinely.

Edwina D'Orsey was branch duty officer for the week, and arrived promptly at 8:30, half an hour before the bank's ponderous bronze doors would swing open to the public. As manager of FMA's flagship branch, as well as a corporate vice-president, she didn't have to do the duty-officer chore. But Edwina preferred to take her turn. Besides, the duty only came around once in ten weeks.

At the building's side door she reached in her handbag for her key. Then, before using it, she checked for a no-ambush signal. The signal was where it should be—a small yellow card, placed inconspicuously in a window. The card would have been put there, minutes earlier, by a porter whose job it was to arrive first each day. If all was in order inside, he placed the signal where arriving staff would see it. But if robbers had broken in during the night and were waiting to seize hostages—the porter first—no signal would be placed, so its absence became a warning. Then later-arriving staff would instantly summon aid. Because of the increasing number of robberies, most banks used a no-ambush signal, its type and location changing frequently.

On entering, Edwina went immediately to a hinged panel in the wall and swung it open. Inside was a push button, which she pressed in code—two long, three short, one long. The Central Security operations room in Headquarters Tower now knew that the door alarm, which Edwina's entry had triggered a moment ago, could be ignored and that an authorized officer was in the bank. The porter, on entering, would also have tapped out his own code. Had either Edwina, as duty officer, or the porter failed to tap out their correct codes, the "ops" room would have alerted police. Minutes later the building would have been surrounded. As with other systems, codes were changed often.

Banks everywhere were finding security in positive signals when all was well, an absence of signals when trouble erupted. That way a bank employee held hostage could convey a warning by merely doing nothing.

By now other officers and staff were coming in, checked by the uniformed porter who had taken command at the side door.

"Good morning, Mrs. D'Orsey." A white-haired bank veteran named Tottenhoe joined Edwina. He was operations officer, in charge of staff and routine running of the branch, and his long, lugubrious face made him seem like an ancient kangaroo. Edwina and Tottenhoe walked together across the bank's main floor, then down a wide, carpeted stairway to the vault. Supervising the vault's opening and closing was the duty officer's responsibility.

While they waited by the vault door for the time lock to switch off, Tottenhoe said gloomily, "There's a rumor that Mr. Rosselli's dying. Is it true?"

"I'm afraid it is." She told him briefly of the meeting yesterday. Last night at home Edwina had thought of little else, but this morning she was determined to concentrate on bank business. Ben would expect it.

She checked her watch. Eight forty. Seconds later a click within the massive steel door announced that the overnight time lock, set before the bank closed the day before, had switched itself off. Only now could the vault combination locks be actuated.

Using another concealed push button, Edwina signaled the Central Security ops room that the vault was about to be opened.

Standing side by side at the door, Edwina and Tottenhoe spun separate combinations. Neither knew the combination setting of the other; thus neither could open the vault alone.

An assistant operations officer, Miles Eastin, had now arrived. He was a handsome young man, usually cheerful, in pleasant contrast to Tottenhoe's glumness. With him was a senior vault teller who would supervise transference of money in and out of the vault for the remainder of the day. Nearly a million dollars in currency and coinage would be under his control during the next six operating hours. Checks passing through the big branch bank that day would represent another twenty million.

As Edwina stood back, the senior teller and Miles Eastin together swung open the huge, precision-engineered vault door. It would remain open until the close of business.

"Just took a phone message," Eastin informed the operations officer. "Scratch two more tellers for today. Flu."

Tottenhoe's look of melancholy deepened. "Then we'll have to empty an executive chair or two. You're the first elected," he said to Miles Eastin, "so get a cashbox and be ready for the public. Do you remember how to count?"

"Up to twenty," Eastin said. "As long as I can work with my socks off."

Edwina smiled. Everything young Eastin touched he did well. When Tottenhoe retired next year, he would be in line for operations officer.

He returned the smile. "Not to worry, Mrs. D'Orsey. I played handball last night and managed to keep score."

Edwina knew, too, of Eastin's other hobby, which was useful to the bank—the study and collection of currencies and coin. It was Miles Eastin who gave orientation talks to new employees, and he liked to toss in historical nuggets such as the fact that paper money and inflation were both invented in China. The first recorded instance of inflation, he would explain, was during the thirteenth century, when the Mongol emperor Kublai Khan was unable to pay his soldiers in coin. So he used a wood printing block to produce worthless paper money. Because of his studies, Eastin was also resident expert on counterfeit money, and doubtful bills which turned up were referred to him for his opinion.

The three of them—Edwina, Eastin, Tottenhoe—ascended the

stairs from the vault to the main banking area. Canvas sacks containing cash were being delivered from an armored truck outside, the money accompanied by two armed guards.

Cash arriving in large volume always came early in the morning, having been transferred earlier still from the Federal Reserve to FMA's own Central Cash Vault. From there it was distributed to branch offices. The reason for the same-day schedule was simple. Excess cash in vaults earned nothing; there were dangers, too, of loss or robbery. The trick, for any branch manager, was never to run short of cash, but not to hold too much.

A large branch bank like FMA's downtown kept a working cash float of half a million dollars in the vault. The money arriving now—another quarter million—was the difference required on an average banking day.

Tottenhoe grumbled to the delivery guards, "I hope you've brought us some cleaner money than we've been getting lately."

"I told them guys over at Central Cash about your beef, Mr. Tottenhoe," one guard said. "Now me," he went on, "I'll take money, clean or dirty."

"Unfortunately," Tottenhoe said, "some customers won't."

New currency, arriving from the Bureau of Engraving and Printing via the Federal Reserve, was keenly competed for by banks. A surprising number of carriage trade customers rejected dirty bills and demanded new or at least clean notes, which bankers called "fit." Fortunately there were others who didn't care, and tellers had instructions to save their fresh bills for those who asked for them.

"Hear there's lots of high-grade counterfeit stuff around. Maybe we could get you a bundle." The second guard winked at his companion.

Edwina told him, "That kind of help we can do without. We've been getting too much of it."

Only last week the bank had discovered nearly a thousand dollars in counterfeit bills, source unknown. More than likely it had come through depositors who had been defrauded themselves and were passing their loss along to the bank, most of them with no idea the bills were counterfeit. U.S. Secret Service agents who had discussed the matter with Edwina and Miles were frankly worried. "Counterfeit money has never been as good as what we're seeing now, and there's never been as much in circulation." Their estimate was that thirty million dollars of bogus money had been produced the previous year. "And a lot more will never get detected."

England and Canada were major supply sources of spurious U.S. currency. The agents also reported that an incredible amount of it was circulating in Europe. "It's not so easily detected there, so warn your friends who go to Europe never to accept American bills. There's a strong chance they could be worthless."

The first armed guard shifted the sacks on his shoulders. "Don't worry, folks! These are genuine greenbacks." Both guards went down the stairway to the vault.

Edwina walked to her desk on the platform. Throughout the bank, activity was increasing. The front doors were open, early customers streaming in. The platform, where by tradition the senior branch officers worked, was raised slightly above the main-floor level and carpeted in crimson. Edwina's desk, the largest and most imposing, was flanked by two flags—behind her and to the right the Stars and Stripes, to her left the state banner. Sometimes, seated there, she felt as if she were on TV.

The bank was lavishly modern, rebuilt a year ago when FMA's adjoining Headquarters Tower was erected. Crimson and mahogany predominated, with an appropriate sprinkling of gold. The result of expert design, it was a combination of customer convenience, excellent working conditions, and opulence.

As Edwina settled into her high-backed swivel chair, she reached for the files of loan applications for amounts greater than other officers in the branch had authority to approve.

Her own authorization to lend money extended to a million dollars in any one instance, providing two other officers in the branch concurred. They invariably did. Amounts in excess were referred to the bank's credit policy unit in Headquarters Tower. In First Mercantile American, as in any banking system, an acknowledged status symbol was the size of a loan which a bank official had power to sanction. It was spoken of as the quality of initial, because an individual's initial put final approval on any loan proposal.

The quality of Edwina's initial was unusually high even for a manager, reflecting her responsibility in running FMA's downtown branch. A manager of a lesser branch might approve loans from ten thousand to half a million, depending on ability and seniority. Quality of initial supported a caste system throughout FMA with attendant privileges. In the Headquarters Tower credit policy unit, for example, an assistant loan inspector, whose authority was limited to a mere fifty thousand dollars, worked at an unimpressive desk, alongside others in a large open office. A loan inspector, whose initial was good for a quarter million dollars, rated a larger desk in a glass-paneled cubicle.

An honest-to-goodness office with door and window was the perquisite of an assistant loan supervisor, whose quality of initial extended higher, to half a million dollars. He also rated a capacious desk, an oil painting on the wall and memo pads printed with his name, a free daily copy of *The Wall Street Journal,* and a complimentary shoeshine every morning. He shared a secretary with another assistant supervisor.

Finally a loan officer vice-president, whose initial was good for a million dollars, worked in a corner office with *two* windows, *two* oil paintings, and a secretary of his own. His name memos were *engraved.* He, too, had a free shoeshine and newspaper, plus magazines and journals, the use of a company car when required for business, and access to the senior officers' dining room for lunch.

As a branch manager Edwina had no office, but she qualified for almost all the other quality-of-initial perquisites. She had never used the shoeshine.

This morning she studied two loan requests, approved one, and penciled some queries on the other. A third proposal stopped her short. Startled, she read through the file again.

The loan officer who had prepared the file answered Edwina's intercom buzz. "Castleman here."

"Cliff, please come over."

"Sure." The loan officer, only half a dozen desks away, looked across at Edwina. "And I'll bet I know why you want me."

As he seated himself beside her desk, he glanced at the open file. "I was right. We get some lulus, don't we?"

Cliff Castleman had a round pink face and soft smile. Borrowers liked him because he was a good listener and sympathetic. But he was also a seasoned loan man with sound judgment.

"Are you serious in proposing to lend this much money for *this* purpose?" Edwina asked him.

"I'm deadly serious—" The loan officer stopped abruptly. "Sorry! That wasn't intended to be gallows humor. But I believe you should approve the loan."

It was all there in the file. A forty-three-year-old pharmaceutical salesman named Gosburne was applying for a loan of twenty-five thousand dollars. He had been married for seventeen years and owned his home except for a small mortgage. The Gosburnes had had a joint account with FMA for eight years—no problems. An earlier, smaller loan had been repaid. Gosburne's employment record and other financial history were good.

The intended purpose of the new loan was to buy a large stainless steel capsule in which would be placed the body of the Gosburnes' daughter, Andrea. She had died six days ago, at age fifteen, from a kidney malignancy. At present Andrea's body was at a funeral home, stored in dry ice. Her blood had been drawn off immediately after death and replaced with a bloodlike "antifreeze" solution. The steel capsule was specially designed to contain liquid nitrogen at a sub-zero temperature. The body, wrapped in aluminum foil, would be immersed in this solution.

A capsule of the type sought, known as a cryocrypt, was available in Los Angeles and would be flown from there if the bank loan was approved. About a third of the intended loan was for prepayment of vault-storage rent for the capsule, and replacement of the liquid nitrogen every four months.

Castleman asked Edwina, "You've heard of cryonics societies?"

"Vaguely."

"Cryonics groups have a big following, and they've convinced Gosburne and his wife that when medicine is more advanced— say fifty or a hundred years from now—Andrea can be thawed out, brought back to life, and cured. The cryonics people have a motto: Freeze—wait—reanimate."

"Horrible," Edwina said.

The loan officer conceded. "Mostly I agree with you. But look at it their way. They believe. Also they're adult, reasonably intelligent people, deeply religious. So who are we to be judge and jury? As I see it, the only question is—can Gosburne repay the loan? I've gone over the figures, and I say he can and will. The guy may be a nut. But the record shows he's a nut who pays his bills."

Reluctantly, Edwina studied the income and expenses figures. "It will be a terrible financial strain."

"The guy insists he can handle it. He's taking on some spare-time work. And his wife is looking for a job."

Edwina said, "They have four younger children. Has anyone pointed out that twenty-five thousand dollars could be put to better use for the living?"

"I did," Castleman said. "But according to him, the whole family talked that over and made their decision. They believe the chance of bringing Andrea back to life someday will be worth the sacrifices. The children also say that when they're older they'll take over responsibility for her body."

"Oh, horror!" Edwina's thoughts went back to yesterday. Ben Rosselli's death, whenever it came, would be dignified. This made death ugly, a mockery. Should Ben's bank's money be used for such a purpose?

"Mrs. D'Orsey," the loan officer said, "I've had this on my desk for two days. My first feeling was the same as yours. But I've thought about it, and in my opinion it's an acceptable risk."

Acceptable risk. Cliff was right. Acceptable risks were what banking was all about. He was also right in asserting that in most personal matters a bank should not be judge and jury.

Of course, this particular risk might not work out, though even if it failed to, Castleman would not be blamed. His record was good, his "wins" far greater than his losses. In fact, a perfect win record was frowned on; a busy loan officer was almost obligated to have a few of his loans turn sour. If he didn't, he could be in trouble when a computer printout warned management he was losing business through excessive caution.

"All right," Edwina said. "But the idea appalls me."

She scribbled an initial. Castleman returned to his desk.

Thus—apart from a loan for a frozen daughter—this day had begun like any other. It stayed that way until early afternoon.

Edwina had just finished lunch with a client in the senior officers' dining room, high in the executive tower, when a waitress brought a message to their table. "Mrs. D'Orsey, Mr. Tottenhoe is on the phone for you. He says it's urgent."

Edwina excused herself and went to the telephone.

"We have a serious cash shortage," Tottenhoe said. He went on to explain. A teller had reported the loss half an hour ago. Checking had been going on continuously since. Edwina asked how much money was involved.

She heard him swallow. "Six thousand dollars."

"I'll be down right away."

Within less than a minute, after apologizing to her guest, she was in the express elevator en route to the main floor.

"As FAR as I can see," Tottenhoe said morosely, "the only thing all of us know for certain is that six thousand dollars in cash is not where it should be."

The operations officer was one of four people seated around Edwina D'Orsey's desk. The others were Edwina; young Miles Eastin, Tottenhoe's assistant; and a teller named Juanita Núñez. It was from Juanita Núñez' cash drawer that the money was missing.

Half an hour had elapsed since Edwina's return from lunch. Now, as the others faced her across the desk, Edwina answered Tottenhoe. "What you say is true, but we can do better. I want us to go over everything again, slowly and carefully."

The time was shortly after 3:00 p.m. Customers had gone. The outer doors were closed. Edwina knew she must remain calm and consider every fragment of information. She wanted to listen carefully to nuances of speech and attitude, particularly those of Mrs. Núñez.

Edwina was aware, too, that very soon she must notify head

office of the apparent heavy cash loss, after which headquarters security would become involved, and probably the FBI. But while there was still a chance of finding a solution without bringing up the heavy artillery, she intended to try.

"If you like," Miles Eastin said, "I'll start, because I was the first one Juanita reported to." He had shed his usual breeziness.

Edwina nodded approval.

A few minutes before 2:00 p.m., Eastin informed the group, Juanita Núñez had approached him and stated her belief that six thousand dollars was missing from her cash drawer. Because of the shortage of tellers, Eastin was working a position only two stations away, and she reported to him there, locking her cash drawer before she did so. Eastin had then locked his own cash drawer and gone to Tottenhoe.

Gloomier than usual, Tottenhoe took up the story. He had talked with Mrs. Núñez at once. He hadn't believed at first that as much as six thousand dollars could be missing, because even if she suspected *some* money was gone, it would have been virtually impossible at that point to know how much. Juanita Núñez had been working all day, having started with slightly more than ten thousand dollars cash from the vault in the morning, and she had been taking in and paying out money for almost five hours, except for a forty-five-minute lunch break. How could she be not only certain that money was missing but know the amount so specifically?

The same question had occurred to Edwina. She studied the young woman. Juanita Núñez was small, dark, provocative in an elfin way, and had a pronounced Puerto Rican accent. It was hard to be sure just what her attitude was. Certainly not cooperative. She had volunteered no information other than her original statement that the money was missing. Since they started, her expression had seemed either sulky or hostile. She was nervous, too, continuously turning a thin gold wedding band on her finger.

Edwina D'Orsey knew from the employment record on her desk that Juanita Núñez was twenty-five, married but separated, with a three-year-old child. She had worked for First Mercantile American for almost two years. What wasn't in the record, but Edwina remembered hearing, was that the Núñez girl supported her child alone and had been, perhaps still was, in financial difficulties because of debts left by the husband who deserted her.

Despite his doubts that Mrs. Núñez could possibly know how much money was missing, Tottenhoe continued, he had relieved her from duty at the counter, after which she was immediately locked up with her cash, standard procedure with a problem of this kind. It simply meant that the teller was placed alone in a small, closed office, along with her cash drawer and a calculator, and told to balance all transactions for the day.

Tottenhoe had waited outside.

Soon afterward she called him in. Her cash, she informed him, was six thousand dollars short.

Tottenhoe summoned Miles Eastin, and together they ran a second check while Juanita Núñez watched. There was cash missing in precisely the amount she stated all along. It was then that Tottenhoe had telephoned Edwina.

"Have any ideas occurred to anyone?" Edwina now inquired.

Miles Eastin volunteered, "I'd like to ask Juanita some more questions, if she doesn't mind."

Edwina nodded.

"At any time, Juanita," Eastin began, "did you make a TX with another teller?"

A TX was a teller's exchange. Tellers often ran short of bills or coins of one denomination. Rather than making a trip to the cash vault, they helped each other by "buying" or "selling" cash, using a TX form to keep a record. But occasionally mistakes were made, so that at the end of the business day one teller would be short on cash, the other long. It would be unlikely, though, for such a difference to be as large as six thousand dollars.

"No," the teller said. "No exchanges. Not today."

"Were you aware of anyone on the staff, at any time, being near your cash so they could have taken some?"

"No."

"When you told me you thought there was some money gone," Eastin said, "how long had you known about it?"

127

"A few minutes."

Edwina interjected, "How long was that after your lunch break?"

The girl hesitated, seeming less sure of herself. "Maybe twenty minutes."

"Let's talk about *before* you went to lunch," Edwina said. "Do you think the money was missing then?"

Juanita Núñez shook her head in a strong negative.

"How can you be sure?"

"I know."

The monosyllabic answers were becoming irritating to Edwina. The hostility she had sensed earlier seemed more pronounced.

Tottenhoe repeated the crucial question. "After lunch, why were you certain not only that money was missing but exactly how much?"

The young woman's small face set defiantly. "I knew."

There was disbelieving silence.

"Do you think that you could have paid six thousand dollars out to a customer in error?"

"No."

Miles Eastin asked, "When you left your teller's position before you went to lunch, Juanita, you took your cash drawer to the cash vault and closed the combination lock. Right?"

"Yes."

"Are you sure you locked it?"

The young woman nodded positively.

The cash drawer Miles Eastin referred to was a portable strongbox on a stand with wheels, light enough to be pushed around easily. It was sometimes called a cash truck. Every teller had one assigned, and the same cash drawer or truck, conspicuously numbered, was normally used by the same individual. A few spares were available. Miles Eastin had been using one today.

All tellers' cash drawers were checked in and out of the vault by a senior vault teller, making it impossible to remove someone else's, deliberately or in error. Each cash drawer had two tamperproof combination locks—one set by the teller, the other by the operations officer. Thus a cash drawer was always opened in the presence of two people—the teller and an operations officer.

Tellers were expected to memorize their combinations and not to confide them to anyone else. The only written record of a teller's combination was in a sealed and double-signed envelope which was kept in a safe-deposit box. The seal on the envelope was only broken in the event of a teller's death, illness, or leaving the bank's employ.

A further feature of the sophisticated cash drawer was a built-in alarm system. When rolled into place at a teller's position, an electrical connection linked each cash drawer with an interbank communications network. A warning trigger was hidden within the drawer, beneath a pile of bills known as bait money. In the event of a holdup this money was to be handed over first. Simply removing the bills released a silent plunger switch, which alerted bank security staff and police. It also activated hidden cameras. Serial numbers of the bait money were on record for use as evidence later.

"When you came back from lunch, was your cash drawer still in the vault, still locked?" Miles asked Juanita.

"Yes."

"Does anyone else know your combination?"

"No."

Edwina asked Tottenhoe, "Was the bait money among the missing six thousand dollars?"

"No," the operations officer said. "It was intact."

Once more Miles Eastin addressed the teller. "Juanita, is there any way you can think of that *anyone at all* could have taken the money out of your cash drawer?"

"No," Juanita Núñez said.

Watching closely as the young woman answered, Edwina thought she detected fear. She no longer had doubts about what had happened to the missing money. The Núñez girl had stolen it. No other explanation was possible. She could have passed it over the counter to an accomplice, or she could have concealed the money and carried it from the bank during her lunch break.

Juanita Núñez must have known that she would lose her job, whether it was proved she had stolen the money or not. Bank tellers were allowed occasional cash discrepancies; such errors were normal and expected. In the course of a year, eight "overs" or "unders" was average, and provided each error was no larger than twenty-five dollars, usually nothing was said. But no one who experienced a major cash shortage kept her job, and tellers knew it.

Of course, Juanita Núñez could have decided that an immediate six thousand dollars was worth the loss of her job, even though she might have difficulty getting another. Either way, Edwina was sorry for the girl. Obviously she must have been desperate.

"I don't believe there's any more we can do at this point," Edwina told the group. As the three got up, she added, "Mrs. Núñez, please stay." The girl resumed her seat.

Edwina was aware of the girl's dark eyes fixed intently on her own. "Juanita, two things must have occurred to you. First, there's going to be a thorough investigation and the FBI will be involved because we're a federally insured bank. Second, there is no way that suspicion cannot fall on you."

Edwina chose her words carefully, avoiding a direct accusation which might rebound in legal trouble.

The girl said emphatically, "I did not take any money."

"I haven't said you did. But if you know something more than you have said already, now is the time to tell me, while we're talking quietly here. After this it will be too late. I'll make a promise. If the money were returned to the bank, let's say no later than tomorrow, there would be no prosecution. Whoever took the money could no longer work here. But nothing else would happen. I guarantee it. Juanita, do you have *anything* to tell me?"

"No, no, no!" The girl's eyes blazed, her face came alive in anger. "I tell you I did not take any money, now or ever."

Edwina sighed. "All right, that's all for now. But please do not leave the bank without checking with me first."

With a shrug, Juanita Núñez rose and turned away.

From her elevated desk Edwina surveyed the activity around her; it was her world, her personal responsibility. The day's transactions were still being balanced. A preliminary check had shown that no teller had a six-thousand-dollar overage. Edwina lifted a telephone and dialed an internal number—the security department. "Mr. Wainwright, please," she said.

NOLAN Wainwright had found it hard, since yesterday, to concentrate on normal work within the bank. He had been deeply affected by Tuesday's session in the boardroom. For over a decade he and Ben Rosselli had achieved both friendship and mutual respect.

It had not always been that way. Yesterday, returning from the boardroom to his modest office, Wainwright had told his secretary not to disturb him. Then he had sat at his desk, sad, brooding, reaching back in memory to his first clash with Ben Rosselli's will.

It was ten years earlier, when Nolan Wainwright was the newly appointed police chief of a small upstate town. Soon after his appointment, Ben Rosselli drove through the outskirts of the town and was clocked at eighty miles per hour. A local patrolman handed him a ticket with a summons to traffic court.

Perhaps because his life was conservative in other ways, Ben Rosselli loved fast cars and drove them with his foot near the floor. Speeding summonses were routine. Back at First Mercantile American headquarters, the state's most powerful man of money sent the summons, as usual, to the bank's security department, with instructions to have it fixed. It was dispatched by courier next day to the FMA branch manager in the town where it was issued. It so happened that the branch manager was also a local councilman and had been influential in Nolan Wainwright's appointment as police chief.

The bank manager–councilman dropped over to police headquarters and amiably suggested that the traffic summons be withdrawn. Nolan Wainwright declined.

The councilman put on his banker's hat and reminded the police chief of his personal application to FMA for a home mortgage loan which would make it possible to bring Wainwright's wife and family to the town. Nolan Wainwright said he could see no relationship between a loan application and a traffic summons.

In due course Mr. Rosselli, for whom counsel appeared in court, was fined heavily for reckless driving and awarded three demerit points, to be recorded on his license—the first in a lifetime. He was exceedingly angry. Also in due course the mortgage application of Nolan Wainwright was turned down by First Mercantile American Bank.

Less than a week later Wainwright presented himself in Rosselli's office, taking advantage of the accessibility on which the bank president prided himself.

When he learned who his visitor was, Ben Rosselli was surprised that he was black. No one had mentioned that. Wainwright spoke coolly. To his credit, Ben Rosselli had known nothing of the police chief's mortgage loan application or its rejection. But he smelled the odor of injustice and sent for the loan file, which he reviewed while Nolan Wainwright waited.

"As a matter of interest," Ben Rosselli said, "if we don't make this loan, what do you intend to do?"

"Fight. I'll hire a lawyer and we'll go to the Civil Rights Commission, for a start. If we don't succeed there, whatever else can be done to cause you trouble, that I'll do."

The banker snapped, "I don't respond to threats."

"I'm not making threats. You asked a question, I answered it."

Ben Rosselli scribbled a signature in the file. He said, unsmiling, "The application is approved."

Before Wainwright left, the banker asked, "What happens now if I get caught speeding in your town?"

"We'll throw the book at you. If it's another reckless driving charge, you'll probably be in jail."

Two years later, when the bank was seeking a security chief who would be—as the personnel head expressed it—"strong and totally incorruptible," Ben Rosselli stated, "I know of such a man."

Since Nolan Wainwright came to work for FMA he and Rosselli had never clashed. The security head did his job efficiently and added to his knowledge by taking night school courses in banking theory. Rosselli, for his part, got his speeding tickets fixed elsewhere. The friendship between the two grew, and after the death of Ben Rosselli's wife, Wainwright frequently would eat dinner with the old man and play chess with him into the night. It had been a consolation for Wainwright, too, for his own marriage had ended

in divorce soon after he went to work for FMA. His new responsibilities, and the sessions with old Ben, helped fill the gap.

They talked at such times about personal beliefs. And it was
Wainwright—though only the two of them ever knew it—who
persuaded the bank president to invest in the Forum East development in the neglected city area where Wainwright had grown up.
Thus Nolan Wainwright had his private memories of Ben Rosselli
and his private sorrow.

Today his depression had persisted. He had stayed at his desk,
avoiding people he did not need to see, keeping only an appointment
with Alex Vandervoort that afternoon.

Their meeting was in the bank's Keycharge credit card division
in the Headquarters Tower. Keycharge—doing a three-billion-
dollar-a-year business—had been pioneered by FMA and now was
operated jointly with a strong group of other banks in the U.S.,
Canada, and overseas. In size, Keycharge ranked third among such
systems. Alex Vandervoort had overall responsibility for the division.

The security chief joined Vandervoort in the Keycharge authorization center. "I always like to see this," Alex said. "Best free
show in town."

In a large, dimly lighted room with acoustic walls and ceilings
to deaden sound, some fifty operators—predominantly women—were
seated at a battery of cathode-ray consoles, similar to TV screens,
with a keyboard beneath each. It was here that holders of the
blue, green, and gold Keycharge cards were given or refused credit.

When a card was presented anywhere in payment for goods or
services, the place of business could accept the card without question
if the amount was below an agreed floor limit, usually between
twenty-five and fifty dollars. For a larger purchase, authorization
was needed, though it took only seconds to obtain.

Calls poured into the authorization center twenty-four hours a
day, seven days a week, from every U.S. state and Canadian province,
while chattering Telex machines brought queries from thirty foreign
countries, including some in the communist orbit.

The approval procedures moved at jet speed. From wherever
they were, merchants and others dialed directly to the Keycharge

nerve center in FMA Headquarters Tower. Automatically each call was routed to a free operator, whose first words were, "What is your merchant number?" As the answer was given, the operator typed the figures, which appeared simultaneously on the cathode-ray screen. Next she asked the card number and amount of credit being sought; this, too, was typed and displayed.

The operator pressed a key, feeding the information to a computer, which instantly signaled ACCEPTED or DECLINED. The first meant that credit was good and the purchase approved, the second that the cardholder was delinquent and credit had been cut off. The operator informed the merchant, the computer recording the transaction. On a normal day fifteen thousand calls came in.

Both Alex Vandervoort and Nolan Wainwright had accepted headsets so they could listen to exchanges between callers and operators. The security chief touched Alex's arm and pointed. A console was flashing a message from the computer—STOLEN CARD.

The operator, speaking calmly, as trained, answered, "The card presented to you has been reported as stolen. If possible, detain the person presenting it and call police. Retain the card. Keycharge will pay you thirty dollars reward for its return."

They could hear a whispered colloquy, then a voice announced, "The creep just ran out of my store. But I grabbed the plastic. I'll mail it in." The storekeeper sounded pleased at the prospect of an easy thirty dollars. For the Keycharge system it was also a good deal, since the card, left in circulation, could have been used fraudulently for a much greater total amount.

Wainwright and Vandervoort removed their headsets. "It works well," Wainwright said, "when we get the information and can program the computer. Unfortunately most of the defrauding happens before a missing card's reported."

"But we still get a warning of excessive purchasing?"

"Right. Ten purchases in a day and the computer alerts us."

Few cardholders ever made more than six or eight purchases during a single day. Thus, a card showing more than normal use could be listed as PROBABLY FRAUDULENT, even though the owner might be unaware of its loss.

Despite all warning systems, however, a lost or stolen Keycharge card, if used cagily, was still good for twenty thousand dollars' worth of fraudulent purchases in the week or so during which most stolen cards stayed unreported.

As both Vandervoort and Wainwright knew, there were devices used by criminals to decide whether a stolen card could be used again or if it was hot. A favorite was to pay a headwaiter twenty-five dollars to check a card out. He could get the answer easily by consulting a weekly confidential warning list issued by the credit card company to merchants and restaurants.

"We've been losing much more than usual through fraud lately," Wainwright said. "It's what I wanted to talk about."

They moved into an office and closed the door. The two men were much in contrast physically—Vandervoort, fair, chunky, non-athletic; Wainwright, black, tall, trim, hard, and muscular. Their personalities differed, too, though their relationship was good.

"This is a contest without a prize," Nolan Wainwright told the executive vice-president. He placed on the office desk eight plastic Keycharge cards, snapping them down like a poker dealer, one by one. "Four of those are counterfeit," the security chief announced. "Can you separate the good ones from the bad?"

"Certainly. The counterfeits always use different typefaces for embossing the cardholder's name and—" Vandervoort stopped. "But these don't! The typeface is the same on every card."

"Almost the same. You can detect slight divergences with a magnifier." Wainwright produced one. He pointed to variations between the embossing on the four genuine cards and the others.

"How do the counterfeits look under ultraviolet?"

"Exactly the same as real ones."

"That's bad."

Following an example set by American Express, a hidden insignia had been imprinted on the face of all authentic Keycharge cards, visible only under ultraviolet light. Now that safeguard, too, had been outflanked.

"It's bad, all right," Nolan Wainwright agreed. "I've four dozen more, intercepted *after* they'd been used successfully in retail outlets, restaurants, for airline tickets, liquor, and other things. And all are the best counterfeits which have ever shown up."

"Arrests?"

"None so far. When people sense a phony card is being queried, they walk out. Besides, even when we do arrest some users, it doesn't follow we'll be near the source. Usually they're sold and resold carefully enough to cover a trail."

Alex Vandervoort picked up one of the fraudulent blue, green, and gold cards. "The plastic seems an exact match, too."

"They're made from authentic plastic blanks that must have been stolen." He motioned to the counterfeits on the desk. "This is the tip of an iceberg. The phony cards we know about can mean a ten-million-dollar loss in charges. But what about others we haven't heard of yet? There could be ten times more."

"Is it likely that there's some kind of ring behind them?"

"Not only likely, it's a certainty. For the product to be this good there has to be an organization. And it's got money behind it, machinery, specialists, a distribution system. Besides, there are other signs. Recently there's been a big increase through the Midwest in counterfeit currency, traveler's checks, other credit cards, stolen and counterfeit securities, forged checks."

"And you believe all these frauds are linked to our losses?"

"Let's say it's possible. We're doing as much as we can, trying to track down every lost or missing Keycharge card. But something like this needs a full-scale investigation, and I don't have either staff or budget to handle it."

Alex Vandervoort smiled ruefully. "I thought we'd get around to budget. You've got proposals and figures, I presume."

Wainwright produced a manila folder. "It's all there. The most urgent need is two more full-time investigators for the credit card division. I'm also asking for funds for an undercover agent to locate the source of these counterfeit cards."

Vandervoort looked surprised. "You think you can get someone?"

Wainwright smiled. "You don't advertise in the Help Wanted columns. But I'm willing to try."

Alex took the manila folder. "I'll do what I can."

"If I don't hear, I'll be along to pound the desk."

Alex left, but Wainwright was delayed by a message. It asked the security chief to see Mrs. D'Orsey at once.

"I've spoken to the FBI," Wainwright informed Edwina. "They'll have two special agents here tomorrow."

"Then can I let the staff go home?" asked Miles Eastin.

"All except the girl. I'd like to talk with her again."

It was early evening, two hours since Wainwright had responded to Edwina's summons and taken over the investigation. He had interviewed Juanita Núñez, Tottenhoe, and Eastin. He had also spoken with tellers who had been working near the Núñez girl.

For privacy, Wainwright had requisitioned a small conference room at the rear of the bank. He was there now with Edwina and Miles Eastin. Nothing new had emerged, and since theft appeared likely, under federal law the FBI must be called in. The law, on such occasions, was not always applied painstakingly. First Mercantile American and other banks often labeled thefts as mysterious disappearances. That way, such incidents could be handled internally, avoiding prosecution and publicity. But the present loss was too large to be concealed.

Edwina and Miles Eastin left the office, and a moment later the small figure of Juanita Núñez appeared at the doorway. "Come in," Nolan Wainwright instructed. "Shut the door. Sit down." He made his tone official and businesslike. Instinct told him that phony friendliness would not deceive this girl. "I want to hear your whole story again. Step by step."

With a sudden flash of spirit Juanita objected. "Three times I have already done that!"

"Then this time will make a fourth, and when the FBI arrive, there'll be a fifth." He kept authority in his voice, but didn't raise it. If he were a police officer, he'd have had to caution her about her rights. But he wasn't, and wouldn't. In a situation like this, private security forces had advantages which police did not.

"You think I will say something different this time," the girl said, "so you can prove that I was lying."

"*Are* you lying?"

"No!"

He read contempt in her eyes. During the earlier questioning he had sensed the girl's attitude as being easier toward him than the others. No doubt because he was black and she was Puerto Rican, she assumed they might be allies. What she didn't know was that, where investigative work was concerned, he was color-blind.

The Núñez girl had been right, of course, about his wanting to catch her out in some variation of her story. But after an hour her version remained identical with what she had stated earlier. Finally, Wainwright said, "All right, that's everything for now. Tomorrow you can take a lie-detector test. The bank will arrange it."

He made the announcement casually, watching for a reaction. What he had not expected was one so fierce. The girl shot upright in her chair. "No! I will not take such a test!"

"Why not?"

"Because it is an insult!"

"Not at all. If you're innocent, the machine will prove it."

"I do not trust the machine. Or you!"

"You've no reason not to trust me. All I'm interested in is getting to the truth."

"You have heard truth! You do not recognize it! You all believe I took the money. It is useless to tell you I did not."

Wainwright stood up. He opened the door for Juanita to go. "Between now and tomorrow," he advised, "I suggest you reconsider. If you refuse to take the test, it will look bad for you."

She looked him fully in the face. "I do not have to take such a test, do I?"

"No."

"Then I will not."

She marched from the office with short, quick steps. Eastin let her out through the street door. "Juanita," he said, "is there anything I can do? Shall I drive you home?"

She shook her head without speaking and went out. Nolan Wainwright, watching from a window, saw her walk to a bus stop across the street. He was convinced the girl did not have the money on her. The cash would be too bulky to conceal. An accomplice must be involved. He had little doubt of her guilt. Her refusal to submit to the lie detector convinced him.

Miles Eastin had relocked the street door and now returned. "Well," he said, "time to head for the showers." He seemed about to say something else, then apparently decided otherwise.

Wainwright asked him, "Something on your mind?"

Again Eastin hesitated, then admitted, "Well, yes. It's a thing I haven't mentioned because it could be just a wild pitch."

"Does it relate in any way to the missing money?"

"I suppose it could. It was mentioned to you—by Mrs. D'Orsey, I think—that Juanita Núñez' husband deserted her."

"I remember."

"When the husband was living with Juanita he used to come in here occasionally. I spoke to him a couple of times. I'm pretty sure his name is Carlos. I believe he was in the bank today."

Wainwright asked sharply, "Are you sure?"

"Fairly sure, though I couldn't swear to it in court. I just noticed someone I thought was him, then put it out of my mind. I was busy. There was no reason to think about it—until later."

"What time of day was it when you saw this man?"

"About midmorning."

"Did you see him go to the counter where she was working?"

"No, I didn't." Eastin's handsome young face was troubled. "The only thing is, if I saw him, he couldn't have been far away from Juanita."

"And that's everything?"

"That's it. I'm sorry it isn't more."

"Thank you for telling me. It could be important." If Eastin were right, Wainwright reasoned, the presence of the husband could tie in with his theory of an outside accomplice. The possibility was certainly something for the FBI to work on.

Across the street, Juanita Núñez—a tiny figure against the soaring city-block complex of First Mercantile American Bank and Rosselli Plaza—was still waiting for a bus. She had seen Wainwright watching her from a window. A cold wind penetrated her thin coat, and she shivered as she waited. The shivering, Juanita knew, was partly from fear, because at this moment she was more frightened than ever before in her life. Terror-stricken. And perplexed.

Perplexed because she had no idea how the money had been lost. Juanita knew that she had neither stolen the money nor handed it across the counter in error, or disposed of it in any other way. The trouble was, no one would believe her.

In other circumstances, she realized, she might not have believed it herself. How *could* six thousand dollars have vanished? It was impossible, *impossible*. And yet it had.

Time after time this afternoon she had searched her recollection to find some explanation. There was none. Using the remarkable memory she knew she possessed, she had thought back over every cash transaction, but no solution came to her. She was positive, too, that she had locked her cash drawer before lunch and that it was still locked when she returned. As to the combination, which Juanita had chosen and set herself, she had never mentioned it or written it down, relying as usual on her memory. And her memory had just added to her troubles. She knew she had not been believed—even by Miles Eastin, who had at least been friendly—when she claimed to know the exact amount of money which was gone. They said it was impossible she should know.

But she *had* known. Just as she *always* knew how much cash she had when she was working as a teller. She was not sure herself how she kept the running tally in her head; it was simply there. For as long as Juanita could remember, adding, subtracting, multiplying, and dividing had seemed as automatic as breathing. It happened without effort as she took money in or paid it out at the bank counter. And she would glance at her cash drawer, checking instantly that the cash on hand was what it should be. Even with coins, she could estimate the amount closely at any time. Occasionally, at the end of a busy day, when she balanced her cash, her mental figure might prove to be in error by a few dollars, but never more.

Where had the ability come from? She had no idea. She had never excelled in school. She had no real grasp of mathematical principles, merely an ability to calculate with lightning speed and carry figures in her head.

At last a crowded bus arrived and Juanita climbed aboard. She grabbed a handhold and continued thinking as the bus swayed through the city streets. Tomorrow the FBI men were coming. The thought filled her with dread, and her face set in tense anxiety—the same expression which Edwina D'Orsey and Nolan Wainwright had mistaken for hostility. She would say as little as possible, just as she had done today after she found that no one was believing her. As to the lie detector, she knew nothing of how such a machine worked, but when no one else would believe her, why would a machine—the bank's machine—be different?

It was a three-block walk from the bus to the nursery school where she had left Estela this morning on her way to work. Juanita hurried, knowing she was late.

The little girl ran toward her as she entered the small school playroom in the basement of a private house. The house was old and dilapidated, but the schoolrooms were clean and cheerful—the reason Juanita had chosen the school, though the cost was high.

Estela was excited, as full of joy as always. "Mommy! Mommy! See my painting. It's a train." She pointed with a paint-covered finger. "There's a bagoose. That's a *man* inside."

She was a small child, even for three, dark like Juanita, with large liquid eyes reflecting her wonder at the fresh discoveries she made every day.

Juanita hugged her. "Caboose, *amorcito.*"

Miss Ferroe, who ran the school, looked at her watch, frowning. "Mrs. Núñez, as a special favor I agreed that Estela could stay after the others, but this is far too late."

"I really am sorry, Miss Ferroe. Something happened at the bank. It won't happen again. I promise."

"Mrs. Núñez, Estela is a sweet child, and we're glad to have her, but may I remind you that last month's bill is not paid."

"It will be on Friday. I'll have my paycheck then. I promise."

"That's two promises, Mrs. Núñez."

"Yes, I know."

"Good night then. Good night, Estela dear."

Despite her starchiness, Miss Ferroe ran an excellent nursery school, and Estela was happy there. The money for the school would have to come out of this week's pay, Juanita decided, though how she would manage until next payday she wasn't sure. After taxes and social security deductions, her take-home pay was eighty-three dollars. Out of that there was food to buy, Estela's school fees, plus rent on their tiny flat at Forum East; also the finance company would demand a payment, since she had missed the last.

Before he walked out a year ago, Juanita had been naïve enough to sign finance papers jointly with her husband. Carlos had bought suits, a used car, a color TV—all of which he took with him. And Juanita was paying, the installments seeming to stretch into a limitless future. She would have to visit the finance company, she thought, and offer them less. They would undoubtedly be nasty, as they had been before, but it would have to be endured.

On the way home Estela skipped happily along, one small hand in Juanita's. In a little while, in the apartment, they would have their evening meal. After supper they usually played and laughed together. Juanita would find it difficult to laugh tonight. Her terror deepened as she considered for the first time what might happen if she lost her job. The probability, she realized, was strong. No other bank would hire her, and other employers would find out about the missing money and reject her. Without a job how could she support Estela?

Abruptly, stopping on the street, Juanita reached down and clasped her daughter to her. She prayed that tomorrow someone would believe her, would recognize the truth.

Someone. But who?

CHAPTER 4

RETURNING from the session with Nolan Wainwright, Alex Vandervoort paced his office suite. Once or twice he stopped to reexamine the counterfeit Keycharge credit cards. Genuine credit cards were also on his mind.

The genuine variety was represented by a set of advertising proofs spread out on his desk. They had been prepared by the Austin Advertising Agency, and their purpose was to encourage Keycharge holders to use their credit and their cards increasingly.

WHY WAIT?
YOU *CAN* AFFORD TOMORROW'S DREAM TODAY!
USE YOUR KEYCHARGE—*NOW!*

There were half a dozen variations on this theme. Alex was uneasy about them all. The general approach had been agreed on by the bank's board of directors. But had the board envisaged a promotional campaign quite so blatantly aggressive?

He shuffled the proofs together and put them in a folder. At home tonight he would reconsider them, and he would hear a second opinion—probably a strong one—from Margot Bracken.

Margot. The thought of her melded with the memory of Ben Rosselli's disclosure yesterday. What had been said was a reminder to Alex of life's brevity, the inevitability of endings. He had been moved and saddened for Ben himself, but also the old man had revived an oft-recurring question: Should Alex make a fresh life for himself and Margot? Or wait? And wait for what? For Celia? That, too, he had asked himself a thousand times.

He sat down and dialed a number which he knew by heart. A woman's voice answered, "Remedial Center."

He identified himself and said, "I'd like to talk with Dr. McCartney."

After a moment a male voice, quietly firm, inquired, "Alex? I intended to call you today and suggest you come to visit Celia."

"The last time we talked you said you didn't want me to. There's been some change?"

"Yes. I wish I could say for the better. Your wife is even more withdrawn. A visit from you might do some good."

"All right, Tim. I'll come this evening."

"Anytime, Alex, and drop in to see me when you do."

The absence of formality, he reflected as he replaced the telephone, was one reason he had chosen the Remedial Center when faced with his despairing decision about Celia nearly four years ago. The atmosphere was deliberately noninstitutional. Another reason was that Dr. Timothy McCartney, young, brilliant, innovative, headed a specialist team which achieved cures of mental illnesses where more conventional treatments failed. The clinic was private; also horrendously expensive, but Celia must have the best of care. That was, he reasoned, the least he could do.

Soon after 6:00 p.m. he left FMA headquarters, giving his driver the center's address. A limousine and chauffeur were perquisites of the executive vice-president's job and Alex enjoyed them.

The Remedial Center had the façade of a large private home, with only a street number to identify it. An attractive blonde, wearing a colorful print dress, let him in. He recognized her as a nurse from a small insignia pin near her left shoulder, the only dress distinction between staff and patients.

He walked with her down a pleasant corridor. Fresh flowers were in niches along the walls. The nurse opened the door of a comfortable private room which contained a studio couch, a deep armchair, a games table, and bookshelves. "Mrs. Vandervoort," the nurse said gently, "your husband is here to visit you."

There was no acknowledgment from the figure in the room. It had been a month and a half since Alex had seen Celia, and though he had been warned of deterioration, her appearance chilled him.

She was seated sideways on the studio couch, facing away from the door. Her shoulders were hunched, her head lowered, arms crossed in front, each hand clasping the opposite shoulder. Her body was curled upon itself, and her legs drawn up with knees together. She was absolutely still.

He put a hand gently on one shoulder. "Hello, Celia. It's me—Alex. I've been thinking about you, so I came to see you." He increased the pressure on the shoulder. "Won't you look at me? Then we can sit together and talk."

The only response was a tightening of the huddled position. Alex saw that her skin was mottled and her fair hair only roughly combed.

Even now her fragile beauty had not entirely vanished, though clearly it would not be long before it did.

"Has she been like this long?" he asked the nurse quietly.

"All of today and part of yesterday. It's best if you take no notice; just sit down and talk."

Alex nodded. The nurse tiptoed out, closing the door.

"I went to the ballet last week, Celia," Alex said. "Do you remember, soon after we were married, when you and I . . ."

How ethereally beautiful she had looked in a pale green chiffon gown, as if a breeze might steal her away. They had been married six months and she was still shy at meeting his friends. Because she was ten years younger, he hadn't minded. Celia's shyness had been one of the reasons he fell in love with her, and he was proud of her reliance on him. Only long after, when she continued to be diffident—foolishly, it seemed to him—had his impatience surfaced, and eventually anger.

How tragically little he had understood! With more perception he would have realized that nothing in her background had prepared her for the active social life he accepted matter-of-factly. She was the only child of reclusive parents of modest means, and had attended sheltered convent schools. Her social experience and responsibilities had been nil. Self-doubts and tensions grew until—as psychiatrists explained—a burden of guilt at failing snapped something in her mind. Alex blamed himself. He had been too busy, ambitious. Perhaps greater understanding would not have helped. But he would never know. He could not feel certain that he had done his best and so could never shed the guilt which haunted him.

"It was *Coppélia*, Celia, and remembering how you loved it made me sorry we weren't seeing it together. . . ."

In fact, he had been with Margot, whom Alex had known now for a year and a half and who zestfully filled a gap in his life which had been empty for so long.

"A sad thing happened at the bank yesterday, Celia. Ben Rosselli, our president, told us he was dying." Alex went on to describe the scene in the boardroom, then abruptly stopped.

Celia had begun to tremble. Her body was rocking back and

forth. A wail, half moan, escaped her. Had his mention of the bank upset her? Or was it his reference to death?

How many years before Celia died? Many, perhaps. She could easily outlive him, could live on like this, the barrier between himself and a full life. His pity evaporated. The angry impatience which had marred their marriage seized him. "For God's sake, Celia, control yourself!"

Her trembling and the moans continued. *She wasn't human anymore.* Celia, whom he had loved. Swept with remorse, his momentary anger spent, he knelt beside her. "Celia, forgive me! Oh, God, forgive me!"

He felt a gentle hand on his shoulder and heard the young nurse's voice. "Mr. Vandervoort, I think you should go now."

In Dr. McCartney's office, Alex, still shaken, listened as the psychiatrist explained, "The general diagnosis remains the same— schizophrenia, catatonic type. You may find this hard to accept, but your wife, despite the way she seems, is relatively happy."

"Yes," Alex said. "I find that hard to believe."

The doctor insisted gently, "Happiness is relative, for all of us. What Celia has is security of a kind, a total absence of responsibility or any need to relate to others."

Alex eyed the other man directly. "Is there any reasonable chance that Celia could recover and lead a normal or near normal life?"

Dr. McCartney sighed, and shook his head. "No."

"Thank you for a plain answer." Alex paused, then went on, "As I understand it, Celia has become—I believe the word is institutionalized. She's withdrawn from the human race. Neither knowing nor caring about anything outside herself."

"You're right about being institutionalized," the psychiatrist said, "but she is not totally withdrawn. She is aware she has a husband, and we've talked about you. But she believes you're entirely capable of taking care of yourself without her help."

"So she doesn't worry about me?"

"On the whole, no."

"How would she feel if I divorced her and remarried?"

Dr. McCartney hesitated, then said, "It would represent a final break from the little outside contact she has remaining. It might drive her over the brink into a totally demented state."

In the ensuing silence Alex leaned forward, covering his face with his hands. Then his head came up. "I guess if you ask for plain answers, you get them. Tim, *what the hell does a man do?*"

Dr. McCartney considered. "Well, he finds out all he can—just as you have. Then he makes decisions based on what he thinks is best for everyone, including himself. He ought to remember two things: if he's a decent man, his guilt feelings are probably exaggerated, because a well-developed conscience has a habit of punishing itself more harshly than it need. The other is that few people are qualified for sainthood."

"And you won't go further? Be more specific?"

Dr. McCartney shook his head. "Only you can make the decision. Those last few paces each of us walks alone."

"WITHOUT doubt," Margot Bracken declared, "that is a collection of chicanery and damn lies."

The object of Margot's censure was the assortment of advertising proofs for Keycharge credit cards, spread out on the living-room rug of Alex's apartment. She pushed back her long chestnut hair in a familiar gesture. An hour ago she had kicked off her shoes and now stood, all five feet two, in stocking feet.

"Look at that!" She pointed to the announcement that began: WHY WAIT? YOU *CAN* AFFORD TOMORROW'S DREAM TODAY! "What it is, is the dishonest, aggressive selling of debt— concocted to entrap the gullible. Tomorrow's dream, for anyone, is sure to be expensive. That's why it's a dream. And *no one* can afford it unless they have the money now or are certain of it soon."

"Shouldn't people make their own judgments about that?"

"No! The people you're trying to influence are the unsophisticated, who believe that what they see in print is true. I know. I get plenty of them as clients in my unprofitable law practice."

"Maybe those aren't the kind of people who have our Keycharge cards."

"Dammit, Alex, you know that isn't true! The most unlikely people

147

nowadays have credit cards because you've all pushed them so hard. The only thing you haven't done is hand them out at street corners, and it wouldn't surprise me if you started that soon."

Alex grinned. He enjoyed these debating sessions with Margot and liked to keep them fueled. "I'll tell our people to think about it, Bracken."

"What I wish other people would think about is that eighteen percent interest all bank credit cards charge."

He took a breath, determined not to let this discussion get out of hand. Even though he disputed some of Margot's views, he found his own thinking aided by her forthrightness and keen lawyer's mind. Her practice, too, brought her contacts which he lacked— among the city's underprivileged, where most of her legal work was done.

He asked, "Another cognac?"

"Yes, please."

It was close to midnight. A log fire had burned low in the hearth of the small, sumptuous bachelor suite. An hour and a half ago they had had a late dinner here, delivered from a restaurant on the apartment block's main floor. Alex replenished their brandy glasses and returned to the argument. "If people pay their credit card bills in full when they get them, there *is* no interest charge."

"But don't most credit card users pay that convenient minimum balance that the statements show?"

"A good many pay the minimum, yes."

"And carry the rest forward as debt—which is what you bankers really want them to do. Isn't that so?"

"True. But banks have to make a profit somewhere."

"I lie awake nights," Margot said, "worrying if banks are making enough profit."

As he laughed, she went on seriously, "Look, Alex, thousands of people who shouldn't are piling up long-term debts by using credit cards. Those small amounts, which ought to be paid by cash, add up to crippling debts, burdening imprudent people for years ahead."

Alex tossed a fresh log on the fire. Some of what Margot said did make sense, he admitted to himself. Credit cards had replaced, to a large extent, small loans. Where individuals used to be dissuaded from excessive borrowing, now they made their own loan decisions, often unwisely.

Of course, doing it the credit card way did swell a bank's profits, even with losses from fraud. And another thing bankers realized was that credit cards were a necessary way station on the route to EFTS—the Electronic Funds Transfer System—which in the not too distant future would replace the present avalanche of banking paper and make existing checks and passbooks as obsolete as the Model T.

"Enough," Margot said. "We're beginning to sound like a shareholders meeting." She came to him and kissed him.

After a while he murmured, "I declare the shareholders meeting closed."

"Well . . . " Margot looked at him mischievously. "There *is* some unfinished business—that advertising, darling. You're not really going to let it go out to the public the way it is?"

"No," he said, "I don't believe I am."

The Keycharge advertising was too strong a sell, and he would use his authority to exercise a veto in the morning. In this, Margot had merely confirmed his own opinion.

The fresh log he had added to the fire was alight and crackling. They sat on the rug before it, watching the rising tongues of flame. Margot leaned her head against his shoulder. "For a stuffy old moneychanger, you're really not too bad."

He put his arm around her. "I love you, too, Bracken."

"Really and truly? Banker's honor?"

"I swear by the prime rate."

"Then love me now."

They held each other, sharing warmth from their bodies and the fire. He had a sense of release and joy, in contrast to the anguish of the day. At last Margot stirred.

"I can't stay much longer. I have to be in court early."

Margot's court appearances were frequent, and she and Alex had met in the aftermath of one of them. She had been defending half a dozen demonstrators who clashed with police during a rally urging amnesty for Vietnam draft evaders. Her spirited defense attracted wide attention. So did her victory—dismissal of all charges. A few days later, at a cocktail party given by Edwina D'Orsey and her husband, Lewis, Margot was surrounded by admirers and critics. She had come to the party alone. So had Alex, who did not know she was Edwina's cousin. He had listened to the debate for a while, then joined forces with the critics.

They were still arguing fiercely when the party ended, and Alex drove Margot home to her apartment. There they found suddenly that physical attraction eclipsed the argument and that something new and vital had entered both their lives.

Now they sat in comfortable companionship before the fire. Margot said, "You saw Celia today, didn't you?"

"How did you know?"

"It always shows. You still blame yourself, don't you?"

"Yes." He told her about his meeting with Celia, and Dr. McCartney's opinion about the probable effect on her of a divorce.

Margot said emphatically, "Then you mustn't divorce her."

"If I don't," Alex said, "there can be nothing permanent for you and me."

"Of course there can! It can be as permanent as we both want to make it. What I won't have on my conscience, or burden you with, is destroying what's left of Celia's sanity."

"What you say makes sense." But his voice lacked conviction.

She assured him softly, "I'm happier with what we have than I've ever been in my life."

THAT evening Roscoe Heyward was at home in his rambling suburban house. He was seated at a leather-topped desk in the room he called his study.

His wife, Beatrice, had retired soon after dinner, shutting her bedroom door, as she had for the past twelve years, since—by mutual consent—they moved into separate sleeping quarters. Long before the separate arrangement their interest in each other had tapered into nothingness. Even in the early years of marriage Beatrice had made plain her distaste for the physical aspect of their union. Heyward had accepted the separation uncomplainingly. Ambition at the bank had, by then, become his driving force. Only now and then did he feel a certain sadness for a portion of his life on which the curtain had fallen too soon.

But in other ways Beatrice had been good for him. She came from an impeccable Boston family and fully shared Roscoe's notions about social position. There had been only one thing her illustrious family lacked—money. At this moment, working on his bills, Roscoe Heyward wished fervently that his wife had been an heiress.

Roscoe and Beatrice's biggest problem was, and always had been, managing to live on his salary. Many people would have scoffed at the idea that $65,000 a year was not ample. For the Heywards it was not. Income taxes cut the gross by more than a third. First and second mortgages on the house required payments of another $16,000 yearly, while municipal taxes ate up a further $2500. That left $23,000—or roughly $450 a week—for food, clothes, insurance, a car for Beatrice, a housekeeper-cook, and an incredible array of smaller items.

The house, Heyward realized, was a serious extravagance. Vandervoort, whose salary was identical, was wiser by far to live in an apartment and pay rent, but Roscoe and Beatrice, who loved their house for its size and prestige, would never hear of that.

The uncomfortable reality was that they had no savings—only a few shares of FMA stock, which might have to be sold soon, though the proceeds would not be enough to offset this year's domestic deficit. Tonight the only conclusion Heyward had reached was that they must hold the line on expenses, hoping for a financial upturn.

There would be one—if he became president of FMA. In First Mercantile American, as with most banks, a wide salary gap existed between the presidency and the next rank down. Ben Rosselli had been paid $130,000 annually. It was a virtual certainty his successor would receive the same. To Roscoe the doubling of his salary would eliminate every problem.

Putting his papers away, he began to dream about it.

CHAPTER 5

FRIDAY morning.

In their penthouse atop fashionable Cayman Manor, Edwina and Lewis D'Orsey were at breakfast.

It was three days since Ben Rosselli's announcement of his impending death, and two days since discovery of the cash loss at First Mercantile American's downtown branch. Of the two events, the cash loss—at this moment—weighed more heavily on Edwina.

Two FBI special agents had questioned the branch staff without tangible result. Juanita Núñez continued to insist that she was innocent and to refuse to submit to the lie detector. The FBI would be in the branch again today; yet there seemed little they could do. What the bank could do was end Juanita Núñez' employment. Edwina knew she must dismiss the girl today.

Across the table, Lewis, hidden behind *The Wall Street Journal*, was growling as usual over the latest lunacy from Washington, where the Under Secretary of the Treasury had declared that the U.S. would never return to the gold standard. Glaring over his steel-rimmed glasses, Lewis D'Orsey flung his newspaper to the floor. "Five centuries after dimwits like him have rotted into dust," he stormed, "gold will still be the world's only sound basis for money!"

Lewis's morning tantrums seldom bothered Edwina. In fourteen years of marriage she had learned they were rarely directed at herself. She also realized Lewis was girding himself for a morning session at his typewriter. His twice-a-month financial newsletter, containing investment advice, provided him with a rich livelihood. His many enthusiastic subscribers felt that if making money was your objective, Lewis was a sound man to follow.

"I wish," Edwina said to him now, "your insight extended to knowing where all that cash of ours went on Wednesday."

"I can't tell you where the money is," Lewis said. "But I'll give you some advice: mistrust the obvious."

As Edwina drove to the bank later, the words "mistrust the obvious" stuck in her mind.

Her midmorning meeting with Wainwright and the two FBI agents was brief and inconclusive. The senior FBI man, whose name was Innes, said, "We've gone as far as we can with our investigation here. We'll be in touch if new facts come to light. There is one item of negative news." The FBI man consulted a notebook. "The Núñez girl's husband—Carlos. One of your people thought he saw him in the bank the day the money was missing."

"That was Miles Eastin," Wainwright said.

"Yes, we questioned Eastin; he admitted he could have been mistaken. Well, we've traced Carlos Núñez to Phoenix, Arizona; he has a job there as a motor mechanic. Our bureau agents in Phoenix have interviewed him. They're satisfied he was at work every day this week, which rules him out as an accomplice."

Wainwright escorted the FBI agents out. Edwina returned to her desk on the platform. Shortly before noon she advised the payroll department that Juanita Núñez' employment would be terminated at the end of the day. Juanita's severance paycheck was on Edwina's desk when she returned from lunch.

Uneasy, Edwina turned the check over in her hand. *Mistrust the obvious.* Think just once more. Go back to the beginning. What were the *obvious* facts? The first was that money was missing. *No room for dispute there.* The second was that the amount was six thousand dollars. *No argument.* The third obvious feature concerned the Núñez girl's assertion that she knew the exact amount of money missing from her cash drawer after almost five hours of transactions and *before* she had balanced out her cash. Everyone who knew about the loss agreed that was impossible. That had been a cornerstone of their belief that Juanita Núñez was a thief.

And yet, was it impossible? A wall clock showed 2:15 p.m. Edwina got up. "Mr. Tottenhoe, will you come with me, please?"

With Tottenhoe glumly trailing, she crossed the floor. Juanita Núñez was accepting a deposit. Edwina said quietly, "Mrs. Núñez, when you've dealt with this customer, please put up your 'position closed' sign and lock your cash drawer."

Juanita Núñez did not speak while transferring a small metal plaque to the counter as instructed. When she turned to close the

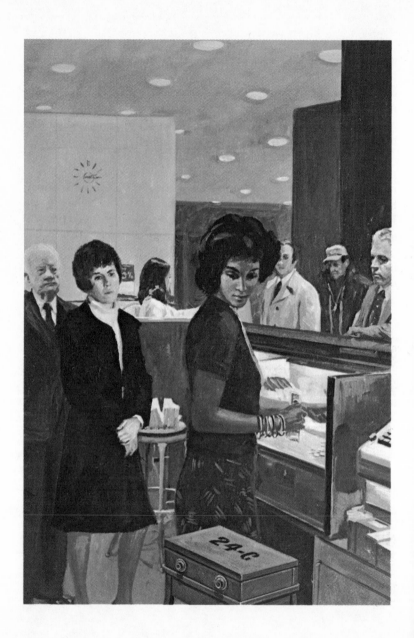

cash drawer, Edwina saw why. The girl was crying silently. The reason was not hard to guess. She had expected to be fired today, and Edwina's sudden appearance confirmed that belief.

Edwina ignored the tears. "Mrs. Núñez, you've been insisting that you always know the amount of cash you have. Do you know how much is in your drawer now?"

The young woman hesitated. Then she nodded, unable to speak.

Edwina handed her a slip of paper. "Write down the amount."

Again visible hesitation. Then Juanita Núñez took a pencil and wrote, "$23,765."

Edwina passed the slip to Tottenhoe. "Please go with Mrs. Núñez and stay with her while she balances out today's cash. Check the result. Compare it with this figure."

Three-quarters of an hour later Tottenhoe reappeared. His hand was shaking. He put the slip of paper on Edwina's desk. The figure which Juanita Núñez had written had a single penciled tick beside it. "If I hadn't seen it myself," he said, "I might not have believed."

"The figure was right?"

"*Exactly* right."

Edwina sat, marshaling her thoughts. Abruptly and dramatically everything concerning the investigation had changed.

"I did know somebody once," Tottenhoe said, "in a little branch upstate, who had that knack of keeping track of cash. It was as if he had a calculating machine inside his head."

Edwina snapped, "I wish your memory had been working sooner." She drew a notepad toward her and began scribbling.

> Núñez. Possibly innocent victim?
> If not Núñez, who?
> Someone who knows procedures, could watch for opportunity.
> Staff? Inside job?
> Motive? Someone who needs money?
> NEEDS MONEY. Examine personal checking/savings accounts, all branch personnel—TONIGHT!

Edwina began leafing quickly through an FMA headquarters phone book, looking for Chief of Audit Service.

ON FRIDAY AFTERNOONS all branches of First Mercantile American Bank stayed open an extra three hours. Thus, at the main downtown branch this Friday, the street doors were closed and locked by a security guard at 6:00 p.m. At 6:05 precisely, a series of sharp, peremptory taps sounded on the outside of the glass door. The guard turned. A young male figure, dressed in a dark topcoat and carrying a briefcase, had tapped with a fifty-cent piece wrapped in a handkerchief. As the guard approached, the man held an identity document flat against the glass. The guard inspected it, unlocked the door, and the young man stepped inside.

Before the guard could close the door a proliferation occurred as remarkable as a magician's trick. Where there had been one individual with briefcase and credentials, suddenly there were six, behind them six more, with still another phalanx at the rear. Swiftly they streamed into the bank. An older man, emanating authority, announced curtly, "Headquarters audit staff."

"Yessir," the security guard said. He had been through this before, and he continued checking the auditors in, twenty of them—sixteen men, four women. All went immediately to various locations in the bank. The older man headed for the platform and Edwina's desk. As she rose to greet him, she regarded the continuing influx with unconcealed surprise. "Mr. Burnside, is this a full-dress audit?"

"It certainly is, Mrs. D'Orsey."

Elsewhere in the bank other staff members groaned and voiced aggrieved comments. "A Friday, of all times to pick!" ... "I had a dinner date!" Tellers knew there would be an extra counting of their cash before they could leave. Accountants would be required to stay until their records were balanced. Senior management staff would be lucky to be away by midnight. The newcomers had already politely taken over all ledgers.

Edwina said, "When I asked for an examination of staff accounts I didn't expect *this*." Normally a branch bank audit took place every eighteen months to two years. A full audit of the main downtown branch had occurred only eight months earlier.

"*We* decide the how and when of audit, Mrs. D'Orsey." As always, Hal Burnside maintained a cool aloofness, the hallmark of a bank examiner. An audit department was an independent watchdog unit with authority like the inspectorate general of an army. Its members were never intimidated by rank.

"I know," Edwina acknowledged. "I'm just surprised you could arrange all this so quickly."

The audit chief smiled. "We have our methods." What he did not reveal was that a surprise audit of another FMA branch had been planned for this evening. Following Edwina's phone call, the earlier plan had been canceled for the present expedition.

Such cloak-and-dagger tactics were not unusual. An essential part of the audit function was to descend without warning. Elaborate precautions were taken to preserve secrecy. For tonight's maneuver the auditors had assembled an hour ago in a salon of a downtown hotel. There they were briefed, then inconspicuously, in twos and threes, they had walked toward the main downtown branch. Until the last few crucial minutes they loitered nearby or browsed store windows. Then, as tradition decreed, the most junior member of the group rapped on the bank door to demand admission. As soon as it was gained, the others, like an assembling regiment, fell in behind him. Now, within five minutes, audit-team members were at every key position, observing everything.

Resigned, regular staff members went on to complete their day's work. The audit process would continue through the following week and part of the next. But the most critical part of the examination would take place within the next few hours.

"Let's get to work, Mrs. D'Orsey," Burnside said. "We'll start with the deposit accounts, both time and demand."

By 8:00 p.m. a notable amount of work had been accomplished. All tellers had left; so had some accountants. Cash had been counted, inspection of other records was well advanced. Among the senior management staff remaining were Edwina, Tottenhoe, and Miles Eastin. Tottenhoe appeared tired, but young Eastin was as fresh and cheerful as when the evening had begun. It was he who arranged for sandwiches and coffee to be sent in for auditors and staff.

Several auditors were concentrating on savings and checking accounts, and from time to time one of this group would bring a note to Burnside at Edwina's desk. In every case he read it and added it to the papers in his briefcase.

At ten minutes to nine he received a lengthier note with several papers clipped to it. This he studied carefully, then announced, "I think Mrs. D'Orsey and I will go out for our supper."

The audit chief escorted Edwina from the building. Outside he apologized. "I'm afraid our supper will have to wait. You and I are on our way to a meeting, but I didn't want it known."

They walked half a block from the bank, then used a pedestrian mall to double back to FMA Headquarters Tower. Edwina pulled her coat tightly around her. The tunnel route would have been shorter and warmer. Why all the mystery?

Inside the bank headquarters building, Hal Burnside signed a night-visitors book, after which a guard accompanied them to the eleventh floor. Nolan Wainwright and the two FBI men were waiting for them in the security department. Almost at once they were joined by another member of the audit team who clearly had followed them from the bank—a youngish man named Gayne, with cool, alert eyes behind severe, heavy-rimmed glasses. It was Gayne who had delivered the several notes and documents to Burnside. Now, at Wainwright's suggestion, they moved into a conference room and seated themselves around a circular table.

Hal Burnside told the FBI agents, "I hope what we've discovered will justify calling you gentlemen out at this hour."

Edwina asked, "Then you *have* discovered something?"

"Unfortunately, more than anyone expected." At a nod from Burnside, Gayne began to spread out papers. "At your suggestion," Burnside stated, "an examination has been made of personal bank accounts of all personnel employed at the main downtown branch, for evidence of financial difficulty. We found it." He turned to the two FBI men. "I should explain that most bank employees maintain their accounts at the branch where they work. Accounts are without service charges, and the employees receive a special low interest rate on loans, usually one percent below prime rate."

Innes, the senior FBI agent, nodded. "Yes, we know that."

"You'll realize, then, that an employee who has borrowed to

the limit on special bank credit and then borrows other sums from an outside source such as a finance company, where interest rates are notoriously high, is in a tenuous financial position. We have a bank employee who has done exactly that." He motioned to Gayne, who handed him several canceled checks.

"These checks are made out to three separate finance companies. We've been able to get in touch by telephone with two, and notwithstanding these payments, both accounts are seriously delinquent. The third company will probably tell us the same story."

Gayne interjected, "And these checks are for the current month only. Tomorrow we'll look at microfilm records for past months."

"One other fact is relevant," the audit chief proceeded. "The individual concerned could not possibly have made these payments on the basis of his bank salary, which we know. Therefore, during the past several hours we have searched for evidence of theft from the bank, and this has now been found."

Edwina's eyes were riveted on the signature on each of the canceled checks—a signature she saw each day, bold and clear. The sight of it appalled and saddened her.

The signature was Eastin's. Young Miles, whom she liked so well—so efficient, so helpful and tireless, even tonight, and whom she had decided to promote when Tottenhoe retired.

The chief of audit service had now moved on. "What our sneak thief has been doing is milking dormant accounts. Once we detected a single fraudulent pattern, others were not hard to find."

Once again Gayne began placing papers on the table.

A dormant account, Burnside explained to the FBI men, was a savings or checking account which had little or no activity. All banks had customers who left accounts untouched, sometimes for years, and with surprisingly large sums in them. Modest interest did accumulate in savings accounts, and some people undoubtedly had that in mind, though others—incredibly—abandoned their accounts entirely. When a checking account was observed to be inactive, with no deposits or withdrawals, banks ceased mailing monthly statements and substituted an annual one. The accounts were segregated; then if a transaction suddenly occurred, it was scrutinized by an operations officer to make sure it was legitimate. *As assistant operations officer, Miles Eastin had authority to approve dormant account transactions. He had used it to cover up the fact that he had been stealing from such accounts himself.*

"Eastin has cleverly selected accounts least likely to cause trouble. We have first a series of forged withdrawal slips, after which the amounts have been transferred into what appears to be a dummy account of his own under an assumed name."

One by one they examined the withdrawal slips, comparing the handwriting with the checks. Although an attempt had been made at disguise, a resemblance was unmistakable.

The second FBI agent, Dalrymple, who was taking notes, asked, "Is there a total figure on the money involved?"

Gayne answered, "So far we've pinpointed close to eight thousand dollars. Tomorrow we'll have access to older records through microfilm and the computer, which may show more."

Edwina asked, "How long has this been going on?"

"At least a year, possibly longer," Gayne informed them.

Edwina turned to Burnside. "So you missed it at the last audit. Isn't inspecting dormant accounts part of your job?"

The audit chief flushed. "Yes, it is. But even we miss things occasionally when a thief has covered his tracks well."

Agent Innes broke the ensuing silence. "This puts us no further ahead so far as Wednesday's missing cash goes."

"Except it makes Eastin the prime suspect," Burnside said. "And he may admit that, too."

"He won't," Nolan Wainwright growled. "He's too smart. Besides, why should he? We still don't know how he did it."

Until now the bank security head had said little, though his face had hardened as the auditors produced their evidence of guilt. Edwina wondered if he was remembering how both of them had put pressure on Juanita Núñez.

Hal Burnside stood up to go, refastening his briefcase. "Here's where audit leaves off and the law takes over."

"We'll require these papers and a signed statement," Innes said.

"Mr. Gayne will stay, and be at your disposal."

"One more question," said Innes. "Do you think that Eastin has any idea he's been found out?"

Gayne shook his head. "I'm certain he doesn't. We were careful not to show what we were looking for, and to cover up we asked for many things we didn't need."

Innes nodded his approval. "Then let's keep it that way. We'll pick him up for questioning. He's still at the bank?"

"Yes," Edwina said. "He'll stay at least until we get back."

Nolan Wainwright cut in, his voice harsh. "*Amend* those instructions. Keep him there as late as possible. After that, let him go home thinking he hasn't been found out."

The eyes of the two FBI men searched Wainwright's face. A message seemed to pass between them. Innes hesitated, then conceded, "All right. Do it that way."

A few minutes later Edwina and Burnside took the elevator down.

Innes said politely to the remaining auditor, "Before we take your statement, I wonder if you'd leave us alone a moment."

"Certainly." Gayne left the conference room.

Innes faced Nolan Wainwright. "You've something in mind?"

"I have. Are you sure you want to know?"

The two had known one another for years and shared a mutual respect. There was a silence, then Agent Dalrymple said, "Tell us as much as you think you should."

"Okay, we've enough to nail Eastin on a larceny rap. What do you think a judge will give him?"

"For a first offense he'll draw a suspended sentence," Innes said. "The court won't worry about the money. They'll figure banks have lots and it's insured anyway."

"Check! But if we can prove he took the six thousand Wednesday, and show he aimed to throw the blame on the girl . . ."

"*If* you could show that, any reasonable judge would send him straight to jail."

"Then don't pick up Eastin tonight. Give me until morning."

"We don't want him to run," Dalrymple cautioned.

"And I don't want a bruised potato either," Innes said.

"He won't run. He won't be bruised. I guarantee it."

Innes glanced toward his colleague, who shrugged. "Okay, then," Innes said. "Until morning. But understand one thing, Nolan—this conversation never took place."

From a list of branch officers in the security department, Wainwright copied Miles Eastin's home address and telephone number. Using a pay phone on Rosselli Plaza, he dialed the number; no one answered. Next he headed for his car in the basement garage. He removed a slim chamois case from the trunk, placing it in an inside coat pocket. Then he drove to Eastin's apartment building.

The time was 10:30. Traffic on the street was light. No pedestrians were near the apartment house. He went in. Next to the mailboxes in the vestibule were three rows of buzzers and a speaker. Wainwright saw the name Eastin beside the buzzer for 2G and pressed the button. As he expected, there was no response.

He pressed a top-floor button. A man's voice rasped, "Yeah, who is it?" The name beside the button was Appleby.

"Western Union," Wainwright said. "Telegram for Appleby."

"Okay, bring it up."

A buzzer sounded and a lock clicked. Wainwright opened the interior door and went in quickly. He saw a stairway to the right and went up it, two steps at a time, to the second floor, reflecting on the astounding innocence of people generally. This night Mr. Appleby would suffer no harm beyond minor puzzlement. He might have fared far worse. Despite repeated warnings, apartment dwellers continued to open up without second thought.

Apartment 2G was near the end of the corridor. Wainwright tried a succession of slim blades from his chamois case, and on the fourth attempt the lock turned. The door swung open and he went in, closing it behind him. He crossed to a window, closed the draperies, and turned on a light switch. The apartment was a single room, orderly and clean. Methodically, as his police training had taught him, he began a thorough search, trying to suppress gnawing self-criticism for the illegal acts he was committing. He did not wholly succeed.

In half an hour he knew that few places remained where anything could be hidden. He had examined cupboards and drawers, probed chairs, removed the back of the TV, taken apart a clock, and riffled through books, noting that an entire shelf was devoted to Eastin's hobby—the study of money through the ages. Of anything incriminating there was no trace. Finally he piled furniture in one corner and rolled up the living-area rug. Then with a flashlight he went over every inch of floorboard.

Without the flashlight he would have missed the carefully sawed board, but two lighter colored lines betrayed where cuts had been made. He gently pried up the foot of board between the lines and found, in the space beneath, a small black ledger and a packet of twenty-dollar bills. Working quickly, he replaced the board, the rug, the furniture. He counted the cash. Six thousand dollars. Then he studied the ledger—a betting record—and whistled at the size and number of amounts involved.

He put the book and the money on a table in front of the sofa, turned out the lights, and sat down to wait. His illuminated watch showed shortly after midnight when he heard the key in the lock. A shadowy figure came in. The door closed and the light came on.

Eastin saw Wainwright at once, and his surprise was total. Blood drained from his face. Wainwright stood up. His voice cut like a knife. "How much did you steal today?"

Before Eastin could answer, Wainwright seized him by the coat lapels, turned him, and pushed. He fell sprawling on the sofa. The young man spluttered, "What the hell do you ..." Then his eyes moved to the money and the ledger, and he stopped.

"I came for the bank's money, or what little is left," Wainwright said harshly. He motioned to the bills stacked on the table. "We know what's there is what you took on Wednesday. And in case you're wondering, we know about the milked accounts."

A convulsive shudder went through Eastin. His head came down, his hands went to his face.

"You've got some talking to do. Start!" Wainwright pulled Eastin's hands free and pushed his head up, though not roughly, remembering his promise to the FBI man. No bruised potato.

If the FBI agents were here, they would have to inform Eastin of his legal right not to answer questions and to have a lawyer

present. Wainwright, not a policeman anymore, had no such obligation. What he was after was Eastin's signed confession.

He sat down facing the younger man, picked up the small black
ledger, and opened it. "Let's start with this." He put his finger
on the list of sums and dates. "These are bets. Right?"

Eastin nodded dully.

"Explain them."

Responses came slowly. The entries covered football and basketball
games. Losses outnumbered winning bets. The minimum bet was
one hundred dollars, the highest three hundred.

"Did you bet alone or with a group?"

"A group. Four other guys. Working. Like me."

"Working at the bank?"

Eastin shook his head. "Other places."

"You made no bets on horses. Why?"

"Everybody knows horse racing is crooked. Football and basketball
are on the level. We worked out a system. With honest games
we figured we could beat the odds." The total of losses showed
how wrong that figuring had been.

"Did you bet with one bookie, or more?"

"One."

"His name?"

Eastin stayed mute.

"The rest of the money you've stolen—where is it?"

The young man answered miserably, "Gone."

"Right now let's talk about *this* money." Wainwright touched
the six thousand dollars. "We know you took it Wednesday. How?"

Eastin hesitated, then shrugged. "I guess you may as well know.
We had people out with flu. I filled in as a teller."

"I know that. Get to what happened."

"Before the bank opened for business, I went to the vault to
get one of the spare cash drawers. Juanita Núñez was there. She
unlocked her regular cash drawer. I was right alongside. Without
Juanita knowing, I watched to see her combination. I memorized
it, and as soon as I could I wrote it down."

With Wainwright prompting, the damning facts multiplied. The vault was large. The vault teller worked in a cagelike enclosure near the door, and was kept busy checking tellers and cash drawers out. While no one could pass him without being seen, once they were inside he took little notice of them. That morning Miles Eastin was desperate for cash. There had been betting losses the week before and he was being pressed for payment of accumulated debts.

Wainwright interrupted. "You owed finance companies. Also the bookie. Did you owe anyone else?"

Eastin nodded.

"A loan shark?"

The younger man hesitated, then admitted, "Yes."

"Was the loan shark threatening you?"

Miles Eastin moistened his lips. "Yes; so was the bookie. They both are, still." His eyes went to the six thousand dollars.

Wainwright motioned to the money. "You promised to pay the shark and the bookie that?"

"Yes."

"When?"

"Tomorrow." Eastin looked nervously at the clock and corrected himself. "Today."

Wainwright prompted, "Go back to Wednesday. So you knew the combination of the Núñez girl's cash drawer. How did you use it?"

It was incredibly simple. He took his lunch break when Juanita did. He wheeled his cash drawer into the vault right after her. The two cash drawers were left there side by side, both locked. Eastin returned from lunch early. The vault teller checked him in, then went on working. No one else was in the vault.

Miles Eastin went directly to Juanita Núñez' cash drawer and opened it, using the combination he had written down. It took only seconds to remove three packages of bills totaling six thousand dollars, then close and relock the box. He slipped the currency into inside pockets; the bulges scarcely showed. He then checked out his own cash drawer and returned to work.

There was a silence; then Wainwright said, "So all the time questioning was going on that day you had the money on you?"

"Yes," Miles Eastin said. As he remembered how easy it had been, a faint smile creased his face.

Wainwright saw the smile. In a single movement he hit Eastin hard on both sides of the face, his open palm for the first blow, the back of his hand for the second. Eastin shrank back on the sofa and blinked tears from his eyes.

"That's to let you know I see nothing funny in what you did to the bank or to Mrs. Núñez." What Wainwright had just learned was that Miles Eastin was afraid of physical violence. "The next order of business," he announced, "is a written statement. In your own handwriting and with everything in it that you've told me."

"No! I won't do that!"

Wainwright shrugged. "In that case there's no point in my staying." He began stowing the six thousand dollars in his pockets. "I'm taking this to the night depository."

Eastin pleaded, "I need it now! Today!"

"Oh, sure, some for the bookie and some for the loan shark. Or the strong-arm guys they'll send." The security chief eyed Eastin with sardonic amusement. "Maybe they'll come together; then they'll break one of your arms and one leg each. They're apt to do that sort of thing. Or didn't you know?"

Real fear showed in Eastin's eyes. "Yes, I do know. You've got to help me! Please!"

Wainwright said coldly, "I'll consider it. *After* you've written that statement."

Miles Eastin collapsed entirely, cooperative and cowed. The security chief dictated the first sentences of the confession.

"I, Miles Broderick Eastin, make this statement voluntarily. I have been offered no inducement to make it. No violence or threat of violence has been used. I confess to stealing from First Mercantile American Bank the sum of six thousand dollars in cash at approximately 1:30 p.m. on Wednesday, October . . ."

While Eastin continued writing, Wainwright telephoned Innes, the FBI man, at his home.

CHAPTER 6

DURING the first week of November, Ben Rosselli's physical condition worsened. While a savage storm beset the city, he was moved to the private pavilion of Mt. Adams Hospital. All control of First Mercantile American had now slipped from him, and a board meeting was set for December 4 to name his successor.

Directors began arriving in the walnut-paneled boardroom shortly before 10:00 a.m., greeting one another with an easy confidence. Each had the patina of a successful businessman in the company of his peers. They were the admirals and field marshals of commerce, as Ben had been, and they knew that business, which kept civilization lubricated, must go on.

A board of directors of any major corporation resembles an exclusive club. Apart from three or four top management executives who are employed full time, the board comprises a score or so of outstanding businessmen from other, diverse fields, who are paid between one and two thousand dollars for every meeting attended, normally ten a year.

Among businessmen it is considered a high honor to be a company director, and the more prestigious the company, the greater the glory. Particularly high in prestige is a directorship of any major bank. First Mercantile American, as befitting a bank among the nation's top twenty, possessed an appropriately impressive board.

Or so they thought. Alex Vandervoort, surveying them as they took seats around the table, decided there was a high percentage of deadwood. There were also conflicts of interest, since some directors, or their companies, were major borrowers of bank money. Among his objectives, if he became president, would be to make the board more representative.

But would he be president? Or would Roscoe Heyward? Today both would expound their views before the directors. Heyward, typically, had armed himself with a prepared text. Seated directly across from Alex, he was studying it now, his gray eyes behind rimless glasses unwaveringly focused on the typewritten words. Alex had deliberated far into last night and decided to speak instinctively, letting thoughts and words fall into place when the moment came.

Across the table, the Honorable Harold Austin slipped into his accustomed seat. Alex nodded. The nod was returned but with noticeable coolness. A week ago the Honorable Harold had dropped by to protest Alex's veto of the Keycharge advertising prepared by Austin's agency. "I'm of two minds," he said, "whether to bring your high-handed action to the attention of the board or not."

Alex was blunt. "I know what the directors decided about Keycharge because I was there, too. What they did *not* agree to was advertising which is misleading and discreditable to the bank. Your people can do better than that, Harold. In fact, they already have. I've seen and approved the revised versions."

Austin had glowered, but decided to drop the subject. Austin Advertising was going to do just as well financially with the revised campaign. But Alex knew he had created an antagonist.

The hum of conversation in the boardroom quieted. Jerome Patterton, vice-chairman of the board, tapped lightly with a gavel and announced, "Gentlemen, the board will come to order."

Patterton, projected into prominence today, was something of a timeserver. He had been acquired as part of a merger with a smaller bank several years ago; as he neared retirement his responsibilities had, by mutual agreement, been diminished. His title of vice-chairman of the board was largely honorary. Alex's assessment of Patterton was that he had an excellent brain, which in recent years he had used minimally.

Patterton began by paying tribute to Ben Rosselli, after which he stressed the need to name, speedily, a new chief executive. He then announced that Roscoe Heyward and Alex Vandervoort would address the board, after which both would leave while their candidacies were discussed. "As to the order of speaking, we'll employ that ancient system—alphabetical precedence. Roscoe, at your convenience, please begin."

"Thank you, Mr. Chairman." Heyward rose and calmly surveyed the nineteen other men around the table. He cleared his throat and began speaking in a precise and even voice.

"Members of the board, I shall be forthright today in emphasizing

what I conceive to be my first responsibility, and this board's—
the profitability of First Mercantile American Bank. Profitability,
gentlemen—our number one priority."

Heyward glanced briefly at his text. "Allow me to elaborate.
In my view, too many banking decisions are being influenced
nowadays by social controversies of our times. Corporate policies
should not be subject to every changing social whim. That kind
of thinking is dangerous for American free enterprise and disastrous
for this bank—lessening our strength, retarding growth, and reducing
profits. In short, we should stay aloof from the sociopolitical scene,
which is none of our concern."

Alex Vandervoort reflected: So Roscoe had decided on a direct
confrontation. Everything he had just said ran contrary to Alex's
own convictions, as well as Ben Rosselli's. It was Ben who had
involved FMA in civic affairs, including projects like Forum East.
But Alex had no delusions. A substantial segment of the board had
been uneasy about Ben's increasing liberalization of the bank and
would welcome Heyward's all-business line.

"I spoke of profit as our principal objective," Roscoe Heyward
was continuing. "The social value of profitability itself is high. All
banks measure profit in terms of earnings per share. While earnings
are strong, confidence in banking continues. But let a few big banks
show decreased per-share earnings and what would happen? Disquiet,
even alarm—a situation in which depositors would withdraw funds
and shareholders their investments, so that bank stocks would tumble,
with the banks themselves imperiled. It happened in 1929. Today,
with banks far larger, the effect would be cataclysmic by comparison.
This is why a bank must remain vigilant in its duty to make money
for itself and its shareholders."

There were murmurings of approval. Heyward read on.

"We do not achieve maximum profit by tying up bank funds
at low rates of yield for many years. I refer, of course, to the
funding of low-income housing. We should not place more than
a minimal portion of bank funds in housing mortgages of any kind,
which are notorious for their low return. For real profitability we
should direct our major thrust elsewhere."

Alex thought, Whatever criticism might be leveled at Heyward, no one could complain later that he had failed to make his viewpoints clear. In a way, his statement was an honest declaration. Yet it was also shrewdly, even cynically, calculated.

"Specifically," Heyward declared, "this bank should depend on its business with American industry, with a proven record of high profits, which will, in turn, enhance our own. I am convinced that First Mercantile American Bank has an insufficient proportion of its funds available for large loans to industry, and we should embark immediately on a program of increasing such lending."

Heyward expanded for some thirty minutes more on his theme. He sat down amid applause.

Jerome Patterton then called on Alex.

"Most of you know me well, as a man and as a banker." Alex stood by the table casually, his tone conversational. "You know that as a banker I am tough—hard-nosed. Proof of this exists in financing I've conducted for FMA, all of it profitable. In banking, like any other business, when you deal from profitability you deal from strength. I'm glad Roscoe brought up this subject, because it gives me an opportunity to declare my own belief in profitability. Ditto for freedom, democracy, love, and motherhood."

Someone chuckled. Alex responded with an easy smile. "For the moment I'd like to stay with beliefs. A belief of my own is that civilization in this decade is changing more quickly than at any time since the Industrial Revolution. What we are seeing is a social revolution of conscience and behavior. The driving force is the determination of a majority of people to improve the quality of life, to stop the spoliation of our environment, and to preserve what's left of resources of all kinds. Because of this, new standards are being demanded of industry and business, so that the name of the game is corporate social responsibility."

Alex moved restlessly in the limited space behind the boardroom table. He decided to meet Heyward's challenge head-on.

"I believe, with Ben Rosselli, that we should share in improving the life of this city and state. An immediate means is through financing of low-rental housing, a commitment this board has already accepted with the early stages of Forum East. As time goes on I believe our contribution should be greater."

He glanced toward Roscoe Heyward. "I realize that housing mortgages are not a high-profit area. Yet there are ways to achieve that involvement with excellent profits, too. One is through large-scale expansion of the savings department. Traditionally, funds for home mortgages are channeled from savings deposits because mortgages are long-term investments, just as savings are stable and long-term. While large commercial banks spurned savings as unimportant, savings and loan associations astutely seized the opportunity and forged ahead of us. But still, in personal savings, gigantic opportunities remain."

He ranged through other bank departments, describing proposed changes. One was to open nine new branches in suburban areas throughout the state. Another was a drastic overhaul of FMA organization to improve efficiency.

Near the end he returned to his original theme. "Our banking relationship with industry should continue to be close. But we should not be so preoccupied with bigness that the importance of small accounts is diminished. This bank was established to serve those of modest means to whom other banking facilities were denied. Neither the founder's son nor his grandson ever lost sight of the precept that smallness multiplied can represent the greatest strength of all. A massive and immediate growth in small savings, which I urge the board to set as an objective, will honor the bank's origins, enhance our fiscal strength, and—in the climate of the times—advance the public good, which is our own."

As they had for Heyward, the board members applauded as Alex sat down. He guessed that the choice could still go either way.

Questioning had occupied half an hour, when an attendant quietly entered the room and approached Jerome Patterton, carrying a small silver tray. On it was a single folded sheet of paper. The vice-chairman unfolded and read it. After a pause he rose to his feet. "Gentlemen," Patterton said, "I grieve to inform you that our beloved president, Ben Rosselli, died a few minutes ago."

The board meeting was adjourned until after the Rosselli funeral.

THE DEATH OF BEN ROSSELLI attracted international press cover-age, with some news writers labeling it an era's end. His departure signaled that the last major American bank to be identified with a single entrepreneur had moved into mid-twentieth-century con-formation, with committee and hired management control.

The funeral took place on Wednesday in the second week of December. The two-day lying-in-state was at St. Matthew's Cathe-dral, appropriate since Matthew—once Levi the tax collector—is considered by bankers a patron saint. Some two thousand people, including a presidential representative, the governor, ambassadors, civic leaders, and bank employees, filed past the open casket.

On the morning of burial an archbishop, a bishop, and a monsignor concelebrated a Mass of Resurrection. Within the cathedral a section near the altar had been reserved for Rosselli relatives and friends. Immediately behind were directors and senior officers of First Mercantile American Bank.

Roscoe Heyward was in the first row of bank mourners, accom-panied by his wife. Alex and Margot Bracken sat two rows behind them with Edwina and Lewis D'Orsey. These four were often together, not just because Edwina and Margot were cousins, but because they found each other's company agreeable.

Alex felt tears spring to his eyes as the coffin was carried from the church. His feeling for Ben, he had realized over the past few days, was close to love. In some ways the old man had been a father figure. His death left a gap in Alex's life which would not be filled. Margot reached gently for his hand.

Outside the cathedral, traffic had been diverted. The coffin was already in a flower-laden hearse. Now relatives and bank officials were getting into limousines. A police motorcycle escort was at the head of the assembling cortege.

While Alex signaled for his car, Lewis D'Orsey, peering at the batteries of cameras, observed, "They'll depress FMA stock again."

Alex murmured uneasy agreement. First Mercantile American shares had fallen five and a half points on the New York Stock Exchange since news of Ben's illness. The death of the last Rosselli, coupled with uncertainty about the course of future management, had caused the most recent drop. Publicity about the funeral could depress the stock still further. "But it won't stay down," Alex said. "Earnings are good and nothing's really changed."

His car from the bank pool moved into the line and the four got in. Lewis addressed Edwina. "I've been meaning to ask the latest about Miles Eastin."

"He appears in court next week, and I have to be a witness. I'm not looking forward to it."

Alex asked, "What about the teller who was involved—Mrs. Núñez? Is she okay?"

"She seems to be. I'm afraid we gave Juanita a hard time."

Margot, only half listening, sharpened her attention. "I know a Juanita Núñez. Nice young woman who lives at Forum East. I believe her husband left her. She has a little girl."

"That sounds like our Mrs. Núñez," Edwina said.

Now the cortege had left the cathedral behind and was passing through city streets. Snow was beginning to fall lightly.

"For my funeral," Lewis mused, "I'd publish a farewell edition of the newsletter. I have a headline for it. 'Bury the U.S. dollar with me! You might as well—it's dead and done for.'"

Alex, on a jump seat in front of the other three, turned. "Lewis, sometimes your gloom about dollars makes sense. But I can't believe everything monetary is falling apart."

"You don't want to believe it; you're a banker," Lewis retorted. "If the money system collapses, you and your bank are out of business. The truth is that the United States *is* close to bankruptcy. The collapse of currencies isn't new. Our century is littered with examples, each one traceable to the same cause—a government which began inflation by printing fiat money unbacked by gold or any other value. For the past fifteen years the U.S. has done precisely that."

"There are more dollars in circulation than there should be," Alex admitted.

Lewis nodded dourly. "Also more debt than can ever be repaid. American governments have spent billions, piled up debits beyond believing, then used the printing presses to create more paper money and inflation. And individuals have followed that example. You, too, Alex, with your credit cards and easy borrowing. Americans have lost what they once had—financial sanity. Savings, pensions, and fixed-interest investments are becoming worthless. Right now it's every man for himself, a time for individuals to scramble for financial life belts."

"Lewis," Alex said, "believing the way you do—that a crash is coming—and assuming you were an ordinary depositor with U.S. dollars, what kind of bank would you want your money in?"

Lewis said unhesitatingly, "A big bank. Small banks are the first to fail. They don't have sufficient cash to survive a run. A few of the big ones will go under, too—those with too many millions locked into big industrial loans, with too high a proportion of international deposits—hot money which can vanish overnight; with too little liquidity when scared depositors want cash. So if I were your mythical depositor, Alex, I'd study the balance sheets of the big banks, then choose one with a low loan-to-deposit ratio and a broad base of domestic depositors."

"Well, that's nice," Edwina said. "It just so happens that FMA fills all of those conditions."

Alex nodded. "At the moment." But the picture could change, he reasoned, if Heyward's plans for new and massive loans to industry were agreed to by the board. The thought was a reminder that the directors would meet again two days from now.

Edwina said suddenly, "It's going to be a white funeral." She was looking out the window at the snow, now falling heavily. The car slowed and stopped. Doors of other cars were opening, figures emerging, hunched against the cold. The coffin was lifted from the hearse. Margot took Alex's arm and, with the D'Orseys, joined in the quiet procession following Ben Rosselli to his grave.

Roscoe Heyward and Alex Vandervoort did not attend the reconvened meeting of the board. Each waited in his office until summoned, shortly before noon. They arrived at the boardroom together and slipped into their seats at the long table.

Harold Austin, the director with the longest service, announced the board's decision. Jerome Patterton, he stated, vice-chairman of

the board, would become president of First Mercantile American Bank immediately. The appointee seemed dazed.

Later, Patterton had separate talks with Heyward and Vandervoort. "I'm an interim pope," he informed each of them. "I didn't seek this job. I'm only thirteen months from retirement. But the board was deadlocked over you two, and choosing me allows them that much time to make up their minds. In the meantime, I intend to do my best and I need the help of both of you. I know I shall get it because that's to your best advantage."

MARGOT Bracken had been involved with Forum East since before it was built. She had been legal counsel first for a citizens group which campaigned to get the project going, and later for a tenants association. She also gave legal aid to families in the development—at little or no cost to them—and therefore she knew many of its occupants, including Juanita Núñez.

Three days after the Rosselli funeral, on a Saturday morning, Margot saw Juanita in a delicatessen, part of a Forum East shopping mall, and invited her to have a cup of coffee.

The Forum East complex had been planned as a whole community with low-cost living accommodation—attractive apartments, town houses, and remodeled older buildings. The buildings completed so far were linked by tree-lined malls and overhead walkways—many of the ideas for which were adapted from San Francisco's Golden Gateway and London's Barbican. Other portions of the project were still under construction or awaiting financing.

On a terrace adjoining the delicatessen, Margot and Juanita sipped espresso and chatted about Estela, who was at a community-sponsored ballet class. Managing was very difficult, Juanita confided. "Everyone has the same problem. Each month our money will buy less. This inflation! Where will it end?"

According to Lewis D'Orsey, Margot reflected, it would end in disaster and anarchy. She kept the thought to herself. "I heard," she said, "that you had some kind of problem at your bank."

Juanita's face clouded. She seemed close to tears as she described the forty-eight-hour nightmare of suspicion and interrogation. As

Margot listened, her anger rose. "They had no right to pressure you without your having legal advice. Edwina D'Orsey is my cousin. I'm going to talk to her about this."

Juanita looked startled. "I didn't know. Please don't! It was Mrs. D'Orsey who found the truth."

"If you don't want me to, I won't. But remember, if you're in trouble again, about *anything,* call me and I'll be there."

"Thank you," Juanita said. "I will. I really will."

The following week Miles Eastin appeared in federal court charged with embezzlement on five counts. Four involved fraudulent transactions at the bank totaling thirteen thousand dollars. The fifth charge related to the six-thousand-dollar cash theft.

Trial was before Judge Winslow Underwood, sitting with a jury. On the advice of an inexperienced young lawyer appointed by the court, a not guilty plea was entered on all counts. A more seasoned lawyer would have urged a guilty plea and perhaps a deal with the prosecutor, rather than have certain details—principally Eastin's attempt to incriminate Juanita Núñez—revealed in court. As it was, everything came out.

Edwina D'Orsey testified, as did Tottenhoe and other bank colleagues. FBI Special Agent Innes introduced as evidence Miles Eastin's signed admission of guilt concerning the cash theft, made at FBI headquarters the night he was arrested. The earlier confession, obtained by Nolan Wainwright, the legality of which might have been challenged, was not needed and not introduced.

The sight of Miles Eastin in court depressed Edwina. He appeared pale and haggard. All his old buoyancy had gone. Edwina's evidence was brief. While being cross-examined, she glanced several times toward Miles, but he declined to meet her eyes.

Juanita Núñez was a reluctant witness for the prosecution. She was nervous, and the court had difficulty hearing her. She demonstrated no antagonism toward Eastin and kept her answers brief. Plainly all she wanted was to have the ordeal over.

It was immediately following Juanita's testimony that defense counsel, after a whispered consultation with his client, requested leave to change Miles Eastin's original plea to guilty. Judge Underwood consented, and Eastin was remanded into custody for sentencing the following week.

Nolan Wainwright, though not required to testify, had been present at the trial. Now, as the bank witnesses filed out, he moved alongside Juanita. "Mrs. Núñez, may I talk with you for a minute?"

She glanced at him with a mixture of indifference and hostility. "It is all finished. Besides, I am going back to work."

"Please, I'd like to walk back with you."

Juanita shrugged. "If you must."

"Look," Wainwright said, "I've never found it easy to say I'm sorry. But I am—for the trouble I caused you, for not believing you were telling the truth when you were and needed help."

"So now you feel better," Juanita said tartly. "You have swallowed your little aspirin? The tiny pain is gone?"

"You don't make it easy."

She stopped. "Did you?" The small elfin face was tilted upward, her dark eyes met his steadily. He was aware of an underlying strength and independence.

"No, I didn't. Which is why I'd like to help now." He told her of the FBI inquiries, tracing her husband to Phoenix and finding him employed as a motor mechanic. "What I had in mind is that you should consult one of our lawyers at the bank. I could arrange that without charge. Under a court order your husband would have to send you money to help take care of your little girl."

"And would that make Carlos a man?"

He wondered if she had properly understood. "Does it matter?"

"It matters that he should not be forced. He knows that I am here and that Estela is with me. If Carlos wanted us to have his money, he would send it. *Si no, para qué?*" she added softly.

He said in exasperation, "I don't understand you."

Unexpectedly, Juanita smiled. "It is not necessary that you should."

They walked toward the bank in silence, Wainwright nursing his frustration. He wished she had thanked him for his offer. If she had, it would have meant that she took it seriously, at least.

"Mrs. Núñez," he said, "if you have a problem, something I might help with, will you call me?"

It was the second such offer she had had. "Maybe."

That was the end of their conversation. Wainwright felt he had done all he could and had other things on his mind. One was planting an undercover informer to track down the source of counterfeit credit cards. As he had told Alex Vandervoort, he had located a man, an ex-convict, known to him only as Vic, who was prepared to take the considerable risk in return for money. Wainwright's hope was to bring the swindlers to justice, as he had Miles Eastin.

The following week Eastin was sentenced to two years.

A few minutes after sentencing, a brief conference took place between Miles and his legal counsel.

"The first thing to remember," the young lawyer said, "is that you'll be eligible for parole in less than a year."

Miles Eastin, wrapped in misery, nodded dully.

"I'm sorry how things came out," the young lawyer went on. "It was your confession that did us in. I know, of course, why you signed that second statement—the FBI one; you thought the first was valid, so another wouldn't make any difference. I'm afraid that security man, Wainwright, tricked you all the way."

The prisoner nodded. "Yes, I know that now."

Next day Miles Eastin was transferred to a federal prison.

Chapter 7

THE first hint of trouble appeared in mid-January. It was a news item in the Sunday paper.

> Anxiety persists amid growing rumors that financial backing may shortly be reduced severely at Forum East, the big rehabilitation project underwritten by a consortium of financial interests spearheaded by First Mercantile American Bank. A spokesman for FMA would make no comment except to say, "An announcement will be forthcoming in due course."

Alex Vandervoort was unaware of the item until Monday morning, when his secretary placed it, ringed in red, on his desk. He summoned Dick French, vice-president for public relations.

"Who was the bank spokesman?" Alex demanded.

"Me," French said. "And I'll tell you right now, I wasn't happy about it, but Mr. Patterton insisted I shouldn't say more."

Alex curbed a rising anger. "Is there a reason I wasn't consulted about any of this?"

The PR head appeared surprised. "I thought you were. When I talked on the phone to Mr. Patterton yesterday, I know Roscoe was with him. I assumed you were there, too."

Alex dismissed French, then instructed his secretary to inquire if Jerome Patterton was free. He was informed that the president would see him at 11:00 a.m.

At 11:00 a.m. Alex walked the few yards to the presidential suite. Jerome Patterton was seated behind his desk, a newspaper folded open to the story which had brought Alex there. On a sofa, in shadow, was Roscoe Heyward.

Patterton said, "I asked Roscoe to stay, because I'd a notion what the subject might be." He touched the paper. "You've seen this, of course."

"I've seen it," Alex said. "I've also had Dick French in. Why wasn't I informed? I'm as involved with Forum East as anyone."

"You should have been informed, Alex." Jerome Patterton seemed embarrassed. "The truth is we got a little rattled when the press calls showed there had been a leak."

"A leak of what?"

It was Heyward who answered. "Of a proposal I'll be making to the money policy committee next Monday. I'm suggesting a fifty percent reduction of the bank's commitment to Forum East."

Astounded, Alex addressed Patterton. "Jerome, do I understand that you are in favor of this incredible piece of folly?"

A flush suffused the president's face. "I've reserved judgment. What Roscoe has been doing is some advance lobbying."

"Let me remind you, Alex," Heyward said, "that on plenty of occasions you took your ideas to Ben in advance of money policy meetings."

"If I did," Alex said, "they made a damn sight better sense than this one."

"That, of course, is solely your opinion."

Jerome Patterton raised his hands. "Will you both please save your arguments for the meeting."

On Monday the bank's money policy committee held its regular session. The committee's purpose was to decide the uses to which bank funds would be put. Roscoe Heyward was the chairman. The other members were Alex and two senior vice-presidents—Tom Straughan and Orville Young. The president of the bank sat in, voting only if necessary to break a tie. So far, Patterton had not contributed to the discussion of Heyward's proposal for a drastic cut in Forum East financing in favor of more profitable investments.

Alex was arguing, "Our profit last year was thirteen percent. That's damned good for any business. This year the prospect's even better—a fifteen percent return on investment, maybe sixteen. Should we strain for more? We should strike a balance between achieving profit and giving service."

Straughan, the bank's chief economist, was consulting his notes. "I intended to bring up the subject of home mortgages, Roscoe. I'd like to point out that only twenty-five percent of our savings deposits are currently in mortgage loans. That's low. We could increase it to fifty percent without harming our liquidity position. I believe we should."

"I'll second that," Alex said. "Our branch managers are pleading for mortgage money. The return on investment is fair, and we know that the risk on mortgages is negligible."

Orville Young objected. "It ties up money for long term—money on which we can earn substantially higher rates elsewhere."

Alex slammed his fist on the table. "Once in a while we've a public obligation to accept lower rates. It's why I object to weaseling out of Forum East."

"There's one more reason not to," Straughan added. "A good many Congressmen would like to see a law similar to Mexico's—one requiring a fixed percentage of bank deposits to be used for financing low-income housing."

"Tom," Roscoe Heyward said, "I'll make a promise. A year from now we'll take a fresh look at mortgages; maybe we'll reopen Forum

East. But not this year. I want this to be a bumper-profit year."
He glanced toward the bank president. "And so does Jerome."

For the first time Alex perceived the shape of Heyward's strategy.
A year of exceptional profit for the bank would make Jerome
Patterton, as president, a hero to its shareholders and directors.
He would go into retirement with glory and the sound of trumpets.
The scenario afterward was easy to guess. Jerome Patterton, grateful
to Roscoe Heyward, would promote the idea of Heyward as his
successor. And because of the profitable year, Patterton would be
in a strong position to make his wishes work.

"There's something else I haven't mentioned," Heyward said. "Not
even to you, Jerome. The probability is strong that we shall shortly
enjoy substantial business with Supranational Corporation. It's another reason I'm reluctant to commit funds elsewhere."

"That's fantastic news," Orville Young said.

Supranational—or SuNatCo—was a multinational giant, the General Motors of global communications. Its prodigious influence with
governments, from democracies through dictatorships, was reportedly
greater than that of any other business complex in history. Until
now SuNatCo had confined its U.S. banking activity to the big
three—Bank of America, First National City, and Chase Manhattan.

"I expect to have more details for our next meeting," Heyward
added. "They may want a substantial credit."

"We still need a vote on Forum East," Tom Straughan said.

"So we do," Heyward acknowledged. He was smiling confidently.

They divided two by two—Vandervoort and Straughan opposed,
Heyward and Young in favor of the cutback of funds. Heads swung
to Patterton. The president hesitated briefly, then announced, "Alex,
on this one I'll go with Roscoe."

On a Thursday evening Margot Bracken's storefront law office
at Forum East was the scene of an executive-committee meeting
of the tenants association. Two days before, FMA had announced
that financing of future Forum East projects was to be cut in half,
effective at once. The meeting now was to determine what could
be done.

The word tenants in the association's name was a loose one. Most members were Forum East tenants. Others were not, but hoped to be. As Deacon Euphrates, a towering steelworker, put it, "There's plenty of us expectin' to be in who ain't gonna make it now." Deacon, his wife, and five children lived in a crowded walk-up in a rat-infested tenement. His name was only midway on a long waiting list for new Forum East housing units, and a construction slowdown was likely to keep it there for a long time.

The FMA announcement had been a shock to Margot, too. Alex, she was sure, would have resisted any cutback proposal, but obviously he had been overruled. For that reason she had not discussed the subject with him yet. Also, the less Alex knew about some simmering plans of Margot's, the better for them both.

"There's no way we can squeeze money out of those banks," Seth Orinda, another member, said. Seth was a black high school teacher, already in at Forum East. But he possessed a keen civic sense. Margot relied a good deal on his stability and help.

"Don't be so sure, Seth." She surveyed the group facing her in the crowded office. They were a dozen or so, blacks and whites. "There *is* a kind of action which I believe will work."

"Miss Bracken." A small figure near the back of the room stood up. It was Juanita Núñez.

"Yes, Mrs. Núñez?"

"I want to help. But I work for the FMA Bank. Perhaps I should not hear what you will tell the others."

Margot said appreciatively, "No, and I should have thought of that." Amid a murmur of understanding, Juanita left the room.

Margot faced the remaining members. As she talked, a smile or two appeared. Near the end, Deacon Euphrates and others were grinning broadly. "Man, oh man!" Deacon said. "That's clever!"

"To make the scheme work," Margot reminded them, "we need at least a thousand people at first, and more as time goes on."

A voice asked, "How long we need 'em?"

"We'll plan on a banking week—five days. If that doesn't work, we should consider going longer. Frankly, I don't believe it will be necessary. Another thing: everyone must be carefully briefed."

"I'll help with that," Seth Orinda volunteered.

Deacon Euphrates said, "I got time comin' to me. I'll take a week off work, an' I can pull in others."

"Good!" Margot said. "I'll have a master plan ready by tomorrow night. You should begin recruiting right away."

Half an hour later the meeting broke up. At Margot's request, Seth Orinda stayed behind. She told him, "Seth, you know that when any action starts I'm usually at the front of it. This time, in a special way, I need your help." The high school teacher beamed. "I don't want my name involved when newspapers and TV start their coverage," Margot continued. "It could embarrass two special friends of mine at the bank. I want to prevent that. Would you front for me? I'll be behind scenes, of course. If there's need to, you can call me, though I hope you won't."

"That's silly," Seth Orinda said. "How could we call you when none of us ever heard your name?"

Two days after the tenants meeting, Margot and Alex were at her apartment—less elegant than Alex's suite, but furnished pleasingly. Alex loved to be there.

"I missed you, Bracken," he said. It was after dinner and he was relaxed in a wing chair; Margot sat on the rug with her head tilted back against his knees, while he gently stroked her hair. It was a week and a half since they had been together, conflicting schedules having kept them apart.

"We'll make up for those lost days," Margot said.

Alex was silent. Then, "You know, I've been waiting all evening for you to fry me on the griddle about Forum East. Instead, you haven't said a word."

Margot asked innocently, "Why should I fry you, darling? The bank's cutback wasn't your idea. I'm sure you opposed it."

Alex regarded her suspiciously. "This isn't like you. You don't accept defeat calmly. It's one of the things I love about you."

"Perhaps some defeats are total. And nothing can be done."

Alex sat up straight. "You're up to something, Bracken! I know it. Now tell me what it is."

Margot considered, then said slowly, "It could be there are certain

184

things it's better you don't know. Something I'd never want to do, Alex, is embarrass you."

He smiled affectionately. "All right, I won't probe. But I'll ask one assurance—that whatever you have in mind is legal."

She said softly, "You know I always operate inside the law."

"Yes, I do." Relaxed once more, he went back to stroking her hair.

Margot stirred, moving closer. "Sometimes the things I do create antagonism. Lots of it. Suppose our names were linked together at a time when you wouldn't want to be associated with me?"

"I'd learn to live with it. Besides, I'm entitled to a private life, and so are you."

"Yes. But I wonder sometimes if you really could live with it. That's if we were together all the time. I wouldn't change, Alex darling. I couldn't ever stop being myself and taking initiatives."

He thought of Celia, who had taken no initiative, ever. He had learned from her that no man is whole unless the woman he loves is free and knows the use of freedom.

Alex dropped his hands to Margot's shoulders. He said gently, "I love you as you are. If you changed, I'd hire some other lady lawyer and sue for breach of loving."

THE sight was so unusual that loan officer Cliff Castleman strolled over to the platform. "Mrs. D'Orsey, have you looked out of a window, by any chance?"

"No," Edwina said. She had been concentrating on the morning mail. "Why should I?" It was 8:55 a.m., Wednesday, at First Mercantile American's downtown branch.

"Well," Castleman said, "there's a lineup outside, the likes of which I've never seen before."

Edwina walked over to one of the large front windows. What she saw amazed her. A long queue of people, four or five abreast, extended the entire length of the building and out of sight beyond. It appeared as if all were waiting for the bank to open.

She stared incredulously. "What on earth . . ."

"They say the line goes halfway across Rosselli Plaza, and more people are joining it all the time," Castleman informed her.

"Has anyone asked what they want?"

"One of the security guards did. They've come to open accounts."

"That's ridiculous! There must be three hundred I can see from here. We've never had that many new accounts in one day."

Tottenhoe joined them at the window. "I've notified Central Security," he said. "They're sending more guards, and Mr. Wainwright's coming over. Also, they're advising the city police."

Edwina commented, "There's no outward sign of trouble. Those people all seem peaceful."

It was a mixed group, about two-thirds women, with a preponderance of blacks. Many of the women were accompanied by children. Among the men, some were in coveralls, as if they had left their jobs or were on the way to them. They were talking to each other animatedly, but no one appeared antagonistic. A few, seeing themselves observed, smiled and nodded to the bank officials.

"Look at that!" Cliff Castleman pointed.

A TV camera crew had appeared. While Edwina and the others watched, it began filming. A flash of insight struck Edwina. "It's Forum East," she said. "I'll bet it's Forum East."

Tottenhoe said, "We should delay opening until the extra guards get here." The clock showed one minute to nine.

"No," Edwina instructed. She raised her voice so that others could hear. "We'll open as usual, on time. Everyone go back to work, please." She returned to her desk on the platform.

From her vantage point she watched the doors swing open and the first arrivals pour in. They paused to look around curiously, then moved forward as others behind pressed in. Within moments the central area of the bank was filled with a chattering crowd. Edwina saw a tall black man wave some dollar bills and declare loudly, "Ah want to put ma money in the bank."

A security guard directed him, "Over there for new accounts." The guard pointed to a desk where a nervous young girl waited. The tall man walked toward her, smiled reassuringly, and sat down. Immediately a press of others formed a ragged line behind him.

The big man leaned back expansively, still holding his dollar bills. His voice cut across the noise of other conversations. "Ah'm in no hurry," he said. "There's some things ah'd like yo' to explain."

Two other desks were quickly manned by other clerks. With equal speed, long lines formed in front of them. Normally three staff members were ample to handle new accounts, but obviously they were inadequate now. Edwina called Tottenhoe on the intercom. "Use more desks for new accounts and take all the staff you can spare to man them."

Tottenhoe grumbled, "You realize we can't possibly process all these people today, and it will tie us up completely."

"I've an idea," Edwina said, "that's what someone has in mind. Just hurry the processing all you can."

She knew, however much they hurried, it would take ten to fifteen minutes to open an account. The paperwork required it—details of residence, employment, social security, a specimen signature, proof of identity. After that the clerk would take all documents to a bank officer for approval and initialing. Finally a savings passbook would be made out or a temporary checkbook issued. Therefore the most new accounts that any bank employee could open in an hour were five. The three clerks presently working might handle ninety in one business day, if going at top speed. Even tripling that number of clerks would permit few more than two hundred and fifty accounts to be opened, yet already the bank was crammed with at least four hundred people, and the line outside, which Edwina rose to check, appeared as long as ever. The noise had increased to an uproar, and the crowd in the central area was preventing access to tellers' counters by regular customers. Edwina could see a few outside, regarding the milling scene with consternation. While she watched, several gave up and walked away.

Inside, some of the newcomers were engaging tellers in conversation, and the tellers, having nothing else to do because of the melee, chatted back. No hostility was evident. Everyone in the jam-packed bank who was spoken to by staff members answered politely, with a smile. It seemed, Edwina thought, as if all had been briefed to be on best behavior.

She decided it was time for her own intervention. With difficulty she made her way to the front door. Signaling two security guards, she instructed, "That's enough people in the bank. Hold everyone else outside, letting a few in as the others leave. Except our regular customers. Allow them to enter, of course."

The older of the two guards put his head close to Edwina's to make himself heard. "That won't be so easy, Mrs. D'Orsey. When anybody arrives they shout, 'Back of the line!' If we play favorites, it could start a riot."

"There won't be any riot. Just do your best."

Turning back, Edwina raised her voice. "I'm the manager of this bank. Would someone tell me why you're all here today?"

"We're opening accounts," a woman with a child beside her said. She giggled. "Nothing wrong with that, is there?"

"You guys put out them ads," another voice injected. "Start one with five dollars, is what they say."

"That's true," Edwina said, "and the bank means it. But there has to be some reason why you all chose to come together."

An elderly man chimed in, "We're all from Forum East."

A younger voice added, "Or want to be."

"Perhaps I can explain, ma'am." A distinguished-looking black man was being shoved forward through the press of people.

"Please do."

At the same moment, Edwina was aware of Nolan Wainwright beside her. She glanced interrogatively at the security chief, who advised, "Go ahead. You're doing okay."

The man who had been thrust forward said, "Good morning, ma'am. I didn't know there were lady bank managers."

"Well, there are," Edwina said. "And getting to be more all the time. I hope you believe in the equality of women, Mr. . . . ."

"Orinda. Seth Orinda, ma'am. And I sure do believe in that, and lots of other things besides."

"Is it one of the other things that brings you here today?"

"In a way you could say that. What we're doing might be called an act of hope." The well-dressed spokesman chose his words carefully. Conversation stilled as the crowd listened.

Orinda went on, "This bank, so it says, doesn't have enough money to go on helping Forum East get built and has cut its lending cash in half. Some of us think that other half will get chopped, too, if someone doesn't take some action."

Edwina said sharply, "And taking action, I suppose, means bringing the business of this entire branch to a standstill." As she spoke, she was aware of several new faces in the crowd and of open notebooks and racing pencils. Reporters had arrived. Obviously someone had alerted the press in advance.

Seth Orinda looked pained. "What we're doing, ma'am, is bringing all the money we can raise to help this bank through its time of trouble."

Nolan Wainwright snapped, "That's nonsense! This bank is not in trouble."

"If it's not in trouble," a woman asked, "why'd it do what it's done to Forum East?"

"The bank's position was made perfectly clear in its announcement," Edwina answered. "It's a question of priorities. Furthermore, it hopes to resume the full financing later." Even to herself the words sounded hollow.

A chorus of jeers erupted. It was the first note of ugliness. Orinda turned sharply, raising a hand. The jeering ceased.

"Whichever way it looks to you folks here," he asserted, "the fact is, we've all come to put some money in your bank. That's what I mean by an act of hope. We figure that when you realize the way we feel, you'll maybe change your minds."

"And if we don't?"

"Then I reckon we'll go on finding more people and more bits of money. We've a lot more good souls coming here today, and tomorrow, and the day after. Just to open an account, of course. To help out this poor bank. Of course," he added innocently, "some of the folks who are putting money in the bank today may have to come and take it out tomorrow, or the next day, or next week. Most haven't got so much that they can leave it in long. But then, soon as we can, we'll be back to put it in again. We aim to keep you busy."

"Yes," Edwina said, "I understand your aim."

A reporter asked, "How much will all of you be depositing?"

"Not much," Seth Orinda replied. "Most have come with just five dollars. That's the smallest amount this bank will take. Isn't that right?" He looked at Edwina, and she nodded.

Some banks required a minimum of fifty dollars to open a savings account, a hundred for checking. A few had no minimums at all. FMA—seeking to encourage small savers—compromised at five dollars. Once an account was accepted, any credit balance would keep the account open. The Forum East people clearly proposed to drown the downtown branch with in-and-out transactions. Nolan Wainwright said to Edwina, "While there's no disturbance, there's nothing we can do except regulate the traffic." He swung toward Orinda and said firmly, "We'll expect all of you to keep this place orderly, inside and out. Our guards will give directions about how many people can come in at once, and where the waiting line should stay."

The other nodded agreement. "Naturally, sir. We don't want any disturbance either. But we shall expect you to be fair. While we're waiting our turn and being patient, we don't expect others to get special treatment. Anybody arriving—no matter who—must go to the back of the line."

"We'll see about that."

"So will we, sir. Because if you do it some other way, it'll be discrimination. Then you'll hear us holler."

Edwina eased her way through to the three new-accounts desks, already supplemented by two more, while a further two were being set up. One of the auxiliary desks was occupied by Juanita Núñez. Edwina remembered that the girl lived at Forum East. Had she known in advance of today's invasion?

The big black man who had come in waving his dollar bills was getting up as Edwina approached. The clerk who had dealt with him, no longer nervous, said, "This is Mr. Euphrates. He just opened an account."

Edwina was offered an enormous hand, which she took. "Welcome to First Mercantile American, Mr. Euphrates."

"Thank you, that's real nice. In fact, I think maybe I'll pop a little more bread in this here account." He examined a handful of small change, selected a quarter and two dimes, and strolled over to a teller.

Edwina asked the clerk, "What was the initial deposit?"

"Five dollars."

"Very well. Just try to keep going as fast as you can."

"I'll do that, Mrs. D'Orsey, but that one took a long time because he asked a lot of questions about withdrawals and interest rates. He had them written out on paper."

"Others will probably have the same thing. Try to get one of the lists and show it to me." It might provide a clue, Edwina thought, as to who had planned and executed this expert invasion.

Something else was emerging: the attempt to inundate the bank would not be limited to opening new accounts. Those who had already opened accounts were now forming lines at tellers' counters, paying in or withdrawing tiny amounts at a glacial pace. Not only would regular customers have difficulty getting into the building but, once inside, they would be further impeded.

She told Nolan Wainwright about the written lists of questions. The security chief nodded. "I'd like to see them, too."

"Mr. Wainwright," a secretary called over, "telephone."

He took the call and Edwina heard him say, "It *is* a demonstration. But it's peaceful and we could make trouble for ourselves by hasty decisions. The last thing we want is a confrontation." He replaced the phone and said, "Word has got to the brass. They're pressing panic buttons over there."

"One thing they could try is restoring funds to Forum East."

A brief smile crossed Wainwright's face. "I'd like to see that, too. But where the bank's money is on the line, outside pressure won't alter a thing."

Edwina was about to say, I wonder, then changed her mind.

While they watched, the crowd monopolizing the bank's central area remained as great; the uproar, if anything, a little louder. Outside, the lengthening line stayed fixedly in place.

It was now 9:45.

Three blocks away, Margot Bracken was operating a command post from an inconspicuously parked Volkswagen. She had intended to remain remote from the execution of her pressure ploy, but in the end, like a war-horse which paws the ground at the scent of battle, she hadn't been able to. A sizable feat of organization had already been carried through, but it was by no means finished.

Initially, it had been essential that there should be a large attendance at the bank to create a strong impression. But some of the volunteers must be relieved periodically. Others were being held in reserve for later that day, or other days. A patchwork communications system had been set up with messengers and heavy use of local pay phones. It was functioning well. And the reports Margot was getting so far were highly satisfactory. She made a calculation, then instructed the latest messenger, "Tell Deacon it looks as if we've enough volunteers for the rest of today. Let some of those standing outside be relieved for a while, though not more than fifty at a time, and warn them to be back to collect their lunches. And tell everyone to make sure there's no litter on Rosselli Plaza and no food or drinks taken into the bank."

At the beginning, money had been a problem. Many of the volunteers lacked a spare five dollars to open an account. Then Margot had telephoned the American Federation of Clerks, Cashiers & Office Workers. Would the union help by lending enough money to provide a five-dollar stake for each volunteer who could not afford it? Union leaders summoned a hasty meeting. The answer was yes. The union also offered to supply lunches.

At 11:45 a.m. Seth Orinda reported personally to Margot. He was grinning broadly and held out an early edition of the afternoon newspaper.

"Wow!" Margot spread the front page wide.

BIG BANK IMMOBILIZED
BY FORUM EASTERS

FIRST MERC AMERICAN IN TROUBLE?
MANY COME TO "HELP"
WITH SMALL DEPOSITS

Pictures and a two-column story followed. "Oh brother!" Margot said. "How FMA will hate *that!*"

192

They did.

Shortly after midday a conference was called in the Tower presidential suite. Jerome Patterton and Roscoe Heyward were there, grim-faced. Alex Vandervoort joined them, as did Tom Straughan. Dick French, vice-president for public relations, strode in carrying the afternoon newspapers, which he slapped down one by one.

" 'First Merc American in Trouble?' " Patterton read, spluttering. "That's a filthy lie! That paper should be sued."

"There's nothing to sue about," French said. "The newspaper hasn't stated it as fact. It's put as a question. Whoever is behind this is good at law *and* public relations. Right now I'll bet this story is on every wire service. It's a David-and-Goliath piece, surefire human interest."

Tom Straughan said quietly, "I can confirm part of that. It *has* been on the Dow Jones news service, and right afterward our stock dropped one more point."

"We may as well brace ourselves for TV tonight," Dick French went on. "My guess is we'll be on all three major networks. If any scripter can resist that bank-in-trouble phrase, I'll swallow my picture tube."

Heyward asked coldly, "Have you finished?"

"Not quite. I'd just like to say that if I'd blown this entire year's PR budget on *just one thing* to make this bank look *bad*, I couldn't have improved on what you guys have done."

"All right," Patterton said, "what do you suggest?"

"You're the ones who pulled the rug out from under Forum East. You're the ones who could put it back."

Patterton turned to Vandervoort. "Alex?"

"You know I was against the cut in funds to begin with," Alex said. "I still am. Some such response could have been foreseen."

Heyward said acidly, "So what you're doing is refusing to stand up to a mob."

Alex shook his head impatiently. "Stop sounding like a small-town sheriff, Roscoe. Sometimes unwillingness to change a decision is plain pigheadedness, nothing more. Besides, those people are not a mob. Every report has made that clear."

"Just the same, Alex," Jerome Patterton ruminated, "I don't like the idea of meekly giving in."

Alex sighed. "If you feel like that, we'd better accept that the downtown branch won't be much use to us for a while."

In the absence of any softening of the bank's attitude, inundation of the downtown branch continued through all of Thursday and Friday. The big branch was almost helpless. And as Dick French predicted, nationwide attention was focused on its plight. Much of the attention was humorous. On the New York Stock Exchange on Friday, FMA closed two and a half points down. Investors were not amused.

On Monday morning the bank capitulated. Dick French announced at a press conference that full Forum East financing would be restored at once.

Behind the capitulation were several cogent reasons. Monday morning the lineup outside the downtown branch was the largest yet. And a second long line appeared at the FMA branch in suburban Indian Hill.

But it was a final factor which clinched the outcome. The union which had loaned money to the Forum East Tenants Association announced that a campaign to unionize the bank's employees would soon begin. All banks feared, even hated, unions. Few organizers had made the slightest headway where bank employees were concerned. If the Forum East situation afforded leverage to a union, then the leverage must be removed.

When the announcement was read to Forum East supporters at both branch banks, there was cheering, after which the groups quietly dispersed. Within half an hour business returned to normal.

The matter might have ended there, except for a newspaper gossip column two days later.

Were you wondering who was behind those Forum Easters who brought the mighty First Mercantile American Bank to heel? It's civil rights lawyer–feminist Margot Bracken. Despite the "bank-in" being her idea, Ms. Bracken stayed out of sight.

Margot's great and good friend, most often seen with her around town, is swinging banker Alexander Vandervoort, exec veep of

First Merc Am. If *you* were Margot and had that connection, wouldn't *you* stay out of sight? Only thing we're wondering: did Alex know and approve the siege of his own home plate?

IT WAS close to midnight. Margot and Alex, meeting for the first time since the siege of FMA's downtown branch, were in Alex's apartment. Margot said, "Alex, I'm sorry! I could skin that columnist alive. At least he didn't mention I'm related to Edwina."

"Not many know that. Anyway, lovers make livelier copy."

She said contritely, "Only a few people knew what I was doing, and I wanted it to stay like that."

He shook his head. "No way. Nolan Wainwright said to me, 'The whole caper has Margot Bracken's handwriting on it.' And he had started to quiz people. Someone would have talked if the news item hadn't appeared first."

"But they didn't have to use *your* name."

Alex smiled. "I rather liked that 'swinging banker' bit." But the smile was false, and Margot knew it. The truth was that the column had jolted him.

"Didn't you have an idea I was involved?" Margot asked.

"Yes. I remembered how you clammed up about Forum East when I expected you to tear me to shreds."

"Did it make things difficult for you—the bank-in?"

He answered bluntly. "Yes. I wasn't sure whether to share what I'd guessed. I kept quiet. It was the wrong decision."

"So now the others believe you knew all the time."

"Roscoe does. Maybe Jerome. I'm not sure about the rest."

"Do you care? Does it matter terribly?"

Alex shrugged. "Not really. I'll survive."

But it did matter very much. Alex's loyalty would, from now on, have an asterisk of doubt beside it. The doubt would be in the directors' minds as they considered the bank presidency.

His dark mood deepened. Margot regarded him, her expression anxious, uncertain. Finally she said, "I've caused you trouble. Quite a lot, I think. So let's stop pretending that I didn't. We've talked about it, knowing it might happen, wondering whether we could

195

remain the kind of people we are—independent—yet stay together."

Without warning, their relationship had reached a crisis.

"It will happen again, Alex. Oh, not with the bank, but with other things. And I want to be sure we can handle it whenever it does, and not just for one time, hoping it will be the last."

He knew this was true. Margot's life was one of confrontations; there would be many, some not remote from his own interests.

"One thing you and I could do," Margot said, "is call it quits while we're ahead. If we stopped being seen together, word would travel quickly. While it wouldn't wipe out what happened at the bank, it could make things easier for you there."

It would, Alex knew. He had a swift temptation to exorcise a complication from his life likely to become greater as years went by. *How much did he want to be president of FMA? Not that much!*

Not for FMA or personal ambition would he surrender, *ever*, his private freedom of action. Or give up Margot.

"The most important thing is, do *you* want to call it quits?"

Margot spoke through tears. "Of course not."

"Then I don't either, Bracken. Nor am I ever likely to. So let's be glad this happened, that we've proved something, and that neither of us has to prove it anymore."

He put out his arms and she came to them.

CHAPTER 8

"ROSCOE, my boy," the Honorable Harold Austin said on the telephone one Saturday afternoon in March. "I've been talking with Big George. He's invited you and me to play golf in the Bahamas next Friday."

It was unnecessary to identify "Big George." G. G. Quartermain, board chairman and chief executive of Supranational Corporation—SuNatCo—was a bravura bull of a man who possessed more power than many heads of state and exercised it like a king.

Heyward had met the SuNatCo chairman once in a Washington, D.C., hotel suite with Harold Austin, whose agency handled national advertising for Hepplewhite Distillers, a SuNatCo subsidiary.

On being introduced to Heyward, Big George observed, "Harold tells me you'd both like your little bank to have a spoonful of our gravy. Well, sometime soon we'll see about it." He then clapped Roscoe across the shoulders and talked of other things.

It was that conversation with G. G. Quartermain which had prompted Heyward, two months ago, to inform the FMA money policy committee that doing business with SuNatCo was a probability.

"Big George is sending his private jet for us," he heard the Honorable Harold say. "A 707. We'll fly from here Thursday at noon, have Friday in Nassau, and be back on Saturday."

As he replaced the telephone in his study, Heyward permitted himself a slight smile. If anything came of this trip, it would enhance his status with the board—something he never lost sight of nowadays.

He was pleased, too, that he would not have to miss an appearance at St. Athanasius', where he was a lay reader and delivered the lesson every Sunday. The thought reminded him of tomorrow's reading. He lifted a heavy family Bible from a bookshelf and turned to a favorite verse in Proverbs: *Righteousness exalteth a nation: but sin is a reproach to any people.*

The following Thursday the 707, identified by a large Q on fuselage and tail, landed at the city's international airport precisely as scheduled. It taxied to a private terminal, where Harold Austin and Roscoe Heyward left the limousine which had brought them from downtown and were whisked aboard.

In a foyer like a miniature hotel lobby, they were greeted by three breathtakingly beautiful young women—a blonde, a brunette, and a redhead—wearing abbreviated hostess uniforms. "Good afternoon, Mr. Heyward," the redhead said. Her voice had a soft, seductive quality. "I'm Avril. If you'll come this way, I'll show you to your room."

As Heyward followed her, surprised by the reference to a room, the Honorable Harold was being greeted by the blonde.

Avril preceded Heyward down a corridor extending along the aircraft on one side and stopped at a doorway. "This is your room, Mr. Heyward." As she spoke, the aircraft moved forward, beginning to taxi. "I'd better strap you in for takeoff. The captain always

197

goes quickly. Mr. Quartermain doesn't like lingering at airports."

The girl led Heyward into a small, sumptuous parlor and strapped him into a comfortable settee. She said, "If you don't mind, I'll stay until we're airborne." She sat down beside him and fastened her own strap.

"No," Roscoe said, dazed. "I don't mind at all."

When they were airborne, Avril released her seat belt and stood up. "If you want Mr. Austin," she said, "he's in the cabin immediately behind. Up forward is the main lounge, where you're invited when you're ready. Mr. Quartermain is having a sauna and massage, and he will join you there later. Then there's a dining room, offices, and Mr. Quartermain's private apartment."

"Thank you for the geography."

"My job on this trip, Mr. Heyward, is to make sure you have everything you want. If you want me for anything, please press button number seven on the telephone."

Had she placed a subtle emphasis on that "anything"? Heyward wondered. If so, the implication was shocking. He answered gruffly, "Thank you, young lady. But I doubt if I'll do that."

"One other thing: on the way to the Bahamas we'll be landing in Washington briefly. The Vice-President is joining us there."

"A vice-president from Supranational?"

Her eyes were mocking. "No, silly. The Vice-President of the United States."

Some fifteen minutes later, in the 707's splendidly appointed main lounge, Quartermain demanded, "Girls taking care of you both?"

"No complaints from this quarter," Austin said. Curled on the rug at his feet was the blonde, who had revealed her name as Rhetta.

Avril, beside Heyward, said sweetly, "We're trying our best."

G. G. Quartermain, fresh from the sauna, was resplendent in a crimson towel robe. He was attended by a hard-faced man in gym whites, presumably a masseur, and still another hostess, her features delicately Japanese.

Physically their host was a mountain of a man—at least six and a half feet in height, his chest, arms, and torso like a village blacksmith's. Yet there was no sign of overweight. Through the enfolding robe, muscles bulged. As to other bigness, his worldwide corporate reach and appetite were reported daily in the business press. And his living style aboard this twelve-million-dollar airplane was unabashedly royal.

"That trouble at your bank." Quartermain addressed Roscoe Heyward. "Demonstrations. Is everything settled? Are you solid?"

"We were always solid. That was never in question."

"The market didn't think so." Big George swung to the petite Japanese hostess. "Moonbeam, get me the latest quote on FMA." She went out by a forward door, returning with a slip of paper. She read out in accented English, "FMA trading now at forty-five and three-quarters."

"There we are," Roscoe Heyward said, "we're up another point."

"But still not as high as before Rosselli bit the bullet." Big George grinned. "Though when word gets out that you're helping finance Supranational, your stock'll soar."

It could happen, Heyward thought. Big George had now declared positively that business *was* to be transacted between FMA and SuNatCo. No doubt they would thrash out details through the next two days. He felt his excitement rising.

Outside, the jet thrum changed to lower tempo. "Washington, ho!" Avril said. She and the other girls began fastening the men into their seats with heavy belts and light fingers.

In less than twenty minutes they had returned to cruising altitude en route to Nassau. Vice-President Byron Stonebridge was installed with the brunette, Krista, an arrangement he patently approved. The Secret Service men guarding the Vice-President had been accommodated at the rear.

Soon after, Big George, now attired in a silk suit, led the way to the airliner's dining room, where they lunched in a style any of the world's great restaurants would have found hard to equal. A few hours later they were at Quartermain's Bahamas mansion.

The Quartermain estate, behind high stone walls, one of half a dozen owned by the Supranational chairman in various countries, was on Prospero Ridge, high above Nassau and with a panoramic view of land and sea.

After dinner they were driven to a gambling casino, where Big George played heavily and appeared to win. Roscoe Heyward, who disapproved of gambling, did not play. Returning at 2:00 a.m., Avril escorted him to his bedroom door. She told him, smiling, "There's an intercom beside the bed. If there's *anything* you want, press button number seven." This time there was no doubt what "anything" meant.

His voice thickened and his tongue seemed oversize as he informed her, "Thank you, no."

But he was finding that ideas and inclinations he knew to be reprehensible were increasingly hard to banish, and he fell on his knees and prayed to God to protect him from sin and relieve him of temptation.

The next day Big George and Heyward shared one electric golf cart, Stonebridge and the Honorable Harold another. Six more carts had been requisitioned by the Vice-President's Secret Service escort. The four were playing a best-ball match—Big George and Heyward against Austin and the Vice-President.

It was as Big George and Roscoe Heyward waited in their cart on the fourteenth hole that the subject Heyward had been hoping for was raised—with surprising casualness.

"So your bank would like some Supranational business."

"The thought had occurred to us." Heyward tried to match the other's manner.

"I'm extending Supranational's foreign communications holdings by buying control of small, key telephone and broadcast companies. Some owned by governments, others private. Supranational provides advanced technology, efficient service, which small countries can't afford, and standardization for global linkage. There's good profitability for ourselves."

"Yes," Heyward agreed, "I can see that."

"From your bank I'd want a credit line of fifty million dollars. Of course, at prime."

"Naturally." Heyward had known that any loan to Supranational would be at the bank's best interest rate. It was axiomatic that the richest corporate customers paid least for borrowed money.

"We would have to review our legal limitation under federal law."

"Legal limitation, hell! There are ways around that, methods used every day. You know it as well as I do."

What both men were speaking of was a U.S. banking regulation forbidding any bank to lend more than ten percent of its capital and paid-in surplus to a single debtor. The purpose was to guard against bank failure and protect depositors from loss. In the case of First Mercantile American, a fifty-million-dollar loan to Supranational would substantially exceed that limit.

"The way to beat the regulation," Big George said, "is to split the loan among our subsidiary companies. Then we'll reallocate it as and where we need."

Roscoe Heyward mused, "It could be done that way." The size of the proposed commitment staggered him. He had envisaged twenty or twenty-five million as a starting point.

As if reading his mind, Big George said flatly, "I never deal in small amounts. If fifty million is bigger than you people can handle, let's forget the whole thing. I'll give it to Chase."

Heyward said emphatically, "No, no. It's not too large." Mentally he reviewed other FMA commitments. Fifty million to SuNatCo would require drastic cutbacks on smaller loans and mortgages, but one large loan to a client like Supranational would be immensely more profitable. "I intend to recommend the line of credit strongly to our board," Heyward said decisively, "and I'm certain they'll agree. Of course, it would strengthen my position if I could inform them that we would have some bank representation on the Supranational board."

Big George drove the golf cart to his ball. "That might be arranged. I'd expect your trust department to invest heavily in our stock. It's time some fresh buying pushed the price up."

"The subject could be explored. Obviously, Supranational will have an active account with us now, and there's the question of a compensating balance. . . ."

G. G. Quartermain said irritably, "Don't bother me with details. My financial man, Inchbeck, will be here today. He'll fly back with us tomorrow. You two can get together then."

Plainly the brief business session was concluded.

Over drinks in the men's locker room at the end of the match, losers Austin and Stonebridge each paid G. G. Quartermain a hundred dollars—a bet they had agreed on before the game. Heyward had refrained from betting. Big George said magnanimously, "I like the way you played, partner." He appealed to the others. "I think Roscoe ought to get some recognition." He slapped his knee. "I got it! A seat on the Supranational board. How's that for a prize?"

Heyward realized that Big George was implementing their earlier conversation. If he agreed, of course, it would mean accepting the other obligations.... His hesitation lasted seconds only. "If you mean it, I'll be delighted to accept."

"It will be announced next week."

The offer was so swift that Heyward had difficulty believing it. To be chosen himself, and personally by G. G. Quartermain, was the accolade of accolades. The SuNatCo board read like a *Who's Who* of business and finance. Big George chuckled. "Among other things, you can keep an eye on your bank's money."

Heyward saw the Honorable Harold glance his way questioningly. As Heyward gave a slight nod, his fellow FMA director beamed.

The second evening all eight of them—the men and girls—shared a relaxed intimacy. Roscoe Heyward was euphoric. The pledge of Supranational business and the dazzling trophy of a seat on the SuNatCo board would enhance his prestige at FMA. His succession to the presidency seemed nearer.

Earlier he had had a short meeting with the Supranational comptroller, Stanley Inchbeck. Apart from that meeting, Inchbeck had been closeted through most of the afternoon with G. G. Quartermain.

Dressing for dinner, Roscoe Heyward had noticed, from the window of his second-floor room, that G. G. Quartermain and Byron Stonebridge were strolling in the grounds, deep in conversation. Big George appeared to be talking persuasively, with the Vice-President interrupting occasionally. Heyward wondered which of Supranational's many interests were being discussed.

Now, after dinner, in the cool, sweet-scented darkness of the terrace beside a colonnaded swimming pool, Krista and Avril, who were drinking champagne, chorused, "Let's have a swimming party!"

Krista set down her glass, kicked off her shoes, unfastened her dress, and let it fall at her feet. She had been wearing nothing else. She walked from the terrace, down steps to the lighted swimming pool, and dived in. She called, "It's glorious! Come in!"

"Dammit!" Stonebridge said. "I will." He tossed off his clothes and joined her. Moonbeam and Rhetta were undressing.

"Hold on!" Harold Austin called. "This sport's coming, too."

Roscoe Heyward found Avril standing beside him. "Rossie, sweetie, undo my zipper." She presented him her back.

Uncertainly he fumbled with the zipper. Her dress fell away. With a graceful movement Avril pivoted. "Coming swimming?" she purred, and kissed him fully on the lips.

He shook his head. His hands were trembling, his eyes riveted on her. She walked away and joined the others in the pool.

But in bed later, sleep eluded him. Despite his best intentions, the focus of his thoughts was Avril. He tried to move his thoughts away—to the loan, the directorship. But Avril was impossible to eclipse. Her lips, her smile, her availability. Twice he made a move toward the intercom. Twice, resolve held him back.

The third time he did not turn back. Decisively and firmly he pressed button number seven.

Chapter 9

Nothing in Miles Eastin's experience had prepared him for the merciless, degrading hell of prison.

It was now four months since his trial and sentencing. In rare moments, when his objectivity prevailed over physical misery and mental anguish, Miles reasoned that, if society had sought to impose savage vengeance on someone like himself, it had succeeded far beyond the knowing of any who had not endured this brutishness. He was striving to hang on to some shards of moral values, to retain some semblance of the best of what he had been before. He would be eligible for parole in four months. *Hold on!* he told himself each day and in the nights. *Hold on* for parole!

The cage at Drummonburg Penitentiary in which he was confined had four bunks clamped to walls, one sink, and a toilet. A group shower was allowed once weekly. It was in the showers, during his second week in prison, that Miles was gang-raped.

One morning when he was emerging from the showers in a group of fifty inmates, Miles felt himself surrounded. His arms were gripped tightly and he was shoved into an adjoining storage room.

"Sir! Sir!" he shouted to a guard. The guard took no notice. Afterward, Miles guessed the man had been bribed.

A fist slammed hard into Miles's ribs. A voice behind him snarled, "Shaddup!"

He cried out again from pain and fear, and another fist thudded home once more. The breath went out of him.

During the horror of the next few minutes Miles's mind began to drift. Consciousness left him totally, then returned. He heard a guard's whistle, the signal to assemble in the yard. He was aware of the others in the room running out. Barely conscious, he staggered to the dressing area and stepped into his rough prison pants. He would have fallen but for an arm which reached out, holding him.

"Take it easy, kid," a deep voice said. "Here, I'll help." The man beside him was huge and black. Later Miles would learn that his name was Karl and that he was serving a life sentence for murder.

Supported by Karl, Miles walked unsteadily out to the yard. Karl asked, "How ya feel, kid?"

Miles shook his head dejectedly. "Awful." He added, "Thanks for what you did."

"It's okay, kid. One thing, though, you gotta figure. They'll be after you again."

"What can I do?" Miles's fear made his voice quaver and his body tremble. The other watched him shrewdly.

"What you need, kid, is a protector. How about me?"

Knowing what the price would be, Miles wanted to be sick. He said bitterly, "Do I have a choice?"

"Put it that way, no, I guess you ain't."

There were no more attacks. Miles was transferred to Karl's cell.

The black giant, Miles discovered, had a gentleness of manner and a sensitive consideration almost feminine. The transfer was obviously the result of money changing hands. Miles asked how he had managed it. The big black chuckled. "Them guys in Mafia Row put up the bread. They like you."

"Like *me?*"

Mafia Row was a segment of cells housing the big wheels of organized crime whose outside influence made them respected and feared. But Miles had had no contact with them, nor was he aware that they knew of his existence.

"They say you're a stand-up guy," Karl told him.

The mystery was resolved a few days later. A weasel-faced prisoner named LaRocca sidled alongside Miles in the prison yard. LaRocca, while not part of Mafia Row, acted as a courier. He told Miles, "Gotta message for ya from Russian Ominsky."

Miles was startled. Igor ("the Russian") Ominsky was the loan shark to whom he still owed several thousand dollars. He realized, too, there must be enormous accrued interest on the debt.

"Ominsky knows ya kept ya trap shut," LaRocca said.

It was true that Miles had not divulged the names of his bookmaker or the loan shark at the time of his arrest. There had seemed nothing to be gained by doing so, perhaps much to lose.

"Because ya buttoned up," LaRocca went on, "Ominsky says to tell ya he stopped the clock while you're inside." That meant that interest on what Miles owed was no longer accumulating during his time in prison. The concession was a large one.

"Tell Mr. Ominsky thanks," Miles said. He had no idea, though, how he could repay the capital sum when he left prison.

LaRocca acknowledged the thought. "Someone'll be in touch before ya get sprung. Maybe we can work a deal."

In the weeks which followed, LaRocca several times sought out Miles's company in the prison yard. He and the other prisoners were fascinated by Miles's knowledge of the history of money. What intrigued LaRocca most was Miles's description of massive counterfeiting, by governments, of other countries' money. "Those have always been the biggest counterfeit jobs," Miles told an interested audience of half a dozen one day. And he described the greatest counterfeit venture of all, when, during World War II, Germany forged millions of pounds in British money as well as large amounts of U.S. dollars, all of highest quality. Rumor said that most of the Allies also printed German money.

LaRocca made it clear that he was relaying Miles's information about counterfeiting to Mafia Row. "Me and my people'll take care of ya outside," he announced. Miles knew that his own release from prison, and LaRocca's, could occur about the same time.

Talking money was a form of mental suspension for Miles, pushing away the horror of the present. He supposed, too, he should feel relief about the stopping of the loan clock. Yet nothing was sufficient to overcome his general wretchedness. In the end only one thing kept him from suicide. He wanted, when his time in prison was done, to tell Juanita Núñez he was sorry.

When he thought about the bank theft now, the betting, the insanity of borrowing from a loan shark—they were like crazy parts of some distemper. As with fever in advanced stages, his mind had been distorted until all values disappeared. How else could he have been guilty of such vileness as to cast blame on Juanita Núñez? Even prison, in all its awfulness, could not pay the debt he owed Juanita. He must seek her out and beg forgiveness.

CHAPTER 10

THE meeting of the board of directors of First Mercantile American Bank in the third week of April was memorable for its intense disagreements.

Two major policy items were the subject of discussion—Roscoe Heyward's Supranational line of credit and Alex Vandervoort's proposed expanding of savings activity and the opening of nine new automated suburban branches.

Heyward, unusually jovial, greeted the other directors at the boardroom door as they arrived. From the cordial responses it was clear that most of them were in favor of the SuNatCo agreement.

Jerome Patterton gaveled for attention. "The first item of business is: loans submitted for board approval. You have in front of you details of our proposed new account with Supranational Corporation. Personally, I'm delighted with the terms and strongly recommend approval. I'll leave it to Roscoe, who's responsible for bringing this business to the bank, to fill in background."

"Thank you, Jerome." Roscoe Heyward leaned forward in his chair. "Gentlemen, in Appendix B of your folders you will find a summary of assets and projected profits of the SuNatCo group, including all subsidiaries. This is based on audited financial statements plus additional data supplied at my request by Supranational's comptroller, Mr. Stanley Inchbeck. As you can see, the corporation has a triple-A credit rating. Our risk is minimal."

Although the recommendations were listed in the folders, Heyward went on to describe the fifty-million-dollar line of credit to be granted to Supranational and subsidiaries immediately, with financial cutbacks in other bank areas, hopefully to be restored at an unspecified future time. Supranational had agreed to a compensating balance of ten percent, which meant that five million dollars of the loan would be kept on deposit in new SuNatCo checking accounts with FMA, available for the bank's use and investment. Heyward concluded his presentation with: "I recommend this package to the board and promise that, in light of it, our profit figures will look very good indeed."

As he leaned back in his chair, Patterton announced, "The meeting is open for questions and discussion."

"Frankly," said Wallace Sperrie, owner of a scientific instrument company, "I see no need for either. I think we're witnesses to a masterstroke of business, and I propose approval."

Several voices called out, "Second!"

"Proposed and seconded," Jerome Patterton intoned. "Are we ready to vote?" His gavel was poised.

"No," Alex Vandervoort said quietly.

Patterton sighed. Alex had warned him of his intentions, but Patterton had hoped that Alex would change his mind. He set the gavel down.

Around the table there was a restless stirring and exclamations of annoyed surprise as Alex reached into his folder and extracted a page of notes. "To begin with," he said, "I object to the *extent* of the commitment to a single account. In my opinion it is fraudulent under the law—"

Roscoe Heyward leaped to his feet. "I object to that word fraudulent. We have made plain that the full commitment is not to Supranational Corporation, but to its subsidiaries: Hepplewhite Distillers, Farview Land Development, Atlas Jet Leasing, Caribbean Funding, and International Bottling."

"You know as well as I do," Alex insisted, "that once the bank's money is in *any* of those subsidiaries, G. G. Quartermain can, and will, move it around any way he chooses."

"Now *hold everything!*" This was Harold Austin. "George is a good friend of mine. I won't hear any accusations of bad faith."

"There was no accusation of bad faith," Alex responded. "What I'm talking about is a fact of conglomerate life."

For the first time Leonard L. Kingswood, Northam Steel chairman, spoke. Last December, Kingswood had been a leader in urging Alex's appointment as president of FMA. "Alex, I'll admit there's some substance to what you say, but frankly, if there's anything to be guilty of with that kind of financing, my own company has been guilty of it, too."

Regretfully, knowing it was costing him a friend, Alex shook his head. "I'm sorry, Len. I still don't believe that it's right. Nor do I think we should leave ourselves open to a conflict-of-interest charge by Roscoe's going on the Supranational board."

Leonard Kingswood's mouth tightened. He said nothing more.

But Philip Johannsen of MidContinent Rubber did. "Could it be, Alex, that you're just a little sore because *you* were not invited to that Bahamas golf game?"

Roscoe Heyward tried, but failed, to conceal a smile.

Alex's face was set grimly. Ignoring Johannsen's remark, he declared, "As bankers we just don't learn. From all sides—including our own customers—we're accused of perpetuating conflict of interest through interlocking directorates. If we're honest with ourselves, most accusations are on target. And the time is close when the bank will have to face that situation squarely and amend it."

Austin growled, "There may be other opinions on that."

Disregarding the growing hostility, Alex plowed on. "Other aspects of the Supranational loan disturb me equally. To make the money available we're to cut back mortgage lending and small loans. In these two areas alone the bank will be defective in its public service. Then there's a third area of cutback which we haven't touched on yet—municipal bonds. In the next six weeks, eleven issues of county and school district bonds within the state will be up for bids. If our bank fails to participate, at least half those bonds are certain to remain unsold." Alex's voice sharpened. "Is it the board's intention to dispense, *so quickly after Ben Rosselli's death*, with a tradition spanning three Rosselli generations?"

Without aid from the state's largest bank, small bond issues might go unmarketed, leaving financial needs of their communities unmet. Returning to communities, in this way, some of the money their own citizenry deposited in FMA was a policy established by the founder.

"Jerome," Leonard Kingswood suggested, "maybe you should take another look at that situation."

Heyward made a swift assessment. "Jerome ... if I may ..."

The bank president nodded.

"I'm certain we can restore a portion of municipal-bond funding without impeding the Supranational arrangements. May I suggest that the board leave details to the discretion of Jerome and myself."

Nods and voices signified agreement.

"That's not a full commitment," Alex objected. "And there's still one other matter. Since negotiation of the Supranational loan, and up to yesterday afternoon, our own trust department has bought one hundred and twenty-three thousand SuNatCo shares with our trust clients' money. The SuNatCo share price has thus risen seven and a half points, which I'm sure was agreed to as a condition—"

Heyward was on his feet again, eyes blazing. "That's a deliberate distortion! SuNatCo is an excellent investment for our trust accounts."

"Whether it is or isn't, I warn you that what is happening may be in violation of the law—"

Half a dozen voices erupted angrily. Knowledge of collusion implied responsibility. The board wanted none of it.

Like it or not, Alex thought, they knew now. He continued firmly, "If we ratify the Supranational loan, we'll regret it." He leaned back in his chair. "That's all."

Moments later the Supranational proposals were approved, with Alex Vandervoort the sole dissenter.

After lunch the directors resumed their meeting, with Alex's savings and branch proposals still to be heard; Philip Johannsen set the mood by pointedly consulting his watch.

Moving to the head of the table, Alex placed a chart in full view of the board members. He said, "I'll be as brief as possible, gentlemen. My intention is to make four points. One, our bank is losing important, profitable business by failing to make the most of opportunities for savings growth. Two, an expansion of savings deposits will improve the bank's stability. Third, the longer we delay, the harder it will be to catch up with our many competitors. Fourth, there is scope for leadership—which we should exercise— in a return to habits of personal, corporate, and national thrift."

He described methods by which First Mercantile American could gain an edge over competitors—offering the top legal savings interest rate; more attractive terms for one- to five-year certificates of deposit; checking facilities for savings depositors, as far as banking law allowed; gifts for opening new accounts; a massive campaign advertising the savings program and the nine new branches to be opened.

Johannsen said, "I'd like to hear Roscoe's view."

Heads turned to Heyward. "One doesn't like to torpedo a colleague," he said blandly, "but board members will observe on the chart that five of the nine suggested branches would be in locations close to savings and loan associations who are large depositors with FMA. If we compete, we risk losing their business."

"I think not," Alex said. "Those locations are where the *people* are. Sure the savings and loans got there first, but it doesn't mean we should stay away forever. There's room for both."

Heyward shrugged. "I dislike the entire idea of storefront branches. Not in keeping with our style. No dignity."

Alex snapped, "They'll be money shops—the branch banks of the future. We'd do better to shed dignity and add business. In ten years half of our present branch banks will have ceased to exist as we know them. The rest will be in less expensive premises, totally automated, with machine tellers, and TV monitors to answer queries—all linked to a computer center. In planning new branches, it's that transition we should be anticipating, and we should do it with flair and fanfare. The advertising and promotion campaign should be massive, saturation coverage."

"Alex," Harold Austin said with a smile, "frankly, I'm impressed. I like the idea of those new branch banks."

Heyward looked startled, then glared at Austin, who ignored him and said to the others, "I think we should look at this with an open mind. Alex, you spoke of a return to personal thrift. Could you expand on that, and on the advantages of savings and the leadership banks like ours might give?"

Alex was not surprised. He knew exactly why Austin had switched sides. *Advertising.* By reason of his directorship at FMA, the Austin agency had a monopoly of the bank's advertising. Austin's action was conflict of interest in its grossest form—the same conflict Alex had attacked over Heyward's appointment to the board of Supranational. Should he say so? Such a confrontation would end his own effectiveness at FMA. The directors were watching him.

"Yes," he said, "I did refer to thrift and a need for leadership, as Harold reminds me. It is often said that the country runs on credit. Today, overwhelming government debt is matched by gargantuan corporate debt. And at a lower financial level, millions of people have followed examples nationally set. National consumer debt is now approaching two hundred billion dollars. In the past six years more than a million Americans have gone bankrupt."

Suddenly the mood of the board had become sober. Responding to it, Alex said quietly, "Savings deposits represent prudence. There *can* be tremendous increases in savings—if we commit ourselves. While personal savings alone will not restore fiscal sanity everywhere, it is one major move toward that end. This is why there is an opportunity for leadership, and why—here and now—I believe this bank should exercise it." Alex sat down. Seconds later he realized he had said nothing about his doubts concerning Austin's intervention.

"I buy that," Harold said. "I intend to vote for the savings and branch-expansion plans. I urge the rest of you to do the same."

For fifteen minutes discussion swirled. Then by an overwhelming majority Alex Vandervoort's proposals were approved.

On his way out of the boardroom, Alex was aware that hostility had not vanished. But this unexpected outcome made him less pessimistic about his role at FMA.

Harold Austin intercepted him. "Alex, when will you move on the savings plan?"

"Immediately. Thank you for your support."

Austin nodded. "I'd like to come in with two or three of my agency people to discuss the campaign."

"Very well. Next week."

The Austin Advertising Agency did good work and could be selected on merit. But Alex was rationalizing and knew it. He wondered what Margot would think.

Roscoe Heyward, leaving the boardroom just ahead of Alex, was accosted by a uniformed bank messenger who handed him an envelope. Heyward ripped it open and took out a folded message. Reading it, he brightened visibly. Alex wondered why.

The note was a simple one. Typed by his trusted senior secretary, Dora Callaghan, it informed him that Miss Deveraux was in town and would like him to call. He recognized the number: the Columbia Hotel. Miss Deveraux was Avril.

They had met twice since the Bahamas trip, both times at the Columbia Hotel. And on each occasion with her, he had begun to realize how much of life's passion and glory he and Beatrice had never known.

He glanced at his watch, smiling. He'd go to Avril as soon as possible. The thought of seeing her made him feel young.

On a few occasions conscience had troubled him. During recent Sundays in church, the text he had read before going to the Bahamas came back to haunt him. But the intoxication of Avril was stronger than any stab of conscience.

Walking back to his office, Heyward reflected, glowing, that a session with Avril would consummate a triumphal day. With the Supranational proposals approved, his professional prestige was at a zenith. Which reminded him—he must make a decision about the additional half million dollars requested by Big George as a further loan to Q-Investments, a small private group headed by Quartermain and including Harold Austin.

A month ago Quartermain had requested a loan of one and a half million dollars to Q-Investments at the same low rate as the Supranational loan, and without a compensating balance. Harold had also urged the loan, bluntly reminding Heyward of a quid pro quo owed for Austin's support at the time of Ben Rosselli's death. In view of the size of Supranational's business with FMA, Heyward had not been too concerned. He had sent Patterton a memo about it, but it was not a large enough loan to require approval by the money policy committee. Therefore, Heyward had initialed approval himself, which he had authority to do.

What he did *not* have authority for was a personal transaction between himself and G. G. Quartermain. During a subsequent telephone conversation, Big George had said, "Been talking to Austin about you, Roscoe. We both think it's time you got involved in our investment group. So what I've done is allot you two thousand shares, fully paid for. They're nominee certificates endorsed in blank—more discreet that way. I'll have 'em put in the mail."

Heyward had demurred. "Thank you, George, but I don't believe I should accept. It would be unethical."

Big George had guffawed. "If it makes you feel better, we'll say the shares are in return for your investment advice."

A day or two later the Q-Investments share certificates arrived in an envelope marked STRICTLY PERSONAL AND CONFIDENTIAL. Even Dora Callaghan hadn't opened that one. At home, studying the financial statement which Big George had also supplied, Heyward realized his shares had a net asset value of twenty thousand dollars. If Q-Investments went public, their worth would be much greater.

Heyward yielded to temptation and put the certificates in his safe-deposit box at FMA's main downtown branch. If Big George chose to make a friendly gift, why be churlish and refuse it? His acceptance still worried him a little, though, especially since Big George had telephoned last week from Amsterdam seeking an additional half million. Reflecting that Supranational shares were soaring on both the London and New York markets, Heyward stifled his qualms. As he entered his outer office, Mrs. Callaghan offered him her usual matronly smile. "The other messages are on your desk, sir." He nodded, but inside pushed the pile aside and dialed the Columbia Hotel.

THAT evening the telephone rang in the sitting room of Avril's suite. She answered it. "It's for you, Rossie."

"For *me?*"

He took the receiver. The voice boomed, "Hi there, Roscoe!"

Heyward asked sharply, "Where are you, George?"

"Washington. Just a friendly call, fella. Checking on arrangements. That Q-Investments credit okayed yet?"

"Not quite. There are formalities."

"Let's move 'em, or I'll have to give some other bank that business, and maybe shift some of Supranational's, too."

The threat did not surprise Heyward. Pressures and concessions were a normal part of banking. "I'll do my best, George."

A grunt. "Lemme talk to Avril."

Heyward passed the phone to her. She listened briefly, said, "Yes, I will," and hung up. She went into the bedroom and a moment later emerged with a large manila envelope. "Georgie said I was to give you this."

It was like the envelope which had contained the Q-Investments share certificates. He considered refusing to accept it, but curiosity was strong.

"Georgie told me to say it's a reminder of our good time in Nassau, but you're not to open it here."

He checked his watch. "I must go, my dear."

"Me, too. I'm flying back to New York tonight." She draped her arms around him. "You're a sugarplum, Rossie. We'll see each other soon."

THE HEADQUARTERS TOWER was deserted when Roscoe Heyward opened the door to his office suite. At his desk he slit the seal of the envelope Avril had given him. Inside were a dozen enlarged photographs. That second night in the Bahamas, when the girls and men had bathed in Big George's pool, the photographer had remained invisible. The photos showed Krista, Rhetta, Moonbeam, Avril, and Harold Austin unclothed. There was a view of Heyward unfastening Avril's dress. Only the back of Vice-President Stonebridge could be seen. Notably, in none of the photographs did Big George appear.

The photos appalled Heyward by their existence. And why had they been sent? Were they some kind of threat? Where were the negatives and other copies? He was beginning to realize that Quartermain was a complex, capricious, perhaps dangerous man.

On the other hand, despite the shock, Heyward found himself fascinated. He studied the photographs. His first impulse had been to destroy them. Now he couldn't do it. Obviously he couldn't take the photos home. What then?

Carefully repacking them, he locked the envelope in a desk drawer where he kept private files. He checked another drawer, where Mrs. Callaghan left current papers when she cleared his desk at night. On top of the pile were those concerning the additional Q-Investments loan. He reasoned, Why delay? The loan was sound, as were G. G. Quartermain and Supranational. Removing the papers, he scribbled "Approved" and added his initials.

CHAPTER 11

DETECTIVE Sergeant Timberwell, who had met Nolan Wainwright by arrangement, walked stolidly beside him down a gloomy passageway of the city morgue. "If the dead guy *is* your man, when was the last time you saw him?"

"Seven weeks ago. Early March. In a bar across town."

"Any idea where he lived?"

Wainwright shook his head. "He didn't want me to know."

Nolan Wainwright hadn't been sure of the man's name either.

All he knew was that Vic was an ex-con who needed money and was prepared to be an undercover informer. At their last meeting it seemed as if he might have stumbled on a lead.

Vic had reported a rumor: a big supply of high-quality bogus twenty-dollar bills was ready for the distributors. Somewhere in the shadows behind the distributors there was said to be a high-powered, competent organization that was into other counterfeit lines, including credit cards. Vic claimed he had been promised a small piece of the action with the counterfeit money. He figured he could work his way deeper into the organization. Wainwright had warned him that this was highly dangerous. Since then Wainwright had not heard from Vic.

Yesterday a small news item about a body found floating in the river caught his attention.

"I should warn you," Detective Sergeant Timberwell said, "that what's left of this guy isn't pretty. The medics figure he was in the water for a week. Also, he's badly cut up."

They entered a brightly lighted, long, low-ceilinged room. The air was chill and smelled of disinfectant. An attendant went to a drawer midway down the room and pulled it out. Wainwright wished he hadn't come. Sick, he studied the corpse. "See anything you can identify?" the detective asked.

"Yes," Wainwright said. A scar was clearly visible on the neck, which Wainwright's trained eye had observed each time he and Vic had met. This was his undercover agent's body.

Timberwell nodded. "We identified him from fingerprints. His real name was Clarence Hugo Levinson. He used several other names, and had a long record, mostly petty stuff."

"The news report said he died of multiple stab wounds."

"That's what the autopsy showed. First he was tortured."

Over strong coffee in a tiny restaurant half a block from the morgue, Detective Sergeant Timberwell asked, "What's the score about counterfeit credit cards now?"

"More and more are being used. Some days it's like an epidemic. It's costing banks like ours a lot of money."

"Is the quality of the cards good?"

"Excellent."

The detective ruminated, "That's what the Secret Service tell us about the phony money that's around. Maybe that guy figured right and the source is the same."

Neither man spoke; then the detective said abruptly, "Whoever cut him up made him talk. You saw him. There's no way he wouldn't have. So you can figure he sang about the deal he had with you."

"Yes, I'd thought of it."

Timberwell nodded. "I don't think you're in any danger yourself, but as far as the people who killed Levinson are concerned, you're poison. If anyone *they* deal with as much as breathes the same air as you, and they find out, he's dead—nastily. I'm not saying you shouldn't send in some other guy. But you stay away from him. You owe him that much."

"Thanks, but I doubt if there'll be anyone else," Wainwright said, thinking about that mutilated body.

JUANITA and Estela were in the kitchen of their tiny but comfortable Forum East apartment preparing dinner. They had both been rolling and shaping dough—Juanita to provide a top for a meat pie, Estela working it with her tiny fingers as imagination prompted. "Mommy! Look, a magic castle!"

They laughed together. Juanita said, "We'll put the castle in the oven with the pie. Then they'll both be magic."

The pie had been in the oven for twenty minutes, with another ten to go, and Juanita was reading a story to Estela, when a knock sounded on the apartment door. Visitors at any time were rare, almost unheard of this late. After a few moments the knock was repeated. Motioning Estela to remain where she was, Juanita went to the door.

Forum East was in an area notorious for muggings and break-ins. At night most occupants bolted themselves in. With her ear pressed against the door, she said, "Who is there?" The answer was another knock, soft, insistent.

She made certain that the inside protective chain was in place, then unlocked the door and opened it a few inches. At first, because of dim lighting, she could see nothing; then a face came into view and a voice asked, "Juanita, may I talk to you? I have to—please! Will you let me come in?"

She was startled. Miles Eastin. But neither the voice nor the face were those of the Eastin she had known. Instead, the figure, which she could see better now, was pale and emaciated, the speech unsure and pleading.

She stalled for time. "I thought you were in prison."

"I was released today on parole."

"Why have you come to *me?*"

"Because all I've thought about for months, all through that time inside, was seeing you, talking to you, explaining . . ."

"There is nothing to explain."

"But there *is!* Juanita, I'm begging you. Don't turn me away! Please!"

Estela's bright voice asked, "Mommy, who is it?"

"Juanita," Miles Eastin said, "there's nothing to be frightened about—for you or your little girl. I've nothing with me except this." He held up a small battered suitcase. "It's just the things they gave me back when I came out."

"Well . . ." Despite her misgivings, her curiosity was strong. Why *did* Miles want to see her? Wondering if she would regret it, she released the chain.

"Thank you." He came in tentatively.

"Hello," Estela said, "are you my mommy's friend?"

For a moment Eastin seemed disconcerted; then he answered, "I wasn't always. I wish I had been."

Now that he was fully in view, Juanita was even more startled by the change in Miles in just eight months. His cheeks were sunken, his crumpled suit hung loosely, as if made for someone twice his size. He looked tired and weak.

"May I sit down?"

"Yes." Juanita motioned to a wicker chair, though she continued to stand, facing him.

Estela asked, "Have you come for dinner? It's meat pie."

He hesitated. . . . "No."

219

Juanita said sharply, "Did you eat today?"

"This morning. I had something at the bus station." The aroma of the almost-cooked pie was wafting from the kitchen. Instinctively he turned his head.

"Then you will join us." She began setting another place at the small table where she and Estela took their meals. As they ate and Estela chattered away to Miles, some of his tension began to leave him. Several times he looked around at the pleasant apartment. Juanita had a flair for homemaking. In the modest living room was a sofa bed she had slipcovered with brightly patterned cotton. The wicker chair which Miles had sat in earlier was painted Chinese red. A primitive painting and some travel posters adorned the walls.

Juanita listened to the other two but said little, within herself still doubtful. But she did not feel antagonism. Time had made Miles's treachery remote. Even originally, when he was exposed, her principal feeling had been relief, not hate.

Miles Eastin sighed as he pushed away his empty plate. "Thank you. That was the best meal in quite some time."

Juanita asked, "What are you going to do?"

"I don't know. Tomorrow I'll start looking for a job." He seemed about to say more, but she motioned him to wait.

"Estelita, vamos, amorcito. Bedtime!*"*

Washed, hair brushed, wearing tiny pink pajamas, Estela came to say good night. Large liquid eyes regarded Miles gravely. "My daddy went away. Are you going away?"

"Yes, very soon."

"That's what I thought." She put her face up to be kissed.

When she had tucked in Estela, Juanita came out of the apartment's single bedroom, closing the door behind her. She sat down facing Miles. "So. You may talk."

Now that the moment had arrived he seemed bereft of words. Then he said, "All this time since I was . . . put away . . . I've been wanting to say I'm sorry. Sorry for everything I did, but mostly for what I did to you. I'm ashamed. In one way, I don't know how it happened. In another, I think I do."

Juanita shrugged. "What happened is gone. Does it matter now?"

"It matters to me. Please, Juanita—let me tell you." Then like a gusher, words flooded out. He spoke of his awakened conscience, and of remorse; worst of all, he told her, was the shame over what he had done to her. That shame had haunted him in prison and would never leave him.

When Miles began speaking, Juanita's strongest instinct was suspicion. Yet as he continued, pity overwhelmed her. She found herself comparing Miles with Carlos. Carlos had been weak; so had Miles. But Miles's willingness to return and face her argued a strength and manhood Carlos never had.

Miles was saying earnestly, "Juanita, I want to ask you something. Will you forgive me?"

She looked at him.

"And if you do, will you say it to me?"

Tears filled her eyes. She had been born a Catholic and she knew the solace of confession and absolution. She rose to her feet.

"Miles," Juanita said. "Stand up. Look at me."

He obeyed, and she said gently, "*Has sufrido bastante.* Yes, I forgive you."

The muscles of his face worked. She held him as he wept.

When he had composed himself and they were seated again, Juanita spoke practically. "Where will you spend the night?"

"I'm not sure. I'll find somewhere."

"You may stay here if you wish." As she saw his surprise, she added quickly, "You can sleep in this room for tonight only. I will be in the bedroom with Estela. Our door will be locked." She wanted no misunderstandings.

"If you really don't mind," he said, "I'd like to do that. And you'll have nothing to worry about."

In the morning she heard Miles stirring early. Half an hour later, when she emerged from the bedroom, he had left. A note was propped up on the living-room table. "Juanita—With all my heart, thank you! Miles."

While she prepared breakfast for herself and Estela, she was surprised to find herself regretting he had gone.

"I WOULDN'T HAVE BELIEVED," Nolan Wainwright said harshly, "that you'd have the nerve to come here."

"I didn't think I would either." Miles Eastin's voice betrayed his nervousness. "I hung around outside for half an hour, getting up courage to come in."

The two men faced each other, both standing, in Nolan Wainwright's private office. They were sharply in contrast: the stern, black, handsome bank vice-president of security, and the ex-convict—pale, unsure, a long way from the bright and affable assistant operations manager.

"Now that you are here," Wainwright said, "what do you want?"

"A job."

"Here? You must be mad." Then curiosity intruded. "Why are you so keen to come back?"

"Because I can't get any kind of work, not *anything*, anywhere else." Miles's voice faltered. "And because I'm hungry."

"You're what?"

"Mr. Wainwright, it's been three weeks since I came out on parole. I've been out of money for more than a week. I haven't eaten in three days." Now his voice cracked. "Coming here . . . guessing what you'd say . . . it was the last . . ."

Some of the hardness left Wainwright's face. He motioned to a chair. "Sit down." He went outside and gave his secretary five dollars. "Go to the cafeteria. Get two roast beef sandwiches and a pint of milk."

When he returned, Miles Eastin was still sitting where he had been told, his body slumped, his expression listless.

"Has your parole officer helped?"

Miles said bitterly, "He has a case load—so he told me—of a hundred and seventy-five parolees. He has to see everybody once a month, and what can he do for even one? There are no jobs."

"If I could do something for you, maybe I would." Wainwright's tone had softened. "But I can't. There's nothing here after your record. Believe me."

Miles nodded glumly. "I guess I knew anyway."

The secretary returned with a paper sack and change. Wainwright took out the milk and sandwiches and set them before Eastin. "You can eat those here if you like."

Miles removed the wrapping from the first sandwich with plucking fingers. Any doubt about his hunger was banished as Wainwright observed the food devoured silently, with speed. While the security chief watched, an idea began to form.

"What will you try next?"

Perceptibly, to Wainwright's ear, Eastin hesitated, then said flatly, "I don't know."

"I think you do know. My guess is that until now you've stayed away from the people you knew in prison. But because you gained nothing here, you've decided to go to them. You'll take a chance on being seen, and on your parole."

"What the hell other kind of chance is there?"

"So you *do* have those contacts."

"If I say yes," Eastin said contemptuously, "the first thing you'll do when I've gone is telephone the parole board."

Wainwright shook his head. "Whatever we decide, I promise I won't do that. There might be something we could work out, if you were willing to run some risks. Big ones. Tell me first about the people you knew inside. I give you my word I won't take advantage of anything you tell me."

Miles sat silent, thinking. Then abruptly he began to talk. He revealed the approach made by the emissary from Mafia Row, the message that Igor (the Russian) Ominsky had stopped the clock on the loan interest while Eastin was inside.

"But now the clock is running again," Wainwright said.

Miles realized that all too clearly. He had been trying not to think about it while he searched for honest work. He had been told where he could make contact with Ominsky: it was the Double-Seven Health Club near the city's center, and the information had been passed to him a few days before leaving Drummonburg. He repeated it now under Wainwright's probing.

"I've heard of the Double-Seven," the security chief mused. "It has the reputation of being a mob hangout."

Miles had also been told that there would be ways outside for him to earn money and begin paying off his debt. He knew that such ways would be against the law. That knowledge, and his dread of a return to prison, had kept him resolutely removed from the Double-Seven. So far.

"I was right, then. You would have gone there from here."

"Oh, God, Mr. Wainwright, I don't want to!"

"Maybe, between us, you can cut it both ways. You've heard of an undercover agent?"

Miles Eastin looked surprised before admitting, "Yes."

"Then listen carefully." The bank security chief explained the counterfeit Keycharge problem and unfolded a plan. Miles would go to the Double-Seven Health Club, making such contacts as he could. He would try to ingratiate himself and take whatever opportunities occurred to earn money. He should be wary of appearing curious. "Don't hurry," Wainwright cautioned. "Let word get around; let people come to you."

Only after Miles was accepted could he begin discreet inquiries about the fake credit cards, seeking to move closer to wherever they were traded. Periodically, Eastin would report to Wainwright. Though never directly. Wainwright then explained bluntly about Vic, omitting no details. He saw Miles Eastin go pale, and remembered when the young man's fear of physical violence had shown so clearly. "Whatever happens," Wainwright said, "I don't want you to think that I didn't warn you of the dangers." He paused, considering. "Now, about money."

If Miles agreed to go undercover on the bank's behalf, the security chief would guarantee five hundred dollars a month to be paid through an intermediary.

"Would I be employed by the bank?"

"Absolutely not." If he ran into trouble and tried to implicate FMA, he would be disowned. "Since you were sent to jail, we haven't heard from you. So what's your answer?"

For a moment the old Miles Eastin humor and good nature flashed. "Heads I lose; tails I lose. I guess I hit the loser's jackpot. Let me ask one thing. If I get the evidence you need, will you help me find a job at FMA afterward?"

Wainwright considered. If it came to it, he could go to Alex Vandervoort and present a case on behalf of Eastin. Success would be worth it. "I'll try. That's *all* I promise."

"All right," Eastin said, "I'll do it."

They discussed an intermediary. "After today," Wainwright warned, "you and I won't meet again directly. It's too dangerous; either one of us may be watched. What we need is someone who can be a conduit for messages—both ways—and money; someone we both trust totally."

Miles said slowly, "There's Juanita Núñez. *If* she'd do it."

Wainwright looked incredulous. "The teller who you . . ."

"Yes. But she forgave me." There was a mixture of elation and excitement in Miles's voice. "I went to see her and heaven bless her, she forgave me!"

"I'll be damned."

"*You* ask her," Miles Eastin said. "There's not a single reason why she should agree. But I just think she might."

CHAPTER 12

ON A Saturday evening Alex Vandervoort and Margot Bracken were guests of Lewis and Edwina's at their elegant penthouse. As they left the dining room, Lewis said to Alex, "How about joining me for a cigar and cognac in my study? Edwina doesn't like cigar smoke."

Excusing themselves, they went to Lewis's sanctum, which was lined with bookcases and racks overflowing with magazines and newspapers. Sipping his brandy, Alex turned the pages of the latest *D'Orsey Newsletter*.

A regular column listed international securities to trade or hold. Alex's eye ran down the list and stopped sharply at: "Supranational—sell immediately at market."

"Lewis, why sell Supranational? And 'immediately at market'? You've listed it for years as a 'long-term hold.'"

His host answered, "I'm uneasy about SuNatCo. I'm getting too many rumors about big unreported losses and sharp accounting practices among subsidiaries. Also, there's an unconfirmed story out of Washington that Big George Quartermain is shopping for a government subsidy. What it amounts to is—maybe—shoal waters ahead. I'm acting on instinct, but I prefer my people out."

On Monday morning Alex was still worried about Lewis's instinct. A sell recommendation in the *D'Orsey Newsletter* was not to be dismissed. The subject was vital to the bank. Yet it was a delicate situation in which Alex would have to move cautiously. If he began asking questions, rumors would fly.

It was possible, of course, that Supranational was merely suffering a temporary cash shortage. Alex hoped that was true. However, as an officer of FMA, he could not afford to sit back and hope. Fifty million dollars of bank money had been funneled into SuNatCo; also the trust department had invested heavily in its shares, a fact which still made Alex shiver.

For some time he sat silently thoughtful at his desk, weighing what to do. Then he pressed an intercom button and said to his secretary, "See if you can locate Miss Bracken."

It was fifteen minutes before Margot's voice said brightly, "This had better be good. You got me out of court on the department-store case." Margot was currently engaged in a class action against a store accused of fraudulent billings.

He wasted no time. "You told me you used a private investigator on that case."

"Yes. Vernon Jax."

"And Lewis had said he'd done work for the SEC?"

"That's right. He has a degree in economics. He's good."

"Where do I find him?"

"I'll find him. Tell me where and when you want him."

"In my office, Bracken. Today—without fail."

In midafternoon a balding, nondescript man was seated opposite Alex in his office. "Mr. Jax," Alex began, "I'm considering having you undertake an inquiry requiring absolute discretion and speed. You've heard of Supranational Corporation?"

"Sure."

"I want a financial investigation of that company. But it will have to be—I'm afraid there's no other word for it—an outside snooping job."

Jax smiled. "Mr. Vandervoort, that's precisely the business I'm in." It would require a month, he estimated. Complete confidentiality concerning the bank's investigative role would be preserved, and nothing illegal would be done. They agreed on a fifteen-thousand-dollar fee.

After Jax had gone, Margot phoned. "Did you hire him?"

"Yes."

"Were you impressed?"

"Not really."

Margot laughed softly. "You will be. You'll see."

THAT night Alex paid one of his periodic visits to Celia at the Remedial Center. He always came away deeply depressed, but continued to go out of a sense of duty. Or was it guilt? He was never sure.

When the nurse who had escorted him to Celia's room had gone, Alex sat talking, chatting in an inane, one-sided conversation about whatever occurred to him. Celia gave no sign of hearing or even an awareness of his presence.

All traces of her former beauty had gone. Her once glorious fair hair was dull and sparse. Watching his wife and continuing to talk, Alex felt compassion, but no sense of attachment or affection anymore. Yet he was tied to Celia, he recognized, by bonds he would not sever.

Tonight he asked himself again if he could, years ago, have saved his young, insecure bride from what she had become. If he had been more a devoted husband, less a devoted banker, he suspected that he might have.

When it was time to leave, he went to Celia, intending to kiss her forehead. But she shrank away, her eyes alert with sudden fear. He sighed and abandoned the attempt.

"Good night, Celia," Alex said.

There was no answer and he went out, leaving his wife to whatever lonely world she inhabited.

NEXT MORNING ALEX SENT for Nolan Wainwright. He told the security chief that the investigator's fee would be remitted through Wainwright's department. Alex didn't state, and Wainwright didn't ask, the nature of Jax's investigation.

Wainwright had a reciprocal report for Alex: his arrangement to use Miles Eastin as an undercover agent for the bank in the counterfeit Keycharge operation.

Alex's reaction was immediate. "No, I don't want that man ever again on our payroll."

"He won't be on the payroll. Any money he'll receive will be in cash, with nothing to show where it came from. If you don't agree, you'll be tying my hands."

They argued heatedly back and forth, and in the end Alex reluctantly conceded. Wainwright felt it was not the time to mention his hope of enlisting Juanita Núñez as an intermediary.

Dusk was settling in the following evening when Nolan Wainwright's Mustang II nosed to the curb outside Juanita's Forum East apartment building. Moments later she climbed in beside him. He said, "Thank you for coming."

"Half an hour," Juanita reminded him. "That's all." She was uneasy about leaving Estela alone. "What is it you want?"

The security chief eased the car into traffic. "I want to know if you'd be willing to help Miles Eastin."

After a pause Juanita asked warily, "What kind of help?"

"Eastin is doing some unofficial investigative work for the bank. If he succeeds, it may help him get rehabilitated."

They had left the bright lights now and were crossing the river. Wainwright turned onto an interstate highway.

"The investigation you speak of. Tell me more about it." Juanita's voice was low, expressionless.

He described how Eastin would operate under cover, using his prison contacts, and the kind of evidence he would search for. "If you were to help, it would keep him safer. For you there'd be virtually no risk. The only contact you'd have would be with Eastin and with me. We'd make sure no one else would know."

"If you are so sure, why are we meeting in this way?"

"Simply a precaution. To make certain we're not seen together and can't be overheard."

Wainwright held the car at a steady forty-five, staying in the right-hand lane. Juanita sat beside him, looking straight ahead.

He was about to break the silence when she turned to face him, eyes blazing. "You must be *mad, mad!* Do you think I am a fool? No risk for me, you say! Of course there is a risk, and I take all of it. And for what? For the glory of Mr. Security Wainwright and his bank—"

"Now wait—"

She brushed aside the interruption. "Am I such an easy target? Does being alone or Puerto Rican qualify me for all the abuses of this world? Do you not care *who* you use, or how? What kind of stupidity is this that you would throw a man's life away for your selfish credit cards?"

"Miles came to me asking for help. I didn't go to him. And it was he who suggested you."

"Then what is wrong with him that he cannot ask me himself? Has he lost his tongue?"

"I get your message," Wainwright said. "I'll take you home." He turned off the highway and headed back toward the city.

Juanita asked him, "So what will you do now?"

"Whatever I decide, I'm certainly not likely to confide in you." His tone was curt, all friendliness gone.

With sudden alarm, Juanita wondered, Would Wainwright retaliate in the bank? Had she put her job in jeopardy—the job she depended on to support Estela? She felt trapped. And something else, if she were honest—regret that she would see no more of Miles. Surprising herself, Juanita said in a flat, small voice, "Very well, I will be—whatever it was—an . . ."

"Intermediary." Wainwright glanced sideways at her. "You're sure?" Some of the friendliness was back.

"*Sí, estoy segura.* I am sure."

A block and a half from Forum East, Wainwright stopped the car. He removed two envelopes from an inside jacket pocket and handed one to Juanita. "That's money for Eastin. Keep it until he gets in touch with you." The envelope contained four hundred and fifty dollars—the agreed monthly payment, less a fifty-dollar advance which Wainwright had given Miles last week.

"Later this week," he added, "Eastin will phone me. Your name will not be mentioned. But he'll know by a code word we've arranged that you've agreed to be the contact."

Juanita nodded, storing the information away.

"After that phone call, all messages will go through you. It would be best if you carried them all in your well-known memory." Wainwright smiled as he said it, and abruptly Juanita laughed. How ironic that her remarkable memory, which was once a cause of her troubles with Wainwright, should be relied on by him now.

"I'll need your phone number. I couldn't find it listed."

"That is because I cannot afford a telephone."

"You'll need one. If you'll have a phone installed immediately, I'll see that the bank reimburses you."

"I will try. But I have heard that phones are slow to be put in at Forum East."

"Let me arrange it. I'll call the phone company tomorrow."

Wainwright opened the second envelope. "When you give Eastin the money, also give him this." It was a Keycharge credit card, made out in the name of H. E. Lyncolp. "Have him sign the card in that name. Point out that the initials and the last letter spell 'help.' That's what the card is for."

He explained that the computer had been programmed to approve any purchase on this card of up to a hundred dollars, but to simultaneously raise an alert which would notify Wainwright that Eastin needed help and where he was.

"Tell him to use the card if he's in danger. He must buy something worth more than fifty dollars; that way the store will be certain to phone in for confirmation. After that phone call he should dawdle as much as he can, to give me time to move."

At Wainwright's request, Juanita repeated his instructions. He looked at her admiringly. "You're pretty bright."

"*De qué me vale, muerta?*"

"What does that mean?"

She hesitated. . . . "What good will it do me if I'm dead?"

Reaching across the car, he gently touched her folded hands. "I promise it'll all work out."

His confidence was infectious. But later, back in her apartment, with Estela sleeping, Juanita's fears returned.

THE Double-Seven Health Club was a boxlike, four-story brown brick building in a decaying dead-end street on the fringe of downtown. Shortly before noon, midweek, Miles Eastin wandered in. A dissonance of raised voices drifted from somewhere in the rear, and Miles walked down a corridor toward the sound. At the end was a semidarkened bar. Two men perched on barstools turned their heads. One said, "This is a private club, buster. If you ain't a member—out!"

Miles told him, "I was looking for Jules LaRocca."

"Milesy baby!" A figure bustled forward through the gloom. The familiar weasel face came into focus. "Come on over. Have a beer." LaRocca seized Miles's arm in pudgy fingers.

"I'm out of bread," Miles said. "I can't buy."

"Forget it. Have a couple on me. Where ya been?"

"Looking for work. I'm all beat, Jules. I need help."

"Sure, sure." They went to a table where two beers were slapped in front of them. LaRocca said, "Before ya make dough, Milesy, ya gotta see the Russian. He knows yer outta the can. Been askin' for ya."

An hour later, in a restaurant booth, Miles had the feeling of being a mouse before a cobra. He sat, sweating, while Ominsky, his diamond-ringed hands moving deftly, continued his meal. LaRocca had strolled discreetly away.

Unexpectedly, Ominsky looked up. "Can you keep books?"

"Bookkeeping? Why, yes; when I worked for the bank . . ."

Cold, hard eyes appraised him. "Maybe I can use you. I need a bookkeeper at the Double-Seven. If I give you work, everything you earn goes to me to pay your loan and interest. In other words, I *own* you. Understand?"

"Yes, Mr. Ominsky."

"You'll get your meals, a room," Ominsky said, "and keep your fingers out of the till, or you'll wish you'd stolen from the bank again, not me." And Miles shivered with awareness of what Ominsky would do to a Judas in his camp.

"Jules will get you set up. That's all." Ominsky dismissed Miles with a gesture and nodded to LaRocca.

THE room at the Double-Seven was a shabbily furnished cubicle on the top floor. Miles didn't mind. It represented a frail beginning but a chance to reshape his life and regain something of what he had lost.

In the next week he concentrated on making himself useful and becoming accepted, as Wainwright had advised. Most of the main floor of the club—apart from the bar—was taken up by a gymnasium and handball courts. On the second floor were steam rooms and massage parlors. The third comprised offices and several other rooms. The fourth floor contained a few more cubicles like Miles's, where club members occasionally slept overnight.

Miles slipped easily into the job. He was good at bookkeeping and tactfully suggested ways of maintaining all club records more efficiently. The manager, an ex-fight promoter named Nate Nathanson, was grateful. He was even more appreciative when Miles offered to do extra chores, such as reorganizing inventory. In return he allowed Miles use of the handball courts, which provided an extra chance of meeting members.

Miles quickly learned that some of the third-floor rooms were used for illegal high-stakes card and dice games. But within a week the night regulars had come to know Miles and were relaxed about him. He began helping out when drinks, sandwiches, and cigarettes had to be carried to the gaming rooms.

He was becoming useful and liked, and some of his old cheerfulness was returning. LaRocca, his sponsor, put him on like a vaudeville act. It was his fund of stories about money and its history which fascinated—it seemed endlessly—Jules's cronies. A favorite item was the saga of the counterfeit money printed by governments.

One night a hulking driver-bodyguard took Miles aside. "Hey, kid, talk about counterfeit, take a look at this." He held out a clean, crisp twenty-dollar bill.

Miles accepted the bill and studied it. "If this is a fake," he said, "it's the best I've ever seen."

"Wanna buy a few?" The man produced nine more. "Gimme forty bucks in real stuff, kid, that whole two hunnert's yours."

It was about the going rate, Miles knew, for high-grade queer. Here was something he could send to Wainwright. He went up to his room, where he had squirreled away forty dollars in small bills from Wainwright's original fifty and from tips he had collected around the club. These he exchanged for the counterfeit two hundred. Some forty-eight hours later he contacted Juanita.

MILES and Juanita had met twice before, during the month he had now been working at the Double-Seven Health Club. The first time—a few days after Juanita's ride with Wainright—had been an uncertain encounter. Miles had not known about Wainwright's installation of the telephone and arrived unannounced at Juanita's apartment. She was frowning as she let him in.

"There was no way to warn you I was coming," he apologized. "But Mr. Wainwright said you'd be expecting me."

"That man! I hate him."

"He isn't my idea of Santa Claus," Miles said. "But I don't hate him, either. I guess he has a job to do."

"Then let *him* do it. Not make use of others."

"If you feel so strongly, why did you agree . . . ?"

Juanita snapped, "Do you think I have not asked myself that? It was an instant's foolishness, to be regretted."

"Nothing says you can't back down." Miles's voice was gentle. "I'll tell Wainwright." He moved toward the door.

Juanita flared at him. "And what of you? Where will you pass your messages?" She shook her head in exasperation. "Were you insane when you agreed to such stupidity?"

"No," Miles said. "I saw it as a chance. In a way the only chance I had, but there's no reason it should involve you. When I suggested that, I hadn't thought it through. I'm sorry."

"Mommy," Estela said, "why are you so angry?"

Juanita reached down and hugged her daughter. "I am angry at life, little one. At what people do to each other." She told Miles abruptly, "Sit!"

He obeyed. "I like your temper, Juanita." Miles smiled, and for a moment, she thought, he looked the way he used to at the bank. He went on, "The real reason I suggested this arrangement was that it would mean I'd have to see you."

"Well, now you have. So make your secret agent's report and I will give it to Mr. Spider Wainwright spinning webs."

Miles told her about the club, his encounters with LaRocca and Russian Ominsky, and his employment at the Double-Seven. "But I'm in," he said, "which is what Wainwright wanted."

"It is easy to get in. Getting out is harder."

Estela had listened gravely. Now she asked Miles, "Will you come again?"

"I don't know." He glanced at Juanita.

She sighed. "Yes, *amorcito*. Yes, he will come."

Juanita went into the bedroom and returned with the two envelopes Nolan Wainwright had given her, one containing money, the other the Keycharge card for H. E. Lyncolp. She explained the purpose of the card—a signal for help. Miles pocketed that, but gave the money back to Juanita. "You take this. If I'm seen with it, someone might become suspicious. Use it for yourself and Estela. I owe it to you."

Juanita hesitated; then she said softly, "I will keep it for you."

THE second encounter had occurred a week and a half later on Saturday afternoon. This time Miles had telephoned in advance, and when he arrived, Juanita and Estela were about to go shopping. He joined them, the three browsing through an open-air market where Juanita bought Polish sausage and cabbage. She told him, "It is for our dinner. Will you stay?"

He assured her he would. While they walked, Estela said suddenly to Miles, "I like you." She slipped her tiny hand into his.

Through dinner there was an easy camaraderie. Later, Estela

went to bed, kissing Miles good night. When he and Juanita were alone he recited his report for Wainwright.

They were seated side by side on the sofa bed. Turning to him, Juanita said, "If you wish, you may stay here tonight."

They stayed silent a moment, listening to the evening hum of traffic and voices from the street outside. Then both began to talk—as friends—until Miles, feeling her body warm beside him, reached for Juanita. She came to him eagerly.

What followed next was a disaster. Miles had wanted Juanita with his mind and—he believed—his body. But despairingly, miserably, he found he could think only of his experience in prison. Sitting bolt upright, his head turned away so as not to meet Juanita's eyes, he told her bluntly the totality of that experience. And then with no word of thanks or farewell, he fled.

Two weeks later it was time to check in again. He wondered if Juanita would want to see him. But the visit was necessary, and when he came she was cool and businesslike, as if the last occasion had been put behind her.

She listened to his report; then he told her of his doubts. "I'm not finding out anything important. Okay, so I deal with LaRocca and the guy who sold me those counterfeit twenties, but both are small fry. I've no more idea than when I started of any bigger people in the rackets."

"You cannot find out everything in a month," Juanita said.

"Perhaps there isn't anything to be found, at least not what Wainwright wants."

"If so, that is not your fault. Besides, it is possible you have discovered more than you know. There is this forged money you have given me. I will get back from Wainwright the forty dollars you paid for that."

"You're taking good care of me."

"It appears someone must."

She was interrupted by Estela, who had been playing with a friend in the next apartment. "Hello," she said to Miles, "are you going to stay again?"

"Not today," he told her. "I'll be leaving soon."

Juanita asked sharply, "Why do you need to?"

"No reason. I just thought . . ."

"Then you will have dinner here. Estela will like it."

"Oh, good," Estela said. "Will you read me a story?" And she brought a book and perched happily on his knee. After dinner, before she went to bed, he read to her again.

"You are a kind person, Miles," Juanita said as she emerged from the bedroom. He had risen to go, but she motioned to him. "No, stay. There is something I wish to say."

As before, they sat beside each other on the sofa bed. Juanita spoke slowly, gently. "Miles, I know that in prison you suffered. How can anyone know—unless they themselves were there—what it might do to them? As to the man—Karl—if he was kind when so much else was cruel, that's what matters most." She raised her eyes and looked at Miles directly. "You loved him, didn't you?"

"Yes . . ." Miles said. His voice was low.

Juanita nodded. "Then it is better said. I do not understand these things—only that love is better, wherever it is found."

Miles saw that she was crying and found his own face wet with tears. His heart too full for speech, tenderly, yearningly, he embraced her. Juanita clasped him to her. "I love you, Miles! My darling, I love you!"

That night Miles Eastin discovered that, through Juanita, he had found his manhood once again.

CHAPTER 13

"How in the name of heaven did you get all this information?" Alex Vandervoort was dazed by what he had just read.

It was quiet outside his office suite. Most of the staff had already gone home. Vernon Jax had read an afternoon paper while Alex studied the seventy-page report on Supranational, including an appendix of photocopied documents.

"I worked for the U.S. Treasury Department for twenty years," Jax said, "most of it as an IRS investigator. I've kept my contacts green, not only there, but in a lot of other places. So what I'm selling is not just financial savvy, but a web of contacts. Some of them might surprise you."

"I've had all the surprises I need today," Alex said. He touched the report in front of him.

When Jax was gone, he studied the report again. It was fraught with the gravest implications for First Mercantile American Bank. The mighty edifice of Supranational Corporation—SuNatCo—was crumbling. Lewis D'Orsey's rumors had been confirmed and much, much more.

The next morning Alex was waiting in the FMA president's suite when Jerome Patterton arrived. Alex filled him in quickly on the Jax report. Then he said, "I want you to give an order to the trust department to sell every share of Supranational we're holding."

"I won't!" Patterton's voice rose. "Who do you think you are, giving orders—"

"I'll tell you who I am, Jerome. I'm the guy who warned the board against in-depth involvement with SuNatCo. I fought against heavy trust department buying of the stock, but no one—including you—would listen. Now Supranational is caving in." Alex leaned across the desk and slammed a fist down hard. "Don't you understand? Supranational can bring this bank down with it."

Patterton was shaken. "But *is* SuNatCo in real trouble? Are you *sure?*"

"If I weren't, do you think I'd be here? I'm giving you a chance to salvage something at least." He pointed to his wristwatch. "It's an hour since the New York stock market opened. Jerome, get on the phone and give that order!"

Muscles around the bank president's mouth twitched nervously. Never decisive, strong influence often swayed him. He hesitated, then picked up the telephone.

"Get me Mitchell in the trust department. . . . Mitch? This is Jerome. Listen carefully. I want you to give a sell order immediately on all the Supranational stock we hold. . . . Yes, *sell*. Every share." Patterton listened, then said impatiently, "Yes, I know what it'll do to the market. And I know we'll take a loss. But sell. . . . Yes,

I know it's irregular." His eyes sought Alex's for reassurance. The hand holding the telephone trembled as he said, "There's no time to hold meetings. So do it! Yes, I accept responsibility."

He hung up and reached for a glass of water. "The stock is already down. Our selling will depress it more. We'll be taking a big beating."

"It's our clients—people who trusted *us*—who will take the beating. And they'd have taken a bigger one still, if we'd waited. Even now we're not out of the woods. A week from now the SEC may disallow those sales. They may rule we had insider knowledge that Supranational was about to be bankrupt, which we should have reported and which would have halted trading in the stock."

"What about our loan to SuNatCo?" Patterton demanded. *"Fifty million."*

"Almost the full extent of the credit has been drawn."

"The compensating balance?"

"Is down to less than a million."

There was a silence. Patterton was suddenly calm. "Tell me the meat of that report again."

"I'll give it to you in five words: Supranational is out of money. For the past three years the corporation has had enormous losses. There's been tremendous borrowing to pay off debts; borrowing again to repay *those* debts; then borrowing still more. What they've lacked is real cash money."

"But they've reported excellent earnings and never missed a dividend."

"It appears the past few dividends have been paid from borrowings. The rest is fancy accounting. In here"—Alex touched the Jax report on the desk between them—"are examples. Among the worst is Farview Land Development, a SuNatCo subsidiary. Farview has big land holdings in Texas, Arizona, Canada—all maybe a generation from development. Farview's been making sales to speculators, accepting small down payments, pushing payments of the full price into the future. On two deals, final payments totaling eighty million dollars are due forty years from now—well into the twenty-first century. Those payments may never be made. Yet on Farview and

Supranational balance sheets, that eighty million is shown as current earnings. There are other exactly similar deals."

"Do we have any idea of the extent of SuNatCo borrowing?"

"Yes. Short-term indebtedness is estimated at a billion dollars. Of that, five hundred million appears to be bank loans. The rest is ninety-day commercial paper, which they've rolled over."

Commercial paper, as both men knew, were IOUs bearing interest, backed only by a borrower's reputation. Rolling over means issuing still more IOUs to repay the earlier ones, plus interest.

"But they're close to the borrowing limit," Alex said. "Buyers of commercial paper are beginning to be wary."

Patterton mused, "It's the way Penn Central fell apart."

"You can add a few more big names since then," Alex said.

The same thought was in both their minds: After SuNatCo, would FMA be on the list?

"Where do we stand?" Patterton made no pretense of leadership now. He was leaning heavily on the younger man.

"If Supranational goes under, there will be investigations. Our bank will not escape attention. Our losses will be news. That kind of news could cause heavy withdrawals."

"You mean a run on the bank! That's unthinkable."

"No, it isn't. If you're a depositor and you think your money might not be safe, you take it out—fast. What I suggest is that you call the money policy committee together immediately and we concentrate, during the next few days, on attaining maximum liquidity. That way, we'll be prepared if there's a sudden drain on cash."

"All right." Patterton nodded. *"Roscoe!"* he said suddenly. *"He* got us into this." He picked up the telephone and snapped, "Tell Mr. Heyward I need him. Now!"

The office door opened and Heyward came in. "They said it was urgent. If it isn't, I've got a client—"

"Tell him about Supranational, Alex," Patterton said.

Heyward's face froze.

Matter-of-factly, Alex repeated the substance of the Jax report. Alex had expected bluster. There was none. Heyward listened quietly.

Alex suspected that Heyward had been told, or guessed at, much of what he was saying.

When Alex was done, Patterton said, "We'll have a meeting of the money policy committee this afternoon to discuss liquidity. Meanwhile, Roscoe, get in touch with Supranational to see what, if anything, we can salvage of our loan."

"It's a demand loan. We can call it anytime."

"Then do so. There isn't much hope they will have fifty million in cash, but we'll go through the motions."

"I'll call George Quartermain at once," Heyward said. "May I take that report?"

"I've no objection," Alex said, "but I'd suggest that the fewer people who know of this, the better."

Back in his office, Heyward settled down to read. Enough rumors had reached him for him to realize that Alex's summary of the report's disastrous highlights had been accurate. What Vandervoort had not mentioned were some details of Quartermain's lobbying in Washington for a government-guaranteed loan to keep Supranational solvent. At one point, the report stated, Quartermain took Vice-President Byron Stonebridge to the Bahamas with the objective of enlisting his support. Later, Stonebridge discussed the possibility at Cabinet level, but the consensus was against it.

Now Heyward knew why the Vice-President had been there. And while Washington had wisely rejected a loan to Supranational, First Mercantile American Bank—on Roscoe's urging—had bestowed one eagerly.

One thing was to the good. There was no reference to Q-Investments. He wished fervently he had returned his bonus Q-Investments shares, but he could get the certificates out of his safe-deposit box and shred them. Fortunately they were nominee certificates, not registered in his name.

Heyward had no illusions about what the collapse of Supranational would do to his standing in the bank. He would be a pariah. But perhaps, even now, if the loan money was regained, he might become a hero.

He asked Mrs. Callaghan to get G. G. Quartermain on the telephone. A minute later she reported, "Mr. Quartermain is out of the country. His office won't say where he is."

"Then get Inchbeck."

Stanley Inchbeck, SuNatCo's comptroller, came briskly on the line. "Roscoe, what can I do?"

"I've been trying to locate George."

"He's in Costa Rica."

"Is there a number I can call?"

"No. He left instructions he doesn't want calls."

"This is urgent."

"Then tell me."

"Very well. We're calling our loan. I'm advising you now, and formal written notice will follow in tonight's mail."

Inchbeck said, "You can't be serious."

"I'm entirely serious. I also believe you wouldn't want me to go into reasons on the telephone."

Inchbeck was silent—in itself significant.

"If the loan were repaid promptly," Heyward said, "any information we have would remain confidential. I'd guarantee that."

"We don't keep fifty million dollars cash on hand."

"Our bank would agree to a series of payments, providing they followed each other quickly." Heyward found himself sweating. Could SuNatCo find the money?

"I'll talk to Big George," Inchbeck said. "But he won't like it."

"When you talk to him, tell him I'd also like to discuss our loan to Q-Investments." Heyward hung up and leaned back, letting the tenseness drain out of him. There was one more thing to do. It took him minutes only to get to his safe-deposit box downstairs in the bank. He removed the Q-Investments certificates and carried them back to the thirty-sixth floor to feed them into a shredding machine personally.

As he walked into his office he had second thoughts. The shares were worth twenty thousand dollars. Was he being hasty? If necessary, he could destroy the certificates at a moment's notice. Changing his mind, he locked them in a desk drawer with other private papers.

THE BIG BREAK CAME when Miles was least expecting it.

On Saturday he had seen Juanita. Late Monday evening at the Double-Seven, Nathanson, the club manager, sent for him.

When Miles entered the manager's office two other men were there. One was Russian Ominsky. The second was a man whom Miles had heard called Tony Bear Marino. Tony Bear had a heavy, powerful body, which suggested an underlying savagery. That he carried authority was evident. Each time he arrived at the Double-Seven Health Club it was in a Cadillac limousine, accompanied by bodyguards.

Ominsky said curtly to the manager, "Wait outside."

"Yes, sir." Nathanson left quickly.

"There's an old guy in a car outside," Ominsky said to Miles. "Mr. Marino's men will help carry him up to one of the rooms near yours. Don't leave him longer than you have to, and when you do go away, lock him in. I'm holding you responsible."

Miles asked uneasily, "I'm to keep him here by force?"

"You won't need force."

Tony Bear added, "The old man knows the score. He won't make trouble. Just remember he's important to us, so treat him okay. But don't let him have booze. Understand?"

Miles asked, "Do you mean he's unconscious?"

"He's dead drunk," Ominsky answered. "He's been on a bender for a week. Your job is to take care of him and dry him out. Do it right, you get another credit."

"I'll do my best," Miles told him. "Does the old man have a name? I'll have to call him something."

"Danny. That's all you need to know."

A few minutes later Tony Bear Marino's two bodyguards and Miles Eastin lifted a filthy, inert figure from the rear seat of a Dodge sedan. All that could be distinguished of their burden was a tangle of gray hair, hollow cheeks stubbled with beard, closed eyes, and a slack mouth revealing toothless gums. They carried the recumbent figure into the club, then up to a cubicle on the fourth floor and dumped him on the bed. "He's all yours, Milesy," one of the men said as he left with his companion.

Stifling his distaste, Miles undressed the old man, then washed and sponged him. He covered him with a sheet and blanket, then gathered up the filthy clothing and began putting it in a plastic bag for cleaning. While doing so, he emptied the pockets. One yielded a set of false teeth. Others held a pair of thick-lensed glasses, several keys on a ring, and—in an inside pocket—three Keycharge credit cards and a billfold packed with money.

Miles rinsed the false teeth and placed them beside the bed in a glass of water. The spectacles he also put close by. Then he examined the credit cards and the billfold.

The cards were made out to Fred W. Riordan, R. K. Bennett, Alfred Shaw. Each card was signed on the back in the same handwriting. Miles checked the dates, which showed that all three were current. As far as he could tell, they were genuine.

In the billfold he found five hundred and twelve dollars, about half in new twenty-dollar bills. The twenties stopped him. Quietly he crossed the corridor to his room, returning moments later with a pocket magnifier, through which he examined the bills. They were counterfeit, and of the same high quality as those he had bought in the Double-Seven.

He reasoned, If the money was counterfeit, wasn't it likely that the credit cards also were? Perhaps, after all, he was close to the source of the false Keycharge cards, which Nolan Wainwright wanted to locate so badly. Miles's excitement rose, along with a nervousness which set his heart pounding.

He needed a record of the new information. Checking to be sure the old man was not stirring, he copied on a paper towel details from the credit cards.

Soon after, Miles turned out the light, locked the door from the outside, and took the billfold and credit cards downstairs to Nate Nathanson to put in the club safe.

He slept fitfully, with his door ajar, aware of his responsibility for the inmate of the cubicle across the hall. Who was this old Danny? What was his relationship to Ominsky and Marino? Tony Bear had declared, "He's important to us." Why?

Miles awoke with daylight. He walked across the corridor and looked in on Danny. He was asleep, snoring gently. Miles gathered the bag of clothing, relocked the door, and went downstairs. He was back in twenty minutes with coffee, toast, and scrambled eggs.

"Danny!" Miles shook the old man's shoulder. "Wake up!"

Two eyes opened warily, inspected him, then hastily closed tight. "Go 'way," the old man mumbled.

"I'm a friend," Miles said. "Tony Bear and Russian Ominsky told me to take care of you."

Rheumy eyes reopened. "Them sons of Sodom found me, eh? That figures. Oh, my suffering head!"

"I brought some coffee. Maybe it will help." Miles put an arm around Danny's shoulders, helping him to sit up.

The old man sipped and grimaced. "Listen, son. What'll set me straight is a hair of the dog. Now you take some money . . ." He looked around.

"Your money's in the club safe. I took it down last night. And there won't be any drinking. I had orders." Miles weighed what he would say, then took the plunge. "Besides, if I used those twenties of yours, I could get arrested."

Danny stiffened in alarm. "Those are good twenties."

"Sure are," Miles agreed. "Some of the best I've seen. Almost as good as the U.S. Bureau of Engraving."

Danny looked at him, interest competing with suspicion. "How come you know so much?"

"Before I went to prison I worked for a bank."

"What were you in the can for?"

"Embezzlement. I'm on parole now."

Danny visibly relaxed. "I guess you're okay. Or you wouldn't be working for Tony Bear and the Russian."

"That's right," Miles said. "I'm okay. The next thing is to get you the same way."

It was like taking care of a child. Miles wrapped Danny in a robe and shepherded him downstairs to the steam rooms. This early the rooms were deserted, so no one was in sight when he escorted the old man back upstairs to bed. He fell asleep almost at once. Carefully, Miles put a towel under his head and shaved him.

In late morning LaRocca appeared. "Got some threads for the old lush." He was carrying a fiberboard suitcase.

Danny, by now, was sitting up in bed. He had put his teeth in and was wearing his glasses.

"Ya useless old bum!" La Rocca said. "Ya always givin' everybody a lotta trouble."

Danny regarded his accuser with distaste. "I'm far from useless. As you and others know. As for the sauce, every man has his little weakness." He motioned to the suitcase. "Do what you were sent for and hang my clothes up."

LaRocca grinned. "Sounds like ya bouncin' back."

"Jules," Miles said, "will you stay here while I go down and get a sunlamp? I think it'll do Danny good."

"Sure."

Miles motioned with his head. "I'd like to speak to you first." LaRocca followed him outside. Keeping his voice low, Miles asked, "Jules, what's this all about? Who is he?"

LaRocca's eyes were suspicious. "Wha' did Tony Bear and Ominsky tell ya?"

"Nothing, except the old man's name is Danny."

"If they wanna tell ya more, they'll tell ya. Not me."

Later, when LaRocca had gone, Miles set up the sunlamp and sat Danny under it briefly. Through the remainder of the day the old man dozed. In the early evening Miles brought dinner from downstairs, most of which Danny ate.

The next day Miles repeated the steam-room and sunlamp treatments, and later the two played chess. They were evenly matched, and Danny clearly enjoyed Miles's company and attentions. During the afternoon the old man wanted to talk.

"Yesterday," he said, "that creep LaRocca said you know a lot about money."

"He tells everybody that." Miles explained about his hobby and the interest it aroused in prison.

Danny asked more questions, then announced, "I'd like my own money now."

"I'll get it for you. But I'll have to lock you in."

245

"If you're worrying about the booze, forget it. I'm over it for this time. Could be months before I'll take a drink again." Miles locked the door just the same.

When he returned, he handed the credit cards and the billfold to the old man. Danny spread the money on the bed, then divided it into two piles. The new twenties were in one, the remaining, soiled bills in another. From the second group Danny selected three ten-dollar bills and handed them to Miles. "That's for the little things, son—like taking care of my teeth, the shave, the sunlamp. I appreciate what you did."

"Listen, you don't have to."

"Take it. And by the way, it's real stuff. Now tell me something. How did you spot that those twenties were homegrown?"

"If you use a magnifier, some of the lines on Andrew Jackson's portrait show up blurred."

Danny nodded sagely. "That's the difference between a government steel engraving and a photo-offset plate. Though a top offset man can come awful close."

"In this case he did," Miles said. "Other parts of the bills are almost perfect."

There was a faint smile on the old man's face. "How about the paper?"

"It fooled me. Usually you can tell a bad bill with your fingers. But not these."

Danny said softly, "People think you can't get the right paper. Isn't true. Not if you shop around. Know the hardest kind of money to reproduce?"

Miles shook his head.

"An American Express traveler's check. It's specially printed in a way that's next to impossible to photograph for an offset printing plate. Nobody with any knowledge would waste time trying, so an Amex check is safer than American money."

"There are rumors," Miles said, "that there's going to be new American money soon, with colors for different denominations—the way Canada has."

" 'Tain't just rumor," Danny said. "Lots of the colored money's already printed and stored by the Treasury. Be harder to copy than anything made yet."

Miles said, "You've asked me questions, Danny. Now I've one for you. Who and what are you?"

The old man pondered, a thumb stroking his chin as he appraised Miles. Frankness struggled against caution; pride mingled with discretion. Then abruptly he made up his mind. "I'm seventy-three years old," he said, "and I'm a master craftsman. Been a printer all my life. I'm still the best there is. Besides being a craft, printing's an art." He pointed to the twenty-dollar bills. "Those are my work. I made the photographic plate. I printed them."

Miles asked, "And the credit cards?"

"Compared with printing money," Danny said, "making those is easy. But yep—I did 'em, too."

IN A fever of impatience to communicate what he had learned to Nolan Wainwright, via Juanita, Miles locked Danny in his cubicle early that evening, then went downstairs to use a pay phone on the club's main floor. Miles put in a dime and dialed Juanita's number. On the first ring her voice answered softly, "Hello."

The pay phone was a wall type near the bar, and Miles whispered so he would not be overheard. "You know who this is. But don't use names."

"Yes," Juanita answered.

"Tell our mutual friend I've discovered something really important here. It's most of what he wanted to know. I can't say more, but I'll come to you tomorrow night."

Miles hung up. Simultaneously, a hidden tape recorder in the club basement, which had switched on automatically when the pay phone receiver was lifted, automatically switched off.

CHAPTER 14

THE first public intimation of Supranational's difficulties was in an AP wire-service story which appeared in afternoon newspapers under a two-column heading halfway down the front page:

SUPRANATIONAL CORP. DISQUIET
HOW SOLVENT IS GLOBAL GIANT?

The next morning amplified reports appeared in *The Wall Street Journal*. At 10:00 a.m., at the New York Stock Exchange, Supranational shares failed to open for trading with the rest of the market. The reason given was "an order imbalance," meaning that the SuNatCo trading specialist was so swamped with requests to sell, that an orderly market in the shares could not be maintained.

The following day the Securities and Exchange Commission announced that it was investigating the affairs of Supranational and that, until its inquiry was completed, all trading in SuNatCo shares would be suspended.

There ensued an anxious wait for SuNatCo stockholders and creditors, whose combined investments and loans exceeded five billion dollars. It was learned later that Big George Quartermain had sold most of his shares, through a nominee, at SuNatCo's all-time high, bailing out early. Among those waiting—shaken and nervous—were officers and directors of First Mercantile American Bank. FMA's fifty-million-dollar loan to SuNatCo could become a write-off, a total loss. If so, for the first time in its history the bank would suffer a substantial operating loss for the year. FMA's next dividend to shareholders might also have to be omitted—another first.

On Thursday the *Times-Register* in the city bannered its page one story:

LOCAL BANK FACES HUGE LOSS
IN WAKE OF SUNATCO DEBACLE

The story had been carried, too, on TV network news shows. Included in all reports was assurance by the Federal Reserve that First Mercantile American Bank was solvent and that depositors need have no cause for alarm. Just the same, FMA was now on the Fed's problem list. Early Thursday morning a team of Federal Reserve examiners had quietly moved in—clearly the first of several such incursions from regulatory agencies.

Alex called a midday strategy meeting of bank officers, including heads of departments responsible for branch-bank administration, since everyone was aware that any lack of public confidence in FMA would be felt in branches first. There had been so far no sign of panic among the bank's customers. Managers of all eighty-four FMA branches had instructions to report promptly if any were observed. A bank survives on its reputation and the trust of others—fragile plants which adversity and bad publicity can wither.

The purpose of today's meeting was to ensure that emergency plans Alex had set up were understood and that communications within the bank were functioning. They were.

At 10:15 the next morning, Fergus W. Gatwick, manager of the First Mercantile American branch at Tylersville, twenty miles upstate, telephoned headquarters. His call was put through to Alex Vandervoort. When the manager identified himself, Alex asked crisply, "What's the problem?"

"A run, sir. This place is jammed with more than a hundred of our regular customers, lined up with passbooks and checkbooks, and more are coming in. They're cleaning out their accounts, demanding every last dollar."

Alex went cold. A bank run was what everyone in top management feared most. Such a run implied public panic, crowd psychology, a total loss of faith. Even worse, once news of a run on a single branch got out, it could sweep through others in the FMA system.

Federal regulations required banks to have only seventeen and a half percent of their demand deposits on hand in liquid cash against possible demand. Penalties for noncompliance were severe. But if deposits were heavier than anticipated, a bank promptly loaned the surplus to other banks that might be short of their reserve requirements. It was poor banking to leave large sums uninvested, even for a day. Thus not even the biggest banking institution ever had enough liquidity to repay the majority of its depositors at once, if all demanded cash. For this reason, if the Tylersville run persisted and spread, cash reserves would be exhausted and FMA obliged to close its doors, perhaps permanently.

The first essential, Alex knew, was to assure those who wanted their money that they would receive it. The second was to localize the outbreak. His instructions to the Tylersville manager were terse. "Fergus, you and your staff are to act as if there is nothing out of the ordinary. Pay out *without question* whatever people ask for and have in their accounts. And don't look worried. Be cheerful."

"I'll try, sir."

"Do *better* than try. At this moment our entire bank is on your shoulders. What's your cash position?"

"We've about a hundred and fifty thousand dollars in the vault," the manager said. "At the rate we're going, we can last an hour, not much more."

"There'll be cash coming," Alex assured him. "Meanwhile, get the money you have out of the vault and stack it up on desks and tables where everyone can see it. Then walk among your customers. Assure them our bank is in excellent shape and that they will all get their money."

Alex hung up and immediately called Tom Straughan, the bank's economist. "Tom," Alex said, "the balloon's gone up at Tylersville. The branch there needs cash—fast. Put Emergency Plan One in motion."

THE municipality of Tylersville was a mixture of bustling market town and rich farmland, turning suburban as the city encroached. Its populace, therefore, was an assortment of conservative farming and local business families and freshly resident commuters, many disgusted with the decaying moral values of the city they had left. The result was an unlikely alliance of real and would-be ruralists, all mistrusting big-business maneuverings, including those of banks.

Unique, too, in the case of the Tylersville bank run, was one gossipy mail carrier. All day Thursday, while delivering letters, he had been handing out the rumor, "Did you hear about First Mercantile American Bank going bust? They say anyone who doesn't get his money out by tomorrow is going to lose everything." Only a few believed him, but the story spread, fueled by evening news reports. Overnight, anxiety grew, so that on Friday the consensus was, Why take a chance? Let's get our money now. By midmorning more and more of the populace was heading for the First Mercantile American branch bank.

At FMA Headquarters Tower, some who had scarcely heard of Tylersville were hearing of it now. On instructions from Tom Straughan a programmer consulted the bank's computer. He tapped a question on a keyboard: "What are the totals of savings and demand deposits at Tylersville branch?" The answer was instantaneous—and up to the minute, since the branch was on-line to the computer:

SAVINGS ACCOUNTS	$26,170,627.54
DEMAND DEPOSITS	$15,042,767.18
TOTAL	$41,213,394.72

The computer was then instructed: "Deduct from this total dormant accounts and municipal deposits." Neither of these was likely to be disturbed, even in a run. The computer responded:

DORMANT & MUNICIPAL	$21,430,964.61
BALANCE	$19,782,430.11

Twenty million dollars, more or less, which depositors in Tylersville could, and might, demand.

The supervisor of Central Cash Vault, a subterranean fortress below the FMA tower, was informed, "Twenty million dollars to Tylersville branch—rush!"

Within the past forty-eight hours—anticipating exactly what was happening now—the normal money supply in Central Cash Vault had been augmented by special drawings from the Federal Reserve, which had approved the FMA emergency plans.

A Midas fortune in currency and coin, already counted and in labeled sacks, was loaded onto armored trucks while armed guards patrolled the loading ramp. There would be six armored trucks in all, and each would travel separately with police escort—a precaution taken because of the unusual amount of cash involved. However, only three trucks would have money in them. The others would be empty—dummies—an extra safeguard against holdup.

Within twenty minutes of the branch manager's call the first armored truck was threading through downtown traffic on its way to Tylersville. Even before that, other bank personnel were en route by private car and limousine, Edwina D'Orsey in the lead. She was to be in charge of the support operation.

Edwina had left her desk at the downtown branch as soon as she got the emergency call, pausing only to collect Cliff Castleman and two tellers, one of whom was Juanita Núñez.

At the same time, Nolan Wainwright, informed of the twenty million dollars cash involved, was on the way with half a dozen armed security guards. State and local police had been alerted.

Alex Vandervoort and Tom Straughan remained in FMA Headquarters Tower. Straughan's office had become a command post. Alex's concern was to keep tabs on the remainder of the branch system and to know instantly if fresh trouble erupted. Jerome Patterton waited tensely with Alex, each mulling the questions: Could they contain the run in Tylersville? Would First Mercantile American make it through the business day without a rash of runs elsewhere?

Until this morning the branch manager, Fergus W. Gatwick, sixtyish, a chubby apple of a man, had been happy at Tylersville, where only one crisis had marred his tenure. A few years ago a woman with an imagined grudge against the bank had rented a safe-deposit box. She had placed in the box an object wrapped in newspaper, then departed for Europe, leaving no address. Within days, a putrid odor had filtered through the bank. Drains were suspected and examined, to no effect, while all the time the stench grew greater. Customers complained, staff were nauseated. Eventually suspicion centered on the safe-deposit boxes, where the awful smell seemed strongest. Then the crucial question arose—which box?

Fergus W. Gatwick, at duty's call, sniffed his way around them all, at length settling on one where the malodor was overpowering. After that, it took four days of legal proceedings before a court order was obtained permitting the bank to drill the box open. Inside were the remains of a large, once fresh sea bass. Sometimes, even now in memory, Gatwick still sniffed traces of that ghastly time.

But today's exigency was far more serious than a fish in a box. Gatwick checked his watch. An hour and ten minutes since he had telephoned headquarters. Though four tellers had been paying out money steadily, the number of people crowding the bank was even greater and still no help had come.

"Mr. Gatwick!" A woman teller beckoned him.

"Yes?" He walked over to her. Across the counter from them, at the head of a waiting line, was the owner of a large poultry farm whom Gatwick knew well. The manager said cheerfully, "Good morning, Steve."

He received a cool nod while silently the teller showed him checks drawn on two accounts totaling twenty-three thousand dollars.

"Those are good," Gatwick said. Taking the checks, he initialed them both.

In a low voice, though audible across the counter, the teller said, "We haven't enough money left to pay that much."

There were angry rumblings down the line. "You hear that! They say they don't have any money."

The farmer leaned forward, his fist clenched. "You better pay those checks, Gatwick, or I'll tear this bank apart!"

"There's no need for any of that, Steve." Gatwick raised his voice, striving to be heard above the suddenly angry scene. "Ladies and gentlemen, a great deal more money will be here soon."

The last words were drowned by shouts. "Get it now!" . . . "How come the bank runs out of money" . . . "Where's the cash?"

Gatwick held up his arms. "I assure you—"

"I want my money now," a smartly dressed woman cried.

"Right!" a man echoed. "That goes for all of us."

People surged forward, voices raised, their faces revealing their alarm. Someone threw a cigarette package, which hit Gatwick in the face. Suddenly, he realized, an ordinary group of citizens, many of whom he knew well, had become a hostile mob. It was the money, of course. It did strange things to human beings, making them greedy, panicky—at times, subhuman. There was genuine dread, too—the possibility of losing everything they had. Violence, which moments ago appeared unthinkable, now loomed close. Gatwick felt physical fear. "Please!" he pleaded. "Please listen!" His voice disappeared under the growing tumult.

Then abruptly the clamor lessened. There seemed to be some activity in the street which those at the rear were craning to see. With a bravura flourish the bank's doors were flung open and a procession marched in.

Edwina D'Orsey headed it. Following her were Cliff Castleman and the two tellers. Behind them was a phalanx of security guards shouldering heavy canvas sacks, escorted by other protective guards with drawn revolvers. Half a dozen more support staff from other FMA branches filed in behind the guards. In the wake of them all—a vigilant lord protector—was Nolan Wainwright.

Edwina spoke clearly across the crowded, now silent bank. "Good morning, Mr. Gatwick. I'm sorry we took so long, but traffic was heavy. I understand you may require twenty million dollars. A third of that is here. The rest is on the way."

While Edwina was speaking, Cliff Castleman and the others continued to the rear of the counters. A newly arrived operations man promptly took charge of incoming cash. Soon plentiful supplies of crisp new bills were being recorded, then distributed to tellers.

Edwina looked over the heads pressed around her and spoke to everyone. "I'm Mrs. D'Orsey, and I'm a vice-president of First Mercantile American Bank. Despite any rumors you may have heard, our bank is sound and has no problems we can't handle. We have ample cash reserves to repay any depositor—in Tylersville or anywhere else."

The smartly dressed woman who had spoken earlier said, "Maybe that's true. Or maybe you're just saying so. Either way, I'm taking my money out today."

"That's your privilege," Edwina said.

Gatwick, watching, sensed that the ugly mood had eased. But it was clear that the run on the bank had not been halted. While the paying out continued, bank guards arrived again with still more loaded canvas sacks.

No one who shared that day at Tylersville would ever forget

the immense amount of money on public view. Even those who worked at FMA had never seen so much assembled at a single time. Under Alex Vandervoort's plan the twenty million dollars brought to fight the bank run was out in the open where everyone could see it. Behind the tellers' counter every desk was cleared; more desks and tables were moved in. Onto them all, great stacks of currency and coin were heaped, while the extra staff who had been brought in kept track of running totals.

Edwina, quietly competent and courteous, supervised everything. But withdrawals continued. Nothing, it seemed, would stop the run at Tylersville.

By early afternoon despondent FMA officials had only one question: How long before the virus spread?

ALEX Vandervoort, who had talked by telephone with Edwina, was already on the way by chauffeured limousine to Tylersville. Margot Bracken rode with him.

Margot had concluded a court case earlier than she expected that morning and joined Alex at the bank for lunch. Afterward, at his suggestion, she stayed on, sharing some of the tensions by then pervading the tower's thirty-sixth floor.

In the car Alex leaned back, savoring the interval which he knew would be brief.

"This year has been hard for you," Margot said.

"Am I showing the strain?"

She reached over, running a finger across his forehead gently. "You've more lines. You're grayer at the temples."

He grimaced. "I'm also older."

"Not that much."

"Then it's the price we pay for living with pressures."

"Alex, are things really bad for FMA?"

"If we have an unstoppable run on Monday," he said, "we'll have to close. A consortium of other banks may then get together to bail us out, after which they'll pick over what's left, and in time, I think, all depositors would get their money. But FMA as an entity would be finished."

255

"It's incredible how it can happen so suddenly."

"It points up," Alex said, "what a lot of people don't fully understand. Banks and the money system are like delicate machinery. Let one component get seriously out of balance because of greed or politics or plain stupidity, and you imperil all the others. If word leaks out, as usually happens, diminished public confidence does the rest. That's what we're seeing now."

There was a silence between them until Alex exclaimed, "God! How I miss Ben Rosselli."

Margot reached out for his hand. "Isn't this rescue operation exactly what Ben would have done himself?"

"Maybe." He sighed. "Except it isn't working. That's why I wish Ben were here."

The chauffeur let down the dividing window and spoke over his shoulder. "We're coming into Tylersville, sir."

"Good luck, Alex," Margot said.

From several blocks away they could see the lineup of people outside the branch. As their limousine pulled up at the curb, a panel truck screeched to a halt across the street and several men and a girl jumped out. On the side of the truck in large letters was WTLC-TV. "That's all we need!" Alex said.

Inside the bank, while Margot looked around her curiously, Alex talked briefly with Edwina and Gatwick, then began to walk down the lines of people, quietly introducing himself.

There were at least two hundred people—a sizable cross section of Tylersville—old, young, middle-aged, well-to-do, poor; women with babies, men in work clothes. Almost everyone showed some degree of nervousness. An elderly woman spoke to Alex on the way out. She had no idea he was a bank official. "Thank heaven! It's been the most anxious day I ever spent. This is my savings—all I have." She held up a dozen or so fifty-dollar bills.

The impression Alex got from everyone he talked to was the same. Maybe First Mercantile American was sound; maybe it wasn't. But no one wanted to take a chance on leaving money in an institution which might collapse. The publicity linking FMA with Supranational had done its work. Details didn't matter. The few people to whom

Alex mentioned Federal Deposit Insurance didn't trust that system, either. FDIC funds, they said, were believed to be inadequate in any major crunch.

And there was something else, Alex realized: people didn't believe anymore what they were told; they had become too accustomed to being deceived and lied to by government officials, politicians, employers, unions. Lied to in advertising. Lied to in financial transactions, including the status of stocks and bonds. The list was endless. Deception had been piled on deception until lying—or, at best, failure to make full disclosure—had become a way of life. So why should anyone believe Alex when he assured them that their money was safe if they left it in FMA? As the afternoon waned, it was clear that no one did.

By late afternoon Alex had become resigned. What would happen would happen; for individuals and institutions, he supposed, there came a point where the inevitable must be accepted. At 5:30, with dusk of the October evening closing in, Nolan Wainwright reported a new anxiety in the waiting crowd.

"They're worried," he told Alex, "because our closing time is six o'clock. They figure in the half hour that's left we can't deal with everybody."

It would be legal, of course, to close the bank on schedule. But Alex hesitated, swayed by his own nature and the remark of Margot's: What Alex was doing, she had said, was exactly what Ben Rosselli would have done. What would Ben have decided about closing? Alex knew.

"I'll make an announcement," he told Wainwright. First he sought out Edwina and gave her some instructions.

Moving to the doorway of the bank, Alex spoke from where he could be heard by those inside and others still waiting on the street. He was conscious of TV cameras directed at him.

"Ladies and gentlemen"—his voice was strong and clear—"I am informed that some of you are concerned about the time of our closing tonight. You need not be. On behalf of the management of this bank I give you my word that we will remain open until we have attended to you all."

There was a murmur of satisfaction and some spontaneous hand-clapping.

"However, there is one thing I urge on all of you—that over the weekend you do not keep large sums of money on your person or in your homes. It would be unsafe. Therefore I advise you to select another bank and deposit there whatever you withdraw from this one. To help you in this, my colleague Mrs. D'Orsey is telephoning other banks, asking them to remain open later than usual in order to accommodate you."

Again there was an appreciative hum.

Nolan Wainwright came to Alex, whispered briefly, and Alex announced, "I am informed that two banks have already agreed to our request. Others are being contacted."

From among those waiting in the street a male voice called, "Can you recommend a good bank?"

"Yes," Alex said. "My own choice would be First Mercantile American. It's the one I know best, the one I'm surest of, and its record has been long and honorable. I only wish all of *you* felt that way." There was a hint of emotion in his voice. A few people smiled or laughed halfheartedly, but most faces watching him were serious.

"Used to feel that way myself," a voice behind Alex volunteered. He turned. The speaker was an elderly man, probably near eighty, wizened, white-haired, stooped, and leaning on a cane. The old man's eyes were clear and sharp, his voice firm. Beside him was a woman of about the same age. Both were tidily dressed in old-fashioned, well-worn clothes. The woman held a shopping bag which contained packages of currency. They had just come from the bank counter.

"The wife and me, we've had an account at FMA for more'n thirty years," the old man said. "Feel kinda bad taking it out."

"Then why do it?"

"Can't ignore all them rumors. Too much smoke for there not to be some truth somewhere."

"There is some truth," Alex said. "Because of a loan to Supranational Corporation, our bank is likely to suffer a loss. But the bank can withstand it, and it will."

The old man shook his head. "If I was younger and working, maybe I'd take a chance on what you say. But what's in there"—he pointed to the shopping bag—"is all we got left until we die. Even that ain't much. Them dollars don't go half as far as when we worked and earned 'em."

"Inflation hits good people like you hardest," Alex said. "But unfortunately, changing banks won't help you there."

"Let me ask you a question, young fellow. If you was me and this here was your money, wouldn't you be doing the same as I am now?"

Alex was aware of others closing in and listening. He saw Margot a head or two away. TV camera lights were on. Someone was leaning forward with a microphone.

"Yes," he admitted. "I suppose I would."

The old man seemed surprised. "You're honest, anyways. Just now I heard your advice about getting to another bank and I appreciate it. I guess we'll go to one."

"Wait," Alex said. "Do you have a car?"

"Nope. Live just a piece from here. We'll walk."

"Not with that money. You might be robbed. I'll have someone drive you to another bank." Alex beckoned Nolan Wainwright and explained the problem. "This is our chief of security," he told the elderly couple.

"Be glad to drive you myself," Wainwright said.

The old man stood looking from one face to the other. "You'd do that for us? When we've just moved our money out of your bank? And we've good as said we don't trust you?"

"Let's say it's all part of our service," Alex said. "Besides, if you've been with us thirty years, we ought to part as friends."

The old man paused. "Maybe we don't have to part. Let me ask you one more question, man to man." The clear, sharp eyes regarded Alex steadily.

"Go ahead."

"You told me the truth once already, young fellow. Now tell me it again, remembering what I said about being old and knowing what them savings mean. Is our money safe in your bank? *Absolutely safe?*"

For measurable seconds Alex weighed the question and all its implications. He knew that many others were watching him intently. The TV cameras were still turning. He caught a glimpse of Margot; she was equally intent, a quizzical expression on her face. He thought of those relying on him—Jerome Patterton, the board, Edwina, more; of the wide and damaging effect if FMA failed, not just at Tylersville but far beyond. Doubt rose. He thrust it down; then he answered crisply and confidently, "I give you my word. This bank is absolutely safe."

"Aw shucks, Freda!" the old man told his wife. "Looks like we been barkin' up a tree about nothing. Let's go put the damn money back."

IN ALL the postmortems over the following weeks, one fact stayed undisputed: the bank run at Tylersville ended when the old man and his wife turned back into the FMA branch and redeposited the money from their shopping bag. Word passed speedily. Almost at once the waiting lines began dispersing, as quickly and mysteriously as they had formed. When the few remaining people in the bank were dealt with, the branch closed—only ten minutes later than was normal on a Friday night.

Nor, on Monday, did a run develop anywhere else. The reason, most analysts agreed, was an honest, moving scene, involving an old couple and a good-looking, open, bank vice-president, as it appeared on weekend television news.

One other postscript developed from that Friday evening in Tylersville. It concerned Juanita Núñez.

Juanita had seen Margot Bracken arrive during the afternoon. When the bank run ended, Juanita left the counter where she had been assisting a regular teller and crossed to the management area. Margot was seated there alone, waiting until Mr. Vandervoort could leave. "Miss Bracken," Juanita said softly, "you once told me that if I had a problem, I could come to you."

"Of course, Juanita. Do you have one now?"

Her small face creased in worry. "Yes, I think so. If you don't mind, could we talk somewhere else?" Juanita was watching Wainwright, on the opposite side of the bank.

"Then come to my office," Margot said.

They agreed on Monday evening.

CHAPTER 15

THE reel of tape retrieved from the Double-Seven Health Club had been lying on the shelf above the test bench for a week while Wizard Wong, an electronics-audio expert, attended to others for his long list of clients. Now, in his sound lab, Wong took the tape from the shelf, put it on a machine, and listened.

A coin was inserted, a number dialed. A ringing tone. One ring only.

A woman's voice (soft, with slight accent): "Hello."

A male voice (whispering): "You know who this is. But don't use names."

The woman's voice: "Yes."

The first voice (still whispering): "Tell our mutual friend I've discovered something really important here. It's most of what he wanted to know. I can't say more, but I'll come to you tomorrow night."

A *click.* The caller had hung up.

Wizard Wong wasn't sure that Tony Bear Marino, who had ordered the bug, would be interested in that portion of the tape. He simply had a hunch. He consulted a private notebook, went to the telephone, and called a number.

On Monday, at the trucking terminal where Marino maintained an office, Wong replayed the tape. Tony Bear Marino, who had a financial interest in the Double-Seven Health Club among his many ventures, and regularly bugged his business partners, scowled savagely. "Judas Priest! You sat on that goddam tape a week before you came here!"

Wong began to sweat. He protested, "I wasn't wasting time, Mr. Marino. I found out some things I thought you'd want to know. I can tell you the number that was called. I have contacts in the phone company—"

"Cut the talk. What's the number? Whose is it?"

"The phone belongs to a Mrs. J. Núñez. She lives at Forum East. Here's the building and apartment number." Wong passed over a slip of paper. "The records show the phone was installed a month ago as a hurry-up job. Normally there's a long waiting list at Forum East, but pressure was applied. By a guy named Nolan Wainwright, who's head of security for First Mercantile American Bank."

Tony Bear was startled. He was aware of the attempt six months ago to plant a stoolie, a creep named Vic, who, after they'd busted his guts, said, "Wainwright." Was there another one now? If so, Tony Bear had a strong idea what action he was after. The caller's voice, a whisper, was unrecognizable. But the other voice had been traced, so whatever was needed they could get from her.

Marino paid Wong off quickly and summoned two musclemen. He gave them the Forum East address and an order. "Pick up the Núñez broad."

"IF EVERYTHING YOU JUST told me turns out to be true," Alex assured Margot, "I'll personally administer the biggest kick that Nolan Wainwright ever had."

They were in Alex's apartment, where Margot had come immediately following her Monday-night talk with Juanita Núñez. Juanita had nervously described the agreement in which she had become the link between Wainwright and Miles Eastin. But recently, Juanita confided, she had begun to realize the risk she was running and her fears had grown, not just for herself but for Estela. At the end, Margot, enraged, had gone directly to Alex.

"I knew about Eastin going under cover." Alex's face was troubled as he paced the living room. "But I swear to you that no arrangement with the Núñez girl was ever mentioned."

"Wainwright probably knew you'd veto it," Margot said.

"Did Edwina know?"

"Apparently not."

Alex stopped pacing. "We'll do something immediately, tomorrow, for Mrs. Núñez. If it means sending her out of town for a while, to be certain she's safe, I'll approve it."

What Alex left unsaid was his intention to order Wainwright to terminate the entire operation. He wished fervently he had stuck with his instincts and forbidden it in the first place. Fortunately it was not too late to remedy the error, since nothing harmful had occurred, either to Eastin or Núñez.

WAINWRIGHT was alone in his office, reviewing progress. Only one more piece. Just one more needed to complete the tantalizing jigsaw. The source of the counterfeit Keycharge credit cards was now known. *But where was the counterfeiters' base?* Wainwright had already informed the FBI and U.S. Secret Service about Danny. The Secret Service had to be included because counterfeiting was their constitutional responsibility. The FBI agents on the case were the same team—Innes and Dalrymple—who had arrested Miles Eastin almost a year ago. They had quickly identified Danny as Daniel Kerrigan, age seventy-three. "Long ago," Innes reported, "Kerrigan had three arrests and two convictions for forgery, but we haven't heard of him in fifteen years. He's either been legit or lucky. Now it looks like he's working for an organization."

As soon as the location of the counterfeiters' headquarters became known, the FBI and Secret Service would close in. High hopes were pinned on Eastin's next report.

As Nolan Wainwright meditated, his telephone jangled. Mr. Vandervoort would like to see him. A few minutes later, in Alex's office, Wainwright was protesting, "You can't be serious!"

"I am serious," Alex said, "though I have trouble believing you were making use of the Núñez girl the way you have. Of all the insane notions. Putting the girl in jeopardy, consulting no one."

"But it worked, Alex. We're close to a breakthrough on the Keycharge frauds. Okay, my judgment was wrong in using Núñez. But it wasn't wrong about Eastin—we've got results to prove it."

Alex shook his head decisively. "Our business here is banking, not crime busting. End the arrangement with Eastin, today if possible. I will not have FMA risking human lives."

"Look, Alex—"

"That's definite, so let's not waste time in further argument."

As Wainwright looked sourly despondent, Alex went on, "The other thing I want is a conference this afternoon between you, Edwina D'Orsey, and me, to discuss how to protect Mrs. Núñez."

A secretary appeared in the office doorway. "Mr. Vandervoort, Miss Bracken's on the line. She said it's extremely urgent."

Alex picked up a phone.

"Alex," Margot's voice said, "Juanita Núñez has disappeared."

"Wait." Alex moved a switch, transferring the call to a speaker phone so that Wainwright could hear. "Go ahead."

"I'm terribly worried. When I left Juanita last night, I arranged to telephone her at work today, hoping to give her some reassurance. Alex, she didn't get to work." Margot's voice sounded strained. "I'm at Forum East now. People in the building say Juanita left this morning at her usual time, to take her little girl to nursery school. I phoned the school. Estela isn't there. Neither she nor her mother arrived this morning. I'm convinced something's terribly, terribly wrong."

"Hold on," Alex told her. "Nolan's here."

Wainwright had hunched forward, listening. Now he straightened and said quietly, "There isn't any doubt of it. Núñez has been picked up."

"By whom?"

"By someone from the Double-Seven crowd. They're probably on to Eastin, too."

"You think they've taken her to that club?"

"No. That's the last thing they'll do. She's somewhere else."

"And whoever it is has the child, too?"

"I'm afraid so." There was anguish in Wainwright's eyes. "I'm sorry, Alex."

"You got us into this," Alex said fiercely. "Now, for God's sake, you've got to get Juanita and the kid out of it!"

Wainwright was concentrating, thinking as he spoke. "The first thing is to see if there's a chance of warning Eastin. If we can get to him, get him out of the club, he might know something which could lead us to the girl." He had a small black notebook open and was already reaching for another phone.

IT HAPPENED so swiftly that car doors had slammed and the big black limousine was moving before Juanita had a chance to cry out. By then she knew it was too late, but screamed just the same. A gloved hand clamped across her mouth. Hearing Estela's shriek of terror alongside her, Juanita went on struggling until a fist slammed savagely into her face.

Juanita lay still, fighting off panic, forcing herself to think through hot knives of pain surging in her head. There were three men in the car, two in the back seat, one in the front. She and Estela were sandwiched together on the car floor, Estela s body heaving in desperate sobs. Juanita moved, trying to hold and comfort her.

"There, *amorcito!* Be brave, little one."

A voice said, "Better gag and blindfold 'em."

Juanita heard a clothlike substance tear. She pleaded, "Please, no! I'll—" Then a wide adhesive tape was slapped over her mouth and pressed down. Moments later a dark cloth covered her eyes;

she felt it being fastened tightly. Next her hands were seized and tied behind her. Cords cut her wrists. From other movements beside her she sensed the same treatment was being meted out to Estela. Tears of rage and frustration filled her eyes. *Mother of God, please save us!*

She was aware of the car stopping and starting as if in traffic, then of a long burst of speed followed by slow twists and turns. After perhaps an hour Juanita felt the force of brakes applied. The car's motor was louder, as if in a confined space. Then the motor stopped. She heard a rumble, as if a heavy door was closing mechanically. Simultaneously the limousine's doors opened, and she was pulled roughly to her feet and impelled forward. She stumbled, but hands seized her. "Dammit, walk!"

Moving clumsily, her fears centered on Estela, she was conscious of her footsteps resounding on concrete. Suddenly she was partly held, partly shoved, downstairs. At the bottom, more walking. Abruptly she was pushed into a hard wooden chair and tied tightly to it. The tape was pulled from her mouth, the blindfold loosened; then Juanita blinked as darkness gave way to a bright light directed into her eyes.

She gasped only, "Where is my—" when a fist struck her.

"Save the singing. When we tell ya, y'll spill plenty."

Unknown to Juanita, Tony Bear Marino was watching her from behind a one-way glass, built into a half wall. Angelo, one of Tony Bear's bodyguards, had been in charge of the pickup operation. An ex-prizefighter who looked like a rhino, he was a bully who enjoyed his work.

He leaned over Juanita. "Okay, start talkin'."

Juanita, who had been straining to look at Estela, tied to a chair beside her, turned her head toward him. *"De qué?* Talk, what about?"

"Da name o' da guy who phoned ya from the Double-Seven."

A flicker of understanding crossed Juanita's face. Tony Bear saw it and knew it would be only a matter of time.

"Animal!" Juanita spat. "I know of no Double-Seven."

Angelo hit her hard. Juanita's head drooped. He seized her hair, holding her face up. "Who phoned ya?"

She answered thickly through swollen lips. "I will tell you nothing until you let my little girl go."

The broad had spirit, Tony Bear conceded. Angelo punched her in the stomach, and Juanita gasped and doubled over as far as her bonds allowed. Estela was sobbing hysterically. The sound annoyed Tony Bear. This was taking too long. He turned to a second bodyguard, Lou, who was watching with him, and whispered, then handed over the cigar he was smoking.

While Lou stepped out past the partition and spoke in an undertone to Angelo, Tony Bear Marino glanced around him. They were in a basement with all doors closed, eliminating the chance of sounds escaping, though it wouldn't matter if they did. The fifty-year-old house stood in its own grounds in a high-class residential district and was protected like a fortress. A syndicate which Marino headed had bought the house eight months ago and moved the counterfeiting operation in. Soon, as a precaution, they would sell it and move on; the new location would have the same innocent-appearing background. That, Tony Bear thought with satisfaction, had been the secret of the long, successful run—frequent moves to quiet, respectable neighborhoods. They had even worked out elaborate precautions for moving from one place to the next: wooden covers, designed to look like household furniture, fitted over every piece of machinery, so to a casual watcher all that was happening was a domestic move. A regular moving van did the job.

The fake-furniture gimmick had been one of Danny Kerrigan's good ideas. A dozen years ago Tony Bear had heard about Kerrigan's reputation as a craftsman and that he had become a skid-row bum. The old man had been rescued, dried out, and put to work for the organization—with spectacular results.

There seemed to be nothing that Danny couldn't print—money, postage stamps, share certificates, drivers' licenses, social security cards. It had been his idea to manufacture bank credit cards. Through a carefully planned raid they had been able to obtain blank plastic sheets from which Keycharge cards were made—enough to last for years. The profit was immense.

But while Danny Kerrigan was important, without the organization's distribution system the old man would have been small time. Therefore it was the threat to the organization which concerned Tony Bear most. Had it been infiltrated by a spy? If yes, how much had he—or she—learned?

His attention swung back to what was happening in the basement. Angelo had the lighted cigar. With the side of his foot he shoved the two chairs so the Núñez woman and her kid now faced each other. Angelo puffed on the cigar until its tip was glowing. Casually he moved to the chair where the child was seated and bound.

Estela looked up, eyes wild with fright. Angelo took her small right hand, lifted it. He removed the glowing cigar from his mouth. Juanita, frantic, weeping, struggling desperately against her bonds, screamed, "No! No! I will tell you."

Angelo waited, the cigar poised, as Juanita gasped, "The man you want . . . is Miles Eastin."

"Who's he work for?"

Her voice a despairing whisper, she answered, "First Mercantile American Bank."

Angelo dropped the cigar and ground it out with his heel. He looked interrogatively at where he knew Tony Bear to be, then went around the partition.

Tony Bear's face was tight. He said softly, "Get him. Go get that fink. Bring him here."

"MILESY," Nate Nathanson said with unusual grouchiness, "whoever your friend is keeps phoning, tell him this place ain't run for the staff; it's for the members."

"What friend?" Miles Eastin had been away from the Double-Seven for part of the morning. Danny had left, and Miles had time for club errands.

"Same guy's phoned four times, asking for you. Wouldn't leave a message." Nathanson handed Miles some papers and a key. "Shipment of canned goods just came in. Cases in the storeroom. Check 'em against the invoices."

On the way to the storeroom, at the rear of the building, Miles wondered about the phone calls. Only three people knew that he was here—his probation officer, Juanita, Nolan Wainwright. The probation officer? Highly unlikely. Juanita? No, Nathanson had said a man. That left Wainwright.

Wainwright would only take the risk of calling if it were something urgent . . . *like a warning?* A warning of what? *That Miles had been exposed as a spy?* Icy fear seized him.

He had pushed the storeroom door open. Now he began to close it to go to the pay phone near the bar to call Wainwright. At that moment he heard several men enter the front lobby. Without knowing why, Miles slipped into the storeroom. He heard someone ask loudly, "Where's that punk Eastin?"

He recognized Angelo's voice. He knew Angelo.

"Up in the office, I guess." That was Jules LaRocca.

"Tony Bear wants . . ." The voices faded as the men hurried upstairs. But Miles had heard enough. He slammed the storeroom door closed and took the key; perhaps the others would waste precious minutes battering the door down.

Then he ran. Through the rear door, down a lane beside a disused factory, across a vacant lot littered with debris. As he reached a railway arch, he heard running feet behind, a shout.

Miles increased his speed, turned sharply left, then right. He was now on the firmer ground of streets and sidewalks. The sounds of running had receded, but that didn't fool him. By now someone in a car was trying to outguess him.

The nature of the area was changing as he ran. Now it was more prosperous; there were several sizable stores. Ahead he could see the city skyline coming into view. Running made him conspicuous.

At an intersection he saw a long black Cadillac cruising slowly. *Marino's.* As the car crossed the street Miles was on, it hesitated, then speeded up, passing quickly out of sight. Miles kept on. He moved close to buildings, slowing his pace as much as he dared. A minute later the Cadillac reappeared. Whoever was in it—most likely Angelo—could now not fail to see him.

Desperately, Miles pushed open a glass door on his left and went in. It was a sporting-goods store. A clerk stepped forward. "Good day, sir. Is there something I can show you?"

"Er . . . yes." He said the first thing that came into his head. "I'd like to see bowling balls."

"Certainly. I'll show you what we have."

He followed the clerk past racks of skis, a display of handguns. Glancing back, Miles saw the silhouette of a single figure peering in the window. Now a second figure joined the first. They stood together, not móving from the storefront.

"This is an excellent ball. It sells for forty-two dollars."

"I'll take it."

"We'll need your hand measurement for the—"

"Never mind."

The clerk looked puzzled, but said, "As you wish, sir. How about a bag for the ball? Perhaps some bowling shoes?"

"Yes," Miles said. "Okay." Scarcely aware of what he was doing, he inspected bags put in front of him, chose one at random, then sat down to try on shoes. It was while slipping on a pair that he remembered it. *The Keycharge card in the name of H. E. Lyncolp—help.*

"How much will all those be?" he asked the clerk.

"Eighty-six dollars and ninety-five cents, plus tax."

"I want to put it on my Keycharge," Miles said. He offered the Lyncolp card, trying to stop his hand from trembling. "I know you need authorization. Go ahead. Phone for it."

The clerk took the card to a glassed-in office area. He was gone several minutes, then returned. "Everything's okay, Mr. Lyncolp."

Miles wondered what was happening now at the Keycharge center in FMA Headquarters Tower. Could it help him? Then he remembered the second instruction relayed by Juanita: After using the card, dawdle. Give Wainwright time to move.

"Sign here, please, Mr. Lyncolp." A Keycharge account slip was filled in for the amount he had spent.

Miles leaned over the counter to add a signature. He felt a hand touch his shoulder lightly. A voice said quietly, "Milesy."

As he turned, Jules LaRocca said, "Don't make no fuss. It won't do no good and you'll get hurt the worse."

Behind LaRocca, their faces impassive, were Angelo and Lou,

271

and a fourth man—another bruiser type—whom Miles hadn't seen before. The four moved around him, seizing him, pinioning his arms. "Move." The order was from Angelo, low-voiced.

The clerk was watching openmouthed. The pressure on Miles's arm tightened. He felt himself propelled helplessly toward the outer door. The bewildered salesclerk ran after them. "Mr. Lyncolp! You've forgotten your bowling ball."

LaRocca told him, "You keep it, buster. This guy won't ever use it."

The black Cadillac was parked a few yards down the street. They pushed Miles roughly into it and drove off.

A FEW minutes before, the call from the sporting-goods clerk had activated a flashing light on a console at the Keycharge authorization center. The operator, seated at a keyboard, spoke into her headset mike. "What is your merchant number, please?"

The clerk gave it. As he did, the operator typed the number. Simultaneously it appeared on her cathode-ray screen. She asked, "Card number and expiration date?"

Another answer, typed. Again, details on the screen.

"Amount of purchase?"

"Ninety dollars, forty-three."

Typed. On screen. The operator pressed a key, alerting a computer several floors below. Within a millisecond the computer digested the information, searched its records, and flashed an answer:

APPROVED.

AUTH. NO. 7416984

URGENT . . . EMERGENCY . . . DO NOT, REPEAT, DO NOT, ALERT MERCHANT . . . ADVISE YOUR SUPERVISOR . . . EXECUTE IMMEDIATELY EMERGENCY INSTRUCTION 17 . . .

"The purchase is approved," the operator told the caller. "Authorization number . . ." She was speaking slowly, deliberately stumbling over the number, as she had been trained to do, to gain time. Emergency signals were not flashed often, but when it happened, there were standard procedures to follow. Murderers had been caught, disappearances solved, stolen art treasures recovered—all because a computer had been alerted to the possibility that a certain credit card might be used.

Before she began talking, the operator had flashed a signal to a supervisor's booth. There another young woman read a duplicate message on her own cathode-ray screen. She reached for a card index, and found emergency instruction 17. It informed her that N. Wainwright, v/p security, was to be advised immediately by telephone that the special Keycharge card issued in the name H. E. Lyncolp had been presented, and where. Using the keyboard, she obtained from the computer the name and location of the store. Then she dialed Wainwright's office, and seconds later, for the Keycharge supervisor, operator, and computer, the brief emergency was over.

Not so for Nolan Wainwright. He had tried four times to reach Miles Eastin at the Double-Seven Health Club to warn him of his danger. The FBI was already investigating the apparent Núñez kidnapping and had alerted city and state police with descriptions of the missing pair. It had been arranged for an FBI team to watch comings and goings at the Double-Seven, though Special Agent Innes agreed with Wainwright that Juanita Núñez and her daughter would not have been taken there. The Secret Service was working the hideout angle, contacting informers, probing for a lead.

When Wainwright received the H. E. Lyncolp alert, he dialed the FBI. Special Agents Innes and Dalrymple, contacted by radio, said they were downtown and would proceed at once to Pete's Sporting Goods store. Wainwright hurried to meet them there.

When he arrived, Innes was questioning bystanders outside the store. Dalrymple was inside, completing a statement by the clerk. "A dry hole," Innes reported glumly. "It was all over when we got here."

Wainwright asked, "Descriptions?"

The FBI man shook his head. "The store guy who served Eastin was so scared he's not sure if there were four men or three. No one outside the store remembers seeing a car."

Wainwright's face was drawn. "So what comes next?"

"You were a cop," Innes said. "You know how it is. We wait, hoping something else will turn up."

SHE heard scuffling and voices. Now she knew they had Miles and were bringing him in.

For Juanita, time had drifted. She had no idea how long it was since she had gasped out Miles Eastin's name, betraying him, to prevent the horror of Estela's torture. Soon after that she had been gagged again and the bonds holding her to the chair were tightened. Then the men left. For a while, she knew, she had dozed.

Alerted by the new noise, her constricted limbs protested agonizingly, so that she wanted to cry out, though the gag prevented it. She willed herself not to panic. She could see Estela, her eyes closed in sleep, her small head drooping. The noises which awakened Juanita were not disturbing her. She, too, was gagged. Juanita hoped that exhaustion would spare her from reality for as long as possible.

The sounds Juanita had been hearing were behind her in an adjoining room, and she guessed a connecting door was open. Briefly she heard Miles's voice protesting, then a thud.

Perhaps a minute passed. She heard a sound like hammer blows, Miles's voice again, this time more distinct. "No! Oh, God, no! Please! I'll—"

Then Tony Bear's voice. "Get me that acid we use for engravings." Miles's words stopped, changing to a high-pitched, piercing, frenzied scream. The screaming, worse than anything she had ever heard, seemed to go on and on."

At last she heard a voice command, "Hold it! All right, stop the damn noise! Start singing."

Miles's screaming turned to racking sobs. "I'll talk! I will! I will!"

Juanita could hear Miles choking out a story. A fresh scream started, then abruptly stilled. Was he dead? she wondered dully, and was aware of new activity in the adjoining room. It sounded as if furniture were being moved; drawers opened and slammed. Then, to her surprise, the man she had heard addressed as Lou appeared and began unfastening her bonds, then Estela's.

"Stand up!" he ordered both of them. Estela, coming awake, began crying softly, the sound muffled by her gag. Juanita wanted to go to her, but could not yet move; she supported her weight against the chair as blood flowed through her cramped limbs.

"You got lucky because of your kid," Lou told Juanita. "The boss is gonna let you go. You'll be blindfolded, taken in a car a long ways from here, and then let out. You won't know where you've been, so you can't bring nobody back. But *if* you tell *anybody anything*, we'll find you wherever you are and kill your kid. Understand?" Juanita nodded. "Then get goin'." Lou pointed to a door. Evidently he was not going to blindfold her yet. Despite her utter exhaustion, she found her mental sharpness coming back.

Partway up a flight of concrete stairs, she leaned against the wall and wanted to be sick. In the outer room they had just passed through, she had seen Miles, his body slumped across a table, his hands a bloody pulp, his face burned with nitric acid. He had stirred slightly and moaned.

"Move it!" Lou urged. They continued up the stairs.

The horror of Miles as she had seen him filled Juanita's mind. What could she do to help him? If she and Estela were released, was there some way she could bring aid back? She had no idea where they were. Yet she must do *something* to expiate—at least a little—her terrible sense of guilt. Whatever the motivation, *she* had brought Miles to this.

The seed of an idea came to her. She concentrated, developing the notion, blotting even Estela from her mind for the moment. It might work. Success depended on the acuity of her senses and her memory. It was also important that she not be blindfolded until *after* getting in the car.

At the head of the stairway they turned right and entered a garage with cement-block walls, looking like any two-car garage belonging to a house. There was one car inside, a dark green Ford. The license number was beyond her view.

In a quick glance around, something puzzled Juanita. Against one wall was a wooden chest of drawers like no chest she had seen before. It had been sawn vertically in half, with the two halves

275

standing separated; the inside was hollow. Beside the chest was a sideboard cut in the same peculiar way. Half the sideboard was being carried out of another doorway by two men.

Lou opened a rear door of the Ford. "Get in," he ordered. In his hands were two thick, dark blindfolds.

Juanita tripped intentionally while getting in and fell forward, grabbing the back of the car's front seat. It gave her the opportunity she wanted—to read the mileage: 25714.8. She closed her eyes, committing the figures to memory.

Estela followed Juanita. Lou came in after them, fastened the blindfolds, and sat in the rear seat. He pushed Juanita's shoulder. "Down on the floor, botha ya. Make no trouble, ya won't get hurt." Squatting on the floor with Estela close beside her, Juanita curled her legs and managed to keep facing forward. She heard someone else get in the car, the motor start, the garage doors rumble open. Then they were moving.

From the instant the car moved, Juanita concentrated as she had never done before. Her intention was to memorize time and direction. She began to count seconds as a photographer friend had once taught her. *A thousand and ONE, a thousand and TWO, a thousand and THREE.* She felt the car reverse and turn, then counted eight seconds while it moved straight forward. Then it slowed almost to a stop. A longish driveway? Probably. The car was again moving slowly, most likely easing out into a street . . . *Turning left. Now faster forward.* She recommenced counting. *Ten seconds. Slowing. Turning right . . . A thousand and ONE, a thousand and TWO. Turning left . . . Speed faster . . . A thousand FORTY-NINE, a thousand FIFTY. Slowing now. A four-second wait, then straight on.* It could have been a traffic light.

Dear God! For Miles's sake help me to remember!

A thousand and NINE, a thousand and TEN. Turning right . . .

Banish other thoughts. React to every movement of the car. Count the time—hoping, praying that the same strong memory that helped her keep track of money at the bank, that once saved her from Miles's duplicity, would now save *him.*

A long straight stretch, smooth road, high speed—she felt her body sway—*the road was curving to the left . . . Stopping.* It had been sixty-eight seconds. *Turning right.* Begin again. *A thousand and ONE, a thousand and TWO . . .*

CHAPTER 16

"THIS is Sergeant Gladstone, Central Communications Bureau, city police," the flat nasal voice on the phone announced. "Says here to immediately notify you people if Juanita Núñez or child Estela Núñez located."

Special Agent Innes sat up. "What do you have, Sergeant?"

"Car radio report just in. Woman and child answering description found near junction of Cheviot Township and Shawnee Lake Road. Officers bringing 'em to Twelfth Precinct."

Innes covered the mouthpiece with his hand. To Nolan Wainwright, seated across the desk at FBI headquarters, he said softly, "City police. They've got Núñez and the kid."

Wainwright gripped the desk edge tightly. "Ask what condition they're in."

"Sergeant," Innes said, "are they okay?"

"Told you all we know, Chief. Want more dope, you better call the Twelfth." Innes dialed the 12th Precinct number. He was connected with a Lieutenant Fazackerly.

"According to our guys, the woman's been beaten up some," Fazackerly said. "No other injuries reported."

Innes relayed the news to Wainwright, who covered his face with a hand as if in prayer.

The lieutenant was speaking again. "Something kind of queer here. Officers in the car say the Núñez woman won't talk. All she wants is pencil and paper. They've given it to her. She's scribbling like mad. Said something about things being in her memory she had to get out."

Special Agent Innes remembered Juanita Núñez' incredible memory. "Radio your car now. Tell your officers not to talk to Núñez, not to disturb her. Help her in any way she wants. And when she gets to the precinct house, let her go on writing if she wants

to. We'll be right there. Handle her like she was something special."
He stopped, then added, "Which she is."

At the precinct house, Juanita's notes amazed them all.

> Short reverse. From garage.
> Forward. 8 secs. Almost stop. (Driveway?)
> Turn left. 10 secs. Med. speed.
> Turn right. 2 secs.
> Turn left. 50 secs. Fast.
> Stop. 4 secs. (Traffic light?)
> Straight on. 10 secs. Med. speed.
> Turn right. Long, straight stretch, high speed.
> Curving to left. Stop. 68 secs.
> Start immed. Turn right . . .

Juanita's summation ran to seven handwritten pages.

They worked intensively for an hour, using large-scale maps. Innes and Dalrymple, Jordan and Quimby of the Secret Service, Nolan Wainwright, and the precinct police. The notes were complete, Juanita maintained, and entirely accurate. She explained she was never confident that what her mind stored away could be recalled—until the moment came to do so. But once the effort had been made, she knew with certainty if her recollections had been correct.

Besides the notes, they had something else to go on. Mileage. The gags and blindfolds had been removed moments before Juanita and Estela were pushed from the car on a lonely suburban road. Again by contrived clumsiness, Juanita had managed to catch a glimpse of the odometer: 25738.5. They had traveled 23.7 miles. But was it a consistent direction, or had the car doubled back, making the journey seem longer than it was, merely to confuse?

Secret Service Agent Jordan drew a series of lines on an area map, representing the most likely directions in which the car would have traveled. Then, around the origins of the lines, he drew a circle. "In there." He prodded with a finger. "Somewhere in there."

"That area," Innes said, "is at least five miles square."

"Then let's comb it," Jordan answered. "In teams, in cars. Our shop and yours, and we'll ask help from the city police."

Lieutenant Fazackerly asked, "And what will we all be looking for, gentlemen?"

"If you want the truth," Jordan said, "damned if I know."

JUANITA Núñez rode in an FBI car with Innes and Wainwright. Wainwright drove, leaving Innes free to work two radios—one which could communicate with the other cars, and the other a regular transmitter-receiver linked to FBI headquarters. They had sectored the area, and five cars were crisscrossing it. Two were FBI, one Secret Service, and two city police.

One thing they were all sure of—where Juanita had been held was the counterfeit center. Instructions to all special units were the same: Report any unusual activity which might relate to an organized-crime center specializing in counterfeiting.

Juanita sat in the rear seat of the FBI car. It was almost two hours since she and Estela had been pushed out of the dark green Ford. Since then Juanita had refused treatment—other than immediate first aid—for her badly bruised face. She knew that if Miles was to be reached in time to save him, everything else must wait, even her own attention to Estela, who had been taken to a hospital for observation. Margot Bracken was with her.

The area within the circle Jordan had drawn—located near the city's eastern edge—included a large industrial tract and several shopping areas. The rest was residential, running from box bungalows to mansion-type dwellings.

To the eyes of the searchers, activity everywhere was routine. At one large house a charity tea was beginning. At another, Alliance Van Lines was loading household furniture. Amid the bungalows a repair crew was fixing a water main.

At the end of an hour Wainwright said, "I've a funny feeling I used to get in police work when I'd miss something right under my nose. Juanita, around the time Eastin stopped crying out, you told us something about there being a lot of noise."

She corrected him. "Noise and *activity*. I could hear people moving, things being shifted, drawers opening and closing—that sort of thing."

"When you were on the way out, did you get any idea what the activity was about?"

Juanita shook her head. "I was too shocked at seeing Miles to see anything else." She hesitated. "Well, there *were* those men in the garage moving that funny furniture."

"Yes," Innes said. "You told us about that. It's odd, but we haven't thought of an explanation."

Wainwright frowned. "That activity Juanita heard . . . supposing they were packing up, preparing to move?"

"Could be," Innes acknowledged. "But what they'd be moving would be printing machines. Not furniture."

"Unless," Wainwright said, "the furniture was a cover. *Hollow* furniture."

"That moving van!" Innes shouted.

Wainwright reversed the car, spinning the wheels in a tight, fast turn. Innes seized the radio. "All special units. Converge on large gray house, stands back near east end Earlham Avenue. Look for Alliance Van Lines moving van. Halt and detain occupants. City units call in all cars in vicinity. Code ten-thirteen."

Code 10-13 meant maximum speed, lights and sirens. Innes switched on their own siren. Wainwright put his foot down hard.

"We went by it twice." Innes sounded close to tears. "And last time they were almost loaded."

"HEAD for the West Coast," Marino was instructing the driver. "Do everything the way you would with a regular load. But keep in touch; you know where to call. You'll get fresh orders in L.A."

"Okay." The driver knew the score. He had done this before, when Tony Bear had kept the counterfeit equipment on the road, moving it around the country like a floating crap game until any heat was off. "I guess I'll roll, Mr. Marino. So long, now."

Tony Bear nodded, feeling relief. Moving out was the smart thing to do, even if they hadn't found the center yet. As usual—ultrasmart. If in doubt, *move*. And now that the loading was done, it was time to get rid of what was left of the stoolie Eastin. Garbage. A detail Angelo would attend to. Meanwhile, Tony Bear decided, it was high time to get the hell away himself. In exceptional good humor, he chuckled. *Ultra*smart.

It was then he heard the sound of converging sirens.

"BETTER move it, Harry!" the young ambulance attendant called to the driver. "This one has no time to spare."

Juanita, on a jump seat, her face intent, asked, "How is he?"

"In bad shape. No sense fooling you." The young paramedic had injected a quarter grain of morphine subcutaneously and now was sloshing water on Miles's face. Despite the morphine, Miles was moaning. "He's in shock. That can kill him, if the burns don't. This water's to wash the acid away, though it's late. As to his eyes . . ." He shook his head. "Say, what went on in there?"

Juanita shook her head. Tears filled her eyes. She pleaded, "Forgive me! Oh, forgive me!"

"He your husband?" the paramedic asked. He began putting splints, secured by bandages, around Miles's hands.

"No."

"Boy friend?"

"Yes." *Was* she his friend? *Need* she have betrayed him? Here and now she wanted forgiveness, as he had once asked it of her.

"Hold this." The attendant placed a mask over Miles's face and handed her an oxygen bottle. She grasped it as if, through her touch, she could communicate as she had wanted to communicate ever since they had found Miles, unconscious, bleeding, burned, hands crushed and nailed to that table.

Juanita and Wainwright had followed the lawmen into the gray mansion, Wainwright holding her back until he made sure there wouldn't be any shooting. There had been no resistance, the people inside having decided they were outflanked and outnumbered.

It was Wainwright who, as gently as he could, pried loose the nails and released Miles's mangled hands. Juanita had been vaguely aware of men lined up and handcuffed, but she hadn't cared. When the ambulance came, she stayed beside the stretcher, followed it into the ambulance, sat as close to Miles as she could get. Now she began praying. *Acordaos, piadosisima Virgen María . . .* that

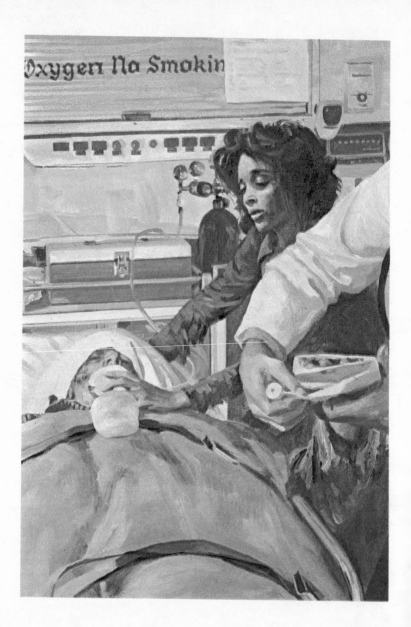

never was it known that anyone who fled to Thy protection, implored Thy help, or sought Thy intercession was left unaided. Inspired by that confidence I fly unto You . . .

Something the paramedic had said played back in her head. *Miles's eyes.* Her voice trembled. "Will he be blind?"

"The specialists will have to answer that. There isn't a lot more I can do right here."

Juanita thought there wasn't anything she could do, either. Except to stay with him, with love and devotion for as long as he needed her. That, and pray. . . . *Virgen Madre de las vírgenes!*

"We're almost there," the attendant said. He had his fingers on Miles's pulse. "He's still alive, anyhow."

CHAPTER 17

IN THE fifteen days since official investigation was begun by the SEC into the labyrinthine finances of Supranational, Roscoe Heyward had prayed for a miracle to avert total catastrophe. But the more deeply investigators probed, the worse the debacle appeared. It seemed probable, too, that criminal charges of fraud would be laid against some of Supranational's officers, including G. G. Quartermain, assuming Big George could ever be enticed back from his Costa Rica hideaway—an unlikely prospect.

In early November a petition of bankruptcy was filed on behalf of SuNatCo. Repercussions were worldwide. Large creditors, associated companies, and many individuals were considered likely to go down the drain along with the corporation. Whether First Mercantile American Bank would be one of them was still an open question.

No longer an open question—as Heyward fully realized—was the subject of his career at FMA. As author of the greatest calamity in the bank's one-hundred-year history, he was finished. What remained at issue was how far he would be legally liable. Yesterday an SEC official, whom Heyward knew well, advised him, "Roscoe, as a friend, I suggest you get yourself a lawyer."

In his office, Heyward's hands trembled as he read *The Wall*

Street Journal's story. He was interrupted by his secretary, Mrs. Callaghan. "Mr. Heyward—Mr. Austin is here."

Without waiting to be told, Harold Austin hurried in. His face was drawn and pale. He wasted no time in preliminaries. "Have you heard *anything* from Quartermain?"

Heyward motioned to the *Journal*. "I know only what I read." In the past two weeks he had tried several times to telephone Big George in Costa Rica, without success. Reports filtering out described him as living in feudal splendor, with a small army of thugs to guard him, and said he had no intention of returning to the United States. It was accepted that Costa Rica would not respond to U.S. extradition proceedings, as other swindlers and fugitives had already proved.

"I'm going down the tube," the Honorable Harold said, his voice breaking. "I put the family trust into SuNatCo and I'm in hock myself for money I raised to buy Q-Investments."

"What *about* Q-Investments?"

"Inchbeck tells me that SOB Quartermain sold out all Q-Investments holdings when the share prices were at their peak. There must have been a swimming pool full of cash."

Including FMA's two million, Heyward thought.

"The bastard transferred everything into shell companies of his own, then moved the money out of them, so all Q-Investments is left with is worthless paper." To Heyward's disgust, Austin began to blubber. "The real money—my money—could be in Costa Rica, the Bahamas, Switzerland. . . . Roscoe, you've got to help me get it back. . . . Otherwise, I'm finished."

Heyward said tersely, "There's no way I can help you, Harold." As quickly as he could, Heyward eased Austin out of the office. He had no sooner gone than Mrs. Callaghan said on the intercom, "There's a reporter calling from the *News*. A Mr. Endicott. He says it's important that he speak to you personally."

"Tell him to call French in the PR department."

Moments later he heard Dora Callaghan's voice again. "I'm sorry, Mr. Heyward, Mr. Endicott asked me to say to you, do you wish him to discuss Miss Avril Deveraux with the PR department?"

Heyward snatched up a phone. "What is all this?"

"I apologize for disturbing you, sir," a quiet voice said. "This is Bruce Endicott of the *News*. We're running a major story on Supranational in tomorrow's paper. Among other things, we're aware of the big loan to SuNatCo by your bank. I've already talked to Dick French about that."

"Then you have all the information you need."

"Not quite, sir. There's a question of when the subject of the loan first came up. Could it have been on a trip you took to the Bahamas in March? With Mr. Quartermain, Vice-President Stonebridge, and some others?"

Heyward hesitated. "It might have been."

"Could you say definitely that it was?"

"Yes, I remember now. It was."

"Thank you, sir. On that particular trip, I believe, you met Miss Avril Deveraux?"

"I may have. The name seems familiar."

"And did you, sir, form a friendship with Miss Deveraux?"

"I suppose you could call it that. She is a charming person."

"Have you met Miss Deveraux subsequently, sir?"

This man Endicott knew. Trying to keep a tremor out of his voice, Heyward insisted, "I've answered all the questions I intend to. I'm extremely busy."

"As you wish, sir. But I think I should tell you that we've talked with Miss Deveraux and she's been extremely cooperative. She's supplied details of her meetings with you, and we have some of the bills from the Columbia Hotel, which Supranational paid. Did such favors have anything to do with the loan from First Mercantile American Bank to Supranational?"

"Certainly not!" Heyward was sweating.

"There's just one other thing, sir. May I ask about a private investment company called Q-Investments? We have copies of some of the records, and you are shown as holding two thousand shares. Is that correct?"

"I have no comment to make."

"Mr. Heyward, were those shares given to you as a payoff for arranging the Supranational loan, and further loans totaling two million dollars to Q-Investments?"

Without speaking, Roscoe Heyward slowly hung up the phone.

"In tomorrow's paper," the man had said. They would print it all, since obviously they had the evidence. He had no illusions about what would follow. Disgrace—total, absolute. Not only at the bank, but among friends, family. At his church. His prestige, influence, pride would be dissolved; for the first time he realized what a fragile mask they were. Even worse was the certainty of criminal prosecution for accepting bribes, the likelihood of other charges, the probability of prison.

A quotation from Genesis came to him: *My punishment is greater than I can bear.* A telephone rang on his desk. He ignored it. There was nothing more to be done here. Ever.

Almost without knowing it, he rose and walked out of the office, past Mrs. Callaghan, who regarded him strangely. He walked down the thirty-sixth-floor corridor, past the boardroom, so short a time ago an arena for his own ambitions. Several people spoke to him. He took no notice. Not far beyond the boardroom was a small door, seldom used. He opened it. There were stairs going upward and he ascended them, climbing steadily, neither hurrying nor pausing on the way.

Once, when FMA Headquarters Tower was new, Ben Rosselli had brought his executives this way. Heyward was one of them, and they had exited by another small door, which he could see ahead. He opened it and went out onto a narrow balcony almost at the building's peak, high above the city.

A raw November wind struck him with blustering force. He leaned against it and found it somehow reassuring, as if enfolding him. It was on that other occasion, he remembered, that Ben Rosselli had held out his arms toward the city and said, "Gentlemen, what was once here was my grandfather's promised land. What you see today is ours. Remember—as he did—that to profit in the truest sense, we must give to it, as well as take." It seemed long ago, in precept as well as time. Now Heyward looked downward. He could see smaller buildings, the winding river, traffic, people moving like ants on Rosselli Plaza far below. The sounds of them all came to him, muted and blended, on the wind.

He put a leg over the waist-high railing separating the balcony from a narrow, unprotected ledge. His other leg followed. Until this moment he had felt no fear, but now all of his body trembled with it, and his hands grasped the railing at his back tightly.

Somewhere behind him he heard agitated voices, feet racing up the stairs. Someone shouted, "Roscoe!"

His last thought was a line from I Samuel: *Go, and the Lord be with thee.* Then, as figures burst through the door behind him, he closed his eyes and stepped forward into the void.

THERE were a handful of days in your life, Alex Vandervoort thought, which, as long as you breathed, would stay sharply and painfully engraved in memory. The day—little more than a year ago—on which Ben Rosselli announced his impending death was one. Today would be another.

It was evening. At home in his apartment, Alex—still shocked by what had happened earlier, uncertain and dispirited—was waiting for Margot. She would be here soon. He mixed himself a drink and tossed a log on the fire, which had burned low.

This morning he had been first through the door to the balcony, having raced up the stairs after hearing worry expressed about Heyward's state of mind, and deducing—from swift questioning of others—where Roscoe might have gone. Alex had cried out as he hurled himself through the doorway, but he was too late.

The sight of Roscoe, seeming to hang for an instant in air, then disappear from view with a terrible scream which faded quickly, left Alex shaking and, for moments, unable to speak. It was Tom Straughan, right behind him, who had taken charge, ordering the balcony cleared.

Returning to the thirty-sixth floor, Alex had pulled himself together and gone to report to Jerome Patterton. After that, the rest of the day was a mélange of events, decisions. Roscoe's wife had been contacted and consoled; police inquiries answered; funeral arrangements overseen; a press statement drafted by Dick French and approved by Alex; and still more questions dealt with or postponed.

Answers to some questions became clearer to Alex in the late afternoon when he received a telephone call from a *News* reporter named Endicott. The reporter seemed upset. He had just read on the AP wire of Roscoe Heyward's apparent suicide. Endicott went on to describe his call to Heyward this morning.

"If I'd had any idea . . ." he ended lamely.

Alex asked, "Is your paper still going to run the story?"

"Yes, sir. The desk is writing a new lead. Apart from that, it will run tomorrow as intended."

"Then why did you call?"

"I guess I just wanted to say—to somebody—I'm sorry."

"Yes," Alex said. "So am I."

This evening Alex reflected again on the conversation, pitying Roscoe for the agony of mind he must have suffered in those final minutes. There was no doubt that the story would do the bank great harm. Despite Alex's success in halting the run at Tylersville, despite also the overwhelming popularity of his new twenty-four-hour branches—where customers inserted plastic identifying cards in auto tellers, which swallowed paper and spat out cash at lightning speed—there had been a public lessening of confidence in First Mercantile American. Nearly forty million dollars in withdrawals had flowed out in the past ten days, and incoming funds were far below their usual level. FMA's share price had also sagged badly on the New York Stock Exchange.

FMA was not alone. Since the news of Supranational's insolvency, a miasma of depression had gripped the business community, sent stock prices on a downhill slide, created fresh doubts about the value of the dollar, and now appeared to some as the last clear warning before the storm of a world recession.

It was, Alex thought, as if the toppling of a giant had brought home the realization that other giants, once thought invulnerable, could topple, too; that neither individuals, nor corporations, nor governments, could escape forever the simplest accounting law of all—that what you owed you must one day pay.

He heard the sound of a key turning. Margot came in, removed her camel's hair coat, and tossed it on a chair. "Alex, I can't get Roscoe out of my mind. How could he do it? *Why?*"

"It seems there were some reasons," he said slowly. "They're beginning to come out. If you don't mind, Bracken, I don't feel like talking about it yet."

"I understand." She came to him. He held her tightly as they kissed.

After a while he said, "Tell me about Eastin, Juanita, the little girl." Margot sat down facing him.

"Miles first. He's out of danger, and the best news is that by a miracle he won't be blind. He must have closed his eyes an instant before the acid hit. Of course, he'll be having plastic surgery for a long time."

"What about his hands?"

"The hospital has been in touch with a surgeon on the West Coast, one of the best hand men in the country. He's agreed to operate next week. I assume the bank will pay."

"Yes," Alex said, "it will."

"I've had a talk," Margot continued, "with Innes of the FBI. He says that, in return for Miles Eastin's testifying in court, they'll offer him protection and a new identity somewhere else in the country. Has Nolan talked to you today?"

Alex shook his head.

"He wants you to help Miles get a job. Nolan says if necessary he'll pound on your desk."

"He won't need to," Alex said. "Our holding company owns consumer finance shops in Texas and California. We'll find something for Eastin in one or the other."

"Maybe they'll hire Juanita as well. She says wherever he goes, she's going with him. Estela, too. The doctor said Estela talked the whole thing out. As a result, she won't bury the experience in her subconscious; she'll remember it only as a nightmare, nothing more."

Alex sighed. At least there would be one happy ending.

The telephone rang and Margot got up and answered it. "It's Leonard Kingswood. For you."

Alex crossed the living room and took the phone.

"I know you're relaxing after a rough day," the Northam Steel chairman said, "and I'm shook up about Roscoe, too. But what I have to say can't wait. There's been a caucus of directors by telephone. A full meeting of the FMA board is being summoned for noon tomorrow. The first order of business will be to accept Jerome's resignation as president. Some of us demanded it. Jerome agreed. I think he was relieved."

Yes, Alex thought, Patterton would be. He clearly had no stomach for the avalanche of problems, along with the critical decisions needed now.

"After that," Kingswood said, "you will be elected president, Alex. To take effect immediately."

While listening, Alex had cradled the telephone against his shoulder and lit his pipe. Now he puffed it while he considered. "At this point, Len, I'm not sure I want the job."

"There was a feeling you might say that, which is why I was elected as the one to call you. We all know you warned us about Supranational. We thought we were wiser. Well, we weren't. Now what you predicted has come true. So we're asking you, Alex—belatedly, I admit—to help us out of this mess. Some of the directors are worried about their personal liability. All of us remember your cautioning about that, too."

"Let me think a minute, Len."

"Take your time."

Alex supposed he should feel some personal satisfaction at being vindicated; a conviction of power at holding—as he knew he did—trump cards. He felt neither of those things. Only a great sadness at the futility and waste, when the best that could happen for a long time to come, assuming he succeeded, was for the bank to regain the state in which Ben Rosselli left it.

Was it worth it? Could the extraordinary effort, deep personal involvement, sacrifice, and strain be justified? And for what? To save a bank, a money machine, from failure. Wasn't Margot's work among the disadvantaged a greater contribution to their times? Yet it wasn't all that simple, because banks were necessary; in their way, as essential as food. Civilization would break down without a money system. Banks, though imperfect, made the system work.

Also, there was a practical consideration. If Alex accepted the leadership of First Mercantile American at this late stage, he might merely preside, ignominiously, over FMA's demise. If so, his reputation as a banker would be liquidated, too. On the other hand, if anyone could save FMA, Alex knew he was the one. As well as ability, he possessed the inside knowledge which an outsider would not have time to learn. Even more important: he believed that he could do it.

"If I accepted," he said, "I'd insist on a free hand to make changes, including changes on the board."

"You'd get your free hand," Kingswood answered. "I personally guarantee it."

Alex drew on his pipe. "Let me sleep on it, Len."

He hung up the phone. Margot regarded him quizzically. "Why didn't you accept? When both of us know you're going to."

"Why are you so certain I'll accept?"

"Because you can't resist the challenge. Because your whole life is banking. Everything else takes second place."

"I'm not sure," he said slowly, "that I want that to be true." It *had* been true, he thought, when he and Celia were together. Was it still? Possibly the answer was yes, as Margot said. Probably, too, no one ever changed his basic nature.

"There's something I've been wanting to ask you," Margot said. "This seems as good a time as any. That night in Tylersville, when the old couple with their life savings in that shopping bag asked you, 'Is our money absolutely safe in your bank?' You answered yes. Were you really sure?"

"I've asked myself that," Alex said. "Right afterward, and since. If I own up, I suppose I wasn't."

"But you were saving the bank. Right? And that came first. Ahead of those old people and all the others; ahead of honesty, even, because business as usual was more important." Suddenly there was emotion in Margot's voice. "You'll go on trying to save the bank, Alex—ahead of everything else. It's the way it was with you and

291

Celia. And," she said slowly, "as it would be—if you had to make a choice—with you and me."

Alex was silent. What could he say, what could anyone say, confronted with the naked truth?

"So in the end," Margot said, "you aren't all that different from Roscoe. Or Lewis, with his harping on gold. Business stability, sound money, high share prices. All those things first. People—especially little, unimportant people—a long way after. It's the big gulf between us, Alex. It will always be there." He saw that she was crying.

A buzzer sounded in the hallway. Alex strode toward an intercom that connected with the doorman. "What is it?"

"Mr. Vandervoort, there's a Mrs. Callaghan asking for you."

"All right. Send her up."

Dora Callaghan was an attractive, well-groomed woman, nearing sixty. She had, Alex knew, worked for FMA for many years, at least ten of them for Roscoe Heyward. Normally she was poised and confident, but tonight she looked tired and nervous. She carried a leather briefcase.

"Mr. Vandervoort, I'm sorry to intrude . . ."

"It's certainly no intrusion, Mrs. Callaghan. Do come in." He introduced Margot.

Alex took her coat, and Margot mixed martinis. "Could you use a drink?"

"I really could."

They all sat by the fire. "You can speak freely in front of Miss Bracken," Alex said.

"Mr. Vandervoort, this afternoon I went through Mr. Heyward's desk. I thought there might be some papers that should be sent to someone else." Her voice thickened and stopped. She whispered, "I'm sorry."

Alex told her gently, "Please don't be. There's no hurry."

As her composure returned, she continued, "There were some locked drawers. Mr. Heyward and I both had keys, though I didn't use mine often. Today I did."

They waited. "In one of the drawers . . . Mr. Vandervoort, I heard there would be more investigators coming tomorrow morning.

I thought . . . that you'd better see what was in there, that you'd know, better than I, what to do."

Mrs. Callaghan opened the briefcase and took out two large envelopes. Alex removed the contents. The first contained share certificates for Q-Investments common stock, signed by G. G. Quartermain. Though they were nominee certificates, there could be no doubt they had belonged to Heyward. Alex remembered the *News* reporter's allegations of this afternoon. This was confirmation. Further proof would be needed, of course, if the matter were pursued, but it seemed certain that Heyward, a trusted, high-ranking officer of the bank, had accepted a sordid bribe. Had he lived, exposure would have meant criminal prosecution.

Alex's earlier depression deepened. He had never liked Heyward. They had always been antagonists. Yet never for an instant had he doubted Roscoe's personal integrity.

Wishing none of this was happening, Alex removed the contents from the second envelope. They proved to be enlarged photographs of a group of people beside a swimming pool—four women and two men in the nude, Roscoe Heyward dressed. They must be from Heyward's much vaunted trip to the Bahamas. Alex spread the prints out on a coffee table while Margot and Mrs. Callaghan watched.

Dora Callaghan's cheeks were red; she was blushing. *Blushing?* He'd thought no one did that anymore. She stood up. "Mr. Vandervoort, I'd better go."

"You were right to bring these things to me," he told her. "I appreciate it, and I'll take care of them personally."

"I'll see you out," Margot said. She retrieved Mrs. Callaghan's coat and went with her to the elevator.

Alex was looking out at the city's lights when Margot returned. "A nice woman," she pronounced. "And loyal."

"Yes," he said, and thought, whatever changes are made, he would see that Mrs. Callaghan was treated considerately. There would be other people to think of, too. Alex would immediately promote Tom Straughan to Alex's own previous post as an executive vice-president. Edwina D'Orsey must move up to senior vice-president in charge of the trust department; it was a post Alex had had in mind for Edwina for some time. Soon he expected her to move higher still. Meanwhile, she must be named, at once, a member of the board.

He realized suddenly he was taking for granted that he would accept the bank presidency. Well, Margot had just told him that. Obviously she was right. He turned away from the window. Margot was standing at the coffee table, looking down at the photographs. Suddenly she giggled, and then he laughed with her.

"Oh, dear," Margot said. "Funny sad!"

When their laughter ended, he collected the prints and returned them to their envelope. He was tempted to throw the package on the fire, but knew he mustn't. It would be destruction of evidence which might be needed. But he would do his best to keep the photos from other eyes—for Roscoe's sake.

"Funny sad," Margot repeated. "Isn't it all?"

"Yes," he agreed, and in that moment knew he needed her, and always would.

He took her hands, remembering what they had been speaking of before Mrs. Callaghan came. "Never mind any gulfs between us," Alex urged. "We have a lot of bridges, too. You and I are good for each other. Let's stay together, Bracken."

She objected. "It probably won't work, or last. The odds are against us."

"Then we'll try to prove them wrong."

"Maybe"—Margot's eyes sparkled mischievously—"if we start out not believing or expecting much, we'll do better than most."

As he took her in his arms, he told her, "Sometimes bankers and lawyers talk too much."

The authenticity that distinguishes every Arthur Hailey novel is not achieved in any casual fashion. Mr. Hailey spends a good year on research for each book; he does the research himself, and he does it in depth. For *Airport* he visited the world's largest and most complex air terminals. *Wheels* took him to Detroit, where he made friends with

Arthur
Hailey

automobile workers on every level. In preparation for *The Moneychangers* he spent hours and days with bank directors, presidents, vice-presidents, as well as branch managers, tellers and accountants, security officers, and guards. It is this direct involvement that enables him to tell his story from the point of view of an insider, and makes readers feel like insiders, too.

From this meticulous foundation Mr. Hailey moves into his writing routine of about six hundred words a day. Though inspiration may come to him at any time—he gets many ideas in the shower—the work itself is slow and painstaking. "I sometimes write a paragraph twenty times until I have it the way I want it," he says. "I never really feel like writing, but like all professional writers, I face that blank page and just get on with it."

Born in England, Arthur Hailey served as a pilot in the RAF, then emigrated to Canada after World War II. Before turning to fiction, he worked as editor of a technical magazine, then in advertising and publishing. He met his wife, Sheila, when they were working for the same publishing company.

The Haileys and their three children left Canada in 1965 and now live on an island in the Bahamas which provides them with a delightful life-style. A morning of work is often followed by a picnic or a swim and a leisurely afternoon on their boat. Readers of *The Final Diagnosis, Hotel, Airport,* and *Wheels* (all Condensed Books selections), and now *The Moneychangers*, will surely agree that a writer who provides so much pleasure deserves some treats for himself.

THE
MASSACRE
AT
FALL
CREEK

A CONDENSATION OF THE BOOK
BY

JESSAMYN
WEST

ILLUSTRATED BY TOM HALL

In Indiana in 1824, red men were still considered fair game for white men's rifles. Then one day two Indian families who camped every sugaring season by Fall Creek were shot down in cold blood. Incredibly, four white men found themselves on trial for murder.

With her rare insight into the human heart, Jessamyn West has woven from the settlers' terrible dilemma a novel as vibrant as the American frontier which forms its backdrop. And in Hannah Cape, the fiery young daughter of Fall Creek's preacher, she has created one of literature's most unforgettable heroines. A major work from the author of *The Friendly Persuasion*.

BOOK ONE

THE CRIME

I

Jud Clasby, hidden in the yet unleafed sassafras clump, watched the work going on in the camp. The three squaws and four children were as pretty as does with their fawns, he thought. He did not actually think—he spoke silently to his listening self. He was a long hunter, alone for months at a time harvesting pelts, and though he never said a word aloud, he continuously commented to himself. Because of this habit, he never knew the loneliness other long hunters spoke of. He talked all day long to the silent self who accompanied him.

The three women were busy, as squaws always were about camp. If Indian men had been half as industrious as their women, the whole country would have been cleared, planted, and built up long ago. And where would he be then? Jud had no more farmer or storekeeping blood in him than an Indian. He was a hunter and trapper. Something knotted pleasurably inside him at the prospect of outwitting—animals *had* wits—and killing an animal. If the government had tried to tie him to a hoe or latch him to a plow the way it had Indians, the government would be in a hard row for stumps. He would move on west ahead of the government. Just what the Indians were doing, too, he supposed.

This was a Seneca camp—though one of the squaws was half white, and old Tall Tree was at least half Miami. The Senecas had been pushed from New York to Pennsylvania and on, until now here they were halfway across Indiana. And the Indian men still weren't planting in the spring and reaping in the fall. They were still hunting; as he was.

The hunters of this party had not had much luck so far; but the season was early, and spring late. Now, in mid-February of 1824, the raccoons were just beginning to leave their holes in the trees; and the Indian bucks, Tall Tree and Red Cloud, had complained to him that whites were springing the traps their squaws set. Jud didn't doubt this was true. There were only ten or twelve white families living around the creek, and if they had all trapped and hunted twelve hours a day seven days a week they wouldn't have skimmed the cream off the game. But the amount of game taken wasn't what bothered the settlers; it was the Indians themselves, moving down from the north to the sugar camp as if they had a right, as in the old days, to go where they pleased.

These particular men and their families had been meek as Moses, not even going into Pendleton, where other Indians were trading pelts and baskets for calico and beads and whiskey. But who knew what went on in an Indian's mind?

Red Cloud's squaw (in her thirties or forties—age was hard to judge in a squaw) was rubbing deer brains into a green hide to cure it. Tall Tree's squaw, no longer young or comely, was chewing a tanned hide to supple it. The young breed was tending a pot of boiling maple sap. Busy as beavers, the lot of them, and the breed pretty. Yank that calico dress over her head, Jud thought, and he'd find skin as white as his own.

Which didn't make her white. There were two ways of being an Indian: to be born one, or to be raised one. This girl was fifty percent the first and a hundred percent the other. That made her a hundred and fifty percent Indian.

The wind that had been blowing into Jud's face was shifting. He had been able to smell the Indians and he supposed they would be able to smell him soon. Smell was as important for a hunter as sound. Only once in his life had he missed Indian smell, and that failure had almost cost him his life.

He had been hunting and trapping far west of the White River valley when half a dozen Sioux began to close in on him, planning to get his hair and his packload of pelts at one swoop. He outmaneuvered them, abandoned his horses, and hid in a canebrake beside some unnamed western river. He was quiet as a coiled snake who had lost his rattle. There was no sound from the Indians, either, which was to be expected. But if they were near, he would have smelled them. There was no smell but of river mud and reeds and of the water itself. Then, between one long breath and another, they were upon him. They hadn't killed him at once because their plan for him was something more entertaining: torture the next day with the whole tribe as audience.

He hadn't been prepared for Indians he couldn't smell. Torture he had been prepared for since he had left home in York state at the age of fifteen. He believed he could make as good a showing when the fire and the slicing started as any brave. So he, knowing what was going to happen, and the Sioux, anticipating it, had traveled south together in comradely fashion.

"Why didn't I smell you?" Jud asked.

They told him. It was an advantage they had counted on. They had been fasting and had ended their religious rite with a session in the steam hut. They were as cleaned out as a wasp nest in winter. "A man smells of what he eats."

It was a truth he knew. "I should have eaten Indian before I started this hunt," he told them, and they laughed, as he had known they would. Their humor was as rough and ready as his own.

"Tomorrow," they said, "we eat you and smell white."

That was no joke. If he was brave, he would be eaten. A man became what he took into his body: the deer made him fleet; the bear, fierce; the courageous enemy, brave.

Clasby didn't hold against them the prospect of being eaten. Every hunter ate what he hunted. He had eaten Indian. Perhaps that accounted for his escape that night. He didn't smell white and he wasn't as noisy as a white. His hands were tied, but he was able on an ember of the still-smoldering fire to burn the thong that bound him. Burned his wrists, but that had been a small price to pay for freedom. He silenced with a knife the one Indian who had been roused; cut his throat too deep for any outcry, then slipped into the river, soundless as an otter.

THE squaws smelled him now. He could tell by the looks they exchanged. He had no wish to make them suspicious. His intention from the first had been to walk in, talk casually, and have a careful look around. But he was a still hunter. He had the habit of sizing up animals before he faced them. He approached a camp or a lodge as carefully as he approached a herd.

Before he was out of his sassafras clump, the two hunters, Tall Tree and Red Cloud, with Black Antler, the Seneca Faithkeeper, returned to the camp. Tall Tree was heavyset in the middle-aged Seneca way. Red Cloud was an Indian in his prime. Black Antler was the shape of Clasby's own father, all beak and Adam's apple.

Black Antler was a follower of Handsome Lake, the Seneca prophet. He preached the longhouse religion, the old faith of the Six Nations. The Seneca had no writing for their scriptures. The prophet's teaching had to be memorized, word for word. Folded Leaf, Red Cloud's son, eleven or twelve, a magpie for picking up words, was being trained to be a faithkeeper.

The men knew at once that Clasby was near. His smell and the women's eyes told them. They knew he would either disappear or come into camp.

The men had returned for their one cooked meal of the day, usually eaten in midmorning, and usually a soupy stew of meat and vegetables. Tall Tree's squaw handed the bowls around, and when Clasby stepped into the camp, he, too, was given a bowl.

Black Antler refused food. "I will teach the boy first."

"Where is Folded Leaf?" Red Cloud asked the women.

"I saw him down by the creek," Clasby told him in their own language. "Playing duck-on-rock with his brother and sisters."

Red Cloud put two fingers in his mouth and gave a blast that Clasby felt inside his nose like a gust of red pepper.

The soup was good. He had tasted and made many a pot like it. "How's the hunting?" he asked.

"Bad. Whites still spring our traps. They want to drive us out."

"You've moved in pretty close to them."

"Close to *them*. We were here before they were born."

Clasby didn't want to waste breath on this old argument. Did the Indians expect white men who had never owned an acre or been allowed to run a deer or even hunt a rabbit to go back hang-dog to an English squire and say, Somebody else was there first? No sirree bob. They couldn't push the squire around, but they'd found that they could push the Indian. And if he wouldn't push, why, shoot him.

Black Antler, when the children returned, took Folded Leaf to one side immediately. While the others ate, Black Antler had Folded Leaf recite what he had memorized the day before. The rigmarole the prophet Handsome Lake had preached took four full mornings to repeat. Clasby had heard enough of it to know it was nine-tenths Indian, one-tenth Christian. Handsome Lake had been influenced by the Pennsylvania Quakers.

Listening now to Folded Leaf made Clasby as uncomfortable as watching a trained bear dance. Let the wild stay wild. He had no stomach for the sight of a young savage mouthing "scriptures." Nevertheless, he could be at least as polite as an Indian. He said thank you for the food he had eaten, and left.

Once Clasby was out of earshot, Talking Crow, Tall Tree's old wife, said, "Watch that one."

Red Cloud answered, "I have known him a long time."

"Watch him."

"It is the other way around. He watches us."

"Like the game he hunts."

Tall Tree asked his wife, "How would you stop him?"

"In the old days, you would not ask that question." Talking Crow's eyes were arrow-shaped. Tall Tree felt the wound of her looking. "We were the Seneca nation, the keepers of the western gate. We keep no gates now. We run."

Red Cloud spoke up. There were truths there was no use raking over. He gestured toward his son, Folded Leaf, his eyes glowing with pride. The boy was a born faithkeeper. "Some of the old ways we keep. Folded Leaf learns the old words. Wherever he goes the words will go with him."

"And you let the whites laugh at the sacred words he speaks."

"Clasby did not laugh."

"Not for you to see. But I saw. Folded Leaf was like a chipmunk to Clasby. Inside, he laughed to hear a chipmunk speak."

"Do you want me to tomahawk Clasby? Have all the men here from the falls with long guns one sun later?"

"No. We have many to their few. Rouse our tribesmen. The river was ours. The falls were ours. Make them ours again."

"You do not understand, Talking Crow. This is a time of peace. We have signed treaties."

Deep out of Talking Crow's throat came a rumble of disgust. "You will die signing treaties." She turned away from him.

Red Cloud watched her enter the lean-to. There was truth in what she said. Twenty-two years ago Handsome Lake, the prophet, spoke to Jefferson, the "Great White Chief of our white brothers," asking him for a "writing on paper" so that "we can hold fast our land against the seizure of our white brothers."

The Great Chief had sent the writing on paper. "I said to you last winter that the land you then held should never go from you except when you should be disposed to sell. . . . We wish you prosperity as brethren should do."

Wishes were not enough. The Seneca had accepted that paper, and their property had vanished. Red Cloud was born a warrior and hunter. He had become a squirrel killer. But Talking Crow need not think it was lack of manhood that kept him from bringing home the dripping scalps of those who were their enemies. It was manhood that caused him to keep his word. He had agreed to the paper of the Great Chief. He could kill an enemy and rejoice. But he would rather die than not keep his word.

And Talking Crow was wrong about Clasby. Clasby owned no land—of theirs or anyone else's. He was a wanderer and hunter, the enemy only of animals whose pelts and skins he needed.

Even so, keeping his word, listening to the quick, sure voice of his son, a sadness filled Red Cloud. He could feel the tension of a pulled bow in his forearms as he heard Folded Leaf repeat after Black Antler, "The Great Spirit has given us a mother: the earth. Our mother we must love. The Great Spirit has given us brothers. To them we must be brotherly. The White Man has Jesus. We have Handsome Lake. If the white man follows Jesus and the red man Handsome Lake, the brothers will dwell in peace."

He was pledged to the way of Handsome Lake, not of Talking Crow.

WHEN Jud Clasby showed up at the Cape house an hour after he left the Indian camp, Hannah Cape lit out to call on the Woods. Actually she was going to court John Wood, Jr. She hoped the others did not know what she was doing. Her mother knew, but her mother approved. Since boys didn't come to court Hannah, the next best thing was to have Hannah court a boy. This was no place for a woman without a man. John Jr. wasn't the man Hannah's mother would have picked. He was seventeen, just Hannah's age, and she had seen mullein stocks with more pith to them than John Jr. had. But Hannah, more than likely, wasn't Mrs. Wood's idea of a perfect daughter-in-law, either. Mrs. Wood probably thought Hannah would wear the pants in the family.

It wouldn't be true. Hannah's husband would wear the pants, if Hannah had to sew them onto him. Hannah wouldn't marry a man she didn't worship. The girl acted as if her brother, Ben, fourteen, were a god. She treated her father as if he were her Creator, with a capital C. Just because she was five feet ten, with a great swag of red hair, people thought she might be feisty. Oh, she wasn't. She'd fetch and carry for the man of her choice, the way she did for her father and Ben. Her size and her hair color might count against her, but she had plenty to count for her. Her face was almost as creamy as her bosom; and her bosom was prominent enough to offset anybody's idea that, because she could use a bucksaw and axe as well as a man, she wasn't womanly.

Her mother wondered why Hannah wasn't courted. Hannah didn't. She knew. The minute a man sashayed up to her, he undermined her faith in his judgment. She wanted a man who dreamed of something better than Hannah Cape, a backwoods girl with a bucksaw. A man who wanted her didn't have his sights set high enough to suit her.

Jud Clasby didn't hide where *his* sights were. His staring made her uncomfortable; and his talk of killing animals and Indians made her queasy.

"I'm going over to the Woods'," she told her mother.

"You set your cap for that milksop boy?" Clasby asked.

"Milksop" made Hannah mad. "No," she said. "It's the old man I've taken a shine to."

This was pert of Hannah, and her mother was sorry to hear her speak that way. It was what people expected of a redhead. But Clasby enjoyed pertness. He leaned his chair back and laughed.

"You going to lose either way. The boy don't want a wife and the old man's got one wife too many already." Old Mr. Wood was a widower remarried not so long ago to Reba Reese, a widow young enough to be his daughter.

Hannah knew that bandying words with Jud Clasby would be like trying to outgrunt a pig. In the first place, he knew more than she did; and in the second, he didn't care what he said.

"Good-by, Mama," she said. "I'll be back before suppertime."

"You better be, or I'll send Ben after you."

"I'll bring her home," Jud said. "I got an errand at the Woods'."

Hannah gave Clasby her bullet stare, but he was too tough for anything but true lead.

HANNAH was bold, but not a bold wooer. She couldn't go to the Woods' without some excuse. When Reba Wood opened the door, Hannah held out a willow basket, its contents neatly covered with a napkin. "Molasses cookies," she said. "Mama sent them."

"Johnny's favorites," Reba said. "How did you ever guess?"

"Everybody likes molasses cookies," Hannah answered coolly.

Mr. Wood was stretched out for a rest on the bed that filled one corner of the room. The Woods had more furniture than most of the people at Fall Creek, because their cabin contained the belongings of two families. The Woods and the Reeses had headed west together after both had been suckered by land agents in York state. On the way west, Hosmer Reese had drowned. A month earlier John Wood's wife, Abbie, had died of a bloody flux. It was the most natural thing in the world for the widow and widower, after they had reached Fall Creek, to combine forces.

Hannah didn't think that lovemaking could have been in Reba Reese's mind when she married John Wood. He looked to be all bone and gristle, his skin as gray as his long beard and hair, his mouth as thin as the cutting edge of an axe. He and Reba didn't get along and made no bones about it, even before company.

Reba would be hard for anybody to get along with, Hannah thought. She was afraid for herself when she looked at Reba. Would she look that way when she was forty? Reba's hair was the red of maple leaves after heavy frost had smirched their color. Her cheeks were cobwebbed with veins. She was sharp and mean to a man old enough to be her father; sharp and mean to the boy she had inherited from Abbie Wood. Was that what happened to pert and saucy girls when they got to be middle-aged?

"I reckon you want to see Johnny?"

"I thought we might read some more together."

The best gift Johnny got from his stepmother was the tin box of books that had belonged to Hosmer Reese. There were spellers and arithmetics in the box—Hosmer had been a schoolteacher—but there were storybooks, too, and these Johnny read aloud to Hannah. She could read all right, faster and with just as much expression; but he liked to read, and Hannah loved to listen to him. It was a good thing. Johnny wasn't much of a talker.

"Do you want to go up and get him?" Reba asked.

The loft was Johnny's bedroom, and Hannah was too well brought up to go alone to a boy's sleeping room. "No. Maybe he's resting up."

"Resting?" Reba exploded. "What's he got to rest up from? He's a spoiled do-nothing. Been carried around on a chip since he was born. That poor old man there does all the chores a boy ought to do." Reba went to the ladder that led to the loft. "Johnny," she shouted, "you've got company."

Everything about Johnny Wood made Hannah's heart ache. Half an orphan, a stepmother who hated him, a father soured on life because of a no-good land deal in York state. Hannah wanted to be both a mother and a father to him—and something else besides, because he was so beautiful.

Johnny came down the ladder from the loft like a man walking onto a stage—though Hannah was his only audience. Reba was stirring up corn pone for supper; the old man still had his eyes closed. Johnny was seventeen, but he might have been twenty-five. Born of old parents, he had maybe come aged from the womb. He was a statue that breathed; all cream ivory, with black carved curls and a narrow, long-limbed body. Was he bashful? Was his mind so occupied with deep thoughts he had no time to talk with her? He liked to read to her, anyway, and she didn't ask for more.

It was too early for candlelighting, so Hannah pulled the bench close to the Dutch door and opened the top half enough of a crack to let in some light, but small enough to keep most of the wind out. Reba was the kind of woman who liked to let people know she was working by making a lot of noise. Her clattering jarred on Hannah at first, but finally the story took over.

They were reading *Ivanhoe*. Had people really lived like that? Worn such rich clothes, fought and died for such noble causes? Was the world going downhill? No shining armor now; nothing but linsey-woolsey and an unfelled forest stretching for untold miles.

One thing hadn't changed: love. Johnny wasn't anything like Ivanhoe; perhaps he was like the man who wrote the book and was silent because his head was full of words he wanted to put on paper. Whether or no, Hannah loved him. He never touched her, but if he did, she would more than likely faint dead away in the last place she'd want to faint: at Reba Wood's feet.

Clasby saved her from such a fate. He came in at twilight as quiet as Reba was noisy. "I've come to fetch Hannah home."

"There was no need," Hannah said.

"I promised your mama, and I want to talk to John and Reba."

Mr. Wood shook himself awake and sat on the bench across the table from Jud Clasby. While the men talked, Johnny read on, but

Hannah couldn't listen, for Clasby was talking about her family.

"Cale Cape thinks because the redskins been hunting in these parts for the past four or five years there's no point getting stirred up about their moving in here now."

"Cale Cape is so kindhearted he'd share his wife with a grizzly," agreed Reba.

Hannah had to bite her tongue at that. Her father was a peaceable, God-fearing man, but he knew right from wrong.

"The reds are treacherous. They'd wait five years to lull our suspicions." Old Mr. Wood was an Indian hater. It was his religion. "Run 'em out," he bellowed.

"Hush up about Indians," Reba ordered her husband. "You'd be the first one under the bed if a redskin doing no more than peddling baskets showed up at the door." She turned to Clasby. "He's all wind and no weather. If you want somebody who means business, go talk to my brother, George Benson. Don't waste your time here. The old man's lost his sap and the boy never had any."

Johnny stopped his reading and quickly stood. He went directly to his stepmother and, with his open book pressed under her chin, pinned her to the wall. "Have I got any sap?" he asked, giving the book a forward shove that brought Reba's pop eyes farther out of their sockets. "Answer me!"

Reba's tongue waggled, but the sounds she made were not speech. Clasby rescued her. He wrenched Johnny away and threw the book onto the table. "You want to kill your stepmother?"

Johnny paid no attention to Clasby, who continued to hold him. "Answer me," he shouted at Reba. "Have I got sap?"

Clasby released Johnny and said, "Junior, if you want a woman to talk to you, don't half choke her to death first." Then he helped Reba to a bench at the table and got her a dipperful of water. Johnny ran up the ladder to the loft.

Restored, Reba said, "Goes up like a monkey, don't he?"

"Best not tease monkeys," Clasby advised, "or a courting boy."

"Courting? The girl's the one doing the courting."

Hannah felt her cheeks flame up like red-hot stove lids. "I visit Johnny," she said. "Is that courting?"

"You want to visit him now? Smooth his feathers?" Reba asked. "Tell him he's full of sap and his mother deserves choking?"

Clasby said, "We'd better be on our way, Hannah. I've got some other visits to make tonight."

"Stop and see George Benson," Reba insisted. "What's on your mind is on his."

Hannah was pulled in more directions at once than were comfortable. How could Johnny, book reader, kind to animals, have turned on his stepmother that way? She wanted to tell him, I don't understand what you did, but whatever you do, I'll love you. She wanted to say to Clasby and the Woods, The Indians haven't done a thing against us.

She'd already been called a courting girl that evening. She didn't want Clasby to shame her for advising them what to do about the Indians with a Yes, General, whatever you order.

Old Mr. Wood made it easy for her to leave. "It was good of you, Hannah, to bring the cookies. They're my favorites."

Kindness in the midst of all she'd heard and seen today was more than she could bear. She ran outside to hide her tears. Jud Clasby followed with her shawl.

WHEN February came, you thought winter's back was broken. The little creek, running downhill to Fall Creek, *sounded* like summer. But winter could still drop down out of a clear sky.

"You aiming to shake yourself to death?" Jud Clasby asked.

"No," Hannah said. "I wasn't even aiming to shake. I didn't know I was. It smells like spring, don't it?"

"You put this on," Clasby said. "No sense not being warm while you smell spring." As he adjusted the shawl over her shoulders his hand brushed lightly across her breast. Hannah started to say something, but shut her mouth. There was no sign Clasby even knew he had touched her. Where was her mind, anyway? First in love with a boy who didn't love her; now thinking that every man who adjusted a shawl for her had other ideas than her comfort in mind. Were other ideas what she wanted him to have?

"Thank you," she said.

"I thought for a minute you were going to bolt."

"Oh, I've worn shawls before." It crossed Hannah's mind that they both might be thinking of the same thing, after all.

"I'd thought to stop at George Benson's and the Bemises' on the way to your place. If you don't want to, I'll take you home first."

"Ora Bemis's my best friend," Hannah said, leaving Benson out of it. She'd as lief visit a bull buffalo as George Benson.

Luther and Ora Bemis lived half a mile up the creek from the Woods. Ora was a couple of years older than Hannah and she was expecting a baby. Some people were surprised when a wandering dandy like Luther Bemis had taken to a girl as swarthy as Ora, with a scar on her face, too. Some weren't. They said that a man who'd spent ten years trapping and hunting far from all whites must've had an Indian wife or two, and that Ora's color and decorations made him feel right at home.

However Ora made Lute feel, he'd been a changed man since he married her. Lute had grown up in Ohio in the same town as Hannah's folks. He had been saved at fifteen, but three years of walking a chalk line had been all his system could stand. At eighteen he broke loose in all directions at once: gave up farming and took up drinking, fighting, and hunting. After he half scalped his stepbrother in a drunken fight, he lit out west.

In the ten years before he reached Fall Creek, he had calmed down considerably. He still looked like a rakehell instead of a Baptist elder, which he'd become since marrying Ora, but pious living, given time, might cure that. He'd given up drink, farmed hard, and hunted only for meat for the table. Whatever he might have felt about Indian girls before, he now had eyes only for Ora.

He'd have been crazy, Hannah thought, otherwise. Ora was as sleek and pretty as a dove, so plump and lustrous she hardly seemed human. And her acts were those of a Christian woman. Hannah's father, who was the nearest to a preacher the settlement had, said that Ora lived in the Light, and Hannah believed him.

The two girls sat together on the deacon's bench beside the fire. The two men faced each other across the table. Lute brought out a jug of cider and poured a mug for each. Jud Clasby swallowed his first mouthful and looked as if he'd had a helping of quinine. "Sweet cider? Ain't you got anything better'n this, Lute?"

"Springwater."

"What's hit you?"

"Common sense's likely the name."

"When I think of the jugs you and me's emptied!"

"I've changed."

"Well, there's nothing so strong as a pretty woman's apron strings to tie a man down." Clasby smiled at Ora, but it was a gibe nevertheless. As if Lute had been more of a man before.

Lute didn't turn a hair. "It's a fact. Tied the strings myself and don't plan to ever unloosen them of my own free will."

Hannah, tied not of her own free will but by touch to Jud Clasby, couldn't keep her mind on Ora's talk. She listened to Jud.

"What I came about," he was saying, "is I need your help in tracking a lost horse of mine. I reckon you can still track."

Lute ignored the soft soap. "Strayed, you mean?"

"Stolen's likely the name for it."

"Got any idea who?"

"The Indians down at Rocky Point. I seen tracks there."

"I'm through fighting Indians."

"Who's talking about fighting? You through helping friends?"

"I ain't reformed that far yet. When do you want to look?"

"The sooner the better. I'm on my way out of here and I need that horse. If you're willing to give me a hand, I'll pick you up tomorrow morning."

HANNAH wouldn't have gone on to the Bensons' with Clasby except that the Bensons lived on her way home. And whatever she thought of George Benson, Sarah and her six children were good neighbors.

At the Bensons', supper was late, and they were asked to join the family meal. The fare was good: stewed squirrel, johnnycake, and hot, sweet sassafras tea.

George Benson was a big-shouldered, heavy-handed man. When he clapped a hand down on the table, the crockery jumped. "Jud, you're just the man I want to see. I could do the job single-handed, but two hands are always better than one—especially if one of the hands has had the practice you've had."

"You mean Rocky Point and the sugar camp?"

"You been thinking about it, too?"

"I been sounding out folks. About got it lined up, I think."

"Wasn't you going to ask me?"

"What do you think I'm here for?"

"Sparking Hannah, maybe. She needs a full-grown man, not that weedy Wood young un."

"George," Sarah Benson warned. "Hannah's company."

Benson gave Hannah's broad shoulder a hearty slap. "Hannah knows I'm teasing her. Why, if I hadn't met you first, Sarah, I'd be courting her myself."

"She's man-shy," Clasby said. "I've found that out."

"What man's she known? Father's nine-tenths a preacher, and John Jr.'s nine-tenths a girl."

Hannah wanted to sail into George Benson, talking that way about her father and Johnny. But she wanted even more to get the talk turned away from herself.

"What are you planning to do at the sugar camp?"

"Break up the camp."

"Break it up? Why? What harm have they done?"

"Harm? If a man asked me that question, I'd flatten him. What harm? They killed my grandfather. They thought I was dead or they would've killed me. They're animals. We kill wolves, who do us less harm. Nothing's safe as long as they lurk around. There's land to spare west of here. They ought to be given their walking papers. And the only walking papers they understand is lead."

"What harm have *these* Indians done?" Hannah persisted.

"They're Indians. That's the harm they've done. If you're so Indian crazy, go be a squaw. You don't belong here."

Hannah slid off the bench. "I'm going home. Don't come with me, Mr. Clasby. It's no more than a step."

Sarah said, "Hannah, don't hold what George said against him. He's out of his senses on that one subject."

"He told me, 'You don't belong here.' And I don't. Good night, Sarah."

"I'll see you across the crick," Clasby said. "Then you can go on home alone. George and me's got more talking to do."

In the middle of the footbridge, Clasby said, "If you make a wish over running water, you'll get it."

"I wish I was home," Hannah said.

At the other side of the bridge, Clasby said, "Use them long legs and you'll have your wish."

Hannah, half crying because of what George Benson had said, was in disarray: her shawl on one side hung almost to her knees. Clasby pulled the shawl even, crossed the ends neatly, then circled each breast with a hand. Hannah's first inclination was to throw herself crying into his arms. But was she going to ask this man, who had said nothing of love, to handle her again in his free and easy way? He could not make her ask that. But she had to do *something*. She hit him, a half shove, half hit. He was on a slope, no more expecting to receive a blow than she was to give one. It was either slide into the creek or sit down. He sat.

"You damn little wildcat. The next time you want to rassle, give me some warning, and we'll have a real tussle."

"I'm not little."

"You damn *big* cat. I'll rassle you to a fare-thee-well."

Then Hannah turned and ran.

The fire was banked and her father and mother were in bed when she got home. She felt her way up the ladder to the loft, where she and Ben slept, he at one end, she at the other. There was a window at her end, a nicety given to her because she was a girl and glass was too precious for everybody to have his own. Now she opened that window and leaned out, trying to put the evening's happenings out of her mind. She wanted to think how small she was under the distant stars. What was the fire Jud Clasby had stirred up in her, compared with them? What was the hurt of Reba's calling her a courting girl and George Benson's calling her a squaw? Stand in somebody else's shoes for a while, she told herself. Love Johnny, forgive Reba, forgive Benson, forget Clasby.

There was a rustling from Ben's cornhusk bed. "Shut that window, Hannah. You want to freeze us to death?"

As she pulled the window shut, an owl hooted.

"It could be an Indian. Ben, could you shoot an Indian?"

"If he was going to shoot me," Ben grunted sleepily.

"But not in cold blood."

"No."

"They're our enemies. Everybody says so, except Papa."

"You can shoot 'em. I'm going to leave them alone."

Hannah wanted to sit down on her brother's bed. She wanted to tell him everything that had happened that night. But Jud Clasby's touch had changed her baby brother; it had made Ben a man. She couldn't, now, throw her arms about his neck and tell him her troubles. They weren't troubles she was proud of.

She put on her nightgown and knelt by her bed. Most times, praying was as natural to Hannah as breathing. But tonight all she could say, over and over, was, "Help me, God. Help me."

THE next day was Saturday. Hannah's mother, Lizzie, with Hannah's help, spent the day cooking. Since there was no church in the settlement, settlers who were churchgoers met at the Cape cabin. It was the one chance of the week to see a face that didn't belong to your own family, and to hear, in addition to whatever news was making the rounds, one of Caleb Cape's hair-raising sermons. It wasn't that Caleb was any hell-and-brimstone preacher (though he didn't let you forget that, either). What Caleb had that made people willing to ride ten miles, fording streams and picking their way around fallen trees, was a God-blessed gift of gab. Listening to him, people thanked God they were alive and living in such a paradise. It was usually a comedown after the preaching to ride home to a lean-to or shanty and all the younger inhabitants bawling their heads off for supper.

Each Sunday Caleb promised his wife that *next* Sunday he would not ask everybody to stay and have a bite. But the next Sunday he did ask them. So Lizzie spent her Saturdays cooking. The neighbors, in any case, had taken to bringing in some food of their own.

315

Lizzie was thirty-four, Caleb thirty-six. They thought of themselves, and so did everybody else, as middle-aged. If Hannah hadn't been so standoffish, they'd have been grandparents by now. Lizzie had no trouble seeing herself as a grandmother. Caleb as a grandfather gave her imagination quite a stretch. He was as pretty as a May apple, but so big and slab-sided you forgave him his long eyewinkers and his glossy locks. If a man wasn't headed toward God, a face like that could get him into a lot of earthly trouble. Lizzie thanked God her husband had turned to Him.

Caleb Cape was a jackanapes, too, a cutup, a clown. There was nothing he liked better than making people laugh. Lizzie endured and Hannah winced when Caleb, drunk with high spirits, started playing the fool. He knew he had this weakness, and held himself on a tight rein, though he didn't think that man, made in God's image, glorified his Maker by going around looking like he'd just bit into a green persimmon. Nor were folks who were holding their sides from laughing in any proper mood for a bath in the Blood of the Lamb. He knew that.

The Sunday feeling began to boil up in Caleb as soon as Saturday dinner was over. By midafternoon Saturday, where they were now, the love of God was fizzing up in him, too high for corking. Since the only congregation he had at hand was Lizzie and Hannah, they got the full force of his pre-Sabbath jubilation. Hannah was taking something in the nature of a pudding from the oven—dried pumpkin, sweetened with maple sugar, thinned down with milk, and thickened up with four precious eggs.

"Never seen a prettier dish," Caleb said. He tasted the venison stew that Lizzie was cooking. "It smells like back home at Thanksgiving time."

He picked up Lizzie, squeezed her tight, and kissed her on the mouth. Lizzie squirmed in his arms like a hooked eel. "Hannah," she reminded him.

Caleb kissed her again. "High time that girl learned that there are worse things in this world than kissing."

Hannah, her cheeks flaming, bent over her pudding.

Caleb was no namby-pamby preacher too delicate for the world the Lord had put him in. He knew Lizzie liked to be kissed; and he hadn't married his wife to suit his daughter. But he was not coarse-grained. He put Lizzie down, didn't say anything further to embarrass Hannah, and went outside. Ben, that softhearted young giant, puffed up from some business of his own back in the woods and said, "Pa, can I go hunting with Johnny Wood?"

"You've had all week to hunt, Ben. I don't like the sound of guns popping off on Sabbath eve."

"Can I go if I don't do any shooting?"

"If you want to go for a run through the woods, I got no objection. Only see you run back in time for supper."

"I'll be back before dark."

He kept his word. It was early twilight and they had just settled down to their supper of milk gravy and corn bread when Ben came in. One look at him stopped all forks in midair. "What happened to you?" his father asked. "You meet a bear?"

"Maybe he met an Injun," Hannah teased.

Ben, who had been about to pull out his stool, jumped like he was bee-stung and ran out the door. All forks at the table were put down at the sound of his dry retching.

"Hannah, take him a dipperful of water," Caleb said.

Hannah carried the water to Ben. He was on his knees, his head resting against a rick of wood, his sides going in and out like a horse with the heaves. "Is it something you ate?" Hannah asked gently. Ben shook his head.

"Come on in. You can't stay out here all night."

"Let me alone," he whispered.

Hannah ran inside. "He's sick, Mama, and he won't get up."

Lizzie half rose. Caleb said, "Best leave him alone."

But when bedtime came, Caleb said, "He'll have to come in, if I have to lug him. Whatever ails him, lung fever won't help."

Lizzie and Hannah half expected some struggle from Ben, but there was none. After a few minutes he walked into the house a step or two ahead of his father.

"What's the trouble, son?" Caleb felt his son's forehead.

"I'm sick."

"You don't feel hot. Touch of the ague, like as not. Now you get up to bed. A night's sleep's the best medicine."

Ben climbed the ladder to the loft without a word.

II

THIS Sunday morning the Sabbath feeling was gone from Caleb's heart. Ben still lay in his bed refusing to move, speak, or eat. Hannah reported he'd cried all night, and wouldn't let her near him. But it wasn't just Ben's sickness, if sickness it was. The day, after a chilly night, had faired off; too warm for February, more like May. He liked nature to hold steady, not make you sweat in February. Such weather brought deaths in March.

His uneasiness caused Caleb to start the morning services off in a quieter manner than customary. Usually, when about half of those expected to attend were in their places, he led them in singing without waiting for the stragglers. Today he hadn't the heart for singing. The senior Woods were there, the Bensons, the Pryces. Luther Bemis, faithful churchgoer, hadn't yet arrived. Jud Clasby, no churchman, but who had come to the meeting (for the home cooking, likely) the last two Sundays, was absent. And four or five families who lived down near the north fork of Fall Creek were not yet here.

Caleb said, "We'll put off our singing until we're all together. Meanwhile, I will read to you the Twenty-third Psalm." He was reading for his own sake, hoping the comforting words would raise his spirits. *"The Lord is my shepherd; I shall not want. He maketh me to lie down in green pastures . . ."* Caleb had his eyes shut. He was praying the psalm rather than reading it. His heavyheartedness was easing up. He forgot he had listeners; he was speaking directly to God. A shout brought him back.

"Get her out of here!"

In the door of the cabin, carried on a quilt held by four men and two women, lay a blood-soaked squaw.

"Get that squaw out of here. Don't you know this is a church meeting?" Benson shouted again.

The North Fork people hesitated; then Caleb, with a voice more carrying than Benson's, said, "Bring her in. She's hurt."

Caleb went to help the men place the woman he knew to be Talking Crow on his and Lizzie's bed. He was sorry for the blood-stains, but he didn't value a coverlet more than a human being. The squaw had a wound near the base of her throat—a gaping bullet hole, by its looks.

Caleb need not have worried about Lizzie's coverlet. The squaw would not stay down, and no one wanted to use force on a woman whose throat bubbled bloody air as she breathed. Talking Crow, gray with loss of blood, rose slowly to her feet.

"You kill me," she said in English. "I not die on your bed."

She faced George Benson. She spat at him, a bloody froth. "Woman killer. Child killer," she said hoarsely.

Benson rose, reaching for a wooden ladle on the table. Caleb wrestled him down to the bench he had risen from. "George, this is a church meeting."

"Not when the savages come in."

The disturbance brought Ben halfway down the ladder from the loft. He looked fully as sick as Talking Crow.

"What's going on?" he asked blankly.

"Nothing you had backbone for," Benson said.

Talking Crow looked at Ben. "You no help Folded Leaf."

Ben did not appear to hear her. He came on down the ladder as if sleepwalking. At the bottom he fell with a sodden thump of flesh onto the floor and lay there, face down.

Talking Crow watched him fall. "You kill me," she told the others. "I not die in your house." She passed her hand over the flowing wound on her throat and pointed a finger dripping blood at Benson. "When you die, you remember."

Slowly but without wavering, the old squaw went out the door and down the two log steps. On the bottom step she gave a last cry, the cry of a brave at death. Then she fell forward.

Some started toward Talking Crow, but Caleb barred the way. "I'll tend to her—if she's still alive." He bent over and studied her. "Her troubles are over," he said.

Hannah, while the others were watching Talking Crow, went to Ben. He was clammy, limp as a dead snake. But alive. She sat on the floor beside him, waiting.

Everyone in the room was talking at once. Hannah tried to sort out the words. The North Fork folks were trying to tell where and how they had found Talking Crow. Each one wanted to tell exactly how he felt. How upsetting it was that Indians as peaceful as those at the sugar camp had been killed. Nobody doubted that settlers had done it. The Indians were crowding in too close. They had to be taught to keep their distance. Indiana was a state now, not a frontier settlement, and had as much right as Massachusetts or old Virginia to cast out the red men. Somebody had done this killing— how or when, who knew? But why was plain to all.

Caleb put an end to the hubbub. "This is not the Tower of Babel," he said. "We need to know what you saw, and one at a time is all we can hear. Ebon Hall, you tell us."

Eb Hall was the right man to call on. He wasn't tongue-tied. Neither was he inclined to make an account of human hapchance sound like God's report of the Creation.

"All of us from up North Fork way was on our way to church. You all know the trace we follow—a hundred yards or so from Rocky Point and the sugar camp there. There was no one around, but I didn't think anything of it. It was along about the old Jessup place that Maggie Bushnell said, 'I hear something.'

"Well, you can always hear something in the woods, but this was a human voice. Sick or hurt. We followed the sound to the Jessup well. The stuff the Jessups had put in it to fill it up when they moved away had sunk. Now it's more sinkhole than well. Kind of a deep saucer. The voice was coming from there. From down under a lot of dead bodies. We pulled them out."

"How many?" a neighbor named Brewster asked.

"Two girls. Two boys. Three women. The woman we brought here was at the bottom of the heap."

"What'd she say when you pulled her out?"

"Not a word. Except for the groaning, I'd of thought she was dead. She didn't come to till we carried her in here."

George Benson got to his feet. "Why did you bring her here? Why didn't you leave her with her own kind?"

Ebon Hall's wife, Phoebe, spoke up. "She's an old woman. When I'm an old woman, I wouldn't want to be left to die like that."

Benson had an answer to that. "She's an old woman for sure. She's the mother and grandmother of men that killed my folks. She's likely hacked white prisoners to death with her own hands. I shot the old squaw, and you'll thank me for it. Next year the redskins'll keep their distance and you'll all breathe easier."

George Benson's sister, Reba Wood, jumped up. "One thing George left out. He didn't do it all single-handed."

"I wasn't meaning to hog the credit, Reba. But in this sort of thing, every man's got the right to speak for himself."

"Well, my husband's one to hang back when it comes to claiming credit. But I want you to know he was right there at Rocky Point, and he done every bit as good as brother George. Young John did his part, too. That boy growed up yesterday. My two men gave every bit as good account of themselves as brother George."

Hannah, who had been huddled over Ben, half hearing, did hear Reba. "What did you say about Johnny?" she called out.

"I said Johnny killed Indians with the best of them."

Hannah, not believing, asked, "Johnny did that?"

"You been doing your best to make a man of him, ain't you, Hannah? Well, he's a man now. He's been blooded."

"I wasn't trying to get him to kill anybody."

"A man finds his manhood the best way he can."

Ben, hearing the argument, if that was what it was, pulled himself, unnoticed, back up the ladder to the loft.

Ebon Hall said, "I ain't concerned about John Jr.'s manhood. What I worry about is what Colonel Johnston, the Indian agent, is going to do when he hears about it."

"Who's in charge of this country?" Benson shouted. "Indians and their softhearted agents, or us? Move in with the redskins if you're so sweet on them, Eb Hall. You'll never be missed."

"We'll all be missed if the tribes to the north take it into their heads they got a little revenge coming."

George Benson erupted like a wounded bear. "I never thought I'd see the day when men of my own country and color would take the side of Indians against me!"

"Let's clear out of here, George," Reba said. "These folks want to have a powwow, not a church meeting."

"You're right, Reba. The place has got an Indian stink."

George and Sarah Benson, their six children, and the two Woods left the meeting—before a prayer had been said.

A hot gush of feeling ran along Hannah's veins. Her father, his church, and God Himself were being discredited. She sprang to her feet and called out, "This has stopped being a church. But it's still Sunday, and if we pray, maybe God will forgive us."

CALEB and Lizzie urged upon their neighbors the food they had brought. But they left it behind, as if it, too, had been sullied by what had been said and done. "We'll pick up the pans later."

The Capes weren't hungry, either. Lizzie had gone up to reason with Ben. They had some idea now of what ailed the boy.

Caleb and Hannah carried Talking Crow to the bed of the wagon. They put the bloody quilt over her.

"We can't leave her here," Hannah said.

"For a while we can," Caleb answered. "I'm going to walk over to Rocky Point. I want to see for myself what happened."

"Can I go with you?" She was too upset to stay home.

"What you'll see won't be very pretty."

"I know that."

It was a three-mile walk, with nothing but the woods, there like they'd always been: oak, walnut, hickory, sycamores, and the sugar maples that brought the Indians back each year. The trees weren't leafed out yet, so they walked through bars of sunshine. It was a day to rejoice in. "It shouldn't have happened on Sunday," Caleb said. Then he took it back. "The day don't matter. The deed makes the day, not the other way round."

Hannah said, "Reba drove Johnny to help Benson. I heard her tell him he was a weakling. She shamed him into it."

"There are other ways of proving your strength."

"That's the way that come up first."

There was no arguing with Hannah about Johnny Wood's reasons for doing what he did. If he did anything. They had nothing but Reba's word for it that he did.

Caleb's mind was split three ways, divided among what had been, was, and would be. He remembered the dying woman, her look and words. While he remembered that, he also saw a raccoon peer out at him from the hollow of a tulip tree. A pair of eagles sat motionless at the top of a lightning-blasted sycamore. But more vivid than either the present he walked through or the morning just past was the imagined scene toward which he advanced.

At the edge of the half-cleared Jessup place, Caleb sighted what he'd come to see: the bodies pulled out of the sinkhole and sprawled where they'd been laid in the haste to get at the woman who still lived. For a minute he couldn't go on. "Well, George didn't lie about what had been done," he said.

Hannah faced away from the bodies, staring at a beech tree as if her life depended on memorizing the number of its limbs.

"There's no call for you to come, Hannah," Caleb said.

She listened to her father's retreating footsteps going away, then ran after him. "I don't want to be left alone."

Hannah had never seen death before. At first sight these dead were as lifeless as boulders, stumps, forest litter to be stepped over. As she came closer they became human beings asleep in awkward positions.

All except Folded Leaf. He was a boy she'd seen playing in the creek. He wasn't a boy anymore. Where his face had been there was a clot of offal like she'd seen at butchering time when the job had been botched. They were tidier with hogs. A pain sharp and sickening went through her. "Ben saw this?"

"Saw it done, maybe."

"Where were the Indian men? Why didn't they help?"

"How do I know?" Caleb was in no mood for talk. The old Jessup place was melancholy enough without dead bodies. Somebody had tried here and given up. They had dug a well to save their girls from the fever that creek water was said to give. And the girls had died from drinking well water. The Jessups had filled in the well to keep wandering livestock from breaking a leg, then backtracked east, defeated. It was a place most people stayed away from, the perfect place in which to hide the dead Indians.

Caleb was sorry for snapping at Hannah. Her questions were natural. He could figure only one answer. "The men must have been ambushed," he told her. "I'm going to take a look around. You don't need to come."

She needed to. She couldn't stay there alone with the dead bodies. But the bodies went with her, filling her mind.

Her father spoke. "There." She followed his pointing finger. Up the trace ahead of them, kneeling, forehead to ground, was a man in prayer. He was dead, his shirt black with dried blood. "It's Tall Tree, shot in the back. Tolled away from camp on some trumped-up excuse so they'd be free to finish off the women and children."

"There were two men," Hannah reminded him.

"The other is probably nearby. Hannah, I can't leave these people lying here like scraps thrown out for dogs. I'm going to put them back in the well. Tomorrow I'll bury them all. You'll have to help me carry Tall Tree. I can't heft a man his size."

Caleb took the bulk of the load; even so, Tall Tree's legs angled downward in Hannah's grasp. A moccasin dropped from his foot. "Papa," Hannah called, then shut her mouth. She staggered under the weight. The effort kept her mind off the burden she carried.

Red Cloud was where her father had thought he might be—in the opposite direction and about the same distance from the camp. He lay on his back, a bullet hole in his stomach, a knife wound in his throat. He was lighter than Tall Tree, easier to carry.

It was full dark when Caleb and Hannah got home, bloodstained and bone-tired. Lizzie didn't pester them with questions until they'd washed and changed. They sat down to the good food that hadn't been eaten at midday, and that they couldn't eat now.

"What did you find?" Lizzie asked when she saw there was going to be no eating.

"Just what George said we would. Dead Indians."

"There was a fight?"

"No signs of that."

"Shot down in cold blood?"

"Worse. Planned. I'm going to bury them in the morning."

"That'll be quite an undertaking, Caleb."

"Ben can help."

"Ben's still sick."

"Try Lute Bemis, Papa," Hannah said. "I was at the Bemises' when he told Jud Clasby he was through fighting Indians. He'd be just the one to help you."

III

CALEB took Hannah's advice. After the supper he couldn't eat, he set out in the cold clear night for the Bemis cabin.

The Bemises had no candles lighted, no fire burning. Caleb thought twice about rousing them if they'd gone to bed. While he was thinking it over, Ora called out sharply, "Who's there?"

"Cale Cape. If you're in bed, I'll come in the morning."

Ora unbolted the door. "Come in. Lute's feeling poorly, but I'm up." She put a couple of sticks on the fire and seated herself in the rocker, hunched up in her wrapper like a bird in cold weather. Lute lay face to the wall, a big bundle of bedclothes.

"Nothing serious, I hope," Caleb said.

"He can't hold anything on his stomach. But he's got no fever. By morning he'll be good as new, I hope."

"I missed you both at church."

"We missed coming. But Lute was in no shape to put in an appearance. And he didn't want me to make the walk by myself."

"It's just as well you didn't try—in your shape. What happened wouldn't have been good for the baby."

"What could hurt a baby at church?"

"We didn't have any church. The folks from North Fork brought in a half-dead squaw from the sugar camp. She said a few words and died. Benson and old Wood, or at least Reba Wood, admitted they'd done it. Boasted about it's nearer the truth. And whoever done it, they're all dead. Men, women, and children."

"You saw it?" Ora asked.

"Hannah and me went up there together."

"Hannah's got a lot of grit for a girl."

"No more per inch, I reckon, than you."

"Did she tell about Clasby being here night before last?"

"That's why I'm here. I'm going to give those folks a resting place underground, not leave them for wolf bait. I come, knowing from Hannah how Lute felt, to get his help."

"He's so poorly—" Ora began, but Lute interrupted her.

"I'll be at your place tomorrow at sunup, Cale."

"If you don't feel like it . . ."

"I'll feel up to it. Did anybody at church mention Clasby?"

"Nobody. Reba was so anxious to claim all the glory for her men, nobody else could get an oar in once she'd started."

"The squaw?"

"She died before she'd had her full say."

Lute, with an unexpected movement, threw all the bedclothes aside and stood tall and white in his long underwear.

"Pray for me, Cale. I missed church today. I ain't so steady in the Light as I'd like to be. I need help."

Caleb said, "There was no church to miss today."

"Where two or three are gathered together in His name," Ora reminded them, "that's church."

So the three had a little church of their own then and there, and Caleb walked home easier in his heart than he'd been all day.

CALEB and Lizzie were at the breakfast table next morning when Ora arrived in a cold drizzle of rain. "I come to tell you Lute's had a setback. He's feverish and got the shakes. I set my foot down against his coming. I'm in no shape to be a widow." She was the only one who laughed at her joke.

She wouldn't eat or linger. She wouldn't hear of anyone walking home with her. "The baby's snug," she assured them, "and Lute needs me. All that talk of killing was too much for him."

"Sounds like Lute and Ben both been hit by the same complaint," Caleb said, as he watched her leave. He put his hand on Lizzie's.

"Ben's going with me this morning. I'll take Hannah, too. This rain'll freeze before it lets up. I don't mind digging wet ground, but frozen ground's something else." He went to the loft ladder. "Ben, Hannah, get down here. We're leaving in fifteen minutes."

They came down at once, Hannah first. Ben's hair hung down, lifeless as a sick cat's. It was combed, though, his shirt buttoned, his back ramrod straight. He looked like a man ready to walk to his own grave. When the corn dodgers and syrup were put in front of him, he shook his head. "My stomach's still unsettled."

"You can't work on an empty stomach, son."

"It'd be empty, anyway, the next minute after I swallowed."

"Ben, you got some reason for not wanting to help me?"

"I want to help you. I'm going to. I never said not."

"Hannah, I'm going to need you, too. Luther Bemis's sick."

CALEB sat on the floor of the wagon beside Talking Crow's body and told Ben to drive. "Up by the old well," he directed.

Before they were there, he saw that branches that he and Hannah had placed over the well lay scattered about. Caleb was out of the wagon before Ben could pull up the horses. He did not find what he expected; animals had not been there. Indians had. There were tracks of moccasins and unshod horses about the sinkhole. All the bodies were gone. The hair on the back of Caleb's neck rose as his skin tightened. Decent burial for a dead Indian was one thing. The presence of live Indians was a different matter.

"Get down in the wagon bed," he yelled to his children.

He peered into the trees. He scanned the ruins of the Jessup place. Was there any movement in there? He thought better of the command he had given Ben and Hannah before the words were cool in his mouth. If redskins were about, better be out in the open. "Hannah, Ben. Come here."

Hannah, there first, exclaimed, "The bodies are gone!"

"I'm glad they're gone," Ben said.

"They didn't just go, Ben. Somebody took them."

"How did they know where they were?" Hannah asked.

"Indians keep pretty good track of each other."

"You got a gun with you, Papa?" Ben asked.

"You know I have. I never leave the house without one. But this is a burying party, not a shooting party. We'll put Talking Crow in the well and cover her up. The Indians'll be back for her."

"Do they know where she is now?" Hannah asked.

"My guess would be they do."

Hannah, while Ben and her father put Talking Crow back where she'd been found, walked up toward the sugar camp. She wasn't frightened by the thought that Indians might be near. Since Friday evening she had felt that the course of her life had gone out of her hands. Two days and a few hours; yet in that time either she was a changed girl or was only becoming acquainted with the girl she really was. On Friday her heart had been engraved on every cookie she gave to Johnny Wood. Two hours later the touch of Jud Clasby's hands had turned her to jelly. On Sunday she had seen a dying squaw spitting blood, then dragged dead men to their graves. Now she'd been told Indians might fall upon them at any minute. Yet she felt calm. If it was to happen, it would.

She stumbled, without noticing where she was walking, onto what she took at first to be a boulder. It was a big deerskin bag stuffed tight and the top held close by a rawhide drawstring. Burned in the skin were the initials J.C. Instinctively Hannah drew her hand across the soft suede bulge of the bag. It was his. She lifted it up; it was heavy. Slowly she carried it back to her father.

Caleb, who never swore, said when he saw her, "In God's name, Hannah, don't go wandering off that way without letting us know. What've you picked up?"

Hannah pointed to the initials. "Jud Clasby's, I reckon."

"Ben, was Clasby there?"

Ben looked at the ground.

Caleb stared at his son. "I can't thrash you into talking. You know that. But the sooner you tell me what you know, the better."

He untied the drawstring. What spilled out were the best peltries of the Indians' trapping, knives, beaded decorations, bowls. Clasby had skinned the camp of its valuables. "Thievery," Caleb said.

Killing Indians was one thing. Benson could boast of that. But "I stole" was a confession nobody was likely to make.

Caleb left the bag and its contents where it had fallen.

"Won't the Indians find it?" Ben said.

"Let them," said Caleb. "It belongs to them. They were likely chasing Clasby when he dropped this."

It was hailing as they drove home.

The horses, Acorn and Oak, so named because one was the father of the other, one little, one big, walked with lowered heads and at a good pace, barn-eager. No one spoke.

Hannah tried to draw herself into a knot of unfeeling flesh—not against the hail, but against memory. On a single day she had been ready to clasp two different men: one a killer, the other a thief and killer. She was riding with her eyes shut. She would not have known that they had turned into their own lane except for her father's wild shout and the sudden jerk of the wagon. She opened her eyes to see him already halfway to their door, in which an arrow was planted, standing straight out.

Hannah leaped out after her father, screaming, "Mama, Mama!"

Lizzie herself opened the door, alarmed by all the commotion. "Caleb, what's happened? What's the trouble? Is somebody hurt?"

Caleb grabbed his wife in his arms. Hannah circled around, patting both. She had something she could cry for now without having to explain, so she sobbed, "Mama, Mama."

"Oh, thank God, praise God," Caleb said. "You're all right?"

"I may have a cracked rib soon if you don't let up your hugging. But I was pretty sound till you got home."

Caleb loosened his arms. "You didn't see or hear anything?"

"I heard the hail. What else was there to see or hear?"

Caleb pulled his wife outside and closed the door. When she saw the arrow, the color went out of her face. "What's the meaning of it, Caleb?"

"I thought I'd find you scalped. I *was* relieved," Caleb said, "when I saw you with your hair." Caleb's tendency, when stirred up, was to joke.

Lizzie looked at the arrow again. "Is there any need for us to be standing out here in the hail?"

"No," said Caleb, "there ain't." It took a hard tug to get the arrow out of the double oak door. It had been sent with force.

When they were all inside, Lizzie, who now was as upset as she had been calm, bolted the door. Caleb stood in front of the fireplace, turning the arrow in his hands. It was an arrow of the old days, feathered with red hawk tail and tipped with chipped quartz. He could not help admiring its beauty. It was the nearest to a bird a man had ever made; but it flew to kill.

"Burn it," Lizzie begged. "Throw it in the fire."

"No, I'm going to keep it, Lizzie. In the first place, the killing part of it wouldn't burn. It will last long after all of us have gone to dust. In the second place, it was sent to us by a friend."

"It was sent to us by an Indian, wasn't it?"

"I judge so. But he sent it as a friend. Indians never been ones to warn you before they take their revenge. But somebody has warned us. Considering what's been done, that's more than we've got any right to expect."

"But we didn't do anything," Hannah said.

"We're part and parcel, as far as Indians are concerned, of the murders at the sugar camp."

"Murders," Hannah repeated, shocked. "Is killing an Indian murder?"

"If all he's doing is boiling a pot of maple sap, I don't know what other word fits."

AFTER an hour's rest and a bowl of hot bean-and-venison soup, Caleb and Ben set out to tell the neighbors that the bodies had been taken from the sugar camp, and that someone had put an arrow in Cale Cape's door. They were home before candlelighting time, and after an early supper Caleb shooed the young ones up to bed. "You've both had a big day," he told them. "Now, scat."

He didn't himself go to bed that night. Oh, he took off his outer clothes and stretched out now and then beside Lizzie. But mostly he stood in front of the fire and rehearsed what had happened and what he thought he should do. After he knew what he thought, he was accustomed to weigh his conclusions against Lizzie's convictions. She was no "as my husband says" woman.

"The Brewsters," he told her, "are already packing to move into Pendleton until this blows over."

"There's no blockhouse there."

"No, but there're two hundred people instead of twenty. Of course, the Bensons and the Woods say that arrow wasn't any warning. Just somebody trying to throw a scare into us."

"Why us instead of them?"

"I reckon they think we scare easier'n them."

"Don't it enter their heads that what they did may stir up the tribes to the north?"

"Nobody except the Brewsters thinks it could come to that. They're all so used to these peaceful sugar-camp, calico-buying Indians, they think some trinkets and a jugful of rum would settle things."

The sleet had let up and now the room was filled with the soft owl-feather swish of falling snow. Lizzie dozed off. When she woke near her usual time—before daylight—Caleb was dressed, had a kettle boiling, and sliced mush frying in the spider.

"No need to be up so early on a day like this, Caleb," she said. "What can you do?"

"I've thought about it all night. I'm going to Piqua. To see the Indian agent. If Brewster's right, Colonel Johnston's likely the only man who can head the Indians off if they're thinking of making a sweep down here."

"Wait till the weather moderates," Lizzie urged. "Piqua's two hundred miles. 'Bout as well stay home and be scalped as go out and die in a snowbank."

Caleb laughed and didn't know why. "No, I'd choose the snowbank any day—and take you with me, if I thought that was the choice. But I'll tell you something, Lizzie. I'm not intended for snowbanks, nor you for scalping. We're going to have to tough it out along more everyday lines."

The mush was overfried and the sassafras tea had steeped too long. Lizzie couldn't swallow a bite and Caleb didn't want to. He filled himself full, anyway. He wasn't going to fizzle out for lack of fuel. When he had finished, he said, "I'm going up and have a few words with Hannah."

Hannah, at the sound of her name, was awake. Caleb sat down on her bed and kept his voice low. No use rousing Ben.

"Hannah, I'm going to ride to Piqua to tell the Indian agent there what happened. I don't think there'll be trouble here. . . ."

"Trouble?" Hannah whispered.

"Indians. If there is, if you get warning, get your mother and Ben into Pendleton. If there's no warning, give up. You and Ben are young; if you don't fight, they'll likely adopt you."

"Make a squaw out of me?"

"There's been more than one child adopted by the Indians who wouldn't go back to their families when they had a chance."

"If we don't fight, what's to become of Mama?" When Caleb didn't answer, Hannah said, "They'll kill her, won't they?"

"They'll kill all of you if you fight. Burn you alive in this house. None of this is likely, Hannah. I wouldn't leave if I thought it was. I told you because I trust your good sense."

Hannah followed her father down the ladder. There, with Lizzie, they knelt before the fire, and Caleb prayed. "May the Lord watch between me and thee while we are absent one from the other," he ended the prayer. Then he folded Lizzie in his arms.

He kissed Hannah and gave her a hearty handshake. "Ben's too young and your mother's too ladylike for the job, so I appoint you man of the house while I'm gone."

A few hours after Caleb left, there was a heavy rapping on the door and George Benson's shout. "You home, Mrs. Cape?"

"We're home," Hannah answered, and opened the door.

Jess Abernathy, a tall man, part Indian himself, people said, who lived a mile or so beyond the Bensons, was with George. The men, wet from the icy drizzle, stood steaming in front of the fire.

"Mrs. Cape," George Benson said, "where's Cale?"

"I don't know."

"On his way to Piqua?"

"Yes."

Benson turned to Abernathy. "You were right. Why would he tell you and not me?"

"He knew you'd raise a ruckus."

"He's gone to ask the agent to quiet the Indians," Lizzie said.

Benson gave the table a slap Lizzie knew he would rather have given her husband. "The agent! All that man Johnston does is baby the Indians. And now Cale runs off to this Indian lover to get help. What he'll do is to get us forbidden to drop a hook in Fall Creek or trap a muskrat on its banks."

"Caleb's risking his own life in this weather to try to save your life," Lizzie said sternly.

Benson snorted. "Preachers would be better off to stay home and pray. Cale's not satisfied to leave matters in the Lord's hands. Oh, no. Cale wants a finger in everybody's pie."

Hannah grabbed the heavy twig broom and swung it in a semi-circle that caught Benson across the side of the head.

"What's going on here?" he shouted. "You lost your senses?"

"You get out of here, or I'll knock *you* senseless."

Benson made a move toward Hannah, but Abernathy held his arm. Hannah, using the broom as a battering ram, shoved Benson toward the door. "You get out of my father's house before you say another word against him."

"I'll get out, but I'll ride after your father and bring him back before he ever lays eyes on Piqua."

Hannah closed the door with a bang, then set the broom in its place by the hearth. "He can't catch Oak. He knows that. He's just talking big," she reassured her mother.

HANNAH was right. Abernathy talked Benson out of trying to follow Caleb. "He'll never make it in this weather, anyway."

Caleb made it; but not in the three or four days he had planned. It was a matter of weeks before he entered Johnston's office in Piqua. Johnston wasn't in. There was only a dark-haired young fellow who looked as if he'd never been out from behind a desk. He was the man, Caleb supposed, who looked after the papers while

334

Johnston was out in the forests looking after the Indians. This clerk would never be able to hold his own in any Indian powwow.

The young man leaped to push a chair toward Caleb. "Have a seat, sir. You look pretty peaked."

"I been sick," Caleb said. "Lung fever. I been in and out of my head for four weeks. I'd of died, except for a family outside Winchester who took me in. I set out in a storm to tell Johnston that nine Indians had been killed at a sugar camp in Fall Creek."

"We got that news right after it happened," the clerk said. "There's been more than Indians killed now."

"Where?" Caleb whispered. "Where? Not at Fall Creek?"

"No, no. Fifty, sixty miles north of there."

"How do you know that?"

"Indian friend of Johnston's, Black Antler, sent a runner. Wanted Johnston to smooth down the Indians up north."

"Can he do it?"

"If he's there, he can. But the news of the sugar-camp killings beat him there. The tribes up north, when they heard that, burned a couple of homesteads and killed everybody in them."

"That's what I want to stop. That's what I came here for."

"You couldn't have done any more good than Black Antler. Johnston himself couldn't, till the government promised that the men who murdered the Indians would be tried and punished the same as if they'd murdered white men."

"Murdered." Caleb remembered Hannah's shock at his use of that word. "Who is promising this trial? The governor?"

"You don't know our governor very good, do you? Woodsies vote. The Indians don't. The governor is not about to call voters murderers. No sirree bob. Not our governor."

Caleb was beginning to think this clerk might not be such a bad man at a powwow after all. "Then who did promise it?"

"Say, how long did you say you'd been sick? The United States Government, that's who. Calhoun, the Secretary of War."

"The Indians have heard a lot of promises."

"They'll believe Johnston. He's never broke his word to them yet, and he says these men are going to be tried. Better a few men in jail than the whole settlement wiped out. Captain Berry didn't have the least trouble getting the accused to jail, either. The burnings up north wasn't wasted on your folks."

"Jail! We ain't got a jail."

"You got one now. Or Pendleton has. They built one on purpose. Trial starts as soon as the circuit court meets there."

"Those men don't have money to hire lawyers."

"Calhoun knows that. Seven thousand dollars have been set aside for this. Four of the best lawyers from Ohio state are on their way to Pendleton to defend them right now. The regular state prosecutors will handle the case against the murderers."

The contents of Caleb's stomach started roiling about. He had come here to save bloodshed, not cause it. "Has any white man ever been convicted of murder for killing an Indian?" he asked.

"Not to my knowledge."

"But that's what Johnston's up there telling the Indians? White men will be tried for murder?"

"Yes."

"And if guilty?"

"You're sick, Mr. Cape. You know what happens when a court finds a man guilty of murder."

Caleb stood, but felt as if he was standing on air and sat down quickly. The clerk's hands bored into his shoulders. Caleb looked up at the man supporting him. "Do I know your name?"

"Hardesty, Jacob Hardesty."

"Thank you, Mr. Hardesty. I was weaker than I thought. I don't know what to think about what I just heard. I didn't want to get my neighbors thrown in jail for murder."

"You didn't do that. Black Antler and Mr. Calhoun did."

The man who killed a man ought to be hanged, Caleb thought. He had never doubted that. But wispy old John Wood? The Wood boy, who had no notion of right or wrong outside a book? Benson, a big ox who needed somebody saying gee-haw and whoa if he was to be kept on any straight path? Hang them? Praying churchgoers? And he the one, no matter who got there first, who went to Piqua to carry the news. What was he? Some kind of a Judas?

BOOK TWO

THE TRIAL

IV

HARDESTY was not exaggerating when he told Caleb that the federal government was supplying the accused men with superior counsel. Up from Ohio to Pendleton came Patrick Conroy, Noah Beazley, Isaac Vickers, and Charles Fort. All were able, eloquent lawyers with every intention of winning a decision for their clients. They were also men of a city called "Queen of the West," a substantial community that had earned its stability, they believed, by conquering the Indian population. If they could help it, no white man was going to be hanged for trying to protect Pendleton in the same way their own forebears had protected Cincinnati.

The federal government had one paramount purpose: *not* to give Indians the impression that this was a powwow called to belittle the red man. The defense lawyers were well known. They had to be. But the prosecution lawyers were famous.

Heading *them* was Senator James Noble, former soldier and Indian fighter. His assistant was his son-in-law, Abel Trask, a young lawyer with the reputation of being able to charm the rings off a raccoon's tail.

Jonathan Armitage, the state's prosecuting attorney, also had an assistant, Oscar Achilles Dilk, a black-haired, bullet-headed young man with a mind like a bear trap. Dilk was obviously headed for the Senate.

The Indian agent, Colonel Johnston, would be present during the entire trial. He had also been instructed to have Indian chiefs present to observe the trial and send the news back to the tribes: "White men are being tried for murder for killing Indians. It is a fair trial. If found guilty, they'll be hanged."

CHARLIE Fort, the youngest of the defense lawyers, twenty-four, had drawn the best lodging in town. Drawn, he knew, was not the right word. He had been offered, by the widow Culligan, the loft room in her Pendleton home because, she told him, "you look like my late son."

Charlie was accustomed to having lonesome widows tell him that he reminded them of their late husbands. "Late son" was more to his liking. He moved into the widow's loft room at once, without wasting pity on his fellow lawyers. They, the senator among them, were piled two in a bed in less commodious lodgings.

He doubted that he looked like the late son. "Charles Fort," he had been told, "you're an oddity." Not a mud-fence, ugly oddity. Kisses had told him that. Just no one else's spit and image. But who needed looks when he had luck? He got good horses at livery stables, helpings from the first serving at boardinghouses, and the best whiskey from bottles usually kept hidden at taverns.

Senator Noble had asked that he come to Pendleton on this historic case. When his family had been killed by Indians as they moved from Kentucky to Ohio, Charlie, the sole survivor, age two, had been found, carried into Cincinnati, and adopted there by the man he thought of as father, Enoch Leverett. Leverett had sent him east to Harvard, where the bright Yankee boys went, planning for him to take over the Leverett newspaper, the *Western Spy*, when he graduated. In spite of himself, Charlie turned out to be a lawyer. A newspaper writer has to tone things down. A lawyer could tell the jury facts that would lose an editor every subscriber. Charlie's mouth wasn't gentled enough for newspaper work. So Leverett made use of what Charlie *could* do: send facts that he could cut, dress up, water down, until they were fit for print.

When Charlie moved into the widow's room, there was a deal table holding the washbowl paraphernalia. He took all this off, moved the table under the window, and had himself a desk. Then he sat down to write Enoch, not a "Dear Pa" letter but a report in what he considered newspaper style of this outlandish place and this outrageous trial.

Extracts from a letter by Charles Fort to Enoch Leverett:

Pendleton is a town of two hundred souls. I made the mistake when I first arrived of calling it a settlement. The Pendletonians wasted no time setting me right. A settlement is a place like Fall Creek, twenty miles upriver—no stores, streets, or taverns there. Pendleton is a town. My idea of a town naturally is Cincinnati. Two theaters, three thousand books in our library, boardwalks, streetlights. I doubt if half a dozen books could be scared up in this entire settlement. Excuse me, I mean town.

Three judges sit here: a presiding judge, appointed by the state legislature, and two elected side judges, who are local. The presiding judge is Amos McGowan. Giddings, a man much respected here, is one of the side judges, as is Omer Oursley, the town blacksmith. Oursley ironed the prisoners after they all climbed over the walls of the prison stockade on the first night of their incarceration. Nobody here, including the prisoners, takes this trial seriously. They look at it as a kind of play-party to impress the Indians. But that Indian agent, Johnston, intends another kind of party. Oursley, a good man with hammer and tongs, can't read or write.

Ezra Fenton, the clerk of the court, can, they say, write his own name. He got himself elected justice of the peace by declaring, "I have been sued on every section of the statute and know all about the law, while the man running against me has never been sued for anything and knows nothing about the law." This apparently made sense to the citizens, and they elected him. Knowledge is knowledge no matter how you come by it, they figure.

Samuel Brady, the sheriff, in buckskins, moccasins, and with a side knife the size of a pigsticker, is a sight to scare wrongdoers before they ever hear the sound of his voice; a sound they say can be heard as far south as the falls of the Ohio. Brady, being bigger than most men, would be an awesome sight in his underwear without the knife. He is actually no different from the others here in dress, in the size of his side knife, or his lack of shoes. Every man, woman, and child is in moccasins. They look at me as I go clip-clopping along in my brogans as if I was half horse.

On my first day here, Judge Giddings invited me to midday dinner. Also present were Jonathan Armitage, the circuit prosecutor, and a friend of his, Dan McGowan, brother of the presiding judge. A very large, nicely browned goose was on the table.

Dan McGowan, after his first bite, said, "Judge, this is a damned fine goose."

Giddings, to my astonishment, replied, "Yes, it is a fine goose, and you are fined a dollar for swearing."

It seems that Pendleton has a statute imposing a fine of one dollar on any person who should "profanely curse, swear, or damn." Not another word was spoken during the entire meal. When we finally pushed back our chairs, the judge said, "Squire McGowan, pay me a dollar."

I was beginning to get some idea of the kind of man I was going to have to plead my case before. Invite a man to dinner and fine him a dollar for complimenting your goose!

After the dinner I went over to talk with my clients, whom I hadn't yet seen. The jail, thrown up in short order since what they have been calling "the massacre" took place, is about what a Buckeye would put up as a shed for animals—square, built of heavy beech logs, with one door and no window. A stockade manned by guards surrounds it. I was let into the stockade and through it into the jail room itself. No furniture, straw on the floor; a bucket in the corner. The prisoners, though heavily ironed, were in good spirits. Old Wood was reading his Bible. Young Wood was reading a novel, obtained God knows where. The guards let them crack the door enough to get a sliver of light for reading.

They were not at all happy to see me. They were not much fazed by being accused of murder. Mad that their neighbors had gone chickenhearted about the possibility of Indian revenge, but not fazed. What really galled them was that the Indian Bureau they all hated took the charges seriously enough to provide them with defenders like myself.

Benson, clanking like a gristmill, strode about, bellowing at me. "What's this country come to? My father was praised for what I done. Now you lock me up for it. Iron me like a mad bull."

I tried to quiet him down. "Mr. Benson, I'm here to get you out of irons. Undoubtedly there was some reason, some reason a jury will understand, for your shooting those Indians. Now if they shot at you first—or threatened you . . ."

"Threaten? Hell, no. Except breeding the way they do."

"So there was no reason for the shooting?"

Benson, in spite of the load of metal he was wearing, jumped a foot in the air. "They were Indians. Fishing in our streams. Killing off the deer. Pushing in right next to our homes. These are facts. Every man you can set on a jury knows it."

George Benson was about like a man who's shot wolves all of his life in the belief that he's protecting himself and his neighbors and who's suddenly told *wolves* must be protected—unless by chance the wolf has got his fangs at your throat. Nothing Calhoun or Colonel Johnston could say was going to change his upbringing.

Wood Sr. was the opposite of Benson: calm, understanding, and seemingly not too put out to be sitting in a straw nest in a jail-house. "After the burnings up north, I guess our neighbors didn't have much choice," he said. "Better for us to have a little spell of setting here than for them heathen to sweep down on our women and children."

"There's going to be a trial," I said. "That's why I'm here."

"I never been in a trial, but I've seen more'n one and I'll know how to handle myself. I've got all my wits about me still."

The boy reading the novel said something like, "Hrrumph."

"That's my son. *He* thinks I lost my wits marrying again."

I wasn't interested in the home affairs of the Wood family.

"I heard down at the tavern that others besides you three were at the shooting," I told Wood.

"Clasby, you mean? He's clear to Texas by now," said Wood.

"Was he the leader in this? Did he put you up to it?"

"What do you mean, put us up to it?" Benson, who had clanked over, asked. "We been fighting Indians all our lives. We're grown men. We don't need anybody to put us up to anything."

Benson gave me strong thoughts about applying for a job with the prosecutor. I ignored him. "Mr. Wood, I heard there was another man there besides Clasby."

"There was one other there," old Mr. Wood said. "A boy. And he didn't have a gun or take any part in it."

"Who was this boy?"

342

Benson replied, "Ben Cape. The preacher's son. Nothing but a soft pile of guts . . ."

Wood Jr. said, "Shh," and Benson, who wouldn't bat an eye at old split-foot himself, said, "Well, speak of the devil!" Not the most courteous way to address your pastor, but Cale Cape, as Benson called him, had lived too long among these rough Indian killers to take offense.

"Well, George," said he, "your body may be in chains but your spirit, I see, is still free and soaring."

Caleb Cape had left Piqua before I passed through there, but I had heard about his ride to bring the news of the killings to Colonel Johnston. He's a tall, lean man. I can see God-searching in his eyes, but there's a sardonic turn to his mouth that looks more like punning than praying to me. He is a preacher only by virtue of the fact that he preaches. But the settlement couldn't hold him in higher regard.

He introduced himself. "Mr. Fort, I understand. I've come over to pray with these men. You're welcome to stay if you like."

I thanked him and said he'd likely prefer to be alone with his parishioners. *I'd* prefer to be absent when Benson prayed.

"My daughter's outside. The guards didn't think the jail a place for a young girl. You might keep her company for a while."

He was right. The jail *wasn't* any place for her. Cape's daughter is a redheaded girl I had caught sight of earlier. The place for her was out in the open, with plenty of cooling air for all. I said who I was and she said who she was. "Hannah Cape."

I just stared, and she stared back. No stubbing her toe or chewing her sunbonnet strings. Girl, I thought, you're hungry for kisses, and I'm the man who can supply you.

Pa, I know the subscribers to the *Western Spy* don't give a tinker's damn as to whether Charlie Fort has or has not fallen in love. And, as a matter of fact, Charlie Fort doesn't know himself. But it seems I can't resist putting my feelings in this story. Well, you'll edit me, anyway.

So this girl, this Hannah Cape, stood there with her red hair flaming like Midsummer Day. I don't know how long the staring match went on. The lawyer wasn't the first to find his tongue, I know that. Hannah said, "Which side are you on?"

The correct answer would have been, "The side of justice." But to Hannah that would sound pompous. With her I wanted everything bedrock simple. "I'm a defense lawyer," I said.

"You're going to get these men off?"

"I'm going to try." She didn't say anything to that. "Do you want them to be hanged?" I asked.

"No."

"I don't think they should be, either."

"The boy in there shouldn't be."

"He your sweetheart?"

"He never kissed me or anything like that. He was just trying to be a man at the sugar camp. His stepmother hounded him into it."

"I had a stepmother." If she pitied boys with stepmothers, she had as well spread some of her tenderheartedness around.

"It didn't hurt *you* any, did it?"

"No."

"I wish you'd talk to my brother."

"He was there, too, wasn't he?"

"Who told you? Benson?"

I nodded yes.

"He didn't do anything. But he saw it all. He's sick from not telling someone."

"He'll have to tell someone. They'll subpoena him."

"What's subpoena?"

"Come to court and tell what you know or go to jail."

"There's something he's ashamed of."

"Everybody has something. Haven't you?"

I shouldn't have asked that. She dropped her head.

"I have, anyway. Most of us have." I took her hand. I didn't want her to be ashamed of anything. She didn't jerk her hand away but let me fold it up in mine like a young kitten. Kisses would have been next in order if her father hadn't come back.

"We're going to have a singing service now and we need your

344

voice, Hannah. The guards say you can come in for that. Mr. Fort, won't you join us?"

My singing, as you know, sounds about like a strangled bull-frog's. So I said I had other business—which was to get over here, write this, and think about Hannah.

End of extracts from a letter by Charles Fort to Enoch Leverett.

V

LIZZIE Cape, having cleaned up after the Sabbath worship and eating, sat in front of the fire with her tired feet on a footstool. If God had listened to that morning's praying, she thought, His head must be spinning. He had been asked to release the imprisoned; to punish the redskins for their killing up north; to bless Colonel Johnston in his efforts to appease the heathen; to have Colonel Johnston scalped; and to have Caleb Cape himself either blessed or shut up.

She was glad to be alone in the house after the morning's turmoil. She hadn't Caleb's faith. Or his high spirits, which made him feel, she believed, that even if God didn't help him he would be able to make out on his own. Caleb had made her a rocker which had as much bump as rock, but the movement was soothing, and in the letdown after the past weeks' worry, she dozed off. She dreamed she heard a voice calling "Lizzie, Lizzie." This did not awaken her, but her own voice answering "Who is it?" did.

"It's Lute, Lizzie. I hope I didn't scare you."

"No, I was only dozing. Come in and warm yourself." Bemis was rubbing his hands like a man bone-cold. "You're not still sick?"

"The only sickness I had, Lizzie, was heartsickness." Lute pulled his bench right up to the edge of the fire.

Lizzie and Lute were at home with each other. They were about of an age, but she couldn't tell herself she felt sisterly toward him. She felt like a woman in the presence of a pleasing man. Perhaps most women felt that way with Lute. She was easy in her feeling because the bond with Caleb was so strong.

Caleb had converted Luther Bemis, seen him settled and married, expecting now a young one born of a Christian marriage.

Lizzie was Caleb's right hand in his work—he himself said so—and in this way they were both Luther Bemis's spiritual parents.

"I came looking for Cale. He around someplace?"

"He and Hannah rode over to visit the men in jail."

"They're still holding them? I thought the government might've come to their senses."

"It makes sense to the government to try the men who did the killing, if that'll stave off an Indian uprising."

"They're our own folks, Lizzie."

"The ones the Indians'd scalp would be our own folks. Us."

"Lizzie, sometime last week the world went round a bend."

"Went round a bend? What happened last week?"

"We suddenly caught sight of a world where an Indian is a human being who can't be killed like a wolf. What's to come's too far ahead to see."

IT WAS full dark when Lizzie heard the horses come into the yard. Both Caleb and Hannah were wet with a drizzle that had started up after Bemis left. Lizzie could feel the tiredness in Caleb as she helped him out of his coat. Hannah was as lit up as if she'd made the whole trip on wings under angel-kindled starlight.

Lizzie pulled her rocker to the fire for Caleb and brought him a cup of hot sassafras tea and a slice of sweet cake. "How are they?" she asked. She didn't need to say who.

"Dry," Caleb said. "That's more than I can say for myself. Could I have a little hot milk with some rum in it?"

"I'll fix it for you, Papa," Hannah said. She swooped to put milk in a saucepan, rum in the milk.

"The ride don't seem to have tired Hannah," Lizzie remarked.

"She don't know she rode. There was a young defense lawyer there too busy making eyes at her to pay much heed to his clients."

After Caleb drank his hot milk and rum, Lizzie told him about Bemis's visit. "I told him you'd be played out."

"I am. But I'll have to go over there."

"You know what's the trouble?"

"I've got an inkling."

Extracts from a letter by Charles Fort to Enoch Leverett:

The town of Pendleton, after building itself a jail, has now also built itself a courthouse. It is, I *suppose*, a courthouse—a log building with two rooms, one for the court, one for the jury. The courtroom is about twenty by thirty feet long with a platform at one end enclosed by a heavy railing. Inside this railing is a bench and table for the judges, a deal table and chair for the clerk. In front of the platform is a long bench for counsel. Here I will sit. Near this bench is a little pen for the defendants.

Feeling, as I need not say, is running very high here. Half the populace is so fearful of retaliation by the Seneca that they would, I verily believe, roast every prisoner alive to calm the Indians down. The other half are friends and relatives of the prisoners and those who believe that trying whites for killing Indians will be taken by the red men as a sign of weakness that will bring upon us the worst massacres ever at their hands. Persons of these convictions would like to free the prisoners, and are prepared to fight off any reprisals, shot for shot.

But the government is very firm in its determination to hold this trial. Colonel Johnston will be back with Indian chiefs to let the people of Madison County understand what will surely happen if there is not due justice. And the employment of Senator Noble to prosecute the accused will convince the Indians that the Great White Father is on their side. We defense lawyers have our work cut out for us.

There are some few who regard this trial like any other. Men have killed men. Let the law prevail. Caleb Cape is no doubt one of these. Black Antler, the Seneca Faithkeeper, doesn't want *any* executions. But I don't expect him to have a hearing.

At the time I met Cape and Hannah, I heard from my clients that her brother, age fourteen, had been at the sugar-camp fracas, though all said he had taken no part in it. So on Wednesday I rode over to Cape's place. If the boy could report some threatening word or gesture by the Indians, my case would be greatly strengthened. Seeing Hannah again didn't go against my grain, either. Though to tell the truth, so overwhelmed was I by this girl that I had been

347

blinded to remembrance of her features. Feeling had covered my eyes like a film. But Hannah or no Hannah, I had to talk to Ben Cape. So I saddled Bay Boy at sunup, and my little pacer stepped off the near to twenty miles in something less than three hours.
Pause in extracts from letter by Charles Fort to Enoch Leverett.

At this point Charlie knew that he wasn't going to be able to stop talking about Hannah. So he took a fresh sheet of paper and prepared to write on, not for the *Spy* at all but just for the pleasure it gave him to talk to his father. His father would laugh and say, This is a story I've heard before, Charlie, but the heroine is new, so spiel on.

Continuation of extracts from a letter by Charles Fort to Enoch Leverett:

I had ridden twenty miles, more or less, to see this girl. Now the minute I saw her a couple of hundred yards away—she was outside in the sunshine making soap—my heart gave such a jump I was half of a mind to turn Bay Boy in his tracks and head back for Pendleton. What if all my heart throbbing had been over a girl with a face like an Irish potato? And would I be any better off if I saw under that bonfire of hair the face that launched the thousand ships? I had my work cut out for me in Pendleton. For my own future, and for those poor fellows set up as sacrificial scapegoats, I intended a great defense. Potato face would be the best for me.

She had the launching face. She also had some boyish straightforwardness that made me jump down and greet her like a teammate, handshake and all. And then I talked. It's our great human cover-up. Nice mess of soap if I ever saw one, said I, staring into a twenty-gallon pot of lye and grease. Sorry for the uproar the trial is bringing to your folks. Was her brother home?

"He's at home. Why do you want to see him? Do you think he can tell you something that will make things easier for Benson and the Woods?"

"I hoped he might."

"He can't. He told me all he knows."

"Then you tell me. Just what he wouldn't mind my hearing."

"I won't. I don't even like him to see us talking."

"Let's walk down to the branch. Can you leave your soap?"

"You don't know anything about soapmaking, do you?"

But she did start to walk toward the branch that circles the knoll the Cape house is built on. We walked in step, not touching. Arm in arm with some girls, you can't keep step. You're as mismatched as a pacer hitched to a trotter. Hannah and I advanced right foot with right foot, left with left.

When we got to the branch, we naturally stopped. Wading wasn't on the program. Soap was a finished subject. She refused to get started on brother Ben. There was nothing to say.

I didn't ask. She didn't offer. When we kissed we were up off the ground for a while, like creatures of air.

End of extracts from letter by Charles Fort to Enoch Leverett.

ORA Bemis arrived at the Cape house soon after Charlie left. She was on foot, downcast, bigger each day with child. Lizzie came to the door. "Ora, you think you should be traipsing around the countryside, as far along as you are?"

"My mind's too uneasy to let me sit still. I came over slow and careful as I could. It's Cale I want to see."

"He's out milking, Ora. He ought to be in any minute."

"What I've got to say is private, Lizzie. I'll go on out to the cowshed now. That'd be all right, won't it?"

"Caleb'd be glad for company."

Caleb was down to stripping the cow when Ora came into the shed. "Sit down," he said, motioning to a mound of hay. "If I don't take all Daisy's got, she'll get the idea she can let up."

"Cale," Ora asked, "have you told anyone? What Lute told you?"

"Not a living soul."

"Not even Lizzie?"

"She's a living soul."

Ora didn't smile. "You think Lute has to go through with it?"

"I think Lute's got to do what he thinks right. You know that. He's God's man. We can't tell him what to do."

"I can pray, can't I?"

"You can pray. But don't ask God to upset His own laws."

"What law has God got about this?"

"About half the Ten Commandments. Don't bear false witness, for one. There're some prayers God can't answer, Ora. Why don't you pray that Lute does what he thinks is right? And ask God to give you the strength to stand by him?"

"Yes. Pray for me, Cale."

Caleb got down on his knees. He didn't know a thing he could ask the Lord but to strengthen Lute, and to comfort Ora in what likely lay ahead. He ended his prayer, "Bless this babe-to-be here in the straw as Thou blessed another Babe born in the straw."

Before he could say amen, Ora was up on her feet. "Don't make a prayer like that for my baby. That Babe was killed. Why do men put killing and dying and blessing so close together?"

"What would you have, Ora?"

"No killing, no killing. Then blessings wouldn't matter."

"We need God's blessing."

"No, we don't. All we need is to love each other. Cale Cape, Lute was a happy man until you started him worrying about his soul. I will pray that Lute forgets he ever laid eyes on you."

She ran out of the shed, and Caleb didn't try to stop her. He picked up the milk pail and went into the house slowly, head lowered. He was heartsick and couldn't use his regular remedy for that disease: tell Lizzie all about it.

NEXT Sunday morning, a couple of hours before sunup, Caleb and Lizzie were still in bed, though planning every minute to get up. Lizzie's head was on Caleb's shoulder, the last comfort she would have that day—the way things were going, perhaps ever.

The fit of man and woman always surprised her. It was a detail you might have thought God wouldn't have had the time to arrange. The heavy bone of a man's big shoulder left a hollow before it reached the bulge of the muscle in his upper arm that just fitted a woman's head. *My* head, Lizzie thought comfortably.

"When was the last time we had a real Sunday, Lizzie? Got to

sleep a little late and could look forward to the peace and fellow-
ship of a church service to follow?" Caleb asked.

"Before the killings," Lizzie said, then wished she hadn't. Now
they'd have to face the day that was ahead of them. "At least the
meeting's not set till eleven," she added.

"The time set ain't going to carry a pennyworth of weight with
folks who want to see this day's meeting. There'll be people here
who've been traveling all night, and some fording cricks and following traces from as far away as Indianapolis this very minute."

"Why is Johnston having the people here at all? Why don't he
take them straight to Pendleton?"

"Here's where it happened, Lizzie. Here's the sore spot—and the
hotheads. If anybody's liable to fly off the handle about the trial,
it's the people here. And if I don't miss my guess, the Indians
Johnston will bring in here will make everybody think twice before
they decide to tangle with them."

"What kind of a man is the colonel?"

"He's nothing special to look at. Not at first glance. Second glance
tells you here's a man that don't back up. He's hewn out of old
rock. The Indians know this. They don't fool with him. They ain't
got no cause to. He's worked for them."

"Couldn't a fight break out? So many men hating the Indians."

"It'll be a fistfight if it does. Nobody's bringing a knife or a gun
into our place. Johnston's got militia down at the foot of the lane
to see to that."

A cock crowed. "Did someone turn into our place?"

"Like as not. But you listen to me, Lizzie. Don't start asking
people in. The house won't hold them, in the first place. In the
second place, the Indians don't want to come inside. They ain't
used to chairs, and much as they trust Johnston, they don't trust us.
They'd think what we had in mind was to get them inside and set
the place on fire—the way we did at—"

Lizzie stopped him before he could finish. "Well, I don't want
Indians in my house, anyway. A lot of them are light-fingered."

"You only know those poor town reds down around Pendleton—
drunks and beggars. They weren't that way till we came along.

Today you'll see Indians we ain't touched yet. Chiefs and braves in furs and skins and warbonnets till we'll all stand chopfallen before them in our calicoes and linsey-woolsies."

"We're all equal in the sight of God," Lizzie said.

Caleb laughed till the bed shook. "God save me from arguing with women."

BEN, who had tried to hide himself from himself, felt at home with the crowd of strangers who were filling the yard. To them he wasn't the Cape boy, who had been at the sugar camp at the time of the killing; to them he could be an onlooker from far down in White River country, or perhaps a Buckeye up from Ohio. No one paid him the least heed, not even Hannah, who usually kept an eye on him. Today she was so busy talking to one of the trial lawyers, she wouldn't have noticed if he'd dropped dead in his tracks.

He knew the Cape yard better than any out-of-state man and had chosen the best place to watch: the angle where barnyard fence met the barn. He had a wall to lean against and a squared-off rail to sit on. In case of any trouble he could be up and into the barn at the first click of a trigger—or war whoop.

Ben was so interested in the crowd, he scarcely noticed that he had been joined on the rail, until he began to feel pushed through the barn wall. The man who had crowded in beside him looked, except for his clothes, like a blacksmith—big, dark, and somehow sooty-looking because of the stub ends of beard under his skin.

"You feeling pinched?" the man asked kindly.

He was, but some soft fiber in him made him hesitate to tell people that they were in the wrong. He was ashamed when he was in the wrong, and he had had too little experience to understand that the world wasn't made up of duplicates of Ben Cape.

"I'm O. A. Dilk," the man said. "I shoved in here on purpose. I'm a lawyer for the state. You're Ben Cape, aren't you?"

There was no way of avoiding a yes to that.

"Who's the beauty over there talking to Charlie Fort?"

"That's my sister, Hannah," Ben had to admit.

Dilk scanned him, searching for a family resemblance that wasn't there. "You know all these people? Are the families of the prisoners here?"

"Mrs. Benson's over there." Ben pointed her out.

"With all those young uns? I'd think they'd stay home."

"They want to see the Indians."

"Their pa didn't have any love of Indians."

"Who told you?"

"Why do you think he's in jail?"

Ben looked at O. A. Dilk. If I was in trouble, I'd like him on my side, not against me, he thought.

"Clasby ought to be in jail," Dilk said. "Your sister, Hannah, found Clasby's saddlebag with stuff he had stolen from the sugar camp. Thieving as well as killing."

"How do you know about that?"

"That's what I'm here for, to find out facts like that. Then to prosecute the guilty. See that they are punished."

Ben didn't say anything. He was hungry, but his father had told him not to be seen with food until the last person had left the place. "We can't feed them all, and there's no use tantalizing them with the sight of food. If your pangs get so you can't stand them, sneak into the barn and have a couple of mouthfuls of chicken food. That'll keep you going till nightfall."

He was thinking about doing that when all the people in the yard turned as if by a single lever. "Here they come."

It was the Indian chiefs who were coming. They moved into the lane where the other visitors had been forbidden to come.

"People aren't supposed to ride in," said Ben.

"*They* can," Dilk told him. "Johnston arranged it. If you were a dozen Indians, would you walk into a crowd of whites after some of them had killed your women and children?"

Ben kept his mouth shut. He wasn't sure what sound would come out if he opened it. Maybe he'd yell a warning like any boy seeing Indians. Maybe the sound would be a whoop for joy, the way it was when geese went over in a shifting V half as big as the sky. Maybe he'd cry for Folded Leaf, who'd never grow up now to ride a horse like this.

"You never seen the like, did you?" Dilk said.

He never had. Fourteen men, not on half-starved Indian nags, but on big, arch-necked stud horses, all colors, all high-stepping, came up the lane. At the head of the line were two white men.

"They squaw men?" Ben asked.

Dilk snorted. "Back here in the woods you think anybody who says howdy to an Indian is a squaw man. You call President Monroe a squaw man? He's talked with Indians. And the first horseman in that line is James Noble, United States senator. You want to call him a squaw man?"

Ben didn't. Senator Noble was thin and straight as a musket.

"Who's that coming next?"

"Colonel Johnston. The agent."

Johnston was as big and heavy as Dilk himself, but colored yellow and white like a miller instead of dark like a smith, his face sharp and his eyes going everywhere.

Behind the white men came the line of Indians, who, because of their headdresses, looked as much like birds or beasts as men. There was no war paint. This wasn't a war party. There were eagle feathers made into a cap and the cap finished off with a beak and glaring eyes. Hawk feathers held in place with a silver band. Owl feathers shaped like a pinwheel. Earrings, shoulder long, swinging. White doeskin. Spotted lynx. Ermine paws.

"Are they all one tribe?" he almost whispered.

"Mostly Senecas. It was Senecas got killed. There's a Miami there. A Winnebago maybe. Oneidas. They're a part of the Six Nations along with the Senecas. There's a breed or two. One of the women killed at the sugar camp was mostly white."

Ben made a sound, soft and broken.

"You choke on something?" Dilk asked.

He had choked on his tears. Better to keep Dilk talking. "How do you know so much about Indians?"

"I'm here to prosecute men for killing Indians. I've got to know something about the men they killed."

The horsemen were all in the yard now, and Ben was able to see the faces under the feathered headdresses: beaks stronger than eagles' beaks and eyes harder than owls'. He wanted to say something about these braves bedecked with beads and feathers.

"They make us look like a bunch of sick muskrats," he said.

"Nonsense," said Dilk. "They're savages. These men you see have eaten dogs. And worse than that. They'll keep a man alive for twenty-four hours just so they can roast him longer. They—"

Ben wouldn't let him finish. "If I was an Indian, I wouldn't have you for my lawyer."

"I'm not *their* lawyer. I'm the state's lawyer, prosecuting men for breaking the law. It's against the law to murder human beings. The law don't say that if the human being ate dogs, or men's livers, he can be murdered."

"Folded Leaf wasn't a savage. He never ate dogs." Ben was crying now. "He didn't even have a gun or a tomahawk. Black Antler taught him not to kill."

"Who's Black Antler?"

"His teacher. I studied with Folded Leaf."

"Studied how to scalp?"

"No. I learned verses like Bible verses, only Indian."

"Well, Folded Leaf made a mistake when he fought the whites."

"He didn't fight the whites. Nobody had any chance to fight the whites. You said you came here to find out what happened. Why don't you ask people who really know?"

"I am," Dilk said. "I'm asking you."

Ben took one look at Dilk, then jumped down from the top rail and pushed his way through the crowd into the barn. He wasn't hungry anymore, but he chomped on corn to ease his feelings. Chomped on corn till his gums bled.

O. A. Dilk wasn't a man who liked to hurt others, but every single thing had to be weighed against every other thing. Better the boy suffer some now, and because of it decide to tell what should be told, than keep the truth from being known.

THE Indian chiefs and the two white men didn't dismount. Down on the ground some shoving might start; and shoving led to blows, and finally what happened at the sugar camp might seem a frolic

355

compared with this. There were no Indians so vengeful as the Seneca. They believed that the spirits of their slain tribesmen would never rest until those responsible for their killing were themselves slain. It was a duty the Seneca accepted with enthusiasm.

Dilk had no idea how Johnston had persuaded these masters of retaliation into letting the white man take care of the punishing. It was possible that to the Indians the nasty business of white men letting other whites dangle at the end of a rope was a revenge sweeter than any they could devise. "They are killing their own." That would be a sight they might like to see.

Johnston was likely the only man whose word they would accept. He had never lied to them. And if he lied this time, there would be nothing to prevent the Indians' carrying out their first plan: burn, scalp, slaughter. Johnston was counting on the settlers to remember this. Dilk was, too.

The agent, for all that he was riding with a senator, was the best mounted there: a fifteen-hand blood bay with a long black switch tail. He sat in front of the band he had gotten together and spoke first, slowly. Every person with two ears and a brain between them could understand what he was saying.

"Most white people can read and write. Because of this we have long records on paper. And all these records tell us how much we have suffered at the hands of the Indians.

"The Indians don't have any way of keeping track of what they have suffered, no records that we can read. And if they did have, we probably wouldn't read them, anyway. But *I* have been keeping records and *I* can tell you they have suffered.

"What has taken place here you all know about. It's not my task to determine who were the killers, or why they killed. A court of law will decide that. The Indians know who the dead are. They know that kin of theirs were killed by men of this neighborhood. Nine people died. Seven of the dead were women and children. They know that.

"They know—you do, too—what happened over in Hancock County a few years back. A Wyandot chief with his wife was on a hunting expedition. Three white men came to his camp and asked to spend the night. The Wyandots were Christians. They shared their camp with those they supposed to be their Christian brothers. They fed them. They said their prayers with them. Then they went to bed. As soon as they were asleep, these white men rose up, killed them, robbed their camp, and stole their horses.

"These murderers were caught and put in prison. But soon after, while the officials were looking the other way, they escaped. And that was all the punishment they had: a few days in jail.

"I have told the chiefs with me that this will not happen here. That if the accused are found guilty and condemned to hang, they will hang, and the hanging will be public. Only because they believe me have these chiefs been able to keep their young men from descending upon you.

"Two of the chiefs will speak to you now. The first is a Seneca. His English name is Sun Fish. Two hundred braves look to him for command. He will speak in his own language; what he says will be interpreted for you. You should listen well."

Sun Fish was a young chief, his face full of pride and his eyes aglitter with hatred. He didn't need to say a word to convince anyone there that, except for Johnston's promises, he and his two hundred braves would avenge the deaths of his kinsmen.

His speech was short, clanged out in a rush of brassy sounds. The translator, his mind trained to retain words, spoke as if the speech were his own. Even his voice had the clang of Sun Fish's.

"There is a treaty between your people and mine. We are not at war. This was not a fight between warriors. There was a time when we called each other brothers. I do not call you brothers today. Brothers do not kill each other's women and children. We have been promised that the murderers will be punished. We have promised that we will wait and see. We are waiting."

The Seneca wheeled his horse and rode slowly down the lane away from the crowd. "One of the men killed is represented here by his uncle," Johnston said. "He is Mingo, son of the great Mingo."

Mingo was a man of forty or more. The grooves from his nose to his mouth were like runnels in clay land after a hard rain. Unlike Sun Fish, he spoke slowly and quietly.

When he had finished, the translator, also speaking slowly and quietly, said, "I was born by the falls below here. This was all Indian country. There was food for all. No man, red or white, was ever turned away from the red man's lodge hungry. The land belonged to all. Then the white settlers came. The land belonged to whatever man could seize it. The Indians were made many promises. We signed many treaties. 'Only this much land and no more.' Pushed back, pushed back. Driven from our own homes. While taking the sugar sap from our own trees, our women and children were killed.

"The agent says you will punish the wrongdoers. If he is right, only the guilty will die. If he is wrong, you must blame yourselves."

Colonel Johnston let the words sink in before he spoke again. "Now we ride to Pendleton to say what we have said here. The chiefs will then depart for their homes and the trial will begin."

The horsemen rode off the Cape place through a quiet crowd. Dilk thought he could hear a sound like that of a hive of disturbed bees: a sound of breaths sucked in, of heart thumps. What could they say, or do? The agent had asked nothing unreasonable. "You made these laws. Keep them." Now the Indians—had they the right?—could say, When you kill us, you murder. Hanging is your way with murderers. Keep to your ways.

The trial would be a mortal tussle, and Dilk felt the power rise in him to win it. He saw the Cape boy, his redheaded sister, and defense lawyer Fort standing together over by the wellhead. He had to see the Cape boy again. And Hannah; he had never expected to find as reward here a girl like Hannah Cape. She would grace any marble staircase, Indiana or Washington.

He introduced himself. "Miss Cape, may I make myself known? I'm O. A. Dilk, lawyer for the prosecution."

Hannah said, "I'm pleased to meet you, Mr. Dilk."

"Oscar, isn't it?" Fort said, not waiting for formalities.

It was. But Dilk preferred to hide it behind initials.

"Those Indian dandies didn't help my cause any," Fort went on.

"What do you consider your cause, Fort?"

"Save white men from being hanged for defending themselves

358

against the savages who have been molesting them for a hundred and fifty years. What's yours?"

"The law. But I'm sure that Miss Hannah doesn't want to have the trial argued here."

"I don't want to have it argued ever," Hannah said.

Dilk smiled. She was a woman. He wouldn't have himself seem a sobersides before her. The trial would be time enough to lock horns with Fort. Leave that for the trial, and let it be seen then who was the better man.

"Miss Hannah," he said, "Ben and I had our talk cut short by the speechmaking. If you'll excuse us, we'll go on with it."

VI

CHARLIE Fort could charm a bird out of a tree. This wasn't his fault, but the ability made some people back off from him. Mrs. Culligan, his landlady, was fully aware of the charm. She was also too honest to fool herself into thinking that her feeling for him was maternal. She *was* able to fool Charlie. In her heart, however, she was a girl in love.

Charlie was eating at eight o'clock on a mild April evening a dish of fresh, tender-grained clabber, which Mrs. Culligan had brought to him with no more than, "I thought this might help you through your evening's work."

He had a long evening's work ahead of him, so he eased into it with his father's letter. It made him laugh.

If you want to write a story called "Hannah, the Hoosier Maiden," I'll try to get it published for you. But readers of the *Spy* generally are not interested in the girls you spark. Now I know you didn't intend parts of your letter for printing; but I tell you, son, it doesn't even make proper reading for me. I'm not trying to stopper you up. Just telling you a fact: the words haven't been invented that'll tell one man what another man feels about a woman.

What I suggest is this. If you have to write about Hannah, put her on a sheet marked personal. Otherwise, if I'm down with the ague, I wouldn't put it past old Ames, who doesn't love either of us, to print the lot just for the fun of seeing your face red. I'm not trying to discourage your writing—or courting. I don't know anything else that's set this town on its ears like that trial in Pendleton. They can't hear enough about it.

Charlie picked up his pen. Pa was right. No more about Hannah.

Extracts from a letter by Charles Fort to Enoch Leverett:

On the day the trial began, Judge McGowan was unable to preside, due to some temporary sickness. One of the side judges, Omer Oursley, took his place. Oursley is the blacksmith who ironed the prisoners. Isaac Vickers, defense attorney, first made a motion that the out-of-state defense lawyers be admitted as attorneys at this bar. "They are regular practitioners," he said, "but they have not brought their licenses with them."

"Let them be sworn," Oursley said. "Nobody but a lawyer would defend a murderer."

Mr. Vickers was naturally taken aback at this kind of talk from a judge in a trial the purpose of which was to decide if anyone had been murdered; and if so, who the murderers were. Fortunately, Judge McGowan recovered sufficiently to assume his rightful position between the two side judges. Matters now went more smoothly.

Judge McGowan ordered the grand jury to be called. The grand jury then brought into court an indictment for murder against each of the defendants. After that the trial jury was chosen.

The trial jurors are all hardy, heavy-bearded fellows. Not one is without a side knife in his belt. The first sight of them gave me considerable confidence. These are men, I thought, who know what it means to stand off the savages; men who have managed to bring Christianity and civilization westward with them.

The courtroom was crowded. Friends and families of the men I will be defending, their faces drawn with anxiety, were there. People I have come to know, clustered together like sheep in a storm, on the front benches with their minister, his wife, and children. Next to the minister sat Luther Bemis and his wife, Ora.

There's more to tell, Pa, much more. But I'm too sleepy tonight. Enough to say now that the defense received a great shock—and setback—in the testimony heard by the court today.

End of extracts from a letter by Charles Fort to Enoch Leverett.

THE courthouse was already crowded when Caleb Cape, with his family and the Luther Bemises, arrived. The turnout for the trial turned Caleb's stomach. It always did. Let a churn be stolen or a coon dog shot and, if the matter came to trial, settlers for miles around traveled to hear the lawyers spiel. It was not to be expected that this trial, the first of its kind ever, would not bring out ten times as many onlookers. Caleb knew that the speechifying of the city lawyers would be in itself a seven-day wonder. And then there were those Indians, upright as trees, at the back of the room, their slit-stone-agate eyes seeing every move that was made. To settlers from lonely crannies of the woods, it was what playacting was to townfolk. Caleb understood all this. Still, he didn't like the flushed, staring faces. This trial was no make-believe. The tears shed would be real tear water. The prisoners and their families were flesh and blood. Was anyone there praying? For the men in jail? For the Indian dead? For the jury that would have to search its heart about right and wrong? Gawking and gaping, that was about the size of it. Caleb reached over, put a hand on Luther Bemis's.

Lute knew what that meant. Armitage was about to call him to the stand, and Caleb was giving him comfort. Or would give him a shove if he saw any signs of faltering.

But Lute wouldn't back down. He kept his eyes on Ora. He wasn't sure what she might do now. She had never denied that what he planned to do was right. But she had never been two-faced enough to pretend (though she knew pleasing God came first with him) that *she* felt at one with God if that meant prison for Lute.

Armitage was asking the court to disregard for the time being the indictment against George Benson, the prisoner scheduled to be tried that day. Armitage wanted to bring another witness.

"Bring on your witness," agreed Judge McGowan.

"Will Luther Bemis please take the stand," said Armitage.

Lute moved through this scene like a man through a dream re-remembered. Ora did not cling to him. Caleb did not have to shove him forward. He floated past faces of neighbors as featureless now as bleached winter cabbages. Only the Indians were truly visible. What he had to say would be said to them.

Fenton, the clerk, asked him to tell the truth, the whole truth, and nothing but the truth. In God's name, did they think he had got up here to tell them some tall tale?

Armitage wanted a conviction. Lute knew that. He intended to tell the truth. If that convicted him, and it would, so be it.

"Mr. Bemis, where were you on the evening before the day of the alleged killings?"

"I was at home."

"Did you have any visitors that evening?"

"I did. Jud Clasby, accompanied by Hannah Cape. He was seeing her home from a visit she had made to the Woods. Our house is between the Woods' and the Capes'."

"So the call was just a social one?"

"For Hannah, it was. Jud was sounding me out about the Indians at the sugar camp."

"What do you mean by sounding you out?"

"He asked me if I didn't think the Indians at the sugar camp ought to be cleared out. He thought they'd stolen his horse."

"What did he mean by cleared out?"

"Killed."

"Did he say so in so many words?"

"I don't remember his exact words. That was his meaning."

"What was your answer?"

"My answer was that I was finished with killing Indians."

"You had killed Indians before?"

"Yes."

"Why?"

"To save my life sometimes. Sometimes because they were Indians. We were pardners, Clasby and me, hunting out west. It don't make sense to wait for a dangerous animal to attack you."

"That's how you considered an Indian? A dangerous animal?"

"Out west when I was younger—yes. Since I came here, I've become a Christian. Mr. Armitage," Bemis said, "it would maybe save time if I'd tell the court what I did and you ask questions only when you think I'm leaving out something."

"Proceed along those lines, Mr. Bemis."

At this point the chief defense counsel got to his feet. "Judge McGowan, may I address a question to the witness?"

"Address your question, Counselor."

"Luther Bemis, did Mr. Armitage promise you that if you gave testimony helpful to the prosecution, he would see that you had a light sentence?"

Luther Bemis's hand instinctively went to his belt, where ordinarily he carried a knife. "That's a damn lie, and you know it."

Judge McGowan gaveled, and the courtroom, which was in an uproar at this exchange, went silent. "Mr. Bemis," the judge said, "you will be held in contempt if there is any more profanity. Defense counsel is trying to help you recognize the facts."

"Judge McGowan," Bemis said, "I am trying to tell the truth."

Caleb Cape rose. "Judge McGowan," he called out.

Caleb was well enough known to be permitted this interruption. "Mr. Cape," the judge said, "you have relevant testimony?"

"I have."

"Step down, Mr. Bemis. Mr. Fenton, call up the witness."

Duly sworn, Caleb said, "Before Luther Bemis ever saw Mr. Armitage, he came to me with the account which he now wishes to give the court. My advice to him was to tell Mr. Armitage what he had told me. It was Mr. Bemis who sought out Mr. Armitage. Not the other way around. No deal was made."

"Mr. Cape," asked McGowan, "why didn't you advise Mr. Bemis to make his report to the defense lawyers?"

"I didn't think the defense lawyers wanted to hear what Luther Bemis had to say. I thought Jonathan Armitage did."

After this interruption, Judge McGowan ordered the questioning of Bemis by Armitage to continue.

"Mr. Bemis," Armitage asked, "what happened after you told Jud Clasby you were finished with killing Indians?"

363

"Jud asked would I just come with him and any others he could roust out to look for his horse. Well, there was no question about my doing that. So the next morning around nine or ten o'clock Jud came to the house and he and I set out."

"Did you take a gun with you, Mr. Bemis?"

"I did," answered Bemis.

"Why?" asked Armitage.

Fort was on his feet at once. "I object. By asking why, Mr. Armitage would like the jury to believe that Mr. Bemis went out armed for the purpose of killing Indians. Mr. Armitage knows as well as I do that no man up here and in his right senses goes five hundred feet from his house without a gun."

"Objection overruled," said McGowan.

Armitage repeated his question. "Why the gun, Mr. Bemis?"

"Habit, mostly," said Bemis. "And good sense."

"Where did you go after leaving the house?"

"We went toward the shack where Clasby has been living since he came back here. On the way he showed me two small piles of corn. Clasby said he figured they had been put there by the Indians to toll the horse away from his place."

"Did you see any tracks around the corn?"

"Yes. Horse and moccasin tracks. At the time I thought the moccasin tracks were Indians'. I think now I was tricked."

"Why? How?"

"I was tricked by somebody's putting that corn there and seeing that some horse come to it. The idea was to make my blood boil at Indian thievery—and it did boil. Then Clasby said, 'Let's go to the sugar camp and see if my horse is there.'

"Before we started out, Clasby asked me into his shack. He got out a bottle and took a pull on it. Then he handed it to me. When I was converted, I gave up drink. I'm not myself when drinking. I do things and afterward I don't know why I done them. But I thought, maybe going without it for so long, whiskey wouldn't work on me the way it used to. I was wrong. If anything, it worked on me harder. I was drunk. While we were still at the shack, Benson, the two Woods, and the Cape boy came along."

"Did these men have guns?"

"All but the Cape boy. He was just traipsing along because young Wood is his friend."

"What happened next?"

"We went to the sugar camp. It was agreed that the others would stay in camp with the women and children, while me and Clasby, with the help of the two Indian bucks, hunted the horse."

"What made you think the Indians would lead you to the horse?"

"We didn't think that. The plan was to kill them."

"Whose plan was this?"

"Clasby's. But I went along with it. I was took in by the corn and the tracks. And by the whiskey. I was thinking the way I did when I was out west and every redskin was my enemy."

"What happened when you got to the sugar camp?"

"First of all, the Indian squaws gave us food. That sobered me up some, but not enough. Clasby told the Indians his horse had strayed. Would the men help us look for it? Tall Tree didn't think much of this plan. But Red Cloud, a leader among the Indians and a man very open and friendly to whites, said they'd be glad to help. So Red Cloud went with me, Tall Tree with Clasby. Clasby had told me what to do. When I heard his gun, it would be a signal that he had killed Tall Tree and that I was to kill Red Cloud."

"Didn't you have any second thoughts about this plan?"

"I did, yes. But by now I was bound. I'd told Clasby what I'd do, and I've never been a man to back down on my word."

"You thought it was better to murder than to break your word?"

"I was drunk. And nobody up to then had ever called killing Indians murder. Keeping my word seemed the right thing to do."

"Mr. Armitage," Judge McGowan intervened, "let's move to what the witness did after he left the camp."

"Well," Bemis resumed, "I let Red Cloud range on up ahead. He was about thirty steps in front of me when I heard my signal— Clasby's shot. At the sound of it Red Cloud turned toward me, and I bungled my shot. I hit him in the belly. I wish I could forget his look. He couldn't believe I'd done it." Bemis, who up to this point had spoken without emotion, buried his face in his hands.

Judge McGowan said, "Mr. Bemis, you'll have to take your hands down so that we can hear what you are saying."

Bemis straightened up at once. His eyes were dry as sandstones. His supply of tears had long since been used up.

"What came next ain't easy to tell. I walked toward Red Cloud. He had sunk to the ground, but was sitting upright. Just sat there, dying like an Indian. They don't beg for mercy. Red Cloud let out only two words. 'Finish me.' I took my knife from my belt, and Red Cloud nodded. He was asking me to do what I done."

"What was it you did?" Armitage asked.

"I cut his throat. And he thanked me with his eyes till they closed. That's one reason I'm here. To say Red Cloud done no wrong. I killed him while drunk, and he died like a brave man."

"Why have you made this confession?" McGowan asked.

"I made it to get some peace with God and my soul."

There hadn't been a sound in the courtroom during Bemis's confession. The listeners held their breaths as if they'd been out there in the woods watching the whole affair—the tracking, the gunshot, the knife at the throat, the closing eyes.

Armitage asked the judge if, in view of Bemis's confession and his expressed desire to share the jail with those already accused, the formality of a grand jury indictment might be waived.

Before McGowan could agree or disagree, Charlie Fort was on his feet. Caleb Cape had also risen, and both began to speak together. Judge McGowan, an old hand at outbreaks in rural courtrooms, pounded his gavel.

"The court is adjourned for two hours for dinner," he said. "Sheriff Brady, take Mr. Bemis into custody."

VII

THE day after Bemis's confession was Thursday. Judge McGowan had come down again with another bout of sickness. At his request, and because they had no wish to stumble through this tangled legal forest without an experienced guide, both side judges moved to postpone the trial until the next morning. A stunned silence lay over Pendleton. People were uncertain what the confession meant and how they felt about it. The postponement heightened this sense of bewilderment. But by Thursday afternoon some of the shock had worn off and the town began to chatter like a family facing a new, unexpected problem.

Charlie Fort had prevailed upon his landlady to provide a little supper for him and Hannah Cape that evening.

"Norry," he said (Mrs. Culligan's name was Norah), "I know you're not running a boardinghouse and that you only took me in out of the kindness of your heart. But I wonder if you could give me and Hannah Cape a little supper tonight?"

"As you said, Charlie, I'm not running a boardinghouse."

"It's this way, Norry. Along with her family and that raft of cousins they're staying with here in town, she now has O. A. Dilk pawing around her like an ox. So my only chance to talk to Hannah alone is here. Or take her out for a little walk in the woods."

Norry's preference would have been to cook a supper that she and Charlie could eat alone together. That being out of the question, why send him traipsing off to the woods with that big redhead? Who would be the gainer by that?

"You courting this girl, Charlie?"

"I haven't asked her to marry me, if that's what you mean."

"That's what I mean."

"Not yet. I don't want to scare her to death."

"I guarantee you won't. What would you like for supper?"

WHAT they had for supper Charlie didn't know. The table was set pretty, not in the kitchen where Norry ate, but in the sitting room in front of a nice little slow-burning fire. Norry had covered the table with a cloth and decorated it with a little jug filled with the first Johnny-jump-ups of spring. A Cincinnati restaurant couldn't have provided a turnout any more stylish.

Hannah made Charlie proud. She wasn't a preacher's daughter for nothing. She was accustomed to putting strangers at their ease. She admired the table, smelled the flowers, helped Norry bring the food from the kitchen.

When the supper was on the table, Norry said, "Now you help yourselves. I've promised to go sit with old Sam Randall for a spell. He's down with a fever and his poor wife hasn't had any rest for a week. If I ain't back before you leave, Hannah, I'm pleased to have met you."

Norry shut the door firmly behind her and went down the path toward the Randalls'. She had done unto others as she would be done by. Die a Christian if not a sweetheart.

When the door closed, Charlie and Hannah, moving slowly, as if carried by a wave, went into each other's arms. They did not kiss. That was too special, too concentrated.

After a time they remembered the table. "What're we going to do with all this food?" Charlie asked.

"It would hurt Mrs. Culligan's feelings to leave it untouched," Hannah said.

They could not unclasp hands. So they ate, or tried to eat, one-handed. Finally Hannah gave up trying and watched Charlie.

She wanted to say, My darling love, you are so beautiful. I will never be separated from you. But he hadn't said I love you yet. A woman who said that first could drive a man off with her forwardness. The game was hide-and-seek, and it was the woman's place to hide and the man's to seek. Otherwise, no game.

Instead she said, "What do you think that row of Indians is standing in the back of the courtroom for?"

"To see that we are keeping our word about having a trial. And don't think Colonel Johnston doesn't want everyone to have a good look at the customers the folks here might have to deal with if the murderers aren't hanged."

"Hanged? They wouldn't hang poor Johnny Wood, would they?"

"If he's found guilty . . ." Charlie put down his fork, took both Hannah's hands in his, and groaned. "Oh, Lord, I've lost my mind. Hanging! I didn't ask you here for any talk like that."

"What kind of talk, then?" Hannah asked, so bold her eardrums pounded with blood.

Charlie closed his eyes and laughed. Then he opened them wide. "You want me to say it?"

"I think so."

"My darling Hannah Cape, I love you."

"I love you, Charlie Fort."

They leaned across the table, ready to kiss now. Charlie's cuff dragged in the gravy bowl.

"We've got to get rid of this damned table," he said.

Hannah's startled look reminded Charlie that he was talking to a preacher's daughter. "I didn't mean the cuss word," he said. "I told you I was out of my mind. Let's carry the table into the kitchen. We'll give the leftovers to the dog."

When they came back from the kitchen, they stood in the sitting room like actors waiting for a cue. They had said "love" and Hannah expected "marry me" next, to which she would instantly say yes; go home, and start plucking geese for feather beds.

He said, "You're the most beautiful girl I've ever seen."

This wasn't a proposal, but it was perhaps the kind of talk that should come before a proposal, like grace before a meal. It made Hannah tongue-tied. She hid her face against Charlie's shoulder—he was tall enough so she could do that. The minute she did so, she didn't care about proposals. Or anyone speaking. Her body spoke, and Charlie's heard and answered.

NORRY came home at ten. There in front of the fire lay Hannah Cape and Charlie Fort, sound asleep and fondly entwined. Norry stared for a time, then closed the door.

What did you expect? she wondered. She sat down at the table where the two had eaten. Tom, Tom, she said to herself, thinking of the husband of her youth, not the Tom dead and in his grave. It was you and me I saw there. She put her head on the white linen tablecloth and cried a big wet splotch of tears. Then she got up. Those two must be roused. Charlie must get Hannah home.

She took the poor cat out of its crib in the woodbox and set her on the step. "Run for your life, Goldie," she said. Scooter could never catch the big cat, but he'd sit under the tree Goldie climbed and bark for an hour. If that didn't wake the young people up, she'd clatter around the kitchen until she did it herself.

Goldie ran, Scooter after her, baying. Norry went behind the springhouse, out of sight from the house. She heard the front door close, then watched as the young people, arms around each other, moved off quickly under the light of a moon growing full.

Inside the house, she went to bed, leaving a night-light burning on the table by the door—as she always did when Charlie came in after her bedtime. She went to sleep at once. The light was gone when sometime later she awakened and turned over.

Upstairs in his loft, Charlie got ready for bed. Tomorrow, he thought, he must write to his father and tell him to prepare to meet a Hoosier daughter-in-law.

ON FRIDAY, Judge McGowan was still sick. Side Judge Giddings's wife was having a baby, their first after eleven years of marriage; he therefore moved that the trial be postponed until Monday. Side Judge Oursley, the blacksmith, was more than willing. Every horse in the township would soon be running barefoot.

Caleb Cape and his family, together with Ora Bemis, left Pendleton Friday morning when the second postponement was announced. Ora wouldn't ride in the same buckboard with Caleb. Except for Caleb's meddling, Lute wouldn't be in jail now, and she alone. Ben and Hannah drove her home in the rig the Bemises had driven over to Pendleton. Ora didn't hold Caleb Cape's making a Christian out of her husband against his children. They would spend the night with her, Ben doing the barn work, Hannah doing housework and keeping Ora company. Ora was within a month of her time, and what she had gone through in the past few days might speed things up.

That night, after Ben had gone to bed, Hannah pulled a stool to Ora's bedside. "Is there anything more I can do?" she asked.

"Bring Lute home," Ora said.

"I was talking to Mr. Fort, the defense lawyer. I think he'll bring Lute home."

"If there were ladies on the jury, I'd banter Mr. Fort could get this case dismissed out of hand if he wanted to."

"You think he's a masher?"

"Maybe not. But when a man's as good-looking as Charlie Fort, women can't keep their hands off him. And men being like they are, Charlie Fort can't help liking that."

"Did Lute ever love anybody besides you?"

"Hannah, Lute left home when he was eighteen. I never laid eyes on him until he was twenty-six. He was out west, a lot of the time with Clasby."

"Is Clasby a masher?"

"He is. You won't catch him settling down with any one woman. He and Lute both had Indian wives. More than one."

"Did they have babies?"

"Of course."

"How soon do babies start to come . . . after you're married?"

"If you don't want one, it comes quick as a wink. If you do, you can wait for years. Look at Judge Giddings and his wife."

"That's not the rule, though."

"There's no rules. It's all hapchance. I think God Himself keeps pretty clear of such matters."

"Aren't you a Christian, Ora?"

"Of course I'm a Christian. That don't mean I blame God for everything that goes on in the world." Ora sighed. "I never thought I'd be able to sleep on a night like this—Lute in prison laying on straw. But I'm dead beat."

Ora slept. Hannah couldn't. She walked in her bare feet up and down the room. Finally she knelt and prayed. "God forgive me" was what she intended to pray. "God, I thank Thee" was the way the prayer came out.

At ten the next morning O. A. Dilk arrived at the Bemis cabin. Hannah answered his knock. For a young girl she looked stately, better turned out at ten on a Saturday morning than many a cabin woman at four on Sunday afternoon. She knew, and Dilk was glad to see it, that appearances counted in this world.

She immediately protected Ora. "Mrs. Bemis is feeling poorly."

"I didn't come to see Mrs. Bemis. I came to see Ben. And you, too, if you'll join us."

"Ben's down at the barn, cleaning out the stable."

"It's such a nice spring day. Isn't there someplace out-of-doors where we could talk? I don't want to upset Mrs. Bemis any more than I have to."

Hannah thought, He talks like a lawyer no matter where he is. It seemed a good trait to her. Nothing two-faced about such a man. "Has something more come up about Lute?" she asked.

"Nothing more about Lute. You can tell his wife that he said this morning that he'd had two of the best nights' rest since the shooting. He feels he's clear with God now."

"I don't know's that's a message she'd like to hear."

"You use your own judgment about what you tell her. I'm going down to get Ben now. I'd like you to be with us when I talk to him. He puts a lot of store in what you say."

Dilk fetched Ben from the barn, and they used upended chunks of logs, sawed but not yet split, for seats. The sun brought out the sweet smell of the freshly cut oak. Frogs down in the branch were tuning up for tadpole time. It was the weather and the place for a picnic, Hannah thought, not a talk about killing.

There were no fireworks about Mr. Dilk. He was steady and thoughtful. Pleasant as a basket of chips, her mother would say. Nor did he have that mortal sweetness that makes folk keep their distance for fear of a heartscald they'd never get over. My heart is already scalded, Hannah thought. She loved and was loved. That made her happy, and happiness made her loving toward everyone. What she and Charlie had done was wrong, and they would never do it again. And yet it was very strange that an action so wicked could make her feel so full of grace; as if she had been somehow sanctified. She was just a moon reflecting Charlie's warmth onto this other lawyer. Anvil-hard, this one seemed to her, however agreeable.

Ben seemed as much changed as a boy as she was as a girl, and with nothing more to help him than some sensible talk with O. A. Dilk. To Ben, the hardness of this man must feel reliable. He was going to do whatever O. A. Dilk wanted. She could tell. Testify in court, if Dilk thought that right.

"I'm not saying it'll be easy," the lawyer told him. "I am saying it'll be simple. Just tell what you saw. It's your duty, and you'll feel better afterward. If they cross-examine you—"

"What's cross-examine?" Ben asked.

"It's what the defense lawyers may do. After you've told your story, they may try to mix you up by asking a lot of questions."

"Why? Don't they want to know the truth?"

"Not if it makes their clients more likely to be convicted."

"Well, they can't mix me up," Ben said. "I'll tell it the same way every time. They'll get sick and tired of hearing me."

"They'll be sick all right," the young prosecutor said.

VIII

Court resumed on Monday morning. Judge and side judges were in place. George Benson, who would be tried that day, was in the prisoners' pen. Ordinarily a florid, heavyset man, he was noticeably thinner and paler. Sitting over there in the jail, cussing and fuming, had worn him down. He was still cussing and fuming, but there was less of Benson for the job.

O. A. Dilk, as assistant to Armitage, wasted no time in asking Ben Cape, the preacher's son, to come to the witness stand. This caused a gasp in the courtroom. Caleb Cape had had a hand in getting Bemis to confess. Was the preacher now going to hear a confession squeezed out of his own son?

Dilk handled young Cape as tenderly as a china dish. He all but carried the big lunk of a boy to the witness stand. Moved his own lips in the swearing in, as if to show Ben anybody could do it. Once under way, the boy didn't need any more help than a sledder going downhill on glazed ice.

"How did you happen to go to the sugar camp on the afternoon in question, Benjamin?" Dilk asked, using the full dignity of the Biblical name.

"Johnny Wood came by our house with a gun. I thought he was going squirrel hunting and I asked if I could go with him. Pa said I could, but not to do any shooting."

"Why not?"

"Saturday afternoon is getting close to Sunday, and Pa thinks that on Saturday afternoon you shouldn't go frolicking."

"But he let you go with Johnny Wood."

"Just to watch and pick up squirrels for him."

"Did you pick up any squirrels?"

"No. Johnny didn't shoot any. He was in a hurry to meet his father and uncle at the sugar camp."

"George Benson and Wood Sr.?"

"Yes, sir."

"Were these men glad to have you with them?"

"No. Old Mr. Wood wanted to send me home. But Johnny's uncle George said, 'Let him stay. It will do him good.'"

"Did he say what it was that would do you good?"

"No, sir."

"Who else was at the sugar camp?"

"The Indians. One was my friend Folded Leaf. I was learning Indian gospel with him from Black Antler, the preacher."

"How did your father feel about your memorizing Indian gospel, Benjamin?"

"He said that what Black Antler preached was about what he preached. Except the names was different."

"Can you remember any of the words you memorized?"

Ben said, "I know by heart lots that Black Antler preached."

"Just a few lines will do," Dilk told him.

"Black Antler said, 'If any man, whatever he may be, will look on the Great Being above us all and do His will on earth, when his days are out and the spirits about find he is a good man they will grant him more days to live in the world, and if he lives a good man, doing no evil in those days, when those days are out, the Great Being will take him to Himself. The like of this—"

Charlie Fort, on his feet, addressed Judge McGowan. "Your Honor, I protest. What is this, a court of law or a camp meeting to convert whites to the religion of the Senecas?"

There were hoots of laughter, the soft thumping of moccasined feet, the high-jinx shouts of play-parties and cornhuskings.

Before Judge McGowan could gavel for silence, there was a

carrying sound from the back of the room: the ominous hoot-owl call of one Indian signaling to another. This silenced the court-room faster than any crack of a gavel. Then, in the muffled drum-roll of a voice that had never had to give a command twice, the words, "Let the boy speak."

All, now looking to the back of the room, saw the largest, most richly dressed of the Indians take a step forward. "Let him speak."

Fort, undaunted, said, "Your Honor, these doctrines have abso-lutely no bearing on the case we are considering."

"Objection overruled," said Judge McGowan.

Ben, rattled by the interruptions, made a couple of false starts, reconsidered, and finally got under way again. "Black Antler taught us, 'Never forget to be thankful to the Great Spirit above us all. We will be good friends here, and when we meet with the Great Being above we will have brighter and happier days.'"

Ben looked apologetically at the Indians. "I know more, but right now I can't seem to remember. The way we always did it, Folded Leaf would say it and I'd follow him."

The chief who had spoken made the Indian sign "We are satisfied."

"Continue with the boy's testimony," McGowan ordered.

"Benjamin," Dilk said, "why did you think Benson and the Woods went to the Indian camp?"

"To visit them."

"What did you think happened to the squirrel hunt?"

"I thought we would hunt after we ate."

"The Indians fed you?"

"Indians always do."

"What happened next?"

"We just talked around for a while . . . till we heard the shots."

"What shots? Where?"

"I can't remember." Ben dropped his head into his arms.

Dilk tried another approach. "Benjamin," he said, "was the first shot from the river side or away from it?"

Ben looked up. "The first shot was from the river side. Then a single shot from the other direction."

"After that, Benjamin?"

"It was then they started killing the women and children."

"Who did the killing?"

"They all did it."

"Did you see anybody in particular?"

"I saw two. First of all, I saw what Johnny Wood did."

Charlie Fort was on his feet at once. "Judge McGowan, we are now considering the case of George Benson. If the boy has any testimony relevant to actions of George Benson on the afternoon in question, let him continue. If not, let him step down."

Dilk turned his anvil face toward defense counsel, then to Judge McGowan. "Your Honor," he spoke harshly, "I ask the court to remember that the witness is a young lad, and the events he witnessed did not happen in any order which Mr. Fort may feel most suited to the defense's case. We will, I assure you, get to Mr. Benson. But I beg of you, Judge McGowan, out of consideration for the boy, and a judicial concern for the most complete account possible of the events of that day, that you permit the witness to tell the court of the happenings in the order that they happened."

"Permission granted, Mr. Dilk. Continue with your witness."

"Benjamin," Dilk said, "you have told me that you can only say positively who was responsible for two deaths at the camp. Now which was the first of these deaths you witnessed and who was the killer?"

"When the shooting started, two squaws and the children fell down right away. Everybody thought they were dead. But one of the squaws wasn't dead. She died at our house the next day."

"There were three Indian women at the camp, Benjamin. Do you know the name of the third, the one who didn't fall down right away?"

"Yes, sir. Wide Eyes. George Benson told Johnny he was leaving her for him because she was younger than the other women."

"Hadn't Johnny done any shooting?"

"No. He hadn't lifted his gun. When Mr. Benson said, 'What are you waiting for, Johnny?' Wide Eyes said, 'I am a Christian. The Lord Jesus Christ is my Saviour. Don't shoot me.' Then Mr.

Benson said, 'She's a redskin, Johnny. Let her have it.' Then Wide Eyes tore open the front of her dress so that all of her skin down to her waist showed. She said, 'Brothers, my skin is white as yours.' And it was. Johnny raised his gun and fired. It hit one side of her chest—right in the center. But she just stood there and not even any blood came out. So Mr. Benson said, 'One more will do it, Johnny.' So Johnny shot her again—on the other side. She went down to her knees like she was going to say her prayers. Then she fell on her face and died. When she died, Johnny raised up his gun and ran at Mr. Benson."

"To shoot him?"

"No, the gun wasn't loaded then. To hit him. But Mr. Benson took hold of the gun and threw Johnny to the ground."

Ben leaned over, his face in his hands. Dilk said quietly, "So all the Indians were then dead?"

Ben shook his head. "Not all."

"Benjamin," Dilk said, "you have already told us that both Benson and Wood Sr. fired at the women and children and that with the exception of Wide Eyes, who was killed by Wood Jr., and of Talking Crow, who died next day at your house, everyone was dead when the firing ceased. Have I misunderstood you?"

Ben sat up with a jerk. His face was glazed with tears. "Everyone looked dead," he said. "But Folded Leaf was alive." On his feet now, he was repeating in a strangled voice, "Alive. He was alive." Then he bolted from the stand and headed for the door. As he passed the bench where the Cape family sat, Caleb shot out an arm and pulled his son down next to him. The crowd murmured, but not enough to require the judge's gavel.

Ben leaned forward in the seat, head to his knees, and rocked soundlessly backward and forward. He could feel his father's arm across his shoulders, supporting him, so his rocking was easier.

"Ben," Caleb whispered, "this is a big test for you. The hardest you've had yet. Now you do what you ought to do here—tell the whole truth. It don't matter what people think. This is between you and Folded Leaf and God. And me. I set some store in you—and what you got the backbone to do. Telling the truth, no matter how much you wish it could be different, will clean the slate. It'll make everybody who loves you proud."

Caleb murmured so low Ben hardly knew whether it was his father or his own mind speaking. Maybe it was Folded Leaf, forgiving him and whispering to him to tell what had happened. The pain in his chest let loose of him and he sat up straight.

Dilk said, "Is the witness ready to resume his testimony?"

Ben's voice had a cracked sound, but it carried. "I am ready."

When Ben had reseated himself in the witness chair, Dilk said, "Benjamin, you have told us that though everyone *looked* dead, one was not. My question for the record is, 'Who was alive?'"

"Folded Leaf. He'd been shot in the leg and was stunned. But when Wide Eyes was shot, he sat up and tried to crawl to her. He couldn't because of his leg. The bone was sticking out. Then Mr. Benson yelled, 'The damned little bastard is alive!'"

"There are ladies present, Benjamin. Bad language has no—"

"I'm keeping back most of the bad language. There was lots."

"Thank you, Benjamin. What did Mr. Benson then do?"

"He started toward Folded Leaf, and Folded Leaf called to me, 'Help me, Ben!' I ran toward him. But Mr. Benson slung me down and said, 'Preacher's boy, if you don't want the same medicine, stay out of here.' Then Folded Leaf called again. But I didn't go. . . ."

"Why?" Dilk asked.

"I was scared. Mr. Benson's eyes were popping and spit ran out of his mouth. He lifted his foot like he was going to kick my teeth out or kick me somewhere."

George Benson, eyes once more bulging, got to his feet. He had been brought into the courtroom ironed, and the chains rattled as he stamped his feet. "That's a lie," he bellowed. "I was trying to save the boy. The redskin was crawling toward him. Ben, you know that's a lie. It was your safety I was thinking of."

"Mr. Benson," Judge McGowan said, "you will be given all the time necessary to tell your story. But now you must sit down and be quiet or I will instruct the sheriff to remove you."

Benson sat down, but he kept talking. "The boy is lying, Judge. He never did like me. I run him off our place once."

"Sheriff," Judge McGowan said, "will you remove the prisoner?" Benson stopped speaking. "Resume, Mr. Dilk," the judge said.

"Benjamin"—Dilk put his hand on Ben's shoulder—"Mr. Benson was right, wasn't he? Folded Leaf tried to kill you."

Ben jerked away. "He didn't, he didn't. I told you, he couldn't move. His leg was shot in two. When Mr. Benson saw he had me buffaloed, he walked over and picked Folded Leaf up by the heels and swung him around in a circle so that he fetched his head up against the trunk of a big beech. Then he swung him the other direction and did the same thing."

"Did this kill the boy?"

"He didn't have any head left. Mr. Benson smashed his head like an egg."

"What did Mr. Benson do then?"

"He threw what was left of Folded Leaf away. Then he said, 'I reckon that finishes the job.'"

"What did you do?"

"When he said that, I got up and run home."

"Did you hear any more shots back at the sugar camp?"

"I couldn't hear anything for a long time but Folded Leaf asking me to help him. And how quiet he was when Mr. Benson picked him up. He didn't beg. He didn't make a sound. But his head made a sound. It made a sound like—"

Judge McGowan said, "You don't need to repeat that. Mr. Dilk, unless you have more questions, ask your witness to step down."

Dilk put his arm around Ben and led him back to his family.

THE courtroom was silent. No one moved. Judge McGowan stared out at the crowd. They had come to see the monkey show. Well, they had seen it. Then he heard George Benson muttering away low enough not to be told to stop, but loud enough to prove no judge could shut him up. McGowan gaveled sharply.

"The court will adjourn for two hours."

The prisoner, his wife and six children trooping behind him, was taken out. Judge McGowan watched him go. Benson would pass through that door someday hearing dreadful words he, Amos

McGowan, had spoken. God in heaven, why did he ever become a judge? He watched the jury leave. Those twelve men had listened to something they could not forget. Finding guilt or innocence was their responsibility. Life or death was his. He wanted to put his head down as that boy had, but he was a man, not a boy, and a judge, to boot; which is hardly a human being, he sometimes thought.

The lawyers, talking, but quiet for lawyers, left together. Then the onlookers filed out, their faces heated and their eyes bright. Judge McGowan had seen this time and time again. Considering the vein of cruelty that pulsed in all men, the love of violence, the fascination with death, it was a wonder so few heads were broken, so few breasts mangled with bullets.

He did not believe the Indians were different in nature from the white men. They, too, were brutal, but their training was different. Their faces were not open books. The Indian boy had not cried out; nor had his kinsmen, hearing the manner of his death. They left the courtroom, their faces as sealed as old tree butts around the living sap that fed them. Amos McGowan envied them.

When he was alone, he did put his arms on the table and his head in his arms. He was not an old man—thirty-eight. But he was not ambitious, like Fort and Dilk. He was judicious by nature. Judicious in practice, he had learned, was another kettle of fish.

A hand on his shoulder roused him.

"Amos, I hope I didn't wake you up."

It was Johnston, the Indian agent. "Will you come eat dinner with me?"

"Thank you, Colonel. I don't feel like eating just now. My stomach turns at the very thought."

"That wasn't a very pretty story."

"That's not what makes me bilious. I've got a troubled mind. No one man can hand out justice the way a judge is asked to."

"No one man is asked to, Amos. Besides the juries, you've got a framework of law and of court practice almost a hundred years old to support you."

"Court practice for the past hundred years won't help me in

this case. You know as well as I do no court has ever handed down a judgment against a white for killing an Indian."

"Don't you think it's about time the law recognized the Indians as human beings?"

"Oh, it's time, all right, Colonel. God knows it's time. But for two hundred years it was time to kill Indians. How were Benson and the Woods to know the time had come to stop?"

"Something told Bemis. This court can teach the others."

"What lesson will the Indians learn?"

"They'll learn there's justice for them, too. They'll learn they don't have to raid and scalp and burn to get it."

"Colonel, it won't be justice that hangs these men. If they hang. It'll be chance. The chance that put an Indian agent like you in the territory at the time of the killings."

"Couldn't chance and justice go together sometimes?"

"I pray they can. In God's name, I pray it, Colonel."

"Leaving justice out of it, Amos, you know what this trial can mean in the matter of saving lives?"

"Oh, I know that. But this court, while I preside, won't be providing victims to appease attackers. I'd rather we'd all be wiped out than sentence any man to save our own necks."

Judge Amos McGowan slumped against the headrest of the tall fanback chair brought in as a judge's bench from somebody's parlor for the trial. He looked up at the chunky colonel. The *colonel's* decision had been made from the minute he heard of the killings. Get the killers hanged and stave off an Indian uprising. Backing up the colonel were the Secretary of War, Calhoun, and Monroe, the President. And what did *he*, McGowan, have? The terrible knowledge that all courts up to this time had ignored the law. And that Benson, the Woods, and Bemis had killed out of their knowledge of this fact.

Charlie Fort didn't feel like eating, either. He didn't know what anyone could have done about the Cape boy's story. In the long run it didn't make much difference how a man died. There was no law providing clemency for tidy killers. But a jury was inclined to find a savage killer guilty faster than one who hadn't bloodied up the landscape. This afternoon, though, when he put Benson on the stand, Charlie had a thing or two to bring out that might undo some of the harm of the morning's testimony.

It was June in April. No June flowers or leaves yet, of course, but June's breath, warm and sweet. Charlie had two hours before he had to be in court. He headed out of the village, past tavern, past the newly made jail, to the Baldwin house, where the Cape family was staying—all sitting outside, eating a cold picnic dinner. Dilk was with them, acting cozy as a member of the family. Hannah was handing out the victuals. When she saw him, he felt in his veins the impulse he knew was in hers to do away with all distance between them. Jump stumps, send fried chicken flying. Clout the sanctimonious Dilk in the process.

Yet Charlie was able to greet them all like a lawyer, not a lover. Congratulate Dilk. Tell Ben that he had done the right thing (he had, though Charlie wished he had kept his mouth shut).

"Have you eaten yet?" Caleb Cape asked. "Join us."

"I thought I'd walk out in the woods. There's a number of things I'd better think over before court this afternoon. The prosecution has put the defense on its mettle."

Lizzie Cape said, "Hannah, fix the poor man some lunch. You can think while you eat, can't you, Mr. Fort?"

"Think better, maybe," Charlie said.

Hannah brought bread, chicken, and sweet cake wrapped in a fringed napkin. "If you don't mind, Mrs. Cape," Charlie said, "I'll take Hannah with me to listen to me practice my plea."

Dilk said, "Pleading's not going to change facts, Charlie."

"The facts are maybe less one-sided than you think, Oscar."

Charlie was talking over his shoulder as he headed himself and Hannah toward the woods. When the trees shielded them from sight, he threw the food away and took Hannah in his arms.

"My love, my Hannah, where have you been?"

"I've only been away three days."

"Does it seem that short to you?"

"No," said Hannah. "It seems forever."

They moved two steps forward, deeper into the woods, then kissed; two more steps, then kissed again.

"Let's sit down and rest," said Charlie.

Sitting down was the last thing Hannah intended. She had already decided how to see and talk to Charlie without encountering the danger of what had already happened once: always stand up.

She was no ignorant backwoods girl who thought that babies were delivered by storks. Ora had taught her more. She had no intention of being pitied because of a watermelon under her apron. There was no way she could stop loving Charlie, but from now on she would stay on her feet when with him. Always. Lying down was when the trouble began.

Charlie didn't ask her to lie down. He simply put his knee into the back crook of hers and she folded up like a jackknife. She went down and Charlie with her, into a nest of leaves. She remembered, Always stand up. But they were nothing but words now.

LATER that day, after court was adjourned, Charlie was back in Norry Culligan's loft, writing his article for the *Western Spy*. He sketched in Ben Cape's testimony of that morning. Then, because he was tired, because he had the notes from which he had spoken, he decided to finish the piece with his own defense of Benson. He wrote of himself in the third person, as lawyer observed, not reporting. It made the writing more objective, he believed; and it would certainly read more impersonally.

Extracts from a letter by Charles Fort to Enoch Leverett:

In the afternoon, when court resumed, George Benson was tried for the first crime for which he had been indicted, the murder of the Indian woman Talking Crow. Before putting Benson on the stand, Charles Fort, for the defense, reminded the jury of facts they must not forget: i.e., that the trial of a white man for killing an Indian could not and must not be separated from the two-hundred-year relationship of these two races. "What happened at the sugar camp cannot be judged except as history," he began, and then quoted Benjamin Franklin as having said, "Our frontier people have been continually butchered by the Indians. We shall never have a firm peace with the Indians until we have drubbed them."

Fort's speech was interrupted at this point by Senator Noble for the prosecution. "Judge McGowan," said he, "I ask that these words, prejudicial to justice, be stricken from the record. We are not here to review the statesmanship of Ben Franklin, or to let silver-tongued lawyers raise our temperatures. Our sole purpose this afternoon is to determine the guilt or innocence of George Benson in the murder of an Indian woman."

Judge McGowan overruled the objection. "In this case I do not believe that it is inappropriate for us to be reminded of the events of the past two hundred years. Continue, Counselor."

Fort thanked the judge. "I would like to recount for the jury a happening within the lifetime of many of you, in the state of Ohio, from which Mr. Benson and I hail. I was given an account of these events by the mother and daughter whose dreadful fate it had been to experience them.

"A family by the name of Ferguson lived on a farm some forty miles from Cincinnati. Adam Ferguson and his fourteen-year-old son were slaughtered by Indians while harvesting the corn crop. Mrs. Ferguson, her babe, and three older children were captured, tied to horses, and made to travel furiously to escape pursuers. The babe began to sob. The Indians, fearing that its cries would alert followers, snatched it from its mother and brained it.

"When the lodges of the Indians were reached, the mother and her two daughters, ages fourteen and sixteen, were bestowed as spoils of war on leading chiefs. They were passed from chief to chief. I will not dwell on their experiences. The youngest girl died in captivity. The seven-year-old boy was taken farther west and never heard from again. Mother and daughter, after three years, escaped. When I was a boy, it was still common for mothers to warn their children against straying too far from the house by saying, 'Remember the Fergusons.'"

After this speech, Fort immediately called George Benson to the stand. Benson, though still in leg irons, had had his handcuffs removed. Mr. Fort had arranged this. It was a strain on that rambunctious man to try to talk without gesturing—and gesturing with his chains rattling was a strain on the listener.

Duly sworn, Mr. Benson was asked by Mr. Fort if he, too, had been warned in his childhood to "remember the Fergusons."

"No," said Mr. Benson. "What the young uns in the Benson family were told was, 'Remember Grandpa.'"

"Did you, when so admonished, 'remember Grandpa?'"

"Nobody had to remind me. I saw it happen to Grandpa."

"What was it you saw?"

"When I was seven years old—that was in 1784—the Benson family was living in Virginia near the banks of a creek called Little Muddy. In October of that year, my grandfather, a man near seventy, was down at that creek, getting a load of dauby mud to use in caulking our log cabin. Pa was nearby, bringing in a load of pumpkins, gun with him, of course. I was playing in the cattails. They was well over my head, so I heard what was happening before I saw it. I heard Pa's gun fire, then I heard him yell to Grandpa, 'Injuns. Run for the house.'"

"Didn't he call to you?"

"He didn't know I was there. And Grandpa was deef and didn't hear anything. Pa made it to the house, but Grandpa didn't have a chance. They put more arrows in him than a porcupine has quills. They scalped him while he was still alive. Then he died."

"How did you get back to the house?"

"After sundown, when all the Indians had left, Pa came down and found me. He thought the Indians had stolen me."

"And you spent most of the day there with the body of your murdered grandfather?"

"Not right with it. I scrunched down in the creek while the redskins were prowling around. I kept hoping Grandpa might come to. But I was afraid to show myself and go to him."

"Did you remember this when you were at the sugar camp?"

"I remember it all the time."

Mr. Fort then turned his witness over to the prosecution for cross-examination. Senator Noble had but few questions.

"Mr. Benson, had your grandfather ever killed any Indians?"

"Of course he had. He had lived on the frontier all of his life. A man don't live there without killing Indians."

"Whose land was he living on?"

"His own."

"Who owned it before he did?"

"Nobody."

"Didn't Indians own it?"

"Indians don't own land. They roam it. Hunting and killing."

"And getting killed."

Mr. Fort here objected. "The means by which the citizens of the United States got a foothold on this continent have no bearing on this case. Mr. Benson is to some degree responsible for the westward march of civilization in this country. But if we turn our attention to that subject, we'll be here till the Fourth of July."

After Fort had spoken, Judge McGowan gave the jury an able charge. They were out no more than twenty minutes when they returned with a verdict of manslaughter. This verdict, after a recess for deliberation, was followed by a sentence from Judge McGowan: "Two years in prison at hard labor."

Patrick Conroy, the leading lawyer for the defense, immediately upon the sentencing sprang to his feet and said, "If the court please, we are ready for the case of Benson for killing the Indian boy in camp."

Judge McGowan, though the state also was ready for a continuation of the trial of Benson, adjourned the court for the day. It was growing late, the hearings had been exhausting, and McGowan had every reason to call for a halt. He instructed the court to reconvene Tuesday afternoon at two.

End of extracts from a letter by Charles Fort to Enoch Leverett.

IX

On Tuesday, though it was noontime, nobody seemed of a mind to eat. The open space around the courthouse had for an hour been filled with many of those who had listened to Monday's proceedings, too restless now to light and stop talking. Was what had happened right? they asked each other. And right or wrong, what would be the outcome for them?

The Indians, impassive in the courtroom, were still impassive as they spoke together. What were they saying? Many in that crowd understood Indian lingo. But these Indians were not now speaking to be heard.

Thomas Gunn, jury foreman, hair sheep-curly and sheep-colored, came up to Charlie. "Mr. Fort," he said, "manslaughter is unpremeditated killing, ain't it? Kind of accidental?"

"That's the way it's defined."

"You want to know why we decided the way we did, Mr. Fort? Way back there when that boy lay in the sedges and saw his grandfather hacked up by the redskins, something took hold of him and was his master. So what he did was manslaughter. No more murder than when a bull tosses a man. It was his nature speaking; nothing he planned. That's the way I seen it, after you put Benson on the stand. And it was the way I persuaded the other jurors to vote."

Before Charlie could thank Gunn, Sarah Benson, with children at her heels, not tall, but buxom enough to envelop Tom Gunn from knees to shoulders, threw her arms around the jury foreman. If a man's character is to be decided by the appearance of his wife, Benson was not a bad man; Sarah would never see forty again, but to judge by her rosy unlined face she had enjoyed the last twenty of those years.

She was crying now, cheeks like plum blossoms in the rain. "Mr. Gunn," she said, "I can't reward you, but God will, for saving my husband's life. Me and my children will forever be in your debt. Oh, Tom Gunn, God bless you."

Charlie, knowing that Benson's troubles were not yet over, turned to Norry Culligan, who was standing close by, as though waiting to speak to him. She said, "I fixed a pickup dinner for you and Hannah, if you want to invite her to the house." Norry didn't expect a miracle, but if Charlie said, I'd like to talk over the trial with a woman of more experience than Hannah, she wouldn't argue. It wasn't the reply she got.

"I haven't seen Hannah," Charlie said.

Norry pointed. Hannah was surrounded by men—her father, Colonel Johnston, a couple of the jurors. Charlie was of two minds about joining the crowd, when Hannah, responding to his wave, came to him.

"Norry has fixed us a bite to eat at her place," he said. "Will you come with me there?"

Norry was heading quickly away. Hannah watched her resolute departure. "Why is that woman so good to us?" she asked.

"She's an old lady without any children left at home," Charlie said. "We take their place."

Hannah looked at Charlie. It was easy for her to see in Charlie what Norry saw. "She's in love with you," Hannah said.

"My God, Hannah," said Charlie, "she's a *grandmother*."

"She don't think of you as a grandson. Likely she had a young husband, just your spit and image. She looks at you and remembers him—and forgets all the time in between."

"I look at her and remember you. And the difference. Come on, let's eat."

Norry had left the food on the table. Custard pie; deviled eggs; pickled beets. Food pretty to look at, but look was all they could do. They sat down, then rose immediately, clasped each other, and kissed away most of the hour they had.

"Charlie," said Hannah, "we mustn't make love anymore."

"Because it is wrong?"

"It *is* wrong. But wrong wouldn't stop me. Besides, afterward, I don't feel like I've done wrong. As I would if I lied . . ."

"Afterward—how do you feel, Hannah?"

"Blessed," she said, startling herself with the holy word.

"We're going to be married, you know, Hannah."

"I don't want to *have* to be married."

"You and I have to be married. There'd be no sense in not. As soon as this trial is over."

"Then we mustn't anymore—until the trial is over."

"No, we mustn't, Hannah. You're right." Charlie held her in his arms. No kissing now. "But you must help me, Hannah."

"I will, Charlie. I'll always help you. You know that."

JUDGE McGOWAN WAS in his tall fanback chair a quarter of an hour before the afternoon session. He leaned his head back and closed his eyes. If people thought he was sleeping, they might let him alone. How a jury had decided that shooting a woman point-blank was manslaughter was beyond him. But a judge didn't override his jury, so he had no choice in his sentencing. Men are not hanged for manslaughter.

A feeling of warmth near him made him open his eyes. Three inches away was the bulk of Black Antler, hot with feeling, trembling with conviction, and with more than the usual amount of lard on his bones to radiate all this. "Judge, you did right not to condemn Benson to die."

"With the verdict what it was, I didn't have much choice."

"No one should be killed for killing. It is not the Indian way. Or the way of Handsome Lake and the old longhouse faith."

"What do you do with your killers?"

"Except in war, we are not killers."

"Sometimes, surely?"

"Sometimes. That man is cast out, not spoken to or fed."

"Doesn't he die?"

"If the Great Spirit wills. We do not kill him."

McGowan nodded toward the Indian line that had once again formed at the back of the room. "Killing is their way."

"With your people, not our own. They have been at war with your people. They want them killed because that is war."

"What if they knew you were here asking me to spare them?"

"They think I am crazy."

"My people would say that you're crazy like a fox. That you'd persuade us not to hang the killers so the tribes up north could claim, 'They did not have a fair trial.' Then they would kill every settler in the Fall Creek valley."

"I know that."

"Then why do you tell me not to hang these men?"

"I say what is right. Right is what you want to do."

"The boy you were teaching was killed. You heard how."

"What Folded Leaf was learning might not die."

"My God, Black Antler, you don't help me much. I can't sentence according to what strikes me or you as right or wrong. I sentence according to law. I have sworn before God to do so. And before God I will do so." McGowan rose and struck the table in front of him with his closed fist.

Black Antler took a seat by himself in the courtroom. The people he knew best had been killed. Neither whites nor reds trusted him. But he sat at ease. He had done what he could.

JUDGE McGowan gaveled the courtroom, already on edge and more stirred up by his seeming dismissal of Black Antler, into silence. Then George Benson, given a new lease on life by the light sentence he had received, was brought to the prisoners' box.

If the court hadn't known for a fact that Benson had spent the night and morning in the straw of the Pendleton jail, they would have been convinced that he was fresh from a tavern and one pony too many of corn whiskey. What was bubbling inside George Benson was stronger than corn—hope, raw, uplifting.

After Armitage had summarized the prosecution's case against Benson, Fort put Benson on the stand. He had no intention of spoiling the effect Benson's account of the death of his grandfather had had on the jury the previous afternoon. He wanted *that* to stay in the jurors' minds, not Benson's admission that he had killed a stripling. He kept his questions brief.

"Mr. Benson, you have been accused of killing the Indian boy named Folded Leaf. Did you do so?"

"I did."

"Wasn't the death of the squaw sufficient revenge?"

"I didn't kill Folded Leaf for revenge."

"What was your motive, then?"

"He was crawling toward me. I wasn't taking no chances."

"So you killed Folded Leaf in self-defense?"

"I did."

Charlie, doubting that Benson would do himself any more good, said, "The defense rests." O. A. Dilk then took over.

Judge McGowan, who had seen many a lawyer perform, felt

sorry for Benson. Dilk was no natural orator like Fort. But he would take that jury over the logical jumps of the killing so smoothly it would end up with "murder" in its mouth without knowing how the word got there.

Dilk made no reference to the verdict—except to praise the jurors for their devotion to duty. They fairly blossomed.

There was not a jot of difference in law between the two killings. McGowan knew it and knew that Dilk knew it. What those jurors knew was hard to say. Benson got healthier-looking by the moment. McGowan tried not to see him.

"Did you kill Folded Leaf?" Dilk was asking.

"I did," said Benson.

Then Dilk produced something from a carpetbag he was carrying. "Do you recognize this garment, Mr. Benson?"

The garment Oscar Dilk held up was a calico blouse. These blouses were much fancied by Indians because of their bright colors. This one had been red, but it was now so stiffened and discolored that little of the original red was visible.

Benson looked but did not speak. Dilk repeated his question.

"No," said Benson. But his face did not say no.

"Could you identify the shirt if you could see the color?"

"Well, I can't see the color."

"Do you know why you can't?"

"The shirt's dirty."

"Do you know what that dirt is?"

Benson sat in silence.

"I'll tell you, Mr. Benson, and the jury, what that dirt is."

Dilk held the blouse, first facing the jury, then the accused. "The rusty brown stains are blood. Great gouts and spurts of blood fell, probably from the head, onto this garment. Notice here, Mr. Benson and gentlemen of the jury, where the color is more gray than rust and the blouse is stiffened. That discoloration is human gray matter, a boy's brains, spilled onto his pretty red blouse. Now, Mr. Benson, do you remember Folded Leaf's red shirt as it looked before you smashed his skull against a tree?"

Benson got to his feet. He was a sick-looking man again. "You know why I killed that boy. I explained it all. My grandfather . . . This boy would grow up and do the same thing."

Dilk, without replying, took from his bag a second garment, a pair of buckskin pantaloons. One leg was intact; the other had been sheared off at thigh height, so that what was left hung in a few tatters of bloodstained buckskin.

"A boy with a leg like this would be a threat?"

"He was crawling toward Ben Cape right then. . . . You heard me say so."

"I heard Ben Cape say he was trying to get some help."

"I killed him out of pity. Yes, I did. He was suffering. I did it to put him out of his misery. I took the quickest way—"

Judge McGowan stopped his ravings. "Sit down, Mr. Benson."

Benson sat and Dilk then addressed himself to the jury.

"Gentlemen of the jury, I see I need not tell you that the case you had to consider yesterday and the one you have to consider today are very different. In the first, you found the prisoner guilty of manslaughter for using his rifle on a grown squaw. In the second, a boy, who went where his parents went, with no choice of his own, was taken by his heels and had his brains knocked out against a tree."

Dilk held up the bloodstained garments again. "Poor helpless child. Taken by his heels like a rabbit and brained. Was this not the act of a brutal murderer?"

Judge McGowan had given the jury a clear charge before it had retired for its verdict on the murder of the squaw. He saw no need of repeating it. He said only, "The charge is as before."

The jury, soft-footed in their moccasins, went into the little room behind the benches where they sat. Dilk left the shirt and pants on the table in front of him. The courtroom was silent.

After an absence of not many minutes, the jury returned, silent as before. "Have you reached a verdict?" asked Judge McGowan.

Gunn, the big Scot with sheep-textured hair, rose. "We have."

"What is the verdict, Mr. Foreman?"

"Guilty of murder in the first degree."

The prisoner was remanded, and the court adjourned.

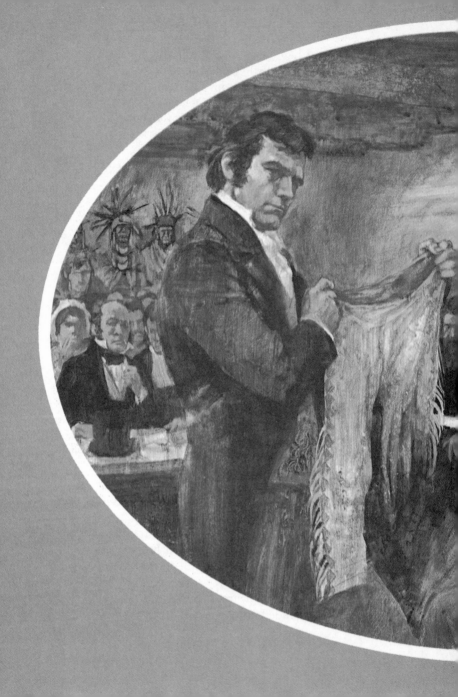

AFTER THAT VERDICT, the strength appeared to have gone out of the onlookers' legs. Many still sat as if felled by a blow. What kind of a sentence could McGowan give after a verdict like that? The boy had died a terrible death; no two ways about it.

The Cape family was strong enough to stand on its feet and start toward the Baldwin home. Hannah knew she should go with them: she was expected to help at her cousins'. Instead she lingered in the courthouse yard, striking up conversations with one person and another, looking for Charlie. She knew she should be feeling sorrow for George Benson, and she did, but at the moment she was grieving more for Charlie. He had done nothing worse than lose a case—his life wasn't at stake—but she loved Charlie, and you hurt where your heart was. And now she couldn't even find him. As soon as her family was out of sight, she searched in earnest.

He was still in the courtroom, backed into a corner with McGowan and Noble. At last he saw her over the heads of his companions and left to join her. "I know a place where we can be alone," Hannah said. "Where we can talk. It's a leaf cave."

Charlie had had his fill of talk. The verdict clanged in his head like a fire bell. Murder. Murder. "What's a leaf cave?"

"Come on and see."

She and her Baldwin cousins had discovered the leaf cave. Fox grapes, climbing a sycamore tree at the edge of a branch, had reached the top limbs, then spilled downward, making a green umbrella clear to the water's edge. "It's a little leaf house," she said. "Look, we marked off the rooms with pebbles."

"Which room is mine?"

"Every one is yours. Lie down. Rest. I'll sit beside you."

He felt like lying down. The land sloped gently toward the branch in the right way for resting. Hannah, with some idea of being a nurse to a man who had suffered a setback, kissed his closed eyes, made him a mustache out of her braid, and finally picked up his head and rocked it against her breasts like a baby.

He forgot there ever had been a trial. Rocked like a baby, he responded like a baby, and Hannah yelled, "You *promised.*" He had her bodice half unbuttoned.

"*You* promised to help me," Charlie said. "Then you lie down with me and hold me and kiss me. What help is that?"

"It is helping you to forget the trial—and Dilk and Benson."

"Dilk and Benson?" he asked. "Who are they?" He unbuttoned and she buttoned. This was becoming less lovemaking and more wrestling. "I love you, Hannah," Charlie said, trying to recall to her the purpose of these embraces.

He, not Hannah, relaxed when he said that. She sat on top of him and looked him in the eye.

"I hate you, Charlie Fort. You are not a man of your word. You are not strong in body or soul. I never want to see you again."

Having said this, Hannah leaped to her feet and ran, hair streaming, out of the house of leaves. Charlie's first impulse was to follow her. Then he thought better of it. If he did catch up with her someplace on the outskirts of Pendleton, what would people think? They'd think that what had not happened had.

He sat in the leaf house and thought, If this branch were big enough, I'd just jump in. He could afford the thought. It wasn't. He started walking home, home being Norry Culligan's house.

Enos Baldwin, Lizzie's brother, had a big family, set a good table, and there was always plenty of slop for the hogs. The washup that evening was big. Caleb helped Hannah carry the scraps to the pen out behind the privy where Spot and Pinky lived.

A pig with his snout in the gruel of dishwater and cabbage leaves may not be the prettiest sight in the world, but it ought not move anyone to tears. Nevertheless, Hannah was crying.

Caleb said, "There ain't been no sentence set yet."

But Hannah wasn't crying about George Benson. She was crying about Charlie. Told he was weak in body and soul. His defense of Benson gone to pieces. She saw him now, stretched out on his attic bed, recalling every painful word that had been spoken that afternoon.

She said, "I'm never going to give any pig I'm going to eat a name. I think if it's going to be meat, you should treat it like meat from the beginning. Not give it a human name, then go out one day, knock it on the head, and fry it. I'll never do that." And she threw her apron over her face and sobbed.

Caleb doubted his daughter was crying her heart out over a pig. "There was no way in the world," he said, "Charlie Fort could have got a decision for Benson in the face of the evidence Dilk showed the jury. Charlie's a good lawyer. But a jury's got to judge by law, not smooth talk."

Hannah uncovered her face. "That's what I told him he was, Papa. Just a smooth talker."

"When did you do all this?"

"This evening—just after the trial was over."

"That was piling the punishment on pretty high."

"I know it. I'm sorry for it now. But he made me mad."

"That temper is going to get you in trouble someday, Hannah."

"I'm in trouble now. Charlie hates me, I think."

"Well, you go tell him you're sorry for what you said, and he'll stop hating you, I expect."

"Tell him right now?"

"It's no more than first dark—and less than a five-minute run to Mrs. Culligan's. You'll feel better, and he will, too, like as not, if you sashay over there and say, 'Charlie, my tongue ran away with me.' Then you can run back home with a clear conscience."

Hannah took off her apron, threw it to her father, and started off. Caleb watched her go—appreciating her clean run, knees not clacking together in the hen run of most women. But he wasn't blind to Hannah's faults. Her height and her quick tongue were enough to scare off most boys. Fortunately Charlie Fort had a tongue of his own and inches to spare.

Caleb went back into the Baldwin hubbub feeling that some things in the world were still headed toward happiness.

THE run went out of Hannah when she saw the glimmer of light at Mrs. Culligan's. It was one thing to know that she'd like to tell Charlie she was sorry. *Charlie, you are not weak. I love you with all my heart.* It was another thing to walk bald-faced up to Mrs. Culligan's door and ask to see Mr. Fort, please. She climbed the porch steps noiselessly, so that, if at the last minute her courage failed, she could turn and run home and no one need be the wiser.

There was no answer to her whisper of a knock, or to the second knock, which was a murmur. Silently she went along the porch to the window of what, besides the kitchen, was the one downstairs room. The glimmer of light she had seen came from a candle set on the night table in that room. At first, in the gloom of its flicker, she saw only dim outlines of furniture. Then, as if they were in a picture filled in little by little by a hand determined that she miss nothing, she saw the two white bodies on Norry Culligan's bed, across from the window. They were male and female. They were Charlie Fort and Norry Culligan.

When Hannah saw this, the entire bed seemed to move to the very edge of the window. Charlie was asleep, lying with no arm or leg extended in affection toward Norry Culligan, and the sight comforted her some. Oh, God, in our extremity what banquets we make of crumbs! If Norry in the light of day was an old lady, in candlelight she didn't show it. Short, plump, and white as a squab. She was on one elbow, her back to the window, watching Charlie.

Hannah crept home. There was no run left in her. She hadn't known anyone could feel so sick without being on his deathbed.

X

THE courthouse was filled an hour before the trial was to begin next morning. The prisoner to be tried that day, Johnny Wood, had not yet been brought over from the jail. Judge McGowan was not yet in his place. The word was around that the judge alternated these days between praying and drinking glasses of water spiked with baking soda. No one envied him his job. The jury, with eleven other jurors to back up each individual juror in his decision, was not in a place so stony lonesome as the judge. It is easier to say "We all did it" than "I did it."

But the defense attorneys were there, having a conference. Charlie Fort had arrived first, hoping to see and talk to Hannah. He saw her, all right, talking to, or being talked to by, O. A. Dilk.

When he caught her eye, she looked at him with a vacant stare. He was glad to give his attention to the problem that faced the defense. Looking at Hannah, he might cry.

Noah Beazley said, "Is there any point getting that Cape boy up here and having him repeat his story?"

"Not for us," Charlie said, "but the prosecution may insist."

"You know Dilk, Charlie. Why don't you ask him if he'll agree to a stipulation that the boy's testimony be made a part of the record and that we spare the boy a repetition of that bloody story? Dilk ought to be willing—looks like he's trying to stand in well with the boy's sister."

Charlie wanted to get away from that subject. "Say they agree to the stipulation," he said, "what's our next move?"

"Put young Wood on the stand. He's got a right to defend himself, however you look at it. That he'd have shot an Indian woman, first in one breast, then the other, don't make good sense."

"He is the unlikeliest-looking murderer I ever saw," Charlie agreed. "The jury's going to have a hard time finding that sweet-faced boy guilty of murder in any degree. Let alone first."

"Then are we of the same mind about putting him on the stand?"

"We are," said Isaac Vickers. "Charlie, you talk to Dilk."

Charlie hoped to talk to Hannah as well, but as he approached, she walked away. Dilk, as Beazley had suggested, was eager to spare the Cape boy any further torment.

"I think I can promise you, Charlie, that the prosecution will agree to the stipulation. You put the Wood boy on the stand now and then we'll cross-examine. But I'd never let a witness like that testify if I was representing him."

"What worse can be said than what we've already heard?"

"Something worse can always be said," Dilk replied.

BEN Cape's testimony as to what he had seen Johnny Wood do at the sugar camp was read into the record. Then Noah Beazley, solid and fatherly, took over for the defense.

Beazley called Johnny to the stand. The boy put down a book he had been reading and was sworn in. Could a young man guilty of murder be that nonchalant? He went into the questioning as if all he had to do was to make his whole story known to be understood and excused.

BEAZLEY: Did you accompany your father and your uncle to the Indian sugar camp?

JOHNNY: Yes, sir.

BEAZLEY: Did you have a gun?

JOHNNY: Yes, sir. I was going squirrel hunting.

BEAZLEY: You didn't take the gun so you could kill Indians?

JOHNNY: No, sir. I was going squirrel hunting. You can ask Ben Cape. I stopped in there to ask him to go with me.

BEAZLEY: We have asked Ben. He says you gave up your squirrel hunt and joined your father and uncle in an Indian hunt.

JOHNNY: No, sir. I never did that.

BEAZLEY: Well, what do you call it, then? You shot and killed an Indian woman.

JOHNNY: No, sir. I never shot and killed any Indian woman.

When Noah Beazley finished his questions, Johnny looked into space, waiting for Mr. Armitage to begin his.

Jonathan Armitage, as if he understood that any rough handling of this soft-spoken stripling would prejudice his case with the jury, talked to Johnny like a kindly uncle.

ARMITAGE: I'm Jonathan Armitage, Johnny. I'd like to talk to you some more about what happened at the sugar camp.

JOHNNY: Yes, sir?

ARMITAGE: You saw some killing there, I believe?

JOHNNY: Yes, I did.

ARMITAGE: How many Indians were killed in all?

JOHNNY: Eight, all together.

ARMITAGE: Eight? There were nine dead bodies at the camp.

JOHNNY: You said Indians. There was one white woman.

ARMITAGE: Who shot the white woman?

JOHNNY: I did.

ARMITAGE: Why?

JOHNNY: I shot her because she was doing what was wrong, and she was trying to get me to do what was wrong. When a woman

401

does that, I know I have to put up a fight. I have to protect myself, or I'll join her in wrongdoing.

ARMITAGE: What wrong were you afraid of doing?

JOHNNY: That woman—

ARMITAGE: Wide Eyes? The Indian woman?

JOHNNY: I don't know her name. But she was white. She showed me she was white. She was no Indian.

ARMITAGE: How did she show you she was white?

JOHNNY: She tore open her dress and did what a woman shouldn't do. Showed me those two things a woman has. I shot one and that didn't stop her. So I shot the other. I seen a woman pointing those things at me once before and I know what she has in mind when she does that. I won't let it happen again.

ARMITAGE: What happened the first time, Johnny?

There was a muffled outcry from the courtroom, and Reba Wood, standing, addressed the prosecutor. "Armitage, you stop hounding my boy. Stop your prying. Johnny ain't no more responsible here for his past life than you are. And I don't reckon you're about to spill all that, are you?"

The courtroom exploded. Even the Indians broke their rigid line to face each other and talk.

Judge McGowan gaveled them into silence. Then he said, "Sheriff Brady, I think you'd better remove the prisoner from the room." Johnny Wood went with Brady as if happy to get out of the limelight and back to his book.

Reba Wood followed. McGowan was inclined to tell her what she had told Armitage: Don't hound that boy anymore. But there was no precedent for a judge to instruct a stepmother about her conduct with her stepson. When the two were out of the room, he gave his charge to the jury.

"You have heard a clear-cut confession of murder. The young man believed he was killing a white woman, though in fact he was shooting a woman who was at least half Miami. She was in no way threatening his life. He believed she was doing something wrong. The law does not empower us to shoot those whose ways are different from ours, or whose conduct we condemn. The law does not give us the right to excuse killing by the conclusion that the killer, if brought up in a different manner, might not have killed.

"The law is very clear on one point. If this was a premeditated killing—not self-defense, not accidental—the defendant is guilty of murder in the first degree. That is all you have to decide."

The jury, given their charge, was not out long. Brady brought the prisoner back into court to hear the verdict. Tom Gunn delivered it: "Guilty of murder in the first degree."

If this meant anything to Johnny Wood, his face didn't show it. The words might have come from the page of a book he was reading. Those in the courtroom had no fault to find with the verdict. A man who thought he had license to shoot loose women—white women—was better punished early than late.

No one knew what the Indians, except Black Antler, thought of the decision. Black Antler was against "murder for murder," and he let everyone know what he felt. Because he was a faithkeeper, the Indians let him talk. The whites believed him crazy.

One other Indian, a Miami chief, the most resplendently dressed Indian at the trials, did make his convictions known. He was named Lone Fawn, and like his tribe's woman Wide Eyes, he had more than a dash of white blood.

Lone Fawn approved wholeheartedly of the death sentence for those who had murdered the Indians at the sugar camp. But what he particularly liked was the method of the punishment. Indians had never used hanging, which, from what he had heard of it, was a manner of killing, slow and dignified. All took place at a height where the hanging could be well viewed—and the punishment, he understood, went on often for as long as ten minutes, with a considerable amount of convulsive twitching and jerking to entertain the onlookers. It was not exactly a religious occasion, but the whites' priests were present and there were prayers for and by the man to be strangled, if he felt like praying.

Lone Fawn, like the other Indians, had been invited to attend the hangings if they took place. It was an event he did not intend to miss. Justice would be done; but, beyond this, Lone Fawn had a natural bent toward the solemn, ceremonious, and fatal.

THAT NIGHT CHARLIE FORT sat at his attic table trying to put together something appropriate for the *Western Spy*. He was determined to keep out of his report everything about his breakup with Hannah. He couldn't, or wouldn't, write his father, Girl thrown me over; case gone to hell.

Hannah, heart of my heart. He tried to prevent himself from rehearsing that last meeting in an effort to create a new scene in which he and Hannah would walk away from that leaf house hand in hand, an engaged couple, as he had planned. Actually, what had he done that was so terrible? Unbutton a few buttons and kiss what the buttoning had covered. What had that fondling girl expected? Whatever it was, he wished he had done it.

The pain had never ceased except for that night, when Norry, nurse and mother and mistress, had made him forget and sleep. Norry kept clear of him now. Food on the table, bed made, but she herself always gone. It would have helped to talk to her.

He finally managed to get onto paper a bare account of Johnny Wood's trial. What was left to report was sad and short.

Extracts from a letter by Charles Fort to Enoch Leverett:

John Wood, Sr., after he learned of his son's testimony and the jury's verdict, refused the services of his lawyers and pleaded guilty.

His speech, addressed to Judge McGowan, was very moving. He said that he was as guilty as his son of killing a squaw; and that if his son had been found guilty of first-degree murder for this act, he should also be found guilty. In fact, he said he was four times as guilty as his son. Johnny had killed one Indian squaw. He had killed one squaw and three Indian children.

He said that he was an old man, that his son was the only tie that he had to life; that his present wife hated him; that he had been able to survive thus far in life in part because he had always fought Indians; and that he would consider his death now, if the judge so decreed, as the often expected termination of many of those fights. What he had never expected was that his death in such a fight would come from the hands of white men. If his countrymen had come to such a pass, he would rather be dead.

The old man was impressive. Tall, thin, gray, his Bible in his hand, his face, as we judge faces, righteous. His lawyers could not have done better for him than he did for himself.

I was glad I was not on that jury, though Wood Sr. was right. The jury could not find for other than first-degree murder. They were out about five minutes. Tom Gunn, the foreman, seemed too dry-mouthed to pronounce the verdict. This God-fearing old man, this Indian fighter from away back, his wife up to God knows what devilishness, and his son guilty of murder as a result—finding him guilty of murder must have seemed more of a blow than any man should be asked to deliver to another.

Gunn croaked a little as he said the words: "Guilty of murder in the first degree." Sheriff Brady led Wood, crying and kissing his Bible, from the courtroom.

Judge McGowan rose, picked up his gavel, but did not use it. He stood turning it over and over in his hand. "Four men," he said finally, "have now been found guilty of murder in the first degree. On Monday at ten in the morning those men will appear before me for sentencing. Until that time the court stands adjourned." Judge McGowan then brought his gavel down with so much force his real desire appeared to be to smash courthouse, lawyers, onlookers, the whole sorry lot.

End of extracts from a letter by Charles Fort to Enoch Leverett.

XI

IT WAS Sunday and Caleb was determined that there should be a regular hour-long meeting for worship. Tomorrow Judge McGowan would pass sentence on four residents of Fall Creek. These four men needed prayers; and Judge McGowan needed prayer perhaps more than any of them. Caleb himself wanted, on his knees, his face hidden from sight, to learn insofar as possible what God's will for him was. So it was going to be church for one full hour, and God have mercy on them all.

Oscar Dilk had made the ride over to the Capes' for two reasons.

First, he wanted to see Hannah. Once this trial was over, he would move on and, he had no doubt, up. His feeling was that Hannah would be the woman to go with him.

She would need a little "gentling," as these Westerners called breaking fractious horses. Slow down her movements, put a little more dignity in her speech. But the girl was naturally a lady. And she was, without being the greatest beauty, the most strikingly beautiful woman he had ever seen. No matter where he went, eyes would not stray from them if that woman was by his side. So the wooing of Hannah Cape was his first reason for coming.

The second was also important: to smell out the settlement's feelings. Here, along this creek, was where the four men lived who were now in jail. If there was to be any attempt at a jailbreak, here is where it would start.

Hannah was already dressed when he arrived an hour before church time. "Your shoes too fancy for a walk, Hannah?" he asked.

Hannah had one pair of shoes, and they were designed for walking. What else? "No, Mr. Dilk. Walking won't hurt them."

"Don't call me Mr. Dilk. My name's Oscar. I don't like it, but it's better than Mr. Dilk."

"Did anyone ever call you Ossie?"

Dilk was delighted. "No one ever did. Would you like to?"

Hannah hadn't the heart to disappoint him. "Yes, Ossie."

Dilk led Hannah to the bridge that crossed the branch below the Capes' house. "If you make a wish over running water, you get your wish, Hannah; did you know that?"

Hannah, remembering when she had stood here with Jud Clasby, thought, What I should wish is that some man like Dilk would fall in love with me and marry me and save me from falling in love with men like Jud Clasby and Charlie Fort. "Yes, I know."

"Have you got a wish?"

"I just wished it."

"Can you tell me?"

"No, of course not. If you tell, it won't come true."

Dilk took one of Hannah's hands and put it solemnly on the left side of the good broadcloth of his jacket.

"Can you feel that, Hannah?"

"Yes," said Hannah. "It is your heart."

"Do you know what it says? It says, 'Ossie loves Hannah.'"

For a second Hannah feared she would laugh. That is your trouble, Hannah, she told herself. You laugh at good men and let mashers have their way with you.

"Does Hannah say she loves Ossie?"

The wish took hold sooner than she had expected.

"I will when I know you better."

That was exactly the kind of answer Dilk wanted. He didn't care for girls who leaped before they looked. Hannah wouldn't say "love" like "good morning" or "pass the salt." When she knew him better, she would say it. But now the Capes' dinner bell, which served on Sundays as church bell, was ringing.

Summer in April was gone that morning. April, too, for that matter. It was now May, which had arrived with a cloudy sky and a raw wind. "A blackberry winter shaping up," they said, that season when freezing weather, or snow itself, matches the creamy blossoms of the berry vines.

Inside, the cabin was crowded, every bench filled, and children either sat on their parents' laps or squatted between their feet. Here sat the families of men who would at ten a.m. on the morrow hear a judgment of life or death.

There were present not only those fearing that the sentencing would be harsh, but those who feared that without death sentences, all of them would die at the hands of the northern tribes.

And Black Antler was there. He had Caleb's permission to preach, after church services were over, his own kind of sermon to as many as would listen. He stood alone against the wall, his austere dress as far from that of the Miami Lone Fawn's as a gray Quaker's from a furbelowed fop's. No headdress, plain moccasins, bare legs, breechclout and apron, and a doeskin jacket.

Caleb stood before them. Last night he had searched his Bible for the right text. Finally God had led him to it. Nothing except the Twenty-third Psalm would speak to the condition of all who were present this morning. The verses had come to him like a gift. Now he poured them forth like a gift. "*Yea, though I walk through the valley of the shadow of death, I will fear no evil: for thou art with me; thy rod and thy staff they comfort me.*" The words filled his mouth like a draft of cool water. The words a man speaks are always more comforting than the words he hears. Caleb knew that. He labored to put the taste of these words on the tongue of every man present. "*Surely goodness and mercy shall follow me all the days of my life.*"

Caleb was never sure whether the words that were in his heart then got spoken or whether they simply thundered in his veins.

"We are met as Christians. We say, *Thy will be done*. We have made laws which we believe will bring the kingdom of heaven nearer to earth. We must abide by them. We must pray for Judge McGowan as well as for the men who await his decision. We must remember that all things work for good for those who love the Lord."

These, he believed, were the words his lips said. Inside, others pounded to the beat of his heart: God, let this hour pass. It is more than we can endure.

Kill for killing. Or refrain from that and be killed for not killing. His final prayer was tears, with a few broken words floating on that tide.

Hannah, seeing the state into which her father had fallen, rose and said, "Let us sing." Many could not. The sides of their throats clung together like slices of meat hung in the sun to dry. Hannah sang. Oscar Dilk, with his lawyer's throat, sang. Lizzie sang. Caleb sat with his head in his hands. He was no true Christian. Why was the prospect of men going home to Jesus so horrifying? It was how they were being sent there.

The singing stopped, and Black Antler, before the congregation could decide that the meeting was over, took the preacher's place in front of the fireplace.

They were against him before he could say a word. His heavy-boned face hung above them like the mask of all the bogeymen they had been taught to fear from childhood days: the Indians! The Indians! Dark, like the devil; slant-eyed. Hair plucked to form

408

a scalp lock—an act of bravado—for easier scalping. And such a one here in a Christian church while white men, because of his kin, were threatened with hanging. And not content to be here listening, but rising to speak of forbearance, long-suffering, forgiveness. Such words in a heathen mouth, in God's name!

From the back of the room a voice called, "You were sent by the northern tribes to talk us into freeing the men in jail. If we do that, you will have an excuse for slaughtering us."

The cry was taken up all over the room. Listening to this red man urge them to become faithkeepers was more than they could stomach. Shouts of "Out, out!" grew to a chant.

Black Antler moved unhurriedly to the yard. He had no intention of staying inside, where his friend's home might be wrecked. Outside, he stood his ground, holding out his arms.

"I offer you myself. I will not run. Strike. You will feel better. I will not be harmed."

"We'll see about that," yelled a huge woodsman, who was carrying an axe handle. But Caleb put himself in front of Black Antler. "Who are the savages here?" he thundered. "Black Antler came because I asked him. He will eat with us. Those who want to join us are asked to. Let us all break bread together and pray for strength for tomorrow."

Oscar Dilk and two families from down near Pendleton stayed. The others left the place at once. Eleven whites and one Indian sat down to a repast prepared by the Capes for half a hundred.

JUDGE McGowan arrived at the courthouse nine o'clock the next morning and closed the door behind him. On the sheets of paper he carried were the sentences he would pronounce. McGowan put the sheets on the table and got onto his knees, with his face on his chair. "God, God," he prayed, "help me."

Outside, the lawyers, defense in one group, prosecutors in another, knotted together, both groups long in the face. The defense believed they had lost. How else read four jury decisions of "murder in the first degree"? The prosecution knew it had won. But what McGowan would do, they did not know. They did know he was honor bound to judge the taking of life, white or red, in the same way. If he did, four men would hear within the hour a sentence of death.

Charlie Fort, whose heart had received its own death sentence, decided to appeal. Hannah, wrapped in a big doeskin cape, was with her family, separated, happily, from Oscar Dilk.

Charlie went to her, greeted her parents and Ben, then said, "Hannah, may I speak to you alone for a few minutes?"

Hannah, the redhead, had her father's gray eyes, and when she looked at him, Charlie drowned in them. He could not speak.

"I am waiting," Hannah said when they had left her parents.

"Hannah, we love each other. We were going to be married."

"We did love each other. We were going to be married."

"What did I do?"

"You know."

"I told you we wouldn't make love again till we were married. We didn't."

"No," said Hannah. "We didn't."

"You don't love Dilk, do you?"

"Not the way I did you. But I can trust him."

"You can trust me."

Hannah's eyes filled with the whole of herself. She was without protection of any kind. "Charlie," she cried.

As she spoke, Oscar Dilk came to her side.

"Charlie trying to appeal his case, Hannah?"

"I'm not the winner today, Oscar. In court or out."

"Maybe your luck will change back in Cincinnati." Dilk turned to Hannah. "Court's opening. Let's not straggle."

Charlie watched the crowd pour into the courtroom. He felt he had already heard the sentence.

THE temperature inside the courtroom was like that inside a body —warm, moist, bloody. The room was so packed there was not enough space to breathe in except when your neighbor breathed out. Judge McGowan rapped his gavel.

"Sheriff Brady," he said, "bring in the prisoners."

When the four men were in front of him, the judge rose. He gazed at them for a long time before he began to speak. And then he spoke, it seemed, less to inform his listeners than to explain himself to himself.

"I have no wish to unnecessarily harrow your feelings," he began. "We are a civilized and Christian people. That is what we call ourselves—Christian, civilized. As such we have sent missionaries to the Indians so that they, too, might become Christian and civilized. There is no record of any hostile act by any Indian against a white before they were mistreated by us.

"How did we mistreat them? You know as well as I do. We took away their land, first of all. Oh, we paid for it sometimes. Not enough. But meanwhile we gave them a taste for whiskey, so we got most of the money back that way. We cut down their forests so that the game their lives depended upon vanished. And even when two families came to boil maple sap in what was their old home, we did not have the heart of decent men, let alone Christians, to say, We have more than enough. It was once yours. Share.

"No. Instead, we fell upon them. We killed women and children. In horrible ways I ask you not to forget.

"These murders would not have been committed, except that the murderers expected the approval of the people of this community. Four men alone will suffer under the law of the land. Everyone here must suffer under the law of heaven for making it possible for those men to believe that it was no sin to kill an Indian."

McGowan sat down in his fanback chair. "Luther Bemis."

Bemis, rigid, white, walked to the judge's bench.

"Luther Bemis, I hereby sentence you, for the murder of the Indian Red Cloud, to be hanged by the neck until dead."

Bemis, head high but staggering a little, returned to his place.

"George Benson."

Benson moved not an inch. The sheriff stepped in his direction, but Judge McGowan shook his head. "Let him alone, Sam. George Benson, for the murder of the boy Folded Leaf, I sentence you to be hanged by the neck until dead."

John Wood, Sr., stepped forward without being summoned.

McGowan's voice trembled for the first time. "John Wood, for the death of three Indian children and the woman Bright Water, I sentence you to be hanged by the neck until dead."

Wood Sr. returned to his fellow prisoners almost jauntily.

"John Wood, Jr., step forward, please."

Johnny looked at his father as if asking, Which direction is that? Wood Sr. gave his son a gentle push forward.

Judge McGowan leaned back momentarily and closed his eyes. Then he leaned forward. "I must speak to you, John. You killed the Indian woman Wide Eyes—"

Johnny interrupted the judge. "She wasn't an Indian."

McGowan said, "You are not to speak, John, but to listen. For the killing of Wide Eyes, the Indian, you are sentenced by this court to be hanged by the neck until dead."

Before this sentence was finished, a woman's scream drowned out the final word. Reba Wood was trying to make her way to McGowan. "Stop it," she shouted. "You can't kill a boy for that."

"Take the woman outside, Sheriff," Judge McGowan said.

Johnny Wood went back to his father's side. "Take her out," he echoed. "She's a bad woman, too."

CALEB Cape received permission to spend the nights before the impending execution, set only ten days in the future, in jail with the prisoners. Caleb could have found no rest away from these men of his church, particularly since one of them, Luther Bemis, would never, except for Caleb's word, have been in jail at all.

He did not know that his presence gave much comfort to anyone except John Wood, Sr., who, brought up in Bible reading and prayer, valued the nearness of his pastor in his final hour.

George Benson paid no heed to Caleb. He had ears for only one thing: the sound of a posse come to set them all free. Restore the country to its rightful ways of thinking. He had depended upon his sister, Reba, to stir up action for the rescue, but something had happened to Reba. He didn't understand what, but he waited for others to take up his cause.

Luther Bemis had not faltered in his belief that he had been right to confess. That hadn't lifted his spirits, however. He thought constantly of Ora and the child, due now at any time.

Caleb gave him what consolation he could. "Lizzie and Hannah are with her," he told Lute, "every minute. And Ben's going over every day to look after the stock. Ora's in good hands."

"They ain't my hands, though," Lute said. "Oh, God, Cale, my son will be born and I will never touch him."

"I had a son," Caleb said. "My firstborn. Died when he was four."

"What was his name?"

"Named for me."

"We plan to . . . we planned to call our first for me. Not that I like juniors much. But Ora wouldn't hear to anything else."

"You might have a girl."

"Ora don't think so from the way the baby kicks."

"Shut up, you two," George Benson said. "The court's robbing us of our lives. You rob us of sleep."

It was a cold night, and there was no means of heating the jail. Caleb wrapped his blanket about him and went as far into his own conscience, his own self-knowledge, as he could.

Greater love hath no man . . . Would he take Lute's place on the gallows if permitted? He thought he could. He'd had more years of life than Lute. Lizzie, with Hannah and Ben, would make out better than Ora alone with a new baby. He thought he could do it. Then he wondered, Could you take his sin on your shoulders? No, I could not. Only one man was able to do that.

He put his hand out to Lute, who was awake, head propped on folded arms. "Let go and sleep will come, Lute."

"I ain't afraid for one minute of the noose. Nobody who's been out in Indian country and fought Indians could be. A twitch at the end of a rope is a play-party game compared with the things they do. But then there was no Ora. There was no son. It's *now* that's tearing my heart out. Now. Now. Why now?"

Caleb turned face down in the straw. He kept silent, he believed, but his shoulders went up and down with his crying.

Bemis reached out a hand to the man who had brought him to God. "I'll tough it out, Cale. I'll tough it out."

413

BOOK THREE

THE VERDICT

XII

O. A. DILK believed in morning constitutionals. Lawyers' work required sharp brains and an iron butt. Those Oscar possessed. But he had no intention of letting legs and lungs rust from nonuse. Also, he'd be stout if he neglected his constitutionals. He wouldn't neglect a thing that might advance him.

All the lawyers, except Noble, who had had to return to Washington, were staying on for the execution. Their presence would dignify the occasion. The defense would stay to show the men they had defended unsuccessfully where their hearts were, the prosecution to see that what they had argued for was carried out. Everyone who had come to town for the trials had stayed, and others had arrived. The trials, whatever the results for the prisoners, were a gold mine for everyone with a loft to rent or a meal to sell.

Oscar, out early for his exercise, had walked a mile into the woods, two thousand paces—he always counted them—when he saw a rider, a long-legged boy on a big roan, approaching at a thundering pace. He thought, They're storming the jail. Find Brady. Oscar began to run. At the edge of the woods he intercepted the rider, who pulled up to avoid running him down. "Hannah," he shouted, "what're you doing here? And in that getup?"

Hannah had on a pair of Ben's buckskin trousers, a little tight in the bottom and short in the leg.

"What getup? Oh. Well, I had to dress in a hurry."

"Surely you had time to put on a skirt? I don't like my sweetheart riding astraddle, legs uncovered for anybody to see."

"Not unless they can see through buckskin. Ossie, something wonderful has happened. Help me to get into the jail."

"You can't get into the jail—with all those men. It wouldn't be decent. And not in that outfit."

"I've got to see my father. Luther Bemis has a new son. I was up

414

all night with Ora. I promised her I'd get the news to Lute as soon as possible."

"You could stop at Mrs. Culligan's and borrow a skirt."

"I don't want her skirt. If you won't help me the way I am, I'll ask the sheriff to get Pa."

Hannah left Oscar gazing after her as she galloped off. He liked spirit in a girl, but britches were a mite too spirited.

SHERIFF Brady was perfectly willing to fetch Caleb Cape for his daughter. If he saw anything unbecoming in a woman in trousers astride a horse, he didn't say so.

"Papa," she said when Caleb reached her, "Lute's baby was born last night. It's a boy, black-haired and big like Lute. I was there all night."

"How's Ora?"

"Fine. She wanted Lute to have the news as soon as possible."

"Lute ought to hear this firsthand."

"Ossie said they wouldn't let me in the jail."

"Ossie?"

"Mr. Dilk."

"So it's Ossie, now? Well, he's probably right. But they ought to let Lute out of the jail into the runway. He can't climb the stockade without help. You could talk to him there."

Sheriff Brady agreed to Caleb's suggestion. Hannah followed Brady inside the stockade and waited there for him to bring Bemis out. Neither she nor Lute spoke until the stockade door slammed on them.

"Ora?"

"Fine. You've got a baby boy."

Luther Bemis clasped Hannah in his arms and rubbed his bearded face against hers. Hannah was startled but knew what he was doing. She was Ora and Luther Bemis, Jr., all rolled into one. She was life, and he was about to lose life. But she was glad that Ossie, who might not understand such things, couldn't see.

"Oh, thank God, Hannah. Thank you for coming. Tell me everything. Did she have a hard time? What's the boy look like?"

"First of all, she said to tell you she loves you. She kissed me and said for me to kiss you and say it was from her." Hannah put her arms around Lute's neck and kissed him on the cheek.

Luther Bemis put his hand to his cheek, holding the kiss close. "Ory. Ory. Did it go hard with her?"

"In the beginning. But she said she'd have this baby in time for me to get the news to you this morning. And she did."

"That Ory! What's the baby look like?"

"He's got your hair, Lute. A big mop of black hair. He's ten pounds and not fat. Ora said to tell you he had your appetite."

"Ory, Ory."

"She's all right. Mama's with her and won't leave her."

"That's about long enough, Hannah," the sheriff called.

Bemis took Hannah's hands in his. "Tell Ory that she's carried my life and that she is my life. And that because of her I'm glad I was born—even to come to this end. I won't send her any kiss. Tell her that what I've got for her is too much for a seventeen-year-old to carry: which is Luther Bemis, body and soul. God bless you, Hannah, for bringing me the word."

Oscar Dilk was waiting with her father when Hannah came outside the stockade. "You go on over to your aunt Rebecca's," Caleb told her. "I'm going to talk with Lute for a while."

Oscar said, "I'll walk you over to the Baldwins'. Your aunt can fix you up with some proper clothes, I expect."

"Who can care about clothes at a time like this? Men going to die. One never to see his son. I wouldn't care if I was naked."

"Now, Hannah, you're overwrought. One reason I've been so proud of you is that you're always so neat about your person."

"Neat about my person?" Hannah repeated. No girl had ever been loved, had she, for being neat about her person?

"Neat about your person," Oscar repeated firmly. "Fastidious, I might say. And where we're going, that'll be important."

Hannah wanted to say, Where *are* we going? But she was too proud to ask. And she was too obstinate to forgo her belief that Ossie was the one man who could save her from running headlong back to a two-timer.

Lute knew what he had to do, and knew that he couldn't do it without help. On the second day after Hannah's visit he asked Caleb to his corner of the room to talk. The room had been divided by choice into individual living areas. The Woods in one corner, Benson in one, Lute and Caleb in the third. The fourth corner held wash bench, pitcher, and water bucket. And a bucket chamber pot, emptied four times a day—not quite often enough.

In Lute's corner, Caleb leaned against the wall and Lute paced in front of him.

"Cale, I've got to see that baby."

"I've been thinking. I don't know if what I've got in mind will work, but this is it. They never put any leg irons on you. You can get over the stockade, but not without help."

Lute took a deep breath. "You mean you'd help me?"

"I'll help you. Not to escape. You keep that in mind. I'm helping you to have one look at your son—then you hotfoot back here. A day for the trip, a day for the visit, a day to return. It'll be hard to come back, Lute."

"It wouldn't be any harder coming back than it was coming in."

"There's the baby to leave now, as well as Ora. And the sentence to face. You didn't have them when you confessed."

"I knew the baby was coming. And what the sentence might be. I ain't changed my mind about what I did. I'll be back."

"We got to get you out first."

Johnny Wood seemed to do all of his living at night. In the daytime he was far away, not in the jail, scarcely in life itself. At night he dreamed, talked to himself, screamed.

The night after Caleb's talk with Bemis, Johnny had one of his screaming dreams. The minute it started, Caleb, disregarding contents, emptied water bucket and chamber pot, ran with them to the jail door, and clanged them together, crying, "Guard. Guard!"

Matt Holmby, the guard on duty, was inside the jailhouse in seconds. "What's going on here?"

Caleb, at his side, said, "The boy is having a fit, Matt. Grab his tongue. He'll choke to death."

Holmby had rushed in without a lantern, and in the dark it was hard to find the boy, let alone his tongue. Holmby's handling awakened Johnny. The screaming stopped; tongue swallowing was no longer a danger.

Caleb was at Holmby's side when Johnny quieted down.

"You all right now, boy?" Holmby asked.

"It was just a bad dream. I'm all right when I wake up."

Holmby said, "Everyone else ready to settle down now?"

Only Benson answered. "Nobody's keeping us awake but you."

Caleb went to the jailhouse door with Holmby, like a courteous host. "Never knew the boy to have such a fit before."

Matt said, "What's he scream about?"

"Something he did in the past, likely."

"The shooting?"

"I couldn't say as to that."

"Well. Good night, Reverend. Get inside. It's freezing."

"Good night, Matt. You maybe saved a life tonight."

Two hours later Benson got up to use the chamber pot. He went bellowing to Caleb's corner. "What did you do with the pot?"

Caleb, sitting up, said, "I'm afraid I left it outside when I went out to rouse up Matt."

"What d'you expect me to do now?" Benson leaned over Caleb menacingly, then straightened up. "Where's Lute?"

Caleb said nothing.

"Where is he, Cale? He sleeps here beside you."

Johnny woke up. "What's wrong? I ain't screaming again, am I?"

"No, you ain't, Johnny, but I am. I'm about to scream my head off." Benson went to the jail door and bellowed, "Matt, Matt. Man loose. Come running, Matt. Man loose."

Matt came running, this time with a lighted lantern in his hand. "What's wrong now?"

"Luther Bemis's gone."

"That can't be. He was here just a while back."

"Well, he ain't here now. Look for yourself."

Holmby looked. He kicked up the loose straw, he shook Bemis's blankets. "He's gone," he finally agreed, and ran to get Brady.

The sheriff was there in ten minutes, nightshirt tucked into his pants and a big bearskin coat on top of his nightshirt. The night was bitter cold and there were occasional splatters of sleet. Brady had a lantern and he, too, had a look around.

"Matt, did you lock the jail door when you came in here?"

"I locked the stockade door. Even if he run outside, that's as far as he'd get."

"It's as far as he'd get without help."

"Who'd help him? Everyone was right under my nose."

Caleb stepped into the circle of lantern light.

"Sheriff, I boosted Bemis up so's he could make the climb."

Holmby said, "Reverend, you're crazy. You was right beside me."

"Matt, while you were hunting around for that boy's tongue, I was outside with Bemis."

"Cale," Brady said, "you know what you've done? Helped a condemned prisoner escape. That's obstructing justice. That's punishable under law. What in God's name got into you?"

"That man come to the jail of his own free will. He'll come back the same way. I helped him so's he could have one look at his newborn son. I couldn't do less for a dying man."

"I reckon God knew what He was doing when He put preachers in the world, Cale. But even He didn't figure on their lacking common sense. Bemis won't be back. Not once he gets a look at his wife and child. I'm going to set men to tracking him right now."

For the first two or three miles Luther Bemis thought he had wings. He didn't notice the weather. All he knew was that he was outside, running home. To Ora and their baby. Ory, my Ory. A man with a good woman oughtn't to get mixed up with God. God and a good woman got in each other's way for a man who wanted to please both.

He'd have to slack up. He'd run three or four miles without being winded. Twenty miles at that pace he couldn't do. He knew the way, all right, but by eye, not by soles of his feet, and in dark like this you could run in circles.

When he slowed down, the cold hit him. He was sweaty from

running, and soaked through by sleety rain. It wouldn't have done much good if he had given a thought to the weather he'd be traveling through. You didn't enter jail with a wardrobe designed for jailbreaking in the middle of a blackberry winter. He had on his moccasins and linsey-woolsey pants, and a deerskin jacket over a calico shirt. The sleet was freezing around his face and butt. He'd have to take a commonsensical pace, slower than he'd been going, but fast enough so he didn't end up an icicle.

There was a trace running between Pendleton and the settlement on the creek. He had started on the trace, then believed he could make faster time in the cutoff through the woods. In daylight, in decent weather, he could have. But now half the effort that should have gone into moving ahead was spent in climbing up and over fallen trees, into and out of creeks that wet him to the knees. He was soaked through and dog-tired when by pure luck he stumbled onto the trace once more and swore never to leave it. He *had* run in circles and, for a minute or two, he thought he might now be traveling in the wrong direction. The idea was so terrible it cheered him up. Run all night and find yourself at morning light right where you'd started from—in jail.

He had covered perhaps another mile when he heard horsemen behind him. There was only one explanation of horsemen here on a night like this: they were hunting him. He got off the trace and back into the woods as quietly as he could. He stumbled to his knees against a fallen tree—a hollow tree, it proved—and he was almost startled into an outcry when a nest of young raccoons ran against him to escape from the log. He explored the opening with his hand. Big enough for him to crawl into.

He didn't know how cold he had been until he got into the dryness of that great fallen beech. He was aware then of an uncontrollable shivering, which meant, he knew, that his body was in danger of freezing. Inside the log, where the chips and leavings of the animals' nesting made him a mattress, the shaking finally stopped. The log wasn't long enough to cover his feet, but some of the warmth that was returning to his body would surely be carried down to them.

He thought he heard more horsemen go by up on the trace. No use exposing himself to another band of searchers. He had as well snuggle down amid the leaves for a little rest.

THE men Brady had dispatched in the search party were back at Pendleton by noon—without Bemis. It was still storming, well below freezing, and the men were gray with cold and weariness.

A dour Brady met them outside the jail. "No luck?"

"Sam," Jim Mullins said, "in this blinding storm we couldn't've seen a buffalo if it didn't bump into us."

"Did you go to his house?"

"We did. His wife had a new baby, but we looked under and in her bed. He wasn't there and hadn't been there."

Brady went directly to Caleb, who was stretched out on his pallet in the jail. "No trace of Bemis," Brady said. "He's given us the slip. I'm taking your word that you believed he'd go home."

"I still believe it."

"It won't make any difference, as far as you're concerned, which way he headed. You helped him escape. There's a prison sentence for that. And that ain't the half of it. We let one condemned man escape and every buck in the Six Nations will claim a right to lift the hair of every white man between here and the Lakes."

"I'm ready to hang in Bemis's place. That ought to satisfy the Indians. Four men sentenced and four men hung."

"And just how do you figure on making the official roll call at hanging time? You plan on mounting that platform, singing the doxology, then saying, 'Me, too, please'?"

"I'll leave the working out of the program to you, Sam."

"If you can get yourself sentenced to hang, I'll hang you. If not, you're going to have to tough it out as a preacher who got the wool pulled over his eyes by one of his backsliding church members." Brady shook his head. "Cale, up to now you were in here through my good-heartedness. You're a prisoner now. The grand jury will meet to indict you for helping a condemned man to escape."

"That's no more than fair."

"It's legal, and that's my lookout."

XIII

Luther Bemis knew exactly where he was when he woke up—and knew that he had slept longer than he had intended. From inside the log he could tell it was no longer night, but there was no sunshine in the day. He was cold and stiff. He had better get out before he was permanently log-shaped and immobile.

He squirmed out of the log, and after he was clear of it he lay still for a few minutes, listening for searchers. The sleet had been replaced by a ground fog, rolled up from the warmer creek. He could hear the drip of water from trees, ice melting, nothing else.

He sat up carefully. He had to move slowly, but he felt no pain. Encouraged, he put his hand to the ground, preparing for the same slow rise to his feet. He was half up, had one foot under him, when he collapsed. His feet were frozen clods, clumps of unfeeling flesh as incapable of supporting him as a cowpat.

He sat there, filled with a sardonic humor. Life hangs upon hinges of chance. He met Caleb Cape and got converted. Converted, he had to confess his sin. Confession put him in jail. Caleb got him out. And here he sat in worse case than bedded down on straw and with death ahead at the end of a quick clean jerk.

He had no way of judging how far he'd traveled toward home—not a landmark to be seen in the smother of ground fog. He was not in pain now, but would be as soon as blood in his calves, blocked off from its regular flow, began to pound in his veins. He could crawl. He didn't have the pants for it. But he *would* crawl. There was still a chance of getting home and seeing that baby.

Animals on all fours can make good time. But not man. Long before nightfall Lute's kneecaps were raw and bleeding. He took his jacket off and tried using it to cushion his way.

The ground fog had thinned out, but a small icy wind had sprung up and went through shirt and skin clear to his heart. He could now make out where the sun was: halfway down the afternoon sky. If tonight was as cold as last night, he'd have lost more than his feet by morning. He wasn't a man to die sitting down. But how could he die any better a mile or two farther and his knee bones scraped clean of flesh?

What had he done wrong? Turned to God? Had a drink? Broke jail? Got a son? Come back to civilization? "Come back to civilization" held about the whole of what was wrong, he reckoned. Out where he'd been, west of the Mississippi, killings didn't have to be confessed, and God hadn't staked out a claim yet. Would he give up Ora and their son, and the warmth in the emptiness of his heart that Caleb's conversion had brought him, to be back west again? Two feet to stand on? No death sentence ahead?

By God, he wouldn't. He'd die crawling. He threw the jacket ahead of him and crawled onto it.

CHARLIE Fort and Norry Culligan sat in Norry's kitchen drinking tea. They, or at least Charlie, had passed beyond self-consciousness, shame. Someone had been kind to him when he was desperately unhappy. Some bond attached him to this woman; he would be hard put to give it a name. Loving-kindness, perhaps.

Norry had a name for what she felt for Charlie: just plain yearning love. But she was a hardheaded Irishwoman, and she had no intention of throwing away what she had in pursuit of what she knew she could never get. Charlie held her hand sometimes, patted it gently in the way he would a kitten. She was at least as smart as a well-trained kitten; she didn't try to climb up his arm.

They were both down in the mouth this afternoon. The weather, which had showed signs of fairing off around noon, had turned arctic again. Fairest sunshine wouldn't have cheered them, though it would have made them more hopeful about Luther Bemis's fate.

Charlie said, "What in God's name got into Cale Cape, do you think, to help Bemis break jail?"

"It's always been there. Milk of human kindness."

"Milk of human kindness is going to get him a jail sentence, unless I do a better job of defending him than I did those others."

"You think you'll get to see Hannah more, defending him."

"It entered my head."

"It's an ill wind," Norry said. "What's she see in that Dilk, anyway? Hannah ain't going to be more than a crutch to him, helping him climb the steps to the statehouse."

"Maybe Hannah'd like to climb some statehouse steps."

Norry looked at the young man with blue eyes still life-filled. "Don't run the girl down just because she gave you the mitten. And if you want to climb statehouse stairs, you can. No need of a crutch, either. I'd like to tell that girl a thing or two."

"There's a thing or two you'd better be quiet about, Norry," Charlie said. He'd gotten that easy with Norry.

BETWEEN losing the case and losing Hannah, Charlie'd about dried up as a source of news for his father. If he wasn't careful, he'd soon add another ache to his miseries: How did I fail my father?

After he left Norry, he set about remedying that one. And in the act of trying to tell his father what was going on in Pendleton, the stone in his chest lightened a little.

Extracts from a letter by Charles Fort to Enoch Leverett:

Perhaps those most outraged by Luther Bemis's escape are the Indians. Lone Fawn, a Miami chief, and Bent Arrow, a Seneca brave, representing the Indians who have gathered here to see that the executions take place per government promises, went to Sheriff Brady and accused him of doing what has been done before in such cases involving the murder of Indians: locking the criminals up for a while, then seeing to it that they get loose. Brady was as mad at this accusation as the Indians were at the escape. What he told them, in unprintable language, was to head for the woods if they thought they could do a better job of finding Bemis than his men had. The two Indians left at once.

Brady is having erected the most impressive gallows ever heard of hereabouts—let alone seen. Platform of oak timbers, twelve feet above the ground. The hanging beam, a walnut timber a foot through, rising about eight feet above the platform. Brady has been scoffed at for the size of it, and for the rope and hangman, both imported from Cincinnati. It is a little odd for the most solid structure in town to be the gallows tree. But the prisoners can be thankful that nobody's going to have to be hanged twice, as has happened before, when beams or ropes break.

The gallows site is a rolling meadow on the north bank of Fall Creek, just above the falls. It is spacious enough to accommodate the more than a thousand spectators who are expected. Rising above the meadow is a low but extensive ridge. Colonel Johnston, the Indian agent, is offering this to his Indian observers, so they can clearly see that the government's word has been kept. He no doubt also wants to keep the Indians and the whites from being elbow to elbow at a time of so much emotion.

Thus matters now stand, with the execution date only four days distant: Clasby vanished; Bemis escaped; the preacher in jail with the three remaining condemned men; the gallows waiting.

End of extracts from a letter by Charles Fort to Enoch Leverett.

CHARLIE put down his pen. The *Western Spy* was now as up-to-date as he was. And he didn't care. He had to face it. All he cared about was Hannah. What *could* he do? She wouldn't listen to a word he had to say. He leaned his face against the window. It might have been ice. He could hear the rising wind in the spruce trees, and floor joints creaking as the cold deepened. If I cried, he thought, my face would freeze to the glass.

NIGHTFALL was at hand. Luther Bemis had given up crawling. His knees were worn down to raw bone. The throb in his feet had passed beyond pain and become a sickness that filled his whole body. He knew what was happening. His feet were dying, and the poison of their death was being passed into his entire body. This was going to be a harder way to die than with a broken neck at the end of a rope. But Ora would know why he had chosen it.

The pain of his knees, or the poison, or lack of food, had caused him to faint—not to the point of unconsciousness, but to the point of leaving his body behind. He could see it stretched out on his jacket, his knees bloody, his eyes sunk into his head. This man is dying, he thought. He floated, but the floating was like seasickness. Now he saw figures he knew were imaginary: two Indians. The sight of them made him glad. It would be easier to endure the pain if he had witnesses to his hardihood.

One of the Indians spoke in English to the body stretched out on the ground, "This would have been your last night, if we hadn't found you." To his companion, a younger man, the Indian spoke in Seneca, and the young man trotted away. The Indian who remained said, "He will bring ice from the stream. I will bind it to your feet with sycamore leaves. You will have less pain."

"Who are you?" Lute asked.

"Lone Fawn."

Lute came down from where he was floating, closer to the Indians—and to the pain in his body. "Miami?"

"Yes."

"Wide Eyes?"

"My niece."

Lute was moving in and out of his sick body. "It should not have happened. Why are you helping me?"

"I want to see you hang." Lone Fawn took off his fur-lined cape and put it around Lute's shoulders. "It is shameful to hang. Killed by your own people. I want my people to see that."

"I am willing."

The younger Indian returned with foam ice held in a cup of leaves. Lone Fawn removed Lute's moccasins and filled each one with the ice and leaves, then shoved Lute's feet back into them. If the Indians hadn't been there he would have screamed. A shoe of red-hot steel couldn't have hurt more. But he was determined from childhood to equal Indians' endurance. Lone Fawn watched him closely. "Your feet will feel better soon."

"You are very kind, Lone Fawn. What's your plan for getting me back to the jail?"

"A travois. We will make one."

They made it before his eyes. Two poles. Lone Fawn's jacket and Bent Arrow's extended between the poles by their sleeves. The two Indians were left in shirt sleeves. Lute was lifted onto the travois and tucked under Lone Fawn's cape as if he were a babe.

"Good night, Mother," Lute said.

Lone Fawn did not smile. "I have said why I am helping you."

The Indians handled him as if he were a featherweight. They carried him smoothly, moving fast even in the darkness.

When they reached the trace and began to pull the travois, the passage was less smooth. The ice around his feet had melted, and he could feel the throb of his shattered knee bones deep in his groin. But he kept his mouth clamped shut.

Lone Fawn stopped and put some jerky in his mouth. "You might have escaped if you had headed in the other direction."

"I know that Clasby went that way, and escaped."

"Clasby is still running. Yes."

"I wanted only to see my son. Then I would come back."

"Why come back?"

"I had done wrong. I was willing to be punished."

"Willing to die?

"Yes."

"How old is your son?"

"One week."

"You kill at the wrong time."

"I was drunk."

"You are as bad as the red man."

"Worse."

"We will bring your woman and boy to you."

Lone Fawn and Bent Arrow returned Luther Bemis to the prison on the morning of the third day before the execution. Bemis's knees were healing, but his feet were dead flesh. Norry, who knew through Charlie of his pain, sent a bottle of painkiller for him to Sam Brady. Sam gave the bottle to Caleb. "It's opium more than likely," Brady said. "Could start him on a craving for it."

"It can't last long if it does start."

The spoonful Caleb gave Lute at noon that day kept him asleep until nightfall. When he awoke, he couldn't remember where he was. "Ory," he said, "I'm better. What time is it?"

"It's Cale, Lute. You're in Pendleton jailhouse. Ora ain't here."

"I was on my way home. I dreamed two Indians carried me."

"It wasn't a dream. They did. And they're going to bring Ora and the baby here to see you."

It all came back to Lute. "Why are they going to do that?"

"Don't ask me to explain Indians to you. They liked the way you talked on the way back, for one thing."

"How they going to get Ory in? She can't climb that wall."

"Brady will let her in. The Indians did him a good turn. Brought you back so he could have a proper hanging. And he don't cotton to the idea that any savage has a kinder heart than Sam Brady."

"But, Cale, what if Ory won't come with the Indians? It's nothing she'd ever do in ordinary times. Nothing I'd let her do. She'll lock the door and shoot one of them through it."

"If I could send Hannah with them, she'd warn Ora. But I can't. I'm as much a prisoner here now as you are."

"What'd you do, Cale?"

"Helped a condemned man escape."

"Me? They put you in prison for that? I wouldn't have done it if . . . Well, I reckon I would. How long'll they keep you in?"

"I don't know. But don't shed any tears. For a spell I figured you weren't coming back at all. Thought I'd end my days here."

"My God, Cale, I'd never run out on you. You know that."

Cale took Lute's hand. "I know that. And I've figured out how to get word to Hannah. Fort's my lawyer now. I got a right to see him, and he'll take the word to Hannah."

"Hannah may be afraid of the Indians herself."

"The shoe'll more likely be on the other foot."

Lute laughed. He'd supposed he'd never laugh again. But he had. He had a wife and a son and a friend. And he'd done the right thing finally, and he didn't doubt the Lord would honor him for it. There were a lot of men laughing with less.

THERE'S no use planning in this world, Charlie thought on his way to the Baldwins'. While he was sitting in his attic room trying to figure out whether his chances would be harmed or helped by seeing Hannah again, fate gave him no choice. He had to see her now. At the Baldwins', the old folks and the young uns, including

429

Oscar Dilk and Hannah, were sitting in a semicircle facing the fire.

After paying his respects to the Baldwins, Charlie said, "I have an urgent message for Hannah from her father."

"Well, what is it, Charlie?" Oscar asked, as if he were empowered to speak for Hannah.

"Hannah's father asked me to talk to her alone. If she'll step outside with me, I'll tell her what he wants her to know."

"Charlie, Hannah and I have an agreement—what concerns one of us concerns the other. I'll just step outside with you two."

"Is this true, Hannah?"

"Yes, it is true. We agreed on that."

"Hannah, since you and Oscar have this agreement, I reckon your father'd be willing for him to hear it, too."

Hannah put on a shawl. Oscar, showing his hardihood, went outside in his shirt sleeves.

"Cale Cape is crazy," Dilk said when he heard the message.

"Don't you say that about my father, Ossie."

"I apologize, Hannah. But your father's too trusting. How's he know what two red men's intentions are toward you?"

"He trusts them, Ossie, just as you said."

"Well, trust apart, how's it look? One girl riding off with two men. It don't *look* good, whatever their intentions may be."

"What do looks matter, Ossie? What matters is that Lute gets a chance to see his wife. I don't care about looks."

"Well, I care. What you do, no matter how good your intentions are, will be judged by how it looks. No, Hannah. I forbid you."

"I am going. You tell Father, Charlie. My mind's made up."

XIV

THE two Indians, with Ora, Ora's baby, and Hannah, rode into Pendleton in the late afternoon the day before the hanging was to be. Sam Brady was outside the jail stockade awaiting them, with the additional guards he had ordered for the night. Brady didn't fear a rescue posse as much as George Benson hoped for one, but he didn't plan to be taken by surprise, either.

Lone Fawn, before either woman could speak, addressed the sheriff in his elegant English. He had made a pause at the Indians' camp outside town to don some of his finery. Beside him, Sam Brady looked like a farmer going squirrel hunting, and both men knew it. Lone Fawn spoke slowly, using simple words, reversing the usual practice of Indian-white conversation.

"Mr. Brady, I have here with me the wife and newborn child of one of your prisoners. We have come in the hope that you would permit the father to step inside the stockade for a few minutes so that he can see his wife and infant son."

Brady understood Lone Fawn's tone and felt his dander rising. "Not a single prisoner is coming outside that jailhouse. Last time that happened, your husband, Mrs. Bemis, made his getaway. I don't figure on letting that happen twice."

"Bemis no longer has feet to walk on," said Lone Fawn.

"I hadn't finished, Lone Fawn, if you'll be kind enough to let me get a word in edgewise. There's no law says I can't let prisoners' wives in. Mrs. Benson is already in there, and has my permission to spend the night with her husband. Mrs. Wood could have been, but her husband didn't want her. You, Mrs. Bemis, can be with your husband tonight—if you want to."

Ora, at that, jumped from her saddle and threw her arms about the sheriff's neck. "God will reward you, Mr. Brady."

Brady said, "After what I've gone through in the last few weeks, I deserve some reward."

The Indians, responsible for this reunion, were left unregarded on the outskirts of the rejoicing. Hannah, the baby in her arms, reined her horse close to them.

"Lone Fawn," she said, "I thank you and Bent Arrow. I will never forget. If I can ever help you, remember that."

"Thank you, Miss Cape. Tell your people that Indians are gentle-folk when they meet whites who are gentlefolk."

"Before I leave the baby for the father to see, I'm taking him to the Baldwins' to wash and feed. They will give you supper."

"We will ride with you, but we will eat at our own camp."

The single street was crowded with people, like sightseers come to a fair. Hannah was glad that the baby she held could not know that these travelers had come to see his father hang.

The three riders—the half-naked Seneca, and Lone Fawn, looking like the Miami chief he was, and the long-legged redhead with a baby in her arms—were not unnoticed in the crowd. One man, his face unsmiling, tipped his hat. Hannah was almost past him before she recognized Oscar. "Ossie," she called. He shook his head and stepped back into the crowd.

"You must say good-by to the red men before your white man will be friends again," said Lone Fawn.

BRADY had bent over backward letting the two women spend the night with their husbands. He hadn't bent far enough to permit candles or lamps. He was determined to have four men to hang in the morning. A candle turned over in that straw and he wouldn't have men, wives, or jail. Or me, Caleb Cape thought. The thing Caleb wished was that the roof was off the jail so that the men could, on this last night, see stars. On *his* last night, he'd want a look at sky and earth.

But what did Luther Bemis care about stars? When Ora had knelt to put that baby in his arms, Lute had made a sound the like of which Caleb had never heard before. Maybe God had made a sound like that when he first saw Adam. Lute nuzzled his face against his son's. Then Ora bent down so their three faces touched.

Caleb had doled out enough medicine to cut down Lute's sharpest pangs, but yet leave him sufficiently awake to know who he was and who was with him. If he forgot where he was, no harm in that.

It was full dark outside as well as in when the guard gave the squalling baby back to Hannah, who came for him in an hour.

"He's hungry," Ora apologized for her son.

"Don't you suckle him, Ory?" Lute asked.

"No. I had a reason not to."

"You never told me."

"No. I will, though. You'll see I was right."

Caleb gave Bemis another small dose. "You don't figure there's enough in there to quiet down Benson, do you?" Lute asked.

"It would take the whole bottle to do the job."

Benson was screaming at the top of his lungs. What he was bellowing against was not the prospect of his death. He could face death. But in jail, condemned to die because his neighbors and friends wouldn't raise a hand to help him, that cut him to the quick. "I'm crying for my country. What's it coming to? God!" He banged his head against the log wall of the jail. Sarah tried to stop him, put her arms around him. But Benson only banged his head more.

Ora came to Caleb, who was leaning against the door where he could catch a whiff of the fresh cold air that blew into the room.

"Cale, I did a wrong thing, but it might help George. I didn't know there'd be medicine for Lute's feet and I knew he'd be in pain, so I brought this." She held up a pint of whiskey.

"How'd you get it in?"

"Hanging on a cord under my skirt. I know it was wrong."

"Ora, there's such a mix-up of wrong and right in this jailhouse tonight, I don't know as God Himself could sort things out. George thinks he's forsaken by all. A remembrance from you would touch his heart. You take it to him. It may quiet him."

It did that. George greeted Ora like the only friend who had kept him in mind, downed the whole bottle, and took Sarah's suggestion to rest his head in her lap and snooze.

Ora talked with Sarah for a minute, then returned to Caleb.

"Cale, I'm not mad at you anymore. Lute's at peace with himself. He never would've been if he'd done what I wanted—run. He'd of hated himself, and me, too, likely, before long. Your words didn't save me, Cale, nor your prayers. Only Lute's example's done that."

"Ora," said Caleb, "don't make me cry. Preachers just preach. But it takes men like Lute, who live out the words, to bring the light home to others." He took the spoon and half-empty medicine bottle from his pocket. "You dole this out to him, Ora, as you think he needs it."

"What're you going to do?"

"Me and John Wood are going to say Bible verses. Have a kind of Bible-verse hoedown. See who knows the most."

Before going to the Woods' corner, Caleb stood again at the crack of the door, where the whiff of the outside world came to him. He, not fated to die in the morning, savored the earth to the bottom of his lungs. He wished he belonged to some church that had thought out long ago words and acts suitable for men's last hours on earth. Words the dying believed in; words that would make a bridge between jail tonight and paradise tomorrow. He felt the need of more than he, with only his memory of the Scriptures and his heartache, could provide. God help me.

Over in the Bemises' corner, Ora was saying, "You let me know when the pain's too great, Lute. There's no sense you bearing it just to show me you can. I know you can do anything."

"Except stay away from the whiskey bottle."

"That's past. Did you like our baby?"

"I never seen his equal. Ory, one thing you got to promise. Don't you stay a widow. You was meant to be a mother."

"I am a mother. And I'll never marry again. I don't want to and it wouldn't be fair to any other man." She put her hand on him. "Lute, I've got to tell you something. You know how easy the baby come."

"Hannah told me. But it wasn't like hearing it from you."

"Oh, I wish you could've been there. You'd have laughed to see him. It was like he was tired of being inside so long."

"But why don't you nurse him? I always figured I'd like to see you nursing our baby."

"I wanted you to give me another baby. A nursing mother can't get in a family way. You know that—except now and then."

"How'd you figure, nursing or not nursing, there'd be any way for me to give you a baby—me locked up in a jailhouse?"

"I knew I'd see you. I trusted in the Lord. I'm a Christian now, Lute. And I'll bring our children up to be Christian."

"Children?"

"Our little boy and our little girl?"

"You even know the denominations?"

"I called the turn last time, didn't I? Lute, we haven't said one word about love."

"When we live it, we don't have to say it."

"We could say it, anyway."

"I can tell you the truth. You're the woman I waited ten years to find. I love you, Ory. The mother of my children."

"You said children."

"That's what I said. Give me a quarter spoonful."

She measured the medicine with great care.

"Ory," Lute said, "I'm man enough for both of us from the knees on up. So if you and the medicine work together, I think I could just about make us an eight-pound girl. You understand, Ory?"

"I understand. What'll the preacher think?"

"In the first place, he can't see you. In the second place, he don't expect you to sleep with all your clothes on."

"Lute . . . Oh, my Lute."

BEFORE he got to Bible verses, old John Wood wanted to do some remembering, and Caleb listened. Wood said, "I reckon I've got a chance to go down in history as the first man to have his neck in a noose for killing an Indian. It'll seem a sudden thing to the rest of the country. Not to me. I been heading for that noose for some time. Ever since I bought that land in York state the developers had cheated the Indians out of. Land that was useless except for trapping and hunting, and we was farmers. Why did we buy it? Because we could get it for next to nothing. We didn't give a passing thought to the Indians we drove out.

"Next I headed west. More easy money. Free land, nothing to do but clear it and kill Indians. I lost my wife on that trip. That's the price I paid for free land. And I married Reba. That was more of the price. I ain't blaming Reba, I'm blaming myself. I went out with brother George to kill Indians to show her I was still as much a man in some lines as anyone else. And she done what she done with John Jr. to show me she was still a woman in some lines.

"For myself, what's to come tomorrow will be a relief. I believe in the Lord Jesus and I believe that He forgives those that believe on Him. Though whether He can forgive me for what I done to John Jr.'s going to test Him some. Cale, you know what Scripture's been going through my head?"

"No, John."

"His birth! All that rejoicing. That's what I'll do tomorrow. Be born again. Rejoice."

Johnny, who had been lying on his pallet, listening but not joining in the conversation, sat up.

"I am going to die tomorrow."

Caleb did not know any honest way of denying this. "Those who believe on Him have everlasting life, Johnny."

"I don't want everlasting life. I've had enough of it. Tomorrow I'm going to go to sleep. I been looking forward to it. What I'd like is one good game of jackstraws before then."

"The verses I've been thinking of," John Sr. repeated, trying, Caleb knew, to turn the talk to something less painful to him than his son's wanderings, "are those of the birth." And old Wood began. *My soul doth magnify the Lord, And my spirit hath rejoiced in God my Saviour. . . ."* And then Johnny joined him.

When they finished, Caleb said, "Johnny, I had no idea you remembered all that."

"I remember everything I read."

"Now," said Wood Sr., "I'm going to get a little sleep."

Caleb told the two Woods good night and returned to the door crack. There Johnny later came to him.

"There's a prayer my mother taught me, my real mother, not the woman living at our house. Say it with me. You'll feel better."

"Maybe I don't know it."

"Everybody knows it.

> *Now I lay me down to sleep.*
> *I pray the Lord my soul to keep.*
> *If I should die before I wake,*
> *I pray the Lord my soul to take.*

"I'm going to sleep now," Johnny said. "You do the same. You've said your prayers. There's nothing more you can do."

Johnny was right. There was nothing more Caleb could do—but he didn't leave the door crack until a knife blade of gray morning came into it. With the light came Matt Holmby.

"The women are to be out in half an hour," he said. "Rouse them up. There'll be a good breakfast for the men. We leave here at eight. The hanging's set for ten."

"Will they let me go with the men?"

"You can go. Say a prayer with each man. But after that you have to come back here till the grand jury meets."

"I was prepared for that."

ORA Bemis didn't need any waking up. She was wide-awake and fully dressed. Lute looked drowsy.

"I gave him enough to see him through the ride out there. He don't want any at the last minute."

When Caleb went to wake the Bensons, Ora said, "Lute, I won't do it if you set your foot down. But I'd like the last thing for you to see to be the look of love in my eyes. And that's the last thing I want to see from you. And I'm going to bring the baby. He won't know what's going on. But afterward I want to tell him he seen how brave his father died. The other'll be there, too."

"You pretty sure about that, Ory?"

"Sure as sure. She's there. I've got her named."

"I'd like to know, if it ain't a secret."

"Laura. That's as near to Luther as I can get for a girl."

"You come then, all of you, if your heart's set on it."

"You just look in my eyes when the time comes, Lute. I'll fix myself where you can. All you'll see is love, then a little wait and we'll all be with you. That's the sum of it."

XV

JUDGE Amos McGowan was at the jailhouse at fifteen of eight. "Cale," he said, "you know I'll have to convene a grand jury for your part in Bemis's escape."

"I know that," Caleb said. "I'm prepared."

"Well, no use being overprepared. The indictment's unlikely. The conviction's unlikely. They could happen, true enough. It's true, too, that a judge hearing the case could suspend sentence."

It took a minute for Caleb to take in all that McGowan was saying. Then he took the hand the judge held out to him.

"You going out to the hanging?" he asked.

"I am. When I sentence a man to hang, I sentence myself to be present at the hanging. It tears me apart. But when I can't observe what I've ordered, I'll resign from my judgeship. What's too much for the law to see is too much for the law to require." He turned abruptly from Caleb. He'd said more than he intended.

McGowan made himself a part of the crowd waiting to see the men come out of the prison. Either Colonel Johnston or the sheriff or both had brought in state militia—around twenty—to see that the proceedings were orderly. There was no telling what spark might light when this rabble caught sight of the gallows.

Judge McGowan was speculating on the possibilities when he was roused by a voice. "I didn't expect to see you here, Judge."

"Fort! I supposed you would have gone back to the civilized comforts of Cincinnati long before this."

"One thing and another has held me. For one thing, if I had had Dilk's power over the jury, these men wouldn't be riding out to the gallows this morning. I feel I belong with them."

"It's the same with me," McGowan said.

A flatbed wagon, pulled by a matched pair of black carriage horses, came through the crowd, which parted silently to let it pass. Matt Holmby and Sam Brady climbed down from the wagon seat. The militia lined up, separating the two men from the crowd, which was pressing in closer. Holmby went inside the stockade. Brady stood, gun in hand, by the wagon.

A few minutes later Holmby and Caleb Cape brought Luther Bemis, seated on a chair, out of the jail.

"My God," said McGowan, "what have they done to the man?"

"He escaped and got his feet frozen. They ought to be amputated. But why cut a man's feet off one day and hang him the next?"

Caleb and Holmby put Lute's chair on the ground, and Sam Brady beckoned to Fort. "We'll need your help to get this chair up onto the wagon, Charlie."

Just before the four of them, Caleb, Holmby, Brady, and Fort, put their backs into the hoist, Brady said to Bemis, "Lute, you can lead off. You're in pain, and I won't keep you waiting."

"Thank you, Sheriff," Lute said. "Charlie, you did your best for me. Don't fash yourself about the way things turned out."

They placed Lute near the tail of the wagon; then Brady and Holmby brought the two Woods through the stockade doors.

John Wood, straight as an arrow, Bible in hand, was everyone's idea of a God-fearing patriarch. When a man like John Wood was headed for the gallows, something had gone amiss with the country. The crowd's murmur became angry, like bees swarming.

Johnny Wood didn't make the crowd any happier. He had a book, too. Not a Bible, but some storybook, and he read as he walked, like a man so caught up in what's happening in the story, he stumbles upstairs to bed not knowing where he's going.

At the wagon, he looked up and saw someone in the crowd he knew. He waved, called, "Good-by, good-by."

Charlie turned to see who was receiving Johnny's farewell. There was Hannah, hat off in spite of the cold, threatening weather, waving, crying, and calling, "Good-by, Johnny. Good-by."

Benson, hands tied behind his back, leg irons on, came out of the stockade next, bucking like a colt who has for the first time felt the touch of leather. For a minute the crowd forgot what was to come, caught up in the excitement of what was happening. How a man so bound and ironed could still manage to plunge and lunge was beyond imagining. They loaded him, with two of Brady's men, deputized for the occasion, on each side of him, and then Caleb got in.

Holmby kept the two mares down to a walk. The militia was ahead, behind, and on both sides. Behind the wagon rode or trudged a hundred or more persons. A few friends and relatives. Many more, those making a day of it.

The road they followed was an old logging track down to where there had once been a stand of ash, the settlers' most valued tree. When they came through the woods to where the stand of ash had been cut, the huge gallows was visible. The wagon proceeded at a

steady pace, but the crowd pulled up at the sight. There was a sound, not angry buzzing, but the sound of a hundred people sucking in their breath at one time.

The men on the wagon bed were faced away from what they were approaching, and, though the crowd must have told them what had come in sight, no man turned his head to have a look.

Charlie and Judge McGowan stood to one side to let the sightseers pass on. The meadow surrounding the gallows was already filled with people. Five or six hundred of them.

"It looks more like a crowd come to a picnic than a deathwatch," Charlie said. Small fires had been lighted to offset the numbing wind and to heat water for tea.

"Up there on the ridge is no picnic," McGowan said.

The ridge above the meadow was a long one. At its top, like rimrocks, stood a double line of Indians, straight, quiet, not talking. They had come to see what none of them had ever seen before: white men punishing white men for the killing of red men.

The wagon had come to a stop at the foot of the gallows when Charlie and the judge reached the meadow. On the gallows platform the Cincinnati hangman was already stationed, black peaked hood, with its cat-slit eyeholes, covering his face.

All the men were walked up the steps to the gallows platform—with the exception of Bemis, who was carried up on his chair.

Near the platform, almost at its edge, Charlie saw Ora Bemis and her baby, Lizzie Cape at her side, Hannah at her mother's elbow, and Oscar A. Dilk at Hannah's elbow. "If you don't mind, Judge," Charlie said, "I think I'll move back a little."

Judge McGowan said, "That suits me to a T. I'll go with you."

THE condemned men knew the order of what was to come. Bemis, old Wood, Benson, young Wood. A prayer for each by Caleb, parting words from each, if anyone had anything to say.

The hangman told Bemis, "We'll set your chair on the trap. When the latch is pulled, you'll go through as smooth as a man standing."

"No," said Bemis. "I don't go to my death on any chair. How long does it take you to pull that latch?"

"One second."

"I can stand for one second." Bemis was white with pain. "Cale, you say the Lord's Prayer. That's what I want to hear. Ory and the baby are right down front. Put the chair on the trap, the noose on my neck. I'll set while you're praying. Then the minute you finish, pull the chair back. I'll stand, and go to my death on my feet, the way a man ought to."

The hangman didn't argue. Who had more right than a dying man for a last request? The chair was moved forward. Lute's hands were tied and the noose's clublike knot was placed just back of his ear.

Caleb's voice was strong and steady. "Our Father, who art in heaven, Hallowed be thy Name."

Lute looked down, as Ora had told him to do, into her eyes, and it was the way she had said it would be: lost in love everlasting. The Lord's Prayer came on, Caleb steady as a pump bolt. "Forgive us our trespasses." As Lute looked, Ora held up the baby. They had told themselves they would say the last words, "For thine is the kingdom, and the power, and the glory, for ever and ever. Amen," together. Their voices mingled with Caleb's.

At "Amen" the chair left him, and Lute did more than stand. He went—up toward God, or out toward Ora—in a kind of swoop before he fell that made the crowd gasp.

"How could he do that? Nothing to stand with?"

Ora answered. "He was a good man going home to God."

Lute, after the fall, hung perfectly still, a young man dead before thirty. Below the platform, in sight of all, the doctor listened for a heartbeat. When he heard none, the militiamen loosened Luther Bemis, born in Ohio, died in Indiana, from the rope and placed him in one of the four coffins that were lined up next to the gallows. Only then did Ora, crying, run to press her face against his. Lizzie, carrying the Bemis baby, went with her.

BIBLE in hand, John Wood walked to the center of the platform. "You don't need to tie my arms behind my back," he told the hangman. "Let me go holding my Bible."

The hangman said, "Nobody can prepare in his head for a noose. Your hands will decide in spite of you to fight for life."

Caleb had an idea. "John, put the Bible over your heart. That's where it belongs, anyway. The belt to your britches will hold it in place. You think God cares where you carry it?"

"No, Cale. God don't care." Caleb took the Bible and placed it inside John Wood's shirt. The hangman tied the old man's hands.

"You want something from the Bible, John? Or a prayer?"

"I'm going to die saying the same words I said last night."

Hands tied, noose adjusted, John Wood, Sr., stepped onto the trapdoor. When the latch was pulled, there was just enough weight to the old man to tauten the rope, but that was enough to kill him.

THE minute John Wood was stretched out in his coffin, George Benson went to the hangman. "Put the rope on me." His hands were already tied behind his back. "Let's get it over with."

"There's time for prayer, George."

"You pray for yourself, Cale, you blasted hypocrite. I wouldn't be here except for that whey-faced boy of yours. Oh, yes, you couldn't keep him off the witness stand, telling his lies."

Benson raised his voice till it carried to everyone in the meadow, over the smoke of the little bonfires and the crawling babies and the hot-eyed red-cheeked backwoodsmen. "Friends and neighbors. I called you that once. I was at your beck and call when you needed me. No man ever asked George Benson for help and got a no. I helped raise your barns, shuck your corn, cut your trees. I was fighting for you at the sugar camp.

"Did the government ever help us? Whose side is the government on today? The redskins'. Look there." Benson nodded toward the coffins. "Two good white men dead as doornails to please men taking their ease in Washington: Calhoun and Monroe—"

The hangman stepped forward. "You've had your say, Benson."

"I'm just started."

"I've got to be in Cincinnati tomorrow."

Benson shouted to the crowd. "The hangman's got a date in Cincinnati tomorrow. He wants to hurry this up."

The crowd responded to that. "Let him wait. A condemned man's got a right to make a speech. Go on, George."

Benson went on. "Here's our chance. A thousand of us here. A hundred of them up there on the ridge. It'd all be over in ten minutes. Let's show those men sitting behind their desks in Washington how we handle things out here in the West."

There was not a whisper from the crowd. Not a movement. Benson listened to the silence. For a half minute, a whole minute.

Then he shouted, "You dirty yellow bastards. You Indian lovers. If ever I called you friends and neighbors, I take it back. You're lower than the red men. They fight for their own. *Love thy neighbor as thyself.* That's what you been preaching, Cale Cape. Let it sink in how much anybody's listened to you. Failed, failed. You've all failed. May God have mercy on your souls. Now, hangman, I've had my say. Spring your trap."

Before the trap dropped for him, George Benson, whose hands had appeared to be tied behind him, brought them up in front of him untied and yanked at the rope around his neck. Before the hangman got to him, his feet were already off the platform.

The crowd screamed. Benson was the underdog, and in the contest between life and death, he was life. Even the Indians on the ridge broke their silence as he grappled with the hangman. The Indians wanted Benson killed. If the whites couldn't manage the affair, they would kill him themselves with pleasure.

Hannah put her hands over her face. "God help him."

"Hannah, what are you saying?" Oscar rebuked her.

"I don't want to see people die."

"Why did you come here?"

"For Johnny's sake. I didn't know it was so terrible."

"Take your hands down. It doesn't look right for the promised wife of one of the prosecuting lawyers to be sobbing because a man he won a verdict against is going to be hanged."

"I'm not sobbing. I'm praying."

"I'm talking about the looks of it—a prosecutor's wife taking on so over a legal execution. Now take your hands down."

She took them down. "I'm not your wife."

George Benson's moment of freedom was a moment only. The combined weight of Brady and the hangman broke his grasp. In an instant Brady had his hands retied, and Benson was sent through the trapdoor, his life three minutes longer than Brady had planned.

One of the four condemned to be hanged still remained alive: young Johnny Wood. Below him in their coffins lay Luther Bemis, and Johnny's father and uncle.

"Why do they keep him waiting, Ossie?"

"There's a rumor the governor may be bringing a pardon."

"If he is, it's cruel to keep Johnny waiting. He's suffered enough, just watching. He can't stand it."

"The governor has other things to do than to save murderers."

A half hour went by. No governor. An hour. No governor. The hangman picked up the black hood, which the other men had refused, and approached Johnny.

"Looks like the pardon's not coming," said Oscar.

At that word, Hannah, moving quickly, left Oscar, scooped the remains of a little bonfire into an empty iron kettle, overlaid the coals with a handful of twigs that had been gathered for tea making, and, with this pot of fire blazing in one hand, ran up the steps of the platform. She was gone before Oscar could forbid her.

On the platform, the twig bonfire leaping above the pot's brim, she faced the Indians on the ridge. "Spare the boy," she screamed, "spare the boy!" She held her hand unflinchingly in the flame, trusting in the Indians' respect for bravery.

"Spare the boy," she pleaded and held the pot higher, so that all on the ridge could see what she was doing. Some on the ridge understood English, she knew. But even if they did not, even if they could not hear, Hannah hoped all would understand her request.

Fort understood. He gave the judge a shove, tripped up a militiaman, and would have knocked down Dilk, except that Dilk, appalled by Hannah's outlandish act, had melted into the crowd.

Charlie snatched the kettle and threw it away. "Lard, lard," he shouted as he took Hannah in his arms. "Bring me some lard."

Neither he nor Hannah saw the Indians on the ledge make their sign, "We are satisfied."

Nor did the governor, who, without much regard for the safety of the crowd, came riding in at a hard gallop, his horse much lathered. The impression he gave—he had done this before—was that of a man sparing neither himself nor his mount to come at breakneck speed to save a human life. The crowd loved their governor. Judge McGowan said under his breath a word he would not permit in the courtroom.

Dismounting, the governor ran up the gallows steps to Johnny. "Young man, do you know who now stands before you?"

"No." Johnny could not take his eyes off the coffins below.

"Well, sir, there are but two persons in the universe who can save you from the noose. One is the great God of heaven; the other is the governor of the sovereign state of Indiana, who now stands before you. Here is your pardon. I have ridden long and hard to bring it to you. Now go, and sin no more."

The governor handed Johnny his pardon. Johnny let the rolled parchment slip from his hand. "What is my sin, sir?"

The governor turned to the sheriff. "Brady, what's wrong with this young man?"

Sam Brady said, "Sir, we've all been through a lot this morning. This boy's father and uncle are lying there below you. Johnny had a long wait, not knowing what was to come next. He's not in his right mind at the minute."

Johnny said, "I know the difference between right and wrong. I resisted, didn't I, Sheriff?"

"Bore him for the simples," the governor said, speaking the language of these backwoodsmen. Then he descended the steps, mounted his horse, and rode slowly through the crowd, taking the salutes of the electorate.

By early afternoon the meadow was almost deserted. Charred remains of fires dotted the meadow. Families had started for their homes. With what they had seen there so recently still in their minds, the meadow had lost its appeal as a place for picnicking.

Lizzie gathered Ora, her baby, and Johnny Wood for the ride back to Pendleton. Oscar Dilk had disappeared, and no one, least

447

of all Hannah, knew whether he had walked back or ridden with others. Charlie Fort would take Dilk's place with her on the return ride.

"I think Black Antler's still on the ridge," Caleb told Lizzie. "I'm going up to talk to him. I promised Brady to go straight back to the jailhouse afterward."

"We'll be all right, Caleb. Charlie's going with us."

Hannah and Charlie, before they climbed in the wagon, drew Caleb a little apart. "Hannah," Caleb asked, "how's your hand?"

Hannah held it up. It was inside a pillow sham filled with pure leaf lard. "It still throbs."

"That was a brave act, Hannah. Charlie, you could use a little lard yourself."

"I haven't had time to think about *my* hand yet. Mr. Cape, Hannah and I've got a favor to ask you. When Hannah's hand is healed enough to wear a wedding ring, will you marry us?"

"Marry you? Hannah, I thought you and Oscar Dilk were keeping company?"

"We were keeping company, but we don't love each other."

"Not much point getting married, then. And you two do?"

"We do," answered Charlie, as if already in the midst of a marriage service. "We had a misunderstanding, but we understand each other now. Isn't that true, Hannah?"

"It is. Papa, I love Charlie and will never marry anyone else."

"That being the case, I guess it's lucky Charlie wants you."

"Papa! You talk that way and he'll change his mind."

Caleb reached out to take Charlie's hand but remembered the burns. "You're a lucky man, Fort. She's the apple of my eye."

On their way to the wagon, walking with their stride that fitted, Charlie said, "Hannah, before you make up your mind once and for all, there's something I've got to tell you."

"I'll listen," Hannah said, "if you're sure it's something you want to talk about."

"I don't want to talk about it. But you've got to know."

"I already know. I saw it."

"My God, my God. Oh, Hannah, I did that to you?"

"What you did was to prove to me I was going to marry you, Charlie, no matter what."

"Hannah," Lizzie called, "you and Charlie can spoon right here in the wagon and not keep the rest of us waiting."

CALEB did want to have a word with Black Antler. But more than that, though he was scarcely aware of it, he wanted to climb out of this valley of death. He wanted to climb above it.

As he neared the top of the ridge, he recognized three of the dozen Indians who had lingered on: Lone Fawn, the powerful Miami; Bent Arrow, the Seneca, and, standing a little apart from his tribesmen, Black Antler.

Caleb greeted them, then addressed himself to the Faithkeeper. "Black Antler, I am sorry you didn't have a chance to speak longer that Sunday at my house. I know that you and followers of Handsome Lake preach against what happened here this morning."

Then he turned to the rest, speaking in Delaware so that none would miss his meaning. "What you saw this morning was ugly. It was right. This will be remembered as a great day both for the red man and the white man. On this day for the first time white men punished their own kind for killing Indians. This day three white men gave their lives so that the killing between whites and reds would be finished. It *is* finished. Now we will live peacefully together. Handsome Lake's prophecy will come true."

Caleb shook hands with all, except Black Antler. To him, Caleb raised his arm in the Indian salute of farewell. Black Antler responded in kind. Then Caleb started down the slope slowly, loath to pass the spot where the price of peace had been paid.

Black Antler spoke to the Indians who remained. "Leave me."

"This is the appointed place," they replied. "He will be here soon. We will leave then, after we hear his message."

Two messengers, not one, arrived. Plains Indians—Osages, well mounted on horses which bore the marks of hard riding.

"We have him trapped at the junction of the Illinois and the Mississippi. He will be caught before you arrive—but they will not begin the feasting until you get there. It was your kin Clasby killed. It is your right before ours to partake of the feast."

Caleb, halfway down the slope, heard the laughter. They have much to rejoice about today, he thought.

BLACK Antler waited silently until Caleb and the Indians were out of sight. He could still see the slow swing of the killing rope. He could still hear the jubilation of the red men in anticipation of the pleasures to come.

He was able to shut both from his mind. For the first time since Folded Leaf's death, tears covered his face. The memory of those two, Handsome Lake, the prophet, and Folded Leaf, the boy who might have outdistanced the master, became one.

Black Antler was bereft, but not alone. The spirits of the boy and the old prophet lived and spoke to him; he replied and he was heard by them. He spoke the words he had first heard from Handsome Lake and had later taught to Folded Leaf.

What remained? The bodies of men vanished, but their words and wisdom lived on. Their spirits did not die. The sun and the earth remained. Sun and earth had mothered and fathered him. The animals, as much as Folded Leaf and Handsome Lake, were his brothers. The willow, the birch, the elder comforted and protected him. He was sad, but not alone.

He knelt and scooped up a handful of sun-warmed earth. He kneaded with it the leaves at hand, aspen and maple and dogwood. He held his two fists clenched on earth, then turned earth's bounty sunward in the old Indian gesture of worship. Black Antler's hands, reaching upward, blotted out the rope. The smell of the crushed leaves was sweet. The sun was warm. He said the two names. "Handsome Lake. Folded Leaf."

The earth his hands held, the names his spirit honored: what else did a man have?

Jessamyn West's extraordinary literary career began almost by accident. A bout with tuberculosis confined her to bed for several years and she took to writing to pass the time. She was thirty-eight when her first book, *The Friendly Persuasion*, was published. It now ranks as a classic. Among her other novels are *Leafy Rivers* (a Reader's Digest Condensed Books selection), *Except for Me and Thee* and *Cress Delahanty*.

Mrs. H. M. McPherson in private life, Jessamyn West was born in Indiana in 1907. She has lived in California since 1913, but returns again and again in her stories to her native territory. This latest book is based on one of the most controversial trials of frontier history, held in Pendleton, Indiana, in 1824.

"It was twenty years ago that I came across a reference to 'The Massacre at Fall Creek'," Miss West recalls. "I remained haunted by it and the dread dilemmas it must have thrust upon whites and Indians alike; the more so perhaps because I had an Indian grandmother."

Jessamyn West

Most of the characters are, Miss West says, her own invention, with a few notable exceptions: Colonel Johnston, the Indian agent; Senator Noble, the prosecutor; and the governor of the state, who did make just such a last-minute appearance. The prophet, Handsome Lake, is also real. He died in 1815 and still has a devoted following.

"So much for the evidence of history," Miss West sums up. "The massacre had no significant impact upon the increasingly violent relationship between whites and Indians. My intention was not to reveal historical facts in a fictional setting, but to open questions of more abiding truths. And that is quite a different matter."

A condensation
of the book
BY SPENCER DUNMORE

ILLUSTRATED BY CECIL VIEWEG

Three pilots, strangers to each other, drawn inexorably together on a collision course . . .

Frank Beatty, middle-aged, reserved, a career pilot for a British airline, bothered for months by dizzy spells. They frightened him, but he couldn't quit flying. It was his life. . . .

Charles Vaughan, attractive, competent, TranState Airlines captain, devoted family man. But when a beautiful, free-spirited girl disrupted his comfortable life, he began to have difficulty concentrating on flying. . . .

Henry Peel, inexperienced but enthusiastic in his tiny Aeronca, daydreaming that he was flying the Atlantic, landing in Paris to a tumultuous reception. He could see the headlines now. . . .

A suspenseful narrative builds dynamically to an explosive climax. *Collision* is as impossible to put down as it is to forget.

Chapter One

THE right main landing gear of a Boeing 747 of Anglo-World Airways cut Lee Chan's general store in half.

The incident took place a few minutes before midnight. The shop was closed, but Lee Chan had remained on the premises to work on his accounts and to tag and display his new shipment of faded Levi's. Lee Chan had been out of faded Levi's for more than a month—a sorry state of affairs, for they sold briskly. Lee Chan was constantly vexed by the inordinate time it seemed to take to move a few goods from London to the west coast of Africa.

It was raining hard, but through the drumming on his sheet-steel roof Lee Chan heard the approaching aircraft. He took no notice. Aircraft were always flying over his shop on their way to or from the international airport. He continued to tag the Levi's. Suddenly he looked up, frowning. The aircraft was making an uncommonly loud din. The roof was shuddering.

Then the 747's undercarriage sliced through the timber and corrugated-iron structure like a razor through butter. Had it not been for the chimney, it might have gone straight through without incurring a great deal of damage. But the chimney was built of solid stone. Thus, when the gear struts encountered the chimney they shattered. A four-foot-diameter landing wheel hurtled free, missed Lee Chan by inches and took out the shop's end wall.

Lee Chan, dazed but unhurt, stood in the wreckage as the 747 hit the ground a thousand yards beyond his shop—five miles short of the runway at the international airport. Blindly, like a suicidal beast, it plunged across the scrub, scything a path through bushes and trees. Three-quarters of a mile later it came to a stop.

The 364 passengers, fifteen cabin crew and three flight crew members were shaken but unhurt.

There was a minimum of panic among the passengers. The fact implies commendable self-control, even heroism. But the truth is that the passengers reacted typically. A few kept their wits about them and were galvanized into instant, intelligent action. Most, however, were benumbed. The total unexpectedness of the whole thing, the shattering bumping, the cacophony, the wreckage, combined to create a momentary stupor. Minds seemed incapable of absorbing the fact that this had really happened. Passengers stared stupidly as crew members dashed through the 747's cavernous hull, exhorting everyone to move, to escape via the chutes and the emergency exits. Some had to be pulled bodily from their seats. And when they were on their feet they had to be restrained from searching for hats and paperback novels.

"Hurry! Please hurry! She might catch fire!"

Everyone, it seemed, came to their senses simultaneously. There was a scrambling. Shoving. Clutching. A woman slipped and fell. A child screamed for his father. At the exits there was courage and there was cowardice—and courtesy too: standing back and permitting the old or the young to jump out first.

At last the enormous jet was empty. She didn't burn. Mute and still, she lay in the dirt, her engines ripped from her wings and scattered. She was bleeding oil. Her ribs were exposed to view. The heavy raindrops hit them with odd ringing thuds.

"I say, it's raining," observed a tall man. He sounded surprised, although he was already drenched. A woman opened her umbrella; for some reason it struck a portly man as hilarious. He laughed unrestrainedly.

Members of the crew hurried among the passengers, assuring them that everything was under control. No need for further alarm.

Everyone was safe. Yes, it was indeed a good show, but, no, it shouldn't be considered a miracle exactly. Transportation would be arriving very soon to take them on to the airport. No, it couldn't be said at this time precisely what caused the whole thing or what Anglo-World Airways might be prepared to do about it.

By now, many passengers were smiling, some laughing. The realization was making its impact: they had survived a disaster that would be read about all over the world. They were celebrities, in a manner of speaking! But there were other reactions. A seventeen-year-old girl suddenly vomited, and a muscular six-foot man fell over in a dead faint. Others kept straying, apparently half asleep. Anxiously, like fretting shepherds, the airliner's crew kept trying to herd them into manageable groups. But the rain was so heavy that it was impossible to see more than a few yards.

A tractor materialized and its driver asked in singsong English if there was some assistance he might be.

"Aye," said a man with a Lancashire accent. "Do you have any petrol? We've run out."

Then the official traffic began to arrive, sirens wailing.

ROGER T. Thorne dabbed at his forehead with a spotted handkerchief. Nervous tension always made him perspire. A plump man, he was Anglo-World's local manager—a job that under normal circumstances was only moderately demanding. Suddenly, however, he had become the most important man in town. All the world's news agencies wanted to talk to him; the local papers wanted to photograph him.

All very flattering, of course, but Thorne knew the drill. No statements to the press until Head Office in London gave the nod. A crash had to be handled like the public relations dynamite it was. The corporation's reputation and the ticket-buying decisions of who knows how many people were at stake. Thank the Lord for the procedure manual. It told a fellow precisely what to do.

"Be helpful to the press," it advised, "but do not permit them to interview members of the crew. Confine your remarks to facts of which there is no doubt. Do not reveal passengers' names."

It was easier said than done, Roger T. Thorne was discovering. Reporters after information were like sharks who have tasted blood.

He scowled at the buzzer on his desk. "Mr. Parrone, Reuters, on line one," said Miss Swayze's voice.

Thorne sighed. "Just tell him we have no more information."

He turned to the man sitting opposite him, a man in a dark blue uniform spattered with mud. "They're absolutely hounding me."

"I'm sorry to cause you so much trouble," murmured the man.

"No trouble, old man. After all, it wasn't *intentional*."

"No, it wasn't intentional."

"Are you feeling all right, old man? You look a bit pale."

"Do I? I often get pale when I crash-land seven forty-sevens."

"I . . . yes, quite." Roger T. Thorne sniffed. Sarcastic sod, this Beatty. No need for it. Didn't help the situation one iota.

The buzzer again. "London on line one," said Miss Swayze.

Thorne cleared his throat and reached for the telephone.

For the first time in ten years Frank Beatty regretted having given up smoking. He was tempted to reach for the cigarettes on Thorne's desk—but no, they would unquestionably taste frightful.

They might even make you sick, he thought.

He rubbed his eyes. Why did his mind persist in dwelling on trivialities? Wasn't his entire future in the balance?

A tall, spare man in his late forties, Beatty had a face that an aunt had once described as patrician, with high cheekbones, and lines of unusual severity framing his regular features. At Anglo-World he was considered a somewhat reserved and caustic individual. The truth was that Frank Beatty was shy, and he tended sometimes to overcompensate for this by speaking directly and curtly. It was known to only a few of his intimates that he possessed a lively sense of humor. He looked younger than his years; only in the sunlight was it noticeable that his thick hair contained as much gray as blond.

They're going to crucify you, he thought. They have no choice. There are no extenuating circumstances. You were in command and you flew the bloody airplane into the ground. It's that simple.

What isn't so simple is *why*. He shook his head. He didn't know.

He did know that airline captains who made mistakes were cancers that had to be sliced from the corporate body as rapidly and cleanly as possible. I wish I had been killed, he thought. Oblivion seemed infinitely preferable to a future full of explanations. Questions. Sidelong glances. There's Beatty. Remember him? Flew a 747 into the deck. Good man in his day, but . . .

He thought, Diane will be an absolute brick. The soul of loyalty, Diane. Not for an instant will she entertain a suspicion that this might have been my fault. She will *know* that I did everything that anyone could conceivably have done. But did I?

He couldn't remember. The events were curiously blurred and foggy; it was hard to separate fancy from reality.

What of Vincent? Would the boys at school make it hard for him, flail him with the sins of the father? Schoolboys were cruel little devils. At least they used to be. These days the kids seemed different, with their long hair and their rock music. They were all wrapped up in *causes*—at *twelve*, for heaven's sake. . . .

He thought of himself at that age. A teacher had asked his pupils' ambitions. "To be an airman," Frank Beatty had replied, and he had never wavered. When the war came, there was no question of his intentions. He progressed through Tiger Moths to Wellingtons. He flew a Halifax on a dozen ops. When the war ended he applied for a permanent commission. He stayed in the air force half a dozen years. In the early 1950s he presented himself and his logbook (a wondrously worn affair detailing some six thousand hours aloft) to Anglo-World Airways. The corporation was pleased to accept him as a probationary pilot. He had to work hard. Endless tests before he progressed to first officer. Seven years ago he had made it to captain at £10,000 a year. He had arrived at the peak.

And now this.

Thorne was earnestly assuring London that everything was being handled the corporation way. By now, Beatty reflected, the powers-that-be would have been informed of the erring captain's identity. In their minds he would have become part of the wreckage that the investigators would examine and cart away.

"Captain Beatty," Thorne was saying, "it's the chairman. He wants to speak to you."

Beatty took the telephone. "Hello, sir. Beatty here."

The voice from London was well tailored and seemingly undismayed by the fact that a £10,000,000 airplane had been written off. Most frightfully sorry. Gratified that no one had been hurt. Hoped that the local authorities were taking care of everything. "And have you been in touch with your wife, Captain?"

"Yes, sir. I spoke to her on the telephone."

"Excellent. I'm sure she was most relieved to hear from you. I believe you are coming back to London tomorrow morning."

"Yes, sir."

"Good, good. Well, the important thing is that everyone is safe. Have they given you something to make you relax? Good. You'll feel as right as rain after a night's rest."

"Yes, sir," said Beatty, suddenly realizing the chairman was unsure what to say next. "Good-by, sir. Thank you."

He hung up. A kind man, the chairman. But it would be naïve to suggest that all would be forgiven.

Beatty massaged his right wrist. It ached. Tomorrow he would be flown back to London. To the questions.

"You've got to think up some bloody answers," he told himself. "You've got to remember."

IT WAS easy to remember the departure from New York. Utterly normal. The preflight routine checks of the aircraft's vitals. Then Anglo-World flight 712 was cleared for takeoff. The brakes were released. The 747 began to roll, three hundred tons propelled by the power of air being compressed, expanded by fuel combustion, then ejected in a furious, bone-snapping stream to the rear. Quickly the enormous machine picked up speed, although from the lofty height of the flight deck the pace still seemed lethargic. A light pressure on the rudder pedal corrected a tendency to wander from the runway's center line.

"Vee-one," said Dowling, the first officer. One hundred and twenty knots. Now or never speed. Time to rotate, to ease the nose wheel off the deck, time to coax the whole colossal contraption into the air. A gentle easing back on the control column, and the rumbling of the main gear ceased. Airborne.

The jet thrust her nose up through the haze and scattered cloud into the clean sunshine. Speed, 250 knots, as required by federal air regulations, up to ten thousand feet. Effortlessly the JT9D engines propelled her to her cruising altitude. Now the aircraft was controlled by a complex of computers, accelerometers and gyroscopes collectively known as the inertial navigation system. On the ground, the INS (the "little black boxes" to the crew) had been fed the latitude and longitude of the starting point, and those of the destination and half a dozen way points between. Armed with these data the INS was able to keep an electronic eye on the autopilot, adjusting heading for wind, compensating for in-path turbulence, maintaining a phenomenally accurate course and altitude.

The three-man flight crew did little more now than supervise the workings of the system. Beatty, the captain, and Oscar Dowling, the first officer, sat side by side in the forward seats. Between them, before them and above them were the dials, levers and switches that controlled the aircraft. Behind the two pilots, facing to starboard, sat Milden, the flight engineer.

Beatty stifled a yawn. He took a deep breath. No time for dozing. He watched the control column moving gently in obedience to the nagging demands of the little black boxes. Insulting, the sheer, damnable efficiency of the things. The truth was that the little black boxes could fly a smoother, more accurate path than any human pilot. And they could land the 747 by themselves, superbly. But sometimes the boxes went wrong. Then the humans had to come in and sort out the mess; they still had their uses.

Beatty was aware of glances from Dowling and pretended not to notice them. He had flown with Dowling before. Nice chap, but loquacious. Give him the slightest encouragement and he would chat the whole way to Africa. Beatty preferred a quiet trip.

Dowling's face was a series of jolly, rather overfed curves. He was a veteran of three decades of flying, a superb craftsman, and at his age he should have been a captain. No one, including Dowling, seemed to know why he wasn't. Perhaps it was his garrulity.

The clouds began to thin. Now the Atlantic could be seen, restless, merciless. As he often did, Beatty spared a thought for the doughty souls of the 1920s and 1930s who had attempted to span the ocean in their underpowered and overloaded crates. Somewhere in the waters below, a sixty-three-year-old lady of noble birth had gone to her death, dressed in a bright blue suede flying suit. Aboard her aircraft she had been carrying half a dozen hatboxes containing the millinery she intended to wear on her triumphal tour of North America as the first woman to fly the Atlantic. Something had gone wrong; they never found a trace of her, her two pilots or her aircraft.

The big jet sped on, becoming lighter at a rate of 470 pounds per minute as the four JT9Ds thirstily consumed their fuel.

The passengers ate, watched a film, then ate again. A man made an indecent proposition to a stewardess. Two dinners were spilled in laps. One wallet crammed with holiday funds was lost. And found. It was a normal trip.

An hour from the African coast Beatty told his passengers that the weather ahead was not very good. "It's been raining all day," he said. "I hope you've all brought your umbrellas. The temperature is ninety-seven degrees Fahrenheit, with a humidity of ninety-four. A trifle sticky, I'm afraid. We expect to be parked in front of the terminal building in fifty-eight minutes."

He released the intercom button on his mike, glad to have the tiresome little PA duty done. He disliked talking to invisible people who didn't respond. But hearing the captain's voice was said to be good for the passengers' peace of mind.

In earlier jet days their peace of mind was assured by personal visits to the passenger cabin from the great man. But during one trip across the Atlantic, a jetliner's autopilot had become disengaged while the captain was aft on his goodwill tour. The first officer, engrossed in a novel, didn't notice the problem until the jet snapped suddenly into a dive. The captain somehow got back to his post and he and the first officer coaxed the machine out of its plunge. Just in time. The tossing waves were said to have slapped the undersides of the jet's wings as it leveled out. From then on, captains were required to remain on the flight deck.

Beatty scanned the instrument panel. It was an automatic procedure. He did not deliberately study each dial and gauge, but had any of them indicated trouble, the fact would have registered on him like a red light.

Another weather report: rain, torrential at times, visibility ranging from five hundred yards to two miles—according to the questionable opinion of the airport officials. And hot as hell. Beatty's eyes prickled with fatigue. He told himself, "You're not the least bit tired." But his body wasn't convinced. Why was it that sometimes one could sleep like a top in a strange bed and at other times it was impossible? Someone who had been flying airliners for twenty years should have become accustomed to it by now. Of course, this time the weather in Hong Kong had delayed the arrival of his aircraft. Then, the maintenance crews' work-to-rule campaign had made fueling a half-day operation. When he took off at last, eighteen hours late, he hadn't slept for thirty-four hours. Well, soon there would be the deck chair by the hotel pool, and rest, hour after delicious hour of it.

Dowling was chatting now to the ground controller in his cheery way, announcing Anglo-World's position and intentions. The controller answered in singsong English, "Visibility half a mile."

Well above the A-W minima—if accurate, Beatty thought. "Anglo-World seven one two," the voice droned on. "Continue on heading one niner five until you intercept the ILS for runway one six. Over."

The Boeing had to be slowed with flaps and air brakes, barriers to interrupt the smooth flow of air over the great wings, since jet aircraft do not lose speed as rapidly as propeller aircraft when their engines are throttled back.

"Tell the passengers we'll probably be encountering some turbulence, will you?"

"Roger," said Dowling as the 747 rocked and swayed in her dignified way. Beatty watched the instrument landing system dial. The vertical needle indicated direction, the horizontal needle represented the angle of the descent toward the runway. The ILS indicator showed a neat cross. Descent rate and direction were bang-on.

"Outer marker," Dowling reported.

"Roger. Undercarriage, please."

"Gear down, sir. Altitude is . . ."

Beatty didn't hear the altitude.

He knew that he wanted to know it. But other matters were capturing his attention. ILS needles wandering, stating with dreadful clarity that the aircraft was pitching and tumbling through the murk. His hands moved to wrest control from the autopilot. Not an instant to lose. He knew it. But there was a gap somewhere. Moments seemed to drift by. Voices were low and languid. The needles danced at a weary tempo. Lights kept flashing, although the mechanism of the flashing was somehow lethargic. And the control column kept exerting back pressure, but it was a gentle, undemanding kind of pressure. Beatty saw Dowling turning, his hands clutching. Sounds faded, almost disappeared, then they returned, amplified, deafening, stupefying.

He saw the building, dead ahead.

Suddenly the noise ceased. He felt the wrenching, twisting thump of impact. Dowling's hand grasped the panel as if he alone could keep the front of the aircraft from exploding upon him. Beatty was aware that his mouth had opened. But no words came. The ground swept up at him. Metal screamed in pain.

A few minutes after eight p.m., eastern standard time, a DC-8 in the eye-catching red and gold livery of TranState Airlines touched down at Toronto International Airport. The passengers disembarked, followed by the crew and the captain, his rank denoted by the four gold rings on his sleeves. Of average height, he moved in the easy, fluid way of one who exercises regularly. The dark blue TranState uniform flattered his trim frame. He had a pleasant face, good-natured rather than handsome; he had a strong, well-formed jaw; his eyes were blue; his dark brown hair was touched by gray at the temples.

His name was Charles Vaughan.

"In my entirely unhumble opinion," Walt Przeczek said to Vaughan, "your average airport has as much gorgeous stuff walking around it as your average Playboy Club." He looked around the terminal building, smiling at females of every age. An astonishingly high proportion of them smiled back.

Walt Przeczek was a large man, over six feet in height, ugly and yet with overwhelming charm. He also was a TranState captain, although junior to Vaughan. At a few hours' notice he had been asked to fly copilot for Vaughan to Chicago, Toronto and New York; the scheduled first officer was down with the flu. The arrangement suited both men; they were old friends and had flown together dozens of times; now they lived within five miles of one another in the San Bernardino mountains near Los Angeles.

Together they made for the office TranState maintained at Toronto. There they heard about Beatty's crash. The TranState aircrew, like those of every other line, felt directly involved. Any accident was the worst possible news, no matter what aircraft was involved. Any crash had the same effect on the traveling public. People by the thousands would suddenly decide to drive or stay home—the same people who seemed able to accept forty or fifty thousand road deaths a year.

"Did anyone get out?" It was the first, urgent question.

"They all did," said Adler, the traffic manager.

"What happened?"

Adler shrugged. "All I heard, the guy undershot and hit a house. I just hope he's got something good and solid to blame it on. Spoiler malfunction or a runaway stabilizer. Something. And can prove it. If not, the poor SOB's in real trouble."

Vaughan agreed. Investigating committees seemed only too eager to heap Everests of blame upon the captains of crashed airliners, especially, it seemed, those who weren't alive to defend themselves. "Pilot error" was their all-too-frequent conclusion.

He handed Adler the flight documents, the waybills and passenger manifest that represented the official existence of flight 12. The flight was due to leave on the last leg of the trip, from Toronto to New York, in fifty-one minutes.

Adler reported that there would be forty-three passengers boarding at Toronto. Vaughan nodded. That would put him well over the magic sixty-two percent occupancy figure, which, according to the sales department, was the point at which TranState started making aviation pay.

According to met, the weather was so-so. The east coast had been hit by severe thunderstorms earlier in the day. There would be rough going in the turbulent air left by the waning storms, but the worst would be over by the time flight 12 reached New York.

Light rain was falling when Vaughan and Przeczek walked out to the DC-8 and commenced their routine external inspection. It was Przeczek who observed the fluid on the underside of the left wing. He touched the stuff and sniffed it. No question. It was jet fuel. The leak appeared to be located in the corner of a small inspection cover. Vaughan examined it. All wings of jetliners tended to leak, especially when they had just been topped up. But it was a question of degree. How much was acceptable?

"Better get in touch with Dispatch," said Vaughan. "Tell them there could be a delay. I'm talking to Maintenance."

Irwin, the chief mechanic, said there was a gunk that would do the trick. "No sweat, Captain. If it was a big leak, we'd have to strip the wing. They'll probably do that when you get back to LA. But in the meantime the gunk'll do just fine."

"What does the manual say?"

"It says use the gunk."

"What happens when the gunk sets? Does it get dry and hard?"

"I guess so. It's a sort of plastic, you know."

"What happens to the plastic patch if the wing flexes more than usual in flight? In turbulence, say."

Irwin pondered. "Reckon the leak could open up again," he admitted. "But I never heard of it. Always worked just great."

Vaughan walked slowly back to the office. "I'm sorry," he told Adler. "I'm canceling. We've got a leak."

Adler clicked his tongue. He seemed to be silently counting the money TranState was going to lose.

Vaughan telephoned the company's flight director in Los Angeles and explained the situation. "Maintenance can only provide a temporary plastic filler to plug the leak."

"And does Maintenance say the stuff will be satisfactory?"

"Yes, sir."

"Then I don't believe I understand your problem, Captain." The flight director had a terse, incisive way of expressing himself. Front-office grapevine had him heading for a vice-presidency.

"Sir, it's turbulent all the way from here to New York. The wing is going to flex more than on an average flight. If it does, and that stuff has hardened, then the leak will open up again."

"Yes, but if Maintenance—"

"Maintenance isn't flying the aircraft, sir, I am."

"If you'll permit me to get a word in edgewise, Captain—*if* Maintenance says the repair is in accordance with the company manual, then my advice would be to take the flight."

Vaughan felt the irritation bubbling within him. "To a guy in a hangar, a leak can easily be classified as minor. But it can look as major as hell to another man thirty thousand feet up in the air. I'm canceling the flight, sir."

After two more telephone calls to Los Angeles, Vaughan emerged from Adler's office feeling drained. Three TranState senior executives in succession had urged him to think of the inconvenience to the passengers, the damage to the company's reputation, the expense of rescheduling. All three had succeeded in implying a threat of disciplinary action.

But Charles Vaughan knew he was right.

Adler went off to inform the passengers that their flight had ceased to exist, while Vaughan completed the cancellation documents. Under Reason for Cancellation Decision he wrote, "Moderate to severe turbulence was to be expected en route. (See met report attached.) This turbulence made temporary repair of wing leak a safety hazard. In my opinion the leak could not be classified as minor. A steady loss of fuel could be seen. Given the weather situation, the possible danger to the aircraft and passengers was unacceptable. C. J. Vaughan, Capt."

He reread it. No pussyfooting. However he'd phrased it, there would be trouble. Airplanes sitting on the ground, management was fond of pointing out, were liabilities, not assets.

In five years, Vaughan had canceled only a dozen flights, each time in circumstances which management couldn't question. But this time the whole thing was open to interpretation. It was essential that he present his side of the matter as forcefully as possible at the inevitable company inquiry. He decided to write it down while it was fresh in his mind.

He was engrossed in this task when Przeczek came bursting into the office, grinning delightedly. "Great news, buddy. I just bumped into a bevy of luscious ladies from Air Canada. One of them is getting married or something. They're having a party. They've invited us!"

Vaughan smiled despairingly. "Can't you ever stop bumping into strange women? Count me out."

"I said you'd come. They particularly asked for the cute captain with the Rock Hudson profile."

"Get lost, Walt."

"I insist that you come, Charles."

"Walt, it's definitely no. Absolutely, irrevocably no!"

THE room was packed. And noisy. And infernally hot. Vaughan put up with it for a couple of hours. Someone trod on his foot; someone else spilled a gin and something down his tunic front. A young man called him sir, which depressed him a little. He wondered what had happened to Walt. He edged toward the door.

"Are you Martin?" A girl was asking the question, a girl with very fair hair that fell straight to her shoulders.

Vaughan shook his head. "I'm not Martin. Sorry."

"I haven't met him yet, you see."

"Nor me," said Vaughan.

"Then you must know Peggy."

"Peggy?"

"She's the one who's marrying Martin." The girl frowned, puzzled. "Are you at the right party, for goodness' sake?"

Vaughan chuckled. "I was invited by proxy. I don't know any-

468

one here except the screwball I came with, and he's vanished."

"She's invited too many guests," said the girl. She had an intriguingly husky quality to her voice. "Typical Peggy. Always overdoing everything. Peggy and I were stews together."

"What line?"

"Air Canada. Is there any other? What's yours?"

"TranState. Out of Los Angeles."

"Do you like flying?"

"It's better than working for a living."

She smiled. She had heard the adage before. Her teeth were white and even, except for the front left incisor, which angled slightly away from its mate. Curiously, the imperfection failed to detract from her looks; it seemed to add a quality.

"You're not a stew anymore?"

"I quit when I realized waitresses on the ground made more money. But I like flying. So I took up gliding."

"Gliding?" Vaughan was intrigued.

"We have a little club about forty miles out of town." She reached into a brown leather purse and withdrew a billfold. The license, issued by the Canadian Department of Transport, was made out to Pringle, Rosalie.

"I've never flown in a glider," Vaughan said.

"If you're willing to part with four dollars, we can fix you up with an introductory flight."

"I might take you up on that, Rosalie."

"Isn't that a hideous name? Everyone calls me Lee." She smiled again. "Do you live in LA?"

"Up in the mountains. A little place called Blue Jay."

"Sounds nice."

"I like it." Why, Vaughan, didn't you say, "We like it?" He asked her, "Do you live in Toronto?"

"Yes. The west end. Near High Park. Do you like Toronto?"

"Sure do. Good places to eat. You can walk around without getting mugged. And there's usually some good jazz in town."

She looked up. "You like jazz?"

"Uh-huh."

469

"Me too."

"No kidding."

"You're surprised."

"I guess I am. Most people who *really* dig jazz are men."

"Typical male." She shook her head reprovingly.

"I apologize. Who do you like on trumpet?"

She grinned. "Testing me, huh? Okay. I dig Miles Davis, Clark Terry and Maynard Ferguson. By the way," she added, "Stan Getz is in town—at the Colonial."

"I just had an idea," said Vaughan.

WHEN Vaughan landed at Los Angeles he was requested to report to the chief pilot. But not immediately. At nine a.m. two days hence. This meant a ninety-minute drive into the city during his off-duty period. The corporate needle was at work.

His white Cougar sat baking in the parking lot where he had left it three days before. At that time, he reflected, you were in good standing with the company. And you weren't an adulterer.

You're a stupid bastard, he thought, starting the engine. "I'm honestly sorry, Susan," he told his wife silently. "I didn't want to hurt you. You don't deserve to be hurt. I really didn't *mean* to do what I did. I didn't set out with the *intention* of doing it." He grimaced. There were no words that would assuage his guilt.

He accelerated into the bunched, speeding traffic of the Harbor Freeway. After the orderly patterns of aerial traffic the freeways always seemed terrifying. Today, preoccupied with the dread of confronting Susan, he was as dangerous a driver as any.

Would she *know*, the instant he walked into the house? Would the guilt in his eyes blurt out the whole sordid story as surely as words?

But it wasn't sordid. What happened was wrong; there could be no denying that. It wasn't sordid, however. But how could he convey that fact to Susan? Should he even try?

He edged across the lanes as the Route 10 exit neared. Was all this really happening to *him*? Square old Chuck Vaughan? The guy whose idea of a big time was to curl up with a Budweiser and the *Journal of the American Aviation Historical Society?* The guy who had been seen to shake his innocent head at the pilots who maintained discreet little pads in Chicago, Atlanta, Montreal.

Now he was an aging lothario, just like the others, and just as despicable. "You're damn nearly old enough to be her father," he said to himself. "But you conveniently neglected to mention that fact, didn't you? She told you she was twenty-four. Did you figure she'd take you for thirty? Thirty-five tops?"

The traffic began to thin. The mountains were near. Blue Jay was six thousand feet above sea level, way above the smog. Vaughan had bought the cottage almost ten years before, soon after Janet's birth, as a weekend escape from the apartment in Inglewood. Then, as tensions in the city mounted, the decision was made. The cottage became a home. Huddled against the hillside, it had doubled in size, sprouting bedrooms, patios, sun decks.

He sped up the mountain road, his tires squealing as the car took the tortuous curves, far exceeding the speed limit all the way to the top. It was as if he craved to hasten the moment of confrontation —and yet his stomach churned in apprehension.

Six-year-old Lynn met him in the driveway. The Carters' cat had had kittens. Could she have one? Vaughan said he would think about it. Lynn sighed and nodded. She had guessed that would be the response.

"Hi, Chuck." Susan was in the doorway, jeans and check shirt in becoming contrast to her dainty features. She wore just a touch of makeup. With her short dark hair she could still turn heads on Wilshire Boulevard. "Good trip?"

He smiled. "Fine." He kissed her. As if nothing had happened, nothing had changed. It was easy. Damnably easy.

Chapter Two

CAPTAIN Fisher, chief pilot for Anglo-World Airways, stoked his pipe, slowly, methodically. Sometimes the act of getting his pipe operational helped to solve problems. This time it did not help a bit. What faced him was a vile job and there was no getting out of it. For so many years, Beatty had been such an excellent fellow in every way. But, dash it all, he had flown the thing into the ground. It was true that conditions were poor. Torrential rain could affect the glide path and localizer beams. But every airline pilot knew of such problems and was ready for them. It was incredible that no one had been killed.

The first officer, Dowling, had been of little help. Busy with his instruments, he had been unaware of any problem until minutes before the aircraft hit. Dowling said he considered Mr. Beatty one of the finest pilots with whom he had ever flown.

Fisher relighted his pipe. Should Beatty's superb record be taken into consideration? No, of course not. Beatty was paid superbly to handle aircraft superbly. In return, a masterful performance was expected at all times. Beatty knew that. He had spoken of extreme fatigue, inadequate sleep. But the corporation rules were straightforward: a pilot had to ground himself if for any reason he felt physically unfit for flying. No excuse to be found there.

But was it possible that fatigue might have affected Beatty's ability to cope with an emergency? Was he, in fact, slow-witted because of lack of sleep?

Let's hope the press doesn't light on that angle, Fisher thought. According to far too many newspapers, the sky was full of jets manned by crews stupefied by exhaustion because they had been flying for impossible numbers of hours without relief.

A knock on the door. Miss Abbott announced that Captain Beatty had arrived.

Fisher didn't respond for a moment. If only the aircraft had had something wrong with it. Something blamable. Damn! He had bitten through his pipestem.

"Ask Captain Beatty to come in, please."

"THEY were really very nice about it," Frank Beatty told his wife. "Couldn't have been fairer, actually. But the fact remains that I have now joined the ranks of the unemployed."

"They are rotters," Diane declared, her fists clenched. "After all the years you've given them ..."

"I've hardly *given* them any years," said Beatty. "They bought them, at a high price. They had no choice but to let me go."

"It's beastly of them," said Diane. "If it hadn't been for you, everyone would have been killed."

"That's a loyal wife speaking. It was because of me that everyone very nearly *was*. You do see that, don't you?"

"If you say so."

"I don't suppose it's any consolation, but I wasn't actually given the sack. They permitted me to resign. They didn't have to do that."

Diane wasn't placated. "It was the least they could do."

She was frightfully worked up. Understandably, of course. The question was, why wasn't *he* worked up? He reminded himself, "It isn't some other poor soul they're sacking; it's you. And your license is revoked for three months. You are grounded. What do you have to say about that?"

The worst had happened. Yet the world tottered on.

Diane asked, "Are you going to the association about it?"

"I don't think so. I haven't been denied any rights. I can't honestly say I've been victimized. The company did what it felt was necessary. Suppose they had kept me on as a captain. Suppose I had another crash. Imagine the headline. BEATTY PRANGS AGAIN. After that, how much confidence would the traveling public have in Anglo-World?"

"It's horrid and unfair. Lord, how I hate big companies!"

He took her hand and held it between both of his. By degrees, her anger evaporated. Then she became the comforter. Everything was going to be all right, she told him. There were hundreds of other airlines. Scores of them would jump at the opportunity of obtaining a captain with his experience and skill. In the long run it would all turn out to be a blessing in disguise. She suggested a drink.

He agreed. The whisky tasted good. Possibly, he thought, this is the first step to a brand-new career as a hopeless alcoholic.

Vincent came in, mumbled hello and dashed upstairs. Beatty wondered whether he would succeed in getting his son to cut his hair before his return to school. He would be at home until early

September—until twenty-nine days before license reinstatement. Funny, Beatty thought, how he had worried over Vincent's reaction to the crash. There had scarcely been a reaction, just a kind of mild annoyance. Father had done something not terribly bright, like taking the wrong turn off the M1. The kid was so unbelievably secure under that idiotic mop of his.

"Another one, darling?"

"Why not?" Why not indeed? He watched her as she poured the drinks. She was tall, five feet ten, and she had a balance and grace that set her apart. Beatty had first noticed her at a corporation Christmas dance. A navigator named Kellaway had brought her. Shortly before midnight he went off to replenish drinks, leaving her alone. Beatty, never at ease with strange females, nevertheless persuaded himself to cross the floor as the band groaned into action. A clearing of throat. Would she care to dance? Yes, it seemed she wouldn't mind at all, thanks very much. After a while he cleared his throat again and said he knew it was a bit of a cheek, but might she care to have a spot of dinner one night? Absurdly, he added that he was sure Kellaway wouldn't mind. Happily, she was amused rather than irked. She would love to have dinner with him, even if Kellaway *did* object.

Seven months later they were married. No flutter-brained kids, they: he was thirty-six, she was twenty-eight. She still carried herself like a queen. Beatty loved her and considered himself lucky to have found her. But it never crossed his mind to tell her.

"I was talking to Mother," Diane said. "She's frightfully sorry about it. She's very fond of you, you know."

"And your father?"

"He said it . . . it was a shame, or something."

"He was right. It is a shame, or something."

Beatty's own parents had died more than ten years before. They had hated his flying. Medicine, they said, was the profession; the world needed doctors and accorded them respect and magnificent livings. You were right, Beatty thought. I won't let Vincent make the same mistake; the hirsute little rock 'n' roller will do as I say.

He smiled to himself. The whisky was working well.

He AWOKE. WHY? He listened. Nothing. He lay still. It was half past four. The vulnerable hour.

"You're grounded," he heard himself say. "Chances are that you'll never fly for an airline again. Never. Ever. You'll keep on applying and they'll keep on turning you down. You can hardly blame them, can you? You pranged. And you're nearly fifty. *Fifty*. When they say old boy they're speaking literally. Damn it! If it hadn't been for that bloody crash landing, you could have expected ten years more of airline flying before reaching mandatory retirement age.

"Ten more years. A lifetime. You've got to do *something*. You've got responsibilities. What then? A job in an office? Who on earth would take you on, at your age, with your experience? Selling cars? Vacuum cleaners? God, no. Instructing? But you don't want to instruct. Then what? Slow but sure decomposition?"

Fear lay on his stomach like a cold hand. His heart pounded. Loud, panicky. In a moment it would disturb Diane.

"How long is a woman supposed to rally behind a total failure? Why did I survive the crash? Why couldn't I have been the one casualty? It would have been so much simpler and neater. Diane would have found herself a moderately rich woman, with the insurance proceeds. And I wouldn't have had to face an utterly bloody future."

To make matters worse, he still didn't know why the crash had happened. Uncertainty, and endless questions, nagged at him like a toothache. There was always a reason for a crash.

He left the house at eight, wearing his track garb. He told Diane he would be back for breakfast in thirty minutes. He headed for his usual route: the path beside the river, then over the bridge, through the wood and back by the railway lines.

It was a fine morning after an overnight shower. The world smelled fresh and good. Beatty set himself an easy pace. He enjoyed jogging; it had been a part of his life since an A-W doctor had observed an increase of seven pounds between the six-month medicals.

His body seemed particularly well balanced today, everything pulling and pushing and pumping in splendid concert. He reached the wooden bridge. Hardly breathing hard. Lungs like a lad of eighteen! With ·constitution to match! Cinders crunched softly beneath his shoes. Still he breathed easily. Not bad for an old chap!

Optimism now warmed him. He *would* get back into flying. Others had bounced back from adversity, hadn't they? Churchill, for example. All washed up, everyone had said back in 1920. But what were they saying twenty years later? Take Bader: smashed up a Bristol Bulldog doing aerobatics at Woodley; lost both legs. Did he let that minor inconvenience prevent him from barging his way back into the RAF and subsequently shooting down twenty or more Jerries? No indeed. Losing one's legs was a damn sight worse than losing one's license for ninety days. Could that fact possibly be denied? Dash it all, airlines *need* competent, experienced people like me, Beatty thought as he jogged. I have lots to offer. It may not be easy to become reestablished, but I shall do it. I shall keep on trying until I do.

He was aware of the sun as he ran. It was strong and it came splashing down through the trees above him. The branches kept interrupting the light. It fell on his face and then vanished, like the flickering light from an old film projector. An instant of glare. An instant of gloom. Glare. Gloom. Light. Darkness. Black. White. Blackwhiteblackwhite. . . . Black.

HE HAD no recollection of falling.

"Did you hurt yourself?" A man with white hair was speaking.

"No," said Beatty. He rubbed his eyes. "I don't think so."

"I'm relieved to hear it," said the man. "Would you like me to help you to your feet?"

"Help me? No . . . no, thank you." An absurd question. Why was it that the man's features were blurred? And why was it necessary to hold on to a tree in order to pull oneself to one's feet? The coarse black bark seemed to pulsate beneath his hands.

"You came quite a cropper. If you are certain you are all right, I shall be on my way."

"What?" Beatty had momentarily forgotten the man's presence. "Yes, of course, thank you. I tripped. I'm okay now."

He watched the old man walk back toward the river. Decent of him to stop. Must have thought I'd dropped dead. Must have tripped. Rest a jiff. Be right as rain. He took half a dozen deep breaths, then attempted a gentle trot. But it was no use. For some extraordinary reason he had been robbed of his strength. He had to walk, slowly.

Diane asked what had happened.

"I fell down," he told her. "I'm all right.".

"I was getting worried. You've been gone over an hour."

"Don't be ridiculous," he snapped.

She frowned, stung by his tone. "I'm not being ridiculous, Frank. It's after nine. Did you go a different way?"

"No," he said. "But I went around twice."

She was smiling now; everything was explained and in order.

He went upstairs to change. All the clocks in the house said the same unbelievable thing. It was an hour and ten minutes since he had left the house. And, despite his explanation to Diane, he knew he had traveled the course only once. Forty-five minutes had been lost somewhere. Evaporated. Vanished.

He was suddenly clammy with fear. Was he losing his mind? How could three-quarters of an hour disappear? Could he have fallen and knocked himself out for forty-five minutes? If so, why didn't his head ache? Why no cuts or bruises? Was it possible to knock oneself out without a mark? It had to be possible. It was the only explanation. Therefore, it had to be what had happened.

Diane called up the stairs; breakfast was ready.

"Be there in a mo!"

All very casual. Not-a-care-in-the-world Beatty. He changed into a sport shirt and slacks and went downstairs. He managed to sniff appreciatively at the bacon and eggs.

But he had no appetite.

VAUGHAN closed the telephone-booth door behind him. He assembled a small heap of nickels, dimes and quarters. No credit-card calls this time, with the evidence itemized on the monthly statements.

"Operator. Can I help you?"

"I want to call Toronto, Canada."

He waited, betting that the phone would be slammed in his ear the moment he identified himself.

But she most likely wouldn't be in. She was an attractive girl, wasn't she? Why wouldn't she be out having a good time? One thing was for sure: she wouldn't have been spending the last three weeks waiting to hear from one Charles Vaughan. If she remembered.

Charles who? Ah, I recall now—the elderly airline pilot.

"That'll be forty-five cents for the first three minutes."

Vaughan injected the coins. Soon the dull, far-off sound of the ringing could be heard.

"Hello."

One word. And he could picture her face in every detail (after twenty-one days of trying to reassemble the parts in his memory).

"Lee?"

"Yes. Chuck? Chuck!" She laughed in her open way. "You jerk! Ever since I met you I've had a crick in my neck looking up at every damned jet that goes by. Are you in town?"

"No, Buffalo."

"Are you coming to Toronto? How long have you got? It's good to hear your voice again, you know that?"

It disintegrated, the whole silly assemblage of apologies and explanations, reasons and protestations.

"I'll rent a car," he said. "How long will it take from here?"

"Hour and a half to two hours. Take the Peace Bridge and just follow the Queen Elizabeth signs to Toronto. But hurry."

FROSTY martinis. Good gin in cheap, thick glasses. Posters for art shows and bullfights. A jungle of plants, tumbling over shelves and tables. Teak and junk furniture in equal proportions. Matisse prints and two earnest original oils. A highway STOP sign over the bed. The warmth of her, her vibrancy, lingered in every corner of the little apartment.

White skin against black velvet cushions. The soft down on her

479

arm. Her hair falling against her breasts. The touch of her long fingers on his back, pressing insistently, urgently.

They lay in silence. Vaughan dozed momentarily. He awoke and kissed her, slowly. "You're marvelous," he said.

She kissed his nose. "You're okay yourself."

She stood up suddenly and walked into the living room. A moment later the sound of piano, bass and drums filled the apartment. Oscar Peterson. Lee had not only a beautiful face and a magnificent body, but splendid taste in music. And she was a glider pilot. A rare and wondrous specimen.

Vaughan found himself thinking how great it would have been had they met thirteen years before. Disloyal. And ridiculous; Lee would have been eleven years old.

She returned with two glasses of cold beer.

"You quit your job at Air Canada," he said. "So what do you do now?"

"Work for an advertising agency. Writing copy."

"Clever girl. Do you like it?"

"Mostly. Except for the dumb things girl copywriters get to work on. One day I'd like to do an ad for a tractor or a Boeing seven forty-seven. Something durable. Everything I write about goes down the drain. Literally."

"Do you have family?"

"My parents are divorced. My mother lives just outside Toronto. My father lives in Calgary. I was married once."

"You were?" He was surprised; he wasn't sure why.

"I was eighteen," she said. "He was twenty-one. A nice-looking weakling. Cute curly hair but no backbone. I despised him after six months. Horrible, isn't it, how you can change?"

Vaughan glanced at her. "I'm married," he said.

"Of course you are," she said quietly. "And you have children."

"Two. I'm also forty years old, or I will be in a few weeks."

"So?"

"So I thought I should tell you. Don't you care?"

"What, about your being forty or being married?"

"About either."

"They're facts," she said. "You're dumb if you try to pretend they don't exist. But you're just as dumb if you let them mess your life up. I'm quite a realistic person. I know you and I aren't going to come to anything. I know it. Okay? It's impossible. So I'm not even thinking beyond tonight." She looked up at him. "I want to tell you something, Chuck. I like you one hell of a lot. And I didn't think I'd ever see you again. I had promised myself that if you called me, I would tell you to get lost."

"Why?"

"Because you were obviously married and you hadn't told me. So you were a lousy prospect."

"I see."

She grinned, showing her bright teeth. "But all my good intentions flew out the window the moment I heard your voice. The very moment!"

"Imagine that," said Vaughan.

IT WAS a sentence, a term to be served. Ninety days of enforced idleness, of petty irritability, of bitter, unreasoning thoughts. Ninety days of shame; of envying the crews of every aircraft that passed over the house.

Faced with similar circumstances, many men might have taken part-time jobs or completed long-delayed projects at home or embarked on courses in Spanish. But Beatty's mind was totally occupied with his profession. Flying was a part of him. Grounded he was incomplete, only partly alive.

Vincent had returned to school (his hair uncut). The leaves turned. The weather cooled. Sluggishly the days passed, wearisome bundles of hours.

Diane, splendid Diane, was courageous. She ignored Beatty's savage moods. She pretended not to hear his insults. She went about her work as if he were not in the house.

During the second-to-last week, Oscar Dowling telephoned. His voice evoked memories of a catastrophe, of questions. "How are you, Frank?"

"I'm well," said Beatty. "Taking it easy, you know."

"Jolly good. Envy you, old man."

Beatty frowned. Did Dowling imagine that he was doing a good turn, cheering up the black sheep?

Dowling said, "Look, this is absolutely none of my business, old man, but I thought I'd give you a tinkle about it anyway." He cleared his throat. "A chap I used to know in the war rang me up; he's starting up a new line and he thought I might be interested. I wasn't—well, you know, I'm a bit of a fixture at A-W now. But I thought of you."

"I see," said Beatty. Flatly. No point in getting eager.

"The chap's name is Amory. A Canadian. Used to run Provincial Airways till the big boys bought him out. Made a good thing of it, I understand. And now he's decided to start a charter business over here. He told me he's got an option on two or three seven oh sevens, and now he's getting his personnel sorted out. If I know old Don, he'll make a success of it. Bit of a rough diamond, of course, but a good type. Anyway, he's in the market for some crews so I thought I'd tell you about it."

"It was thoughtful of you," Beatty said. "I'm much obliged."

"Don't mention it, old man."

"Of course, I have feelers out with several lines, but nothing has been signed. No harm in having a chat with your Mr. . . ."

"Amory."

"Yes. Amory. Where can I get in touch with him?"

"He's at the Savoy. Nothing but the best for old Don. I took the liberty of mentioning you, so he's expecting a call from you."

AMORY was a craggy-faced man in his fifties with broad shoulders and gigantic hands. He greeted Beatty at the door of his suite, wearing a striped bathrobe. His feet were bare; his thinning hair was rumpled; he needed a shave. "Eaten lunch yet?"

Beatty said he had.

"I haven't. You mind if I eat while we talk?"

"Not at all."

Amory telephoned room service and ordered a steak and two pots of coffee. "So you're the guy who piled up with old Ossie, eh?"

"Yes, sir, the actual circumstances—"

"I know all about the circumstances," said Amory with a smile that was surprisingly warm. "I don't talk to people until I've done some checking. You were with A-W a long time."

"Twenty years."

"When do you get your license back?"

"Next week."

"Do you figure you were unfairly treated?"

"Not really. I think if it were possible to unearth *all* the facts, it might be found that I was unfairly treated. But under today's investigative conditions, no. They could find no mechanical failure, therefore the pilot was blamed. It's the rules of the game. I knew them and so did everyone else. But the fact that my license was revoked for only ninety days is an indication, I believe, how doubtful the decision was."

"You figure you did everything possible to prevent the crash?"

"Yes, I think so, sir."

"So does old Ossie. He thinks highly of you. Did he tell you I'm planning a charter operation?"

"He did, sir."

"There's a lot of business around. I've already got some lined up. May have to do some subcontracting; depends on how soon we can get things rolling on our own. You want to show me your logbook?"

Amory studied it in silence. "You've got a lot of air time, mister. You think you'd be interested in working for me?"

"I . . . I think I might, sir. I'd have to consider . . ."

"Not too sure about it?"

"It's just that . . . there are a couple of other companies . . ."

Amory raised a hand as if to express complete understanding. "Sure, after flying for Anglo-World for twenty years, a little charter operation seems like real small potatoes."

"It's not exactly that, sir."

"Lots of prestige, I guess, working for A-W. And now there's a wild man from the colonies with no offices, nothing but a whole lot of talk. I know how you feel. But remember, I've been a pretty successful guy in my time. In the end you might wind up farther ahead than if you'd stuck with A-W. Then again"—he smiled—"it could turn out to be a real stinkin' bust."

When Beatty left the hotel an hour later he was simultaneously elated and alarmed. It was marvelous to think that he might be flying again in a mere matter of days. But for whom? And for how long? It might last only a few months. And it would mean flying in the right-hand seat for a while, according to Amory. From captain on a 747 to copilot on a 707. Marvelous, he thought bitterly. What a bloody success story. But Amory was offering a *job*, which was more than anyone else was.

He walked along the Strand. In Trafalgar Square the inevitable tourists were feeding the inevitable pigeons. The sun appeared and played on damp stone lions. Deep in thought, Beatty strolled up Charing Cross Road. It became warm. He took off his raincoat and carried it on his arm.

He had told Amory that he wanted until Friday to think the offer over. But was there really anything to think over? Letters from the airlines had been arriving in a steady stream, all with the same message. Thank you, Mr. Beatty, but no, thank you. The simple truth was that he was branded. You've no choice, chum, not if you want to fly. He took a deep breath. All right. Nothing to be ashamed of, flying for a smaller line. Lots of chaps spent their entire careers doing it.

As he walked, his enthusiasm grew. Yes, it was going to be all right. Amory would succeed brilliantly with his UK charter, just as he had in Canada. And everyone involved would prosper.

He turned up Coventry Street. Cheerful now, he strolled in a leisurely manner—something he realized he hadn't done for ages. It was warm enough to sit awhile on a bench in Leicester Square, savoring the autumn sun, the satisfaction within. Good old Amory; good old Oscar Dowling.

It will be a breeze to convert back to 707s, he thought. He spent a few enjoyable moments, trying to recall the exact positions of the instruments on the panel: ASI, Machmeter, compass comparator, horizon switch. . . .

He seemed to doze. The instrument panel became rubbery, the dials went floating away, wandering, bumping into one another.

Pressure. Something was crushing his shoulder. Something heavy, insistent. He opened his eyes. An empty cigarette packet, a dead match, yesterday's evening paper.

"Go home and sleep it off, chum."

"What?" A burning pain seared through his skull. The light of the sun hurt his eyes.

"Come on, now, let's not have any trouble with you."

Beatty discerned a policeman, a young fellow with a kind face. "Trouble?" He moved his shoulder but the policeman's hand remained. "What do you mean, Officer?"

"You know full well what I mean."

Curtly, Beatty told him to talk sense.

The policeman stooped lower. "Now you've 'ad one or two too many, sir, 'aven't you?" His tone was less assured.

Beatty snapped, "I haven't been drinking, for God's sake."

"Are you ill then, sir?"

"My head hurts like hell."

"I'll call for an ambulance."

"No!" Beatty shook his head. "I simply fell asleep."

The policeman nodded gravely. "You were almost on the ground, sir, you were, lolling half off the bench. I really did think you'd had a couple too many. But . . . if not, I beg pardon."

Beatty swallowed. His stomach churned. "It was good of you to be concerned, Constable."

"You'll be all right now, sir?" the constable persisted.

"I'm sure I shall. I'll take a taxi."

"There's a stand over there. I'll walk over with you, sir."

"No, thank you. I'm perfectly capable of walking there alone."

Reluctantly the policeman moved off. Beatty stood up. For a frightening instant, the world revolved. He caught hold of the bench arm and steadied himself. A deep breath and he began to walk. His legs felt oddly disconnected, as if they belonged to someone else. Sweat beaded his forehead. He longed to collapse, but no, damn it, he wouldn't give in. "Nothing the matter," he kept telling himself. "All that happened was that I fell asleep. . . ." Then he remembered the man with the white hair.

I wonder, he thought, whether I'm going mad.

Chapter Three

HENRY Peel had an almost overwhelming desire to smile. But a guy had to look serious when he was embarking on his very first flying lesson. Above all, he couldn't burble about how gratifying it was to get into the pilot's seat of a Piper Cherokee after all those years of waiting.

Henry Peel was nineteen.

"You got to be comfortable and relaxed."

"I am . . . really."

"Okay. Put your hand over the dashboard. Feel the grip? Grab it and pull yourself forward until your feet set on the rudder pedals. That's better. You're not driving a sports car."

The instructor's name was Joe Machin. His face was weathered like old stone; he looked old enough to have fought over the Western Front in a Jenny. His mouth was set in a long-suffering pout at the ineptitude of his pupils. But his voice was gentle.

"See, the wheel moves the ailerons out there on the wings. One goes up, the other goes down. Pull the wheel back and it raises the elevator on the tail and the aircraft goes up. Push it forward, the elevator is depressed. Down she goes. Whole idea of flying an airplane is to keep her balanced. Kind of like a bicycle."

Henry nodded gravely, as if absorbing brand-new information. In fact, however, he knew it all by heart. He had read it ten thousand times. For as long as he could remember, Henry had wanted nothing in the world more than to fly.

"We'll take a little ride," said Machin. "See how you like it."

"I'll like it," said Henry fervently. And the smile popped onto his lips like a nervous twitch.

Expertly, Machin's fingers danced over the instrument panel. "See the ignition switch? Just turn it to the right, through the two magneto settings to ignition. Now push her. Okay."

The engine heaved, caught and sent the propeller hurtling into motion. Machin called the tower for permission to taxi. "The brake's under the dash," he told Henry. "Press the button to release it and away we go. You steer with the rudder pedals. No need to hang on to the wheel; it's done with your feet. Try it."

For a moment it seemed impossible; Henry found himself reaching for the control yoke. Then he discovered that steering by feet was easy.

"Okay," said Machin. "Ease off the throttle a little as you get near the runway. Make sure your door's latched. Okay, now ask the tower if we can take off."

He showed Henry how to apply pressure on the right rudder pedal during the takeoff run in order to correct a tendency to swing to the left, how to ease back on the yoke to get the nose wheel off the ground. "See, she just floats off herself. Up she goes."

At three thousand feet over southern Ontario, Henry took control of an aircraft in flight for the first time. He noted the time; he would record it later. Machin told him to fly straight and level, to try to keep the horizon in the same place.

It was a delicious hour; it escaped in great chunks, ten and fifteen minutes at a time.

"Fantastic," said Henry when they landed.

"You want to get your license?" Machin asked.

"More than anything," said Henry. "You think I'll be able to?"

"Sure. You have a good feeling for the controls. You figure on making a career in aviation?"

"I might; I don't know. I just know I want to fly. I've been saving up. By the time I get my license I'll have enough to buy a small plane. Would you be able to advise me what to buy?"

Machin nodded his grizzled head. "I think we should be able to handle that for you. Wednesday at eight a.m.?"

"I'll be here," Henry said.

POSSIBLY it was pure luck; more probably, however, Flight Scheduling arranged it intentionally, on orders from above. For most pilots it would have been a drag: a late Saturday night trip

487

into Toronto with a layover until Monday afternoon. For Vaughan it could hardly have been better.

Sunday dawned bright and mild. Lee's little MG whisked them to Brockton, a small field with a single hangar, a clubhouse, and an assortment of gliders leaning sideways into the wind. Two Piper Cubs, for towing the gliders, were the only powered aircraft in evidence. The club members, ranging in age from sixteen to sixty, comprised a congenial group and talked endlessly of cumulus clouds "popping" and "rates of sink." They all knew Lee.

Lunch was a soggy, grilled-cheese sandwich in a tiny shack of a restaurant, sharing the table with a burly man who was building his own sailplane, a college kid still on dual instruction, and a youthful Air Canada second officer named Larry who flew tow-planes for fun on weekends. There was only one subject of conversation: soaring. Through the window the towplanes and the student glider pilots could be seen wobbling into the air.

After lunch, Vaughan strapped himself into the front seat of a metal Blanik. Lee climbed into the rear seat. The canopy closed over their heads like a transparent coffin lid, and the towline was fastened beneath the Blanik's nose. Arms waved; the Cub tow-plane wormed forward. Then a burst of throttle, a jerk as the line took the strain. As the Blanik started its roll, Lee eased the stick forward to get the tail off the ground and balance the sailplane on its central wheel. For a few yards the wingman ran alongside, supporting one wing. He let go. A moment's wobble, then, almost immediately, the rumbling of the wheel ceased. Airborne.

"We get off before the towplane," said Lee, "but we have to stay close to the ground or we'll drag his tail up and he'll be in trouble."

Vaughan nodded, his eyes on the rocketing ground just inches away and the Cub careering along the bumpy grass strip. Then up, into the sparkling fall sunshine, obediently following the Cub, always turning in a wider arc to keep the towline taut. Lee flew well, with the smooth assurance of the natural pilot. What a girl.

At two thousand feet she asked him to release the towline. The umbilical line went snaking away behind the turning Cub. Suddenly it was quiet but for the sighing of the wind against the canopy.

"Like it?"

"Great," he assured her.

She found a modest thermal which won them 450 feet. Vaughan tried the controls and promptly lost the thermal.

"Keep turning tightly," she told him.

But it was too late. Laughing at his incompetence, they turned gently over the flat countryside, in perfect peace. They landed ten minutes later, sideslipping in to a gentle touchdown. The Blanik rolled for only a few yards before settling onto one wing tip. Vaughan unfastened his harness, twisted around in the narrow seat and kissed her. She squirmed, laughing, aware of interested onlookers.

They drove to Niagara-on-the-Lake, saw a Shaw play and ate at The Pillar and the Post. They talked. There was so much to tell each other: likes, dislikes, memories, fears, hopes. The words tumbled out and the hours slipped by, filled with a marvelous intensity. The air was crisp and fresh for the drive back to Toronto. There seemed to be another dimension to being alive, and only they were privy to its secret. It was a charmed night.

T. Roydon Goodall, M.D., F.R.C.P., M.R.C., Psych., arranged his pen, calendar and appointment book in a perfectly straight line along the far edge of the desk. Then he positioned his note pad firmly in the center. He often reflected that his passion for tidiness was in all probability a subconscious reaction to the extreme untidiness of most of his patients' lives.

Dr. Goodall's person, although short and distinctly overweight, was as neat as his desk. His white shirt was crisp; his suit was a black pinstripe. His kind, round face was clean-shaven; he wore the remnants of his dark hair brushed smoothly across his skull in a gallant, if not totally successful, attempt to cover it.

Mrs. Latham buzzed. "Mr. Carter," she announced.

Carter. New patient. Telephoned yesterday for the first appointment. Dr. Goodall rose and crossed to the door. Through the reflective glass panel he was able to have a leisurely look at Mr. Carter without Mr. Carter's knowledge. He seemed a well-set-up fellow, nothing lolling or drooping. Dr. Goodall frowned. There was something familiar about this man. He opened the door and asked Mr. Carter to enter.

They exchanged good-mornings. Carter spoke well, firmly, but he seemed ill at ease. He wore a good quality blazer and striped silk tie. His hair was well trimmed. One might take him for a military type in mufti, Dr. Goodall reflected. And, by George, there *was* something familiar about him.

"You are aware that I'm a psychiatrist, Mr. Carter? I mention it only because people have been known to come and see me in regard to everything from gallstones to gout."

Mr. Carter's smile was brief. "I know you're a psychiatrist. You don't recognize me, do you?"

Dr. Goodall shrugged, smiling vaguely.

"At school I used to call you Hoke—but I can't remember why."

"Good Lord!" Suddenly, Dr. Goodall knew. "Frank Beatty! I should have known at once. How extraordinarily nice to see you."

Then he frowned to himself, alarmed. Why was Frank calling himself James Carter? Was he a criminal? A spy? A slight squeakiness affected Dr. Goodall's voice as he asked Frank about the name Carter.

"I'll explain it in a minute, Hoke. It's quite simple."

"I'm sure it is." Dr. Goodall smiled in what he hoped was a casual way. But apprehension had formed a lump in his stomach.

"And Hoke, have no fear. I'm not here to sell you anything or touch you for a loan. The fact of the matter is, I need your professional services, or rather, I think I do."

"I see." Dr. Goodall's lump began to dissolve. Good chap, Frank, always was. "Perhaps we ought to start out with a spot of personal background. Helps one get the full picture. You went into the RAF, didn't you? You were jolly keen on airplanes."

"You remember, do you? Yes, I was in the RAF for a few years."

"And what do you do now?"

"Now? I'm . . . a commercial traveler."

"A salesman."

"What? Oh, yes. That's right, a salesman."

"What do you sell?"

"Aircraft parts, systems, electronics, that sort of thing."

"Interesting. Are you married, Frank—sorry, Mr. Carter?"

"Yes, and I have a son of twelve. Hoke, will you be a friend and put me down on your records as James Carter?"

Dr. Goodall had been considering the question. No law stated that a chap had to demand proof of identity from private patients. On the other hand, in a court of law a chap could hardly claim that he didn't know the true identity of a patient who had been a close chum at school. . . .

Frank said, "The reason I want to use a pseudonym, Hoke, is my employers. They're rather a sticky lot, if you know what I mean. Now, if there's nothing wrong with me, I'd rather they never knew I had been to see you. If there is something wrong, it really won't matter much because I probably won't be able to continue working for them. You see the pickle I'm in, don't you?"

"Of course," said Dr. Goodall, relieved that Frank had provided a reason that a chap could defend. He placed his fingertips together. "Perhaps you should tell me about your . . . problem."

Frank nodded. "I'll try, Hoke. It's a bit difficult because I don't quite know what I'm talking about, but I'm afraid I may be heading for some sort of mental breakdown."

"What makes you say that?"

"A couple of times I seem to have . . . well, faded away. I've woken up to find that I've been *out*. Once I was jogging. I found that I had fallen down. And yesterday I almost fell off a bench in Leicester Square. A policeman thought I was drunk."

"Well, one does tend to doze more, Frank, the older one gets."

"It's more than a doze, Hoke. It's a sort of . . . *cutting off*."

"Have you consulted your family doctor?"

"No."

"Your wife?"

"No. I don't want to worry her needlessly."

Dr. Goodall nodded thoughtfully. "First, it might be well if I quickly checked your heart, lungs, blood pressure, that sort of thing. Odd, how frequently a problem in one location is associated with a symptom in another. . . ."

AMORY answered the telephone with a characteristic "Yup?"

"It's Frank Beatty, Mr. Amory."

"Sure. How are you? And what's the good word?"

"Fine, sir. I would, er, like to take you up on your offer."

Amory's heavy chuckle sounded metallic over the telephone. "You decided in our favor, eh? When can you start?"

"Whenever you want me, sir."

"How about tomorrow morning?"

"First-rate."

"Okay. Gatwick Airport. Nine a.m. Just ask for my office."

"Yes, sir, I will. Thanks very much."

"See you," was the breezy farewell.

Beatty hung up, grinning. He had a job. Of sorts. Good old Amory. He hailed a taxi.

"Sloane Square, please."

Hoke had failed to find anything wrong with him. Indeed he had remarked upon his good health. "My guess," Beatty told himself, "is that the whole thing will turn out to be some idiotic virus and that it's already gone forever." Admittedly, another appointment had been set for some tests; Hoke had said there were a few questions that had to be answered. But Beatty was convinced that all was well; he had never felt better.

He met Diane at the entrance to Peter Jones. She wore a bright green coat that she had just bought. It suited her admirably.

"Do you like it?" she asked. "Really?"

"You look gorgeous," he told her. "And, by the way, in case I haven't mentioned it for a while, I love you."

She glowed. "You haven't mentioned it for about ten years. Your business must have gone well. Are you going with Amory?"

"I start tomorrow morning. So tonight we celebrate. The old man's working again. It's dinner at the Café Royal for us!"

"Frank, that's terribly extravagant!" She laughed, drawing close

493

to him as they walked. It was a moment of happiness without res-
ervation, after three bleak months. Frank was an entire person once
more! He would be flying again.

BEATTY spent three hours at the controls of one of Amory's
Boeing 707s. A pilot named Williams flew with him, first in the
left-hand seat, then in the copilot's position. Williams was an
Australian, an excellent pilot and Amory's senior man.

"You seem to remember the thing pretty good," Williams observed as Beatty performed a faultless engine-failure procedure.

Beatty nodded, smiling. He had done more than three thousand
hours in 707s. He had a high regard for the aircraft. It was superbly
designed. This particular one had seen thirteen years of service,
according to Williams. Amory had purchased it from a French
company and had had it repainted in gray with maroon trim, with
the legend AMORY INTERNATIONAL on the fuselage. The main cabin
had been redecorated. Only the flight deck revealed the machine's
age. The crew's seats were worn; the metal of the control column
was dented; paint had been rubbed from switches and levers by
years of contact.

"Did Mr. Amory buy all three of his aircraft from the same company?" Beatty asked.

Williams shook his head. "The other two came straight from the
States. They're good aircraft, all of them. Amory knows what he's
doing when he's buying airplanes."

Beatty agreed. The 707 handled well. Clearly it had been expertly maintained. Airplanes were as individual as people. Some
plodded through the sky like old, dour men. Some were unpredictable; some were gentle and forgiving. And some cockpits
seemed to have been designed by individuals who had never
flown. In fact, most pilots agreed that no aircraft in the world had
a thoroughly good cockpit layout. Since there was no attempt at
standardization among manufacturers, important levers might
operate forward in one machine, backward in another; even the
same model might differ if different airlines had ordered them.
Each line had its own ideas of what constituted the correct ar-

rangement of instruments and switches. And no flight deck had sufficient room to stow the crew's collection of bags, hats, tunics, manuals, checklists and signal books.

Amory was waiting on the ramp. "How do you like her, Beatty?"

"She's no chicken, but she seems sound in wind and body."

Amory grinned. "Good to be flying again?"

"Marvelous," said Beatty.

"Good. You'll be flying copilot with Mr. Williams here for your first few trips. It's Athens for you on Saturday. Okay?"

"Okay, sir," said Beatty with enthusiasm.

IT WAS indeed a surprise party. "Honestly," Vaughan said, "Sue made me put on a clean shirt and pants. I thought she wanted me to take her to a movie! And suddenly the place is full of people. A birthday party for me!"

"For your fortieth birthday!" someone yelled. "Don't forget that, old-timer. It's not just a run-of-the-mill birthday!"

Everyone chuckled. Susan's ploy had succeeded. The catering firm had delivered the food to the Arlens; the extra liquor had gone to the Gregorys.

"You're a lucky man, Chuck," Maureen Biggin said between nibbles at bacon and chicken liver hors d'oeuvres. "There's a hell of a lot of work arranging one of these things. You men never realize just how much."

Lloyd Foreman babbled about life beginning at forty.

Peter McIlvray said, "When I got to be forty I had a *wake*. In honor of the sudden and untimely death of my goddam youth!"

Soon the guests stopped talking about Charles Vaughan and his birthday and drifted back to the old topics of prices, politicians and relatives. As the bottles emptied, the guests became louder and their jokes, apparently, funnier.

The last guests finally departed. The last car doors slammed. Mellow and pleasantly tired, Vaughan latched the front door. He went back into the living room to find Susan sitting beside the window that overlooked the lake.

"A wonderful party," he told her. "You were a doll to go to all that trouble. It must have been a hell of a lot of work." He leaned down and kissed her cheek.

"I wanted to arrange the party," said Susan, still gazing at the lake, "because I thought you would be grateful and think kindly of me."

"I *am* grateful. Of course I'm grateful. But what do you mean, think kindly of you?"

"It's really rather funny," she said, turning to him. "I went to all this trouble for a reason. And the reason was that I felt frightened and insecure. I thought if I did all this it might solve my problem. And now, because of what I did, I've consumed enough alcohol to face the thing that was bothering me in the first place. That's funny, isn't it, Chuck?"

"Very," said Vaughan, but he felt the heat rising in his face.

"I *know*," she said.

"Know? Know what?"

"Please don't insult my intelligence by denying it. You're seeing another woman. You have been for some time. I know it."

"Susan . . ." The glow from the coffee-table lamp highlighted her cheekbones. Only a slight fullness beneath the chin suggested that this wasn't the profile of a girl in her early twenties. Vaughan groped for words. He wanted to apologize, but he couldn't.

"Who . . . No, I don't want to know. Just tell me where."

"Toronto," he said.

"For how long?"

He shrugged. "I don't know. . . . A few weeks."

"Longer than that," she said. "Did you really think I was unaware that anything was going on?"

"Why didn't you say something sooner?"

"I guess for the same reason that someone with a suspicious pain puts off going to the doctor. You hope the trouble will go away by itself. And I thought I could maybe help make it go away by doing things for you, like arranging this stupid party."

"It was a good party."

"I don't know how long I might have gone on saying nothing. Years, maybe. I guess some women never say anything. Probably half the women at this party have had the same problem sometime or other. But somehow I never thought I'd have it."

"I'm sorry," he said. "I didn't mean it to happen."

Susan looked at him with furious contempt.

Numbly, Vaughan watched a powerboat streak across the lake, its light probing the darkness ahead like some great antenna.

"Do you love her?"

"What do you mean?"

"You know perfectly well what I mean." Susan reached for the Scotch bottle and poured herself a drink. "Well? Can't you speak?"

"No, I don't love her . . . not the way you mean."

"The way I mean? What way do I mean, for God's sake?"

Vaughan said, "I don't love her the way I love you."

She turned and laughed in his face. "That's for sure."

It was a nightmare. He rubbed the flesh above his eyebrows. His fingers seemed to burn into his skull. "I was telling the truth," he said, "when I told you I didn't mean it to happen."

"Helpless in the storm of flaming passion. But it damn well did happen, didn't it? So what are you going to do about it?"

"I'll . . . I'll give her up."

"Why didn't you give her up months ago?"

"I tried. Honestly, I did try."

"That was big of you, Charlie boy. But you couldn't make it."

"No. . . ."

"She must be a dish. Tell me about her. Blond? Brunette? Nice legs? Tell me what she *does*, Charlie."

"Please, Susan. . . ." He leaned toward her—but she shrank away.

"No. It sounds like a cliché, but I don't want you to touch me."

"I'm sincerely sorry."

"You keep saying that. I'm sincerely sorry too. Sorry as hell."

The telephone rang. Vaughan took it. "Yes?"

"Captain Vaughan?"

"Speaking."

"It's Mangione, Captain, from the office. I'm sorry to have to tell you, but there's been an accident. It was Captain Przeczek."

God. "Is he . . ."

"Yeah. I don't think there were any survivors."

"Have you told his wife?"

"No. We thought, maybe, as you and he were friends like . . ."

"All right," said Vaughan, icily calm now. "I'll tell her."

"Thanks, Captain."

Vaughan hung up. He turned to Susan. "It's Walt Przeczek," he said. "He crashed. He's dead."

"Oh, no," she said softly.

"I've got to tell May."

"I understand," she said, nodding in an almost mechanical way. Her eyes were bright with tears. "Oh, not Walt. . . . Poor May."

HOURS of anger and agony began. Hours in which tiny worlds were smashed forever. May wanted to know precisely what had happened. Vaughan couldn't tell her. The official word didn't come until shortly before dawn. After an apparently normal lift-off from runway 32 of a midwestern city the aircraft had suddenly plunged vertically into the median of an interstate highway.

"Those rich bastards have killed him," May declared.

Vaughan knew the airport well. If an aircraft flew straight out after taking off from runway 32, it would find itself over the city's swankiest new subdivision. The residents of the subdivision had pull at city hall. They objected to the noise. Soon the federal word was transmitted to all pilots using runway 32. Turn left to 290 degrees as soon as practicable after lift-off; intercept Brewer beacon, then make another left turn at 2500 feet to intercept Markton beacon. The maneuvers guided the aircraft around the subdivision. Provided everything was working properly and the weather was reasonable, they were not difficult maneuvers. But something had gone wrong with Walt Przeczek's aircraft in foggy, wet conditions.

"He told me about that stinking runway, Chuck," May said. "He knew he was going to run into trouble one day. He'd have been all right if they'd let him fly straight out, wouldn't he?"

May began to sob silently. Susan tried to comfort her. Vaughan watched the pale light creeping along the walls of the neighboring houses. Soon it would be the new day, the day that Walt and his passengers would never see. Walt. So full of life. Walt, dead. Sick at heart, Vaughan shook his head. What went wrong? What did he think in those horrific miniseconds? Did he believe to the very last that he was going to get out of it, as he had gotten out of all the other near things? There was, it seemed, a useful device attached to the brains of pilots that refused to permit the acceptance of inevitable death. Vaughan had heard tapes from flight recorders recovered from wrecks; the voices were calm and confident right up to impact. No screams. No prayers. Only an occasional apology, in mild tones, for having done something inexcusably stupid.

Susan was beside him. "I'm going to make some more coffee," she said softly, and Vaughan nodded.

"Hi."

Vaughan turned. It was six-year-old John, tousled from sleeping. Delighted to see Uncle Chuck and Auntie Sue. Wanting to know why his mother was up and about before him. Before either adult could respond, he pattered into the kitchen to the refrigerator.

"I'm not going to tell him," May said.

"You have to," Vaughan told her.

"No," May said. "Why Walt, Chuck? Why?"

"God knows."

"He was a bastard at times. But he was good, and gentle too, and I loved him very much. I'm going to miss him like hell."

"I am too," Vaughan said. "I know how you feel."

She looked at him and shook her head. "No, you don't, Chuck, you don't know at all."

TAKEOFFS weren't too hard, in Henry Peel's limited experience; landings, however, were quite another matter. While the aircraft would float good-naturedly into the air, given sufficient power and enough runway, she seemed positively cantankerous when the time came to return to terra firma.

Joe Machin was patient. "People get uptight about landings," he said, "but all you're doing is flying her back to earth and then slowing her up until she can't stay in the air anymore. You fly straight and level down the runway two or three feet up. Then cut

499

the power and keep on pulling up the nose when she starts to settle. This slows her progressively so she won't be able to stay up anymore. She'll stall onto the ground."

Henry nodded soberly. He knew the theory. The problem lay in converting theory into action. Since taking up flying, he had discovered that air is seldom still, rarely reliable. Trees, buildings and hills create treacherous currents close to the ground, lying in wait for the unwary like icy patches on city streets. And, he had learned, aircraft could be willful, like spirited animals. They loved to wander off to the left or right when they thought you weren't paying attention. In Machin's hands the Cherokee was docile and obedient, settling onto the runway with an obsequious little sigh. When Henry landed, she wallowed into the ground in a semi-drunken manner.

"You're getting the hang of it," said Machin, chewing his gum with determination after a particularly bumpy arrival.

"I don't think I am."

"Sure. Just practice. Let's go around again. I'll look after the flaps and trim. Away you go."

Henry eased the throttle forward. The aircraft rolled; the runway began to unwind. It was a moment that never ceased to thrill. He, Henry Peel, was at the controls of an aircraft rushing at breakneck speed. Right foot on the rudder pedal to keep her heading straight. Gentle heave back on the yoke.

At once the Cherokee soared. Her left wing dropped a few degrees. Henry applied right aileron control. But too much. Up; down; at last she was level. Three hundred feet. Flaps up; lever to the floor. Fuel pump to off; fuel pressure still okay.

A glance over the side. Two kids standing outside a store, ignoring the Piper. Why weren't they staring up, envying him?

"Always keep an eye out for other traffic," said Machin as the Cherokee soared into the air. "Old pilots are pilots who've spent a lot of time looking around for other traffic."

"Right," said Henry. He eased the Cherokee's nose down and looked from left to right. Nothing to be seen but flat land.

Machin pointed. "Two o'clock," he said.

Henry looked at his watch. Automatically. Idiotically. He cursed himself. Holy cow, you bloody *groundling!*

Two o'clock means off the right beam a bit. You had to imagine the nose as the hand of a clock pointing to twelve.

"See her?" Machin asked.

"Well . . ." Henry stared.

Machin said, "She's turned off. A one fifty."

Henry had caught not even a glimpse of the other aircraft. Until he had started flying he had no idea how difficult it was to see other machines in the sky. Now he wondered about all those stories he had read about sharp-eyed heroes in Spads spotting enemy Albatroses five miles away and ten thousand feet below. They must have had infrared eyesight.

Machin raised a languid hand and indicated the left. Henry nodded. It was time to turn into the crosswind leg of the circuit. Check speed. Damn! Too fast! He felt the nervous sweat sticking his shirt to his body. Please behave, he begged the Cherokee.

"Watch your height," Machin murmured.

Jeepers! Two hundred feet too high! Throttle lever back. He was flying the downwind leg of his circuit, parallel to the runway on which he would land. In a moment it would be time to turn onto the base leg.

"Landing checks," said Machin with a yawn.

Landing checks. What were they? For a moment his brain seized solid. Ah, yes. Fuel. Left tank. Almost full. Fuel pump on. Carburetor heat on. Reduction in revs? Yes, thank God. No ice. Keep looking out for traffic. And listen to Machin suggesting that it might be nice to let the tower know his intentions.

God, yes! He grabbed for the mike fastened to the window post, dropped it, fumbled for it and gabbled the message. "Turning left base for a touch and go on runway zero six."

Now he was too close. He would have to turn onto final at once. But he was still traveling at well over one hundred miles per hour. If only the bloody airplane would stop for a moment and let a guy sort things out. At last he got the nose of the Cherokee pointed at the runway. It sped toward him. Important-looking lights poked their heads a few inches above the ground. The runway unrolled beneath him, a mile-long carpet of gray concrete. Keep your eyes on a spot forty or fifty yards ahead, Machin had said again and again. The speed began to drop, but simultaneously the Cherokee developed an inclination to wander off to the left. Rudder, thought Henry desperately. Use some rudder.

But the Cherokee had already landed. On one main wheel. She bounced to the other. Then onto the nose wheel. At last, shaking herself, she ran along on all three wheels.

Henry cursed under his breath.

"I've seen worse," said Machin.

"Honestly?"

"Sure," said Machin, "though not without some blood."

BEATTY discovered that charter flying had a character all its own. For one thing, it was maximum-capacity business all the time. And charter passengers were a breed apart, good-natured and noisy, given to visiting throughout the aircraft, and far more philosophical about delays than their scheduled brethren. Charter flights were holiday flights. An hour or two made little difference. Day after day they trooped aboard Amory's aircraft: members of social clubs, athletic clubs, glee clubs, church clubs, servicemen's clubs. And almost without fail, they burst into spontaneous applause the moment the jets touched down at journey's end.

Because Amory's 707s usually flew to airfields where the company had no service facilities, they carried a substantial inventory of spare parts. They also carried a fourth crew member, a flight engineer, who, unlike most flight engineers, was a qualified aviation mechanic who could tackle major repair jobs.

Like most organizations, the Amory company seemed to take on some of the characteristics of the headman. There was a brash, pioneering air about everything. Amory kept promising to get stationery printed with the company name but did not. Supplies of company checks ran out one week; Amory paid the staff in cash. Schedules had a habit of becoming badly scrambled; shortly before Christmas, Beatty found that he was supposed to fly to Nice,

France, and Montreal, Canada, the same morning. There were times when not one member of the crew had even seen the destination before; often, when briefed, they were unsure just where it was. Such flights were illegal on scheduled services. More than once, Amory himself flew as second·officer; no one had the nerve to ask him if his license was still valid.

When Diane asked her husband how he enjoyed his new job, he said, truthfully, that he had never enjoyed flying more.

HOKE seemed a little testy. "Frank, I do wish you'd try not to cancel appointments at half an hour's notice. It's really not playing the game. This is the third one in a row."

Beatty smiled into the telephone. Hoke sounded so plaintive. "I'm most awfully sorry, old man. It's this job of mine. I . . . have to go out of the country unexpectedly at times."

"I see."

"Besides, I've been feeling so much better, Hoke."

"Quite so. But I do think those tests we talked about are advisable. They won't take too long, and they could be important."

"You really think I should have them, do you, Hoke?"

"Most definitely. I'm going to make an appointment with a hospital lab. Now, do you wish to make it in the name of Carter?"

"Yes, I suppose so."

"When will you be back in this country?"

"Next week. Thursday."

"I'll make it for Friday. Now do be a good fellow and keep it. It could be important."

Two hours after the takeoff from Gatwick, the intercom signal buzzed. A stewardess reported a problem. One of her passengers had gone berserk; he was convinced the aircraft would crash.

"Shall I see what I can do?" Beatty asked Captain Hallman.

Hallman nodded, relieved. "Good show."

Beatty eased himself out of the right-hand seat and put on his tunic and cap. Full uniform often helped in this sort of situation.

He opened the flight-deck door. The troublemaker stood at the rear of the cabin, his legs apart, his arms folded tightly over his chest. He was about twenty-five, thin and sallow-faced. His eyes bulged with terror. He was screaming that the plane was going to crash. Occupants of the rear seats now stood jammed in the center aisle, frightened and confused.

"I can't do a thing with him," the stew told Beatty. "He just suddenly went potty. His name is Birdlett."

"Has he a wife on board?"

"No, he's traveling alone."

"Damn." Beatty drew a deep breath and made his way along the packed aisle until he stood a few feet from passenger Birdlett. The man was trembling. Sweat poured down his gray-toned face.

"Everything's all right, old man," said Beatty in a chatty tone.

"We're all going to die. We're all doomed!"

Beatty smiled. "I can assure you we're not. It's quite safe. . . ." He took a pace forward and Birdlett swung at him wildly. Beatty ducked, but the blow caught him on the shoulder. He plunged forward, trying to pin Birdlett's arms. A thin, bony fist thudded into his cheek. Angered, he hit back. He clutched at Birdlett. Both men went down, Birdlett's head cracking against the toilet door. Clumsily they scuffled.

Now there were dozens of hands, eagerly helping. Beatty rescued his cap from among excited feet as he got up again.

"Are you all right, Mr. Beatty?"

Beatty nodded at the stew.

"He hit you."

"Not too seriously."

They tied Birdlett down on a crew seat, and a passenger named Forbes, who said he was a policeman, volunteered to do guard duty until the aircraft landed.

Beatty returned to the flight deck. He closed the door behind him. Then he passed out.

It was easily explained. A nasty scuffle. Vicious blows from a deranged passenger. A shock to the system. Passing out wasn't all that surprising when you thought about it. So said the crew. So said the doctor at the airport.

BRISK FINGERS CLEANSED the skin with alcohol. A solution of pyroxylin in acetone formed tiny transparent patches of secondary skin which secured the electrodes in position. Each electrode was the terminal for a slender wire leading to a control panel.

"Not nearly as complicated as the airplane systems you deal with, Mr. Carter, but quite interesting. The object of the exercise, you see, is to detect and record rhythmic changes in the electrical potential of the brain. We can learn quite a lot about the brain if we can study its electrical discharges. So we attach the electrodes to various areas of the scalp. When you are fully plugged in, so to speak, we can measure the impulses." The hospital technician chattered on. . . .

"PLEASE sit down, Frank."

"You mean Carter, don't you, old man?"

"What? Oh, yes, of course, Carter." Hoke didn't smile. He rubbed his chin as if it ached. "How have you been feeling?"

"On top line, except for one little incident."

"Incident?"

"I got into a bit of a scuffle. A chap hit me. I sort of flaked out afterward, but I don't think that counts as a *spell*, do you?"

"Possibly not. But you feel quite well now?"

"Perfectly. Don't look so disappointed, Hoke."

Hoke appeared not to have heard. "I have the results of your EEG, Frank. Mind you, they are not absolutely conclusive, but they do indicate an abnormality."

Beatty cleared his throat, feeling his insides chill and contract. "An abnormality? What sort of abnormality?"

"This really isn't my field, Frank. It's a sort of . . . well, electrical problem, neurological rather than psychiatric. It's my understanding, however, that this type of condition can frequently be treated very successfully, although there's a great deal that isn't yet known about it."

Beatty said, "What is the condition called?"

"It's a form of epilepsy, Frank."

"God."

505

"You see, the disease comes in many forms." Hoke tumbled over the words in his anxiety to get them out. "People hear epilepsy and think of frightful, uncontrollable fits. But it isn't always like that. And it's not in your case, Frank. I believe you have a mild form of what is known as psychomotor or temporal lobe epilepsy. It's characterized by short losses of consciousness such as you have been experiencing."

"You're sure, Hoke? There's no doubt at all?"

"I think not. But I do want you to see a neurologist."

"Bloody incredible." Beatty shook his head as if unable to comprehend the truth. *Why me, why, why?*

"I'm going to make an appointment with the neurologist."

"No, I'm not going to anyone else."

"But you must, Frank. This is outside my field."

"If I do nothing, will the attacks continue much as they have?"

"I have no way of knowing. Frank, please . . . I'm a psychiatrist."

"Yes, but you're a doctor too. I bet you got jolly good marks in epilepsy classes, didn't you?"

"Frank . . ."

"Tell me all about it, Hoke. I'm really interested. It's nice to know what's happening to one's brain, I always say."

Hoke frowned unhappily. "Well, the medical term is cerebral dysrhythmia. It's the result of disturbances in the electrical discharges from the brain. Attacks can be triggered by such things as changes in the chemical balance of the blood, by hypoglycemia—which is a very low glucose level in the blood—by exhaustion, or psychological stresses, or by something as innocent as a stroboscopically flashing light."

"Which," Beatty said, "might be caused by running under a long line of trees when the sun was streaming through the branches."

"What? Yes, I suppose so. Treatment varies, Frank. Phenobarbital and phenytoin are often used successfully, I believe. Mind you, there can be side effects if the dosage is heavy: drowsiness, lethargy, that sort of thing."

A minor inconvenience for an airline pilot.

"But, Frank," Hoke went on earnestly, "people under this sort of treatment usually manage awfully well. Often their friends have no idea that there's anything wrong."

"Except when they do odd things such as cutting off ears and posting them to girl friends."

"Pardon?"

"Isn't that what van Gogh did? And wasn't he an epileptic? I read that in a paperback sitting in Boston waiting for the weather to clear. Funny, I never thought for a moment . . ."

Funny as hell.

BEATTY walked for three hours. Through Hyde Park, along Piccadilly, down to Trafalgar Square, along the Strand. He had Hoke's prescription (for Mr. J. Carter) filled at a chemist's shop. "To be taken four times a day or as required." He walked on, to find himself at last somewhere east of the City. It was raining now in a sullen and insistent manner. He had a cup of tea in a grubby little café and swallowed one of Hoke's pills.

"Anything to eat, mister?" A doleful black man.

"No, thanks." The black man shrugged.

"Don't look so glum," Beatty told him silently. "You're not an epileptic." Epileptic. How he hated even the sound of the word.

He rested his fingertips against his forehead. Inside, he thought, the electricity is hard at work and operating properly, according to the manual. But for how long? Odd to think that the thing might have been lurking in one's head, waiting for the right moment to strike. Nice of it to pick the moment when one was bringing in a jet to land.

The fact of the matter is, he thought, you have to find another line of work. But the choice of employment must be a bit limited for forty-nine-year-old epileptics who have never done anything but fly airplanes.

Must look the problem squarely in the eyes. But it isn't the end of the world. So said Hoke. Who doesn't happen to have the problem. Anger surged within him. It was as unfair as hell. His license would be permanently revoked the instant the authorities knew of his condition. "You no longer have a profession," he told himself.

"You can claim insurance against the loss of your license on medical grounds. But you can't live on that forever. You have to do something else. Think positively: there are thousands of ways for a chap to make a living."

He ordered more tea.

Whenever he thought of employment on the ground he seemed to see herds of gray-faced, cheerless people streaming out of underground stations, waiting at bus stops, piling into office buildings that looked like colossal coffins on their ends. Always hurrying and pushing. Worrying about being late. Fretting their lives away.

"I want to keep on flying," he said, as if he had only himself to persuade. It was his life; a hell of a life when you came to think of it. Hard, unrelenting work. But Beatty wanted no other.

Rain dribbled disconsolately down the café window.

He was due for his next medical in three weeks, before which he was scheduled to fly about a dozen trips. He would be flying them as copilot; therefore, any landings and takeoffs he performed would be under the supervision of the captain in command. Hell, there really wasn't any danger, was there? Even in the unlikely event that he began to feel woozy while actually flying, the captain could take over at once. That was one of the reasons for having two pilots, wasn't it?

Just a few more trips. It wasn't much to ask.

Then he would go to his medical. The doctor would discover that all was not on top line. Beatty would express surprise. No need to mention Hoke. No need to admit to any symptoms. No need to do a bloody thing except stand still to be stamped unfit.

God, how he would enjoy those last trips.

MR. COX disappeared into the attic, to reappear moments later with the suitcases. They were indeed dusty, but, Mrs. Cox reckoned, since they had been up in the attic since the summer of 1948, the year before Joycie went off to live in Canada, it was hardly surprising.

When he had successfully negotiated the steps, Mr. Cox examined the cases. He was relieved to find them sound; at his time of life, he didn't want to be buying expensive new luggage. "They'll see us to Toronto and back all right," he affirmed.

His wife giggled girlishly. "I can't hardly believe we're really going, I really can't."

"Course we're going," said Mr. Cox, as if a transatlantic trip were the most usual thing in the world.

Mr. and Mrs. Cox were due to fly to Toronto via Amory International in four months and two days.

Chapter Four

VAUGHAN watched Lee as she slid the meat out of the crab legs. She tackled the job in the total way she did everything. Recently she had purchased a guitar; now she practiced as much as five hours a day. Lee hurled herself headlong into the business of being alive. And damn the torpedoes.

She dipped the last morsel of crab into the drawn butter. "Heavenly." She wiped her fingers on the damp cloth supplied. "Is it on my face? I feel as if I've been wallowing in the stuff."

"A smidgen right there." He touched the corner of her mouth.

She thanked him, then looked at him for a moment, steadily. "My antenna tells me you have something to say, Chuck."

"Your antenna could be wrong."

"Could be. But isn't."

The waiter materialized. Vaughan ordered coffee and Hennessey.

"Nothing's wrong," he said.

"I didn't say anything was wrong. I just said you have something on your mind."

"I haven't."

"Okay." A gentle little shrug.

She couldn't have made it any easier for him to tell her. Why the hell didn't he? It wouldn't be any surprise. Secret revealed. Wife irked. Decision in her favor. The kids. The end. Deep regrets. But uttering the words had become as unthinkable as thrusting a knife into her heart. He was suspended in a maddening limbo, wanting her, yet wishing he had the courage to break with her.

The conversation over coffee and brandy became politely automatic. At last, her eyes roaming his face as if committing every feature to memory, she said, "Your wife knows, doesn't she?"

He turned the cognac in his glass and nodded.

"Why didn't you say so?"

"I couldn't. I don't know why. It was impossible."

Her eyes glistened. "I knew it had to happen. Sometime. I mean, it was inevitable, wasn't it? I wasn't kidding myself. I just hoped it might last a bit longer."

"I'm sorry," he said inadequately.

"Poor Chuck." She smiled, her lips trembling. "He has to apologize to two women. It must have been rough for you. I guess she was bloody sore about it."

"Yes, she was sore."

Her eyes searched his face again. "I don't blame her," she said. "I'd be bloody sore too, in her position. You're a nice man. And there aren't that many nice men around. It's a hell of a job replacing them when they go."

He touched her hand. "You sound as if you're talking about spark plugs."

Her tone became falsely bright. "Is this it? End of the line? That sounds like a song title, doesn't it? I just want to know where I stand, Chuck. The next move is up to you. Hell, more song titles. I can't stop it." She poured too much cream into her coffee. "We both knew it couldn't last forever. You know, that's another one. How the hell does a girl turn herself off? Maybe this is the beginning of a new career for me. Sad song specialist."

Vaughan heard himself saying, "I don't want it to end, Lee. You matter too much. I just can't imagine life without you."

"You're not playing fair, Chuck. You're saying dangerous things. The sort of things that build up a girl's hopes."

"I'm being honest," he said. "I won't let you go."

"Please don't say things you don't mean."

"I'm not." He took her hand. "I don't know what the hell I'm going to do. I don't know what's going to happen. But I do know I love you and I'm not going to give you up."

A FEW HUNDRED yards away a gray-haired, innocuous-looking couple named Hardcastle walked out of a Toronto department store. Mr. Hardcastle carried two large cans of paint. He planned to start painting the spare bedroom the very next morning. It was only a matter of weeks until his sister would be occupying the room; she was booked on a charter flight from Gatwick to Toronto.

Mr. Hardcastle eagerly awaited his sister's arrival; he hadn't seen her for more than twenty years. He hoped she would like the room. He and his wife, after more than an hour of wondering, had selected a pale shade of pink. It didn't strike either of them as strange that they should take so much trouble to select a color for someone who had been blind since birth.

ACCORDING to flight-deck etiquette it was an unforgivable faux pas. Captains bestowed the privilege of landings and takeoffs upon their copilots; a copilot was never expected to ask. But Beatty did. As the English coast came into view, he turned to Williams and asked for the landing.

Williams smiled, puzzled. "Any particular reason?"

"I'm due for my medical tomorrow," Beatty told him. "This may be my last chance."

"Do you think you'll fail your medical?"

"I hope not. But there's always the chance." A bloody enormous chance, he thought.

Had Beatty been a run-of-the-mill junior copilot and not a former 747 captain, he would unquestionably have been ticked off for being cheeky. Instead, Williams nodded. "She's all yours."

"Thanks very much. Good of you."

Autopilot off. Beatty wanted to fly her, feel the life of her through the controls. He settled himself. Time to concentrate completely. No matter how skilled and experienced, a pilot could never permit himself to relax during a landing; too much could happen too rapidly.

The ether was full of chattering voices: voices from other aircraft reporting positions, intentions; voices from the ground requesting descents to certain heights, turns to certain headings. The nearer the airport, the more complex the patterns. Somewhere in the gray sky were Lord knows how many jets, arriving, departing, climbing, descending. *Hurtling.* The men on the ground had to keep them in their proper places, safely apart. Down to the next aerial story, recently vacated by another five-hundred-mile-per-hour occupant. Turn. Circle. Descend.

"Clear to descend. Advise established inbound on ILS."

Beatty glanced at the ILS dial to ensure that the tiny failure flag hadn't appeared. Pilots had been known to fly to their deaths faithfully following the directions of an instrument that had failed and was trying desperately to tell them so.

"Flaps fifty," Beatty reported. "Runway in sight."

The aircraft was docile in his hands as she descended smoothly toward the concrete strip. The ground rolled beneath him: damp, shiny fields, a road packed with toy cars, tiny houses, antlike people. A bang-on approach, a steady, progressive settling down of one hundred tons of machinery and humanity at seven hundred feet per minute. In 120 seconds the 707 would be whooshing over the threshold of the runway, her bunches of main wheels reaching for the ground. Runway number clearly visible. Brisk crosswind to be handled with aplomb.

My farewell performance, ladies and gentlemen. No encores, I regret, due to technical difficulties.

The skill in landing lay in knowing just when to apply the elevator to bring the machine out of its descent and send it skimming along the runway at an altitude of an inch or two.

Beatty relished the challenge of every landing. This one, he decided, would be a greaser, a triumph with which to terminate his career. The passengers would never know the precise moment they ceased to fly. One moment airborne, the next trundling sweetly along the strip.

Beatty frowned slightly as he became totally absorbed in his task, scanning the runway ahead, mentally computing height, distance and speed. Now the ground was rushing at him. This was the moment. Ease back on the yoke. The runway leveled. Power down. He felt the aircraft's tendency to wander to the left because a strong wind was pressing on her flank. He made her resist by angling her nose and lowering one wing a degree or two. Her speed fell off. Irresistibly the forces of gravity worked on her; her wheels touched the runway. Barely a bump. The nose plopped down, the wheel smack on the center line.

"Reverse thrust, please."

The 707 slowed. She was behaving like a lady, without pitching and bouncing as she sometimes did. At this point in every landing there was a temptation to cancel the reverse thrust too soon. An aircraft that has been traveling at 125 knots seems to be moving quite slowly when its speed is down to eighty-five. Beatty waited until the speed was down to fifty knots before canceling the reverse thrust. Thus the brakes and tires were not unduly worked.

He parked at the terminal, the aircraft's main exit neatly in line with the ramp.

Williams said, "Good luck with your medical."

"Thanks very much. Thanks for the landing too."

"Don't mention it. It was a dandy."

As he collected his cap, tunic and flight bag, Beatty reflected that this would almost certainly be the last time he stood on a flight deck. He looked around. It was cramped and ugly. But there was nothing quite like it, and he would miss it dreadfully.

"So long," he said silently.

THIRTY-SIX hours later, Frank Beatty swung his car out of a parking space near Baker Street and drove off smiling. He felt like a prisoner granted a reprieve on the morning of his execution. Glee bubbled within him. I passed my medical! I'm not dreaming this, am I? No, I'm officially fit to fly.

No doubt about it. He had a slip of paper to prove it.

Admittedly, he had lied to the doctor. When asked about his general state of health, he had said he had no problems. If they're going to ground me, let them find out for themselves. The doctor had accepted the statement. Heart, lungs, hearing, vision, all had been tested and found fit. Nothing had led the doctor to question the workings of Beatty's brain.

Lots of chaps lie at medicals. He felt the box of pills in his pocket. They would keep him out of trouble. Good old Hoke.

The sun broke through the overcast as he drove along Oxford Street. He beamed up at it. Life had the funniest habit of plunging him into the depths and then, just as rapidly, hurling him to the heights. He had telephoned the Amory office to report and had been put through to Mr. Amory himself.

"Passed your medical okay?"

"Yes, sir."

"Glad to hear it. I just bought a couple more aircraft. Need captains. Interested in stepping up in the world?"

"Hell, yes! Er, that is . . ."

Amory had chuckled in his throaty way. "That's okay, feller, I know how you feel. I got to be made captain myself once. I goofed. Did a perfect landing at Toronto. It was a hazy day, though, and for some reason or other I came down on the wrong airfield. The two airports in Toronto are pretty close, you know. Anyway, my employers came to the conclusion they could get along just fine without my services. Well, so much for ancient history. You're hereby promoted to the dizzy rank of captain in Amory International Airways. Which isn't saying a hell of a lot right now, but it may be one day, eh? We'll talk about dough the next time you're in the office."

"Right, sir. And thank you very much indeed."

Beatty had then telephoned Diane—loyal, long-suffering Diane, on whom he had vented his anxiety that very morning.

"You sound better," she had said. "I gather you passed."

"Yes. Er, sorry I was a bit of a bear this morning."

"Don't mention it," she replied. "I'm used to it by now, just like any well-behaved airline pilot's wife."

He grinned. "I would appreciate it, madam, if you would have a modicum of respect for my rank. Be so good as to address me as captain from this moment on."

Diane had shrieked with delight.

He felt marvelous. Never better. And intensely grateful to Amory and Hoke.

ON THE MORNING OF April 19, after ten hours and twelve minutes of dual instruction, Henry Peel flew solo. It was a brief flight: takeoff, turn to the left, downwind leg, another left turn to base leg, then one more left turn onto final.

Joe Machin stood beside the runway, chewing gum. He looked bored, but he was nervous. You could never tell what a kid might do the first time he got up in an aircraft by himself.

Thump. Henry Peel was down. And if his first solo landing was something slightly less than perfection, it had at least deposited him on the runway the right way up and facing in the right direction. And that, in Joe Machin's experience, was considerably better than the way many a first solo had ended up. He sent Henry off to do more circuits.

FOURTEEN minutes after Henry Peel touched down on his first solo landing, a man in Santa Ana, California, named Earl Gasparac told his wife about the trip he had arranged. New York by Tran-State, then Providence, Boston, and Portland, Maine, by auto. "After that," he announced, "we head toward New Hampshire and Vermont—and then New York State and a joint called—"

"Utica!" she cried, delighted.

They laughed. Mrs. Gasparac had been born in Utica, New York, thirty-one years before, but it was almost ten years since she had been back east. For this trip Earl Gasparac would have to borrow heavily from the credit union. His salary as a telephone company repairman, while adequate, had its limitations. But the trip couldn't be delayed. Dr. Malcolm had made it horribly clear: if Mrs. Gasparac didn't make the trip before the end of summer, she would never make it at all.

A WOMAN in Des Moines, Iowa, named Lillian Dumont counted the money she had been stealing from her husband and her employer, Associated Security Services, manufacturers of Ever-Watchful television equipment for stores and offices. It came to seventeen thousand dollars. Amazing, how little bits out of petty cash, housekeeping and the savings account can mount up.

THE VISIT TO May Przeczek was an ordeal. She was still in semi-shock. There was so much to say and yet there were no words. Talk was little more than a respite from silence. May and Susan made tentative plans for shopping expeditions, bridge parties, and picnics for the kids, knowing that none of them would take place.

When it was time to leave, Vaughan and Susan said they would come again soon, guilty with the relief they felt at parting.

"I think old Walt was laughing like hell at us," said Vaughan as he accelerated away from the house.

"Why?"

"Because we were such phonies. We weren't honest with each other. Walt respected honesty above all things."

Susan said, "He didn't deserve May."

"Why do you say that?"

"He had other women."

"How do you know that?"

"May told me. And he made a pass at me. Several, in fact."

"Walt couldn't resist women," Vaughan said. "He loved to be in their company. And flirting was as natural as breathing."

"Why don't you ask me what happened? You don't give a damn."

"It's not that. The man's dead. And if you'd had an affair with him, I don't think you'd want to talk about it now."

"You sound damned sure of yourself," she said angrily.

"No," said Vaughan, "I'm not sure at all. But I think it might be better if we dropped the subject."

Susan was silent for a couple of miles. Then she said, "You're still seeing that female in Canada."

He lied. Too easily. "No, it's all over. I told you."

"I don't believe you." She huddled against the passenger door, her shoulders jerking spasmodically. Vaughan pictured her eyes full of bitter tears, her mouth trembling. She hated him. And he didn't blame her.

The substance of his world was disintegrating. And it was his fault. He wanted to take Susan in his arms and tell her, convince her, that everything was going to be all right. She *deserved* to hear it. God, what *was* he becoming, loving two women equally. His hands tightened on the steering wheel. You are a despicable SOB.

Vaughan found himself cursing Lee for plunging into his life, destroying its balance and its direction. What an unholy idiot he had been! Was there still time to salvage the wreck of his marriage? Still time to be forgiven? All he had to do was call Lee and tell her good-by. He swallowed, remembering the time he had stopped at the phone booth on Wilshire Boulevard, determined to end it there and then. But even as he had lifted the receiver he seemed to hear her voice and see her face. Hopelessly he had let the receiver drop.

You're no damned good at this. Your wife is broken up because she knows you're being unfaithful and you may leave her. Lee is no better off because she thinks you won't. Why, he wondered, did I have to let her think there might be some sort of permanent relationship? What right did I have to do that? None! Zero!

"Stop at the grocery store," said Susan, "if you don't mind. I have to get a loaf of bread."

Vaughan nodded. No matter what the crisis, the domestic machinery still had to function.

It was a strange time in the Vaughans' lives, full of silences, full of television. Vaughan would go off on long walks alone, wondering how to put his life back in order. Inevitably the situation touched Janet and Lynn. They sensed the tension between their parents with the sure instinct of the young, and they reacted, taking their mother's part. Yet, through it all, the family still somehow functioned. The annual trip to Disneyland took place and Lynn's birthday was celebrated as usual by dinner at the Fox and Hounds. There was brave talk of a summer vacation. Sometimes there was laughter—but it tended to stop in midflight.

In early May they drove to Carmel to visit Susan's parents. "We've got to," she said. "It's been more than three months. They'll think something's wrong." Vaughan was of the opinion that a visit would remove all doubt, but he kept silent.

The Jearards' house overlooked the Pacific; it was a pleasant, tranquil spot. Harold Jearard was a retired steel mill vice-president, a slim, stooped man with tired eyes and a wry sense of humor. Susan's mother was plump and warm and a superb cook.

The visit turned out to be remarkably successful. In the company of her parents Susan seemed to soften, as if calling a silent truce. When Sunday came, Vaughan prepared for the return drive in a relaxed mood, glad that the visit had been made. He was due to fly to Miami the following morning. Soon after breakfast he asked Susan what time she wanted to leave.

"I'm not leaving," she said.

He looked up from his packing. "What?"

"I'm staying here." Her voice sounded brittle. She avoided his eyes. "So are Janet and Lynn. You know why."

"What about their school?"

"There are schools in Carmel. Besides, it's almost vacation."

Vaughan shook his head. Why was his first reaction to wonder about the girls' school? "What do you want from me?"

"You know."

"I told you; it's all over."

"Please don't lie to me."

"I mean it, Susan. . . ."

"Yes, I know you do, Chuck, when you're with me." There was the hint of a sad smile on her lips. "I think you're sincere when you say such things to me. But you haven't been able to make them happen, have you? I guess it must be hell for you. But it's up to you to work it out. It's your problem." She went to the door. "You'd better come up," she called to her parents. "We may as well get this over with."

And then her parents were in the room. For ghastly moments there was silence. No one looked at anyone else.

At last Susan said, "I've told Charles I'm staying."

Suddenly all eyes were on Vaughan.

"I'm sorry," he said. "It's as embarrassing for you as for me. I don't know why Susan had to bring you into this."

Mrs. Jearard said something which became sobs. Mr. Jearard said, "Susan, why don't you take your mother into her room and give her a glass of water or something?"

Vaughan swallowed. He felt slightly sick. What now?

When the door had closed, Mr. Jearard said, "I agree that Susan

should not have brought us into this. It makes the situation more painful. There are times when it is much the best course to side-step the truth. All of us, I think, would have felt better if we had pretended that you had to return for business reasons."

"I suppose you know why she did it," said Vaughan. He tossed socks into his bag. The sooner he left the better.

"I just want to tell you," said Mr. Jearard, "that I think I understand something of the ordeal you're going through. Of course, I deplore what it is doing to my daughter's happiness, but I doubt that you went looking for the problem you found."

"Maybe if I was the sort who went looking, I'd be able to get out a hell of a lot easier."

"I think you're right, Chuck. Your handicap is that you are, I believe, a man with a vigorous conscience. You try to avoid hurting. And by so doing, you hurt more. But now, I suggest, is a time you must hurt. Because I truly am convinced that you are far better to stay with Susan than go with . . . let's say anyone else. There are also the children to consider. And me. I'm very fond of you. I would be most upset to lose you as a son-in-law."

Vaughan smiled. "Nice of you to say so."

"I mean it. And you mustn't think for a moment that Susan or her mother will fail to forgive you. Of course they will. Indeed they will probably think the higher of you."

"Higher?"

"Certainly. The prodigal son syndrome."

"I doubt it applies in this sort of situation."

"Oh, but I can assure you it does," said Mr. Jearard. "And I can assure you of something else—though it may seem presumptuous— but I can assure you that you will recover from the blow of giving up . . . *her*. Indeed you will relish her memory the more keenly for it. A morsel or two of memory is good for a man as he approaches middle age. Believe me, I know."

DR. T. ROYDON Goodall munched a lunchtime sandwich as he listened to Sibelius on the FM radio. The buzzer sounded. He sighed long-sufferingly. Would Mrs. Latham never learn that lunchtime was sacred? Then he remembered: Mrs. Latham was on holiday; Mrs. Whatever-her-name-was had taken her place.

"It's Mr. Carter. I told him you were having your dinner"—Dr. Goodall winced—"but he said it was very important."

"Carter, you say?" Oh, Lord. Beatty. "All right, put him on."

Frank's voice had a jovial quality that was oddly mechanical. "Hoke, old man, awfully sorry to disturb your lunch. The fact of the matter is, I need a few more of those pills."

"Pills?"

"The ones you prescribed. They're just the job. Not a hint of a spell since I started taking them." Frank spoke as if he had learned the speech by heart.

"You mustn't think those pills are a cure," Hoke cautioned. "All they do is tend to nullify the symptoms; you see—"

"I understand. But I need a prescription for more."

Hoke sighed. "Frank, I recommended a man. . . . You haven't been to see him."

A chuckle, a trifle hollow. "I'd rather give you the business."

"As I told you, your condition is outside my field of competence. Do I gather your employer still knows nothing of it?"

"I haven't passed on the good news yet, Hoke. I have a few things to wrap up before I do. You see, they'll remove me from the scene the moment they know what's wrong with me. Now be a good chap . . ."

As he hung up the telephone, Frank Beatty grimaced. Rotten business, deceiving Hoke. But what could one do? Glumly he wondered which would give out first: the pills or Hoke's patience.

MRS. Latham felt better the instant the jet's wheels touched the runway. Her stomach settled back in her abdominal cavity. She could cease eyeing the paper bag in the seat pocket before her and look out the window instead. England looked gray and wet after the dazzling sunshine of Bermuda, but she decided she was rather pleased. It would have been irksome to have returned from a costly two-week holiday only to be told that it had been just as sunny and hot at home.

She passed easily through customs and walked on through the terminal building. Then she stopped dead. "Why, Mr. Carter!"

"No, you're mistaken. My name's not Carter."

"And with that he dashed off," Mrs. Latham told Dr. Goodall the following morning. "It was definitely Mr. Carter."

Dr. Goodall shrugged. "I understand he travels a great deal." He glanced at his watch. He faced a busy day.

Mrs. Latham smiled. "Travels a great deal?" She paused a moment for dramatic effect. "I imagine he does. He's an airline pilot."

Dr. Goodall stared. "He can't be."

"He had the uniform, the cap, everything. He was walking along with two other pilots. It was definitely Mr. Carter."

"Good God!" Dr. Goodall rubbed his chin. "What airline, did you notice?"

"It was a blue uniform with a peaked cap."

"I think they all wear that." Dr. Goodall leaned back in his chair. "He never intimated for a moment that he was . . . flying."

"Taking people up in the sky! Why, he might have flown me to Bermuda. It's criminal in his condition."

"I think that we must contact Mr., er, Carter and tell him in the most forcible manner that he must, er, I think the expression is ground himself."

"You're right there," said Mrs. Latham, "but the crafty beggar hasn't given us an address or a phone number. There's nothing in your file. I can't think where you planned to send the bill."

Dr. Goodall was tempted to reveal Carter's identity so Mrs. Latham could tackle the tedious business of finding him. But upon reflection it seemed prudent to do it himself. It was more than an hour before he tracked Frank to Amory International, only to be told that his man was in Rome and would be back on Wednesday.

"Please ask him to telephone Dr. Goodall. It's rather important."

"Certainly, Doctor," said a most agreeable girl.

But Frank didn't call on Wednesday. Or Thursday. Or Friday. Hoke rang the airline once more. Frank telephoned a week later.

"Hullo, Hoke. I understand you've been calling me."

His offhand tone wasn't convincing. Hoke felt the warmth of

righteous anger in his plump cheeks. Dash it all, one's patience did have limits. Couldn't Frank realize what a wretchedly invidious position he was putting a chum in? Didn't he care?

"So it was your nurse at the airport."

"Yes. Good God, Frank . . . you're a *pilot*, of all things."

"As far as your files are concerned, Hoke, I'm a traveling salesman named Carter. You're not involved. That was the whole idea. I used a false name for that very reason."

"Frank, it's absolutely out of the question for you to keep flying. It's most frightfully dangerous."

"Hoke, listen to me. There's no danger at all because I'm not doing any landings or takeoffs. I'm giving them all to my first officers. And the amusing thing is, I've told each to keep quiet about it because he's the only one getting such privileged treatment. So you see, there's really no danger."

"But if your employers knew . . ."

"They will soon enough, Hoke. Airline pilots have to take regular medicals. I just want to keep on flying as long as possible. I happen to enjoy it enormously."

"I know you do. But you must," Hoke said fervently, "give it up. I consider it my duty, Frank, to instruct you to . . . er, ground yourself immediately."

"Are you going to tell Amory about me?"

"No. It's up to you, Frank. So when will you tell them?"

"Soon, Hoke, soon."

THE man from the Medical Defense Union said, "I take it you have advised your patient to resign his position."

"In the strongest possible terms," Hoke said. "But he's reluctant. Do you think I should tell his employers?"

"Under the circumstances, yes, quite definitely yes."

Unhappily, Hoke said, "I was taught that information given one during treatment was privileged."

"True," said the MDU man, "but from time to time we are faced with situations such as yours in which physicians have a moral or even *legal* duty to break secrecy in order to prevent foreseeable harm to others. My advice to you, Doctor, is to inform your patient that if he fails to tell his employers the truth, you will be obliged to do so."

Hoke thanked the man. He would write tomorrow to Frank, put it to him straightforwardly; tell him he had a week (possibly two) to advise Amory; a deadline.

BEATTY flew, delivering planeload after planeload of holiday-makers to Nice, Rome, Montreal, Lisbon, Miami. He worked hard, often exceeding the legal monthly maximums of on-duty hours. He welcomed the extra work for he was reveling in his craft as never before. The knowledge that his flying days were strictly numbered added a singular keenness. He knew he had been incredibly lucky to pass his last medical. Such luck couldn't hold. Those doctors weren't fools. Eventually one of them would spot his problem. Then there would be batteries of questions. Puzzled, bewildered, he would declare that he had never felt better. But the game would unquestionably be up. And it would almost certainly happen at his very next medical. Everyone would be full of regrets and be most awfully sorry. He wouldn't mention having been to see Hoke. As far as anyone would be concerned officially, James Carter would simply vanish. Case closed.

HENRY Peel taxied to the ramp. He parked with care, lining up his wing tip with that of the next aircraft on the line. Brake on. Radio off. Mixture to lean. The propeller slowed and gurgled to a halt. Ignition to off. Master switch to off. He mopped his dripping brow.

The man in the right-hand seat scribbled something on his clipboard, then sniffed and unlatched the door. He was halfway out before he spoke. "I guess you passed," he said.

Henry felt a shameful tear spring to his eye. He had done it; he had actually done it. He was a licensed pilot.

Within the hour he was on the telephone to a man in St. Catharines who had advertised a dainty little yellow and white Aeronca for sale.

Chapter Five

LEE arrived at Brockton shortly before noon on a bright Sunday morning. She turned her green MG into the members' parking lot, got out and strolled toward the flight line. The day promised good soaring, but the cumulus clouds which provided the essential up-currents of air would not be popping for an hour or two.

She sat in the long grass beyond the landing strip. The sun was warm and it was good to be alone. It was time for rumination. To cut free or become more and more entangled.

Larry, the Air Canada second officer who doubled as a club tow pilot, interrupted her. What was she doing all by herself?

"Wondering why we don't spend all our lives soaring. It's only when we come down to earth that things get nasty."

He smiled. "Very philosophical, aren't we? You flying today?"

"I will when the thermals pick up."

"The Cu are beginning. Look."

Tiny white clouds were indeed appearing against the blue, like balls of cotton. "Larry, take me up to five thousand, will you?"

"Five? It's above club's limits."

"I don't care. Will you take me?"

"Sure."

The freshening wind nudged the slender sailplanes as they sat waiting in their lopsided way; ailerons and elevators moved against safety locks, signaling that they wanted to be free.

Someone held the Blanik's nose down while Lee clambered into the cockpit, bulky in her parachute, which was mandatory for solo flights. She sorted out the harness straps—two for the shoulders, two lap straps—all meeting in a buckle at the waist. It felt good when they were snugly adjusted; you became part of the aircraft, a comrade of all the other components. She tested the controls: all okay. The canopy closed over her. The world tilted as a handler raised the grounded wing.

Minutes later she was in the air, her eyes fixed on Larry's Cub, anticipating its turns. Her movements of the stick and rudder were smooth and instinctive. Up, up.

At five thousand feet Larry explored the air for a minute, seeking the elusive upcurrent of warm air. His wing waggled. Success! Time to release. Lee leaned forward and tugged on the lever. The line went wriggling away. The noise of the Cub receded. She was on her own. A gentle wind enfolded the Blanik, pressing on the canopy, shouldering the broad wings.

Lee smiled. Soon there would be a flurry of activity on the field, but for the moment she had the sky to herself. She was the queen, soaring, turning, her slim craft sparkling in the sun. Six thousand feet, seven, eight, almost nine, before the vigor of the lift began to wane. It was utterly peaceful. Her mind wandered. A sailplane was a good vantage point from which to study your life. You saw it in perspective. She thought about Charles Vaughan.

There was a chance—a real chance—that he might leave his wife and children for her. Would that solve all problems? Or would it simply create a whole new batch? Runaway husbands sometimes came to regret it and began hating their new partners. Then there was the age thing, which might matter later on.

But, she thought, if there is such a thing as love, I think this has to be it. He's a wonderful guy, the nicest, gentlest man in the whole crummy world. Only I have to give him up.

It wasn't a noble decision. She acknowledged the fact. Indeed it was selfish. She refused to settle for a future that was jeopardized even before it began. This one wouldn't work. The odds were stacked too high. She would write him a letter. . . .

Suddenly she noticed the altimeter. She had descended almost three thousand feet. Her thermal had long since abandoned her and she had drifted God knows how many miles. Okay, no need to panic. There's the lake to the north. The wind was blowing from the west, so you've strayed to the east. Okay, so just keep heading west, you're bound to find the field sooner or later. Make it sooner, please, she thought.

"Anyway," she said aloud, her voice assuming an odd quality in the enclosed cockpit, "I can put her down in any field. No sweat, girl." All she had to do was look out for power lines and barbed-wire fences. The sailplane could alight in a few yards.

The Blanik descended gently but steadily. The sky seemed devoid of cumulus. No welcoming signs of lift for lonely girl glider pilots. Her stomach was knotted. "Don't get all atwitter," she told herself. Now the altimeter was showing less than two thousand feet. And nothing below looked familiar. She eased back on the stick and pulled the nose up more, the instinctive action of the glider pilot stretching the glide. The Blanik's speed was hovering around the stall mark.

Then Lee smiled. Two specks, definitely gliders—presumably right over the field. Now she could see the orange hangar and the wind sock. "I'm coming straight in!" she chortled. "So anyone else had better get out of the way!"

The field was tantalizingly close now—but it hardly seemed to move. And then, as if she had drawn a diagram of the distance and measured the speed and the rate of sink and the strength of the wind, she knew without a doubt that she wouldn't make it.

"Okay," she said, swallowing, "then I must put her down. Now."

But below, it was all fences and sheds. Biting her lip, Lee turned. No. Power lines. Could she get under them? Make your dumb mind up, Lee.

There it was—a little strip of plowed land, just beyond the road. The wind was blowing across her path, but this was no time to be choosy about wind direction. With her hand on the spoiler lever, she angled the nose to the left. She felt the Blanik's side sway as the wind pressed against her.

"That's it," she said. "Between the trees, over the road and you've got it made."

Her approach was good. There was no reason why she shouldn't have made a safe landing—except for the wires stretching between the tall elms. She couldn't see them, but they caught her wing as she banked. There was a snapping, a screeching, a crumpling. The Blanik swerved, shuddering. Lee saw the white lines of the road rushing up at her. Her hands and feet still moved the controls in a perfectly futile attempt to straighten out in time. But there was no more time. As the wing thudded into the road, she heard the squeal of brakes.

THIRTY-SEVEN MILES away, Henry Peel touched down on his private landing field: eight hundred feet of the family farm that had been carefully leveled. The yellow and white Aeronca bounced gently, then settled down. With a burst of throttle, Henry turned and taxied to his hangar, formerly an implement barn.

His parents were waiting for him there, shaking their heads and saying they never thought they'd see the day when a member of the family would be flying his own airplane.

IT HAD drizzled all day. On the way to Gatwick, Diane said she hoped the weather would improve for Vincent's holidays—he was due home from school in two days. Beatty said he wished he could be there.

"Gosh no," said Diane, "it would be too much of a shock for the poor lad if he came home and found his father there."

Beatty smiled. "Actually I don't think he was too keen on it when I was at home more or less permanently. I was too much competition for your attention."

"Flatterer." She grinned. She had slipped her reading glasses on. Her private logbook was open and her pen poised. "How long will you be in Toronto?"

"Six hours. We leave at twenty-two forty local for Belfast."

"And you get there at . . ."

"Eight in the morning your time."

"And off to Lisbon that afternoon?"

"Correct. And home Thursday evening with luck."

Over the years Diane had filled several notebooks with particulars of her husband's journeyings. His whereabouts could always be known by telephoning the line. But she preferred to keep her own records, mentally flying with him wherever he went.

At the terminal building he stopped the Rover and took his bag from the back seat. Diane took the wheel.

"Drive carefully," he told her. "It's a bit slippery in spots."

She nodded. "You drive carefully too."

He stooped and kissed her through the car's open window. She touched his cheek; her fingertips were cool and soft.

"Have a nice trip. Don't forget to put your wheels down." It was her stock farewell.

Beatty gripped her hand for a moment, then he let go and watched her as she put the Rover in gear and drove away.

Jordan, the flight engineer, met him in Dispatch.

"Sorry, number four's unserviceable. Temperature."

"Damn," said Beatty. "How long?"

"Don't know yet. Could be the thermostat spring. We're looking into it."

"Okay. Keep me posted, will you?"

"Roger." He headed for the ramp, a stocky, vaguely untidy figure, his cap set at a jaunty angle. A good engineer, Jordan; he would get the recalcitrant engine working if anyone could.

Beatty joined Webb, the navigator; together they examined the charts giving the wind and weather patterns over the North Atlantic. Each trip was a matter of planning the best route and height, then finding out whether they were free. Often another aircraft had already claimed the one they asked for. The North Atlantic was heavily traveled; thus each aircraft was allotted a block of airspace, and, in theory, it should never be less than 120 miles from the next aircraft. In practice, it occasionally worked out to be rather less.

On the captain fell the responsibility for a number of crucial decisions at this point. How much fuel should the aircraft carry? What alternate airports should be selected? What runway should be used on takeoff?

Mr. AND Mrs. Frederick Cox had found themselves a window seat in the cafeteria. Over a nice cup of tea they could watch the airplanes landing and taking off. It was deliciously exciting to think that they would soon be inside one of those monsters, high over the Atlantic. Neither had flown before.

A thin young man wearing cowboy boots and faded jeans sat down a dozen feet away. Len Sparrow was twenty and was on his way to spend three weeks with a married brother who lived in Ontario. As he lit a cigarette he caught a hazy reflection of himself in the glass door. It pleased him. The lean, lone stranger. The silent

man with a secret. He would have been deeply hurt to know that
the few people who noticed him saw an undernourished, nervous-
looking youth in desperate need of a haircut and a shampoo.

As A rule Miss Hardcastle was a patient individual—you learn
patience when you have been blind since birth. But today, waiting
at Gatwick, when her flight to Toronto was announced as delayed
one hour she had a quite absurd desire to stand up and shout, "Oh,
do hurry up, will you!" She had looked forward to this day for too
long. It would be her first trip abroad, her first opportunity to
experience *foreignness*, and she wasn't at all sure just what was
in store for her. She felt the wallet in her handbag: passport, ticket,
traveler's checks were safe. An amiable young lady from the airline
had found this seat and had assured Miss Hardcastle that she would
return the moment the Toronto flight was called, to guide her
through the formalities and onto the aircraft. VIP service. It was
like being a celebrity.

Miss Hardcastle amused herself by listening to the airport noises.
They struck her as essentially happy noises. People sounded as if
they were pleased to be going wherever they happened to be going. Such was not the case at railway and bus stations, where a
great many negative sounds could be heard.

Miss Hardcastle was aware of someone sitting down on the bench
beside her. Someone light-sounding. And smelling rather delightful. Obviously the someone had commendable taste. Was she as
pretty as her presence suggested?

Had Miss Hardcastle asked Len Sparrow, she would have received an enthusiastically affirmative reply. Seated a few feet away,
he studied the girl's profile. She was unquestionably a bit of all
right. Len lit another cigarette. Our paths have crossed, girl. No use
fightin' fate. This thing is bigger than both of us.

BEATTY told Amory that the number four temperature problem
had been solved, but now trouble was being experienced with the
transponder, the secondary radar system which enables ground
controllers to identify individual aircraft on their radar screens.

"This isn't my day," said Amory. Beatty followed him out into the drizzle.

Slattery, the chief mechanic, said the transponder was working satisfactorily when they had tested it earlier in the day. He had a flat, measured way of talking. "We're checking back through the circuit as fast as we can, Mr. Amory. And the longer you talk to me, the less I'm getting done."

"You insolent SOB, you're fired," said Amory.

"Okay," said Slattery with a grin. "I'll get it going soon as I can."

"Thanks," said Amory.

Back in his office, he slumped in his chair, still wearing his damp raincoat. "Sit down, Frank; take the weight off." He scowled at the rain through the office window. "We've got to get that flight off the ground, Frank. You've got a tight schedule and it's important you stick to it. I've got a lot of money riding on you, my friend." He punched the palm of his left hand. "That transponder could just as well have gone in the air as on the ground. You'd simply advise ground control, right?"

"Right." Beatty nodded. "And that's what you'd like me to do."

"Correct."

"I'm the one who stands to lose my license for taking off in an aircraft I know to be improperly equipped."

"I know that," said Amory. "But it's important that this flight goes. If you hold it up any longer, you'll compound the problem in Belfast, then in Lisbon. I can't afford to let that happen, Frank. I mean that. Literally."

"Is a few hours really going to make that much difference?"

Amory rubbed his eyes. "I'm afraid so." He sounded tired and dispirited. "To tell you the truth, Frank, I'm out on a financial limb. Just bought new aircraft. New crews to fly them. Bigger payroll. I'm overextended, Frank. It's going to be all right in a little while. There's a lot of business lined up and the new aircraft will more than pay for themselves, in time. In time. But right now, I can't have any more problems, not until the heat's off."

Beatty felt as embarrassed as if his father had confessed some sin. "I'm very sorry to hear you have problems, sir."

Amory shrugged. "It's business, Frank. I don't know why I don't keep out of it. I know what it's like. Juggling payrolls and bills and contracts and interest payments. It's a dumb way to live. The trouble is, you feel like Napoleon when you win!" He laughed. "So what I'd like you to do is to load your seven oh seven up and get the hell to Toronto."

"I'd be less than honest if I didn't tell you that I'm reluctant to fly without a transponder. There is an element of risk."

"Of course there is," said Amory. "There's an element of risk every time you get into an airplane. Radar and all the navaids are great. But all they mean in the end is that the pilot's job gets tougher because you have to fly in worse conditions. Sure, we cut down the risks as much as possible, but equipment fails, machines break down. And so we rely on the pilot to get us out of the mess. Usually he does. And you are one hell of a good pilot, Frank."

Beatty smiled, shaking his head. "After that, how can I refuse?"

"Thanks, Frank," said Amory. "You won't regret this."

I hope not, Beatty thought.

THE voice over the PA was bright and cheerful.

"Amory International apologizes for the delay in the departure of flight ten ten; that flight is now ready for boarding. . . ."

Miss Hardcastle was already on her way through Passport Control, the courteous hand of the Amory official steering her.

Len Sparrow eased himself out of his seat. The pretty girl was gathering her belongings. Could it be that she was catching the Amory flight too? Struth, he thought.

"THE transponder is unserviceable," Beatty told Corfield, his first officer for the trip. "But we're going anyway."

"Roger," said Corfield, an uncommonly cheerful individual.

The four-man flight crew sat at their stations on the flight deck while the passengers were boarding. Through the window panel at his left, Beatty could glimpse them as they moved along the walkway to the forward entrance door. Most of them peered inquisitively into the cockpit and marveled at the maze of instruments, after which they glanced at him. The order was invariably the same: the instruments, then the pilot. Did they expect someone looking like a composite of John Wayne, Charlton Heston and Jack Hawkins? Were they disappointed?

Beatty ran his eye over the instrument panel. The aircraft was one of Amory's new acquisitions, a 707-320B; it was in excellent condition. He rolled up his shirt sleeves and loosened his tie. Only actors in aviation epics and models for airline advertisements wear tunics and caps on the flight deck.

The light on the interphone glowed.

"Passengers all loaded, sir." The girl had a soft Scottish accent. "Doors and chutes are secured."

"Thank you." He turned to Corfield. "Stand by for engine start."

VAUGHAN walked from room to empty room. The windows were firmly latched and the television sets and radios and electric blankets were unplugged. He wrote notes for the milkman and the paper man. No deliveries until further notice, thanks.

His packed bag sat at the front door like a patient hound. It had been there an hour. Outside, he met the mailman.

"Hi there, Mr. Vaughan. Where to this time?"

"New York."

"Can't say as I envy you. Just one today. Have a good trip."

Vaughan took the envelope. The childish scrawl was Janet's. She was having a nice vacation in Carmel but she missed him and wished he would finish his work and come and stay with them and Lynn threw up in a store and Grandpa caught a cold.

Vaughan replaced the letter in its envelope. His eyes had suddenly become prickly. As he backed the Cougar down the driveway, he knew he had to end the affair. He loved Susan and the kids. And he missed them. Alone, he was only half alive. He put the car into drive and sped away.

A MAN named Hobbs was also driving to the airport at that moment. Grant Hobbs had for some years made a prosperous living by sending invoices to selected companies all over the United

533

States and Canada. The invoices covered listings in various business directories—which were never published. A remarkably high percentage of companies sent in their checks. Grant Hobbs always cashed them.

Hobbs was moving—something he found it necessary to do from time to time. The trick lay in knowing when to move on. A man couldn't last a dozen years in such an enterprise without knowing. Thin, wearing a perpetual frown, Hobbs was heading east for a vacation. Later on he would set up operations near Hartford, though he regretted leaving the Coast; the weather agreed with him.

IN SANTA Ana, Earl Gasparac poured a second cup of coffee for his wife. She had had a bad night; the pain must have been savage; you could see the evidence around her mouth and eyes. Her smile, merry as hell, didn't fool him. Neither did her eager chatter about the trip to see all the old places again. Anger seethed within him, impotent fury at a fate that could condemn an innocent to lingering death. How could anyone believe in *anything?*

TRANSTATE's flight-planning department was full of Teletype machines that clattered and telephones that jangled. Vaughan turned from checking his flight's weight load as a young man with corn-colored hair and an anxious-to-please look in his eyes introduced himself.

"Er, Captain, I'm Garten. I'm your copilot, sir."

Vaughan nodded. "How are you?" He knew he sounded terse and disinterested. "How long have you been with TranState?"

"Two months, sir. I finished the course last Friday."

"And this is your first line ride?"

"Yes, sir."

Vaughan nodded again, mechanically. He wanted to welcome the young pilot to the line; it was the nice thing to do; today, however, he seemed incapable of doing anything nice.

Cutshall, the navigator, was already at the met desk. "Looks pretty good, Captain, until we get near Detroit. There's some stuff building up around there."

The airmen studied the met charts. Conditions looked good, except possibly on the last lap. Thunderstorms were brewing east of the Mississippi, but it was hard to predict just how severe they might turn out to be and just where they might form.

"Anything reported en route?"

"A Northwest flight reported some CAT at thirty thousand."

"Okay." Vaughan decided to stay well away from that altitude; clear-air turbulence could be thoroughly unpleasant and dangerous. He would request air-traffic control to route him at a minimum of 35,000 feet, flight level 350.

Garten was making notes of the conditions at Chicago, Toronto and New York and calculating the amount of fuel required for the trip—an amount that had to include reserves for emergencies.

It always made sense to carry as much fuel as possible. You never knew when you might need it. A famous case in point was the DC-6 that took off from a field in Africa bound for the United States, with scheduled refueling stops at the Azores and Gander, Newfoundland. The first stop was made without a hitch, but before reaching the midway point between the Azores and Newfoundland, a radio message was received: dense fog had closed Gander Airport. There was nothing for it but to head back to the Azores. No sweat. But now came another shock. A radio message from the Azores regretted that fog now blanketed that airport also. The nearest fog-free landing place was Casablanca. According to the fuel-gauge needles, the tanks were empty when the aircraft finally landed; upon inspection it was found that only a gallon or two still sloshed around. And Casablanca was the point from which the flight had started many hours before. The moral was: Always pump in as much fuel as you can lift.

In the crew lounge, the cabin crew awaited Vaughan: six girls in the pale blue pantsuits that were TranState's current uniform for stews. Jane Meade, the chief stew for the trip, had flown with Vaughan many times. She greeted him with the easy respect of one veteran for another. Vaughan recognized only three of the others. Stews rarely stayed on the job much more than a year.

"Mr. Garten will be the first officer and Mr. Cutshall is our navigator," he said. "The trip should be pretty smooth to Chicago. After that we might run into some rough stuff."

As he spoke, he found himself wondering what the girls knew about him and his private life. He remembered with a shock that Walt Przeczek's carryings-on had been common gossip at Tran-State. Had they been giggling about him moments before he entered the lounge? Anger flared in his cheeks.

Testily he insisted that the girls demonstrate their knowledge of the DC-8's emergency procedures. Two of them became flustered and made mistakes. Irritably, Vaughan told Jane Meade to make them study their manuals before flight time. "I don't want amateurs in my crew."

Jane colored but said nothing.

Outside the lounge, Vaughan was contrite. Why take it out on those kids? he thought. Why make Jane look bad? In all probability the stews knew nothing about Lee or Susan. But he couldn't go back now and apologize. It would only make a bad situation worse. Better they thought of him as a martinet than a mental case.

Garten said, "Shall I do the external now, sir?"

Vaughan nodded. "I think I'll come with you. I could use some fresh air."

Garten smiled nervously. Vaughan thought, Now he thinks I don't trust him. I'm doing a great job of instilling confidence and team spirit in this crew.

The DC-8 stood by the terminal building, connected to it by the umbilical-like tube through which the passengers would shortly enter. The baggage-compartment doors were open, waiting. It was cool beneath the broad, swept-back wings. Vaughan looked up at the ailerons and flap linkages, the great engine pods that dangled from the wings on the slender mountings. Nothing appeared to be loose or leaking. He inspected the aircraft's tires, each of which cost roughly $250 and was good only for about seventy-five landings. Plenty of tread left on these; no nails or sharp stones embedded in the rubber. Above him, the two-hundred-foot-long fuselage blotted out the sky. He saw Garten peering studiously at the underside of the wing.

"Everything looks just fine, Captain," he announced. He looked as if he were about to salute in his eagerness.

"You figure she's safe to fly?"

"Yes, *sir*."

"Captain Vaughan?" Vaughan turned. Wills, one of the flight-planning men, was at the office doorway. "Air Canada's on the phone for you, Captain."

"Air Canada?" Vaughan went in and took the telephone.

A girl said, "We've received a Telex from Toronto. They asked us to call you."

"Toronto?" Vaughan caught his breath.

"Yes, Captain. Here's the message."

Vaughan listened. When it was over he asked the girl to repeat it. The words had to mean something different. But they didn't.

" 'Lee hurt in glider mishap. In St. Michael's Hospital, Hamilton. Sorry. Larry.' "

Larry. The towplane pilot.

"That's all?"

"Yes, sir, that's it."

"Okay, thank you."

It seemed to take an hour for the operator to put him through. At last a woman's voice announced, "St. Michael's."

Vaughan said, "I'm inquiring about a patient. Her name is Lee—no, Rosalie Pringle."

"Pringle. One moment, sir." The voice again. "Mrs. Pringle is in intensive care, sir. I'll give you ICU."

Intensive care! His fingers tightened on the phone. "Look, ma'am, I'm calling from Los Angeles, California. . . ."

"Are you a relative, sir?"

What the hell difference . . . "No, a friend of the family."

"I'm sorry. The line to ICU is busy at the moment."

"I'll call back," said Vaughan. His mouth was dry and bitter.

Amory International flight 1010 sliced up through the murky clouds. The sun suddenly bounced all over the bright metal of the wings, dazzling many an eager eye.

Mr. and Mrs. Cox had held hands during the takeoff. It had all seemed rather breakneck and frantic, that enormous, trembling contraption, God knows how many tons of it, hurling itself head-long at the London to Brighton railway line. But with a great heave it had gone zooming up—almost vertically, it had seemed. Mr. Cox realized that he had been holding his breath since the beginning of the run. He heard his wife say "Well, I never" several times. He patted her hand and smiled at her. She smiled back. But it wasn't a genuine smile of pleasure or contentment. Definitely a bit on the forced side.

Miss Hardcastle had been led aboard the aircraft ahead of the other passengers. The stewardess found her a seat beside a window and immediately in front of a toilet. Soon other passengers came clattering along the aisle. A young girl's voice said hello—followed at once by the inevitable intake of air. It was, Miss Hardcastle supposed, a bit of a shock to discover that one is talking to a blind person.

She suggested that the girl take her seat by the window; it was, after all, completely wasted on someone unable to see out. Julie (for that was the girl's name) was much obliged for the offer. This was her first long trip by air and she wanted to see everything there was to see. Soon the two of them were chatting like old friends. Julie was going to Canada to visit an aunt and uncle and decide whether to emigrate. Miss Hardcastle said she was going to visit her brother in Toronto. They settled down to enjoy a pleasant trip in congenial company.

They were blissfully unaware of the irritation boiling within the third occupant of their row of seats. In Len Sparrow's opinion, fate had delivered him a low blow. When the flight had been called he had slipped into the queue right behind the bird with the nice profile. (She smelled nice too.) Peeping over her shoulder, he had seen that her seat number was 8E. Accordingly he had asked for 8D. Hopes high, he had followed the mob into the plane—but would you believe it, when he got inside, he found the bird changing places! Now he was stuck next to an old blind bint with dark glasses. What a turnup!

FLYING THE ATLANTIC was not particularly demanding. It was largely a matter of guiding the aircraft to the correct altitude and heading, then trimming it and handing it over to the automatic pilot. Thereafter, the job was handled by gyros and accelerometers. At 35,000 feet there was little for the pilot to look at. The clouds lay far below. The ocean, when it was visible, looked like a gray motionless pond. In theory a pilot at that altitude can see about two hundred miles. In practice the sky is rarely clear enough to see anything like that far.

This is a problem for jet pilots, for the speed of their aircraft makes their eyes a poor safeguard against midair collisions. Before a speck of dirt on the windscreen is identified as an approaching aircraft, it may be too late. Heavy jet airliners are not noted for nimbleness. Their speed and weight create colossal momentum. They need distance to change direction. Distance means time— and that is precisely what they do not have when another aircraft is dead ahead.

Beatty listened as Corfield sent the latest position report: evidence for the record keepers that at the correct time flight 1010 was in the correct position at the correct height and heading in the correct direction.

"Captain?"

Beatty turned. Jordan, the engineer, stood between the two pilots, his elbows resting on the backs of their seats.

"Yes?"

"Troubles. That bloody temperature in number four."

THE DC-8 streaked upward; the sprawling city of Los Angeles seemed to shrink beneath its trembling wings. Despite the twenty-one square feet of window on three sides of the flight deck, the crew could see little but sky. The nose section blotted out their view and would continue to do so until 35,000 feet, when the aircraft reached the cruising altitude reserved for it and leveled off. Climb-out completed. Autopilot on.

The DC-8 had consumed nearly ten thousand pounds of fuel. At cruising speed it would burn kerosene at approximately twelve thousand pounds per hour. The computer announced that the aircraft was traveling at a ground speed of 478 knots and would arrive at the next checkpoint in eight minutes. At the navigator's table, Cutshall methodically entered the figures on the company route sheets.

It was superb weather. CAVU—ceiling and visibility unlimited. Far below, the Rockies slid away, the colossal peaks and valleys no more than sand castles on a beach. Ahead lay the endless prairies that had seen dogged convoys of covered wagons groaning westward, measuring their progress in miles per day. Hurtling eastward, the DC-8 gobbled up the miles, one every six seconds.

Jane came in, taking orders for coffee. Vaughan shook his head, not looking at her. I'll talk to her later, he thought. She'll understand. He noticed Garten glancing at him from the right-hand seat. He seemed a little apprehensive, which wasn't too surprising. The poor guy had probably been told he was lucky to have drawn Vaughan for his first line flight. Now he must be wondering how the others can be worse.

What about Lee? What the hell did *hurt* mean? Did she break a leg? Get a black eye? Was he worrying needlessly? Chances are she's sitting up in bed drinking beer and reading *Playboy*.

In intensive care? What did that mean? Is this a punishment?

Vaughan winced. No, that was absurd. A lot of old superstition. Lee hadn't sinned, anyway. If anyone should be punished, it should be him.

Perhaps I am being punished, he thought.

He glanced at the panel clock. In an hour and a half they would be landing at O'Hare. He would call the hospital again from there.

Please have good news for me, he thought. Please.

He stared ahead through the two-and-a-half-inch-thick windshield. The sky was losing its clarity. The horizon had become fuzzy. Below, the ground seemed to be slowly sinking, its tones progressively muted as the stratum of moisture particles settled.

He turned to Garten. "You want to take her into O'Hare?"

Garten beamed. "Sure thing, Captain, thanks."

"Okay. I'm your copilot now. She's all yours."

In Toronto the revised weather forecast advised that there was a strong possibility of moderate to severe thunderstorms developing during the afternoon and evening.

"Reducing the power won't help," said Jordan. "The oil's cooled by the fuel. Anyway," he added, "I'm just about sure it's the bloody gauge. But I can't be a hundred percent sure until we get on the ground."

"So we shut down number four."

"Fraid so, Skipper."

Gander was 890 miles ahead. Beatty told Corfield to call and advise them of the problem. "But we're not declaring an emergency," he said. "Piece of cake getting there on three engines." He glanced at his watch. Poor old Amory's timetables were becoming properly screwed up. Thank the Lord, Gander was in Canadian territory. Canadians were usually fairly unemotional about three-engine landings. On a British or American field, emergency procedure would be mandatory, complete with expensive fire engines and ambulances. All very comforting, of course, but hardly necessary in this case.

"Overcast at Gander," Corfield reported. "No problem, though."

The passengers were unaware of the shutdown of number four. There was no sensation of sudden power loss. And no telltale stationary propeller stood guard before the stilled engine.

Beatty cleared his throat and pressed the PA button. "This is the captain speaking. I'm sorry to have to tell you that we'll be making an unscheduled stop. A minor problem has occurred, nothing to get the slightest bit alarmed about, but we want to look into it. So we'll be touching down at Gander, Newfoundland, in slightly more than an hour. No extra charge for letting you have a quick visit to Newfoundland; all part of the Amory service." He groaned to himself; he really wasn't good at this sort of thing.

"Amory ten ten, you are clear for a straight-in approach."

The 707 touched down, incurring landing fees of approximately one thousand dollars for Amory International, plus some three hundred dollars for such necessities as the provision of steps and ground power.

At that moment TranState flight 738 was 2114 miles away, approaching Des Moines, Iowa.

ON THE ground in Gander, Jordan cut a shim out of a small piece of aluminum. It was, he pointed out with justifiable pride, worth about twopence, but it would do the work of the thermostat spring that had been causing all the trouble. The crew ran up the engines; everything checked out. Beatty ordered the aircraft's tanks refilled. Everything was under control.

Five minutes later he was clinging to the towel dispenser in the washroom. His limbs were as heavy as lead. He gasped in air. The room began to revolve, then steadied itself like an aircraft coming out of a spin. Everything okay in a minute, Beatty thought.

It was. Strength traveled slowly along every nerve and through every bone. He stood up. Weak but steady. You're all right now.

But the truth was, he felt sick and wobbly. Why, he wondered, didn't the pills work this time? Did he need a stronger variety now? Had he outgrown these? He would have to see Hoke about it the moment he got back to London.

He shook his head, pained by his own delusions. "You've had it," he told himself. "Grounded. Here? In Newfoundland? No!" He wouldn't fly, though. He would take another pill and play copilot. If he dropped dead, it wouldn't make any difference. Corfield was a thoroughly competent chap.

He felt better. He would telephone Amory from Toronto and explain the situation. Amory could replace him far more readily in Toronto than here in Newfoundland.

The passengers filed back across the windswept concrete to the aircraft, thankful to be on their way.

For the majority of them, Gander was their first glimpse of North America. And a dismaying glance it was. Len Sparrow was one of the very few who had welcomed the unscheduled stop. Perhaps at last he would get an opportunity to work a spot of the old fatal charm on the bird with the profile. But the old bint hadn't let go of the poor kid for an instant. So his hands had been tied, figuratively speaking. He was irked.

As the crew strapped themselves in for takeoff, Beatty turned to Corfield. "You're the skipper. Take us to Toronto, there's a good fellow."

It was sultry in Chicago, the air still and heavy with warm, clammy moisture. Vaughan eased himself out of the captain's seat. "See you back here in twenty minutes."

The crew acknowledged, glancing at their watches.

The terminal building was thronged with irritable people laden with baggage or children. Was it the Fourth of July? A holiday? Vaughan couldn't remember the date. He swore as he looked for a telephone that was free. He stationed himself behind a stocky man in a crumpled tropical suit who was explaining to someone, presumably his boss, why the business had gone to the competition. Hanging up the phone, the man looked drained and weary. He glanced at Vaughan's uniform. "Sure wish I could fly airplanes for a living."

"It's better than working for a living," said Vaughan automatically, and reached for the phone.

He slipped the dime into the slot and told the operator his credit-card number and the number of the hospital in Hamilton, Ontario.

The hospital switchboard answered. He was, he explained, calling regarding the condition of a patient named Rosalie Pringle.

"One moment, please." Then, "Are you the gentleman who called from California?"

"That's right. Now I'm calling from Chicago, Illinois."

Pause. "Are you a relative?"

"Yes. An uncle. From Winnipeg."

"I see." Another pause. Then, "Sir, I'm not supposed to reveal information of . . . but as you're calling from so far . . . Sir, Mrs. Pringle passed away at one twenty-five."

"One twenty-five," he said.

"Yes, sir."

"Thank you."

"You're welcome, sir."

He hung up while the PA crackled something about Memphis and New Orleans.

"How about a cup of coffee?" The salesman in the crumpled suit was still there, swaying slightly.

"What?" Vaughan looked at the man without seeing him. He turned back to the telephone, dazed, as he searched in his wallet for the note bearing the Carmel number. Be in, please be in.

Susan's father answered.

"I have to talk to Susan," Vaughan said.

Mr. Jearard sensed the urgency. "Hold on, Chuck."

Somewhere in the house a TV set was playing a rerun of a "Beverly Hillbillies" episode. Cackles and canned laughter.

"Yes?" Crisp. Curt.

"She's dead, Susan."

Silence.

"Susan?"

"Yes, I'm here."

"Did you hear what I said?"

"Yes, I heard." Her voice softened. "I'm sorry, Chuck. . . . I don't know what to say. I honestly don't."

"I had to call you."

"I'm glad you did. What . . . what happened?"

"It was an accident in a glider. I don't *know* what happened."

"I'm sorry." She added, "Yes, I am sorry because she was young and . . . I mean it, but . . ."

"I know you mean it," he said.

"How are you?"

"I'm . . ." He thought, rubbing his forehead. "I'm kind of stunned. I don't know really how I am. Do you understand?"

"Of course I do. Where are you calling from, Chuck?"

"O'Hare. I'm due out in a few minutes. Toronto, then New York. I'm coming back to the Coast tomorrow, Susan. Will you . . ."

"Do you want us to be there?"

"Of course I do. Please come home. I'll be getting in around six, LA time. I can be home around eight, eight thirty."

"We'll be there," she said.

"Susan. I know it's . . . crazy, my calling you . . . to tell you . . . you know what I mean."

Susan said, "I don't think it's crazy at all, Chuck." She sounded as if her eyes were full of tears. "In a way it's . . . rather lovely that you called me. At least that's the way I'm reacting. I don't know if I'm supposed to react that way, but I am."

"I'm glad. Thank you."

She said, "Don't fly, Chuck. They can get someone else."

"Not at such short notice. Besides, I'm okay. Really. Don't worry. Give my love to the girls, and see you tomorrow."

"Yes," she said. "Good-by."

"Good-by."

The man in the crumpled suit was still there, but Vaughan walked past him, unaware. Dead? Was Lee really dead? Had he just had a totally unbelievable conversation with Susan?

He sat down on a bench and stared at the headline of a *Tribune* someone had dropped. Meaningless words. Not about Lee.

"Are you a pilot, mister?" A small boy was asking the question.

Vaughan nodded. "Yes, son."

"D'you fly jumbo jets?"

"No. DC-eights."

"They're okay too," said the boy gravely. "I've been up in a jumbo. I'm going to fly one when I grow up."

"Then you must take care not to call them jumbos."

"Why?"

"Because jumbos make you think of elephants, don't they? And the Boeing seven forty-seven doesn't look like an elephant. Only people who don't know much about airplanes call them jumbos."

The boy promised to remember that.

"Cap'n Vaughan, sir?"

Vaughan looked up. Garten stood there, perspiring freely.

"It's thirteen forty-five, sir."

"What?" Vaughan stared at his watch. "Sorry," he said. "I didn't realize it was so late." It would be necessary, he thought numbly, to complete a Reason for Delayed Departure form.

545

"Are you okay, sir? Sitting here ... alone?"

The little boy and his mother had gone. He hadn't noticed. "I'm fine," he told Garten. "Dozed off, I guess."

"I've completed the external, sir."

Vaughan nodded. "Good. So let's go."

GRANT Hobbs habitually traveled economy despite the fact that the income from his invoice enterprise exceeded $100,000 a year (approximately $80,000 of which he studiously neglected to report to the Internal Revenue Service). He appreciated the anonymity of economy—in first class people noticed you. Flying scared him. He preferred to drive, but today some instinct commanded him to depart the state of California by the most rapid means available. He had purchased a ticket on TranState flight 738 only minutes before departure time. When he boarded he had asked the stewardess to point out the emergency exits, then to explain the workings of the exit handles. It was comforting to find out such things; survival was, after all, largely a matter of planning ahead.

On reentering the DC-8 at Chicago, Hobbs again checked the exit. He then opened his book, but before he could start to read, a bright red head appeared above the seat in front of him and an equally bright voice declared that he didn't need to worry himself about the emergency exits, these airplanes were safe as houses.

"Thank you very much for your information," mumbled Mr. Hobbs, and he began to read.

Lillian Dumont turned to the front, a smile on her lips. The quiet little guy had class. You could always tell class. Perhaps he'd strike up a conversation after takeoff. An encounter was needed just about now to get the big adventure off to a swinging start. In a few minutes she would be on her way out of Chicago, away from Des Moines, Iowa, out of the United States. She held her purse tightly. It contained $16,821.37. She had left a note for Herman, saying it was a shame, but she found him a drag and that went for his mother too. She had slammed the door so hard that the mailbox fell off the wall. At the airport she bought a ticket to Toronto. One way. She had never been to Toronto, but she had heard that it was groovy and there would be no problem at the border if you said you were visiting a cousin for a week or two.

Half a dozen rows forward, Earl Gasparac was helping his wife with her seat belt. She was smiling and chatting, but it was obvious that she was going through hell. There should be a medal, Earl Gasparac thought bitterly, for people who suffer uncomplainingly. For inconceivable gallantry day after stinking day.

Briskly the stewardesses strode down the aisle. Seat belts were fastened; the overhead racks contained no briefcases or movie cameras to injure or even kill if tossed off the rack during a bumpy flight. The toilets were empty, the emergency chutes secure, the doors fastened and latched. TranState flight 738 was ready for departure. It was twenty-two minutes behind schedule.

Chapter Six

THERE were 10,304 aircraft flying in the skies over North America when TranState flight 738 took off from Chicago. One was Amory International flight 1010, which was crossing the border between Maine and New Brunswick. Another was Henry Peel's tiny yellow and white Aeronca. He had just made a low pass over the farmhouse; now he was zooming off to Niagara Falls. Utterly content, he circled the huge waterfall, his wing tip slicing its rising mist. Below, the streets were jammed with cars full of hot, uncomfortable people. Henry looked down at them with amused pity.

He felt the urge to wander. Was there any happiness greater in the world than being at the controls of your very own aircraft? Perhaps he should get a bigger aircraft and try to break a record or two. Why not? LONE EAGLET HENRY PEEL LANDS IN PARIS. He was laughing out loud at himself as the diminutive Welland airport appeared through the summer haze. He knew Welland well. It had no control tower and was therefore open to aircraft without radio. He touched down in a thoroughly professional three-pointer. With a tank full of fuel, he then took off again and headed north, following the ship canal toward Lake Ontario. The air was bumpy, which was usual at this time of year, Henry had learned. His little machine bounced and swayed as it cut through the upcurrents.

At Welland, Henry Peel hadn't taken the time to check on the weather. If he had, he might have headed for home.

THERE was a tightness around the eyes and a feeling of strain in the throat. A few minutes earlier, Beatty had taken another pill. "I'll be all right in a minute," he kept telling himself. But he knew it was pointless. The pills were no cure-all. Montreal below. He glanced at his watch. In less than an hour the trip would be over. So would his career. Finis. Right now Corfield was in command. And he was doing admirably.

Webb, the navigator, had news of the weather. "Toronto is reporting thunderstorm activity, severe in spots. At the moment it's not affecting the field itself, but they think it will before we get there."

"Roger," said Corfield. "Let's check again in fifteen minutes."

Ahead, ground and sky merged in haze. Typical summer conditions for this part of the world: moisture and heat—with cooler air on the way to stir up trouble. Beatty reflected that from now on the air and its restless movements would merely be of academic interest to him. He would never again have to see and feel it as an airman does: the ever mobile masses of air roaming over the earth, umpteen tons of it, cold, warm, moist, dry, sometimes tranquil, sometimes angry; billions of molecules, always on the move, shunted and shoved by ceaseless winds that stream from the areas of high pressure to those of low pressure.

An airman learns to know and respect the air, the shape of a cloud, the color of the moon, just as a sailor discovers the vagaries of the sea. It is the sixth sense—the one that takes over when the instruments fail; the conviction that *that* is the way back to the field, that *now* is the time to slip down through that fog. Beatty frowned. He didn't like the look of the weather ahead.

TRANSTATE flight 738 was already feeling the turbulence in the air. Invisible fists struck at her as she sped by, jolting her, sending stresses speeding through her one-tenth-inch-thick skin. Her passengers were drawn to the disquieting sight of her huge wings flexing as they took the loads. None of them knew that the wing was capable of flapping as much as nine feet without damage.

"Seat-belt sign, please," Vaughan told Garten. "And look after the PA, will you? Tell them we're encountering turbulence and they should put on their belts for their own safety."

Garten nodded. "Okay, sir."

Vaughan scanned the instrument panel. Speed, altitude, course, temperatures, pressures: all okay. But it was getting bumpier by the minute. Behind the dials, needles shivered and vibrated.

Lee, Lee. I can't believe you're dead. I can't, I can't.

The ground had almost vanished beneath a blanket of haze. Lake Erie was ahead. Detroit lay beneath a layer of brown-tinted air that looked incapable of sustaining any form of life.

"The stuff's building over there," he said to Garten, pointing.

"It sure is, sir." Garten wasn't about to disagree on anything.

Before them, the sky was dominated by gigantic, blue black clouds piling themselves one upon the other, as if attempting to build a wall before flight 738 reached them.

It HAD been a sweltering day in the northeastern United States and the adjoining Canadian provinces. The air was heavy with heat, saturated heat. Nerves and tempers of groundlings suffered accordingly. But, so said the news media, relief was on the way: a cold front was edging down from the north.

Because cold air is heavier than warm air, the front clung to the earth as it moved. It was an invisible wedge that pried the warm, damp air from the surface of the ground and sent it rolling skyward on the back of more cool air that came piling in behind. TEMPERATURES DUE TO DIVE, said the newspapers. They were correct. A second front of even cooler air was following on the heels of the first.

Meanwhile, the warm, humid air kept rising, pushed relentlessly from below. Soon it found itself ten, fifteen, even twenty thousand feet high. And suddenly the air became cold. Like steam from a kettle, the moisture in the air underwent a rapid transformation.

It became visible: tiny droplets of water that clustered together to become clouds. Cumulus. Cumulonimbus.

Nature was busily setting the scene for the storm.

IN THE 1930s five German glider pilots flew deliberately into a thunderstorm to study its effects at close quarters. They were brave men, but foolhardy. Within minutes their gliders were being tossed around like feathers; soon they began to break up. The pilots jumped for their lives. But they made the mistake of opening their parachutes too soon. The storm's violent upcurrents took their open chutes and sent the men hurtling upward. They were powerless. Gasping for air, they found themselves becoming coated with ice. Now, heavy with layers of the stuff, they plunged earthward, until the uprushing torrent of warm air found their chutes and sent them up again. Incredibly, one of the five men survived, though he was horribly frostbitten. The others continued to be playthings of the storm until at last it subsided. Then, finally, they returned to earth: human hailstones strapped to ripped parachutes.

Thunderstorms commanded the utmost respect from pilots, for they were killers, capable of generating awesome energy. By far the most sensible thing to do was to avoid them. To that end, passenger airliners carried radar capable of detecting storm precipitation up to two hundred miles ahead.

THE cells of the storm that Vaughan and Beatty both saw building sped upward. Behind them swept tides of air. By now water particles were being propelled to such great altitudes that they promptly froze. They fell. They melted. And then, as water droplets again, they went careering upward once more. And once more they froze. And fell. And again stronger, newer updrafts of warm air packed with moisture halted their tumbling and sent them spinning toward the heavens. And at last the ice particles were so heavy that even the strongest upcurrent could not stay them. Down went billions of them, at speeds of up to 120 miles per hour. They were an avalanche that smashed its way down through the warm upcurrents, dragging wave after wave of frigid air in its wake.

It was the storm's catalyst. Now the winds began their battle. As if someone had pressed a button, abruptly they shifted. As hail thrashed the earth, the sky became a battleground. Updrafts and downdrafts fought in deadly proximity, creating wind shears like guillotines that were capable of slicing an airplane's wing from its body.

"HOLY Mother," said Henry Peel loudly and distinctly.

He gulped, frozen in horror at the sight. The clouds were enormous. Blue black. Seething with anger. How could he not have noticed them forming? He had been looking out over the lake, thinking of it as the Atlantic, imagining himself flying it, becoming a famous hero, lionized in every city. . . .

The sun disappeared. It was night. Never had he felt so tiny, so inadequate, so completely, utterly alone. There was no one in the entire world who could help him. He had no radio, no means of contacting anyone until he landed. *If* he landed. He clasped a hand over his mouth. I may be dead in a few minutes!

The storm clouds had formed a huge mobile wall bent on forcing him out over Lake Ontario, but he couldn't let it. He *had* to turn inland. Ten o'clock direction. Over there the sky seemed a bit lighter. With a morsel of luck he might find somewhere to land.

He pushed the stick forward. The tiny aircraft bounced and tilted, bravely pushing through the hostile air. He passed over the shoreline with its ribbon of busy highway. Hurrying traffic. Headlights on. Expecting the worst. But the ground was still dry. The storm hadn't really begun, but Henry could feel its anger already.

No field in sight. Where the hell was he? Why in heaven's name hadn't he paid attention? Wandering around the bloody sky like a hobo . . . He flew over rows of houses, and roads on which people walked, their feet sensibly planted on good, solid earth. A shopping plaza: cars in dense, neat rows, the store lights defying the gargantuan shadow above. It was densely built up. Nowhere to land. It must be Toronto. There was no other city of this size in the area. Lord, how he had wandered. "You goddam idiot."

The first drops of rain hit the windshield. Almost simultaneously a giant hand grabbed Henry and his Aeronca. Up he went. Madly. Suicidally.

He opened his mouth as if to protest. Nothing, absolutely nothing he did made the slightest difference. Stick fully forward. Rudder pedals hard left, then right. Throttle forward. Back. All futile. The elevators *had* to raise the tail; the rudder *had* to turn the nose. It was what he had learned. But it was no longer true. The Aeronca was unable to escape the upcurrent. She zoomed upward on a torrent of boiling air. The ground vanished. Above was nothing but blue blackness.

"God . . . oh, God." Now the Aeronca was almost vertical. Stupefied with fear, Henry found himself looking straight at another world: a world of black seething cloud.

It was the end. It had to be. Henry felt his body banging against the side of the cockpit. Something hit him on the head. Was he upside down? He was sure he wasn't. Then he wasn't sure at all. Of anything. The air had turned on him. He had thought it to be his friend, his companion in adventure; now it was doing its level best to kill him.

With the realization that he was utterly helpless came a kind of peace. He could do absolutely nothing but wait for the end. In all probability the aircraft would shortly come apart in bits. A thousand fragments would flutter down to the ground. He would be one.

"It's going to be all right," Frederick Cox assured his wife, patting her hand that had become a fist. "A few air pockets, that's all. Nothing to get het up about."

She groaned. "Fred, make him put this thing on the ground."

"Make who?"

"The driver."

"Can't do that, old girl. He's got his hands full up there, you know. We don't want to interfere with his work, do we?"

Len Sparrow was thinking what a godsend this rough weather would have been if only he had been sitting in the right seat! A bit of the old strong silent comforter would have worked wonders. No, don't mind a bit if you want to put your head on my shoulder. You go on and . . . Without the slightest warning Len Sparrow's lunch came up. He heard the girl say, "Oh, you poor little chap!" Aggrieved, ashamed, he rushed for the toilet.

"Is he all right?" Miss Hardcastle inquired.

"He was sick," said Julie. "It's quite bumpy."

Miss Hardcastle smiled. "Yes, I did notice."

Julie blushed. "Of course you did. How absolutely stupid of me."

VAUGHAN took a deep breath as he gazed at the dark mountains in the sky. Toronto was reporting bands of severe thunderstorms, heavy rain and hail, winds gusting up to fifty knots.

"Toronto, TranState seven three eight. We'd like to orbit until the worst of this stuff has gone through."

"Roger, TranState seven three eight. Stand by, please." A minute later the controller called again, advising the flight to orbit the Ash beacon, where the storm was not active.

Soon the aircraft's path became smoother. Nearby, the sun sparkled on the choppy waters of Lake Ontario. Vaughan turned the yoke and applied gentle rudder. Towns on the far shore appeared in the windshield panels, then slid away as the turn was maintained. Ahead lay a hundred miles of water; the Canadian shore huddled beneath glowering storm clouds. Occasionally lightning flashes streaked jaggedly between sky and ground.

Vaughan pressed the PA button. "This is the captain speaking. I'm sorry to have to tell you that we're going to be a few minutes late landing at Toronto. They're experiencing some rough weather there, but it should be through the area shortly. We apologize for the delay, but we think you'd rather be a few minutes late than . . ."

Than what? Dead? Like Lee? He winced. He hadn't intended to say that. He thumbed the PA button again. "Er, we'll let you know just as soon as we have clearance to land. Thank you."

Lake Ontario turned smoothly below.

There was no way for anyone to know that it would almost certainly have been safer to have tried a landing during the storm.

BEATTY SAT BACK and watched as Corfield guided the 707 between the towering thunderheads, gently banking in order to avoid sudden movements. The shapely wing tips sliced the churning clouds like rapiers, then darted out over air that was clear almost to the ground. Through the haze Beatty could see the eastern extremities of Lake Ontario; then cloud obscured his vision.

Beatty was feeling fine again. It was curious how extravagantly well he could feel after a bout with whatever it was. Three rousing cheers after all for Dr. Hoke's "magic" pills.

Lewis, the chief steward, came in, balancing himself with the assurance of one who has spent a major part of his adult life walking around aircraft in flight.

"How are the passengers?" Beatty inquired.

Lewis grimaced. "There's a bit of puking going on back there, sir, but we're coping."

"We should be down in about thirty minutes," Beatty told him.

Webb handed Beatty a card on which he had written his estimate of the aircraft's landing weight and the correct power setting in case of an overshoot. Jordan was busy with cabin depressurization and fuel balance. Descending toward Toronto, the 707 passed through the eighteen-thousand-foot level.

THE radar operator frowned. Was that an echo? It vanished, reappeared, vanished. The operator shook his head. It was impossible to sort things out with storms popping off all around. If it was an echo, it would be from a small aircraft. But no small aircraft were in the vicinity—at least none had announced its presence on the Toronto advisory frequency, 119.3.

THE voice from the ground battled with the static. "Amory ten ten, you are clear to descend to and maintain fifteen thousand. Over."

Beatty repeated the instructions. The aircraft was descending at a rate of two thousand feet per minute, slicing through the turbulent air. The thunderheads loomed on either side. "What are your intentions?" he asked Corfield.

Corfield thought a moment. "The visibility is almost down to minimums on the ground. The storms are severe. I heard a couple of aircraft saying they intended to wait it out. I say we should do the same."

Beatty said, "Thunderstorms can go on for a hell of a long time in this part of the world. We're badly behind schedule."

"I realize that, sir," Corfield said, reddening. "But if conditions make it dangerous . . ."

"Don't you think we should plan on landing until it becomes absolutely obvious that we can't?"

Corfield swallowed. "I don't feel I have sufficient experience of conditions like this, sir. I'd rather you took control."

Beatty nodded. "Very well."

Corfield abruptly raised his hands from the yoke, as if it had become too hot to hold, and stared ahead rigidly. The TranState flight was correct to wait out the storm, he thought. It was the sensible, cautious decision. But gallant Captain Beatty was undeterred. Press on regardless. Those old bomber command types were all the same.

Beatty smiled to himself. He knew how the poor blighter felt. He was probably thinking fierce thoughts about captains who give a chap command and then take it away again on a whim. He sympathized and silently told Corfield, "We've all had to go through it, old chap."

Toronto said, "Amory ten ten, we're not reading your transponder squawk." Which, thought Beatty, is hardly surprising since Amory 1010 was flying with a defective one. He made a show of switching to the backup transponder. Predictably, the ground controller reported a continued lack of response. His task was now to make sure which of the flickering dots on the screen was the Amory 707.

"Turn on a heading of three three zero. . . . Okay, Amory ten ten, we have you identified now. Please advise your intentions."

"Landing Toronto."

"Roger. Stand by."

Beatty scratched the tip of his nose. He felt absolutely confident of his ability to land the aircraft—or, if airport conditions were impossible, he would know when to abandon the attempt.

"Let's have the preliminary checklist, shall we?"

One by one the aircraft's systems were checked. No problems—except for the unserviceable transponder. Even that was no longer a problem; Toronto radar had identified the Amory flight. The flickering dot on the screens now had an identity.

Time had no meaning. If Henry Peel had been asked to state how long he had been tossed by the storm, he might have said half an hour. In fact, it was less than three minutes. For much of that merciless interlude he was upside down. At one point he emerged through a wall of cloud and saw a blur of sky. Then, without warning, it was dark again. Dark and wet and lonely. And cold. He was holding on to the rim of the instrument panel. The instruments had gone mad, the needles spinning. Hail caked his tiny world with a layer of frost. Moments later the frost melted and flew away in jagged chunks. There was no sign of the ground. Did it still exist? Was this, Henry wondered, the end of the world?

Suddenly, gloriously, he was free. And the beautiful earth was below, full of gorgeous human beings. "Good God," he said.

A kick somewhere in the region of the stabilizer reminded him that the storm was still close by. And still angry. The little Aeronca was in a tight turn. He discovered that if he didn't do something about the turn at once, he would simply fly back into the cloud. He kicked the rudder and jammed the stick to one side. The Aeronca obediently righted herself. Throttle right forward. Escape!

He came to the conclusion that it was remarkably cold. He looked at the altimeter. The needles were no longer spinning. It took him moments to absorb the significance of their positions.

"Good God," he said again. He was at seventeen thousand feet.

His consciousness was swimming. He could hear his own voice instructing himself to shove the stick forward. "The reason," his voice explained, "is that you are in the process of flaking out from oxygen starvation. The doctor told you all about it at ground school. If you don't do something about it, you will die."

And yet it was a shame to leave. Up near the heavens the colors were soft and the sounds sweet. Then his eyes began to focus on something. It was difficult because the something refused to stay still. He blinked. It was a layer of cloud. Hurtling at him. It looked solid enough to shatter the Aeronca. Then he realized that he was through that layer of cloud and that, below him, there were more and more layers. Reality returned with each breath of denser air. One by one, as if there were all the time in the world, the facts of his situation thrust themselves upon him. He was diving. If he didn't pull out, he would be killed. The joystick pumped against his hand and Henry discovered that the engine was blasting away at full throttle. He pulled the throttle back to idle.

Now the little aircraft began to come out of her dive. Soon she was almost on the level again and still retaining her wings. Through the clouds Henry caught glimpses of the ground and the lake. But which lake? He looked around for a landmark. Instead he saw a Boeing 707.

THE tiny Aeronca suddenly popped out from behind the cloud like some suicidally dangerous toy. It was there, mere feet away—a flimsy thing, wobbling in the air. Inside, clearly visible, sat a young man in a bright check shirt. His face was turned toward the hurtling 707. He looked disbelieving.

Corfield had time to utter a strangled croak of warning.

Beatty had already jammed on aileron and rudder. But there was so little time. In a fragment of an instant, the jet had consumed the space between the two machines. The Aeronca loomed in the windshield, insanely huge and close. And then it was gone.

In the passenger cabin, Len Sparrow was just emerging from the toilet, where he had once again been vomiting. He was closing the door when, without warning, everything tipped over. Len was tossed back into the toilet to sprawl, dazed and sickly, on the seat.

A stewardess was also on her feet when Beatty threw the 707 into a violent bank. Instinctively her hands grasped for something, encountered Mr. Cox.

"We're crashing," gasped Mrs. Cox.

"No . . . quite normal maneuver just before landing," her husband muttered bravely but unconvincingly.

The 707 plummeted.

"Give me a hand, man!"

Corfield nodded jerkily, his eyes bright with horror. His hands gripped the yoke. Together the two pilots fought the aircraft's plunge. Every muscle, every fiber was concentrated on the task of forcing the 707 back to level flight before it smashed into Lake Ontario. Layers of cloud rushed past. Somewhere a radio voice was yelling something in agitated tones. Someone in the aircraft was calling out altitudes. Jordan. Sensible chap.

Beatty didn't know whether he had hit the Aeronca. Would a frail little thing like that make any sort of impact? Why was the stupid bastard *there, then?*

"Easy. Don't force her." Corfield was pulling too energetically. In his eagerness to live, he was practically guaranteeing an early demise.

Oh, God be praised, thought Beatty, we *might* make it. He saw the waters of the lake tipping, then straightening.

"Bloody marvelous!" yelled Corfield, beaming. "Good girl! Good girl!" He kept patting the instrument panel as if it were the back of a faithful hound.

Ahead there was a shaft of sunlight piercing the clouds like a searchlight. Beatty realized he was smiling. How many lives did he have left now? "Are the bloody wings still on?"

Corfield elaborately gazed out of the windows. "All wings present and accounted for, sir. Better luck next time."

"What's that din?" Webb, the navigator, said.

"Undercart horn. Shut it off, will you?"

It screeched at the crew like a cantankerous old fishwife, telling them that the undercarriage was still retracted, although they had brought the aircraft down almost to ground level.

The control column heaved against Beatty's hand. Gentle back pressure. Up a bit, old girl. We need a spot of height.

"Would someone go and see how the passengers are coping? And tell them it was a near-miss. . . ." Near-missmissmissmissmiss . . .

The dials on the instrument panel began to move like amoebas beneath a scientist's microscope. Beatty had time to think, I'm going to have another attack, and mumble, "Take over," to Corfield, and then the world became a blur of revolving lights and shadows and dull, insistent sounds.

THE controller's face was ashen. His radarscope was a nightmare. The bright green blips—each representing a jet packed with humanity—were like willful creatures bent on self-destruction.

Frantically he tried to create a perspective of the situation—and what it would be in ten seconds and thirty seconds. The errant blip on the left side of the screen had to be Amory. But what had caused it to dive? Now it was streaking out across the lake. And climbing.

Mother of God! "Amory ten ten, make an immediate left turn!"

HE'S had a bloody heart attack, Corfield thought. He was gazing at Beatty's mouth and its pathetic attempts to form sounds.

Then Jordan snapped, "Control is calling us!"

"What?"

Precious, irreplaceable seconds slipped by.

The controller's voice cut through the static a second time, harsh with urgency. "TranState seven three eight, make an immediate right turn! *Immediate!*"

VAUGHAN heard the controller's order. But for an instant he didn't react. The words of the controller had somehow become part of what Lee was saying. Her voice was sharp and urgent. She was reaching out to him. And he wanted somehow to answer her and tell her that there was meaning in it all, that it wasn't just a mindless sexual ritual; there was significance in what had happened.

An instant. Then he was thrusting control yoke and rudder hard over, obeying the "immediate" command, hurling the big machine toward a gigantic wall of cloud.

"TranState seven three eight, turning ninety to the right." The cloud enfolded them. A second later, they were in the sunlight.

And then Amory flight 1010 hit them.

SIMULTANEOUSLY SCORES of people saw different things happen. Grant Hobbs saw a row of seats in front of him rise as if lifted by giant hands. A fraction of an instant later there was a shuddering bang that exploded out of the very walls of the aircraft. At the same moment he saw a second wing suddenly materialize beneath that of the DC-8. Absurdly the thought flashed through his mind that the aircraft had become a biplane. Then, frantically, his hand was reaching for the emergency-exit handle.

Jane Meade, the chief stewardess, opened her mouth to scream, but stopped herself. The DC-8 seemed to have been halted in mid-flight. It was coming to pieces before her eyes. The deck had reared up and broken; the seats spilled passengers who were not strapped in; those who were tried to free themselves.

Earl Gasparac saw the sides of the aircraft bend and buckle. He clutched his wife and buried her head in his chest. He saw a stewardess emerge from the flight deck at the moment the Amory aircraft collided. The girl's legs gave way and she slammed into the floor. She skidded along the aisle, her arms and legs flopping as if the bones had turned to rubber.

An emergency exit—a great doorlike panel—suddenly opened beside Lillian Dumont. Shocked, she turned. She saw Grant Hobbs, but only for an infinitesimal fragment of time. He was suspended in midair, a few feet from the aircraft. His thin face wore an expression of mild surprise. His hand still gripped the emergency-exit handle. Then he vanished. Lillian screamed as a tidal wave of air grabbed at her. Her seat belt held her securely, but her purse, with $16,821.37, was snatched by the boiling gale and rocketed away from the aircraft. Inconsequentially she thought, I wish I'd spent the goddam money in Des Moines.

Aboard the Amory aircraft, the passengers were already strapped in their seats. It was fortunate, for the impact caused them to half rise, their heads involuntarily bobbing, toward the roof that was abruptly crumpling in upon them.

There was a horrifying din, a grinding and smashing, an end-of-the-world eruption of sound.

Mr. Cox looked up to see a section of the roof disappear, exposing the underside of another airplane. It was a dreadful-looking tangle of metal and, incongruously, baggage. The impact had opened up the DC-8's luggage compartment. The flimsy material of a nightdress fluttered like a threadbare flag. It was entangled in a smart blue and white tie.

"Good gracious," exclaimed Miss Hardcastle. "Whatever has happened?"

"I think we . . . hit another airplane." Julie looked up through her window to find an enormous shimmering mass of metal, bearing bright red letters spelling TranState.

In front of Mr. Cox the wall separating the 707's flight deck from the passenger cabin folded and collapsed. He saw four men sitting in the cockpit.

Corfield suddenly realized something appalling.

The instruction to turn right had been given to a TranState aircraft, not to Amory 1010. He had obeyed the wrong orders. He had turned right instead of left.

He was to blame.

VAUGHAN held up his arms to protect his head as the floor of the DC-8's flight deck heaved and broke in a confusion of metal, wires, switches and levers. Part of the nose section broke away. An icy hurricane tore through the flight deck. Garten, in the right-hand seat, tried to shield his eyes from the blast.

Vaughan felt the wind tearing at his earphones. He looked down. "God help us," he breathed. The torn wing of the Boeing 707 looked close enough to touch.

A midair. It had happened to him.

But why was the aircraft still flying? Why wasn't everything exploding and burning and tumbling?

Cutshall, the navigator, was crouching beside him, his eyes blinking in the torrent of air. Vaughan leaned back out of the wind. "Check the damage."

Cutshall nodded. Vaughan turned back to the controls. No time to wonder about passengers or cabin crew. The only thing that mattered was getting the aircraft down safely. First, find out what still worked. He clutched the control yoke. It was loose. He touched the thrust levers but dared not move them. The rudder pedals were jammed.

Vaughan swallowed. His brain reasoned: Of course the controls are useless; the linkages of the hydraulic-boost system run through the floor beams, under the flight deck. How could they be expected to work? Icy panic grabbed him. He had no controls. He was powerless. In a moment the whole goddam aircraft would come apart.

But, incredibly, the ground and sky remained in their proper places as moment succeeded moment.

DAZED, groggy, Beatty thought the aircraft had hit something on the ground. He kept seeing a West African village store cut in half by the right main landing gear unit of an Anglo-World 747.

"Midair," Corfield was croaking. "We've had a midair."

Beatty struggled with his consciousness. "What did you say?"

"We hit another bloody airplane! Look behind you."

Then, through the side window, Beatty saw the unbelievable sight of the DC-8's wing snuggling up to the 707's wing, the tips almost touching. The metal was torn and folded back, curiously, neatly, as if done with great care. Fuel poured out in a wind-battered mist.

"You passed out," said Corfield accusingly.

"He hit us," said Webb.

"No, we hit him," said Jordan.

The flight-deck roof was a shambles. It sagged over their heads. Beatty saw that the bulkhead at the rear of the flight deck had disappeared. The passengers could be seen: rows of faces, white and terrified, with eyes imploring him to do something. Quickly he turned forward, as if chastised by them. Then he heard the voice of the TranState pilot on the VHF radio.

BY SHEER miraculous chance, the two aircraft had been traveling in almost exactly the same direction and at similar speeds when they collided. Angled upward a degree or two, the 707 had thudded into the belly of the DC-8. Thus the roof of one aircraft slithered along the underside of the other. Contact was relatively gentle. But speed exacerbated its effect. Sections of metal plating crumpled and fluttered away, flimsy mementos of the contact. A great section of the Amory aircraft's wing folded and snapped amid a haze of escaping fuel.

At last the awesome forces of momentum were tamed. Joined by a tangle of tortured metal, the two aircraft had become one.

They had become a monster. An aeronautical aberration. A sagging, heaving catastrophe that had no right to remain in the air but for the single fact that its wings were still capable of creating power from the speeding air. The monster lacked lateral stability, and kept wobbling, on the point of tumbling. But fuel continued to pour to the engines that still functioned. They provided thrust. And the monster staggered toward the shore.

THE passenger cabin of the DC-8 had become a nightmare of screaming wind. The wind swept into the hull, snatching at anything movable, hurling it down the length of the cabin. You ducked these objects if you could. Earl Gasparac was knocked unconscious by a section of metal paneling. Lillian Dumont clung to the arms of her seat, not daring to move.

The TranState stewardesses had been well trained. They knew that passengers in an emergency urgently need leadership and liberal doses of reassurance. But it was impossible to provide either, because you couldn't talk to anyone in this fiendish hurricane; it was hard enough even to stand up.

Jane Meade managed to half drag, half push an injured girl to an unoccupied row of seats. She kept telling her that everything was going to be all right. She wondered whether she was really talking to the girl or to herself. She wondered how long it would be until the aircraft tore itself into pieces and whether she would be brave in the moments before she died. She felt sick and weak with fear; her self-control was impossibly stretched. But in the meantime the girl had to be helped.

Earl Gasparac was only dimly conscious of the icy wind that

battered his face. But he could feel his wife's fingers pressing insistently on the side of his head. He knew something heavy had hit him, had cut him badly. But his wife was tending him. She knew what to do; she had been a nurse.

"I have no aileron or elevator control," Vaughan reported.

"How about rudder?" asked the ground controller. He sounded calm and matter-of-fact.

"Negative. Jammed."

"Roger. Your controls, Amory?"

"Our controls seem to be working, after a fashion." Beatty and Corfield had the control yoke hard over to the left, compensating for the missing wing section, persuading the confused forces to balance. It was odd to think that the TranState pilot was only a few feet away. "Amory to TranState," Beatty said. "We seem to be temporarily wedded. If you've got an idea how we might get this thing down, let's hear it."

"Negative, Amory. She's all yours. All I can do is watch."

The 707's airspeed indicator registered 250 knots. What, Beatty wondered, is the stalling speed of two crashed jetliners?

There was so much to decide, and so little time. The airport, shrouded in fitful rain showers, was only a few miles distant.

Beatty felt the sweat trickling over his forehead. Why was the thing still flying? It was appallingly unstable. The turbulent air kept trying to tip the whole contraption off-balance and send it tumbling out of the sky like the mountain of junk it was.

"TranState to Amory. You're doing a great job. Wish I could help."

Beatty thanked him. He sounded incredibly casual about the whole thing. Typical Yank. "I'm just aiming it at the airport and I plan to plunk it down as rapidly as I can."

"Roger, Amory. We can maybe help you with a little power if necessary. I haven't tried the engines yet, but they may be okay."

"Thanks, TranState. I'll let you know if we need more power."

Ground control reported all clear for emergency landing. There was not, however, time to foam the runways.

"Anything else we can do?" asked the controller.

Webb said flatly, "Ask him if he knows a good prayer."

"Shut your bloody mouth!" snapped Corfield.

"Go aft," Beatty told Webb. "See if you can do anything for the passengers."

The speed was falling off. Gently he edged the nose down. To apply more power was dangerous; it was liable to drag the Amory aircraft free of the DC-8. And the DC-8 had no controls. It would simply tumble several thousand feet to the ground.

He felt dizzy from the effort of holding the controls hard over. The monster wanted to roll up and die. It had had enough of this idiotic game. It was tired of pretending to be an airplane.

"The bloody fuel's simply pouring out!" Jordan yelled from the other side of the flight deck. He sounded as if he were commenting on an interesting phenomenon, a fascinating sight they all should see. But the poor sod knew only too well the horrifying probability of everything suddenly becoming a giant bonfire in the sky.

Fast though; it'll be bloody fast.

Beatty pressed the PA button. He cleared his throat; the right words were important. "This is the captain speaking. I don't have to tell you what has happened. I *am* telling you, however, that we have control of the aircraft and we are heading straight in for a landing. But it could be rough, so prepare yourselves and obey the cabin crew's instructions. We'll be touching down in a few minutes. Everything will be okay provided you do as you are instructed. Thank you."

What, he wondered, am I thanking them for? For not storming the flight deck and lynching me for being criminally dangerous?

He called the TranState pilot. "I think my undercarriage and flaps will still work. I'm going to leave them until the last possible moment, though."

"I understand," said the American. "If we try it before, we might stall out, uh?"

"Exactly. She's frightfully wobbly even now." For the first time it occurred to Beatty that their conversation was being heard on the ground. Indeed it was at this moment being taped, every word recorded for posterity and the accident investigators.

The rain stopped in the typically abrupt manner of a North American summer storm. A patch of blue sky appeared.

Heading in from the lake was an incredible sight: two big jets in what appeared to be the tightest formation in the history of aviation.

In the control tower, binoculars were suddenly in short supply. One controller hastily loaded his camera. On the field, emergency vehicles cruised warily along deserted runways, their crews watching and wondering, a curious tension apparent everywhere.

"No," SAID Mrs. Cox, "I won't. If I'm going to die, it's going to be with me teeth in."

Moments before, the pale-faced stewardesses had hurried from seat to seat, instructing their passengers to fasten their seat belts over their hips rather than across their stomachs. "Hold your arms under your knees," were the orders. "Protect your head with a pillow. Take off your shoes and glasses. Loosen your collars. Remove pens and other sharp objects from your pockets. And take dentures from your mouths."

"Suppose you lose them," said Mr. Cox. "Suppose we hit the ground with a bit of a bang—I'm not saying we will, mind; I'm just saying we might—anyway, your dentures will go flying out of your mouth. And then someone might tread on them. And then where would you be?"

"What d'you mean?" his wife asked.

"You'd be facing your daughter without any teeth. Bare gums!"

She paled. "It never crossed me mind. I'll take 'em out."

"Good girl," he said approvingly.

"WE HAVE you in sight," the ground controller announced. "You are cleared for a straight-in approach to runway three two."

"Good," said Vaughan, "because we sure as hell can't do a circuit of the field."

"The wind," said the controller levelly, as if this were a normal, everyday landing, "is two eight degrees at twenty knots."

"Roger," said Vaughan. "Okay, Amory?"

"Piece of cake," came the Englishman's voice.

Vaughan gazed ahead. It was weird to see a runway and be powerless to control the approach. His flying had started to resemble his life: all he could do was watch; he was no longer directly in control of anything.

Suddenly the Englishman's voice cut through his ruminations. "We're sinking too fast! Have to have some more power!"

"Okay." Vaughan's hand was on the thrust levers. His heart pounded. If a surge of power tore the two aircraft apart . . . The end was too horribly clear. Gingerly he pushed the levers forward. It took time. Three seconds, four, five. Row upon row of houses wobbled nearer. Then, with a terrifying heave, the engines began to deliver more power. You could hear the metal groaning and stretching. The monster tottered precariously, trying to tear itself in two.

Vaughan said aloud, "Hang in there, baby. For God's sake, hang in there. Please."

A pungent smell seeped up from the shattered electrical and radio compartment beneath the flight deck. Garten had emptied a portable extinguisher into it, but still it smoked. Hydraulic fluid sloshed over the floor, and the hurricane of air still screamed in through the torn nose.

Jane Meade appeared between the two pilots, hair plastered flatly across her grimy forehead. She reported that the passengers were in crash-landing positions.

"How are they?"

"Pretty good," she yelled. "But it's as drafty as hell back there. Mind if we close the window?"

Vaughan smiled. "Good girl," he said.

"Still there, old boy?" The British voice sounded as if it were taking orders for whiskys and soda.

"Affirmative. But only just."

"I think we might bleed off a little of that power now."

"Okay." He's one hell of a fine pilot, Vaughan thought. Somehow he's bringing this airborne abortion in on a reasonable facsimile of a final landing approach.

EARL GASPARAC REALIZED that he was dying. He had known he was hurt, but that he might die hadn't occurred to him. Now life was dissolving within him. He accepted the fact without regret. He was content. He managed to squeeze his wife's hand.

She looked down at him. Her eyes were gentle, brimming with love. Without speaking she was able to tell him that she knew he was happy. And she understood why.

Len Sparrow came to his senses. Where the hell was he? What was he doing in a box? Everything was rattling. Then he remembered. He was in the toilet in the jet. What had happened to it? It looked sort of squashed and creased. He reached for the door. The handle turned, but the door wouldn't budge. He was trapped.

Mr. Cox grasped his wife's hand and braced himself. "In case we don't get out of this, er, in one piece, if you know what I mean, I just want to say . . . I've always loved you, old girl."

She nodded. "Me too, Fred. You've been a good husband and father. I couldn't have asked for better."

"Good of you to say so, old girl."

"And," said Mrs. Cox, "that business with George Harris didn't mean anything at all, really."

"Course it didn't," said Mr. Cox comfortingly. Then, as the unfamiliar terrain of southern Ontario appeared in the cabin window, his eyes grew big. Had he heard aright? *What* business with George Harris?

THE nearer to touchdown, the more viciously the monster fought, twisting, nosing, one instant dipping a torn, trembling wing, the next skidding like an overloaded truck on an icy road.

Beatty felt weak. I must not pass out, he thought.

The runway was dead ahead.

"Fifteen hundred feet," said Corfield.

"Will we . . ."

"Piece of cake," Beatty made himself say. He thumbed the transmit button. "TranState, let's peel off some more power, shall we?"

"Sure thing," came the reply.

Beatty grinned wryly. Both he and the American were trying to sound quite unconcerned by the catastrophe and its impending consequences, and neither man was fooling the other. Beatty thanked God he had the controls. He couldn't imagine how the DC-8 could simply sit there and wait, powerless to do a thing except work the throttles.

Below, cars breezed along neat roads as if all were well with the world. It will all be over, Beatty thought, in a few moments, one way or the other, win or lose. He spoke to the aircraft. "Please behave for another few seconds. I know it's a hell of a thing to ask, but please, just a few seconds more."

The window panel at his left shoulder began to vibrate, shivering as if terrified by the imminent return to earth.

"Stand by!" As he uttered the words he wondered what they meant. Surely the crew didn't have to be reminded that touchdown was only seconds away.

The American said, "Real nice, buddy, right on the button."

"Roger," said Beatty. "Flaps and undercarriage coming. Good luck, old boy."

"Same to you!"

Corfield's hands were on the flap and undercarriage levers. Beatty nodded. "Now!" He grimaced as the monster bucked and swung. Oh God, he thought, only half the flaps are working. Controls hard over and forward. Power off on one side. The ground tilted and swayed. The strip of dark gray concrete swept toward him, a sword plunging into him. He thought, When the speed drops off another few knots, the wing will suddenly drop. The poor thing can't do anything else. And when it does, we'll cartwheel all over the bloody airport, which is singularly unhealthy under any circumstances whatsoever.

Whereupon he corrected, even before the wing began to drop. At his side, Corfield thought he had gone mad; he tried to cancel out the control movements.

Beatty shook his head. "We've got to," he explained as the ground whirled past. "I know I'm right," he added quite mildly.

The monster wobbled threateningly. And then its wheels touched the concrete. The tires held for approximately five seconds before they blew in rapid succession, and an instant later the nose wheel and the right main undercarriage unit collapsed. The monster slued off the runway in an explosion of dirt and turf. A JT3D engine snapped off and tumbled end over end.

Simultaneously the TranState DC-8 tore herself free, thrusting forward as the 707 dipped. For a fragment of time, the two aircraft were bridged by an afterbirth of torn metal, tubing, cables and wires. Then they separated.

The DC-8 hit the ground tail first. A wing snapped cleanly and spun sideways, as if flicked away by a giant finger. To horrified watchers it appeared that the wing of the 707 had sliced into the TranState machine; in fact, the two aircraft missed each other by several feet. The 707 skidded in a virtually straight line over the sodden grass, shedding sections of wing and fuselage, while fuel cascaded from the torn wing tanks. The DC-8 ground-looped. There was nothing that either pilot could do to control his aircraft. The tools of control—ailerons, elevators, rudders, flaps, spoilers, slots—were now just so much more weight to charge the relentless impetus.

Inside each plane, passengers and crew members huddled in their seats, stupefied by the battering and the din. It was merciless, incredible, beyond imagination. Muscles turned to jelly, eyes popped out of shivering sockets. All the world's dustbin lids were beaten simultaneously by lead pipes; a billion drummers were hitting a billion cymbals.

And then, suddenly, miraculously, the world was quiet.

Chapter Seven

THE wind, damp and unseasonably chilly, pulled at the somber clothes of the mourners. Dr. T. Roydon Goodall shivered. He felt sick at heart, as he had for days, since he had read the appalling news of the crash at Toronto. MAJOR AERIAL DISASTER . . . DEATH IN THE SKIES . . . BRITISH AND U.S. JET AIRLINERS COLLIDE. Wincing, he had scanned the story for the name he intuitively knew was there. He was correct, horribly correct. "The British aircraft was a 707 charter belonging to Amory International, piloted by Captain F. N. Beatty, 49, of Royston, Herts," said *The Times*.

Now, cold and miserable, he stood amid a hundred strangers at the graveside. The service ended, and Hoke watched as the minister spoke to the widow and her son. Hoke wondered whether he should go and speak to her. But what could he say? One felt so helpless at such times. He observed a man speaking to her, a man in an airline pilot's uniform. Someone said it was the pilot of the American jet. He was tanned, a pleasant-looking individual. The papers had quoted him. His name was Vaughan, if Hoke remembered correctly. He had spoken of Beatty's amazing feat of piloting in managing to coax the two airliners back to the ground.

Hoke shivered as, for the umpteenth time, he imagined Frank's aircraft smashing across the field on its belly, fire gobbling at the torn wings, the crew hurling open doors and hatches, inflatable escape chutes prancing out like great dangling tongues, passengers and crew slithering down them to land in piles in the mud. And then the frenzy to run from the flames. Hurrying, slipping, stumbling, crawling. And after the passengers, the crew, choking, coughing: the stewardesses, hair awry, pretty faces smudged; the men with white shirts singed and bloody. . . .

"Everyone escaped within minutes," *The Times* reported, "except for Captain Beatty and a passenger, twenty-year-old Leonard Sparrow, of Streatham, who had become trapped in the wreckage and been overlooked by the crew. Captain Beatty, without regard for his own safety, remained inside the burning, smoke-filled hull in order to assist Mr. Sparrow from the plane."

The words evoked dreadful images in Hoke's mind. Frank tearing at the scorching metal with his bare hands, dragging the lad free, then shoving him to safety down the escape chute.

The papers said that Leonard Sparrow was in satisfactory condition in Toronto General Hospital, suffering the effects of smoke inhalation, minor burns, cuts and contusions.

The papers also rued the fact that Captain Beatty didn't make his escape at the same time. "He returned to the interior of the hull, presumably searching for more passengers." They had no inkling that Captain Beatty would undoubtedly have remained in the burning plane even if there had been no one to rescue, thought Hoke.

The papers had no definite information as to why the two machines collided. One account hinted at electronic problems, possibly caused by the severe storm conditions. Another speculated that a third aircraft might have been involved. A full-scale investigation was being initiated by the Canadian authorities.

What would it uncover? Hoke didn't care. The reason for Frank's death seemed unimportant now; only the fact of it mattered.

The cars moved away. Only a handful of people remained. His hands in his overcoat pockets, Hoke walked slowly along the gravel path. On the way he passed two men in airline uniform. One said that Frank Beatty was a good pilot, a damned good pilot.

Hoke was inclined to agree; Frank had indeed been damned.

ADVERTISEMENT in *Canadian Aviation:*

FOR SALE

Aeronca 7AC-468. Clean. No reasonable offer refused.

Apply:

H. Peel, R. R. #3, Filden, Ontario.

Spencer Dunmore, born and educated in England, now lives with his wife in Hamilton, Ontario, where he is an advertising executive during the day, an author in the evenings, and a private pilot on weekends. Upholding the theory that truth is stranger than fiction, Mr. Dunmore explains:

Spencer
Dunmore

My novel is founded on fact, or rather a series of facts, dating back to the first midair collision between scheduled airliners. Near Paris one overcast day in 1922 two aircraft, navigating by the elementary means of following a main road, collided head-on.

Today, with radar, such collisions should never take place. However, equipment fails; human beings err; and inexperienced pilots in private aircraft roam more or less at will. Result: hundreds of near-misses a year. And from time to time luck runs out.

But people *can* survive midairs. On a clear day in the 1950s a Cessna descended upon a DC-3. The Cessna pilot had been showing his passengers a view of their home; the DC-3 crew, preoccupied with landing checks, suddenly found they had a private aircraft astride their fuselage. Damaged but still airworthy, the monster landed safely. More recently, one aircraft flew into the rear of another while both were on final approach to an Illinois airport. Again there was a safe landing of two interlocked planes. The important fact in each case, of course, is that the two planes were traveling in the same direction at the moment of impact.

The ability of the Boeing 707 to fly without major portions of wing was dramatically demonstrated when a 707 collided with a Constellation over North Salem, New York, in 1965. The 707 lost twenty feet of the port wing plus one engine. All praise to the awesome skill of the airmen who set those craft down safely.

ACKNOWLEDGMENTS

Page 3: *Held Up*, an oil painting by Newbold Trotter, is used by courtesy of the Smithsonian Institution.